A master storyteller, Sidn[...] eighteen novels (which h[...] copies), over 200 televi[...] scripts, twenty-five major motion pictures and six Broadway plays, ranking him as one of the world's most prolific writers. His first book, *The Naked Face*, was acclaimed by the *New York Times* as 'the best first mystery novel of the year' and subsequently each of his highly popular books have hit No. 1 on the *New York Times* bestseller list. His latest bestseller, *Are You Afraid of the Dark?*, cements Sheldon's reputation as the master of the unexpected.

For more about Sidney Sheldon, visit his website at www.sidneysheldon.com.

For automatic updates on Sidney Sheldon visit HarperCollins.co.uk/sidneysheldon and register for AuthorTracker.

By the same author

SIDNEY SHELDON

Bloodline

Nothing Lasts Forever

HARPER

HarperCollins*Publishers*
77–85 Fulham Palace Road,
Hammersmith, London W6 8JB

www.harpercollins.co.uk

This omnibus edition 2008

Bloodline
Copyright © Sheldon Literary Trust 1978

Nothing Lasts Forever
Copyright © Sidney Sheldon 1994

Sidney Sheldon asserts the moral right to
be identified as the author of this work

A catalogue record for this book is available from the British Library

ISBN 978-0-00-783976-6

Printed and bound in Great Britain by Clays Ltd, St Ives plc

Mixed Sources
Product group from well-managed
forests and other controlled sources
www.fsc.org Cert no. SW-COC-1806
© 1996 Forest Stewardship Council
FSC

FSC is a non-profit international organisation established to promote the
responsible management of the world's forests. Products carrying the FSC
label are independently certified to assure consumers that they come
from forests that are managed to meet the social, economic and
ecological needs of present and future generations.

Find out more about HarperCollins and the environment at
www.harpercollins.co.uk/green

Bloodline

For Natalie with love

ACKNOWLEDGEMENTS

While this is a work of fiction, the backgrounds are authentic, and I wish to express my gratitude to those who so generously contributed to my research. If, in adapting their information to the requirements of a novel, I have found it necessary to expand or contract certain time elements, I take full responsibility. My deepest appreciation goes to:

Dr Margaret M. McCarron
Associate Medical Director
Los Angeles County, University of Southern California

Dean Brady, USC Pharmacy School

Dr Gregory A. Thompson
Director, Drug Information Center
Los Angeles County, University of Southern California

Dr Bernd W. Schulze
Drug Information Center
Los Angeles County, University of Southern California

Dr Judy Flesh
Urs Jäggi, Hoffman-La Roche & Co. A.G., Basel

Dr Gunter Siebel, Schering A.G., Berlin

The Criminal Investigation Divisions of Scotland Yard, Zurich and Berlin

Charles Walford, Sotheby Parke Bernet, London

And to Jorja, who makes all things possible.

*The physician will carefully
prepare a mixture of crocodile
dung, lizard flesh, bats' blood
and camels' spit . . .*

from a papyrus listing
811 prescriptions used
by the Egyptians in
1550 BC

BOOK ONE

BOOK ONE

ONE

Istanbul
Saturday, September 5
10 p.m.

He was seated in the dark, alone, behind the desk of Hajib Kafir, staring unseeingly out of the dusty office window at the timeless minarets of Istanbul. He was a man who was at home in a dozen capitals of the world, but Istanbul was one of his favourites. Not the tourist Istanbul of Beyoglu Street, or the gaudy Lalezab Bar of the Hilton, but the out-of-the-way places that only the Moslems knew: the *yalis*, and the small markets beyond the *souks*, and the Telli Baba, the cemetery where only one person was buried, and the people came to pray to him.

His waiting had the patience of a hunter, the quiet stillness of a man in control of his body and his emotions. He was Welsh, with the dark, stormy good looks of his ancestors. He had black hair and a strong face, and quick intelligent eyes that were

3

a deep blue. He was over six feet tall, with the lean, muscular body of a man who kept himself in good physical condition. The office was filled with the odours of Hajib Kafir, his sickly sweet tobacco, his acrid Turkish coffee, his fat, oily body. Rhys Williams was unaware of them. He was thinking about the telephone call he had received from Chamonix an hour earlier.

'. . . A terrible accident! Believe me, Mr Williams, we are all devastated. It happened so quickly that there was no chance to save him. Mr Roffe was killed instantly . . .'

Sam Roffe, president of Roffe and Sons, the second largest pharmaceutical company in the world, a multi-billion-dollar dynasty that girdled the globe. It was impossible to think of Sam Roffe as being dead. He had always been so vital, so full of life and energy, a man on the move, living in aeroplanes that raced him to company factories and offices all over the world, where he solved problems others could not deal with, created new concepts, pushed everyone to do more, to do better. Even though he had married, and fathered a child, his only real interest had been the business. Sam Roffe had been a brilliant and extraordinary man. Who could replace him? Who was capable of running the enormous empire he had left? Sam Roffe had not chosen an heir apparent. But then he had not planned to die at fifty-two. He had thought there would be plenty of time.

And now his time had run out.

The lights in the office suddenly flashed on and Rhys Williams looked towards the doorway, momentarily blinded.

'Mr Williams! I did not know anyone was here.'

It was Sophie, one of the company secretaries, who was assigned to Rhys Williams whenever he was in Istanbul. She was Turkish, in her middle twenties, with an attractive face and a lithe, sensuous body, rich with promise. She had let Rhys know in subtle, ancient ways that she was available to bring him whatever pleasures he wished, whenever he desired them, but Rhys was not interested.

Now she said, 'I returned to finish some letters for Mr Kafir.' She added softly, 'Perhaps there is something I can do for you?'

As she moved closer to the desk, Rhys could sense the musky smell of a wild animal in season.

'Where is Mr Kafir?'

Sophie shook her head regretfully. 'He has left for the day.' She smoothed the front of her dress with the palms of soft, clever hands. 'Can I help you in some way?' Her eyes were dark and moist.

'Yes,' Rhys said. 'Find him.'

She frowned. 'I have no idea where he could –'

'Try the Kervansaray, or the Mermara.' It would probably be the former, where one of Hajib Kafir's mistresses worked as a belly dancer. Although you never knew with Kafir, Rhys thought. He might even be with his wife.

Sophie was apologetic. 'I will try, but I am afraid I –'

'Explain to him that if he's not here in one hour, he no longer has a job.'

The expression on her face changed. 'I will see what I can do, Mr Williams.' She started towards the door.

'Turn out the lights.'

Somehow, it was easier to sit in the dark with his thoughts. The image of Sam Roffe kept intruding. Mont Blanc should have been an easy climb at this time of the year, early September. Sam had tried the climb before, but storms had kept him from reaching the peak.

'I'll plant the company flag up there this time,' he had promised Rhys, jokingly.

And then the telephone call a short while ago as Rhys was checking out of the Pera Palace. He could hear the agitated voice on the telephone. '. . . They were doing a traverse over a glacier . . . Mr Roffe lost his footing and his rope broke . . . He fell into a bottomless crevasse . . .'

Rhys could visualize Sam's body smashing against the unforgiving ice, hurtling downward into the crevasse. He forced his mind away from the scene. That was the past. There was the present to worry about now. The members of Sam Roffe's family had to be notified of his death, and they were scattered in various parts of the world. A press announcement had to be prepared. The news was going to travel through international financial circles like a shock wave. With the company in the

6

midst of a financial crisis, it was vital that the impact of Sam Roffe's death be minimized as much as possible. That would be Rhys's job.

Rhys Williams had first met Sam Roffe nine years earlier. Rhys, then twenty-five, had been sales manager for a small drug firm. He was brilliant and innovative, and as the company had expanded, Rhys's reputation had quickly spread. He was offered a job at Roffe and Sons and when he turned it down, Sam Roffe bought the company Rhys worked for and sent for him. Even now he could recall the overwhelming power of Sam Roffe's presence at their first meeting.

'You belong here at Roffe and Sons,' Sam Roffe had informed him. 'That's why I bought that horse-and-buggy outfit you were with.'

Rhys had found himself flattered and irritated at the same time. 'Suppose I don't want to stay?'

Sam Roffe had smiled and said confidently, 'You'll want to stay. You and I have something in common, Rhys. We're both ambitious. We want to own the world. I'm going to show you how.'

The words were magic, a promised feast for the fierce hunger that burned in the young man, for he knew something that Sam Roffe did not. There was no Rhys Williams. He was a myth that had been created out of desperation and poverty and despair.

He had been born near the coalfields of Gwent and Carmarthen, the red, scarred valleys of Wales where layers of sandstone and saucer-shaped beds of limestone and coal puckered the green earth. He grew up in a fabled land where the very names were poetry: Brecon and Pen-y-fan and Penderyn and Glyncorrwg and Maesteg. It was a land of legend, where the coal buried deep in the ground had been created 280 million years before, where the landscape was once covered with so many trees that a squirrel could travel from the Brecon Beacons to the sea without ever touching the ground. But the Industrial Revolution had come along and the beautiful green trees were chopped down by the charcoal-burners to feed the insatiable fires of the iron industry.

The young boy grew up with the heroes of another time and another world. Robert Farrer, burned at the stake by the Roman Catholic Church because he would not take a vow of celibacy and abandon his wife; King Hywel the Good, who brought the law to Wales in the tenth century; the fierce warrior Brychen who sired twelve sons and twenty-four daughters and savagely put down all attacks on his kingdom. It was a land of glorious histories in which the lad had been raised. But it was not all glory. Rhys's ancestors were miners, every one of them, and the young boy used to listen to the tales of hell that his father and his uncles recounted. They talked of the terrible times when there was no work, when the rich coalfields of Gwent and Carmarthen had been closed in a bitter fight between the companies and the miners, and the miners were debased by a poverty that eroded ambition and pride, that sapped a man's spirit and strength and finally made him surrender.

When the mines were open, it was another kind of hell. Most of Rhys's family had died in the mines. Some had perished in the bowels of the earth, others had coughed their blackened lungs away. Few had lived past the age of thirty.

Rhys used to listen to his father and his ageing young uncles discussing the past, the cave-ins and the cripplings and the strikes; talking of the good times and the bad, and to the young boy they seemed the same. All bad. The thought of spending his years in the darkness of the earth appalled Rhys. He knew he had to escape.

He ran away from home when he was twelve. He left the valleys of coal and went to the coast, to Sully Ranny Bay and Lavernock, where the rich tourists flocked, and the young boy fetched and carried and made himself useful, helping ladies down the steep cliffs to the beach, lugging heavy picnic baskets, driving a pony-cart at Penarth, and working at the amusement park at Whitmore Bay.

He was only a few hours away from home, but the distance could not be measured. The people here were from another world. Rhys Williams had never imagined such beautiful people or such glorious finery. Each woman looked like a queen to him and the men were all elegant and splendid. This was the world where he belonged, and there was nothing he would not do to make it his.

By the time Rhys Williams was fourteen, he had saved enough money to pay for his passage to London. He spent the first three days simply walking round the huge city, staring at everything, hungrily drinking in the incredible sights and the sounds and the smells.

His first job was as a delivery boy at a draper's shop. There were two male clerks, superior beings both, and a female clerk, who made the young Welsh boy's heart sing every time he looked at her. The men treated Rhys as he was meant to be treated, like dirt. He was a curiosity. He dressed peculiarly, had abominable manners and spoke with an incomprehensible accent. They could not even pronounce his name. They called him Rice, and Rye, and Rise. 'It's pronounced Reese,' Rhys kept telling them.

The girl took pity on him. Her name was Gladys Simpkins and she shared a tiny flat in Tooting with three other girls. One day she allowed the young boy to walk her home after work and invited him in for a cup of tea. Young Rhys was overcome with nervousness. He had thought this was going to be his first sexual experience, but when he began to put his arm around Gladys, she stared at him a moment, then laughed. 'I'm not giving none of that to you,' she said. 'But I'll give you some advice. If you want to make somethin' of yourself, get yourself some proper clothes and a bit of education and learn yourself some manners.' She studied the thin, passionate young face and looked into

Rhys's deep blue eyes, and said softly, 'You're gonna be a bit of all right when you grow up.'

If you want to make somethin' of yourself . . . That was the moment when the fictitious Rhys Williams was born. The real Rhys Williams was an uneducated, ignorant boy with no background, no breeding, no past, no future. But he had imagination, intelligence and a fiery ambition. It was enough. He started with the image of what he wanted to be, who he intended to be. When he looked in his mirror, he did not see the clumsy, grubby little boy with a funny accent; his mirror image was polished and suave and successful. Little by little, Rhys began to match himself to the image in his mind. He attended night school, and he spent his weekends in art galleries. He haunted public libraries and went to the theatre, sitting in the gallery studying the fine clothes of the men seated in the stalls. He scrimped on food, so that once a month he could go to a good restaurant, where he carefully copied the table manners of others. He observed and learned and remembered. He was like a sponge, erasing the past, soaking up the future.

In one short year Rhys had learned enough to realize that Gladys Simpkins, his princess, was a cheap Cockney girl who was already beneath his tastes. He quit the draper's shop and went to work as a clerk at a chemist's shop that was part of a large chain. He was almost sixteen now, but he looked older. He had filled out and was taller.

Women were beginning to pay attention to his dark Welsh good looks and his quick, flattering tongue. He was an instant success in the shop. Female customers would wait until Rhys was available to take care of them. He dressed well and spoke correctly, and he knew he had come a long way from Gwent and Carmarthen, but when he looked in the mirror, he was still not satisfied. The journey he intended to make was still ahead of him.

Within two years Rhys Williams was made manager of the shop where he worked. The district manager of the chain said to Rhys, 'This is just the beginning, Williams. Work hard and one day you'll be the superintendent of half a dozen stores.'

Rhys almost laughed aloud. To think that that could be the height of anyone's ambition! Rhys had never stopped going to school. He was studying business administration and marketing and commercial law. He wanted more. His image in the mirror was at the top of the ladder; Rhys felt he was still at the bottom. His opportunity to move up came when a drug salesman walked in one day, watched Rhys charm several ladies into buying products they had no use for, and said, 'You're wasting your time here, lad. You should be working in a bigger pond.'

'What did you have in mind?' Rhys asked.

'Let me talk to my boss about you.'

Two weeks later Rhys was working as a salesman at the small drug firm. He was one of fifty salesmen, but when Rhys looked in his special mirror, he knew that that was not true. His only competition was himself. He was getting closer to his image now, closer to the fictitious character he was creating. A man who was intelligent, cultured, sophisticated and charming. What he was trying to do was impossible. Everyone knew that one had to be born with those qualities; they could not be created. But Rhys did it. He became the image he had envisaged.

He travelled around the country, selling the firm's products, talking and listening. He would return to London full of practical suggestions, and he quickly began to move up the ladder.

Three years after he had joined the company, Rhys was made general sales manager. Under his skilful guidance the company began to expand.

And four years later, Sam Roffe had come into his life. He had recognized the hunger in Rhys.

'You're like me,' Sam Roffe had said. 'We want to own the world. I'm going to show you how.' And he had.

Sam Roffe had been a brilliant mentor. Over the next nine years under Sam Roffe's tutelage Rhys Williams had become invaluable to the company. As time went on, he was given more and more responsibility, reorganizing various divisions, troubleshooting in whatever part of the world he was needed, coordinating the different branches of Roffe and Sons, creating new concepts. In the end

Rhys knew more about running the company than anyone except Sam Roffe himself. Rhys Williams was the logical successor to the presidency. One morning, when Rhys and Sam Roffe were returning from Caracas in a company jet, a luxurious converted Boeing 707-320, one of a fleet of eight planes, Sam Roffe had complimented Rhys on a lucrative deal that he had concluded with the Venezuelan government.

'There'll be a fat bonus in this for you, Rhys.'

Rhys had replied quietly, 'I don't want a bonus, Sam. I'd prefer some stock and a place on your board of directors.'

He had earned it, and both men were aware of it. But Sam had said, 'I'm sorry. I can't change the rules, even for you. Roffe and Sons is a privately held company. No one outside the family can sit on the board or hold stock.'

Rhys had known that, of course. He attended all board meetings, but not as a member. He was an outsider. Sam Roffe was the last male in the Roffe bloodline. The other Roffes, Sam's cousins, were females. The men they had married sat on the board of the company. Walther Gassner, who had married Anna Roffe; Ivo Palazzi, married to Simonetta Roffe; Charles Martel, married to Hélène Roffe. And Sir Alec Nichols, whose mother had been a Roffe.

So Rhys had been forced to make a decision. He knew that he deserved to be on the board, that one day he should be running the company. Present circumstances prevented it, but circumstances had a way of changing. Rhys had decided to stay, to wait and see what happened. Sam had taught him patience. And now Sam was dead.

The office lights blazed on again, and Hajib Kafir stood in the doorway. Kafir was the Turkish sales manager for Roffe and Sons. He was a short, swarthy man who wore diamonds and his fat belly like proud ornaments. He had the dishevelled air of a man who had dressed hastily. So Sophie had not found him in a nightclub. Ah, well, Rhys thought. A side-effect of Sam Roffe's death. Coitus interruptus.

'Rhys!' Kafir was exclaiming. 'My dear fellow, forgive me! I had no idea you were still in Istanbul! You were on your way to catch a plane, and I had some urgent business to –'

'Sit down, Hajib. Listen carefully. I want you to send four cables in company code. They're going to different countries. I want them hand-delivered by our own messengers. Do you understand?'

'Of course,' Kafir said, bewildered. 'Perfectly.'

Rhys glanced at the thin, gold Baume & Mercier watch on his wrist. 'The New City Post Office will be closed. Send the cables from Yeni Posthane Cad. I want them on their way within thirty minutes.' He handed Kafir a copy of the cable he had written out. 'Anyone who discusses this will be instantly discharged.'

Kafir glanced at the cable and his eyes widened.

'My God!' he said. 'Oh, my God!' He looked up at Rhys's dark face. 'How – how did this terrible thing happen?'

'Sam Roffe died in an accident,' Rhys said.

Now, for the first time, Rhys allowed his thoughts to go to what he had been pushing away from his consciousness, what he had been trying to avoid thinking about: Elizabeth Roffe, Sam's daughter. She was twenty-four now. When Rhys had first met her she had been a fifteen-year-old girl with braces on her teeth, fiercely shy and over-weight, a lonely rebel. Over the years Rhys had watched Elizabeth develop into a very special young woman, with her mother's beauty and her father's intelligence and spirit. She had become close to Sam. Rhys knew how deeply the news would affect her. He would have to tell her himself.

Two hours later, Rhys Williams was over the Mediterranean on a company jet, headed for New York.

TWO

Anna Roffe Gassner knew that she must not let herself scream again or Walther would return and kill her. She crouched in a corner of her bedroom, her body trembling uncontrollably, waiting for death. What had started out as a beautiful fairy-tale had ended in terror, unspeakable horror. It had taken her too long to face the truth: the man she had married was a homicidal maniac.

Anna Roffe had never loved anyone before she met Walther Gassner, including her mother, her father and herself. Anna had been a frail, sickly child who suffered from fainting spells. She could not remember a time when she had been free of hospitals, nurses, or specialists flown in from far-off places. Because her father was Anton Roffe, of Roffe

17

and Sons, the top medical experts flew to Anna's bedside in Berlin. But when they had examined her and tested her and finally departed, they knew no more than they had known before. They could not diagnose her condition.

Anna was unable to go to school like other children, and in time she had become withdrawn, creating a world of her own, full of dreams and fantasies, where no one else was allowed to enter. She painted her own pictures of life, because the colours of reality were too harsh for her to accept. When Anna was eighteen, her dizziness and fainting spells disappeared as mysteriously as they had started. But they had marred her life. At an age when most girls were getting engaged or married, Anna had never even been kissed by a boy. She insisted to herself that she did not mind. She was content to live her own dream life, apart from everything and everyone. In her middle twenties suitors came calling, for Anna Roffe was an heiress who bore one of the most prestigious names in the world, and many men were eager to share her fortune. She received proposals from a Swedish count, an Italian poet and half a dozen princes from indigent countries. Anna refused them all. On his daughter's thirtieth birthday, Anton Roffe moaned, 'I'm going to die without leaving any grandchildren.'

On her thirty-fifth birthday Anna had gone to Kitzhübel, in Austria, and there she had met Walther Gassner, a ski instructor thirteen years younger than herself.

The first time Anna had seen Walther the sight of him had literally taken her breath away. He was skiing down the *Hahnenkamm*, the steep racing slope, and it was the most beautiful sight Anna had ever seen. She had moved closer to the bottom of the ski run to get a better look at him. He was like a young god, and Anna had been satisfied to do nothing but watch him. He had caught her staring at him.

'Aren't you skiing, *gnädiges Fräulein?*'

She had shaken her head, not trusting her voice, and he had smiled and said, 'Then let me buy you lunch.'

Anna had fled in a panic, like a schoolgirl. From then on, Walther Gassner had pursued her. Anna Roffe was not a fool. She was aware that she was neither pretty nor brilliant, that she was a plain woman, and that, aside from her name, she had seemingly very little to offer a man. But Anna knew that trapped within that ordinary façade was a beautiful, sensitive girl filled with love and poetry and music.

Perhaps because Anna was not beautiful, she had a deep reverence for beauty. She would go to the great museums and spend hours staring at the paintings and the statues. When she had seen Walther Gassner it was as though all the gods had come alive for her.

Anna was having breakfast on the terrace of the Tennerhof Hotel on the second day when Walther Gassner joined her. He did look like a young god.

He had a regular, clean-cut profile, and his features were delicate, sensitive, strong. His face was deeply tanned and his teeth were white and even. He had blond hair and his eyes were a slate grey. Beneath his ski clothes Anna could see the movement of his biceps and thigh muscles, and she felt tremors going through her loins. She hid her hands in her lap so that he could not see the keratosis.

'I looked for you on the slope yesterday afternoon,' Walther said. Anna could not speak. 'If you don't ski, I'd like to teach you.' He smiled, and added, 'No charge.'

He had taken her to the *Hausberg*, the beginners' slope, for her first lesson. It was immediately apparent to them both that Anna had no talent for skiing. She kept losing her balance and falling down, but she insisted on trying again and again because she was afraid that Walther would despise her if she failed. Instead, he had picked her up after her tenth fall and had said gently, 'You were meant to do better things than this.'

'What things?' Anna had asked miserably.

'I'll tell you at dinner tonight.'

They had dined that evening and breakfasted the next morning, and then had lunch and dinner again. Walther neglected his clients. He skipped skiing lessons in order to go into the village with Anna. He took her to the casino in Der Goldene Greif, and they went sleigh-riding and shopping and hiking, and sat on the terrace of the hotel hour after hour, talking. For Anna, it was a time of magic.

20

Five days after they had met, Walther took her hands in his and said, 'Anna, *liebchen*, I want to marry you.'

He had spoiled it. He had taken her out of her wonderful fairyland and brought her back to the cruel reality of who and what she was. An unattractive, thirty-five-year-old virginal prize for fortune-hunters.

She had tried to leave but Walther had stopped her. 'We love each other, Anna. You can't run away from that.'

She listened to him lying, listened to him saying, 'I've never loved anyone before,' and she made it easy for him because she wanted so desperately to believe him. She took him back to her room, and they sat there, talking, and as Walther told Anna the story of his life, she suddenly began to believe, thinking with wonder, It is really the story of my own life.

Like her, Walther had never had anyone to love. He had been alienated from the world by his birth as a bastard, as Anna had been alienated by her illness. Like her, Walther had been filled with the need to give love. He had been brought up in an orphanage, and when he was thirteen and his extraordinary good looks were already apparent, the women in the orphanage had begun to use him, bringing him to their rooms at night, taking him to bed with them, teaching him how to please them. As a reward the young boy was given extra food and pieces of meat, and desserts made with real sugar. He received everything but love.

21

When Walther was old enough to run away from the orphanage, he found that the world outside was no different. Women wanted to use his good looks, to wear him as a badge; but it never went any deeper than that. They gave him gifts of money and clothes and jewellery, but never of themselves.

Walther was her soul-mate, Anna realized, her *doppelgänger*. They were married in a quiet ceremony at the town hall.

Anna had expected her father to be overjoyed. Instead, he had flown into a rage. 'You're a silly, vain fool,' Anton Roffe screamed at her. 'You've married a no-good fortune-hunter. I've had him checked out. All his life he's lived off women, but he's never before found anyone stupid enough to marry him.'

'Stop it!' Anna cried. 'You don't understand him.'

But Anton Roffe knew that he understood Walther Gassner only too well. He asked his new son-in-law to come to his office.

Walther looked around approvingly at the dark panelling and the old paintings hanging on the walls. 'I like this place,' Walther said.

'Yes, I'm sure it's better than the orphanage.'

Walther looked up at him sharply, his eyes suddenly wary. 'I beg your pardon?'

Anton said, 'Let's cut out the *Scheiss*. You've made a mistake. My daughter has no money.'

Walther's grey eyes seemed to turn to stone. 'What are you trying to tell me?'

'I'm not trying to tell you anything. I'm telling you. You won't get anything from Anna because she hasn't got anything. If you had done your homework more thoroughly, you would have learned that Roffe and Sons is a close-held corporation. That means that none of its stock can be sold. We live comfortably, but that's it. There is no big fortune to be milked here.' He fumbled in his pocket, drew out an envelope and threw it on the desk in front of Walther. 'This will reimburse you for your trouble. I will expect you to be out of Berlin by six o'clock. I don't want Anna ever to hear from you again.'

Walther said quietly, 'Did it ever cross your mind that I might have married Anna because I fell in love with her?'

'No,' Anton said acidly. 'Did it ever cross yours?'

Walther looked at him a moment. 'Let's see what my market price is.' He tore open the envelope and counted the money. He looked up at Anton Roffe again. 'I value myself at much higher than twenty thousand marks.'

'It's all you're getting. Count yourself lucky.'

'I do,' Walther said. 'If you want to know the truth, I think I am very lucky. Thank you.' He put the money in his pocket with a careless gesture and a moment later was walking out of the door.

Anton Roffe was relieved. He experienced a slight sense of guilt and distaste for what he had done and yet he knew it had been the only solution. Anna would be unhappy at being deserted by her groom, but it was better to have it happen now than later.

He would try to see to it that she met some eligible men of her own age, who would at least respect her if not love her. Someone who would be interested in her and not her money or her name. Someone who would not be bought for twenty thousand marks.

When Anton Roffe arrived home, Anna ran up to greet him, tears in her eyes. He took her in his arms and hugged her, and said, 'Anna, *liebchen*, it's going to be all right. You'll get over him –'

And Anton looked over her shoulder, and standing in the doorway was Walther Gassner. Anna was holding up her finger, saying, 'Look what Walther bought me! Isn't it the most beautiful ring you've ever seen? It cost twenty thousand marks.'

In the end, Anna's parents were forced to accept Walther Gassner. As a wedding gift they bought them a lovely Schinkel manor-house in Wannsee, with French furniture mixed with antiques, comfortable couches and easy chairs, a Roentgen desk in the library, and bookcases lining the walls. The upstairs was furnished with elegant eighteenth-century pieces from Denmark and Sweden.

'It's too much,' Walther told Anna. 'I don't want anything from them or from you. I want to be able to buy you beautiful things, *liebchen*.' He gave her that boyish grin and said, 'But I have no money.'

'Of course you do,' Anna replied. 'Everything I have belongs to you.'

Walther smiled at her sweetly and said, 'Does it?'

At Anna's insistence – for Walther seemed reluctant to discuss money – she explained her financial situation to him. She had a trust fund that was enough for her to live on comfortably, but the bulk of her fortune was in shares of Roffe and Sons. The shares could not be sold without the unanimous approval of the board of directors.

Anna told him. Walther could not believe it. He made her repeat the sum.

'And you can't sell the stock?'

'No. My cousin Sam won't let it be sold. He holds the controlling shares. One day . . .'

Walther expressed an interest in working in the family business. Anton was against it.

'What can a ski bum contribute to Roffe and Sons?' he asked.

But in the end he gave in to his daughter, and Walther was given a job in administration with the company. He proved to be excellent at it and advanced rapidly. When Anna's father died two years later, Walther Gassner was made a member of the board. Anna was so proud of him. He was the perfect husband and lover. He was always bringing her flowers and little gifts, and he seemed content to stay at home with her in the evening, just the two of them. Anna's happiness was almost too much for her to bear. *Ach, danke, lieber Gott*, she would say silently.

Anna learned to cook, so that she could make Walther's favourite dishes. She made *choucroute*, a bed of crunchy sauerkraut and creamy mashed potatoes heaped with a smoked pork chop, a frankfurter and a Nuremberg sausage. She prepared fillet of

25

pork cooked in beer and flavoured with cumin, and served it with a fat baked apple, cored and peeled, the centre filled with *airelles*, the little red berries.

'You're the best cook in the world, *liebchen*,' Walther would say, and Anna would blush with pride.

In the third year of their marriage, Anna became pregnant.

There was a great deal of pain during the first eight months of her pregnancy, but Anna bore that happily. It was something else that worried her.

It started one day after lunch. She had been knitting a sweater for Walther, day-dreaming, and suddenly she heard Walther's voice, saying, 'My God, Anna, what are you doing, sitting here in the dark?'

The afternoon had turned to dusk, and she looked down at the sweater in her lap and she had not touched it. Where had the day gone? Where had her mind been? After that, Anna had other similar experiences, and she began to wonder whether this sliding away into nothingness was a portent, an omen that she was going to die. She did not think she was afraid of death, but she could not bear the thought of leaving Walther.

Four weeks before the baby was due, Anna lapsed into one of her day-dreams, missed a step and fell down an entire flight of stairs.

She awakened in the hospital.

Walther was seated on the edge of the bed, holding her hand. 'You gave me a terrible scare.'

In a sudden panic she thought, The baby! I can't

feel the baby. She reached down. Her stomach was flat. 'Where is my baby?'

And Walther held her close and hugged her.

The doctor said, 'You had twins, Mrs Gassner.'

Anna turned to Walther, and his eyes were filled with tears. 'A boy and a girl, *liebchen*.'

And she could have died right then of happiness. She felt a sudden, irresistible longing to have them in her arms. She had to see them, feel them, hold them.

'We'll talk about that when you're stronger,' the doctor said. 'Not until you're stronger.'

They assured Anna that she was getting better every day, but she was becoming frightened. Something was happening to her that she did not understand. Walther would arrive and take her hand and say goodbye, and she would look at him in surprise and start to say, 'But you just got here . . .' And then she would see the clock, and three or four hours would have passed.

She had no idea where they had gone.

She had a vague recollection that they had brought the children to her in the night and that she had fallen asleep. She could not remember too clearly, and she was afraid to ask. It did not matter. She would have them to herself when Walther took her home.

The wonderful day finally arrived. Anna left the hospital room in a wheelchair, even though she insisted she was strong enough to walk. She actually felt very weak, but she was so excited that nothing mattered except the fact that she was going to see her babies. Walther carried her into the house, and he started to take her upstairs to their bedroom.

'No, no!' she said. 'Take me to the nursery.'

'You must rest now, darling. You're not strong enough to –'

She did not listen to the rest of what he was saying. She slipped out of his arms and ran into the nursery.

The blinds were drawn and the room was dark and it took Anna's eyes a moment to adjust. She was filled with such excitement that it made her dizzy. She was afraid she was going to faint.

Walther had come in behind her. He was talking to her, trying to explain something, but whatever it was was unimportant.

For there they were. They were both asleep in their cribs, and Anna moved towards them softly, so as not to disturb them, and stood there, staring down at them. They were the most beautiful children she had ever seen. Even now, she could see that the boy would have Walther's handsome features and his thick blond hair. The girl was like an exquisite doll, with soft, golden hair and a small, triangular face.

Anna turned to Walther and said, her voice choked, 'They're beautiful. I – I'm so happy.'

'Come, Anna,' Walther whispered. He put his arms around Anna, and held her close, and there was a fierce hunger in him, and she began to feel a stirring within her. They had not made love for such a long time. Walther was right. There would be plenty of time for the children later.

The boy she named Peter and the girl Birgitta. They were two beautiful miracles that she and Walther had made, and Anna would spend hour after hour in the nursery, playing with them, talking to them. Even though they could not understand her yet she knew they could feel her love. Sometimes, in the middle of play, she would turn and Walther would be standing in the doorway, home from the office, and Anna would realize that somehow the whole day had slipped by.

'Come and join us,' she would say. 'We're playing a game.'

'Have you fixed dinner yet?' Walther would ask, and she would suddenly feel guilty. She would resolve to pay more attention to Walther, and less to the children, but the next day the same thing would happen. The twins were like an irresistible magnet that drew her to them. Anna still loved Walther very much, and she tried to assuage her guilt by telling herself that the children were a part of him. Every night, as soon as Walther was asleep, Anna would slip out of bed and creep into the nursery, and sit and stare at the children until dawn started filtering into the room. Then she would turn and hurry back to bed before Walther awoke.

Once, in the middle of the night, Walther walked

into the nursery and caught her. 'What in God's name do you think you're doing?' he said.

'Nothing, darling. I was just –'

'Go back to bed!'

He had never spoken to her like that before.

At breakfast Walther said, 'I think we should take a holiday. It will be good for us to get away.'

'But Walther, the children are too young to travel.'

'I'm talking about the two of us.'

She shook her head. 'I couldn't leave them.'

He took her hand and said, 'I want you to forget about the children.'

'Forget about the children?' There was shock in her voice.

He looked into her eyes and said, 'Anna, remember how wonderful it was between us before you were pregnant? What good times we had? How much joy it was to be together, just the two of us, with no one else around to interfere?'

It was then that she understood. Walther was jealous of the children.

The weeks and months passed swiftly. Walther never went near the children now. On their birthdays Anna bought them lovely presents. Walther always managed to be out of town on business. Anna could not go on deceiving herself for ever. The truth was that Walther had no interest in the children at all. Anna felt that perhaps it was her fault, because she was *too* interested in them. *Obsessed* was the word

Walther had used. He had asked her to consult a doctor about it, and she had gone only to please Walther. But the doctor was a fool. The moment he had started talking to her, Anna had shut him out, letting her mind drift, until she heard him say, 'Our time is up, Mrs Gassner. Will I see you next week?'

'Of course.'

She never returned.

Anna felt that the problem was as much Walther's as hers. If her fault lay in loving the children too much, then his fault lay in not loving them enough.

Anna learned not to mention the children in Walther's presence, but she could hardly wait for him to leave for the office, so that she could hurry into the nursery to be with her babies. Except that they were no longer babies. They had had their third birthday, and already Anna could see what they would look like as adults. Peter was tall for his age and his body was strong and athletic like his father's. Anna would hold him on her lap and croon, 'Ah, Peter, what are you going to do to the poor fräuleins? Be gentle with them, my darling son. They won't have a chance.'

And Peter would smile shyly and hug her.

Then Anna would turn to Birgitta. Birgitta grew prettier each day. She looked like neither Anna nor Walther. She had spun-gold hair and skin as delicate as porcelain. Peter had his father's fiery temper and sometimes it would be necessary for Anna to spank him gently, but Birgitta had the disposition of an angel. When Walther was not around, Anna played records or read to them. Their favourite book was *101 Märchen*. They would insist that Anna read them the tales of ogres and goblins and witches over and over again, and at night Anna would put them to bed, singing them a lullaby:

Schlaf, Kindlein, schlaf,
Der Vater hüt't die Schaf . . .

Anna had prayed that time would soften Walther's attitude, that he would change. He did change, but for the worse. He hated the children. In the beginning Anna had told herself that it was because Walther wanted all of her love for himself, that he was unwilling to share it with anyone else. But slowly she became aware that it had nothing to do with loving her. It had to do with hating her. Her father had been right. Walther had married her for her money. The children were a threat to him. He wanted to get rid of them. More and more he talked to Anna about selling the stock. 'Sam has no right to stop us! We could take all that money and go away somewhere. Just the two of us.'

She stared at him. 'What about the children?'

His eyes were feverish. 'No. Listen to me. For both our sakes we've got to get rid of them. We must.'

It was then that Anna began to realize that he was insane. She was terrified. Walther had fired all the domestic help, and except for a cleaning woman who came in once a week, Anna and the children were alone with him, at his mercy. He needed help. Perhaps it was not too late to cure him. In the fifteenth century they gathered the insane and imprisoned them for ever on houseboats, *Narrenschiffe*, the ships of fools, but today, with modern medicine, she felt there must be something they could do to help Walther.

Now, on this day in September, Anna sat huddled on the floor in her bedroom, where Walther had locked her, waiting for him to return. She knew what she had to do. For his sake, as well as hers and the children's. Anna rose unsteadily and walked over to the telephone. She hesitated for only an instant, then picked it up and began to dial 110, the police emergency number.

An alien voice in her ear said, '*Hallo. Hier ist der Notruf der Polizei. Kann ich Ihnen helfen?*'

'*Ja, bitte!*' Her voice was choked. '*Ich –*'

A hand came out of nowhere and tore the receiver from her, and slammed it down into the cradle.

Anna backed away. 'Oh, please,' she whimpered, 'don't hurt me.'

Walther was moving towards her, his eyes bright, his voice so soft that she could hardly make out the words. '*Liebchen*, I'm not going to hurt you. I love you, don't you know that?' He touched her, and she could feel her flesh crawl. 'It's just that we don't want the police coming here, do we?' She shook her head from side to side, too filled with terror to speak. 'It's the children that are causing the trouble, Anna. We're going to get rid of them. I –'

Downstairs the front doorbell rang. Walther stood there, hesitating. It rang again.

'Stay here,' he ordered. 'I'll be back.'

Anna watched, petrified, as he walked out of the bedroom door. He slammed it behind him and she could hear the click of the key as he locked it.

I'll be back, he had said.

Walther Gassner hurried down the stairs, walked to the front door and opened it. A man in a grey messenger's uniform stood there, holding a sealed manila envelope.

'I have a special delivery for Mr and Mrs Walther Gassner.'

'Yes,' Walther said. 'I will take it.'

He closed the door, looked at the envelope in his hand, then ripped it open. Slowly, he read the message inside.

DEEPLY REGRET TO INFORM YOU THAT SAM ROFFE WAS KILLED IN A CLIMBING ACCIDENT. PLEASE BE IN ZURICH FRIDAY NOON FOR AN EMERGENCY MEETING OF THE BOARD OF DIRECTORS.

It was signed 'Rhys Williams'.

THREE

Rome
Monday, September 7
6 p.m.

Ivo Palazzi stood in the middle of his bedroom,
the blood streaming down his face. '*Mamma mia!*
Mi hai rovinato!'

'I haven't begun to ruin you, you miserable *figlio*
di putana!' Donatella screamed at him.

They were both naked in the large bedroom of
their apartment in Via Montemignaio. Donatella
had the most sensuous, exciting body Ivo Palazzi
had ever seen, and even now, as his life's blood
poured from his face, from the terrible scratches
she had inflicted on him, he felt a familiar stirring
in his loins. *Dio*, she was beautiful. There was an
innocent decadence about her that drove him wild.
She had the face of a leopard, high cheekbones
and slant eyes, full ripe lips, that nibbled him and
sucked him and – But he must not think of that

now. He picked up a white cloth from a chair to staunch the flow of blood, and too late he realized that it was his shirt. Donatella was standing in the middle of their huge double bed, yelling at him. 'I hope you bleed to death! When I've finished with you, you filthy whoremonger, there won't be enough left for a *gattino* to shit on!'

For the hundredth time Ivo Palazzi wondered how he had got himself into this impossible situation. He had always prided himself on being the happiest of men, and all his friends had agreed with him. His *friends? Everybody!* Because Ivo had no enemies. In his bachelor days he had been a happy-go-lucky Roman without a care in the world, a Don Giovanni who was the envy of half the males in Italy. His philosophy was summed up in the phrase *Farsi onore con una donna* – 'Honour oneself with a woman.' It kept Ivo very busy. He was a true romantic. He kept falling in love, and each time he used his new love to help him forget his old love. Ivo adored women, and to him they were all beautiful, from the *putane* who plied their ancient trade along the Via Appia, to the high-fashion models strutting along the Via Condotti. The only girls Ivo did not care for were the Americans. They were too independent for his tastes. Besides, what could one expect of a nation whose language was so unromantic that they would translate the name of Giuseppe Verdi to Joe Green?

Ivo always managed to have a dozen girls in various states of preparation. There were five stages. In stage one were the girls he had just met. They received daily phone calls, flowers, slim volumes of erotic poetry. In stage two were those to whom he sent little gifts of Gucci scarves and porcelain boxes filled with Perugina chocolates. Those in stage three received jewellery and clothes and were taken to dinner at El Toula, or Taverna Flavia. Those in stage four shared Ivo's bed and enjoyed his formidable skills as a lover. An assignation with Ivo was a production. His beautifully decorated little apartment on the Via Margutta would be filled with flowers, *garofani* or *papaveri*, the music would be opera, classical or rock, according to the chosen girl's taste. Ivo was a superb cook, and one of his specialities, appropriately enough, was *pollo alla cacciatora*, the hunter's chicken. After dinner, a bottle of chilled champagne to drink in bed . . . Ah, yes, Ivo loved stage four.

But stage five was probably the most delicate of them all. It consisted of a heartbreaking farewell speech, a generous parting gift and a tearful *arrivederci*.

But all that was in the past. Now Ivo Palazzi took a quick glance at his bleeding, scratched face in the mirror over his bed and was horrified. He looked as though he had been attacked by a mad threshing machine.

'Look at what you've done to me!' he cried. '*Cara*, I know you didn't mean it.'

He moved over to the bed to take Donatella in his arms. Her soft arms flew around him and as he started to hug her, she buried her long fingernails in his naked back and clawed him like a wild animal. Ivo yelled with pain.

'Scream!' Donatella shouted. 'If I had a knife, I'd cut off your *cazzo* and ram it down your miserable throat.'

'Please!' Ivo begged. 'The children will hear you.'

'Let them!' she shrieked. 'It's time they found out what kind of monster their father is.'

He took a step towards her. '*Carissima* –'

'Don't you touch me! I'd give my body to the first drunken syphilitic sailor I met on the streets before I'd ever let you come near me again.'

Ivo drew himself up, his pride offended. 'That is not the way I expect the mother of my children to talk to me.'

'You want me to talk nice to you? You want me to stop treating you like the vermin you are?' Donatella's voice rose to a scream. '*Then give me what I want!*'

Ivo looked nervously towards the door. '*Carissima* – I can't. I don't have it.'

'Then get it for me!' she cried. 'You promised!'

She was beginning to get hysterical again, and Ivo decided the best thing for him to do was to get out of there quickly before the neighbours called the *carabinieri* again.

'It will take time to get a million dollars,' he said soothingly. 'But I'll – I'll find a way.'

He hastily donned his underpants and trousers, and socks and shoes, while Donatella stormed around the room, her magnificent, firm breasts waving in the air, and Ivo thought to himself, My God, what a woman! How I adore her! He reached for his bloodstained shirt. There was no help for it. He put it on, feeling the cold stickiness against his back and chest. He took a last look in the mirror. Small pools of blood were still oozing from the deep gashes where Donatella had raked her fingernails across his face.

'*Carissima*,' Ivo moaned, 'how am I ever going to explain this to my wife?'

Ivo Palazzi's wife was Simonetta Roffe, an heiress of the Italian branch of the Roffe family. Ivo had been a young architect when he had met Simonetta. His firm had sent him to supervise some changes in the Roffe villa at Porto Ercole. The instant Simonetta had set eyes on Ivo, his bachelor days were numbered. Ivo had got to the fourth stage with her on the first night, and found himself married to her a short time later. Simonetta was as determined as she was lovely, and she knew what she wanted: she wanted Ivo Palazzi. Thus it was that Ivo found himself transformed from a carefree bachelor to the husband of a beautiful young heiress. He gave up his architectural aspirations with no regrets and joined Roffe and Sons, with a magnificent office in EUR, the section of Rome started with such high hopes by the late, ill-fated Duce.

Ivo was a success with the firm from the beginning. He was intelligent, learned quickly and everyone adored him. It was impossible not to adore Ivo. He was always smiling, always charming. His friends envied him his wonderful disposition and wondered how he did it. The answer was simple. Ivo kept the dark side of his nature buried. In fact, he was a deeply emotional man, capable of great volatile hatreds, capable of killing.

Ivo's marriage with Simonetta thrived. At first, he had feared that marriage would prove to be a bondage that would strangle his manhood to death, but his fears proved to be unfounded. He simply put himself on an austerity programme, reducing the number of his girl friends, and everything went on as before.

Simonetta's father bought them a beautiful home in Olgiata, a large private estate twenty-five kilometres north of Rome, guarded by closed gates and manned by uniformed guards.

Simonetta was a wonderful wife. She loved Ivo and treated him like a king, which was no more than he felt he deserved. There was just one tiny flaw in Simonetta. When she became jealous, she turned into a savage. She had once suspected Ivo of taking a female buyer on a trip to Brazil. He was righteously indignant at the accusation. Before the argument was over, their entire house was a shambles. Not one dish or piece of furniture was left intact, and much of it had been broken over Ivo's head. Simonetta had gone after him with a butcher's knife, threatening to kill him and then herself, and it had taken all of Ivo's strength to wrest the knife from her. They had wound up fighting on the floor, and Ivo had finally torn off her clothes and made her forget her anger. But after that incident Ivo became very discreet. He had told the buyer he could not take any more trips with her, and he was careful never to let the faintest breath of suspicion touch him. He knew that he was the luckiest man in the world. Simonetta was young and beautiful and intelligent and rich. They enjoyed the same things and the same people. It was a perfect marriage, and Ivo sometimes found himself wondering, as he transferred a girl from stage two to stage three, and another from stage four to stage five, why he kept on being unfaithful. Then he would shrug philosophically and say to himself, Someone has to make these women happy.

Ivo and Simonetta had been married for three years when Ivo met Donatella Spolini on a business trip to Sicily. It was more of an explosion than a meeting, two planets coming together and colliding. Where Simonetta had the slender, sweet body of a young woman sculpted by Manzù, Donatella had the sensuous, ripe body of a Rubens. Her face was exquisite and her green, smouldering eyes set Ivo aflame. They were in bed one hour after they had met, and Ivo, who had always prided himself on his prowess as a lover, found that he was the pupil and Donatella the teacher. She made him rise to heights he had never achieved before, and her body did things to his that he had never dreamed possible. She was an endless cornucopia of pleasure, and as Ivo lay in bed, his eyes closed, savouring incredible sensations, he knew he would be a fool to let Donatella go.

And so Donatella had become Ivo's mistress. The only condition she imposed was that he had to get rid of all the other women in his life, except his wife. Ivo had happily agreed. That had been eight years ago, and in all that time Ivo had never been unfaithful to either his wife or his mistress. Satisfying two hungry women would have been enough to exhaust an ordinary man, but in Ivo's case it was exactly the opposite. When he made love to Simonetta he thought about Donatella and her ripe, full body, and he was filled with lust. And when he made love to Donatella, he thought of Simonetta's sweet young breasts and tiny *culo* and he performed like a wild man. No matter which woman he was with, he felt that he was cheating the other. It added enormously to his pleasure.

Ivo bought Donatella a beautiful apartment in Via Montemignaio, and he was with her every moment that he could manage. He would arrange to be away on a sudden business trip and, instead of leaving, he would spend the time in bed with Donatella. He would stop by to see her on his way to the office, and he would spend his afternoon siestas with her. Once, when Ivo sailed to New York on the *QE 2* with Simonetta, he installed

42

Donatella in a cabin one deck below. They were the five most stimulating days of Ivo's life.

On the evening that Simonetta announced to Ivo that she was pregnant, Ivo was filled with an indescribable joy. A week later Donatella informed Ivo that *she* was pregnant, and Ivo's cup ran over. Why, he asked himself, are the gods so good to me? In all humility, Ivo sometimes felt that he did not deserve all the great pleasures that were being bestowed upon him.

In due course Simonetta gave birth to a girl and a week later Donatella gave birth to a boy. What more could any man ask? But the gods were not finished with Ivo. A short time later, Donatella informed Ivo that she was pregnant again, and the following week Simonetta also became pregnant. Nine months later, Donatella gave Ivo another son and Simonetta presented her husband with another daughter. Four months later, both women were pregnant again and this time they gave birth on the same day. Ivo frantically raced from the Salvator Mundi, where Simonetta was ensconced, to the Santa Chiera Clinic where Ivo had taken Donatella. He sped from hospital to hospital, driving on the Raccordo Anulare, waving to the girls sitting in front of their little tents along the sides of the road, under pink umbrellas, waiting for customers. Ivo was driving too fast to see their faces, but he loved them all and wished them well.

Donatella gave birth to another boy and Simonetta to another girl.

Sometimes Ivo wished it had been the other way round. It was ironical that his wife had borne him daughters and his mistress had borne him sons, for he would have liked male heirs to carry on his name. Still, he was a contented man. He had three children with outdoor plumbing, and three children with indoor plumbing. He adored them and he was wonderful to them, remembering their birthdays, their saints' days, and their names. The girls were called Isabella and Benedetta and Camilla. The boys were Francesco and Carlo and Luca.

As the children grew older, life began to get more complicated for Ivo. Including his wife, his mistress and his six children, Ivo had to cope with eight birthdays, eight saints' days, and two of every holiday. He made sure that the children's schools were well separated. The girls were sent to Saint Dominique, the French convent on the Via Cassia, and the boys to Massimo, the Jesuit school in EUR. Ivo met and charmed all their teachers, helped the children with their homework, played with them, fixed their broken toys. It taxed all of Ivo's ingenuity to handle two families and keep them apart, but he managed. He was truly an exemplary father, husband and lover. On Christmas Day he stayed home with Simonetta, Isabella, Benedetta and Camilla. On *Befana*, the sixth of January, Ivo dressed up as the *Befana*, the witch, and handed

44

out presents and *carbone*, the black rock candy prized by children, to Francesco, Carlo and Luca.

Ivo's wife and his mistress were lovely, and his children were bright and beautiful, and he was proud of them all. Life was wonderful.

And then the gods spat in Ivo Palazzi's face.

As in the case of most major disasters, this one struck without any warning.

Ivo had made love to Simonetta that morning before breakfast, and then had gone directly to his office, where he did a profitable morning's work. At one o'clock he told his secretary – male, at Simonetta's insistence – that he would be at a meeting the rest of the afternoon.

Smiling at the thought of the pleasures that lay ahead of him, Ivo circled the construction that blocked the street along the Lungo Tevere, where they had been building a subway for the past seventeen years, crossed the bridge to the Corso Francia, and thirty minutes later was driving into his garage at Via Montemignaio. The instant Ivo opened the door of the apartment, he knew something was terribly wrong. Francesco, Carlo and Luca were clustered around Donatella, sobbing, and as Ivo walked towards Donatella, she looked at him with an expression of such hatred on her face that for a moment Ivo thought he must have entered the wrong apartment.

'*Stronzo!*' she screamed at him.

Ivo looked around him, bewildered. '*Carissima* –

children – what's wrong? What have I done?'

Donatella rose to her feet. 'Here's what you've done!' She threw a copy of the magazine *Oggi* in his face. 'Look at it!'

Bewildered, Ivo reached down and picked up the magazine. Staring out from the cover was a photograph of himself, Simonetta and their three daughters. The caption read: *Padre di Famiglia*.

Dio! He had forgotten all about it. Months before, the magazine had asked permission to do a story about him and he had foolishly agreed. But Ivo had never dreamed that it would be given this prominence. He looked over at his sobbing mistress and children, and said, 'I can explain this . . .'

'Their schoolmates have already explained it,' Donatella shrieked. 'My children came home crying because everybody at school is calling them bastards!'

'*Cara*, I –'

'My landlord and the neighbours have treated us like lepers. We can't hold up our heads any more. I have to get them out of here.'

Ivo stared at her, shocked. 'What are you talking about?'

'I'm leaving Rome, and I'm taking my sons with me.'

'They're mine too,' he shouted. 'You can't do it.'

'Try to stop me and I'll kill you!'

It was a nightmare. Ivo stood there, watching his three sons and his beloved mistress in hysterics, and he thought, This can't be happening to me.

But Donatella was not finished with him. 'Before we go,' she announced, 'I want one million dollars. In cash.'

It was so ridiculous that Ivo started to laugh. 'A million –'

'Either that, or I telephone your wife.'

That had happened six months earlier. Donatella had not carried out her threat – not yet – but Ivo knew she would. Each week she had increased the pressure. She would telephone him at the office and say, 'I don't care how you get the money. Do it!'

There was only one way that Ivo could possibly obtain such a huge sum. He had to be able to sell the stock in Roffe and Sons. It was Sam Roffe who was blocking the sale, Sam who was jeopardizing Ivo's marriage, his future. He had to be stopped. If one knew the right people, anything could be done.

What hurt Ivo more than anything was that Donatella – his darling, passionate mistress – would not let him touch her. Ivo was permitted to visit the children every day, but the bedroom was off limits.

'After you give me the money,' Donatella promised, 'then I will let you make love to me.'

It was out of desperation that Ivo telephoned Donatella one afternoon and said, 'I'm coming right over. The money is arranged.'

He would make love to her first and placate her later. It had to work out that way. He had managed to undress her, and when they were both naked, he had told her the truth. 'I don't have the money yet, *cara*, but one day soon –'

It was then that she had attacked him like a wild animal.

Ivo was thinking of these things now, as he drove away from Donatella's apartment (as he now thought of it) and turned north on to the crowded Via Cassia, towards his home at Olgiata. He glanced at his face in the rearview mirror. The bleeding had lessened, but the scratches were raw-looking and discoloured. He looked down at his shirt, stained with blood. How was he going to explain to Simonetta the scratches on his face and his back? For one reckless moment Ivo actually considered telling her the truth, but he dismissed the thought as quickly as it came into his head. He might – just might – have been able to confess to Simonetta that in a moment of mental aberration he had gone to bed with a girl and got her pregnant, and he might – he just *might* – have got away with a whole skin. But *three children?* Over a period of *three years?* His life would not be worth a five-lire piece. There was no way he could avoid going home now, for they were expecting guests for dinner, and Simonetta would be waiting for him. Ivo was trapped. His marriage was finished. Only San Genaro, the patron saint of miracles, could help him. Ivo's eye was caught by a sign at the side of the Via Cassia. He suddenly slammed on the brakes, turned off the highway and brought the car to a stop.

Thirty minutes later, Ivo drove through the gates

of Olgiata. Ignoring the stares of the guards as they saw his torn face and bloodstained shirt, Ivo drove along the winding roads, came to the turn that led to his driveway, and pulled up in front of his house. He parked the car, opened the front door of the house and walked into the living-room. Simonetta and Isabella, their eldest daughter, were in the room. A look of shock came over Simonetta's face as she saw her husband.

'Ivo! What happened?'

Ivo smiled awkwardly, trying to ignore the pain it cost, and admitted sheepishly, 'I'm afraid I did something stupid, *cara* –'

Simonetta was moving closer, studying the scratches on his face, and Ivo could see her eyes begin to narrow. When she spoke, her voice was frosty. 'Who scratched your face?'

'Tiberio,' Ivo announced. From behind his back he produced a large, spitting, ugly grey cat that leaped out of his arms and raced off. 'I bought it for Isabella, but the damned thing attacked me while I was trying to put it in its basket.'

'*Povero amore mio!*' Instantly, Simonetta was at his side. '*Angelo mio!* Come upstairs and lie down. I'll get the doctor. I'll get some iodine. I'll –'

'No, no! I'm fine,' Ivo said bravely. He winced as she put her arms around him. 'Careful! I'm afraid he's clawed my back, too.'

'*Amore!* How you must be suffering!'

'No, really,' Ivo said. 'I feel good.' And he meant it.

The front doorbell rang.

'I'll go,' Simonetta said.

'No, I'll go,' Ivo said quickly. 'I – I'm expecting some important papers from the office.'

He hurried to the front door and opened it.

'Signor Palazzi?'

'*Sì.*'

A messenger, dressed in a grey uniform, handed him an envelope. Inside was a teletype from Rhys Williams. Ivo read the message rapidly. He stood there for a long, long time.

Then he took a deep breath and went upstairs to get ready for his guests.

FOUR

Buenos Aires
Monday, September 7
3 p.m.

The Buenos Aires autodrome on the dusty out-skirts of Argentina's capital city was crammed with fifty thousand spectators who had come to watch the championship classic. It was a 115-lap race over the almost four-mile circuit. The race had been running for nearly five hours, under a hot, punishing sun, and out of a starting field of thirty cars only a handful remained. The crowd was seeing history being made. There had never been such a race before, and perhaps never would be again. All the names that had become legend were on the track this day: Chris Amon from New Zealand, and Brian Redman from Lancashire. There was the Italian Andrea di Adamici, in an Alfa-Romeo Tipo 33, and Carlos Maco of Brazil, in a March Formula 1. The prize-winning Belgian

Jacky Ickx was there, and Sweden's Reine Wisell in a BRM.

The track looked like a rainbow gone mad, filled with the swirling reds and greens and black and white and golds of the Ferraris and Brabhams and McLaren M19-As and Lotus Formula 3s.

As lap after gruelling lap went by, the giants began to fall. Chris Amon was in fourth place when his throttle jammed open. He sideswiped Brian Redman's Cooper before he brought his own car under control by cutting the ignition, but both cars were finished. Reine Wisell was in first position, with Jacky Ickx close behind the BRM. On the far turn, the BRM gearbox disintegrated and the battery and electrical equipment caught fire. The car started spinning, and Jacky Ickx's Ferrari was caught in the vortex.

The crowd was in a frenzy.

Three cars were outpacing the rest of the field, Jorje Amandaris from Argentina, driving a Surtees; Nils Nilsson from Sweden in a Matra; and a Ferrari 312 B-2, driven by Martel of France. They were driving brilliantly, daring the straight track, challenging the curves, moving up.

Jorje Amandaris was in the lead, and because he was one of them, the Argentinians cheered him madly. Close behind Amandaris was Nils Nilsson, at the wheel of a red and white Matra, and behind him the black and gold Ferrari, driven by Martel of France.

The French car had gone almost unnoticed until

the last five minutes, when it had started gaining on the field. It had reached tenth position, then seventh, then fifth. And it was coming on strongly. The crowd was watching now as the French driver started moving up on number two, driven by Nilsson. The three cars were travelling at speeds in excess of 180 miles an hour. That was dangerous enough at carefully contoured race tracks like Brands Hatch or Watkins Glen, but on the cruder Argentine track it was suicide. A red-coated referee stood at the side of the track, holding up a sign: FIVE LAPS.

The French black and gold Ferrari attempted to pass Nilsson's Matra on the outside, and Nilsson inched over, blocking the French car's way. They were lapping a German car on the inside track, moving up on it fast. Now it was opposite Nilsson's car. The French car dropped back and edged over so that it was positioned in the tight space behind the German car and Nilsson's Matra. With a quick burst of acceleration the French driver made for the narrow slot, forcing the two cars out of its way and shooting ahead into the number two spot. The crowd, which had been holding its breath, roared its approval. It had been a brilliant, dangerous manoeuvre.

It was Amandaris in the lead now, Martel second and Nilsson in third position, with three laps remaining. Amandaris had seen the move. The French driver is good, Amandaris told himself, but not good enough to beat me. Amandaris intended to win this race. Ahead of him he saw the sign being flashed – TWO LAPS. The race was almost over, and it was his. Out of the corner of his eye he could see the black and gold Ferrari trying to pull up alongside him. He got a glimpse of the driver's goggled, dirt-streaked face, tight and determined. Amandaris gave an inward sigh. He regretted what he was about to do, but he had no choice. Racing was not a game for sportsmen, it was a game for winners.

The two cars were approaching the north end of the oval, where there was a high banking turn, the most dangerous in the track, the scene of a dozen crashes. Amandaris shot another quick look at the French driver of the Ferrari and then tightened his grip on the wheel. As the two cars started to approach the curve, Amandaris imperceptibly lifted his foot from the accelerator, so that the Ferrari began to pull ahead. He saw the driver give him a quick, speculative look. Then the driver was abreast of him, falling into his trap. The crowd was screaming. Jorje Amandaris waited until the black and gold Ferrari was fully committed to passing him on the outside. At that moment Amandaris opened his throttles wide and started to move towards the right, cutting the French driver's path to the straight, so that the only choice was to head up the embankment.

Amandaris saw the sudden, dismayed expression on the French driver's face and silently said, *Salaud!* At that instant the driver of the French car turned the wheel directly into Amandaris's Surtees. Amandaris could not believe it. The Ferrari was on a crash course with him. They were only three feet apart and at that speed Amandaris had to make a split-second decision. *How could anyone have known that the French driver was completely loco?* In a swift, reflex action, Amandaris swung the wheel sharply to the left, trying to avoid the thousand pounds of metal hurtling at him, and braked hard, so that the French car missed him by a fraction of an inch, and shot past him towards the finish line. For a moment Jorje Amandaris's car fishtailed, then went out of control into a spin, flinging itself wildly across the track, rolling over and over until it burst into a tower of red and black flames.

But the crowd's attention was riveted on the French Ferrari, roaring across the finishing line to victory. There were wild screams from the spectators as they ran towards the car, surrounding it, cheering. The driver slowly stood up and took off the racing goggles and helmet.

She had wheat-coloured hair, cut short, and her face was sculptured with strong, firm features. There was a classic cold beauty about her. Her body was trembling, not with exhaustion, but with excitement, the memory of the moment when she had looked into Jorje Amandaris's eyes as she sent him to his death. Over the loudspeaker the announcer was excitedly yelling, 'The winner is Hélène Roffe-Martel, from France, driving a Ferrari.'

Two hours later, Hélène and her husband, Charles, were in their suite in the Ritz Hotel in downtown

Buenos Aires, lying on the rug in front of the fireplace, and Hélène was naked on top of him in the classic position of *la diligence de Lyon*, and Charles was saying, 'Oh, Christ! Please don't do that to me! Please!'

And his begging increased her excitement and she began to put on more pressure, hurting him, watching the tears come to his eyes. I'm being punished for no reason, Charles thought. He dreaded to think what Hélène would do to him if she ever found out about the crime he had committed.

Charles Martel had married Hélène Roffe for her name and for her money. After the ceremony she had kept her name, along with his, and she had kept her money. By the time Charles found out he had made a bad bargain, it was too late.

Charles Martel was a junior attorney in a large Paris law firm when he first met Hélène Roffe. He had been asked to bring some documents into the conference room, where a meeting was taking place. In the room were the four senior partners in the firm, and Hélène. Charles had heard of her. Everyone in Europe had. She was an heiress to the Roffe pharmaceutical fortune. She was wild and unconventional, and the newspapers and magazines adored her. She was a champion skier; flew her own Learjet, had led a mountain-climbing expedition in Nepal, raced cars and horses, and changed men as casually as she changed her wardrobe. Her photograph was constantly appearing in *Paris-Match* and

Jours de France. She was in the law office now because the firm was handling her divorce. Her fourth or fifth, Charles Martel was not sure which, nor was he interested. The Roffes of the world were out of his reach.

Charles handed the papers to his superior, nervous, not because Hélène Roffe was in the room – he hardly glanced at her – but because of the presence of the four senior partners. They represented Authority, and Charles Martel respected Authority. He was basically a retiring man, content to make a modest living, reside in a little apartment in Passy and tend to his small stamp collection.

Charles Martel was not a brilliant attorney, but he was a competent one, thorough and reliable. He had a stiff *petsec* dignity about him. He was in his early forties and his physical appearance, while not unattractive, was certainly far from prepossessing. Someone had once said that he had the personality of wet sand, and the description was not an unjust one. It was with a good deal of surprise, therefore, that the day after he had met Hélène Roffe, Charles Martel received a summons to go to the office of M. Michel Sachard, the senior partner, where he was told, 'Hélène Roffe wishes you to assume personal charge of her divorce case. You will take over at once.'

Charles Martel was stunned. He asked, 'Why me, Monsieur Sachard?'

Sachard looked him in the eye and replied, 'I can't imagine. See that you service her well.'

Being in charge of Hélène's divorce action made it necessary for Charles to see her frequently. Too frequently, he felt. She would telephone him and invite him to dinner at her villa in Le Vésinet to discuss the case, and to the opera and to her house in Deauville. Charles kept trying to explain to her that it was a simple case, that there would be no problem in obtaining the divorce, but Hélène – she insisted that he call her Hélène, to his acute embarrassment – told him she needed his constant reassurance. Later he was to think back on that with bitter amusement.

During the weeks that followed their first meeting, Charles began to suspect that Hélène Roffe was interested in him romantically. He could not believe it. He was a nobody, and she was a member of one of the great families, but Hélène left him in no doubt as to her intentions. 'I'm going to marry you, Charles.'

He had never thought of getting married. He was not comfortable with women. Besides, he did not love Hélène. He was not even certain he liked her. The fuss and attention that attended her wherever they went discomfited him. He was caught in the limelight of her celebrity and it was a role he was not accustomed to. He was also painfully aware of the contrast between them. Her flamboyance was an irritant to his conservative nature. She set fashion styles and was the epitome of glamour, while he – well, he was a simple, ordinary, middle-aged lawyer. He could not understand what Hélène Roffe saw in him. Nor could anyone else. Because of her well-publicized participation in dangerous sports that were normally the exclusive province of men, there were rumours that Hélène Roffe was an advocate of the women's liberation movement. In fact, she despised the movement, and had only contempt for its concept of equality. She saw no reason why men should be allowed to become the equal of women. Men were handy to have around, when required. They were not particularly intelligent, but they could be taught to fetch and light cigarettes, run errands, open doors and give satisfaction in bed. They made excellent pets, dressed and bathed themselves and were toilet-trained. An amusing species.

Hélène Roffe had had the playboys, the daredevils, the tycoons, the glamour boys. She had never had a Charles Martel. She knew exactly what he was: *Nothing*. A piece of blank clay. And that was precisely the challenge. She intended to take him over, mould him, see what she could make of him. Once Hélène Roffe made up her mind, Charles Martel never had a chance.

They were married in Neuilly and they honeymooned in Monte Carlo, where Charles lost his virginity and his illusions. He had planned to return to the law firm.

'Don't be a fool,' his bride said. 'Do you think I want to be married to a law clerk? You'll go into the family business. One day you'll be running it. *We'll* be running it.'

Hélène arranged for Charles to work in the Paris branch of Roffe and Sons. He reported to her on everything that went on and she guided him, helped him, gave him suggestions to make. Charles's advancement was rapid. He was soon in charge of the French operation, and a member of the board of directors. Hélène Roffe had changed him from an obscure lawyer to an executive of one of the largest corporations in the world. He should have been ecstatic. He was miserable. From the first moment of their marriage Charles found himself totally dominated by his wife. She chose his tailor, his shoemaker and his shirtmaker. She got him into the exclusive Jockey Club. Hélène treated Charles like a gigolo. His salary went directly to her, and she gave him an embarrassingly small allowance. If Charles needed any extra money, he had to ask Hélène for it. She made him account for every moment of his time, and he was at her constant beck and call. She seemed to enjoy humiliating him. She would telephone him at the office and order him to come home immediately with a jar of massage cream, or something equally stupid. When he arrived, she would be in the bedroom, naked, waiting for him. She was insatiable, an animal. Charles had lived with his mother until he was thirty-two, when she had died of cancer. She had been an invalid for as long as Charles could remember, and he had taken care of her. There had been no time to think about going out with girls or getting married. His mother had been a burden and when she died, Charles thought he would feel a sense of freedom. Instead, he felt a sense of loss. He had no interest in women or sex. He had, in a naïve burst of candour, explained his feelings to Hélène when she had first mentioned marriage. 'My – my libido is not very strong,' he had said.

Hélène had smiled. 'Poor Charles. Don't worry about sex. I promise you, you'll like it.'

He hated it. That only seemed to add to Hélène's pleasure. She would laugh at him for his weakness, and force him to do disgusting things that made Charles feel degraded and sick. The sex act was debasing enough. But Hélène was interested in experimenting. Charles never knew what to expect. Once, at the moment he was having an orgasm, she had put crushed ice on his testicles, and another time she had shoved an electric prod up his anus. Charles was terrified of Hélène. She made him feel that she was the male and he was the female. He tried to salvage his pride but, alas, he could find no area in which Hélène was not superior to him. She had a brilliant mind. She knew as much about the law as he did, and much more about business. She spent hour after hour discussing the company with him. She never tired of it. 'Think of all that power, Charles! Roffe and Sons can make or break more than half the countries in the world. I should be running the company. My great-grandfather founded it. It's part of me.'

After one of these outbursts Hélène would be sexually insatiable, and Charles was forced to satisfy her in ways that did not bear thinking about. He came to despise her. His one dream was to get away from her, to escape. But for that he needed money.

One day, over lunch, a friend of his, René Duchamps, told Charles about an opportunity to make a fortune.

'An uncle of mine who owned a large vineyard in Burgundy has just died. The vineyard is going to be put up for sale – ten thousand acres of first-class *Appelation d'origine contrôlée*. I have the inside track,' René Duchamps continued, 'because it's my family. I don't have enough to swing the deal by myself, but if you came in with me, we could double our money in one year. At least, come and look at it.'

Because Charles could not bear to admit to his friend that he was penniless, he went to the rolling red slopes of Burgundy to view the land. He was deeply impressed.

René Duchamps said, 'We'll each put in two million francs. In a year we'll each have four million.'

Four million francs! It would mean freedom, escape. He could go away to some place where Hélène could never find him.

'I'll think about it,' Charles promised his friend. And he did. Day and night. It was the chance of a life-time. But *how*? Charles knew that it would be impossible for him to try to borrow money without Hélène immediately learning about it. Everything was in her name, the houses, the paintings, the cars, the jewellery. The jewellery . . . those beautiful, useless ornaments she kept locked up in the safe in the bedroom. Gradually, the idea was born. If he could get hold of her jewellery, a little at a time, he could replace the pieces with copies and borrow money on the real jewellery. After he had made his killing in the vineyard, he would simply return the jewels. And have enough money to disappear for ever.

Charles telephoned René Duchamps and said, his heart pounding with excitement, 'I've decided to go in with you.'

The first part of the plan filled Charles with terror. He had to get into the safe and steal Hélène's jewellery.

The anticipation of the terrible thing he was about to do made Charles so nervous that he was barely able to function. He went through each day like an automaton, neither seeing nor hearing what was happening around him. Every time Charles saw Hélène he began to sweat. His hands would tremble at odd times. Hélène was concerned about him, as she would have been concerned about any pet. She had the doctor examine Charles, but the doctor could find nothing wrong. 'He seems a bit tense. A day or two in bed, perhaps.'

Hélène looked long at Charles, lying in bed, naked, and smiled. 'Thank you, doctor.'

The moment the doctor left, Hélène began getting undressed. 'I – I'm not feeling very strong,' Charles protested.

'I am,' Hélène replied.

He had never hated her more.

Charles's opportunity came the following week. Hélène was going to Garmisch-Partenkirchen to ski with some friends. She decided to leave Charles in Paris.

'I want you home every night,' Hélène told him. 'I'll telephone you.'

Charles watched her speed away, at the wheel of her red Jensen, and the moment she was out of sight he hurried to the wall safe. He had watched her open it often, and he knew most of the combination. It took him an hour to figure out the rest of it. With trembling fingers he pulled the safe open. There, in velvet-lined boxes, sparkling like miniature stars, lay his freedom. He had already located a jeweller, one Pierre Richaud, who was a master at duplicating jewellery. Charles had begun a long, nervous explanation about why he wanted the jewels copied, but Richaud said, matter-of-factly, 'Monsieur, I am making copies for everyone. No-one with any sense wears real jewellery on the streets these days.'

Charles gave him one piece at a time to work on, and when the copy was ready, he substituted it for the real piece. He borrowed money on the real jewellery from the Crédit Municipal, the state-owned pawnshop.

The operation took longer than Charles had anticipated. He could only get into the safe when

Hélène was out of the house, and there were unforeseen delays in copying the pieces. But finally the day came when Charles was able to say to René Duchamps, 'I'll have all the money for you tomorrow.'

He had accomplished it. He was half-owner of a great vineyard. And Hélène had not the slightest suspicion of what he had done.

Charles had secretly begun to read up on the growing of vines. And why not? Was he not a vintner now? He learned about the different vines: *cabernet sauvignon* was the principal vine used, but others were planted alongside it: *gros cabernet, merlot, malbec, petit verdot*. The desk drawers of Charles's office were filled with pamphlets on soil and wine pressing. He learned about fermentation and pruning and grafting. And that the worldwide demand for wine kept growing.

He met regularly with his partner. 'It's going to be even better than I thought,' René told Charles. 'Prices for wine are sky-rocketing. We should get three hundred thousand francs a *tonneau* for the first pressings.'

More than Charles had dreamed! The grapes were red gold. Charles began to buy travel pamphlets on the South Sea Islands and Venezuela and Brazil. The very names had a magic about them. The only problem was that there were few places in the world where Roffe and Sons did not have offices, where Hélène could not find him. And if she found him, she would kill him. He knew that, with an absolute

65

certainty. Unless he killed her first. It was one of his favourite fantasies. He murdered Hélène over and over again, in a thousand delicious ways.

Perversely, Charles now began to enjoy Hélène's abuse. All the time she was forcing him to do unspeakable things to her, he was thinking, I'll be gone soon, you *convasse*. I'll be rich on your money and there's nothing you can do about it.

And she would command, 'Faster now,' or 'Harder,' or 'Don't stop!' and he would meekly obey her.

And smile inside.

In vine-growing, Charles knew the crucial months were in the spring and summer, for the grapes were picked in September and they had to have a carefully balanced season of sun and rain. Too much sun would burn the flavour, just as too much rain would drown it. The month of June began splendidly. Charles checked the weather in Burgundy once, then twice a day. He was in a fever of impatience, only weeks away from the fulfilment of his dream. He had decided on Montego Bay. Roffe and Sons had no office in Jamaica. It would be easy to lose himself there. He would not go near Round Hill or Ocho Rios, where any of Hélène's friends might see him. He would buy a small house in the hills. Life was cheap on the island. He could afford servants, and fine food, and in his own small way live in luxury.

And so in those first days of June, Charles Martel was a very happy man. His present life was an ignominy, but he was not living in the present: he was living in the future, on a tropical, sun-bathed, wind-caressed island in the Caribbean.

The June weather seemed to get better each day. There was sun, and there was rain. Perfect for the tender little grapes. And as the grapes grew, so did Charles's fortune.

On the fifteenth day of June it began to drizzle in the Burgundy region. Then it began to rain harder. It rained day after day, and week after week, until Charles could no longer bring himself to check the weather reports.

René Duchamps telephoned. 'If it stops by the middle of July, the crop can still be saved.'

July turned out to be the rainiest month in the history of the French weather bureau. By the first of August, Charles Martel had lost every centime of the money he had stolen. He was filled with a fear such as he had never known.

'We're flying to Argentina next month,' Hélène had informed Charles. 'I've entered a car race there.'

He had watched her speeding round the track in the Ferrari, and he could not help thinking: *If she crashes, I'm free.*

But she was Hélène Roffe-Martel. Life had cast her in the role of a winner, just as it had cast him in the role of a loser.

Winning the race had excited Hélène even more than usual. They had returned to their hotel suite in Buenos Aires, and she had made Charles get undressed and lie on the rug, on his stomach. When he saw what she had in her hand as she straddled him, he said, 'Please, no!'

There was a knock on the door.

'*Merde!*' Hélène said. She waited, silent, but the knocking was repeated.

A voice called, 'Señor Martel?'

'Stay here!' Hélène commanded. She got up, whipped a heavy silk robe about her slim, firm body, walked over to the door and pulled it open. A man in a grey messenger's uniform stood there, holding a sealed manila envelope.

'I have a special delivery for Señor and Señora Martel.'

She took the envelope and closed the door.

She tore the envelope open and read the message inside, then slowly read it again.

'What is it?' Charles asked.

'Sam Roffe is dead,' she said. She was smiling.

FIVE

London
Monday, September 7
2 p.m.

White's Club was situated at the top of St James's
Street, near Piccadilly. Built as a gambling club in
the eighteenth century, White's was one of the oldest
clubs in England, and the most exclusive. Members
put their sons' names down for membership at
birth, for there was a thirty-year waiting list.

The façade of White's was the epitome of dis-
cretion. The wide bow-windows looking out on St
James's Street were meant to accommodate those
within rather than to satisfy the curiosity of the outsiders passing by. A short flight of steps led to the
entrance but, aside from members and their guests,
few people ever got past the door. The rooms in the
club were large and impressive, burnished with the
dark, rich patina of time. The furniture was old and
comfortable – leather couches, newspaper racks,

priceless antique tables and deep, stuffed armchairs that had held the posteriors of half a dozen Prime Ministers. There was a backgammon room with a large, open fireplace behind a bronze-covered rail, and a formal curved staircase led to the dining-room upstairs. The dining-room ran across the entire breadth of the house, and contained one huge mahogany table which seated thirty persons, and five side tables. At any luncheon or dinner the room contained some of the most influential men in the world.

Sir Alec Nichols, Member of Parliament, was seated at one of the small corner tables, having lunch with a guest, Jon Swinton. Sir Alec's father had been a baronet, and his father and grand-father before him. They had all belonged to White's. Sir Alec was a thin, pale man in his late forties, with a sensitive aristocratic face and an engaging smile. He had just motored in from his country estate in Gloucestershire, and was dressed in a tweed sports jacket and slacks, with loafers. His guest wore a pin-stripe suit with a loud, checked shirt and a red tie, and seemed out of place in this quiet, rich atmosphere.

'They really do you proud here,' Jon Swinton said, his mouth full, as he chewed the remains of a large veal chop on his plate.

Sir Alec nodded. 'Yes. Things have changed since Voltaire said, "The British have a hundred reli-gions and only one sauce."'

Jon Swinton looked up. 'Who's Voltaire?'

Sir Alec said, embarrassed, 'A – a French chap.'

'Oh.' Jon Swinton washed his food down with a swallow of wine. He laid down his knife and fork and wiped a napkin across his mouth. 'Well, now, Sir Alec. Time for you and I to talk a little business.'

Alec Nichols said softly, 'I told you two weeks ago I'm working everything out, Mr Swinton. I need a bit more time.'

A waiter walked over to the table, balancing a high stack of wooden cigar boxes. He skilfully set them down on the table.

'Don't mind if I do,' Jon Swinton said. He examined the labels on the boxes, whistled in admiration, pulled out several cigars which he put in his breast-pocket, then lit one. Neither the waiter nor Sir Alec showed any reaction to this breach of manners. The waiter nodded to Sir Alec, and carried the cigars to another table.

'My employers have been very lenient with you, Sir Alec. Now, I'm afraid, they've got impatient.' He picked up the burned match, leaned forward and dropped it into Sir Alec's glass of wine. 'Between you and I, they're not nice people when they're upset. You don't want to get them down on you, you know what I mean?'

'I simply don't have the money right now.'

Jon Swinton laughed loudly. 'Come off it, chum. Your mum was a Roffe, right? You've got a thousand-acre farm, a posh town house in Knightsbridge, a Rolls-Royce and a bloody Bentley. You're not exactly on the dole then, are you?'

Sir Alec looked around, pained, and said quietly, 'None of them is a liquid asset. I can't –'

Swinton winked and said, 'I'll bet that sweet little wife of yours, Vivian, is a liquid asset, eh? She's got a great pair of Bristols.'

Sir Alec flushed. Vivian's name on this man's lips was a sacrilege. Alec thought of Vivian as he had left her that morning, still sweetly asleep. They had separate bedrooms, and one of Alec Nichols's great joys was to go into Vivian's room for one of his 'visits'. Some times, when Alec awakened early, he would walk into Vivian's bedroom while she was asleep and simply stare at her. Awake or asleep, she was the most beautiful girl he had ever seen. She slept in the nude, and her soft, curved body would be half exposed as she curled into the sheets. She was blonde, with wide, pale blue eyes and skin like cream. Vivian had been a minor actress when Sir Alec had first met her at a charity ball. He had been enchanted by her looks, but what had drawn him to her was her easy, outgoing personality. She was twenty years younger than Alec, and filled with a zest for living. Where Alec was shy and introverted, Vivian was gregarious and vivacious. Alec had been unable to get her out of his mind, but it had taken him two weeks to summon up nerve enough to telephone her. To his surprise and delight Vivian had accepted his invitation. Alec had taken her to a play at the Old Vic, and then to dinner at the Mirabelle. Vivian lived in a dreary little basement flat in Notting Hill, and when Alec had brought her home, she had said, 'Would you like to come in then?' He had stayed the night, and it had changed his whole life. It was the first time that any woman had been able to bring him to a climax. He had never experienced anything like Vivian. She was velvet tongue and trailing golden hair and moist, pulsing, demanding depths that Alec explored until he was drained. He could become aroused simply thinking about her.

There was something else. She made him laugh, she made him come alive. She poked fun at Alec because he was shy and a bit stodgy, and he adored it. He was with her as often as Vivian would permit it. When Alec took Vivian to a party, she was always the centre of attention. Alec was proud of that, but jealous of the young men gathered around her, and he could not help wondering how many of them she had been to bed with.

On the nights when Vivian could not see him because she had another engagement, Alec was frantic with jealousy. He would drive to her flat and park down the block, to see what time she came home, and whom she was with. Alec knew that he was behaving like a fool, and yet he could not help himself. He was in the grip of something too strong to break.

He realized that Vivian was wrong for him, that it was out of the question for him to marry her. He was a respected Member of Parliament, with a brilliant future. He was part of the Roffe dynasty, on the board of directors of the company. Vivian had no background to help her cope with Alec's world. Her mother and father had been second-rate music-hall artists, playing the provincial circuit. Vivian had had no education except for what she had picked up in the streets, or backstage. Alec knew that she was promiscuous and superficial. She was shrewd but not particularly intelligent. And yet Alec was obsessed with her. He fought it. He tried to stop seeing her, but it was no use. He was happy when he was with her, and he was miserable when he was without her. In the end he proposed to her because he had to, and when Vivian accepted, Sir Alec Nichols was ecstatic.

His new bride moved into the family home, a beautiful old Robert Adam house in Gloucestershire, a Georgian mansion with Doric columns and a long sweeping driveway. It was set amid the green of a thousand acres of lush farmland, with its own private shooting, and running streams to fish. At the back of the house was a park that had been laid out by 'Capability Brown'.

The interior of the house was stunning. The large front hall had a stone floor and walls of painted wood. There were pairs of old lanterns and marble-topped Adam gilt-wood tables and mahogany chairs. The library had original eighteenth-century built-in bookcases, and a pair of pedestal tables by Henry Holland, and chairs designed by Thomas Hope. The drawing-room was a mixture of Hepplewhite and Chippendale, with a Wilton carpet, and a pair of Waterford glass chandeliers. There was a huge dining-room that could seat forty guests, and a smoking-room. On the second floor were six bedrooms, each with an Adam fireplace, and on the third floor were the servants' quarters.

Six weeks after she had moved into the house, Vivian said, 'Let's get out of this place. Alec.'

He looked at her, puzzled. 'You mean you'd like to go up to London for a few days?'

'I mean I want to *move* back to London.'

Alec looked out of the window at the emerald-green meadows, where he had played as a child, and at the giant sycamore and oak trees, and he said hesitantly, 'Vivian, it's so peaceful here. I –'

And she said, 'I know, luv. That's what I can't stand – the fucking peace!'

They moved to London the following week.

Alec had an elegant four-storey town house in Wilton Crescent, off Knightsbridge, with a lovely drawing-room, a study, a large dining-room, and at the back of the house, a picture window that overlooked a grotto, with a waterfall and statues and white benches set amid a beautiful formal garden. Upstairs were a magnificent master suite and four smaller bedrooms.

Vivian and Alec shared the master suite for two weeks, until one morning Vivian said, 'I love you, Alec, but you do snore, you know.' Alec had not known. 'I really must sleep alone, luv. You don't mind, do you?'

Alec minded deeply. He loved the feel of her soft body in bed, warm against him. But deep inside, Alec knew that he did not excite Vivian sexually the way other men excited her. That was why she did not want him in her bed. So now he said, 'Of course I understand, darling.'

At Alec's insistence, Vivian kept the master suite, and he moved into one of the small guest bedrooms.

In the beginning, Vivian had gone to the House of Commons and had sat in the Visitors' Gallery on days when Alec was to speak. He would look up at her and be filled with a deep, ineffable pride. She was undoubtedly the most beautiful woman there. And then came the day when Alec finished his speech and looking up for Vivian's approval, saw only an empty seat.

Alec blamed himself for the fact that Vivian was restless. His friends were older than Vivian, too conservative for her. He encouraged her to invite her young companions to the house, and brought them together with his friends. The results were disastrous.

Alec kept telling himself that when Vivian had a child, she would settle down and change. But one day, somehow – and Alec could not bear to know how – she picked up a vaginal infection and had to have a hysterectomy. Alec had longed for a son. The news had shattered him, but Vivian was unperturbed.

'Don't worry, luv,' she said, smiling. 'They took out the nursery, but they left in the playpen.'

He looked at her for a long moment, then turned and walked away.

Vivian loved to go on buying sprees. She spent money indiscriminately, recklessly, on clothes and jewellery and cars, and Alec did not have the heart to stop her. He told himself that she had grown up in poverty, hungry for beautiful things. He wanted to buy them for her. Unfortunately, he could not afford it. His salary was consumed by taxes. His fortune lay in his shares of stock in Roffe and Sons but those shares were restricted. He tried to explain that to Vivian but she was not interested. Business discussions bored her. And so Alec let her carry on.

He had first learned of her gambling when Tod Michaels, the owner of Tod's Club, a disreputable gambling place in Soho, had dropped in to see him.

'I have your wife's IOUs here for a thousand pounds, Sir Alec. She had a rotten run at roulette.'

Alec had been shocked. He had paid off the IOUs and had had a confrontation with Vivian that evening. 'We simply can't afford it,' he had told her. 'You're spending more than I'm making.'

She had been very contrite. 'I'm sorry, angel. Baby's been bad.'

And she had walked over to him and put her arms around him and pressed her body against his, and he had forgotten his anger.

Alec had spent a memorable night in her bed. He was sure now that there would be no more problems.

Two weeks later Tod Michaels had come to visit Alec again. This time Vivian's IOUs were five thousand pounds. Alec was furious. 'Why did you let her have credit?' he demanded.

'She's your wife, Sir Alec,' Michaels had replied blandly. 'How would it look if we refused her?'

'I'll – I'll have to get the money,' Alec had said. 'I don't have that much cash at the moment.'

'Please! Consider it a loan. Pay it back when you can.'

Alec had been greatly relieved. 'That's very generous of you, Mr Michaels.'

It was not until a month later that Alec learned that Vivian had gambled away another twenty-five thousand pounds, and that he was being charged interest at the rate of ten per cent a week. He was horrified. There was no way he could raise that much cash. There was nothing that he could even sell. The houses, the beautiful antiques, the cars, all belonged to Roffe and Sons. His anger frightened Vivian enough so that she promised not to gamble any more. But it was too late. Alec found himself in the hands of loan sharks. No matter how much Alec gave them, he could not manage to pay off the debt. It kept mounting each month, instead of getting smaller, and it had been going on for almost a year.

When Tod Michael's hoodlums first began to

press him for the money, Alec had threatened to go to the police commissioner. 'I have connections in the highest quarters,' Alec had said.

The man had grinned. 'I got connections in the lowest.' Now Sir Alec found himself sitting here at White's with this dreadful man, having to contain his pride, and beg for a little more time.

'I've already paid them back more than the money I borrowed. They can't –'

Swinton replied, 'That was just on the interest, Sir Alec. You still haven't paid the principal.'

'It's extortion,' Alec said.

Swinton's eyes darkened. 'I'll give the boss your message.' He started to rise.

Alec said quickly, 'No! Sit down. Please.'

Slowly Swinton sat down again. 'Don't use words like that,' he warned. 'The last chap who talked like that had both his knees nailed to the floor.'

Alec had read about it. The Kray brothers had invented the punishment for their victims. And the people Alec was dealing with were just as bad, just as ruthless. He could feel the bile rising in his throat. 'I didn't mean that,' Alec said. 'It's just that I – I don't have any more cash.'

Swinton flicked the ash from his cigar into Alec's glass of wine, and said, 'You have a big bundle of stock in Roffe and Sons, don't you, Alec baby?'

'Yes,' Alec replied, 'but it's non-saleable and non-transferable. It's no good to anyone unless Roffe and Sons goes public.'

Swinton took a puff on his cigar. 'And is it going public?'

'That's up to Sam Roffe. I've – I've been trying to persuade him.'

'Try harder.'

'Tell Mr Michaels he'll get his money,' Alec said. 'But please stop hounding me.'

Swinton stared. 'Hounding you? Why, Sir Alec, you little cocksucker, you'll know when we start hounding you. Your fucking stables will burn down, and you'll be eating roast horsemeat. Then your house will burn. And maybe your wife.' He smiled, and Alec wished he had not. 'Have you ever eaten cooked pussy?'

Alec had turned pale. 'For God's sake –'

Swinton said soothingly, 'I'm kidding. Tod Michaels is your friend. And friends help each other, right? We were talking about you at our meeting this morning. And do you know what the boss said? He said, "Sir Alec's a good sort. If he hasn't got the money, I'm sure he'll think of some other way to take care of us."'

Alec frowned. 'What other way?'

'Well, it's not hard for a bright chap like you to work something out, is it? You're running a big drug company, right? You make things like cocaine, for example. Just between you and I, who'd ever know if you happened to accidentally misplace a few shipments here and there?'

Alec stared at him. 'You're insane,' he said. 'I – I couldn't do that.'

'It's amazing what people can do when they have to,' Swinton said genially. He rose to his feet. 'You either have our money for us, or we'll tell you where to deliver the merchandise.'

He ground his cigar out on Alec's butter plate. 'Give my regards to Vivian, Sir Alec. Ta.'

And Jon Swinton was gone.

Sir Alec sat there alone, unseeing, surrounded by all the familiar, comfortable things that were so much a part of his past life, that were now threatened. The only alien thing was the obscene, wet, cigar butt on the plate. How had he ever allowed them to come into his life? He had permitted himself to be manoeuvred into a position where he was in the hands of the underworld. And now he knew that they wanted more than money from him. The money was merely the bait with which they had trapped him. They were after his connections with the drug company. They were going to try to force him to work with them. If it became known he was in their power, the Opposition would not hesitate to make capital of it. His own party would probably ask him to resign. It would be done tactfully and quietly. They would probably exert pressure on him to apply for the Chiltern Hundreds, a post that paid a nominal salary of a hundred pounds a year from the Crown. The one barrier to being an MP was that you could not be in receipt of pay from the Crown or the Government. So Alec would no longer be allowed to serve in Parliament. The reason could not be kept secret, of course. He would be in disgrace. Unless he could come up with a large sum of money. He had talked to Sam Roffe again and again, asking him to let the company go public, to let the shares of stock be marketed.

'Forget it,' Sam had told him. 'The minute we let outsiders in, we have a lot of strangers telling us how to run our business. Before you know it, they'll take over the board, and then the company. What's the difference to you, Alec? You have a big salary, an unlimited expense account. You don't *need* the money.'

For a moment Alec had been tempted to tell Sam how desperately he needed it. But he knew it would do no good. Sam Roffe was a company man, a man without compassion. If he knew that Alec had in any way compromised Roffe and Sons, he would have dismissed him without a moment's hesitation. No, Sam Roffe was the last person to whom he could turn.

Alec was facing ruin.

The reception porter at White's walked towards Sir Alec's table with a man dressed in a messenger's uniform, carrying a sealed manila envelope.

'Excuse me, Sir Alec,' the porter apologized, 'but this man insists that he has instructions to deliver something to you personally.'

'Thank you,' Sir Alec said. The messenger handed him the envelope, and the porter led him back to the door.

Alec sat there a long time before he reached for the envelope and opened it. He read the message through three times, then he slowly crumpled the paper in his fist, and his eyes began to fill with tears.

SIX

New York
Monday, September 7
11 a.m.

The private Boeing 707-320 was making its final
approach to Kennedy Airport, gliding out of the
stacked-up traffic pattern. It had been a long,
tedious flight and Rhys Williams was exhausted,
but he had been unable to sleep during the night.
He had ridden in this plane too often with Sam
Roffe. His presence still filled it.

Elizabeth Roffe was expecting him. Rhys had
sent her a cable from Istanbul, merely announcing
that he would arrive the following day. He could
have broken the news of her father's death over
the telephone but she deserved more than that.

The plane was on the ground now, taxiing
towards the terminal. Rhys carried very little luggage, and he was quickly ushered through Customs.
Outside, the sky was grey and bleak, a foretaste of

the winter to come. A limousine was waiting at the side entrance to drive him to Sam Roffe's Long Island estate, where Elizabeth would be waiting.

During the drive Rhys tried to rehearse the words that he would say to her to try to soften the blow, but the moment Elizabeth opened the front door to greet him the words flew out of his head. Each time Rhys saw Elizabeth her beauty caught him by surprise. She had inherited her mother's looks, the same patrician features, midnight black eyes framed by long, heavy lashes. Her skin was white and soft, her hair a shiny black. Her figure was rich and firm. She was wearing an open-necked, creamy silk blouse and a pleated grey-flannel skirt and fawn-coloured pumps. There was no sign of the awkward little girl Rhys had first met nine years earlier. She had become a woman, intelligent and warm and completely unselfconscious about her beauty. She was smiling at him now, pleased to see him. She took his hand and said, 'Come in, Rhys,' and led him into the large oak-panelled library. 'Did Sam fly in with you?'

There was no way to break it gently. Rhys took a deep breath and said, 'Sam had a bad accident, Liz.' He watched the colour drain from her face. She waited for him to go on. 'He was killed.'

She stood there frozen. When she finally spoke, Rhys could barely hear her. 'What – what happened?'

'We don't have any of the details yet. He was climbing Mont Blanc. A rope broke. He fell into a crevasse.'

'Did they find –'

She closed her eyes for a moment, then opened them.

'A bottomless crevasse.'

Her face had turned white. Rhys felt a quick sense of alarm. 'Are you all right?'

She smiled brightly, and said, 'Of course. I'm fine, thank you. Would you like some tea or something to eat?'

He looked at her in surprise and started to speak, and then he understood. She was in shock. She was rattling on, making no sense, her eyes unnaturally bright, her smile fixed.

'Sam was such a great athlete,' Elizabeth was saying. 'You've seen his trophies. He always won, didn't he? Did you know he climbed Mont Blanc before?'

'Liz –'

'Of course you did. You went with him once, didn't you, Rhys?'

Rhys let her talk, anaesthetizing herself against the pain, trying to build an armour of words to ward off the moment when she would have to face her own anguish. For an instant, as he listened to her, he was reminded of the vulnerable little girl he had first known, too sensitive and shy to have any protection against brutal reality. She was dangerously wound up now, tense and brittle, and there was a fragility about her that worried Rhys.

'Let me call a doctor,' he said. 'He can give you something to –'

'Oh, no. I'm really quite all right. If you don't mind, I think I'll lie down for a while. I'm feeling a bit tired.'

'Would you like me to stay?'

'Thank you. That won't be necessary.'

She walked him to the door, and as he started to get into the car Elizabeth called, 'Rhys!'

He turned.

'Thank you for coming.'

Jesus Christ.

Long hours after Rhys Williams had gone, Elizabeth Roffe lay in her bed, staring at the ceiling, watching the shifting patterns painted by the pale September sun.

And the pain came. She had not taken a sedative, because she wanted the pain. She owed that to Sam. She would be able to bear it, because she was his daughter. And so she lay there, all day and all night, thinking of nothing, thinking of everything, remembering, feeling. She laughed, and she cried, and she supposed that she was in a state of hysteria. It did not matter. There was no one to hear her. In the middle of the night, she suddenly became ravenously hungry and went down into the kitchen and devoured a large sandwich and then threw it up. She felt no better. Nothing could ease the pain that filled her. Her mind kept going back, back over the years with her father. Through her bedroom window she watched the sun rise. Some time later, one of the servants knocked at the door, and Elizabeth sent her away. Once the phone rang, and her heart leaped and she reached for it, thinking, It's Sam! Then she remembered, and snatched her hand away.

He would never call her again. She would never hear his voice again. She would never see him again.

A bottomless crevasse.

Bottomless.

Elizabeth lay there, letting the past wash over her, remembering, remembering it all.

SEVEN

The birth of Elizabeth Rowane Roffe was a double tragedy. The minor tragedy was that Elizabeth's mother died on the delivery table. The major tragedy was that Elizabeth was born a girl.

For nine months, until she emerged from the darkness of her mother's womb, she was the most eagerly awaited child in the world, heir to a colossal empire, the multi-billion-dollar giant, Roffe and Sons.

Sam Roffe's wife, Patricia, was a dark-haired woman of surpassing beauty. Many women had tried to marry Sam Roffe, for his position, his prestige, his wealth. Patricia had married him because she had fallen in love with him. It had proved to be the worst of reasons. Sam Roffe had been looking for a business arrangement, and Patricia had suited his requirements ideally. Sam had neither the time nor the temperament to be a family man. There was no room in his life for anything but Roffe and Sons. He was fanatically dedicated to the company, and he expected no less from those around him. Patricia's importance to him lay solely in the contribution she could make to the image of the company. By the time Patricia came to a realization of what kind of marriage she had made, it was too late. Sam gave her a role to play, and she played it beautifully. She was the perfect hostess, the perfect Mrs Sam Roffe. She received no love from her husband and in time Patricia learned to give none. She served Sam, and was as much an employee of Roffe and Sons as the lowliest secretary. She was on call twenty-four hours a day, ready to fly wherever Sam needed her, capable of entertaining a small company of world leaders or serving a gourmet dinner to a hundred guests at a day's notice, with crisp, heavily embroidered table cloths, gleaming Baccarat crystal, heavy Georgian silverware. Patricia was one of Roffe and Sons' unlisted assets. She worked at keeping herself beautiful, and exercised and dieted like a Spartan. Her figure was perfect, and her clothes were designed for her by Norell in New York, Chanel in Paris, Hartnell in London, and young Sybil Connolly in Dublin. The jewellery Patricia wore was created for her by Jean Schlumberger and Bulgari. Her life was busy and full and joyless and empty. Becoming pregnant had changed all that.

Sam Roffe was the last male heir of the Roffe dynasty, and Patricia knew how desperately he wanted a son. He was depending on her. And now she was the queen mother, busy with the baby within her, the young prince, who would one day inherit the kingdom. When they wheeled Patricia into the delivery room, Sam clasped her hand and said, 'Thank you'.

She was dead of an embolism thirty minutes later, and the only blessing about Patricia's death was that she died without knowing that she had failed her husband.

Sam Roffe took time off from his gruelling schedule to bury his wife, and then turned his attention to the problem of what he should do with his infant daughter.

One week after Elizabeth was born, she was taken home and turned over to a nanny, the beginning of a long series of nannies. During the first five years of her life, Elizabeth saw very little of her father. He was barely more than a blur, a stranger who was always arriving or leaving. He travelled constantly and Elizabeth was a nuisance who had to be carted along, like a piece of extra luggage. One month Elizabeth would find herself living at their Long Island estate, with its bowling alley, tennis court, swimming pool and squash court. A few weeks later, her nanny would pack Elizabeth's clothes and she would be flown to their villa in Biarritz. It had fifty rooms and thirty acres of grounds and Elizabeth kept getting lost.

In addition, Sam Roffe owned a large duplex penthouse apartment on Beekman Place, and a villa on the Costa Smeralda in Sardinia. Elizabeth travelled to all these places, shunted from house to apartment to villa, and grew up amid all the lavish elegance. But always she felt like an outsider who had wandered by mistake into a beautiful birthday party given by unloving strangers.

As Elizabeth grew older, she came to know what it meant to be the daughter of Sam Roffe. Just as her mother had been an emotional victim of the company, so was Elizabeth. If she had no family life, it was because there was no family, only the paid surrogates and the distant figure of the man who had fathered her, who seemed to have no interest in her, only in the company. Patricia had been able to accept her situation, but for the child it was torment. Elizabeth felt unwanted and unloved, and did not know how to cope with her despair, and in the end she blamed herself for being unlovable. She tried desperately to win the affection of her father. When Elizabeth was old enough to go to school, she made things for him in class, childish drawings and watercolour paintings and lopsided ashtrays, and she would guard them fiercely, waiting for him to return from one of his trips, so that she could surprise him, please him, hear him say, *It's beautiful, Elizabeth. You're very talented.*

When he returned, Elizabeth would present her love offering, and her father would glance at it absently and nod, or shake his head. 'You'll never be an artist, will you?'

Sometimes Elizabeth would awaken in the middle of the night, and walk down the long winding staircase of the Beekman Place apartment and through the large cavernous hall that led to her father's study. She would step into the empty room as if she were entering a shrine. This was *his* room, where he worked and signed important pieces of paper and ran the world. Elizabeth would walk over to his enormous leather-topped desk and slowly rub her hands across it. Then she would move behind the desk and sit in his leather chair. She felt closer to her father there. It was as though by being where he was, sitting where he sat, she could become a part of him. She would hold imaginary conversations with him, and he would listen, interested and caring as she poured out her problems. One night, as Elizabeth sat at his desk in the dark, the lights in the room suddenly came on. Her father was standing in the doorway. He looked at Elizabeth seated behind his desk, clad in a thin nightgown, and said, 'What are you doing here alone in the dark?' And he scooped her up in his arms and carried her upstairs, to her bed, and Elizabeth had lain awake all night, thinking about how her father had held her.

After that, she went downstairs every night and sat in his office waiting for him to come and get her, but it never happened again.

No one discussed Elizabeth's mother with her, but there was a beautiful full-length portrait of Patricia Roffe hanging in the reception hall, and Elizabeth would stare at it by the hour. Then she would turn to her mirror. Ugly. They had put braces on her teeth, and she looked like a gargoyle. No wonder my father isn't interested in me, Elizabeth thought.

Overnight she developed an insatiable appetite, and began to gain weight. For she had arrived at a wonderful truth: if she were fat and ugly, no one would expect her to look like her mother.

When Elizabeth was twelve years old, she attended an exclusive private school on the East Side of Manhattan, in the upper seventies. She would arrive in a chauffeur-driven Rolls-Royce, walk into her class and sit there, withdrawn and silent, ignoring everyone around her. She never volunteered to answer a question. And when she was called upon, she never seemed to know the answer. Her teachers soon got into the habit of ignoring her. They discussed Elizabeth among themselves and unanimously agreed that she was the most spoiled child they had ever seen. In a confidential year-end report to the headmistress, Elizabeth's teacher wrote:

We have been able to make no progress with Elizabeth Roffe. She is aloof from her classmates and refuses to participate in any of the group activities, but it is difficult to tell if this is because she makes no effort, or because she is unable to handle the assignments. She is arrogant and egotistical. Were it not for the fact that her father is a major benefactor of this school, I would strongly recommend expelling her.

The report was light-years from the reality. The simple truth was that Elizabeth Roffe had no protective shield, no armour against the terrible loneliness that engulfed her. She was filled with such a deep sense of her own unworthiness that she was afraid to make friends, for fear they would discover that she was worthless, unlovable. She was not arrogant, she was almost pathologically shy. She felt that she did not belong in the same world that her father inhabited. She did not belong anywhere. She loathed being driven to school in the Rolls-Royce, because she knew she did not deserve it. In her classes she knew the answers to the questions the teachers asked, but she did not dare to speak out, to call attention to herself. She loved to read, and she would lie awake late at night in her bed, devouring books.

She day-dreamed, and oh! what lovely fantasies. She was in Paris with her father, and they were driving through the Bois in a horse-drawn carriage, and he took her to his office, an enormous room something like Saint Patrick's cathedral, and people kept walking in with papers for him to sign, and he would wave them away and say, 'Can't you see I'm busy now? I'm talking to my daughter, Elizabeth.'

She and her father were skiing in Switzerland, moving down a steep slope side by side, with an icy wind whipping past them, and he suddenly fell and cried out with pain, because his leg was broken, and she said, 'Don't worry, Papa! I'll take care of you.' And she skied down to the hospital and said, 'Quickly, my father's hurt,' and a dozen men in white jackets brought him there in a shiny ambulance and she was at his bedside, feeding him (it was probably his arm that was broken, then, not his leg), and her mother walked into the room, alive somehow, and her father said, 'I can't see you now, Patricia. Elizabeth and I are talking.'

Or they would be in their beautiful villa in Sardinia, and the servants would be away, and Elizabeth would cook dinner for her father. He would eat two helpings of everything and say, 'You're a much better cook than your mother was, Elizabeth.'

The scenes with her father always ended in the same way. The doorbell would ring and a tall man, who towered over her father, would come in and beg Elizabeth to marry him, and her father would plead with her, 'Please, Elizabeth, don't leave me. I need you.'

And she would agree to stay.

Of all the homes in which Elizabeth grew up, the villa in Sardinia was her favourite. It was by no means the largest, but it was the most colourful, the friendliest. Sardinia itself delighted Elizabeth. It was a dramatic, rock-bound island, some 160 miles south-west of the Italian coast, a stunning panorama of mountains, sea and green farmland. Its enormous volcanic cliffs had been thrown up thousands of years ago from the primal sea, and the shoreline swept in a vast crescent as far as the eye could follow, the Tyrrhenian Sea framing the island in a blue border.

For Elizabeth the island had its own special odours, the smell of sea breezes and forests, the white and yellow *macchia*, the fabled flower that Napoleon had loved. There were the *corbeccola* bushes that grew six feet high and had a red fruit that tasted like strawberries, and the *guarcias*, the giant stone oaks whose bark was exported to the mainland to be used for making corks for wine bottles.

She loved to listen to the singing rocks, the mysterious giant boulders with holes through them. When the winds blew through the holes, the rocks emitted an eerie keening sound, like a dirge of lost souls.

And the winds blew. Elizabeth grew to know them all. The mistral and the *ponente*, the tramontana and the *grecate* and the levanter. Soft winds and fierce winds. And then there was the dreaded sirocco, the warm wind that blew in from the Sahara.

The Roffe villa was on the Costa Smeralda, above Porto Cervo, set high atop a cliff overlooking the sea, secluded by juniper trees and the wild-growing Sardinian olive trees with their bitter fruit. There was a breathtaking view of the harbour far below, and around it, sprinkled over the green hills, a jumble of stucco and stone houses thrown together in a crazy hodgepodge of colours resembling a child's crayon drawing.

The villa was stone, with huge juniper beams inside. It was built on several levels, with large, comfortable rooms, each with its own fireplace and balcony. The living-room and dining-room had picture windows that gave a panoramic view of the island. A free-form staircase led to four bedrooms upstairs. The furniture blended perfectly with the surroundings. There were rustic refectory tables and benches, and soft easy chairs. Across the windows were fringed white wool curtains that had been hand-woven on the island, and the floors were laid with colourful *cerasarda* tiles from Sardinia and other tiles from Tuscany. In the bathrooms and bedrooms were native wool carpets, coloured with vegetable dyes in the traditional way. The house was ablaze with paintings, a mixture of French Impressionists, Italian masters and Sardo primitives. In the hallway hung portraits of Samuel Roffe and Terenia Roffe, Elizabeth's great-great-grandfather and grandmother.

The feature of the house that Elizabeth loved most was the tower room, under the sloping tile roof. It was reached by a narrow staircase from the second floor, and Sam Roffe used it as his study. It contained a large work desk and a comfortable, padded swivel chair. The walls were lined with bookcases and maps, most of them pertaining to the Roffe empire. French windows led to a small balcony built over a sheer cliff, and the view from there was heart-stopping.

It was in this house, when she was thirteen years

old, that Elizabeth discovered the origins of her family, and for the first time in her life felt that she belonged, that she was part of something.

It began the day she found the Book. Elizabeth's father had driven to Olbia, and Elizabeth had wandered upstairs to the tower room. She was not interested in the books on the shelves, for she had long since learned that they were technical volumes on pharmacology and pharmacognosy, and on multinational corporations and international law. Dull and boring. Some of the manuscripts were rare, and these were kept in glass cases. There was a medical volume in Latin called *Circa Instans*, written in the Middle Ages, and another called *De Materia Medica*. It was because Elizabeth was studying Latin and was curious to see one of the old volumes that she opened the glass case to take it out. Behind it, tucked away out of sight, she saw another volume. Elizabeth picked it up. It was thick, bound in leather, and had no title.

Intrigued, Elizabeth opened it. It was like opening the door to another world. It was a biography of her great-great-grandfather, Samuel Roffe, in English, privately printed on vellum. There was no author given, and no date, but Elizabeth was sure that it was more than one hundred years old, for most of the pages were faded, and others were yellowed and flaking with age. But none of this was important. It was the story that mattered, a story that brought life to the portraits hanging on the wall downstairs. Elizabeth had seen the pictures of her great-great-grandparents a hundred times: paintings of an old-fashioned man and woman, dressed in unfamiliar clothes. The man was not handsome, but there was great strength and intelligence in his face. He had fair hair, high Slavic cheekbones and keen, bright blue eyes. The woman was a beauty. Dark hair, a flawless complexion and eyes as black as coal. She wore a white silk dress with a tabard over the top, and a bodice made of brocade. Two strangers who meant nothing to Elizabeth.

But now, alone in the tower room, as Elizabeth opened the Book and began to read, Samuel and Terenia Roffe became alive. Elizabeth felt as though she had been transported back in time, that she was living in the ghetto of Krakow in the year 1853, with Samuel and Terenia. As she read deeper and deeper into the Book, she learned that her great-great-grandfather Samuel, the founder of Roffe and Sons, was a romantic and an adventurer.

And a murderer.

EIGHT

Samuel Roffe's earliest memory, Elizabeth read, was of his mother being killed in a pogrom in 1855 when Samuel was five years old. He had been hidden in the cellar of the small wooden house the Roffes shared with other families in the ghetto of Krakow. When the rioting was finally over, endless hours later, and the only sound left was the weeping of the survivors, Samuel cautiously left his hiding place and went out into the streets of the ghetto to look for his mother. It seemed to the young boy that the whole world was on fire. The entire sky was red from the blazing wooden buildings that burned on every side, and clouds of thick black smoke hung everywhere. Men and women were frantically searching for their families, or trying to save their businesses and homes and meagre possessions. Krakow, in the mid-nineteenth century, had a fire department, but it was forbidden to the Jews. Here in the ghetto, at the edge of the city, they were forced to fight the holocaust by hand, with water drawn

101

from their wells, and scores of people formed bucket brigades to drown the flames. Samuel saw death wherever he looked, mutilated bodies of men and women tossed aside like broken dolls; naked, raped women and children, bleeding and moaning for help.

Samuel found his mother lying in the street, half conscious, her face covered with blood. The young boy knelt down at her side, his heart pounding wildly. 'Mama!'

She opened her eyes and saw him, and tried to speak, and Samuel knew that she was dying. He desperately wanted to save her, but he did not know how, and even as he gently wiped the blood away, it was already too late.

Later, Samuel stood there watching as the burial party carefully dug up the ground under his mother's body: for it was soaked in her blood, and according to the Scriptures, it had to be buried with her so that she could be returned to God whole.

It was at that moment that Samuel made up his mind that he wanted to become a doctor.

The Roffe family shared a three-storey, narrow, wooden house with eight other families. Young Samuel lived in one small room with his father and his Aunt Rachel, and in all his life he had never been in a room by himself or slept or eaten alone. He could not remember a single moment when he could not hear the sound of voices, but Samuel did not crave privacy, for he had no idea that it existed. He had always lived in a crowded maze.

Each evening Samuel and his relatives and friends

were locked into the ghetto by the gentiles, as the Jews penned up their goats and cows and chickens.

At sundown the massive double wooden gates of the ghetto were closed and locked with a large iron key. At sunrise the gates were opened again, and the Jewish merchants were permitted to go into the city of Krakow to conduct business with the gentiles, but they were required to be back inside the ghetto walls before sunset.

Samuel's father had come from Russia, where he had fled from a pogrom in Kiev, and he had made his way to Krakow, where he had met his bride. Samuel's father was a stooped, grey-haired man, his face worn and wrinkled, a pushcart pedlar who hawked his wares of potions and trinkets and utensils through the narrow, winding streets of the ghetto. Young Samuel loved to roam the crowded, bustling, cobblestoned streets. He enjoyed the smell of fresh-baked bread mingled with the odours of drying fish and cheeses and ripening fruit and sawdust and leather. He liked to listen to the pedlars singing out their wares, and the housewives bargaining with them in outraged, grieved tones. The variety of goods that the pedlars sold was staggering: linens and laces, ticking and yarn, leather and meats and vegetables and needles and soft soap and plucked whole chickens and candies and buttons and syrups and shoes.

On Samuel's twelfth birthday his father took him into the city of Krakow for the first time. The idea of going through the forbidden gates and seeing Krakow itself, the home of the gentiles, filled the boy with an almost unbearable excitement.

At six o'clock in the morning Samuel, wearing his one good suit, stood in the dark next to his father in front of the huge closed gates of the city, surrounded by a noisy crowd of men with crude, homemade pushcarts, wagons or barrows. The air was cold and raw, and Samuel huddled into his threadbare sheep's-wool coat.

After what seemed hours, a bright orange sun peeped over the eastern horizon and there was an expectant stir from the crowd. Moments later, the huge wooden gates began to swing open and the merchants started to pour through them like a stream of industrious ants, heading towards the city.

As they approached the wonderful, terrible city, Samuel's heart began to beat faster. Ahead he could see the fortifications towering over the Vistula. Samuel clung to his father more tightly. He was actually in Krakow, surrounded by the feared goyim, the people who locked them up every night. He stole quick, frightened glances at the faces of the passers-by and he marvelled at how different they looked. They did not wear *payves*, earlocks, and *bekeches*, the long black coats, and many of them were clean-shaven. Samuel and his father walked along the Plante towards the Rynek, the crowded market-place, where they passed the enormous cloth hall, and the twin-towered Church of Saint Mary. Samuel had never seen such magnificence. The new world was filled with wonders.

First of all, there was an exciting feeling of freedom and space that left Samuel breathless. The houses on the streets were all set apart, not jumbled together, and most of them had a small garden in front. Surely, Samuel thought, everyone in Krakow must be a millionaire.

Samuel accompanied his father to half a dozen different suppliers, where his father bought goods which he tossed into the cart. When the cart was filled, he and the boy headed back towards the ghetto.

'Can't we stay longer?' Samuel begged.

'No, son. We have to go home.'

Samuel did not want to go home. He had been outside the gates for the first time in his life, and he was filled with an elation that was so strong it almost choked him. That people could live like *this*, free to walk wherever they pleased, free to do whatever they wanted . . . Why could he not have been born outside the gate? Instantly, he was ashamed of himself for having such disloyal thoughts.

That night when Samuel went to bed, he lay awake for a long time, thinking about Krakow and the beautiful houses with their flowers and green gardens. He had to find a way to get free. He wanted to talk to someone about the things he felt, but there was no one who would understand him.

Elizabeth put the Book down and sat back, closing her eyes, visualizing Samuel's loneliness, his excitement, his frustration.

It was at that moment that Elizabeth began to identify with him, to feel that she was part of him, as he was a part of her. His blood ran in her veins. She had a wonderful, heady sense of belonging.

Elizabeth heard the sound of her father's car coming up the driveway, and she quickly put the Book away. She had no further chance to read it during her stay there, but when she returned to New York the Book was hidden at the bottom of her suitcase.

NINE

After the warm winter sunshine of Sardinia, New York seemed like Siberia. The streets were filled with snow and slush, and the wind blowing off the East River was frigid; but Elizabeth did not mind. She was living in Poland, in another century, sharing the adventures of her great-great-grandfather. Every afternoon after school, Elizabeth would rush up to her room, lock the door and take out the Book. She had thought of discussing it with her father, but she was afraid to, for fear he would take it away from her.

In a wonderful, unexpected way, it was old Samuel who gave Elizabeth encouragement. It seemed to Elizabeth that they were so much alike. Samuel was a loner. He had no one to talk to. Like me, thought Elizabeth. And because they were almost the same age – even though a century apart – she could identify with him.

Samuel wanted to be a doctor.

Only three physicians were allowed to take care

of the thousands of people crowded into the insanitary, epidemic-ridden confines of the ghetto; and of the three, the most prosperous was Dr Zeno Wal. His house stood among its poorer neighbours like a castle in the midst of a slum. It was three storeys high, and through its windows could be seen freshly washed and starched white-lace curtains and glimpses of shining, polished furniture. Samuel could visualize the doctor inside, treating his patients, helping them, curing them: doing what Samuel longed to do. Surely, if someone like Dr Wal took an interest in him, Samuel thought, he could help him to become a doctor. But as far as Samuel was concerned, Dr Wal was as inaccessible as any of the gentiles living in the city of Krakow, outside the forbidden wall.

From time to time Samuel would catch glimpses of the great Dr Zeno Wal walking along the street, engaged in earnest conversation with a colleague. One day, as Samuel was passing the Wal house, the front door opened and the doctor came out with his daughter. She was about Samuel's age, and she was the most beautiful creature Samuel had ever seen. The moment Samuel looked at her, he knew she was going to be his wife. He did not know how he was going to manage that miracle, he only knew that he had to.

Every day after that, Samuel found an excuse to be near the house, hoping to get another glimpse of her.

One afternoon, as Samuel was walking by the

Wal house on an errand, he heard piano music coming from inside, and he knew that *she* was playing. He had to see her. Looking around to make sure no one was observing him, Samuel walked to the side of the house. The music was coming from upstairs, directly above his head. Samuel stepped back and studied the wall. There were enough handholds for him to climb it, and without a moment's hesitation he started up. The second floor was higher than he had realized, and before he reached the window he was ten feet above the ground. He looked down and felt a momentary sense of dizziness. The music was louder now, and he felt as if she were playing for him. He grabbed another handhold so that he could peer over the sill. He found himself looking into an exquisitely furnished parlour. The girl was seated before a gold and white piano, playing, and behind her in an armchair, reading a book, was Dr Wal. Samuel had no eyes for him. He could only stare at the beautiful vision just a few feet away from him. He loved her! He would do something spectacular and daring so that she would fall in love with him. He would – So engrossed was Samuel in his daydream that he loosened his grip and began to fall into space. He let out a cry and saw two startled faces staring at him just before he plunged to the ground.

He woke up on an operating table in Dr Wal's office, a spacious room fitted with medical cabinets and an array of surgical equipment. Dr Wal was holding an awful-smelling piece of cotton under Samuel's nose. Samuel choked and sat up.

'That's better,' Dr Wal said. 'I should remove your brain but I doubt if you have one. What were you planning to steal, boy?'

'Nothing,' Samuel replied indignantly.

'What's your name?'

'Samuel Roffe.'

The doctor's fingers began to probe Samuel's right wrist, and the boy cried out with pain.

'Hm. You have a broken wrist, Samuel Roffe. Maybe we should let the police fix it.'

Samuel groaned aloud. He was thinking about what would happen when the police brought him home in disgrace. His aunt Rachel's heart would be broken; his father would kill him. But, even more important, how could he ever hope to win Dr Wal's daughter now? He was a criminal, a marked man. Samuel felt a sudden, agonizing jerk on his wrist, and looked up at the doctor in shocked surprise.

'It's all right,' Dr Wal said. 'I've set it.' He went to work putting a splint on it. 'Do you live around here, Samuel Roffe?'

'No, sir.'

'Haven't I seen you hanging about?'

'Yes, sir.'

'Why?'

Why? If Samuel told the truth, Dr Wal would laugh at him.

'I want to become a doctor,' Samuel blurted out, unable to contain himself.

Dr Wal was staring at him in disbelief. '*That's* why you climbed the wall of my house like a burglar?'

Samuel found himself telling his entire story. He told about his mother dying in the streets, and about his father, about his first visit to Krakow and his frustration at being locked inside the ghetto walls at night like an animal. He told how he felt about Dr Wal's daughter. He told everything, and the doctor listened in silence. Even to Samuel's ears his story sounded ridiculous; and when he was finished, he whispered. 'I – I'm sorry.'

Dr Wal looked at him for a long time, and then said, 'I'm sorry, too. For you, for me, and for all of us. Every man is a prisoner, and the greatest irony of all is to be the prisoner of another man.'

Samuel looked up at him, puzzled. 'I don't understand, sir.'

The doctor sighed. 'One day you will.' He rose to his feet, walked over to his desk, selected a pipe and slowly and methodically filled it. 'I'm afraid this is a very bad day for you, Samuel Roffe.'

He put a match to the tobacco, blew it out and then turned to the boy. 'Not because of your broken wrist. That will heal. But I'm going to have to do something to you that may not heal so quickly.' Samuel was watching him, his eyes wide. Dr Wal walked over to his side, and when he spoke his voice was gentle. 'Very few people ever have a dream. You have two dreams. And I'm afraid I am going to have to break both of them.'

'I don't –'

'Listen to me carefully, Samuel. You can never be a doctor – not in our world. Only three of us are allowed to practise medicine in the ghetto. There are dozens of skilled doctors here, waiting for one of us to retire or to die so that they can take our place. There's no chance for you. None. You were born at the wrong time, in the wrong place. Do you understand me, boy?'

Samuel swallowed. 'Yes, sir.'

The doctor hesitated, then went on. 'About your second dream – I'm afraid that one is just as impossible. There is no chance of your ever marrying Terenia.'

'Why?' Samuel asked.

Dr Wal stared at him. '*Why?* For the same reason you can't become a doctor. We live by the rules, by our traditions. My daughter will marry someone of her own class, someone who can afford to keep her in the same style in which she has been raised. She will marry a professional man, a lawyer, a doctor or a rabbi. You – well, you must put her out of your mind.'

'But –'

The doctor was ushering him towards the door. 'Have someone look at that splint in a few days. See that the bandage is kept clean.'

'Yes, sir,' Samuel said. 'Thank you, Dr Wal.'

Dr Wal studied the blond, intelligent-looking boy before him. 'Goodbye, Samuel Roffe.'

* * *

Early the next afternoon, Samuel rang the front doorbell of the Wal house. Dr Wal watched him through the window. He knew that he should send him away.

'Send him in,' Dr Wal said to the maid.

After that, Samuel came to Dr Wal's house two or three times a week. He ran errands for the doctor, and in exchange Dr Wal let him watch as he treated patients or worked in his laboratory, concocting medicines. The boy observed and learned and remembered everything. He had a natural talent. Dr Wal felt a growing sense of guilt, for he knew that in a way he was encouraging Samuel, encouraging him to be something he could never be; and yet he could not bring himself to turn the boy away.

Whether it was by accident or design, Terenia was almost always around when Samuel was there. Occasionally he would get a glimpse of her walking past the laboratory, or leaving the house, and once he bumped into her in the kitchen, and his heart began to pound so hard that he thought he would faint. She studied him for a long moment, a look of speculation in her eyes, then she nodded coolly and was gone. At least she had noticed him! That was the first step. The rest was only a matter of time. There was not the slightest doubt in Samuel's mind. It was fated. Terenia had become a major part of Samuel's dreams about the future. Where once he had dreamed for himself, he now dreamed for the two of them. Somehow he would get them both out of this terrible ghetto, this stinking, over-crowded prison. And he would become a great success. But now his success would not be for him alone, but for both of them.

Even though it was impossible.

Elizabeth fell asleep, reading about old Samuel. In the morning when she awakened, she carefully hid the Book and began to get dressed for school. She could not get Samuel off her mind. How did he marry Terenia? How did he get out of the ghetto? How did he become famous? Elizabeth was consumed by the Book, and she resented the intrusions that tore her away from it and forced her to return to the twentieth century.

One of the classes that Elizabeth had to attend was ballet, and she loathed it. She would stuff herself into her pink tutu, and stare at her image in the mirror and try to tell herself that her figure was voluptuous. But the truth was there for her to see. She was fat. She would never be a ballet dancer.

Shortly after Elizabeth's fourteenth birthday, Mme Netturova, her dance teacher, announced that in two weeks the class would give its yearly dance recital in the auditorium, and that the students were to invite their parents. Elizabeth was in a state of panic. The mere thought of getting upon a stage in front of an audience filled her with dread. She could not go through with it.

A child was running across a street in front of a car. Elizabeth saw her, raced out and snatched

the child from the jaws of death. Unfortunately,
ladies and gentlemen, Elizabeth Roffe's toes were
crushed by the wheels of the automobile, and she
will not be able to dance at the recital this evening.

A careless maid left a bar of soap at the top of
the stairs. Elizabeth slipped and fell down the long
flight, breaking her hip. Nothing to worry about,
the doctor said. It will heal in three weeks.

No such luck. On the day of the performance, Elizabeth was in perfect health, and in a state of hysteria. Again, it was old Samuel who helped her. She remembered how frightened he had been, but he had gone back to face Dr Wal. She would not do anything to disgrace Samuel. She would face up to her ordeal.

Elizabeth had not even mentioned the recital to her father. In the past she had often asked him to school meetings and parties which parents were requested to attend, but he had always been too busy.

On this evening, as Elizabeth was getting ready to leave for the dance recital, her father returned home. He had been out of town for ten days.

He passed her bedroom, saw her and said, 'Good evening, Elizabeth.' Then, 'You've put on some weight.'

She flushed and tried to pull in her stomach. 'Yes, Father.'

He started to say something, then changed his mind. 'How's school coming along?'

'Fine, thank you.'

'Any problems?'

'No, Father.'

'Good.'

It was a dialogue they had had a hundred times over the years, a meaningless litany that seemed to be their only form of communication. How's-school-coming-along-fine-thank-you-any-problems-no-Father-good. Two strangers discussing the weather, neither listening nor caring about the other's opinion. Well, one of us cares, Elizabeth thought.

But this time Sam Roffe stood there, watching his daughter, a thoughtful expression on his face. He was used to dealing with concrete problems and although he sensed that there was a problem here, he had no idea what it was, and if anyone had told him, Sam Roffe's answer would have been, 'Don't be a fool. I've given Elizabeth everything.'

As her father started to leave, Elizabeth heard herself say, 'My – my – ballet class is giving a recital. I'm in it. You don't want to come, do you?'

And even as she said the words, she was filled with a sense of horror. She did not want him there to see her clumsiness. Why had she asked him? But she knew why. Because she was the only girl in the class whose parents would not be in that auditorium. It doesn't matter, anyway, she told herself, because he's going to say no. She shook her head, furious with herself, and turned away. And behind her, incredibly, she heard her father's voice saying, 'I'd like that.'

The auditorium was crowded with parents, relatives and friends, watching the students dance to the accompaniment of two grand pianos on either side of the stage. Mme Netturova stood off to one side, counting the beat aloud as the children danced, calling the attention of the parents to herself.

A few of the children were remarkably graceful, and showed signs of real talent. The others went through their performances determined to substitute enthusiasm for ability. The mimeographed programmme announced three musical excerpts from *Coppélia, Cinderella* and, inevitably, *Swan Lake*. The *pièce de résistance* was to be the solos, when each child would have her moment of glory, alone.

Backstage, Elizabeth was in an agony of apprehension. She kept peering through the side curtain, and each time she saw her father sitting in the second row centre, she thought what a fool she had been to ask him. So far during the show, Elizabeth had been able to lose herself in the background, hidden behind the other dancers. But now her solo was coming up. She felt gross in her tutu, like something in a circus. She was certain they would all laugh at her when she came out on the stage – and she had *invited* her father to watch her humiliation! Elizabeth's only consolation was that her solo lasted for only sixty seconds. Mme Netturova was no fool. It would all be over so quickly that no one would even notice her. All Elizabeth's father had to do was to glance away for a minute, and her number would be finished.

Elizabeth watched the other girls as they danced,

one by one, and they seemed to her like Markova, Maximova, Fonteyn. She was startled by a cold hand on her bare arm, and Mme Netturova hissed, 'On your toes, Elizabeth, you're next.'

Elizabeth tried to say, 'Yes, madame,' but her throat was so dry that no words came out. The two pianists struck up the familiar theme of Elizabeth's solo. She stood there, frozen, incapable of moving, and Mme Netturova was whispering, 'Get out there!' and Elizabeth felt a shove against her back, and she was out on the stage, half naked, in front of a hundred hostile strangers. She did not dare look at her father. All she wanted was to get this ordeal over with as quickly as possible and flee. What she had to do was simple, a few pliés and jetés and leaps. She began to execute the steps, keeping time to the music, trying to think herself thin and tall and lithe. As she finished, there was a smattering of polite applause from the audience. Elizabeth looked down at the second row, and there was her father, smiling proudly and applauding – applauding her, and something inside Elizabeth snapped. The music had stopped. But Elizabeth kept on dancing, doing pliés and jetés and battements and turns, carried away, transported beyond herself. The confused musicians began to pick up her beat, first one pianist, then the other, trying to keep up with her. Backstage, Mme Netturova was signalling to Elizabeth wildly, her face filled with fury. But Elizabeth was blissfully unaware of her, transported beyond herself. The only thing that mattered to her was that she was onstage, dancing for her father.

'I am sure you understand, Mr Roffe, that this school simply cannot tolerate that type of behaviour.' Mme Netturova's voice was trembling with anger. 'Your daughter ignored everyone else and took over, as though – as though she were some kind of *star*.'

Elizabeth could feel her father turn to look at her, and she was afraid to meet his eyes. She knew that what she had done was unforgivable, but she had been unable to stop herself. For one moment on that stage she had tried to create something beautiful for her father, had tried to impress him, make him notice her, be proud of her. Love her.

Now she heard him say, 'You're absolutely right, Madame Netturova. I will see to it that Elizabeth is suitably punished.'

Mme Netturova gave Elizabeth a look of triumph, and said, 'Thank you, Mr Roffe. I will leave it in your hands.'

Elizabeth and her father were standing outside the school. He had not said a word to her since leaving Mme Netturova's office. Elizabeth was trying to compose a speech of apology – but what could she say? How could she ever make her father understand why she had done what she had done? He was a stranger, and she was afraid of him. She had heard him vent his terrible anger on others for making mistakes, or for having disobeyed him.

Now she stood there waiting for his wrath to fall upon her.

He turned to her and said, 'Elizabeth, why don't we drop in at Rumpelmayer's and get a chocolate soda?'

And Elizabeth burst into tears.

She lay in her bed that night, wide awake, too stimulated to go to sleep. She kept replaying the evening over and over in her mind. The excitement of it had been almost more than she could bear. Because this was no made-up daydream. It had happened, it was real. She could see herself and her father, seated at the table at Rumpelmayer's surrounded by the large, colourful stuffed bears and elephants and lions and zebras. Elizabeth had ordered a banana split, which had turned out to be absolutely enormous, and her father had not criticized her. He was talking to her. No how's-school-coming-along-fine-thank-you-any-problems-no-Father-good. But really *talking*. He told her about his recent trip to Tokyo, and how his host had served chocolate-covered grasshoppers and ants as a special treat for him, and how he had had to eat them in order not to lose face.

When Elizabeth had scooped up the last drop of the ice cream, her father suddenly said, 'What made you do it, Liz?'

She knew that everything was going to be spoiled now, that he was going to reprimand her, tell her how disappointed he was in her.

She said, 'I wanted to be better than everyone else.' She could not bring herself to add, *For you.*

He looked at her for what seemed a long time, and then he laughed. 'You certainly surprised the hell out of everybody.' There was a note of pride in his voice.

Elizabeth felt the blood rushing to her cheeks, and she said, 'You're not angry with me?'

There was a look in his eyes that she had never seen before. 'For wanting to be the best? That's what the Roffes are all about.' And he reached over and squeezed her hand.

Elizabeth's last thoughts as she drifted off to sleep were: My father likes me, he really likes me. From now on, we'll be together all the time. He'll take me on trips with him. We'll talk about things and we'll become good friends.

The following afternoon her father's secretary informed her that arrangements had been made to send Elizabeth away to a boarding-school in Switzerland.

TEN

Elizabeth was enrolled in the International Château Lemand, a girls' school situated in the village of Sainte-Blaise, overlooking the Lake of Neuchâtel. The ages of the girls ranged from fourteen to eighteen. It was one of the finest schools in the excellent Swiss educational system.

Elizabeth hated every minute of it.

She felt exiled. She had been sent away from home, and it was like some dire punishment for a crime she had not committed. On that one magic evening she had felt that she was on the verge of something wonderful, discovering her father, and her father discovering her, and their becoming friends. But now he was farther away than ever.

Elizabeth was able to keep track of her father in the newspapers and magazines. There were frequent stories and photographs of him meeting with a Prime Minister or a President, opening a new pharmaceutical plant in Bombay, mountain climbing, dining with the Shah of Iran. Elizabeth pasted all the stories in a scrapbook which she constantly pored over. She hid it next to the book of Samuel.

Elizabeth remained aloof from the other students. Some of the girls shared rooms with two or three others, but Elizabeth had asked for a room by herself. She wrote long letters to her father, then tore up the ones that revealed her feelings. From time to time she received a note from him, and there were gaily wrapped packages from expensive stores on her birthday, sent by his secretary. Elizabeth missed her father terribly.

She was going to join him at the villa in Sardinia for Christmas, and as the time drew nearer, the waiting became almost unbearable. She was sick with excitement. She made a list of resolutions for herself and carefully wrote them down:

Do not be a pest.

Be interesting.

Do not complain about anything, especially school.

Do not let him know you are lonely.

Do not interrupt while he is speaking.

Be well groomed at all times, even at breakfast.

Laugh a lot so that he can see how happy you are.

The notes were a prayer, a litany, her offering to the gods. If she did all these things, maybe – maybe – Elizabeth's resolutions merged into fantasies. She would make profound observations about the Third World and the nineteen developing nations, and her father would say, 'I didn't know you were so interesting' (rule number two). 'You're a very bright girl, Elizabeth.' Then he would turn to his secretary and say, 'I don't think Elizabeth needs to go back to school. Why don't I keep her here with me?'

A prayer, a litany.

A company Learjet picked Elizabeth up at Zurich and flew her to the airport at Olbia, where she was met by a limousine. Elizabeth sat in the back of the car, silent, forcing her knees together to keep them from trembling. No matter what happens, she thought fiercely, I won't let him see me cry. He mustn't know how much I've missed him.

The car drove up the long, winding mountain highway that led to the Costa Smeralda, then turned off on to the small road that wound to the top. This road had always frightened Elizabeth. It was very narrow and steep, with the mountain on one side and a terrifying abyss on the other.

The car pulled up in front of the house, and Elizabeth stepped out and began walking towards the house and then running, her legs carrying her as fast as they could. The front door opened and Margherita, the Sardinian housekeeper, stood there smiling. 'Hello, Miss Elizabeth.'

'Where's my father?' Elizabeth asked.

'He had to go to Australia on some emergency. But he left a lot of pretty presents for you. It's going to be a lovely Christmas.'

ELEVEN

Elizabeth had brought the Book with her. She stood in the hallway of the villa, studying the painting of Samuel Roffe, and next to him, Terenia, feeling their presence as though they had come to life. After a long time Elizabeth turned and climbed up the ladder to the tower room, taking the Book. She spent hours every day in the tower room, reading and rereading, and each time she felt closer to Samuel and Terenia, the century that separated them disappearing . . .

Over the next few years, Elizabeth read, Samuel spent long hours in Dr Wal's laboratory, helping him mix ointments and medicines, learning how they worked. And always in the background was Terenia, haunting, beautiful. The very sight of her was enough to keep alive Samuel's dream that one day she would belong to him. Samuel got along well with Dr Wal, but Terenia's mother was another story. She was a sharp-tongued virago, a snob, and she hated Samuel. He tried to keep out of her way.

Samuel was fascinated by the many drugs that could heal people. A papyrus had been found that listed 811 prescriptions used by the Egyptians in 1550 BC. Life expectancy at birth then was fifteen years and Samuel could understand why when he read some of the prescriptions: crocodile dung, lizard flesh, bats' blood, camels' spit, lions' liver, toe of a frog, unicorn powder. The *Rx* sign on every prescription was the ancient prayer to Horae, the Egyptian god of healing. Even the word 'chemistry' derived from the ancient name of Egypt, the land of Kahmi, or Chemi. The priest-physicians were called magi, Samuel learned.

The apothecaries' shops in the ghetto and in Krakow itself were primitive. Most of the bottles and jars were filled with untested and untried medicinal items, some useless, some harmful. Samuel became familiar with them all. There was castor oil, calomel and rhubarb, iodine compounds and codeine and ipecac. You could purchase panaceas for whooping cough, colic and typhoid fever. Because no sanitary precautions were taken, it was common to find ointments and gargles filled with dead insects, roaches, rat droppings and bits of feather and fur. The majority of patients who took the remedies died either of their diseases or from the remedies.

Several magazines were printed that were devoted to apothecary news, and Samuel read them all avidly. He discussed his theories with Dr Wal.

'It stands to reason,' Samuel said, his voice ringing with conviction, 'that there must be a cure for every disease. Health is natural, disease is unnatural.'

'Perhaps,' Dr Wal said, 'but most of my patients won't even let me try the new medications on them.' He added dryly, 'And I think they're wise.'

Samuel devoured Dr Wal's sparse library on pharmacy. And when he had read and reread those books, he felt frustrated by the unanswered questions that lay between the covers.

Samuel was fired by the revolution that was taking place. Some scientists believed that it was possible to counteract the cause of diseases by building up a resistance that would destroy the illness. Dr Wal tried it once. He took the blood of a patient with diphtheria, and injected it into a horse. When the horse died, Dr Wal gave up his experiments. But young Samuel was sure that Dr Wal had been on the right track.

'You can't stop now,' Samuel said. 'I know it will work.'

Dr Wal shook his head. 'That's because you're seventeen, Samuel. When you're my age, you won't be as sure of anything. Forget about it.'

But Samuel was not convinced. He wanted to continue his experiments, but for that Samuel needed animals, and there were few available except for the stray cats and rats that he was able to catch. No matter how minute the doses that Samuel gave them, they died. They're too small, Samuel thought. I need a larger animal. A horse or a cow or a sheep. But where was he going to find one?

One late afternoon when Samuel arrived home, an ancient horse and cart stood in front of the house. On the side of the cart a crudely lettered sign read: 'ROFFE & SON.' Samuel stared at it unbelievingly, then raced into the house to find his father. 'That – that horse out there,' he said. 'Where did you get it?'

His father smiled at him proudly. 'I made a deal. We can cover more territory with a horse. Maybe in four or five years we can buy another horse. Think of it. We'll have *two* horses.'

That was the extent of his father's ambition, owning two broken-down horses pulling carts through the dirty, crowded streets of the Krakow ghetto. It made Samuel want to weep.

That night when everyone was asleep, Samuel went out to the stable and examined the horse, which they had named Ferd. As horses went, this one was without question one of the lowest of the species. She was a very old horse, swaybacked and spavined. It was doubtful whether she could move much faster than Samuel's father. But none of that mattered. What was important was that Samuel now had his laboratory animal. He could do his experiments without having to worry about catching rats and stray cats. Of course, he would have to be careful. His father must never find out what he was doing. Samuel stroked the horse's head. 'You're going into the drug business,' he informed Ferd.

Samuel improvised his own laboratory, using a corner of the stable in which Ferd was kept.

He grew a culture of diphtheria germs in a dish of rich broth. When the broth turned cloudy, he removed some of it to another container and then weakened it, first by diluting the broth, then by heating it slightly. He filled a hypodermic needle with it and approached Ferd. 'Remember what I told you?' Samuel whispered. 'Well, this is your big day.'

Samuel plunged the contents of the hypodermic into the loose skin of the horse's shoulder, as he had seen Dr Wal do. Ferd turned to look at him reproachfully, and sprayed him with urine.

Samuel estimated that it would take about seventy-two hours for the culture to develop in Ferd. At the end of that time Samuel would give her a larger dose. Then another. If the antibody theory was right, each dose would build up a stronger blood resistance to the disease. Samuel would have his vaccine. Later, he would have to find a human being to test it on, of course, but that should not be difficult. A victim of the dread disease should be only too happy to try something that might save his life.

For the next two days Samuel spent almost every waking moment with Ferd.

'I've never seen anyone love an animal so much,' his father said. 'You can't keep away from her, can you?'

Samuel mumbled an inaudible reply. He felt a sense of guilt about what he was doing, but he knew what would happen if he even mentioned it to his father. However, there was no need for his father to know. All Samuel had to do was extract enough blood from Ferd to make up a vial or two of serum, and no one would ever be the wiser.

On the morning of the third and crucial day, Samuel was awakened by the sound of his father's voice from in front of the house. Samuel got out of bed, hurried to the window and looked out. His father was standing in the street with his cart, bellowing at the top of his lungs. There was no sign of Ferd. Samuel threw on some clothes and raced outside.

'*Momser!*' his father was yelling. 'Cheat! Liar! Thief! Thief!'

Samuel pushed past the crowd that was beginning to gather round his father.

'Where's Ferd?' Samuel demanded.

'I'm glad you asked me,' his father moaned. 'She's dead. She died in the streets like a dog.'

Samuel's heart sank.

'We're going along as nice as you please. I'm tending to business, not rushing her, you understand, not whipping her, or pushing her like some of the other pedlars I could name. And how does she show her appreciation? She drops dead. When I catch that *gonif* who sold her to me, I'll kill him!'

Samuel turned away, sick at heart. More than Ferd had passed away. Samuel's dreams had died. With Ferd went the escape from the ghetto, the freedom, the beautiful house for Terenia and their children.

But a greater disaster was to befall.

The day after Ferd died, Samuel learned that Dr Wal and his wife had arranged for Terenia to marry a rabbi. Samuel could not believe it. Terenia belonged to *him*! Samuel raced over to the Wal house. He found Dr and Mrs Wal in the parlour. He walked up to them, took a deep breath and announced, 'There's been a mistake, Terenia's mistake, Terenia's going to marry *me*.'

They stared at him in astonishment.

'I know I'm not good enough for her,' Samuel hurried on, 'but she won't be happy married to anyone but me. The rabbi's too old for –'

'*Nebbich*! Out! Out!' Terenia's mother was apoplectic.

Sixty seconds later Samuel found himself standing out in the street, forbidden ever to enter the Wal house again.

In the middle of the night Samuel had a long talk with God.

'What do you want from me? If I can't have Terenia, why did you make me love her? Haven't you any feelings?' He raised his voice in frustration and yelled, 'Can you hear me?'

And the others in the crowded little house yelled back, 'We can all hear you, Samuel. For God's sake, shut up and let us get some sleep!'

The following afternoon, Dr Wal sent for Samuel. He was ushered into the parlour, where Dr and Mrs Wal and Terenia were gathered.

'It seems we have a problem,' Dr Wal began.

'Our daughter can be quite a stubborn young lady. For some reason she's taken a fancy to you. I cannot call it love, Samuel, because I don't believe that young girls know what love is. However, she has refused to marry Rabbi Rabinowitz. She thinks she wants to marry you.'

Samuel sneaked a glance at Terenia, and she smiled at him and he almost burst with joy. It was short-lived.

Dr Wal was going on. 'You said that you love my daughter.'

'Y – y – yes, sir,' Samuel stammered. He tried it again, his voice stronger. 'Yes, sir.'

'Then let me ask you something, Samuel. Would you like Terenia to spend the rest of her life married to a pedlar?'

Samuel instantly saw the trap, but there was no way out of it. He looked at Terenia again and said slowly, 'No, sir.'

'Ah. Then you see the problem. None of us wants Terenia to marry a pedlar. And you're a pedlar, Samuel.'

'I won't always be, Dr Wal.' Samuel's voice was strong and sure.

'And what *will* you be?' Mrs Wal snapped. 'You come from a family of pedlars, you'll remain a family of pedlars. I will not allow my daughter to marry one.'

Samuel looked at the three of them, his mind filled with confusion. He had come here with trepidation and despair, had been lifted to the heights of joy, and now he had been plunged into a black abyss again. What did they want from him?

'We've agreed on a compromise,' Dr Wal said. 'We're going to give you six months to prove that you're more than just a pedlar. If, by the end of that time, you cannot offer Terenia the kind of life she is accustomed to, then she is going to marry Rabbi Rabinowitz.'

Samuel stared at him, aghast. 'Six months!'

No one could become a success in six months! No one, certainly, who lived in the ghetto of Krakow.

'Do you understand?' Dr Wal asked.

'Yes, sir.' Samuel understood only too well. He felt as if his stomach were filled with lead. He did not need a solution, he needed a miracle. The Wals would only be content with a son-in-law who was a doctor or a rabbi, or who was wealthy. Samuel quickly examined each possibility.

The law forbade him to become a doctor.

A rabbi? One had to start studying for the rabbinate by thirteen, and Samuel was almost eighteen now.

Wealthy? That was out of the question. If he worked twenty-four hours a day peddling his wares in the streets of the ghetto until he was ninety, he would still be a poor man. The Wals had set an impossible task for him. They had seemingly given in to Terenia by allowing her to postpone her marriage to the rabbi, while at the same time setting conditions that they knew would be impossible for Samuel to meet. Terenia was the only one who believed in him. She had confidence that he could find some kind of fame or fortune in six months. She's crazier than I am, Samuel thought in despair.

The six months began, and time flew. Samuel's days were spent as a pedlar, helping his father. But the moment the shadows of the setting sun began to fall on the walls of the ghetto, Samuel would hurry home, gulp down a bite to eat, and then go to work in his laboratory. He made hundreds of batches of serums, and injected rabbits and cats and dogs and birds, and all the animals died. They're too small, Samuel thought desperately. I need a larger animal.

But he had none, and time was racing by.

Twice a week Samuel would go into Krakow to replenish the merchandise that he and his father sold from the cart. He would stand inside the locked gates at dawn, surrounded by the other pedlars, but he neither saw nor heard them. His mind was in another world.

As Samuel stood there one morning, daydreaming, a voice yelled, 'You! Jew! Move on!'

Samuel looked up. The gates had been opened and his cart was blocking the way. One of the guards was angrily motioning for Samuel to move. There were always two guards on duty in front of the gate. They wore green uniforms and special insignia and were armed with pistols and heavy clubs. On a chain around his waist one of the guards carried a large key that opened and locked the gates. Alongside the ghetto ran a small river spanned by an old wooden bridge. Across the bridge was the police garrison where the ghetto guards were stationed. More than once, Samuel had witnessed a hapless Jew being dragged across the bridge. It was always a one-way trip. Jews were required to be back inside the ghetto by sundown, and any Jew caught outside the gates after dark was arrested and deported to a labour camp. It was the nightmare of every Jew that he might be caught outside the ghetto after sunset.

Both guards were supposed to remain on duty, patrolling in front of the gates, all night; but it was common knowledge inside the ghetto that after the Jews were locked in, one of the guards would slip away for a night of pleasure in the city. Just before dawn he would return to help his partner open the gates for the new day.

The two guards that were usually stationed there were named Paul and Aram. Paul was a pleasant man with a genial disposition. Aram was an entirely different matter. He was an animal, swarthy and stockily built, with powerful arms and a body like a beer keg. He was a Jew-baiter, and whenever he was on duty, all the Jews outside the gates made sure that they returned early, because nothing delighted Aram more than to lock a Jew out, club him senseless and drag him across the bridge to the dreaded police barracks.

It was Aram now who stood yelling at Samuel to move his cart. He hurriedly went through the gates and headed for the city, and he could feel Aram's eyes boring into his back.

Samuel's six-months grace period quickly dwindled to five months and then to four months, then three. There was not a day, not an hour, when Samuel was not thinking about a solution to his problem, or feverishly working in his tiny laboratory. He tried to speak to some of the wealthy merchants of the ghetto, but few had time for him, and those who had time offered him useless advice.

'You want to make money? Save your pennies, boy, and one day you'll have enough to buy a fine business like mine.'

That was easy enough for them to say – most of them had been born into wealthy homes.

Samuel thought of taking Terenia and running away. But where to? At the end of the journey would lie another ghetto, and he would still be a penniless *nebbich*. No, he loved Terenia too much to do that to her. That was the real trap in which he was caught.

Inexorably the clock ran on, and the three months became two, and then one. Samuel's only consolation during that time was that he was allowed to see his beloved Terenia three times a week, chaperoned, of course, and each time Samuel saw her, he loved her more deeply. It was a bitter-sweet feeling, for the more often he saw her, the closer he was coming to losing her. 'You'll find a way,' Terenia kept assuring him.

But now there were only three weeks left, and Samuel was no closer to a solution than when he had started.

Late one night Terenia came to see Samuel at the stable. She put her arms around him and said, 'Let's run away, Samuel.'

He had never loved her so much as he loved her at that moment. She was willing to disgrace herself, give up her mother and father, the wonderful life she lived, for him.

He held her close and said, 'We can't. Wherever we went, I'd still be a pedlar.'

'I don't mind.'

Samuel thought of her beautiful home with the spacious rooms and the servants, and he thought of the tiny squalid room he shared with his father and his aunt, and he said, '*I* would mind, Terenia.'

And she turned and left.

The following morning Samuel met Isaac, a former schoolmate, walking down the street, leading a horse. It had one eye, suffered from acute colic, was spavined and deaf.

'Morning, Samuel.'

'Morning, Isaac. I don't know where you're going with that poor horse, but you'd better hurry. It doesn't look like it's going to last much longer.'

'It doesn't have to. I'm taking Lottie to a glue factory.'

Samuel eyed the animal with a sudden, quickened interest. 'I shouldn't think they'd give you much for her.'

'I know. I just want a couple of florins to buy a cart.'

Samuel's heart began to beat faster. 'I think I can save you a trip. I'll trade you my cart for your horse.'

It took less than five minutes to conclude the bargain.

Now all Samuel had to do was build another cart and explain to his father how he had lost the old one, and how he had come into possession of a horse that was on its last legs.

Samuel led Lottie to the barn where he had kept Ferd. On closer examination the horse was an even more discouraging sight. Samuel patted the animal and said, 'Don't worry, Lottie, you're going to make medical history.'

A few minutes later Samuel was at work on a new serum.

Because of the crowded and insanitary conditions of the ghetto, epidemics were frequent. The latest plague was a fever that produced a choking cough, swollen glands and a painful death. The doctors did not know what caused it, or how to treat it. Isaac's father went down with the disease. When Samuel heard the news, he hurried over to see Isaac.

'The doctor has been here,' the weeping boy told Samuel. 'He said there's nothing to be done.'

From upstairs they could hear the terrible sounds of a racking cough that seemed to go on for ever.

'I want you to do something for me,' Samuel

said. 'Get me a handkerchief of your father's.'

Isaac stared at him. '*What?*'

'One that he's used. And be careful how you handle it. It will be full of germs.'

An hour later Samuel was back at the stable, carefully scraping the contents of the handkerchief into a dish filled with broth.

He worked all that night and all the next day and the following day, injecting small doses of the substance into the patient Lottie, then larger doses, fighting against time, trying to save the life of Isaac's father.

Trying to save his own life.

In later years Samuel was never sure whether God was looking out for him or for the old horse, but Lottie survived the gradually increased doses, and Samuel had his first batch of antitoxin. His next task was to persuade Isaac's father to let him use it on him.

As it turned out, it needed no persuasion. When Samuel reached Isaac's house, it was filled with relatives, mourning the dying man upstairs.

'He only has a little time left,' Isaac told Samuel.

'Can I see him?'

The two boys went upstairs. Isaac's father was in bed, his face flushed with fever. Each racking cough sent his wasted frame into a spasm that left him weaker. It was obvious that he was dying.

Samuel took a deep breath and said, 'I want to talk to you and your mother.'

Neither of them had any confidence in the little glass vial that Samuel had brought, but the alternative was death. They took a chance simply because there was nothing to lose.

Samuel injected Isaac's father with the serum. He waited at the bedside for three hours, and there was no change. The serum had no effect. If anything, the coughing spells seemed more frequent. Finally Samuel left, avoiding Isaac's eyes.

At dawn the next day Samuel had to go into Krakow to buy goods. He was in a fever of impatience to get back to see whether Isaac's father was still alive.

There were large crowds at all the markets, and it seemed to Samuel that it took for ever to make his purchases. It was late afternoon by the time his cart was finally filled and he headed back towards the ghetto.

When Samuel was still two miles away from the gates, disaster struck. One of the wheels of the cart broke in half and the merchandise began to spill on to the pavement. Samuel was in a terrible dilemma. He had to find another wheel somewhere, and yet he did not dare leave the cart unguarded. A crowd had begun to gather, eyeing the spilled merchandise with avid eyes. Samuel saw a uniformed policeman approaching – a gentile – and he knew that he was lost. They would take everything away from him. The policeman pushed his way through the crowd and turned to the frightened boy. 'Your cart needs a new wheel.'

'Y – yes, sir.'

'Do you know where to find one?'

'No, sir.'

The policeman wrote something on a piece of paper. 'Go there. Tell him what you need.'

Samuel said, 'I can't leave the cart.'

'Yes, you can,' the policeman said. He cast a stern eye over the crowd. 'I'll be right here. Hurry!'

Samuel ran all the way. Following the directions on the piece of paper, he found himself in a blacksmith's shop, and when Samuel explained the situation, the blacksmith found a wheel that was the right size for the wagon. Samuel paid for the wheel out of the small bag of money he carried. He had half a dozen guldens left.

He raced back to his cart, rolling the wheel before him. The policeman was still there, and the crowd had dispersed. The merchandise was safe. With the policeman helping him, it took another half-hour to get the wheel on and secure it. Once more he started for home. His thoughts were on Isaac's father. Would Samuel find him dead or alive? He did not think he could stand the suspense of not knowing a moment longer.

He was only a mile from the ghetto now. Samuel could see the high walls rising against the sky. And even as he watched, the sun set on the western horizon, and the unfamiliar streets were bathed in darkness. In the excitement of what had happened, Samuel had forgotten about the time. It was past sundown and he was outside the gates! He began to run, pushing the heavy cart ahead of him, his heart pounding until it felt ready to burst. The ghetto gates would be closed. Samuel recalled all the terrible stories he had heard about Jews who were locked out of the ghetto at night. He began running faster. There would probably be only one guard on duty now. If it were Paul, the friendly one, then Samuel might have a chance. If it were Aram – Samuel could not bear to think about it. The darkness was thickening now, closing in on him like a black fog, and a light rain began to fall. Samuel was nearing the ghetto walls, only two blocks away, and suddenly the huge gates loomed into view. They were locked.

Samuel had never seen them closed from the outside before. It was as though life had suddenly been turned inside out, and he shivered with terror. He was shut away from his family, from his world, from everything that was familiar. He slowed down, approaching the gates warily, looking for the guards. They were not in sight. Samuel was filled with a sudden wild hope. The guards had probably been called away on some emergency. Samuel would find a way to open the gates, or to scale the walls without being seen. As he reached the gates, the figure of a guard stepped out of the shadows.

'Keep coming,' the guard commanded.

In the darkness Samuel could not see his face. But he recognized the voice. It was Aram.

'Closer. Come here.'

Aram was watching Samuel approach, a thin grin on his face. The boy faltered.

'That's it,' Aram called encouragingly. 'Keep walking.'

Slowly, Samuel moved towards the giant, his stomach churning, his head pounding. 'Sir,' Samuel said. 'Please let me explain. I had an accident. My cart –'

Aram reached out with his hamlike fist, grabbed Samuel by the collar and lifted him into the air. 'You dumb son-of-a-bitch of a Jew,' he crooned softly. 'Do you think I care why you're out? You're on the wrong side of the gates! Do you know what's going to happen to you now?'

The boy shook his head in terror.

'Let me tell you,' Aram said. 'We got a new edict last week. All Jews caught outside the gates after sundown are to be shipped to Silesia. Ten years of hard labour. How do you like that?'

Samuel could not believe it. 'But I – I haven't done anything. I –'

With his right hand Aram hit Samuel hard across the mouth, then let him drop heavily to the ground. 'Let's go,' Aram said.

'Wh – where?' Samuel asked. His voice was choked with terror.

'To the police barracks. In the morning you'll be shipped out with the rest of the scum. Get up.'

Samuel lay there, unable to bring his mind into focus. 'I – I have to go inside to say goodbye to my family.'

Aram grinned. 'They won't miss you.'

'Please!' Samuel pleaded. 'Let me – let me at least send them a message.'

The smile died on Aram's face. He stood over Samuel menacingly. When he spoke his voice was soft. 'I said get up, Jew shit. If I have to say it once more, I'll kick your balls in for you.'

Slowly, Samuel rose to his feet. Aram took his arm with an iron grip and started walking him towards the police barracks. *Ten years of hard labour in Silesia!* No one ever returned from there. He looked up at the man holding his arm, pulling him towards the bridge that led to the barracks.

'Please don't do this,' Samuel pleaded. 'Let me go.'

Aram squeezed his arm tighter, so that the blood seemed to stop flowing. 'Keep begging,' Aram said. 'I love to hear a Jew beg. Have you heard about Silesia? You'll be just in time for the winter. But don't worry, it's nice and warm underground in the mines. And when your lungs get black with coal and you start coughing them up, they'll leave you out in the snow to die.'

Ahead of them across the bridge, barely visible in the rain, was the stark building that served as the police barracks.

'Faster!' Aram said.

And suddenly Samuel knew that he could not let anyone do this to him. He thought of Terenia and his family and Isaac's father. No one would take his life from him. Somehow he had to escape, to save himself. They were crossing the narrow bridge now, the river running noisily below, swollen by the winter rains. There were only thirty yards left to go. Whatever was going to be done had to be done now. But how could he escape? Aram had a gun and even without it the enormous guard could have killed him easily. He was almost twice as big as Samuel and much more powerful. They had reached the other side of the bridge now, and the barracks lay just ahead of them.

'Hurry up,' Aram growled, pulling Samuel along. 'I've got other things to do.'

They were so close to the building now that Samuel could hear the laughter of the guards coming from inside. Aram tightened his grip and started to drag the boy across the cobblestoned yard that led to the police station. There were only seconds left. Samuel reached into his pocket with his right hand and felt the bag with the half-dozen guldens in it. His fingers closed around it, and his blood began to course with excitement. Carefully, he pulled the bag out of his pocket with his free hand, loosened the drawstring and dropped the bag. It landed on the stones with a loud tinkle of coins.

Aram stopped suddenly. 'What was that?'

'Nothing,' Samuel replied quickly.

Aram looked into the boy's eyes and grinned. Holding Samuel tightly, he took a step back, looked down at the ground and saw the open bag of money.

'You won't need money where you're going,' Aram said.

He reached down to pick up the sack, and Samuel reached down at the same time. Aram snatched the sack of money away from him. But it was not the sack that Samuel was after. His hand closed on one of the large cobblestones lying on the ground, and as Samuel straightened up, he smashed it into Aram's right eye with all his strength, turning it into a red jelly, and he kept pounding at him, again and again. He watched the guard's nose cave in, and then his mouth, until the face was nothing but a gout of red blood. And still Aram stood there on his feet, like some blind monster. Samuel looked at him, sick with fear, unable to hit him again. Then, slowly, the giant body began to collapse. Samuel stared down at the dead guard, unable to believe what he had done. He heard the voices from the barracks and he became suddenly aware of the terrible danger he was in. If they caught him now, they would not send him to Silesia. They would flay him alive and hang him in the town square. The penalty for even *striking* a policeman was death. And Samuel had killed one of them. He must get away quickly. He could try to flee across the border, but then he would be a hunted fugitive for the rest of his life. There had to be another solution. He stared down at the faceless corpse and suddenly he knew what he had to do. He reached down and searched the guard's body until he found the large key that opened the gates. Then, overcoming his revulsion, Samuel grabbed Aram's boots and began pulling the guard towards the river bank. The dead man seemed to weigh a ton. Samuel kept pulling, spurred by the sounds coming from the barracks. He reached the river bank. He stopped a moment to regain his breath, then shoved the body over the edge of the steep embankment and watched it roll into the coursing waters below. One hand stuck to the side of the bank for what seemed an eternity, and then the body was slowly washed downstream, out of sight. Samuel stood there, hypnotized, filled with horror at what he had done. He picked up the rock he had used and threw it into the water. He was still in great danger. He turned and ran back across the bridge towards the huge, locked gates of the ghetto. There was no one around. With trembling fingers Samuel placed the giant key in the lock and turned it. He pulled against the great wooden gates. Nothing happened. They were too heavy for him to move. But on that night nothing was impossible for Samuel. He was filled with a strength that came from outside and he pulled the huge gates open. He shoved the cart inside, then closed the gates behind him, and ran towards his house, pushing the cart ahead of him. The tenants of the house were gathered in the living-room, and when Samuel walked in, they stared at him as if he were a living ghost.

'They let you come back!'

'I – I don't understand,' his father stammered. 'We thought you –'

Quickly, Samuel explained what had happened, and their looks of concern turned to expressions of terror.

'Oh, my God!' groaned Samuel's father. 'They'll murder us all!'

'Not if you listen to me,' Samuel said. He explained his plan.

Fifteen minutes later Samuel and his father and two of their neighbours stood at the gates of the ghetto.

'Suppose the other guard comes back?' Samuel's father whispered.

Samuel said, 'We have to take that chance. If he's there, I'll take all the blame.'

Samuel pushed open the huge gates and slipped outside, alone, expecting to be pounced upon at any moment. He put the huge key in the lock and turned it. The gates of the ghetto were now locked from the outside. Samuel tied the key around his waist, and walked a few yards to the left of the gates. A moment later a rope slithered down the wall like a thick snake. Samuel clung to it while on the other side his father and the others began to haul him up. When Samuel reached the top of the wall, he made a noose of one end of the rope, fastened it to a projecting spike and lowered himself to the ground. When he was safely down, he shook the rope loose.

'Oh, my God!' his father was mumbling. 'What's going to happen at sunrise?'

Samuel looked at him and replied. 'We're going

to be pounding on the gates, telling them to let us out.'

At dawn the ghetto was swarming with uniformed police and soldiers. They had had to locate a special key to open the gates at sunrise for the merchants who were yelling to be let out. Paul, the second guard, had confessed to leaving his post and spending the night in Krakow, and he had been placed under arrest. But that still did not solve the mystery of Aram. Ordinarily the incident of a guard disappearing so close to the ghetto would have been a perfect excuse to start a pogrom. But the police were baffled by the locked gate. Since the Jews were safely locked up on the *inside*, they obviously could not have harmed him. In the end they decided that Aram must have run off with one of his many girl friends. They thought he might have thrown away the heavy, cumbersome key, and they searched for it everywhere, but they could not find it. Nor would they because it was buried deep in the ground, under Samuel's house.

Exhausted physically and emotionally, Samuel had fallen into his bed and was asleep almost instantly. He was awakened by someone yelling and shaking him. Samuel's first thought was: *They've found Aram's body. They've come to get me.*

He opened his eyes. Isaac was standing there in a state of hysteria. 'It's stopped,' Isaac was screaming. 'The coughing's stopped. It's a *bracha*! Come back to the house.'

Isaac's father was sitting up in bed. The fever had miraculously disappeared, and the coughing had stopped.

As Samuel walked up to his bedside, the old man said, 'I think I could eat some chicken soup,' and Samuel began to cry.

In one day he had taken a life and saved a life.

The news about Isaac's father swept through the ghetto. The families of dying men and women besieged the Roffe house, pleading with Samuel for some of his magic serum. It was impossible for him to keep up with the demand. He went to see Dr Wal. The doctor had heard about what Samuel had done, but he was sceptical.

'I'll have to see it with my own eyes,' he said. 'Make up a batch and I'll try it out on one of my patients.'

There were dozens to choose from, and Dr Wal selected the one he felt was closest to death. Within twenty-four hours the patient was on his way to recovery.

Dr Wal went to the stable where Samuel had been working day and night, preparing serum, and said, 'It works, Samuel. You've done it. What do you want for your dowry?'

And Samuel looked up at him and replied wearily, 'Another horse.'

That year, 1868, was the beginning of Roffe and Sons.

Samuel and Terenia were married and Samuel's

dowry was six horses and a small, well-equipped laboratory of his own. Samuel explained his experiments. He began to distil drugs from herbs, and soon his neighbours began coming to the little laboratory to buy remedies for whatever ills bothered them. They were helped, and Samuel's reputation spread. To those who could not afford to pay, Samuel would say, 'Don't worry about it. Take it away.' And to Terenia, 'Medicine is for healing, not for profit.'

His business kept increasing, and soon he was able to say to Terenia, 'I think it's time to open a small apothecary's shop where we can sell ointments and powders and other things besides prescriptions.'

The shop was a success from the beginning. The rich men who had refused to help Samuel before came to him now with offers of money.

'We'll be partners,' they said. 'We'll open a chain of shops.'

Samuel discussed it with Terenia. 'I'm afraid of partners. It's our business. I don't like the idea of strangers owning part of our lives.'

Terenia agreed with him.

As the business grew and expanded into additional shops, the offers of money increased. Samuel continued to turn them all down.

When his father-in-law asked him why, Samuel replied, 'Never let a friendly fox into your henhouse. One day he's going to get hungry.'

As the business flourished, so did the marriage

of Samuel and Terenia. She bore him five sons – Abraham, Joseph, Anton, Jan and Pitor – and with the birth of each son Samuel opened a new apothecary's shop, each one larger than the one before. In the beginning Samuel hired one man to work for him, then two, and soon he had more than two dozen employees.

One day Samuel received a visit from a government official. 'We're lifting some of the restrictions on Jews,' he told Samuel. 'We would like you to open an apothecary's shop in Krakow.'

And Samuel did. Three years later he had prospered enough to erect his own building in downtown Krakow and to buy Terenia a beautiful house in the city. Samuel had finally achieved his dream of escaping from the ghetto.

But he had dreams far beyond Krakow.

As the boys grew older, Samuel hired tutors for them, and each of the boys learned a different language.

'He's gone crazy,' Samuel's mother-in-law said. 'He's the laughing-stock of the neighbourhood, teaching Abraham and Jan English, Joseph German, Anton French and Pitor Italian. Who are they going to speak to? No one here speaks any of those barbaric languages. The boys won't even be able to talk to one another!'

Samuel merely smiled and said patiently, 'It's part of their education.' He knew to whom his sons would be talking.

By the time the boys reached their middle teens,

they had all travelled to different countries with their father. On each of his trips Samuel laid the groundwork for his future plans. When Abraham was twenty-one years old, Samuel called the family together and announced, 'Abraham is going to America to live.'

'America!' Terenia's mother shouted. 'It's filled with savages! I will not let you do this to my grandson. The boy is staying here where he will be safe.'

Safe. Samuel thought of the pogroms and Aram, and of his mother's murder.

'He's going abroad,' Samuel declared. He turned to Abraham. 'You'll open a factory in New York and be in charge of the business there.'

Abraham said proudly, 'Yes, Father.'

Samuel turned to Joseph. 'On your twenty-first birthday you will go to Berlin.' Joseph nodded.

Anton said, 'And I will go to France. Paris, I hope.'

'Just watch yourself,' Samuel growled. 'Some of those gentiles are very beautiful.'

He turned to Jan. 'You will go to England.'

Pitor, the youngest son, said eagerly, 'And I'm going to Italy, Papa. How soon can I leave?'

Samuel laughed and replied. 'Not tonight, Pitor. You'll have to wait until you're twenty-one.'

And thus it worked out. Samuel accompanied his sons abroad and helped them establish offices and factories. Within the next seven years, there were branches of the Roffe family in five foreign countries. It was becoming a dynasty, and Samuel had his lawyer set it up so that while each company was independent, it was at the same time responsible to the parent company.

'No strangers,' Samuel kept warning the lawyer. 'The stock must never leave the family.'

'It won't,' the lawyer assured him. 'But if your sons can't sell their stock, Samuel, how are they going to get along? I'm sure you'll want them to live in comfort.'

Samuel nodded. 'We'll arrange for them to live in beautiful homes. They'll have generous salaries and expense accounts, but everything else must go back into the business. If they ever want to sell the stock, it must be unanimous. The majority of the stock will belong to my eldest son and his heirs. We're going to be bigger than the Rothschilds.'

Over the years Samuel's prophecy became a reality. The business grew and prospered. Though the family was widely scattered, Samuel and Terenia saw to it that they remained as closely-knit as possible. Their sons returned home for birthdays and high holidays. Their visits were more than festive occasions, however. The boys would closet themselves with their father and discuss business. They had their own private espionage system. Whenever one son in one country heard about a new drug development, he would dispatch couriers to report it to the others, and they would begin manufacturing it themselves, so that in this way they kept constantly ahead of their competitors.

*   *   *

154

As the wheel of the century turned, the boys married and had children and gave Samuel grandchildren. Abraham had gone to America on his twenty-first birthday, in the year 1891. He had married an American girl seven years later and in 1905 she gave birth to Samuel's first grandchild, Woodrow, who sired a son named Sam. Joseph had married a German girl, who bore him a son and a daughter. The son in his turn married a girl, who bore a daughter, Anna. Anna married a German, Walther Gassner. In France, Anton had married a French girl, by whom he had two sons. One son committed suicide. The other married and had one daughter, Hélène. She married several times but had no children. Jan, in London, had married an English girl. Their only daughter had married a baronet named Nichols and had a son whom they christened Alec. In Rome, Pitor had married an Italian girl. They had a son and daughter. When the son, in his turn, married, his wife gave him a daughter, Simonetta, who fell in love with and married a young architect, Ivo Palazzi.

These then were the descendants of Samuel and Terenia Roffe.

Samuel lived long enough to see the winds of change that swept across the world. Marconi created wireless telegraphy and the Wright brothers launched the first aeroplane at Kitty Hawk. The Dreyfus affair captured the headlines and Admiral Peary reached the North Pole. Ford's Model Ts were in mass production; there were electric lights and telephones. In medicine, the germs that caused tuberculosis and typhoid and malaria were isolated and tamed.

Roffe and Sons, a little less than half a century after it had been founded, was a multi-national behemoth that circled the globe.

Samuel and his broken-down horse, Lottie, had created a dynasty.

When Elizabeth had finished reading the Book for perhaps the fifth time, she quietly returned it to its place in the glass case. She no longer needed it. She was a part of it, just as it was a part of her.

For the first time in her life, Elizabeth knew who she was, and where she had come from.

TWELVE

It was on her fifteenth birthday in the second term of her first year at school that Elizabeth first met Rhys Williams. He had dropped in at the school to bring Elizabeth a birthday present from her father.

'He wanted to come himself,' Rhys explained, 'but he couldn't get away.' Elizabeth tried to conceal her disappointment but Rhys was quick to see it. There was something forlorn about the young girl, a naked vulnerability, that touched him. On an impulse he said, 'Why don't you and I have dinner together?'

It was a terrible idea, Elizabeth thought. She could visualize the two of them walking into a restaurant together: him, incredibly good-looking and suave, and her, all braces and pudge. 'Thank you, no,' Elizabeth said stiffly. 'I – I have some studying to do.'

But Rhys Williams refused to accept no for an answer. He thought of the lonely birthdays he had spent by himself. He got permission from the head-mistress to take Elizabeth out for dinner. They got into Rhys's car and started heading towards the airport.

'Neuchâtel is the other way,' Elizabeth said.

Rhys looked at her and asked innocently, 'Who said we were going to Neuchâtel?'

'Where are we going?'

'Maxim's. It's the only place to celebrate a fifteenth birthday.'

They flew to Paris in a private jet, and had a superb dinner. It began with pâté de foie gras with truffles, lobster bisque, crisp duck à l'orange and Maxim's special salad, and ended with champagne and a birthday cake. Rhys drove Elizabeth down the Champs-Élysées afterwards, and they returned to Switzerland late that night.

It was the loveliest evening of Elizabeth's life. Somehow Rhys had managed to make her feel interesting, and beautiful, and it was a heady experience. When Rhys dropped Elizabeth off at school, she said, 'I don't know how to thank you. I – it's the nicest time I've ever had.'

'Thank your father.' Rhys grinned. 'It was all his idea.'

But Elizabeth knew that that was not true.

She decided that Rhys Williams was the most wonderful man she had ever met. And without doubt the most attractive. She got into her bed that night thinking about him. Then she rose and went to the small desk under the window. She took out a piece of paper and a pen, and wrote, 'Mrs Rhys Williams'.

She stared at the words for a long time.

Rhys was twenty-four hours late for his date with a glamorous French actress, but he was not concerned. They wound up at Maxim's, and somehow Rhys could not help thinking that his evening there with Elizabeth had been more interesting.

She would be someone to reckon with, one day.

Elizabeth was never certain who was more responsible for the change that began in her – Samuel or Rhys Williams – but she began to take a new pride in herself. She lost the compulsion to eat constantly, and her body began to slim down. She began to enjoy sport and started to take an interest in school. She made an effort to socialize with the other girls. They could not believe it. They had often invited Elizabeth to their pyjama parties, and she had always declined. Unexpectedly, she appeared at a pyjama party one night.

The party was being held in a room shared by four girls, and when Elizabeth arrived the room was crammed with at least two dozen students, all in pyjamas or robes. One of the girls looked up in surprise and said, 'Look who's here! We were betting you wouldn't come.'

'I – I'm here.'

The air was filled with the pungent, sweet aroma of cigarette smoke. Elizabeth knew that many of the girls smoked marijuana, but she had never tried any. Her hostess, a French girl named Renée Tocar, walked up to Elizabeth, smoking a stubby brown cigarette. She took a deep puff, then held it out to Elizabeth. 'You smoke?'

It was more of a statement than a question.

'Of course,' Elizabeth lied. She took the cigarette, hesitated a moment, then put it between her lips and inhaled. She could feel her face going green, and her lungs rebelling, but she managed a smile and gasped, 'Neat.'

The moment Renée turned away, Elizabeth sank down on to a couch. She experienced a dizziness, but in a moment it passed. Experimentally she took another puff. She began to feel curiously light-headed. Elizabeth had heard and read about the effects of marijuana. It was supposed to release inhibitions, take you out of yourself. She took another puff, deeper this time, and she began to feel a pleasant floating sensation, as if she were on another planet. She could see the girls in the room and hear them talking, but somehow they were all blurred, and the sounds were muted and far away. The lights seemed very bright, and she closed her eyes. The moment she did she was floating off into space. It was a lovely feeling. She could watch herself drifting over the roof of the school, up and up, over the snowy Alps into a sea of fluffy white clouds. Someone was calling her name, calling her back to earth. Reluctantly, Elizabeth opened her eyes. Renée was leaning over her, a look of concern on her face.

'Are you all right, Roffe?'

Elizabeth gave her a slow, contented smile, and said fuzzily, 'I'm just wonderful.' And in her infinite, euphoric state, she confessed, 'I've never smoked marijuana before.'

Renée was staring at her. 'Marijuana? That's a Gauloise.'

On the other side of the village of Neuchâtel was a boys' school, and Elizabeth's classmates sneaked away for trysts at every opportunity. The girls talked about the boys constantly. They talked about their bodies and the size of their penises and what they allowed the boys to do to them, and what they did to the boys in turn. At times it seemed to Elizabeth that she was trapped in a school full of raving nymphomaniacs. Sex was an obsession with them. One of the private games at school was *frôlage*. A girl would completely strip, and lie in bed on her back while another girl stroked her from her breasts to her thighs. The payment was a pastry bought in the village. Ten minutes of *frôlage* earned one pastry. By the end of ten minutes the girl usually reached orgasm, but if she had not, the one administering the *frôlage* would continue and earn an additional pastry.

Another favourite sexual *divertissement* was to be found in the bathroom. The school had large, old-fashioned bathtubs, with flexible hand showers that could be removed from the hook on the side of the wall. The girls would sit in a tub, turn on

161

the shower, and then with the warm water gushing out, they would push the head of the shower between their legs and rub it gently back and forth.

Elizabeth indulged in neither *frôlage* nor the shower head, but her sexual urges were beginning to get stronger and stronger. It was at about this time that she made a shattering discovery.

One of Elizabeth's teachers was a small, slim woman named Chantal Harriot. She was in her late twenties, almost a schoolgirl herself. She was attractive-looking, and when she smiled she became beautiful. She was the most sympathetic teacher Elizabeth had, and Elizabeth felt a strong bond with her. Whenever Elizabeth was unhappy, she would go to Mlle Harriot and tell her her problems. Mlle Harriot was an understanding listener. She would take Elizabeth's hand and stroke it, and give her soothing advice and a cup of hot chocolate and cakes, and Elizabeth always felt better immediately.

Mlle Harriot taught French and also taught a class in fashion, in which she emphasized style and harmony of colours, and the proper accessories.

'Remember, girls,' she would say, 'the smartest clothes in the world will look terrible if you wear the wrong accessories.' 'Accessories' was Mlle Harriot's watchword.

Whenever Elizabeth lay in the warm tub, she found that she was thinking of Mlle Harriot, of the look on her face when they talked together, and of the way Mlle Harriot caressed her hand, softly and tenderly.

When Elizabeth was in other classes, she would find her mind drifting towards Mlle Harriot, and she would remember the times that the teacher had put her arms around her, consoling her, and had touched her breasts. At first Elizabeth had believed that the touches were accidental, but they had happened more and more often, and each time Mlle Harriot would give Elizabeth a soft, questioning look as though waiting for some response. In her mind Elizabeth could see Mlle Harriot, with her gently swelling breasts, and her long legs, and she would wonder what she looked like naked, in bed. It was then that the full realization stunned Elizabeth.

She was a Lesbian.

She was not interested in boys, because she was interested in girls. Not the kind of silly little girls who were her classmates, but someone sensitive and understanding, like Mlle Harriot. Elizabeth could visualize the two of them in bed together, holding and comforting each other.

Elizabeth had read and heard enough about Lesbians to know how difficult life was for them. Society did not approve. Lesbianism was considered a crime against nature. But what was wrong, Elizabeth wondered, in loving someone tenderly and deeply? Did it matter whether it was a man or a woman? Was it not the love itself that was the important thing? Was it better to have a loveless heterosexual marriage than a loving homosexual one?

Elizabeth thought about how horrified her father was going to be when he learned the truth about her. Well, she would just have to face up to it. She would have to readjust her thinking about the future. She could never have a so-called normal life like other girls, with a husband and children. Wherever she went, she would always be an outcast, a rebel, living outside the mainstream of society. She and Mlle Harriot – Chantal – would find a little apartment somewhere, or perhaps a small house. Elizabeth would decorate it beautifully in soft pastels, with all the proper accessories. There would be graceful French furniture and lovely paintings on the walls. Her father could help – no, she must not expect any help from her father. In all probability he would never even speak to her again.

Elizabeth thought about her wardrobe. She might be a Lesbian, but she was determined not to dress like one. No tweeds or slacks, tailored suits or vulgar mannish hats. They were the lepers' bells of emotionally crippled women. She would try to look as feminine as possible.

Elizabeth decided that she would learn to be a great cook so that she could prepare Mlle Harriot's – Chantal's – favourite dishes. She visualized the two of them sitting in their apartment, or small house, enjoying a candle-lit dinner that Elizabeth had prepared. First, there would be vichyssoise, followed by a lovely salad, then perhaps shrimps or lobster, or a Chateaubriand, with delicate ices for dessert. After dinner they would sit on the floor before a blazing fire in the hearth, watching the soft snowflakes fall outside. *Snowflakes*. So it would be winter. Elizabeth hastily revised the menu. Instead of a cold vichyssoise she would prepare a nice, hearty onion soup, and perhaps make a fondue. The dessert could be a soufflé. She would have to learn to time it so that it would not fall. *Then* the two of them would sit on the floor before a warming fire, and read poetry to each other. T. S. Eliot, perhaps. Or V. J. Rajadhon.

> *Time is the enemy of love,*
> *The thief that shortens*
> *All our golden hours.*
> *I have never understood then*
> *Why lovers count their happiness*
> *In days and nights and years,*
> *While our love can only be measured*
> *In our joys and sighs and tears.*

Ah, yes, Elizabeth could see the long years stretching out before the two of them, and the passage of time would begin to melt into a golden, warm glow.

She would fall asleep.

Elizabeth had been expecting it, and yet when it happened it caught her by surprise. She was awakened one night by the sound of someone entering her room and softly closing the door. Elizabeth's eyes flew open. She could see a shadow moving across the moon-dappled room towards her bed, and a ray of moonlight fell across Mlle Harriot's – Chantal's – face. Elizabeth's heart began to beat wildly.

Chantal whispered, 'Elizabeth,' and, standing there, slipped off her robe. She was wearing nothing underneath. Elizabeth's mouth went dry. She had thought of this moment so often, and now that it was actually happening, she was in a panic. In truth she was not sure exactly what she was supposed to do, or how. She did not want to make a fool of herself in front of the woman she loved.

'Look at me,' Chantal commanded hoarsely. Elizabeth did. She let her eyes roam over the naked body. In the flesh Chantal Harriot was not quite what Elizabeth had envisioned. Her breasts looked a little like puckered apples, and they sagged a bit. She had a tiny potbelly, and her derrière seemed – this was the only word Elizabeth could think of – underslung.

But none of that was important. What mattered was what lay underneath, the soul of the woman, the courage and the daring to be different from everyone else, to defy the whole world and to want to share the rest of her life with Elizabeth.

'Move over, *mon petit ange*,' she was whispering.

Elizabeth did as she was told, and the teacher slipped into bed beside her. There was a strong, feral smell about her. She turned towards Elizabeth and put her arms around her, and said, 'Oh, *chérie*, I have dreamed of this moment.' And she kissed Elizabeth on the lips, forcing her tongue into Elizabeth's mouth, and making quick, groaning noises.

It was, without doubt, the most unpleasant sensation Elizabeth had ever experienced. She lay there in shock. Chantal's – Mlle Harriot's – fingers were moving across Elizabeth's body, squeezing her breasts, slowly sliding down her stomach towards her thighs. And all the time her lips were on Elizabeth's, slobbering, like an animal.

This was it. This was the beautiful magic moment. *If we were one, you and I, together we would make a universe to shake the stars and move the heavens.*

Mlle Harriot's hands were moving downward, caressing Elizabeth's thighs, starting to reach between her legs. Quickly, Elizabeth tried to conjure up the candle-lit dinners and the soufflé and the evenings before the fireplace, and all the wonderful years the two of them would share together; but it was no use. Elizabeth's mind and flesh were repelled; she felt as though her body was being violated.

Mlle Harriot moaned, 'Oh, *chérie*, I want to fuck you.'

And all Elizabeth could think of to say was, 'There's a problem. One of us has the wrong accessories.'

And she began to laugh and cry hysterically, weeping for the beautiful candle-lit vision that had died, and laughing because she was a healthy, normal girl who had just learned that she was free.

The next day Elizabeth tried the shower nozzle.

THIRTEEN

In the Easter holiday, in her final year at school, when she was eighteen, Elizabeth went to the villa in Sardinia to spend ten days. She had learned to drive, and for the first time she was free to explore the island on her own. She took long drives along the beaches and visited tiny fishing villages. She swam at the villa, under the warm Mediterranean sun, and at night lay in her bed listening to the mournful sound of the singing rocks, as the wind gently blew through them. She went to a carnival in Tempio, where the entire village dressed up in national costume. Hidden behind the anonymity of domino masks, the girls invited the boys to dance, and everyone felt free to do things they would not dare do at any other time. A boy might *think* he knew which girl he made love to that night, but the next morning he could not be certain. It was, Elizabeth thought, like an entire village playing *The Guardsman*.

She drove to Punta Murra and watched the

Sardos cook small lambs on open fires. The native islanders gave her *seada*, a goats' cheese covered in a dough, with hot honey over it. She drank the delicious *selememont*, the local white wine that could be had nowhere else in the world because it was too delicate to travel.

One of Elizabeth's favourite haunts was the Red Lion Inn at Porto Cervo. It was a little pub in a basement, with ten tables for dining, and an old-fashioned bar.

Elizabeth dubbed that holiday the Time of the Boys. They were the sons of the rich, and they came in swarms, inviting Elizabeth to a constant round of swimming and riding parties. It was the first move in the mating rite.

'They're all highly eligible,' Elizabeth's father assured her.

To Elizabeth they were all clods. They drank too much, talked too much and pawed her. She was sure they wanted her not for herself, because she might be an intelligent or worthwhile human being, but because she was a Roffe, heiress to the Roffe dynasty. Elizabeth had no idea that she had grown into a beauty, for it was easier to believe the truth of the past than the reflection in her mirror.

The boys wined and dined her and tried to get her into bed. They sensed that Elizabeth was a virgin, and some aberration in the male ego deluded each boy into the conviction that if he could take away Elizabeth's virginity, she would fall madly in love with him and be his slave for ever. They refused to give up. No matter where they took Elizabeth, the evenings always ended up the same. 'Let's go to bed.' And always she politely refused them.

They did not know what to make of her. They knew she was beautiful, so it followed that she must be stupid. It never occurred to them that she was more intelligent than they. Who ever heard of a girl being both beautiful *and* intelligent?

And so Elizabeth went out with the boys to please her father, but they all bored her.

Rhys Williams came to the villa, and Elizabeth was surprised at how excited and pleased she was to see him again. He was even more attractive than she had remembered.

Rhys seemed glad to see her. 'What's happened to you?' he asked.

'What do you mean?'

'Have you looked in your mirror lately?'

She blushed. 'No.'

He turned to Sam. 'Unless the boys are all deaf, dumb and blind, I have a feeling Liz isn't going to be with us much longer.'

Us! Elizabeth enjoyed hearing him say that. She hung around the two men as much as she dared, serving them drinks, running errands for them, enjoying just looking at Rhys. Sometimes Elizabeth would sit in the background, listening as they discussed business affairs, and she was fascinated. They spoke of mergers and of new factories, and products that had succeeded and others that had failed, and why. They talked about their competitors, and planned strategies and counter-strategies. To Elizabeth it was all heady stuff.

One day when Sam was up in the tower room, working, Rhys invited Elizabeth to lunch. She took him to the Red Lion and watched him play darts with the men at the bar. Elizabeth marvelled at how much at home Rhys was. He seemed to fit in anywhere. She had heard a Spanish expression that she had never understood, but she did now as she watched Rhys. *He's a man easy in his skin.*

They sat at a small corner table with a red and white tablecloth, and had shepherd's pie and ale, and they talked. Rhys asked her about school.

'It's really not too bad,' Elizabeth confessed. 'I'm learning how little I know.'

Rhys smiled. 'Very few people get that far. You finish in June, don't you?'

Elizabeth wondered how he had known. 'Yes.'

'Do you know what you want to do after that?'

It was the question she had been asking herself. 'No. Not really.'

'Interested in getting married?'

For one quick instant her heart missed a beat. Then she realized that it was a general question. 'I haven't found anyone yet.' She thought of Mlle Harriot and the cosy dinners in front of the fireplace and the snow falling, and she laughed aloud.

'Secret?'

'Secret.' She wished she could share it with him, but she did not know him well enough. The truth was, Elizabeth realized, that she did not know Rhys at all. He was a charming, handsome stranger who had once taken pity on her and flown her to Paris for a birthday dinner. She knew that he was brilliant in business and that her father depended on him. But she knew nothing about his personal life, or what he was really like. Watching him, Elizabeth had the feeling that he was a many-layered man, that the emotions he showed were to conceal the emotions he felt, and Elizabeth wondered if anyone really knew him.

It was Rhys Williams who was responsible for Elizabeth losing her virginity.

The idea of going to bed with a man had become more and more appealing to Elizabeth. Part of it was the strong physical urge that sometimes caught her unawares and gripped her in waves of frustration, an urgent physical ache that would not leave. But there was also a strong curiosity, the need to know what *it* was like. She could not go to bed with just anyone, of course. He had to be someone special, someone she could cherish, someone who would cherish her.

On a Saturday night Elizabeth's father gave a gala at the villa.

'Put on your most beautiful dress,' Rhys told Elizabeth. 'I want to show you off to everyone.'

Thrilled, Elizabeth had taken it for granted that she would be Rhys's date. When Rhys arrived, he had with him a beautiful blonde Italian princess.

Elizabeth felt so outraged and betrayed that at midnight she left the party and went to bed with a bearded, drunken Russian painter named Vassilov.

The entire, brief affair was a disaster. Elizabeth was so nervous and Vassilov was so drunk that it seemed to Elizabeth that there was no beginning, middle or end. The foreplay consisted of Vassilov pulling down his pants and flopping on to the bed. At that point Elizabeth was tempted to flee, but she was determined to punish Rhys for his perfidy. She got undressed and crawled into bed. A moment later, with no warning, Vassilov was entering her. It was a strange sensation. It was not unpleasant, but neither did the earth shake. She felt Vassilov's body give a quick shudder, and a moment later he was snoring. Elizabeth lay there filled with self-disgust. It was hard to believe that all the songs and books and poems were about *this*. She thought of Rhys, and she wanted to weep. Quietly, Elizabeth put on her clothes and went home. When the painter telephoned her the next morning, Elizabeth had the housekeeper tell him that she was not in. The following day Elizabeth returned to school.

She flew back in the company jet with her father and Rhys. The plane, which had been built to carry a hundred passengers, had been converted into a luxury ship. It had two large, beautifully decorated bedrooms in the rear, with full bathrooms, a comfortable office, a sitting-room amidship, with paintings, and an elaborately equipped galley up front. Elizabeth thought of it as her father's magic carpet.

The two men talked business most of the time. When Rhys was free, he and Elizabeth played a game of chess. She played him to a draw, and when Rhys said, 'I'm impressed,' Elizabeth blushed with pleasure.

The last few months of school went by swiftly. It was time to begin thinking about her future. Elizabeth thought of Rhys's question, *Do you know what you want to do with your life?* She was not sure yet. But because of old Samuel, Elizabeth had become fascinated by the family business, and knew that she would like to become a part of it. She was not sure what she could do. Perhaps she could start by helping her father. She remembered all the tales of the wonderful hostess her mother had become, how invaluable she had been to Sam. She would try to take her mother's place.

It would be a start.

FOURTEEN

The Swedish Ambassador's free hand was squeezing Elizabeth's bottom, and she tried to ignore it as they danced round the room, her lips smiling, her eyes expertly scanning the elegantly dressed guests, the orchestra, the liveried servants, the buffet heaped with a variety of exotic dishes and fine wines, and she thought to herself with satisfaction, It's a good party.

They were in the ballroom of the Long Island estate. There were two hundred guests, all of them important to Roffe and Sons. Elizabeth became aware that the Ambassador was pressing his body closer to hers, trying to arouse her. He flicked his tongue in her ear and whispered, 'You're a beautiful dancer.'

'So are you,' Elizabeth said with a smile, and she made a sudden mis-step and came down hard on his toe with the sharp heel of her shoe. He gave a cry of pain and Elizabeth exclaimed contritely, 'I'm so sorry, Ambassador. Let me get you a drink.'

She left him and threaded her way towards the bar, making her way easily through the guests, her eyes moving carefully around the room, checking to see that everything was perfect.

Perfection – that was what her father demanded. Elizabeth had been the hostess for a hundred of Sam's parties now, but she had never learned to relax. Each party was an event, an opening night, with dozens of things that could go wrong. Yet she had never known such happiness. Her girlhood dream of being close to her father, of his wanting her, needing her, had come true. She had learned to adjust to the fact that his needs were impersonal, that her value to him was based on how much she could contribute to the company. That was Sam Roffe's only criterion for judging people. Elizabeth had been able to fill the gap that had existed since her mother's death. She had become her father's hostess. But because Elizabeth was a highly intelligent girl, she had become much more than that. She attended business conferences with Sam, in aeroplanes and in foreign hotel suites and factories and at embassies and palaces. She watched her father wield his power, deploying the billions of dollars at his command to buy and sell, tear down and build. Roffe and Sons was a vast cornucopia, and Elizabeth watched her father bestow its largesse on its friends, and withhold its bounty from its enemies. It was a fascinating world, filled with interesting people, and Sam Roffe was the master of it all.

As Elizabeth looked around the ballroom now,

she saw Sam standing at the bar, chatting with Rhys, a Prime Minister and a Senator from California. Her father saw Elizabeth and waved her over. As Elizabeth moved towards him, she thought of the time, three years earlier, when it had all begun.

Elizabeth had flown home the day of her graduation. She was eighteen. Home, at the moment, had been the apartment at Beekman Place in Manhattan. Rhys had been there with her father. She had somehow known that he would be. She carried pictures of him in the secret places of her thoughts, and whenever she was lonely or depressed or discouraged, she would take them out and warm herself with her memories. In the beginning it had seemed hopeless. A fifteen-year-old schoolgirl and a man of twenty-five. Those ten years might as well have been a hundred. But through some wonderful mathematical alchemy, at eighteen the difference in years was less important. It was as though she was growing older faster than Rhys, trying to catch up with him.

Both men rose as she walked into the library where they were talking business. Her father said casually, 'Elizabeth. Just get in?'

'Yes.'

'Ah. So school's finished.'

'Yes.'

'That's fine.'

And that was the extent of her welcome home. Rhys was walking towards her, smiling. He seemed genuinely pleased to see her. 'You look wonderful, Liz. How was the graduation? Sam wanted to be there but he couldn't get away.'

He was saying all the things her father should have been saying.

Elizabeth was angry with herself for being hurt. It was not that her father did not love her, she told herself, it was just that he was dedicated to a world in which she had no part. He would have taken a son into his world; a daughter was alien to him. She did not fit into the Corporate Plan.

'I'm interrupting.' She moved towards the door.

'Wait a minute,' Rhys said. He turned to Sam. 'Liz has come home just in time. She can help with the party on Saturday night.'

Sam turned to Elizabeth, studying her objectively, as though newly assessing her. She resembled her mother. She had the same beauty, the same natural elegance. A flicker of interest came into Sam's eyes. It had not occurred to him before that his daughter might be a potential asset to Roffe and Sons. 'Do you have a formal dress?'

Elizabeth looked at him in surprise. 'I –'

'It doesn't matter. Go and buy one. Do you know how to give a party?'

Elizabeth swallowed and said, 'Certainly.' Wasn't that one of the advantages of going to a Swiss finishing-school? They taught you all the social graces. 'Of course I know how to give a party.'

'Good. I've invited a group from Saudi Arabia. There'll be about –' He turned to Rhys.

Rhys smiled at Elizabeth and said, 'Forty. Give or take a few.'

'Leave everything to me,' Elizabeth said confidently.

The dinner was a complete fiasco.

Elizabeth had told the chef to prepare crab cocktails for the first course, followed by individual cassoulets, served with vintage wines. Unfortunately the cassoulet had pork in it, and the Arabs touched neither shellfish nor pork. Nor did they drink alcoholic beverages. The guests stared at the food, eating nothing. Elizabeth sat at the head of the long table, across the room from her father, frozen with embarrassment, dying inside.

It was Rhys Williams who saved the evening. He disappeared into the study for a few moments and spoke into the telephone. Then he came back into the dining-room and entertained the guests with amusing stories, while the staff began to clear the table.

In what seemed no time at all, a fleet of catering trucks drove up, and as if by magic a variety of dishes began appearing. Couscous and lamb en brochette and rice and platters of roast chicken and fish, followed by sweetmeats and cheese and fresh fruit. Everyone enjoyed the food except Elizabeth. She was so upset that she could not swallow a bite. Each time she looked up at Rhys, he was watching her, a conspiratorial look in his eyes. Elizabeth could not have said why, but she was mortified that Rhys should not only witness her shame but save her from it. When the evening finally ended, and the last of the guests had reluctantly departed in the early hours of the morning, Elizabeth and Sam and Rhys were in the drawing-room. Rhys was pouring a brandy.

Elizabeth took a deep breath and turned to her father, 'I'm sorry about the dinner. If it hadn't been for Rhys –'

'I'm sure you'll do better next time,' Sam said flatly.

Sam was right. From that time on, when Elizabeth gave a party, whether it was for four people or for four hundred, she researched the guests, found out their likes and dislikes, what they ate and drank, and what type of entertainment they enjoyed. She kept a catalogue with file cards on each person. The guests were flattered to find that their favourite brand of wine or whisky or cigars had been stocked for them, and that Elizabeth was able to discuss their work knowledgeably.

Rhys attended most of the parties, and he was always with the most beautiful girls there. Elizabeth hated them all. She tried to copy them. If Rhys brought a girl who wore her hair pinned up at the back, Elizabeth did her hair the same way. She tried to dress the way Rhys's girls dressed, to act the way they acted. But none of it seemed to make any impression on Rhys. He did not even seem to notice. Frustrated, Elizabeth decided that she might as well be herself.

On the morning of her twenty-first birthday, when Elizabeth came down to breakfast, Sam said, 'Order some theatre tickets for tonight. Supper afterwards at "Twenty-one".'

Elizabeth thought. He remembered, and she was inordinately pleased.

Then her father added, 'There'll be twelve of us. We'll be going over the new Bolivian contracts.'

She said nothing about her birthday. She received telegrams from a few former schoolmates, but that was it. Until six o'clock that evening, when an enormous bouquet of flowers arrived for her. Elizabeth was sure it was from her father. But the card read: 'What a lovely day for a lovely lady.' It was signed 'Rhys'.

Her father left the house at seven o'clock that evening on his way to the theatre. He noticed the flowers and said absently, 'Got a beau, huh?'

Elizabeth was tempted to say, 'They're a birthday present,' but what would have been the point? If you had to remind someone you loved that it was your birthday, then it was futile.

She watched her father leave, and wondered what she would do with her evening. Twenty-one had always seemed such an important milestone. It signified growing up, having freedom, becoming a woman. Well, here was the magic day, and she felt no different from the way she had felt last year, or the year before. Why couldn't he have remembered? Would he have remembered if she were his son?

The butler appeared to ask her about dinner.

Elizabeth was not hungry. She felt lonely and deserted. She knew she was feeling sorry for herself, but it was more than this uncelebrated birthday she was regretting. It was all the lonely birthdays of the past, the pain of growing up alone, without a mother or a father or anyone to give a damn.

At ten o'clock that night she was dressed in a robe, sitting in the living-room in the dark, in front of the fireplace, when a voice said, 'Happy birthday'.

The lights came on and Rhys Williams stood there. He walked over to her and said reprovingly, 'This is no way to celebrate. How many times does a girl have a twenty-first birthday?'

'I – I thought you were supposed to be with my father tonight,' Elizabeth said, flustered.

'I was. He mentioned that you were staying home alone tonight. Get dressed. We're going to dinner.'

Elizabeth shook her head. She refused to accept his pity. 'Thank you, Rhys. I – I'm really not hungry.'

'I am, and I hate eating alone. I'm giving you five minutes to get into some clothes, or I'm taking you out like that.'

They ate at a diner on Long Island, and they had hamburgers and chili and French-fried onions and root beer, and they talked, and Elizabeth thought it was better than the dinner she had had at Maxim's. All Rhys's attention was focused on her, and she could understand why he was so damned attractive to women. It was not just his looks. It was the fact that he truly liked women, that he enjoyed being with them. He made

Elizabeth feel like someone special, that he wanted to be with her more than with anyone else in the world. No wonder, Elizabeth thought, everyone fell in love with him.

Rhys told her a little about his boyhood in Wales, and he made it sound wonderful and adventurous and gay. 'I ran away from home,' he said, 'because there was a hunger in me to see everything and do everything. I wanted to be everyone I saw. *I* wasn't enough for me. Can you understand that?'

Oh, how well she understood it!

'I worked at the parks and the beaches and one summer I had a job taking tourists down the Rhosili in coracles, and –'

'Wait a minute,' Elizabeth interrupted. 'What's a Rhosili and what's a – a coracle?'

'The Rhosili is a turbulent, swift-flowing river, full of dangerous rapids and currents. Coracles are ancient canoes, made of wooden lathes and water-proof animal skins, that go back to pre-Roman days. You've never seen Wales, have you?' She shook her head. 'Ah, you would love it.' She knew she would. 'There's a waterfall at the Vale of Neath that's one of the beautiful sights of this world. And the lovely places to see: Abereiddi and Caerbwdi, Porthclais, Kilgetty and Llangwm Uchaf,' and the words rolled off his tongue like the lilt of music. 'It's a wild, untamed country, full of magical surprises.'

'And yet you left Wales.'

Rhys smiled at her and said, 'It was the hunger in me. I wanted to own the world.'

What he did not tell her was that the hunger was still there.

Over the next three years Elizabeth became indispensable to her father. Her job was to make his life comfortable, so that he could concentrate on the thing that was all-important to him: the Business. The details of running his life were left entirely to Elizabeth. She hired and fired servants, opened and closed the various houses as her father's needs required, and entertained for him.

More than that, she became his eyes and ears. After a business meeting Sam would ask Elizabeth her impression of a man, or explain to her why he had acted in a particular fashion. She watched him make decisions that affected the lives of thousands of people and involved hundreds of millions of dollars. She heard heads of state plead with Sam Roffe to open a factory, or beg him not to close one down.

After one of those meetings Elizabeth said, 'It's unbelievable. It's – it's as though you're running a country.'

Her father laughed and replied, 'Roffe and Sons has a larger income than three-quarters of the countries in the world.'

In her travels with her father Elizabeth became reacquainted with the other members of the Roffe family, her cousins and their husbands or wives.

As a young girl Elizabeth had seen them during holidays when they had come to one of her father's houses, or when she had gone to visit them during brief school holidays.

Simonetta and Ivo Palazzi, in Rome, had always been the most fun to be with. They were open and friendly, and Ivo had always made Elizabeth feel like a woman. He was in charge of the Italian division of Roffe and Sons, and he had done very well. People enjoyed dealing with Ivo. Elizabeth remembered what a classmate had said when she had met him. 'You know what I like about your cousin? He has warmth and charmth.'

That was Ivo, warmth and charmth.

Then there was Hélène Roffe-Martel, and her husband, Charles, in Paris. Elizabeth had never really understood Hélène, or felt at ease with her. She had always been nice to Elizabeth, but there was a cool reserve that Elizabeth had never been able to break through. Charles was head of the French branch of Roffe and Sons. He was competent, though from what Elizabeth had overheard her father say, he lacked drive. He could follow orders, but he had no initiative. Sam had never replaced him, because the French branch ran very profitably. Elizabeth suspected that Hélène Roffe-Martel had a great deal to do with its success.

Elizabeth liked her German cousin, Anna Roffe Gassner, and her husband, Walther. Elizabeth remembered hearing family gossip that Anna Roffe had married beneath her. Walther Gassner was reputed to be a black sheep, a fortune-hunter, who had married an unattractive woman years older

185

than himself, for her money. Elizabeth did not think her cousin was unattractive. She had always found Anna to be a shy, sensitive person, withdrawn, and a little frightened by life. Elizabeth had liked Walther on sight. He had the classic good looks of a movie star, but he seemed to be neither arrogant nor phony. He appeared to be genuinely in love with Anna, and Elizabeth did not believe any of the terrible stories she had heard about him.

Of all her cousins, Alec Nichols was Elizabeth's favourite. His mother had been a Roffe, and she had married Sir George Nichols, the third baronet. It was Alec to whom Elizabeth had always turned when she had a problem. Somehow, perhaps because of Alec's sensitivity and gentleness, he had seemed to the young child to be her peer, and she realized now what a great compliment that was to Alec. He had always treated her as an equal, ready to offer whatever aid and advice he could. Elizabeth remembered that once, in a moment of black despair, she had decided to run away from home. She had packed a suitcase and then, on a sudden impulse, had telephoned Alec in London to say goodbye. He had been in the middle of a conference, but he had come to the phone and talked to Elizabeth for more than an hour. When he had finished, Elizabeth had decided to forgive her father and give him another chance. That was Sir Alec Nichols. His wife, Vivian, was something else. Where Alec was generous and thoughtful, Vivian was selfish and thoughtless. She was the most self-centred woman Elizabeth had ever known.

Years ago, when Elizabeth was spending a weekend in their country home in Gloucestershire, she went on a picnic by herself. It had begun to rain, and she had returned to the house early. She had gone in by the back door, and as she had started down the hallway, she had heard voices from the study raised in a quarrel.

'I'm damned tired of playing nursemaid,' Vivian was saying. 'You can take your precious little cousin and amuse her yourself tonight. I'm going up to London. I have an engagement.'

'Surely you can cancel it, Viv. The child is only going to be with us another day, and she –'

'Sorry, Alec. I feel like a good fuck, and I'm getting one tonight.'

'For God's sake, Vivian!'

'Oh, shove it up your ass! Don't try to live my life for me.'

At that moment, before Elizabeth could move, Vivian had stormed out of the study. She had taken one quick look at Elizabeth's stricken face, and said cheerily, 'Back so soon, pet?' And strode upstairs.

Alec had come to the doorway. He had said gently, 'Come in, Elizabeth.'

Reluctantly she had walked into the study. Alec's face was aflame with embarrassment. Elizabeth had wanted desperately to comfort him, but she did not know how. Alec had walked over to a large refectory table, picked up a pipe, filled it with tobacco and lit it. It had seemed to Elizabeth that he took for ever.

'You must understand Vivian.'

Elizabeth had replied, 'Alec, it's none of my business. I –'

'But in a sense it is. We're all family. I don't want you to think harshly of her.'

Elizabeth could not believe it. After the incredible scene she had just heard, Alec was defending his wife.

'Sometimes in a marriage,' Alec had continued, 'a husband and a wife have different needs.' He had paused awkwardly, searching for the right phrase. 'I don't want you to blame Vivian because I – I can't fulfil some of those needs. That's not her fault, you see.'

Elizabeth had not been able to stop herself. 'Does–does she go out with other men often?'

'I'm rather afraid she does.'

Elizabeth had been horrified. 'Why don't you leave her?'

He had given her his gentle smile. 'I can't leave her, dear child. You see, I love her.'

The next day Elizabeth had returned to school. From that time on, she had felt closer to Alec than to any of the others.

Of late, Elizabeth had become concerned about her father. He seemed preoccupied and worried about something, but Elizabeth had no idea what it was. When she asked him about it, he replied, 'Just a little problem I have to clear up. I'll tell you about it later.'

He had become secretive, and Elizabeth no longer

had access to his private papers. When he had said to her, 'I'm leaving tomorrow for Chamonix to do a little mountain climbing,' Elizabeth had been pleased. She knew he needed a rest. He had lost weight and had become pale and drawn-looking.

'I'll make the reservations for you,' Elizabeth had said.

'Don't bother. They're already made.'

That, too, was unlike him. He had left for Chamonix the next morning. That was the last time she had seen him. The last time she would ever see him . . .

Elizabeth lay there in her darkened bedroom, remembering the past. There was an unreality about her father's death, perhaps because he had been so alive.

He was the last to bear the name of Roffe. Except for her. What would happen to the company now? Her father had held the controlling interest. She wondered to whom he had left the stock.

Elizabeth learned the answer late the next afternoon. Sam's lawyer had appeared at the house. 'I brought a copy of your father's will with me. I hate to intrude on your grief at a time like this, but I thought it best that you know at once. You are your father's sole beneficiary. That means that the controlling shares of Roffe and Sons are in your hands.'

Elizabeth could not believe it. Surely he did not expect *her* to run the company. 'Why?' she asked. 'Why me?'

The attorney hesitated, then said, 'May I be frank, Miss Roffe? Your father was a comparatively young man. I'm sure he didn't expect to die for many years. In time, I'm confident he would have made another will, designating someone to take over the company. He probably had not made up his mind yet.' He shrugged. 'All that is academic, however. The point is that the control now rests in your hands. You will have to decide what you want to do with it, who you want to give it to.' He studied her for a moment, then continued, 'There has never before been a woman on the board of directors of Roffe and Sons, but – well, for the moment you're taking your father's place. There's a board meeting in Zurich this Friday. Can you be there?'

Sam would have expected it of her.

And so would old Samuel.

'I'll be there,' Elizabeth said.

BOOK TWO

FIFTEEN

Portugal
Wednesday, September 9
Midnight

In the bedroom of a small rented apartment in Rua dos Bombeiros, one of the winding, dangerous back alleys of Alto Estoril, a motion-picture scene was being filmed. There were four people in the room. A cameraman, and on a bed the two actors in the scene, the man in his thirties and a young blonde girl with a stunning figure. She wore nothing except a vivid red ribbon tied round her neck. The man was large, with a wrestler's shoulders and a barrel-shaped, incongruously hairless chest. His phallus, even in detumescence, was huge. The fourth person in the room was a spectator, seated in the background, wearing a black broad-brimmed hat and dark glasses.

The cameraman turned to the spectator, questioningly, and the spectator nodded. The cameraman pressed a switch and the camera began to whir. He said to the actors, 'All right. Action.'

The man knelt over the girl and she took his penis in her mouth until it began to grow hard. The girl took it out and said, 'Jesus, that's big!'

'Shove it in her,' the cameraman ordered.

The man slid down over the girl and put his penis between her legs.

'Take it easy, honey.' She had a high, querulous voice.

'Look as though you're enjoying it.'

'How can I? It's the size of a fucking watermelon.'

The spectator was leaning forward, watching every move as the man entered her. The girl said, 'Oh, my God, that feels wonderful. Just take it slow, baby.'

The spectator was breathing harder now, staring at the scene on the bed. This girl was the third, and she was even prettier than the others.

She was writhing from side to side now, making little moaning noises. 'Oh, yes,' she gasped. 'Don't stop!' She grasped the man's hips and began pulling them towards her. The man began to pump harder and faster, in a frantic, pounding motion. Her movements began to quicken, and her nails dug into the man's naked back. 'Oh, yes,' she moaned. 'Yes, yes, yes! I'm coming!'

The cameraman looked towards the spectator, and the spectator nodded, eyes glistening behind the dark glasses.

'Now!' the cameraman called to the man on the bed.

The girl, caught in her own furious frenzy, did not even hear him. As her face filled with a wild ecstasy, and her body began to shudder, the man's huge hands closed round her throat and began to squeeze, closing off the air so that she could not breathe. She stared up at him, bewildered, and then her eyes filled with a sudden, terrified comprehension.

The spectator thought: *This is the moment. Now! Jesus God! Look at her eyes!* They were dilated with terror. She fought to tear away the iron bands around her throat, but it was useless. She was still coming, and the deliciousness of her orgasm and the frantic shudder of her death throes were blending into one.

The spectator's body was soaked with perspiration. The excitement was unbearable. In the middle of life's most exquisite pleasure the girl was dying, her eyes staring into the eyes of death. It was so beautiful.

Suddenly it was over. The spectator sat there, exhausted, shaken with spasms of pleasure, lungs filled with long, deep breaths. The girl had been punished.

The spectator felt like God.

SIXTEEN

Zurich
Friday, September 11
Noon

The world headquarters of Roffe and Sons occupied sixty acres along the Sprettenbach on the western outskirts of Zurich. The administration building was a twelve-storey modern, glass structure, towering over a nest of research buildings, manufacturing plants, experimental laboratories, planning divisions, and railway spurs. It was the brain centre of the far-flung Roffe and Sons empire.

The reception lobby was starkly modern, decorated in green and white, with Danish furniture. A receptionist sat behind a glass desk, and those who were admitted by her into the recesses of the building had to be accompanied by a guide. To the right rear of the lobby was a row of lifts, with one private express lift for the use of the company president.

On this morning the private lift had been used by the members of the board of directors. They had arrived within the past few hours from various parts of the world by plane, train, helicopter and limousine. They were gathered now in the enormous, high-ceilinged, oak-panelled boardroom: Sir Alec Nichols, Walther Gassner, Ivo Palazzi and Charles Martel. The only non-member of the board in the room was Rhys Williams.

Refreshments and drinks had been laid out on a sideboard, but no-one in the room was interested. They were tense, nervous, each preoccupied with his own thoughts.

Kate Erling, an efficient Swiss woman in her late forties, came into the room. 'Miss Roffe's car has arrived.'

Her eyes swept round the room to make sure that everything was in order: pens, note pads, a silver carafe of water at each place, cigars and cigarettes, ashtrays, matches. Kate Erling had been Sam Roffe's personal secretary for fifteen years. The fact that he was dead was no reason for her to lower his standards, or hers. She nodded, satisfied, and withdrew.

Downstairs, in front of the administration building, Elizabeth Roffe was stepping out of a limousine. She wore a black, tailored suit with a white blouse. She had on no make-up. She looked much younger than her twenty-four years, pale and vulnerable.

The press was waiting for her. As she started

into the building, she found herself surrounded by television and radio and newspaper reporters, with cameras and microphones.

'I'm from *L'Europeo*, Miss Roffe. Could we have a statement? Who's going to take over the company now that your father –?'

'Look this way, please, Miss Roffe. Can you give our readers a big smile?'

'Associated Press, Miss Roffe. What about your father's will?'

'New York *Daily News*. Wasn't your father an expert mountain climber? Did they find out how –?'

'*Wall Street Journal*. Can you tell us something about the company's financial –?'

'I'm from the London *Times*. We're planning to do an article on the Roffe –'

Elizabeth was fighting her way into the lobby, escorted by three security guards, pushing through the sea of reporters.

'One more picture, Miss Roffe –'

And Elizabeth was in the lift, the door closing. She took a deep breath and shuddered. Sam was dead. Why couldn't they leave her alone?

A few moments later, Elizabeth walked into the boardroom. Alec Nichols was the first to greet her. He put his arms around her shyly and said, 'I'm so sorry, Elizabeth. It was such a shock to all of us. Vivian and I tried to telephone you but –'

'I know. Thank you, Alec. Thank you for your note.'

Ivo Palazzi came up and gave her a kiss on each

cheek. '*Cara*, what is there to say? Are you all right?'

'Yes, fine. Thank you, Ivo.' She turned. 'Hello, Charles.'

'Elizabeth, Hélène and I were devastated. If there is anything at all –'

'Thank you.'

Walther Gassner walked over to Elizabeth and said awkwardly, 'Anna and I wish to express our great sorrow at what has happened to your father.'

Elizabeth nodded, her head high. 'Thank you, Walther.'

She did not want to be here, surrounded by all the reminders of her father. She wanted to flee, to be alone.

Rhys Williams was standing off to one side, watching Elizabeth's face, and he was thinking, If they don't stop, she's going to break down. He deliberately moved through the group, held out his hand and said, 'Hello, Liz.'

'Hello, Rhys.' She had last seen him when he had come to the house to bring her the news of Sam's death. It seemed like years ago. Seconds ago. It had been one week.

Rhys was aware of the effect it was costing Elizabeth to keep her composure. He said, 'Now that everyone's here, why don't we begin.' He smiled reassuringly. 'This won't take long.'

She gave him a grateful smile. The men took their accustomed places at the large, rectangular oak table. Rhys led Elizabeth to the head of the table and pulled out a chair for her. My father's chair, Elizabeth thought. Sam sat here, chairing these meetings.

Charles was saying, 'Since we do not have a –' He caught himself and turned to Alec. 'Why don't you take over?'

Alec glanced round, and the others murmured approval. 'Very well.'

Alec pressed a button on the table in front of him, and Kate Erling returned, carrying a notebook. She closed the door behind her and pulled up a straight chair, her notebook and pen poised.

Alec said, 'I think that under the circumstances we can dispense with the formalities. All of us have suffered a terrible loss. But' – he looked apologetically at Elizabeth – 'the essential thing right now is that Roffe and Sons show a strong public face.'

'*D'accord*. We have been taking enough of a hammering in the press lately,' Charles growled.

Elizabeth looked over at him and asked, 'Why?'

Rhys explained, 'The company is facing a lot of unusual problems just now, Liz. We're involved in heavy lawsuits, we're under government investigation, and some of the banks are pressing us. The point is that none of it is good for our image. The public buys pharmaceutical products because they trust the company that makes them. If we lose that trust, we lose our customers.'

Ivo said reassuringly, 'We have no problems that can't be solved. The important thing is to reorganize the company immediately.'

'How?' Elizabeth asked.

Walther replied, 'By selling our stock to the public.'

Charles added, 'In that way we can take care of all our bank loans, and have enough money left –' He let the sentence trail off.

Elizabeth looked at Alec. 'Do you agree with that?'

'I think we're all in agreement, Elizabeth.'

She leaned back in her chair, thoughtful. Rhys picked up some papers, rose and carried them to Elizabeth. 'I've had all the necessary documents prepared. All you have to do is sign.'

Elizabeth glanced at the papers lying before her. 'If I sign these, what happens?'

Charles spoke up. 'We have a dozen international brokerage firms ready to form a consortium to underwrite the stock issue. They will guarantee the sale at a price we mutually agree upon. In an offering as large as this one, there will be several institutional purchasers, as well as private ones.'

'You mean like banks and insurance companies?' Elizabeth asked.

Charles nodded. 'Exactly.'

'And they'll put their people on the board of directors?'

'That's usual . . .'

Elizabeth said, 'So, in effect, they would control Roffe and Sons.'

'We would still remain on the board of directors,' Ivo interposed quickly.

Elizabeth turned to Charles. 'You said a consortium of stockbrokers is ready to move ahead.'

Charles nodded. 'Yes.'

'Then why haven't they?'

He looked at her, puzzled. 'I don't understand.'

'If everyone is in agreement that the best thing for the company is to let it get out of the family and into the hands of outsiders, why hasn't it been done before?'

There was an awkward silence. Ivo said, 'It has to be by mutual consent, *cara*. *Everyone* on the board must agree.'

'Who didn't agree?' Elizabeth asked.

The silence was longer this time.

Finally Rhys spoke up. 'Sam.'

And Elizabeth suddenly realized what had disturbed her from the moment she had walked into this room. They had all expressed their condolences and their shock and grief over her father's death, and yet at the same time there had been an atmosphere of charged excitement in the room, a feeling of – strangely, the word that came into her mind was *victory*. They had had the papers all drawn up for her, everything ready. *All you have to do is sign.* But if what they wanted was right, then why had her father objected to it? She asked the question aloud.

'Sam had his own ideas,' Walther explained. 'Your father could be very stubborn.'

Like old Samuel, Elizabeth thought. Never let a friendly fox into your hen-house. One day he's going to get hungry. And Sam had not wanted to sell. He must have had good reason.

Ivo was saying, 'Believe me, *cara*, it is much better to leave all this to us. You don't understand these things.'

Elizabeth said quietly, 'I would like to.'

'Why bother yourself with this?' Walther objected. 'When your stock is sold, you will have an enormous amount of money – more than you'll ever be able to spend. You can go off anywhere you like and enjoy it.'

What Walther said made sense. Why *should* she get involved? All she had to do was sign the papers in front of her, and leave.

Charles said impatiently, 'Elizabeth, we're simply wasting time. You have no choice.'

It was at that instant that Elizabeth knew she did have a choice. Just as her father had had a choice. She could walk away and let them do as they pleased with the company, or she could stay and find out why they were all so eager to sell the stock, why they were pressuring her. For she could feel the pressure. It was so strong it was almost physical. Everyone in that room was *willing* her to sign the papers.

She glanced over at Rhys, wondering what he was thinking. His expression was non-committal. Elizabeth looked at Kate Erling. She had been Sam's secretary for a long time. Elizabeth wished she could have had a chance to speak to her alone. They were all looking at Elizabeth, waiting for her to agree.

'I'm not going to sign,' she said. 'Not now.'

There was a moment of stunned silence. Then Walther said, 'I don't understand, Elizabeth.' His face was ashen. 'Of course you must! Everything is arranged.'

Charles said angrily, 'Walther's right. You must sign.'

They were all speaking at once, in a confused and angry storm of words that beat at Elizabeth.

'*Why* won't you sign?' Ivo demanded.

She could not say: *Because my father would not sign. Because you're rushing me.* She had a feeling, an instinct that something was wrong, and she was determined to find out what it was. So now she merely said, 'I'd like a little more time to think about it.'

The men looked at one another.

'How much time, *cara*?' Ivo asked.

'I don't know yet. I'd like to get a better understanding of what's involved here.'

Walther exploded. 'Damn it, we can't –'

Rhys cut in firmly, 'I think Elizabeth is right.'

The others turned to look at him. Rhys went on, 'She should have a chance to get a clear picture of the problems the company is facing, and then make up her own mind.'

They were all digesting what Rhys had said.

'I agree with that,' Alec said.

Charles said bitterly, 'Gentlemen, it doesn't make any difference whether we agree with it or not. Elizabeth is in control.'

Ivo looked at Elizabeth. '*Cara* – we need a decision quickly.'

'You'll have it,' Elizabeth promised.

They were all watching her, each busy with his own thoughts.

One of them was thinking, Oh, God. *She's going to have to die too.*

SEVENTEEN

Elizabeth was awed.

She had been in her father's Zurich headquarters often, but always as a visitor. The power belonged to him. And now it belonged to her. She looked round the huge office and felt like an impostor. The room had been magnificently decorated by Ernst Hohl. At one end stood a Roentgen cabinet with a Millet landscape over it. There was a fireplace, and in front of it a chamois leather couch, a large coffee-table and four easy chairs. Around the walls were Renoirs, Chagalls, Klees and two early Courbets. The desk was a solid block of black mahogany. Next to it, on a large console table, was a communications complex – a battery of telephones with direct lines to company headquarters around the world. There were two red phones with scramblers, an intricate intercom system, a ticker-tape machine and other equipment. Hanging behind the desk was a portrait of old Samuel Roffe.

A private door led to a large dressing-room, with cedar closets and lined drawers. Someone had removed Sam's clothing, and Elizabeth was grateful. She walked through a tiled bathroom that included a marble bath and a stall shower. There were fresh Turkish towels hanging on warming racks. The medicine chest was empty. All the daily paraphernalia of her father's life had been taken away. Kate Erling, probably. Elizabeth idly wondered whether Kate had been in love with Sam.

The executive suite included a large sauna, a fully equipped gymnasium, a barber's shop, and a dining-room that could seat a hundred people. When foreign guests were being entertained, a little flag representing their country was placed in the floral centrepiece on the table.

In addition, there was Sam's private dining-room, tastefully decorated with murals.

Kate Erling had explained to Elizabeth, 'There are two chefs on duty during the day, and one at night. If you are having more than twelve guests for luncheon or dinner, they need two hours' notice.'

Now Elizabeth sat at the desk, piled high with papers, memoranda, and statistics and reports, and she did not know where to begin. She thought of her father sitting here, in this chair, behind this desk, and she was suddenly filled with a sense of unbearable loss. Sam had been so able, so brilliant. How she needed him now!

Elizabeth had managed to see Alec for a few moments before he returned to London.

'Take your time,' he had advised her. 'Don't let anyone pressure you.'

So he had sensed her feelings.

'Alec, do you think I should vote to let the company go public?'

He had smiled at her and said awkwardly, 'I'm afraid I do, old girl, but then I've got my own axe to grind, haven't I? Our shares are no good to any of us until we can sell them. That's up to you now.'

Elizabeth was remembering that conversation as she sat alone in the huge office. The temptation to telephone Alec was overpowering. All she had to say was, 'I've changed my mind.' And get out. She did not belong here. She felt so inadequate.

She looked at the set of intercom buttons on the console. Opposite one of them was the name RHYS WILLIAMS. Elizabeth debated a moment, then flicked down the switch.

Rhys was seated across from her, watching her. Elizabeth knew exactly what he must be thinking, what they were all thinking. That she had no business to be there.

'That was quite a bomb you dropped at the meeting this morning,' Rhys said.

'I'm sorry if I upset everyone.'

He grinned. '"Upset" is hardly the word. You put everyone in a state of shock. It was all supposed to have been cut and dried. The publicity releases were ready to send out.' He studied her a moment. 'What made you decide not to sign, Liz?'

How could she explain that it was nothing more than a feeling, an intuition? He would laugh at her. And yet Sam had refused to let Roffe and Sons go public. She had to find out why.

As though reading her thoughts, Rhys said, 'Your great-great-grandfather set this up as a family business, to keep away outsiders. But it was a small company then. Things have changed. We're running one of the biggest drugstores in the world. Whoever sits in your father's chair has to make all the final decisions. It's one hell of a responsibility.'

She looked at him and wondered whether this was Rhys's way of telling her to get out. 'Will you help me?'

'You know I will.'

She felt a rush of relief and she realized how much she had been counting on him.

'The first thing we'd better do,' Rhys said, 'is take you on a tour of the plant here. Do you know about the physical structure of this company?'

'Not much.'

That was not true. Elizabeth had been at enough meetings with Sam over the past few years to have picked up a good deal of knowledge about the workings of Roffe and Sons. But she wanted to hear it from Rhys's point of view.

'We manufacture much more than drugs, Liz. We make chemicals and perfumes and vitamins and hair sprays and pesticides. We produce cosmetics and bio-electronic instruments. We have a food division, and a division of animal nitrates.' Elizabeth was aware of all that, but she let Rhys go on. 'We publish magazines for distribution to doctors. We make adhesives, and building protection agents and plastic explosives.'

Elizabeth could sense that he was becoming caught up by what he was saying; she could hear the undertone of pride in his voice, and she was oddly reminded of her father.

'Roffe and Sons owns factories and holding companies in over a hundred countries. Every one of them reports to this office.' He paused, as though to make sure that she understood the point. 'Old Samuel went into business with a horse and a test tube. It's grown to sixty factories around the world, ten research centres and a network of thousands of salesmen and detail men and woman.' They were the ones. Elizabeth knew, who called on the doctors and hospitals. 'Last year, in the United States alone, they spent over fourteen billion dollars on drugs – and we have a healthy share of that market.'

And yet Roffe and Sons was in trouble with the banks. Something was wrong.

Rhys took Elizabeth on a tour of the company's headquarters factory. In actuality, the Zurich division was a dozen factories, with seventy-five buildings on the sixty acres of ground. It was a world in microcosm, completely self-supporting. They visited the manufacturing plants, the research departments, the toxicology laboratories, the storage plants. Rhys brought Elizabeth to a sound stage, where they made motion pictures for research and for their world-wide advertising and product divisions. 'We use more film here,' Rhys told Elizabeth, 'than the major Hollywood studios.'

They went through the molecular biology department, and the liquid centre, where fifty giant, stainless steel, glass-lined tanks hung suspended from the ceiling, filled with liquids ready to be bottled. They saw the tablet-compression rooms, where powders were formed into tablets, sized, stamped with ROFFE AND SONS, packaged and labelled, without anyone ever touching them. Some of the drugs were ethical products, available only on prescription, others were proprietary items, sold over the counter.

Set apart from the other buildings were several small buildings. These were for the scientists: the analytical chemists, biochemists, organic chemists, parasitologists, pathologists.

'More than three hundred scientists work here,' Rhys told Elizabeth. 'Most of them are PhDs. Would you like to see our hundred-million-dollar room?'

Elizabeth nodded, intrigued.

It was in an isolated brick building, guarded by a uniformed policeman with a gun. Rhys showed his security pass, and he and Elizabeth were permitted to enter a long corridor with a steel door at the end of it. The guard used two keys to open the door, and Elizabeth and Rhys entered. The room contained no windows. It was lined from floor to ceiling with shelves filled with every variety of bottles, jars and tubes.

'Why do they call this the hundred-million-dollar room?' Elizabeth asked.

'Because that's what it cost to furnish it. See all those compounds on the shelves? None of them have names, only numbers. They're the ones that didn't make it. They're the failures.'

'But a hundred million –'

'For every new drug that works, there are about a thousand that end up in this room. Some drugs are worked on for as long as ten years, and then abandoned. A single drug can cost five or ten million dollars in research before we find out that it's no good, or that someone else has beaten us to it. We don't throw any of these things away because now and then one of our bright young men will back into a discovery that can make something in this room valuable.'

The amounts of money involved were awesome.

'Come on,' Rhys said. 'I'll show you the Loss Room.'

It was in another building, this one unguarded, containing, like the other room, only shelves filled with bottles and jars.

'We lose a fortune here too,' Rhys said. 'But we plan it that way.'

'I don't understand.'

Rhys walked over to a shelf and picked up a bottle. It was labelled 'Botulism'. 'Do you know how many cases of botulism there were in the United States last year? Twenty-five. But it costs us millions of dollars to keep this drug in stock.' He picked up another bottle at random. 'This is an antidote for rabies. This room is full of drugs that are cures for rare diseases – snakebites, poisonous plants. We furnish them free to the armed forces and to hospitals, as a public service.'

'I like that,' Elizabeth said. Old Samuel would have liked it too, she thought.

Rhys took Elizabeth to the capsule rooms, where empty bottles were carried in on a giant conveyor belt. By the time they had crossed the room, the bottles had been sterilized, filled with capsules, labelled, topped with cotton, and sealed. All done by automation.

There was a glass-blowing factory, an architectural centre to plan new buildings, a real estate division to acquire the land for them. In one building there were scores of writers turning out pamphlets in fifty languages, and printing presses to print them.

Some of the departments reminded Elizabeth of George Orwell's *1984*. The Sterile Rooms were bathed in eerie ultraviolet light. Adjoining rooms were painted in different colours – white, green or blue – and the workers wore uniforms to match. Each time they entered or left the room, they had to go through a special sterilizing chamber. Blue workers were locked in for the entire day. Before they could eat or rest or go to the toilet, they had

213

to undress, enter a neutral green zone, put on other clothes, and reverse the process when they returned.

'I think you'll find this interesting,' Rhys said.

They were walking down the grey corridor of a research building. They reached a door marked 'RESTRICTED – DO NOT ENTER'. Rhys pushed the door open, and he and Elizabeth walked through. They went through a second door and Elizabeth found herself in a dimly lit room filled with hundreds of cages containing animals. The room was hot and humid, and she felt as if she had suddenly been transported to a jungle. As her eyes grew accustomed to the half-light, she saw that the cages were filled with monkeys and hamsters and cats and white mice. Many of the animals had obscene-looking growths protruding from various parts of their bodies. Some had their heads shaven, and were crowned with electrodes that had been implanted in their brains. Some of the animals were screaming and gibbering, racing around in their cages, while others were comatose and lethargic. The noise and the stench were unbearable. It was like some kind of hell. Elizabeth walked up to a cage that contained a single white kitten. Its brain was exposed, enclosed in a clear plastic covering through which protruded half a dozen wires.

'What – what's going on here?' Elizabeth asked.

A tall, bearded young man making notes in front of a cage explained. 'We're testing a new tranquillizer.'

'I hope it works,' Elizabeth said weakly. 'I think

I could use it.' And she walked out of the room before she could be sick.

Rhys was at her side in the corridor. 'Are you all right?'

She took a deep breath. 'I – I'm fine. Is all that really necessary?'

Rhys looked at her and replied. 'Those experiments save a lot of lives. More than one third of the people born since nineteen fifty are alive only because of modern drugs. Think about that.'

Elizabeth thought about it.

It took six full days to tour the key buildings, and when Elizabeth had finished, she was exhausted, her head spinning with the vastness of it. And she realized she was seeing just one Roffe plant. There were dozens of others scattered around the world.

The facts and figures were stunning. 'It takes between five and ten years to market a new drug, and out of every two thousand compounds tested, we'll average only three products . . .'

And '. . . Roffe and Sons has three hundred people working here in quality control alone.'

And '. . . Worldwide, Roffe and Sons is responsible for over half a million employees . . .'

And '. . . our gross income last year was . . .'

Elizabeth listened, trying to digest the incredible figures that Rhys was throwing at her. She had known that the company was large, but 'large' was such an anonymous word. Having it actually translated into terms of people and money was staggering.

That night as Elizabeth lay in bed, recalling all the things she had seen and heard, she was filled with an overpowering feeling of inadequacy.

Ivo *Believe me*, cara, *it is much better to leave all this to us. You don't understand these things.*

Alec *I think you should sell but I have an axe to grind.*

Walther *Why bother yourself with this? You can go off anywhere you like and enjoy your money.*

They were right, all of them, Elizabeth thought. I'm going to get out and let them do what they like with the company. I do not belong in this position.

The moment she made the decision, she felt a deep sense of relief. She fell asleep almost immediately.

The following day, Friday, was the beginning of a holiday weekend. When Elizabeth arrived at the office, she sent for Rhys to announce her decision.

'Mr Williams had to fly to Nairobi last night,' Kate Erling informed her. 'He said to tell you he would be back on Tuesday. Can anyone else help you?'

Elizabeth hesitated. 'Put in a call to Sir Alec, please.'

'Yes, Miss Roffe.' Kate added, a note of hesitation in her voice, 'A package for you was delivered this morning by the police department. It contains the personal belongings your father had with him at Chamonix.'

The mention of Sam brought back that sharp sense of loss, of grief.

'The police apologized because they could not give it to your messenger. It was already on its way to you.'

Elizabeth frowned. 'My messenger?'

'The man you sent to Chamonix to pick it up.'

'I didn't send anyone to Chamonix.' It was obviously some bureaucratic mix-up. 'Where is it?'

'I put it in your closet.'

There was a Vuitton suitcase, containing Sam's clothes, and a locked attaché case with a key taped to it. Probably company reports. She would let Rhys handle them. Then she remembered that he was away. Well, she decided, she would go away for the weekend too. She looked at the attaché case and thought, Perhaps there's something personal belonging to Sam. I'd better look at it first.

Kate Erling buzzed. 'I'm sorry, Miss Roffe. Sir Alec's out of the office.'

'Leave a message for him to call me, please. I'll be at the villa in Sardinia. Leave the same message for Mr Palazzi, Mr Gassner and Mr Martel.'

She would tell them all that she was leaving, that they could sell the stock, do as they pleased with the company.

She was looking forward to the long weekend. The villa was a retreat, a soothing cocoon, where she could be alone to think about herself and her future. Events had been flung at her so rapidly that she had had no chance to put things into any kind of perspective. Sam's accident – Elizabeth's mind tripped over the word 'death'; inheriting the controlling stock of Roffe and Sons; the urgent pressure from the family to let the company go public. And the company itself. The awesome heartbeat of a behemoth whose power spanned the world. It was too much to cope with all at once.

When she flew to Sardinia late that afternoon, Elizabeth had the attaché case with her.

EIGHTEEN

She took a taxi from the airport. There was no one at the villa because it had been closed, and Elizabeth had not told anyone she was coming. She let herself in and walked slowly through the large familiar rooms and it was as if she had never been away. She had not realized how much she had missed this place. It seemed to Elizabeth that the few happy memories of her childhood had been here. It felt strange to be alone in this labyrinth where there had always been half a dozen servants bustling around, cooking, cleaning, polishing. Now there was only herself. And the echoes of the past.

She left Sam's attaché case in the downstairs hallway and carried her suitcase upstairs. With the habit of long years, she started to head for her bedroom in the centre of the hallway, then stopped. Her father's room was at the far end. Elizabeth turned and walked towards it. She opened the door slowly, because while her mind understood the reality, some deep, atavistic instinct made her half expect to see Sam there, to hear the sound of his voice.

The room was empty, of course, and nothing had changed since Elizabeth had last seen it. It contained a large double bed, a beautiful tallboy, a dressing-table, two comfortable upholstered chairs, and a couch in front of the fireplace. Elizabeth put down her suitcase and walked over to the window. The iron shutters had been closed against the late September sun, and the curtains were drawn. She opened them wide and let the fresh mountain air flow in, soft and cool with the promise of fall. She would sleep in this room.

Elizabeth returned downstairs and went into the library. She sat down in one of the comfortable leather chairs, rubbing her hands along the sides. This was where Rhys always sat when he had a conference with her father.

She thought about Rhys and wished that he were here with her. She remembered the night he had brought her back to school after the dinner in Paris, and how she had gone back to her room and had written 'Mrs Rhys Williams' over and over. On an impulse Elizabeth walked over to the desk, picked up a pen and slowly wrote 'Mrs Rhys Williams'. She looked at it and smiled. 'I wonder,' she mocked herself aloud, 'how many other idiots are doing the same thing right now?'

She turned her thoughts away from Rhys, but still he was at the back of her mind, pleasantly comforting. She got up and wandered around the house. She explored the large, old-fashioned kitchen, with its wood-burning stove, and two ovens.

She walked over to the refrigerator and opened it. It was empty. She should have anticipated that, with the house shut down. Because the refrigerator was empty, she became suddenly hungry. She searched the cupboards. There were two small cans of tuna fish, a half-filled jar of Nescafé, and an unopened packet of biscuits. If she was going to be here for a long weekend, Elizabeth decided, she had better do some planning. Rather than drive into town for every meal, she would shop at one of the little markets in Cali di Volpe and stock enough food for several days. A utility jeep was always kept in the carport and she wondered if it was still there. She went to the back of the kitchen and through the door that led to the carport, and there was the jeep. Elizabeth walked back into the kitchen, where, on a board behind the cupboard, were hooks with labelled keys on them. She found the key to the jeep and returned to the carport. Would there be petrol in it? She turned the key and pressed the starter. Almost immediately the motor sparked into life. So *that* problem was eliminated. In the morning she would drive into town and pick up whatever groceries she needed.

She went back into the house. As she walked across the tiled floor of the reception hall, she could hear the echo of her footsteps, and it was a hollow, lonely sound. She wished that Alec would call, and even as she was thinking it the telephone rang, startling her. She walked to it and picked it up. 'Hello.'

'Elizabeth. It's Alec here.'

Elizabeth laughed aloud.

'What's so funny?'

'You wouldn't believe me if I told you. Where are you?'

'Down in Gloucester.' And Elizabeth felt a sudden, urgent impulse to see him, to tell him her decision about the company. But not over the telephone. 'Would you do me a favour, Alec?'

'You know I will.'

'Could you fly down here for the weekend? I'd like to discuss something with you.'

There was only the slightest hesitation, and then Alec said, 'Of course.'

Not a word about what engagements he would have to break, how inconvenient it might be. Just 'Of course.' That was Alec.

Elizabeth forced herself to say, 'And bring Vivian.'

'I'm afraid she won't be able to come. She's – ah – rather involved in London. I can arrive tomorrow morning. Will that do?'

'Perfect. Let me know what time, and I'll pick you up at the airport.'

'It will be simpler if I just take a taxi.'

'All right. Thank you, Alec. Very much.'

When Elizabeth replaced the receiver, she was feeling infinitely better.

She knew she had made the right decision. She was in this position only because Sam had died before he had had the time to name his successor.

Elizabeth wondered who the next president of Roffe and Sons would be. The board could decide that for themselves. She thought about it from Sam's point of view, and the name that sprang instantly to mind was Rhys Williams. The others were competent in their own areas, but Rhys was the only one who had a working knowledge of the company's complete global operation. He was brilliant and effective. The problem, of course, was that Rhys was not eligible to be president. Because he was not a Roffe, or married to a Roffe, he could not even sit on the board.

Elizabeth walked into the hallway and saw her father's attaché case. She hesitated. There was hardly any point in her going through it now. She could give it to Alec when he arrived in the morning. Still, if there *was* something personal in it . . . She carried it into the library, set it on the desk, untaped the key and opened the little locks on each side. In the centre of the case lay a large manila envelope. Elizabeth opened it and removed a sheaf of typewritten papers lying loosely in a cardboard cover labelled:

Mr Sam Roffe
Confidential
No copies

It was obviously a report of some kind, but without anyone's name on it so that Elizabeth could not know who had drawn it. She started to skim through the report, then slowed down, then stopped. She could not believe what she was reading. She carried the papers over to an armchair, kicked off her shoes, curled her legs up underneath her and turned to page one again.

This time she read every word, and she was filled with horror. It was an astonishing document, a confidential report of an investigation into a series of events that had occurred over the past year.

In Chile a chemical plant owned by Roffe and Sons had exploded, sending tons of poisonous materials spouting over a ten-square-mile area. A dozen people had been killed, hundreds more had been taken to hospitals. All the livestock had died, the vegetation was poisoned. The entire region had had to be evacuated. The lawsuits filed against Roffe and Sons had run into hundreds of millions of dollars. But the shocking thing was that the explosion had been deliberate. The report read 'The Chilean government's investigation into the accident was cursory. The official attitude seems to be: the Company is rich, the people are poor, let the Company pay. There is no question in the minds of our investigating staff but that it was an act of sabotage, by a person or persons unknown, using plastic explosives. Because of the antagonistic official attitude here, it will be impossible to prove.'

Elizabeth remembered the incident only too well. Newspapers and magazines had been full of horror stories complete with photographs of the victims, and the world's press had attacked Roffe and Sons, accusing it of being careless and indifferent to human suffering. It had damaged the image of the company badly.

The next section of the report dealt with major research projects that Roffe and Sons' scientists had been working on for a number of years. There were four projects listed, each of them of inestimable potential value. Combined, they had cost more than fifty million dollars to develop. In each case a rival pharmaceutical firm had applied for a patent for one of the products, just ahead of Roffe and Sons, using the identical formula. The report continued: 'One isolated incident might have been put down as coincidence. In a field where dozens of companies are working in related areas, it is inevitable that several companies might be working on the same type of product. But four such incidents in a period of a few months force us to the conclusion that someone in the employ of Roffe and Sons gave or sold the research material to the competitive firms. Because of the secret nature of the experiments, and the fact that they were conducted in widely separated laboratories under conditions of maximum security, our investigation indicates that the person, or persons, behind this would need to have access to top security clearances. We therefore conclude that whoever is responsible is someone in the highest executive echelon of Roffe and Sons.'

There was more.

A large batch of toxic drugs had been mis-labelled and shipped. Before they could be recalled there were several deaths, and more bad publicity for the company. No-one could learn where the wrong labels had come from.

A deadly toxin had disappeared from a heavily guarded laboratory. Within an hour an unidentified person had leaked the story to the newspapers and started a scare.

The afternoon shadows had long since lengthened into evening, and the night air had turned chilly. Elizabeth remained totally absorbed in the document she held in her hands. When the study became dark, she switched on a lamp and continued to read, the horror piled on horror.

Not even the dry, terse tone of the report could conceal the drama in it. One thing was clear. Someone was methodically attempting to damage or destroy Roffe and Sons.

Someone in the highest echelon of the company. On the last page was a marginal note in her father's neat, precise handwriting. 'Additional pressure on me to let the company go public? Trap the bastard.'

She remembered now how worried Sam had been, and his sudden secrecy. He had not known whom to trust.

Elizabeth looked at the front page of the report again. 'No copies.'

Elizabeth was sure the report had been done by an outside investigative agency. So in all probability no one had been aware of this report but Sam. And now herself. The guilty person had no idea he was under suspicion. Had Sam known who he was? Had Sam confronted him before his accident? Elizabeth had no way of knowing. All she knew was that there was a traitor.

Someone in the highest echelon of the company.

No one else would have the opportunity or the ability to carry out so much destruction on so many different levels. Was that why Sam had refused to let the company go public? Was he trying to find the guilty person first? Once the company was sold, it would be impossible to conduct a secret investigation, with every move being reported to a group of strangers.

Elizabeth thought about the board meeting, and how they had urged her to sell. All of them.

Elizabeth suddenly felt very alone in the house. The loud ringing of the telephone made her jump. She walked over to it and picked it up. 'Hello?'

'Liz? It's Rhys. I just received your message.'

She was glad to hear his voice, but she suddenly remembered why she had called him. To tell him that she was going to sign the papers, let the company be sold. In a few short hours everything had completely changed. Elizabeth glanced out into the hallway, at the portrait of old Samuel. He had founded this company and had fought for it. Elizabeth's father had built it up, helped turn it into a giant, and lived for it, dedicated himself to it.

'Rhys,' Elizabeth said, 'I'd like to have a board

meeting Tuesday. Two o'clock. Would you please arrange for everyone to be there?'

'Tuesday at two o'clock,' Rhys agreed. 'Anything else?'

She hesitated. 'No. That's all. Thank you.'

Elizabeth slowly replaced the receiver. She was going to fight them.

She was high on a mountain with her father, climbing at his side. *Don't look down*, Sam kept saying, and Elizabeth disobeyed, and there was nothing below but thousands of feet of empty space. There was a loud rumble of thunder, and a bolt of lightning came hurtling towards them. It hit Sam's rope and set it on fire, and Sam started falling through space. Elizabeth watched her father's body tumble end over end, and she began to scream, but her screams were drowned by the roar of the thunder.

Elizabeth awakened suddenly, her nightgown drenched with perspiration, her heart pounding wildly. There was a loud clap of thunder, and she looked towards the window and saw that it was pouring outside. The wind was driving the rain into the bedroom through the open French doors. Quickly, Elizabeth got out of bed, crossed to the doors and pushed them tightly shut. She looked out at the storm clouds that filled the sky, and at the lightning flashes across the horizon, but she was not seeing them.

She was thinking about her dream.

*   *   *

In the morning the storm had passed over the island, leaving only a light drizzle. Elizabeth hoped that the weather would not delay Alec's arrival. After reading the report she desperately needed someone to talk to. In the meantime she decided it would be a good idea to put it away in a secure place. There was a safe up in the tower room. She would keep it there. Elizabeth bathed, put on a pair of old slacks and a sweater, and went down into the library to get the report.

It was gone.

NINETEEN

The room looked as though a hurricane had swept through it. The storm had blown open the French doors during the night, and the wind and the rain had wreaked havoc, scattering everything before it. A few loose pages of the report lay on the wet rug, but the rest of the pages had obviously been carried away by the wind.

Elizabeth stepped to the French windows and looked out. She could see no papers on the lawn, but the wind could easily have blown them over the cliff. That must have been what happened.

No COPIES. She must find out the name of the investigator Sam had hired. Perhaps Kate Erling would know. But Elizabeth could not be sure now that Sam had trusted Kate. This had become like a terrible game, where no one could trust anybody. She would have to move very carefully.

Elizabeth suddenly remembered that there was no food in the house. She could shop at Cala di Volpe and be back before Alec arrived. She went to the hall closet and got her raincoat and a scarf for her hair. Later, when the rain let up, she would search the grounds for the missing papers. She went into the kitchen and took the key to the jeep from the key rack. She walked out the back door that led to the carport.

Elizabeth started the engine and carefully backed the jeep out of the carport. She turned it round and headed out of the private driveway, braking to slow down because of the wet surface. At the bottom of the driveway she turned right, on to the narrow mountain road that led to the little village of Cala di Volpe below. There was no traffic on the road at this hour, but there seldom was, for few houses had been built up this high. Elizabeth glanced down to her left and saw that the sea below had become dark and angry, swollen with the night storm.

She drove slowly, for this part of the road became treacherous. It was narrow, with two lanes that had been cut into the side of the mountain, along a sheer precipice. On the inside lane was the solid rock of the mountain, and on the outside, a drop of hundreds of feet to the sea below. Elizabeth kept as close as she could to the inside lane, braking to fight the momentum of the steep mountain gradient.

The car was approaching a sharp curve. Automatically, Elizabeth put her foot on the brakes to slow the jeep down.

The brakes were dead.

It took a long moment to register. Elizabeth

pressed again, harder, pushing down on the pedal with all her strength, and her heart began to pound as the jeep kept gathering speed. It took the curve and was moving faster now, racing down the steep mountain road, gaining momentum with each second. She pressed down on the brakes again. They were useless.

Another curve lay ahead. Elizabeth was afraid to take her eyes off the road to look at the speedometer, but out of the corner of her eye she could see the needle racing upward and she was filled with an icy terror. She reached the curve and skidded round it, much too fast. The back wheels slid towards the edge of the precipice, then the tyres found their traction and the jeep plunged forward again, hurtling down the steep road ahead. There was nothing to stop it now, no barriers, no controls, only the swift roller-coaster ride down, and the deadly, beckoning curves ahead.

Elizabeth's mind raced frantically, seeking some escape. She thought of jumping. She risked a quick look at the speedometer. She was doing seventy miles an hour now, and building up speed every moment, trapped between the solid mountain wall on one side and the deadly drop into space on the other. She was going to die. And in an instant revelation Elizabeth knew that she was being murdered, and that her father had been murdered. Sam had read the report, and he had been killed. As she was going to be killed. And she had no idea who her murderer was, who hated them enough to do this terrible thing. Somehow she could have borne it better if it had been a stranger. But it was someone she knew, someone who knew her. Faces flashed through her mind. Alec . . . Ivo . . . Walther . . . Charles . . . It had to be one of them. *Someone in the highest echelon of the company*.

Her death would be listed as an accident, as Sam's had been. Elizabeth was crying now, silently, her tears mixing with the fine mist of rain that was falling, but she was not even aware of it. The jeep was beginning to skid out of control on the wet surface, and Elizabeth fought to keep the wheels on the road. She knew it was only a matter of seconds before she hurtled over the cliff, into oblivion. Her body became rigid, and her hands were numb from gripping the steering-wheel. There was nothing in the universe now but herself, careering down the mountain road, with the roaring wind tugging at her, saying *Come join me*, tearing at the car, trying to push it over the brink of the cliff. The jeep started into another skid, and Elizabeth fought desperately to straighten it out, remembering what she had been taught. *Steer into the skid, always into the skid*, and the rear wheels straightened out and the car continued racing downhill. Elizabeth stole another quick glance at the speedometer . . . eighty miles an hour. She was catapulting towards a steep hairpin curve ahead, and she knew she was not going to make this one.

Something in her mind seemed to freeze, and it was as if there was a thin veil between her and

233

reality. She heard her father's voice saying, *What are you doing down here alone in the dark?* and he was picking her up and carrying her to bed and she was on stage dancing and turning and turning and she could not stop, and Mme Netturova was screaming at her (or was it the wind?) and Rhys was there, saying, *How many times does a girl have her twenty-first birthday?* And Elizabeth thought, I'll never see Rhys again, and she screamed his name and the veil disappeared, but the nightmare was still there. The sharp curve was looming closer now, the car speeding towards it like a bullet. She would go over the cliff. *Let it happen quickly*, she prayed silently.

At that moment, to the right, just before the hairpin curve, Elizabeth caught a glimpse of a small firebreak trail that had been cut through the rock, going up the mountainside. She had to make a decision in a split second. She had no idea where the trail led. All she knew was that it went *upward*, that it might slow her momentum, give her a chance. And she took it. At the last instant, as the jeep reached the trail, Elizabeth swung the wheel hard to the right. The rear wheels started to skid, but the front wheels were on the gravel road and the momentum gave them enough traction to hold. The jeep was now hurtling upward, and Elizabeth was fighting the wheel, trying to keep the car on the narrow trail. There was a thin line of trees and their branches were slashing at her as she raced by them, tearing at her face and her hands. She looked ahead, and to her horror, she could see the Tyrrhenian Sea below. The path had merely led to the other side of the cliff. There was no safety here at all.

She was getting closer and closer to the brink now, moving too fast to jump from the jeep. The edge of the cliff was just ahead of her, the sea hundreds of feet below. As the jeep hurtled towards the edge, it went into a wild skid, and the last thing Elizabeth remembered was a tree looming up in front of her and then an explosion that seemed to fill the universe.

After that the world became still and white and peaceful and silent.

TWENTY

She opened her eyes and she was in a hospital bed and the first thing she saw was Alec Nichols.

'There's nothing in the house for you to eat,' she whispered, and started to cry.

Alec's eyes filled with pain, and he put his arms around her and held her close. 'Elizabeth!'

And she mumbled, 'It's all right, Alec. Everything is fine.'

And it was. Every inch of her body felt bruised and beaten, but she was alive, and she could not believe it. She remembered the terror of that drive down the mountain, and her body went cold.

'How long have I been here?' Her voice was weak and hoarse.

'They brought you in two days ago. You've been unconscious since then. The doctor says it was a miracle. According to everybody who saw the scene of the accident, you should be dead. A service crew came across you and rushed you in here. You have a concussion and a hell of a lot of bruises, but, thank the Lord, there's nothing broken.' He looked at her, puzzled, and said, 'What were you doing up there on that firebreak road?'

Elizabeth told him. She could see the horror on his face as he lived through the terrible ride with her. He kept repeating, 'Oh, my God,' over and over. When Elizabeth had finished, Alec was pale. 'What a stupid, terrible accident!'

'It wasn't an accident, Alec.'

He looked at her, puzzled. 'I don't understand.'

How could he? He had not read the report. Elizabeth said, 'Someone tampered with the brakes.'

He shook his head incredulously. 'Why would anyone do that?'

'Because –' She could not tell him. Not yet. She trusted Alec more than she trusted anyone else, but she was not ready to talk. Not until she felt stronger, not until she had had time to think.

'I don't know,' she said evasively. 'I'm just sure someone did.'

She watched him and she could read the changing expressions on his face. They went from disbelief to puzzlement to anger.

'Well, we're certainly going to find out.' His voice was grim.

He picked up the telephone, and a few minutes later he was talking to the Chief of Police in Olbia. 'This is Alec Nichols,' he said. 'I – Yes, she's fine, thank you . . . Thank you. I'll tell her. I'm calling about the jeep she was driving. Could you tell me where it is? . . . Would you keep it there, please?

And I'd like you to get hold of a good mechanic. I'll be there in half an hour.' He replaced the receiver. 'It's in the police garage. I'm going over.'

'I'm coming with you.'

He looked at her in surprise. 'The doctor said you must stay in bed for at least another day or two. You can't –'

'I'm coming with you,' she insisted stubbornly.

Forty-five minutes later Elizabeth checked her bruised and swollen body out of the hospital over a doctor's protests, and was on her way to the police garage with Alec Nichols.

Luigi Ferraro, the Chief of Police of Olbia, was a swarthy, middle-aged Sardo, with a large stomach and bandy legs. Next to him was Detective Bruno Campagna, who towered over his chief. Campagna was a muscularly built man in his fifties, with an air of solid competence. He stood next to Elizabeth and Alec, watching a mechanic examine the underside of a jeep that was raised on a hydraulic hoist. The left front fender and radiator had been smashed, and they were streaked with the sap of the trees they had crashed into. Elizabeth had felt faint at her first sight of the car, and she had had to lean on Alec for support. He looked at her with concern. 'Are you sure you're up to this?'

'I feel fine,' Elizabeth lied. She felt weak and terribly tired. But she had to see for herself.

The mechanic wiped his hands on a greasy cloth and walked over to the group. 'They don't build them like that no more,' he said.

Thank God, Elizabeth thought.

'Any other car woulda been in bits and pieces.'

'What about the brakes?' Alec asked.

'The brakes? They're in perfect condition.'

Elizabeth felt a sudden sense of unreality engulfing her. 'What – what do you mean?'

'They're workin' fine. The accident didn't hurt them at all. That's what I meant when I said that they don't build –'

'That's impossible,' Elizabeth interrupted. 'The brakes were not working on that jeep.'

'Miss Roffe believes that someone tampered with them,' Chief Ferraro explained.

The mechanic shook his head. 'No, sir.' He walked back to the jeep and pointed to the underside. 'There's only two ways you can *fregare* –' He turned to Elizabeth. 'Excuse me, signorina – screw up the brakes on a jeep. You can either cut the brake links or you can loosen this nut' – he indicated a piece of metal on the underside – 'and let the brake fluid run out. You can see for yourself that this link is solid, and I checked the brake drum. It's full.'

Chief Ferraro said to Elizabeth soothingly, 'I can understand how in your condition it could –'

'Just a moment,' Alec interrupted. He turned to the mechanic. 'Isn't it possible that those links were cut and then replaced or that someone drained the brake fluid and then filled it again?'

The mechanic shook his head stubbornly. 'Mister, those links ain't been touched.' He took his rag again and carefully wiped off the oil around the nut that held the brake fluid. 'See this nut? If anyone had loosened it, there'd be fresh wrench marks on it. I'll guarantee that no one's touched it in the last six months. There's not a thing wrong with these brakes. I'll show you.'

He walked over to the wall and pulled a switch. There was a whirring sound and the hydraulic lift began to lower the jeep to the floor. They watched as the mechanic got in it, started the engine and backed the jeep up. When it was touching the back wall, he put the jeep in first gear and pressed down on the accelerator. The car raced towards Detective Campagna. Elizabeth opened her mouth to scream, and at that instant the jeep jerked to a stop an inch away from him. The mechanic ignored the look the detective gave him and said, 'See? These brakes are perfect.'

They were all looking at Elizabeth now, and she knew what they were thinking. But that did not change the terror of that ride down the mountain. She could feel her foot pressing on the brakes, and nothing happening. Yet the police mechanic had proved that they worked. Unless he was in on it. And that meant the Chief of Police probably knew too. I'm becoming paranoiac, Elizabeth thought.

Alec said helplessly, 'Elizabeth —'

'When I drove that jeep, those brakes were not working.'

Alec studied her for a moment, then said to the mechanic, 'Let's suppose that someone did arrange it so that the brakes on this jeep wouldn't work. How else could it have been done?'

Detective Campagna spoke up. 'They could have wet the brake lining.'

Elizabeth could feel an excitement stirring in her. 'What would happen if they did that?'

Detective Campagna said, 'When the brake lining pressed against the drum, it would have no traction.'

The mechanic nodded. 'He's right. The only thing is –' He turned to Elizabeth. 'Were your brakes working when you started driving?'

Elizabeth remembered using the brakes to back out of the carport, and braking again later when she came to the first curves. 'Yes,' she said, 'they were working.'

'There's your answer,' the mechanic said triumphantly. 'Your brakes got wet in the rain.'

'Hold on,' Alec objected. 'Why couldn't someone have wet them before she started?'

'Because,' the mechanic said patiently, 'if anyone had wet them before she started, she wouldn'ta had no brakes at all.'

The Chief of Police turned to Elizabeth. 'Rain can be very dangerous, Miss Roffe. Particularly on these narrow mountain roads. This sort of thing happens all too often.'

Alec was watching Elizabeth, not knowing what to do next. She felt like a fool. It *had* been an accident after all. She wanted to get out of here. She looked at the Chief of Police. 'I – I'm sorry to have put you to all this trouble.'

241

'*Please*. It is a pleasure. I mean – I am distressed about the circumstances, but it is always a pleasure to be of service. Detective Campagna will drive you back to your villa.'

Alec said to her, 'If you don't mind my saying so, old girl, you look ghastly. Now, I want you to hop into your bed and stay there for a few days. I'll order some groceries by telephone.'

'If I stay in bed, who's going to cook?'

'I am,' Alec declared.

That evening he prepared dinner and served it to Elizabeth in bed.

'I'm afraid I'm not a very good cook,' he said cheerfully, as he set a tray down in front of Elizabeth.

It was the understatement of the year, Elizabeth thought. Alec was a terrible cook. Every dish was either burned, underdone or oversalted. But she managed to eat, partly because she was starving, and partly because she did not want to hurt Alec's feelings. He sat with her, making careful small talk. Not a word about what a fool she had made of herself at the police garage. She loved him for it.

The two of them spent the next few days at the villa, with Elizabeth remaining in bed, and Alec fussing over her, cooking all the meals, reading to her. During that time it seemed to Elizabeth that the telephone never stopped ringing. Ivo and Simonetta called every day to see how she was, and Hélène and Charles, and Walther. Even Vivian called. They all offered to come and stay with her.

'I'm really all right,' she told them. 'There's no reason for you to come. I'll be returning to Zurich in a few days.'

Rhys Williams called. Elizabeth had not realized how much she had missed him until she heard the sound of his voice.

'I hear you decided to give Hélène some competition,' he said. But she could hear the concern in his voice.

'Wrong. I only race on mountains, downhill.' It was incredible to her that she could joke about it now.

Rhys said, 'I'm glad you're all right, Liz.'

His tone, as much as his words, warmed her. She wondered if he was with another woman now, and who she was. It would be someone beautiful, of course.

Damn her.

'Did you know you made the headlines?' Rhys asked.

'No.'

'"Heiress narrowly escapes death in car accident. Only a few weeks after her father, the well-known –" You can write the rest of the story yourself.'

They spoke on the phone for half an hour, and when Elizabeth hung up she was feeling much better. Rhys seemed so genuinely interested in her, and concerned. She wondered whether he made every

243

woman he knew feel that way about him. It was part of his charm. She remembered how they had celebrated her birthday together. *Mrs Rhys Williams*.

Alec walked into the bedroom. He said, 'You look like the Cheshire cat.'

'Do I?'

Rhys had always been able to make her feel that way. Perhaps, she thought, I should tell Rhys about the confidential report.

Alec had arranged for one of the company planes to fly them back to Zurich.

'I hate to take you back so soon,' he said apologetically, 'but there are some rather urgent decisions that have to be made.'

The flight to Zurich was uneventful. There were reporters at the airport. Elizabeth made a brief statement about her accident, and then Alec had her safely inside the limousine and they were on their way to the company headquarters.

She was in the conference room with all the members of the board, and Rhys, present. The meeting had been going on for the past three hours, and the air was stale with cigar and cigarette smoke. Elizabeth was still shaken from her experience, and she had a pounding headache – *Nothing to be concerned about, Miss Roffe. When the concussion wears off, the headaches will go away.*

She looked round the room, at the tense, angry faces. 'I've decided not to sell,' Elizabeth had told them. They thought she was being arbitrary and stubborn. If they only knew how close she had come to giving in. But now it was impossible. Someone in this room was an enemy. If she quit now, it would be his victory.

They had all tried to convince her, each in his own fashion.

Alec said reasonably, 'Roffe and Sons needs an experienced president, Elizabeth. Particularly now. For your own sake, as well as everyone else's, I would like to see you walk away from this.'

Ivo used his charm. 'You're a beautiful young girl, *carissima*. The whole world is yours. Why do you want to become a slave to something as dull as business when you could be out, having a wonderful time, travelling –'

'I've travelled,' Elizabeth said.

Charles used Gallic logic. 'You happen to hold the controlling stock through a tragic accident, but it makes no sense for you to try to run the company. We have serious problems. You will only make them worse.'

Walther spoke bluntly. 'The company is in enough trouble. You have no idea how much trouble. If you do not sell now, it will be too late.'

Elizabeth felt as though she were under siege. She listened to them all, studying them, evaluating what they were telling her. Each of them based his argument on the good of the company – yet one of them was working to destroy it.

One thing was clear. They all wanted her to get

out, to let them sell their stock, and bring in outsiders to take over Roffe and Sons. Elizabeth knew that the moment she did that, her chances of finding out who was behind this were finished. As long as she stayed here, on the inside, there was the possibility that she could learn who was sabotaging the company. She would stay only as long as she had to. She had not spent the last three years with Sam without learning something about the business. With the help of the experienced staff he had built up, she would continue to carry out her father's policies. The insistence from all the board members that she get out now only made her more stubbornly determined to remain.

She decided it was time to end the meeting.

'I've made my decision,' Elizabeth said. 'I don't plan to run this company alone. I'm aware of how much I have to learn. I know I can count on all of you to help me. We'll deal with the problems one by one.'

She sat at the head of the table, still pale from her accident, looking small and defenceless.

Ivo threw up his hands helplessly. 'Can't anyone talk some logic into her?'

Rhys turned to Elizabeth and smiled. 'I think everyone's going to have to go along with whatever the lady wants to do.'

'Thank you, Rhys.' Elizabeth looked at the others. 'There's one thing more. Since I'm taking my father's place, I think it would be best to make it official.'

Charles stared at her. 'You mean – you want to become president?'

'In effect,' Alec reminded him dryly, 'Elizabeth is already president. She's merely showing us the courtesy of letting us handle the situation gracefully.'

Charles hesitated, then said, 'All right. I move that Elizabeth Roffe be nominated president of Roffe and Sons.'

'I second the motion.' Walther.

The motion was carried.

It was such a bad time for presidents, he thought sadly. *So many were being assassinated.*

TWENTY-ONE

No-one was more aware than Elizabeth of the enormous responsibility she had assumed. As long as she was running the company, the jobs of thousands of people depended upon her. She needed help, but she had no idea whom she could trust. Alec and Rhys and Ivo were the ones she most wanted to confide in, but she was not ready yet. It was too soon. She sent for Kate Erling.

'Yes, Miss Roffe?'

Elizabeth hesitated, wondering how to begin. Kate Erling had worked for Elizabeth's father for many years. She would have a sense of the undercurrents that flowed beneath the deceptively calm surface. She would know about the inner workings of the company, about Sam Roffe's feelings, his plans. Kate Erling would make a strong ally.

Elizabeth said, 'My father was having some kind of confidential report drawn up for him, Kate. Do you know anything about it?'

Kate Erling frowned in concentration, then

shook her head. 'He never discussed it with me, Miss Roffe.'

Elizabeth tried another approach. 'If my father had wanted a confidential investigation, to whom would he have gone?'

This time the answer was unhesitating. 'Our security division.'

The last place Sam would have gone to. 'Thank you,' Elizabeth said.

There was no-one she could talk to.

There was a current financial report on her desk. Elizabeth read it with growing dismay, and then sent for the company comptroller. His name was Wilton Kraus. He was younger than Elizabeth had expected. Bright, eager, an air of faint superiority. The Wharton School, she decided, or perhaps Harvard.

Elizabeth began without preamble. 'How can a company like Roffe and Sons be in financial difficulty?'

Kraus looked at her and shrugged. He was obviously not used to reporting to a woman. He said condescendingly, 'Well, putting it in words of one syllable –'

'Let's begin with the fact,' Elizabeth said curtly, 'that up until two years ago Roffe and Sons had always done its own capital financing.'

She watched his expression change, trying to adjust. 'Well – yes, ma'am.'

'Then why are we so heavily indebted to banks now?'

He swallowed and said, 'A few years ago, we went through a period of unusually heavy expansion. Your father and the other members of the board felt that it would be wise to raise that money by borrowing from banks on short-term loans. We have current net commitments to various banks for six hundred and fifty million dollars. Some of those loans are now due.'

'Overdue,' Elizabeth corrected him.

'Yes, ma'am. Overdue.'

'We're paying the prime rate, plus one per cent, plus penalty interest. Why haven't we paid off the overdue loans and reduced the principal on the others?'

He was beyond surprise now. 'Because of – er – certain unfortunate recent occurrences, the company's cash-flow position is considerably less than we had anticipated. Under ordinary circumstances we would go to the banks and ask for extensions. However, with our current problems, the various litigation settlements, the write-offs in our experimental laboratory, and . . .' His voice trailed off.

Elizabeth sat there, studying him, wondering whose side he was on. She looked down at the balance sheets again, trying to pinpoint where things had gone wrong. The statement showed a sharp decline over the past three quarters, largely because of the heavy lawsuit payoffs listed under the column 'Extraordinary Expenses (Non-recurring)'. In her mind's eye she saw the explosion in Chile, the cloud of poisonous chemicals spouting into the air. She could hear the screams of the victims. A dozen people dead. Hundreds more taken to hospitals. And in the end all the human pain and misery had been reduced to money, to Extraordinary Expenses (Non-recurring).

She looked up at Wilton Kraus. 'According to your report, Mr Kraus, our problems are of a temporary nature. We are Roffe and Sons. We're still a first-class risk for any bank in the world.'

It was his turn to study her. His supercilious air was gone, but he was wary now.

'You must realize, Miss Roffe,' he began cautiously, 'that a drug firm's reputation is as important as its products.'

Who had said that to her before? Her father? Alec? She remembered. Rhys.

'Go on.'

'Our problems are becoming too well-known. The business world is a jungle. If your competitors suspect that you've been wounded, they move in for the kill.' He hesitated, then added, 'They're moving in for the kill.'

'In other words,' Elizabeth replied, 'our competitors bank with our bankers, too.'

He gave her a brief congratulatory smile. 'Exactly. The banks have a limited amount of funds to loan out. If they're convinced that A is a better risk than B –'

'And *do* they think that?'

He ran his fingers through his hair, nervously. 'Since your father's death I've had several calls from

Herr Julius Badrutt. He heads the banking consortium we're dealing with.'

'What did Herr Badrutt want?' She knew what was coming.

'He wanted to know who was going to be the new president of Roffe and Sons.'

'Do you know who the new president is?' Elizabeth asked.

'No, ma'am.'

'I am.' She watched him try to conceal his surprise. 'What do you think will happen when Herr Badrutt learns the news?'

'He'll pull the plug on us,' Wilton Kraus blurted out.

'I'll talk to him,' Elizabeth said. She leaned back in her chair and smiled. 'Would you care for some coffee?'

'Why, that's – that's very kind of you. Yes, thank you.'

Elizabeth watched him relax. He had sensed that she had been testing him, and he felt that he had passed the test.

'I'd like your advice,' Elizabeth said. 'If you were in my position, Dr Kraus, what would you do?'

That faintly patronizing air was back. 'Well,' he said confidently, 'that's very simple. Roffe and Sons has enormous assets. If we sold off a substantial block of stock to the public, we could easily raise more than enough money to satisfy all our bank loans.'

She knew now whose side he was on.

TWENTY-TWO

Hamburg
Friday, October 1
2 a.m.

The wind was blowing from the sea, and the early-morning air was chill and damp. In the Reeperbahn section of Hamburg the streets were crowded with visitors eager to experience the forbidden pleasures of the city of sin. The Reeperbahn catered for all tastes impartially. Drinks, drugs, girls or boys – they were all available at a price.

The garishly lighted hostess bars were on the main street, while the Grosse Freiheit featured the lewd strip shows. The Herbertstrasse, one block away, was for pedestrians only, and both sides of the street were lined with prostitutes sitting in the windows of their flats, displaying their wares through flimsy, soiled nightgowns that concealed nothing. The Reeperbahn was a vast market, a human butcher shop, where you could select any piece of meat you could afford to pay for. For the strait-laced there was simple sex, missionary style; for those who enjoyed a bit of variety there was cunnilingus and analingus and sodomy. On the Reeperbahn you could buy a twelve-year-old boy or girl, or get into bed with a mother and daughter. If your tastes ran that way, you could watch a woman being serviced by a Great Dane, or get yourself whipped until you achieved orgasm. You could hire a toothless crone to perform fellatio on you in a busy alley or buy yourself an orgy in an elaborately mirrored bedroom with as many girls or boys as your libido required. The Reeperbahn prided itself on having something for everyone. Younger whores in short skirts and tight-fitting blouses cruised the pavements, propositioning men, women and couples impartially.

The cameraman walked down the street slowly, the target for a dozen girls and brightly rouged boys. He ignored them all until he came to a girl who looked to be no more than eighteen. She had blonde hair. She was leaning against a wall, talking to a girl friend. She turned as the man approached, and smiled. 'Would you like a party, *liebchen*? My friend and I will give you a good time.'

The man studied the girl and said, 'Just you.'

The other girl shrugged and moved off.

'What's your name?'

'Hildy.'

'Would you like to be in the movies, Hildy?' the cameraman asked.

The young girl studied him with cold eyes. '*Herrgott!* You're not going to give me that old Hollywood *Scheiss*?'

He smiled reassuringly. 'No, no. This is a genuine offer. It's a porno film. I make them for a friend of mine.'

'It will cost you five hundred marks. In advance.'

'*Gut.*'

She regretted instantly that she had not asked for more. Well, she would find some way to get a bonus out of him. 'What do I have to do?' Hildy asked.

Hildy was nervous.

She lay sprawled out naked on the bed in the small, shabbily furnished apartment, watching the three people in the room, and thinking, There's something wrong here. Her instincts had been sharpened on the streets of Berlin and Munich and Hamburg. She had learned to rely on them. There was something about these people she did not trust. She would have liked to have walked out before it started, but they had already paid her five hundred marks, and promised her another five hundred if she did a good job. She would do a good job. She was a professional and she took a pride in her work. She turned to the naked man in bed beside her. He was strong and well-built; his body was hairless. What bothered Hildy was his face. He was too old for this sort of film. But it was the spectator who sat quietly at the back of the room who disturbed Hildy the most. The spectator wore a long coat, a large hat and dark glasses. Hildy could not even tell if it was a man or a woman. The vibrations were bad. Hildy fingered the red ribbon tied around her neck, wondering why they had asked her to wear it. The cameraman said, 'All right. We're ready now. Action.'

The camera began whirring. Hildy had been told what to do. The man was lying on his back. Hildy went to work.

She started with a trip around the world, skilfully using her tongue and lips on the man's ears and neck, moving down across his chest and stomach and belly, lightly flicking her tongue in quick butterfly strokes against his groin and penis, then each leg, down to his toes, slowly licking each toe, watching his erection begin. She rolled him over on his stomach, and her tongue began to work its way back up his body, moving slowly, expertly, finding all the erotic crevices and sensitive areas and exploring them. The man was fully aroused now, rock-hard.

'Get inside her,' the cameraman said. The man rolled her over and was on top of her, forcing her thighs apart, his penis swollen to an enormous tumescence, and as he entered her, Hildy forgot her earlier fear. It felt wonderful.

'Shove it in me, *liebchen*!' she cried.

The man was deep, deep inside her, rocking back and forth, and Hildy started to move with him, her hips writhing in quickening spasms. In the back of the room the spectator was leaning forward, watching every movement. The girl on the bed closed her eyes.

She was spoiling it!

'Her eyes!' the spectator shouted.

The director called out, '*Offne die Augen!*'

Startled, Hildy opened her eyes. She watched the man on top of her. He was good. It was the kind of sex she liked. Hard and thrusting. He was moving faster now, and she began to respond to him. Usually she did not have orgasms, except with her girl friend. With customers she always faked it, and they never knew the difference. But the cameraman had warned her that if she did not have an orgasm, she would not be paid the bonus. And so now she relaxed and let herself think about all the beautiful things she was going to buy with the money, and she felt herself beginning to climax.

'*Schneller!*' she cried. '*Schneller!*'

Her body began to shudder. '*Ah, jetzt!*' she screamed. '*Es kommt! Es kommt!*'

The spectator nodded, and the cameraman cried, 'Now!'

The man's hands moved up towards the girl's neck. His enormous fingers closed over her windpipe and squeezed. She looked up into his eyes and saw what was there, and she was filled with terror. She tried to scream, but she was unable to breathe. She fought desperately to fight free, her body jerking in great, orgiastic spasms, but he had her pinned down. There was no escape.

The spectator sat there drinking it in, feasting

on it, looking into the dying girl's eyes, watching her being punished.

The girl's body shuddered once, and then was still.

TWENTY-THREE

Zurich
Monday, October 4
10 a.m.

When Elizabeth arrived at her office, a sealed envelope marked 'CONFIDENTIAL', with her name on it, was lying on her desk. She opened it. In it was a report from the chemical laboratory. It was signed 'Emil Joeppli'. It was full of technical terms, and Elizabeth read it through without understanding it. Then she read it again. And again. Each time more slowly. When finally she had grasped its significance, she said to Kate, 'I'll be back in an hour.' And she went to find Emil Joeppli.

He was a tall man, about thirty-five, with a thin, freckled face, and a scalp that was bald except for a tonsure of bright red hair. He fidgeted uncomfortably, as though unused to having visitors in his little laboratory.

'I read your report,' Elizabeth told him. 'There's

a great deal in it that I don't understand. I wonder if you would mind explaining it to me.'

Instantly, Joeppli's nervousness vanished. He leaned forward in his chair, sure and confident, and began to speak rapidly. 'I've been experimenting with a method of inhibiting rapid differentiation of the collagens, by using mucopolysaccharides and enzyme blocking techniques. Collagen, of course, is the fundamental protein basis of all connective tissue.'

'Of course,' Elizabeth said.

She did not even try to understand the technical part of what Joeppli was saying. What Elizabeth did understand was that the project he was working on could retard the ageing process. It was a breathtaking concept.

She sat there, silent, listening, thinking about what this could mean in terms of revolutionizing the lives of men and women all over the world. According to Joeppli, there was no reason why everyone could not live to be a hundred, or a hundred and fifty, or even two hundred years old.

'It would not even be necessary to have injections,' Joeppli told Elizabeth. 'With this formula the ingredients could be taken orally in a pill or a capsule.'

The possibilities were staggering. It would mean nothing less than a social revolution. And billions of dollars for Roffe and Sons. They would manufacture it themselves, and license it out to other companies as well. There was no one over fifty years of age who would not take a pill that would keep him or her young. It was difficult for Elizabeth to conceal her excitement.

'How far along are you on this project?'

'As I wrote in my report, I've been doing tests with animals for the last four years. All the recent results have been positive. It's just about ready for testing on human beings.' She liked his enthusiasm.

'Who else knows about this?' Elizabeth asked.

'Your father knew. It's a Red Folder project. Top security. That means that I report only to the president of the company and to one member of the board.'

Elizabeth suddenly felt chilled. 'Which member?'

'Mr Walther Gassner.'

Elizabeth was silent for a moment. 'From this time on,' she said, 'I want you to report directly to me. And only to me.'

Joeppli looked at her in surprise. 'Yes, Miss Roffe.'

'How soon could we have this on the market?'

'If everything goes well, eighteen to twenty-four months from now.'

'Fine. If you need anything – money, extra help, equipment – let me know. I want you to move as quickly as possible.'

'Yes, ma'am.'

Elizabeth rose, and instantly Emil Joeppli jumped to his feet.

'It's a pleasure meeting you.' He smiled, and added shyly, 'I liked your father.'

'Thank you,' Elizabeth said. Sam had known about this project. Was that another reason he refused to sell the company?

At the door Emil Joeppli turned to Elizabeth.

'It's going to work on people!'

'Yes,' Elizabeth said. 'Of course it will.'

It had to.

'How is a Red Folder project handled?'

Kate Erling asked, 'From the beginning?'

'From the beginning.'

'Well. As you know, we have several hundred new products in various experimental stages. They –'

'Who authorizes them?'

'Up to a certain amount of money, the heads of the different departments involved,' Kate Erling said.

'What amount of money?'

'Fifty thousand dollars.'

'And after that?'

'There must be board approval. Of course, a project does not come into the Red Folder category until it has passed its initial tests.'

'You mean until it looks like it has a chance of being successful?' Elizabeth asked.

'That's right.'

'How is it protected?'

'If it's an important project, all the work is transferred to one of our high-security laboratories. All the papers are removed from the general files and put into a Red Folder file. Only three people have access to that. The scientist in charge of the project, the president of the company, and one member of the board.'

'Who decides who that member will be?' Elizabeth asked.

'Your father selected Walther Gassner.'

The moment the words were out of her mouth, Kate realized her mistake.

The two women looked at each other, and Elizabeth said, 'Thank you, Kate. That will be all.'

Elizabeth had made no mention of Joeppli's project. Yet Kate had known what Elizabeth was talking about. There were two possibilities. Either Sam had trusted her and told her about Joeppli's project, or she had learned about it on her own. For someone else.

This was too important to allow anything to go wrong. She would check on the security herself. And she had to speak to Walther Gassner. She reached for the telephone, then stopped. There was a better way.

Late that afternoon Elizabeth was on a commercial airliner to Berlin.

Walther Gassner was nervous.

They were seated at a corner booth in the upstairs dining-room of the Papillon on the Kurfürstendamm. Whenever Elizabeth had visited Berlin in the past, Walther had always insisted that Elizabeth have dinner at his home, with Anna and him. This time there had been no mention of that. He had suggested instead that they meet at this restaurant. And he had come without Anna.

Walther Gassner still had the clear-cut, boyish, movie-star handsomeness, but the surface gloss had begun to crack. There were lines of tension in his face, and his hands never stopped moving. He seemed to be under some extraordinary tension. When Elizabeth asked about Anna, Walther was vague. 'Anna's not feeling well. She couldn't come.'

'Is it anything serious?'

'No, no. She'll be fine. She's at home, resting.'

'I'll call her and –'

'Better not to disturb her.'

It was a puzzling conversation, totally unlike Walther, whom Elizabeth had always found so open and outgoing.

She brought up the subject of Emil Joeppli. 'We need what he's working on very badly,' Elizabeth said.

Walther nodded. 'It's going to be big.'

'I've asked him not to report to you any more,' Elizabeth told him.

Walther's hands suddenly went very still. It was like a shout. He looked at Elizabeth and asked, 'Why did you do that?'

'It has nothing to do with you, Walther. I would have done exactly the same thing with any other board member working with him. I simply want to handle this in my own way.'

He nodded. 'I see.' But his hands remained motionless on the table. 'You have a right, of course.' He forced a smile and she could see what it was costing him. 'Elizabeth,' he said, 'Anna has a lot of stock in the company. She can't sell it unless you vote yes. It's very important. I –'

'I'm sorry, Walther, I can't let the stock be sold now.'

His hands suddenly began to move again.

TWENTY-FOUR

Herr Julius Badrutt was a thin, brittle man who resembled a praying mantis in a black suit. He was like a stick figure drawn by a child, with angular arms and legs, and a dry, unfinished face sketched on top of his body. He was seated stiffly at the conference table of the Roffe and Sons boardroom, facing Elizabeth. There were five other bankers with him. They all wore black suits with waistcoats, white shirts and dark ties. They appeared, Elizabeth thought, not so much *dressed* as in uniform. Looking round at the cold, impassive eyes at the table, Elizabeth was filled with a sense of misgiving. Before the meeting had begun, Kate had brought in a tray of coffee and delicious, freshly baked pastries. The men had all declined. Just as they had declined Elizabeth's invitation to come to lunch. She decided it was a bad sign. They were there to get the money that was owed them.

Elizabeth said, 'First of all, I wish to thank all of you for coming here today.'

There were polite, meaningless murmurs in response.

She took a deep breath. 'I asked you here to discuss an extension on the loans owed to you by Roffe and Sons.'

Julius Badrutt shook his head in tiny, jerky movements. 'I am sorry, Miss Roffe. We have already informed –'

'I haven't finished,' Elizabeth said. She glanced round the room. 'If I were you, gentlemen, I would refuse.'

They stared at her, then looked at one another in confusion.

Elizabeth continued, 'If you were concerned about the loans when my father was running this company – and he was a brilliant businessman – why would you extend them for a woman who is inexperienced in business?'

Julius Badrutt said dryly, 'I think you have answered your own question, Miss Roffe. We have no intention of –'

Elizabeth said, 'I haven't finished.'

They were eyeing her more warily now. She looked at each of them in turn, making sure she had their full attention. They were Swiss bankers, admired, respected and envied by their lesser colleagues in other parts of the financial world. They were leaning forward now, listening carefully, their attitude of impatience and boredom replaced by curiosity.

'You have all known Roffe and Sons for a long time,' Elizabeth went on. 'I am sure most of you knew my father and, if you did, you must have respected him.'

There were nods of agreement from some of the men.

'I imagine,' Elizabeth continued, 'that you gentlemen must have choked over your morning coffee when you learned that I was taking his place here.'

One of the bankers smiled, then laughed aloud, and said, 'You are quite right, Miss Roffe. I do not mean to be ungallant, but I think I am speaking for the rest of my colleagues when I say that – what were your words? – we choked over our morning coffee.'

Elizabeth smiled ingenuously. 'I don't blame you. I'm sure I would have reacted in exactly the same way.'

Another banker spoke up. 'I am curious, Miss Roffe. Since we are all in agreement about the outcome of this meeting' – he spread his hands expressively – 'why are we here?'

'You're here,' Elizabeth said, 'because in this room are some of the greatest bankers in the world. I can't believe that you became so successful by looking at everything only in dollars and cents. If that were true, then any of your bookkeepers could run your business for you. I am sure that there is much more to banking than that.'

'Of course there is,' another banker murmured, 'but we're businessmen, Miss Roffe, and –'

'And Roffe and Sons is a business. It's a great business. I didn't know how great until I sat behind my father's desk. I had no idea how many lives this company has saved in countries all over the world. Or of the enormous contributions we've made to medicine. Or how many thousands of people depend on this company for their livelihood. If –'

Julius Badrutt interrupted. 'That is all very commendable, but we seem to be getting off the point. I understand that it has been suggested to you that if you release the company stock, there will be more than sufficient monies to satisfy our loans.'

His first mistake, Elizabeth thought. *I understand that it has been suggested to you.*

The suggestion had been made in the privacy of a board of directors' meeting, where everything was confidential. Someone at that meeting had talked. Someone who was trying to put pressure on her. She intended to find out who, but that would have to come later.

'I want to ask you a question,' Elizabeth said. 'If your loans are repaid, would it matter to you where the money came from?'

Julius Badrutt studied her, his mind circling the question, looking for a trap. Finally he said, 'No. Not as long as we receive the money due to us.'

Elizabeth leaned forward and said earnestly, 'So it doesn't matter whether you're paid from the sale of company stock to outsiders, or from our own financial resources. All of you know that Roffe and Sons isn't going out of business. Not today. Not tomorrow. Not ever. All I'm asking is the courtesy of a little extra time.'

Julius Badrutt smacked his dry lips and said, 'Believe me, Miss Roffe, we are most sympathetic. We understand the terrible emotional stress you have gone through, but we cannot –'

'Three months,' Elizabeth said. 'Ninety days. With your getting additional penalty interest, of course.'

There was a silence around the table. But it was a negative silence. Elizabeth could see their cold, hostile faces. She decided on one last desperate gamble.

'I – I don't know whether it's proper for me to reveal this,' she said with deliberate hesitation, 'and I must ask you to keep it confidential.' She looked around and saw that she had their interest again. 'Roffe and Sons is on the verge of a breakthrough that's going to revolutionize the entire pharmaceutical industry.' She paused to heighten the suspense. 'The company is about to reveal a new product that our projections show will *far outsell every drug available on the market today.*'

She could feel the change in the atmosphere.

It was Julius Badrutt who rose to the bait first. 'What – er – type of –?'

Elizabeth shook her head. 'I'm sorry, Herr Badrutt. Perhaps I've already said too much. I can only tell you that it will be the biggest innovation in the history of this business. It will require a tremendous expansion of our facilities. We'll have to double them, perhaps triple them. Of course, we'll be looking for new financing on a large scale.'

The bankers were glancing at one another,

exchanging silent signals. The silence was broken by Herr Badrutt. 'If we *were* to give you a ninety-day extension, we would naturally expect to act as the prime bankers for Roffe and Sons in all future transactions.'

'Naturally.'

Another exchange of meaningful looks. It's like a form of jungle drums, Elizabeth thought.

'In the meantime,' Herr Badrutt said, 'we would have your assurance that at the end of ninety days all your outstanding notes will be met in full?'

'Yes.'

Herr Badrutt sat there, staring into space. He looked at Elizabeth, then looked around at the others, and received their silent signals. 'For my part, I am willing to agree. I do not think a delay – with penalty interest – will do any harm.'

One of the other bankers nodded. 'If you think we should go along, Julius . . .'

And it was done. Elizabeth leaned back in her chair, trying to conceal the feeling of relief flooding through her. She had gained ninety days.

She would need every minute of that time.

TWENTY-FIVE

It was like being in the eye of a hurricane.

Everything flowed across Elizabeth's desk from the hundreds of departments at headquarters, from the factories in Zaire, the laboratories in Greenland, the offices in Australia and Thailand, from the four corners of the earth. There were reports on new products, sales, statistical projections, advertising campaigns, experimental programmes.

There were decisions to be made on building new factories, selling old ones, acquiring companies, hiring and firing executives. Elizabeth had expert advice on every phase of the business, but all final decisions had to be made by her. As they had once been made by Sam. She was grateful now for the three years she had worked with her father. She knew much more about the company than she had realized, and much less. Its very scope was awesome. Elizabeth had once thought of it as a kingdom, but it was a *series* of kingdoms, run by viceroys, with the president's office as the throne room. Each of her cousins had charge of his own domain, but in addition they supervised other overseas territories, so that they were all travelling constantly.

Elizabeth soon learned that she had a special problem. She was a woman in a man's world, and she discovered that it made a difference. She had never really believed that men subscribed to the myth of the inferiority of women, but she quickly learned better. No-one ever put it into words or acted overtly, but Elizabeth was faced with it every day. It was an attitude born of ancient prejudices and it was inescapable. The men did not like taking orders from a woman. They resented the idea of a woman questioning their judgements, trying to improve on their ideas. The fact that Elizabeth was young and attractive made it worse. They tried to make her feel that she should be at home, in a bed or kitchen, and that she should leave serious business matters to the men.

Elizabeth scheduled meetings with different department heads every day. Not all were hostile. Some were predatory. A beautiful girl sitting behind the president's desk was a challenge to the male ego. Their minds were easy to read: If I can fuck her, I can control her.

Like the grown-up version of the boys in Sardinia.

The men went after the wrong part of Elizabeth. They should have gone after her mind, because in the end that was where she controlled them. They underestimated her intelligence, and that was their mistake.

They miscalculated her capacity to assume authority, and that was another error.

And they misjudged her strength, and that was their greatest mistake. She was a Roffe, with the bloodline of old Samuel and her father in her, and she had their determination and spirit.

While the men round her were trying to use Elizabeth, she used them. She tapped the knowledge and the experience and the insights that they had accumulated, and she made them her own. She let the men talk, and she listened. She asked questions, and she remembered the answers.

She learned.

Every night Elizabeth took home two heavy briefcases filled with reports to be studied. Sometimes she worked until four in the morning. One evening a newspaper photographer snapped a picture of Elizabeth walking out of the building with a secretary carrying her two briefcases. The photograph appeared in the newspapers the next day. The caption read: 'Working Heiress'.

Elizabeth had become an international celebrity overnight. The story of a beautiful young girl inheriting a multi-billion-dollar corporation and then taking command was irresistible. The press jumped at it. Elizabeth was lovely, intelligent, and down-to-earth, a combination they rarely came across in celebrities. She made herself available to them whenever possible, trying to build up the damaged image of the company, and they appreciated it.

When she didn't know the answer to a reporter's question, she was not afraid to pick up a telephone and ask someone. Her cousins flew into Zurich once a week for meetings and Elizabeth spent as much time with them as possible. She saw them together, and one at a time. She talked to them and studied them, searching for a clue as to which one of them had allowed innocent people to die in an explosion, had sold secrets to competitors, and which one of them was trying to destroy Roffe and Sons. One of her cousins.

Ivo Palazzi, with his irresistible warmth and charmth.

Alec Nichols, a correct and proper gentleman, and gentle man, always helpful when Elizabeth had needed him.

Charles Martel, a dominated, frightened man. And frightened men could be dangerous when cornered.

Walther Gassner. The All-German boy. Beautiful-looking and friendly on the outside. What was he like on the inside? He had married Anna, an heiress, thirteen years his senior. Had he married for love or money?

When Elizabeth was with them, she watched, and listened, and probed. She mentioned the explosion in Chile and studied their reactions, and she talked about the patents that Roffe had lost to other companies, and she discussed the impending government lawsuits.

She learned nothing. Whoever it was, he was

too clever to give himself away. He would have to be trapped. Elizabeth recalled Sam's marginal note on the report. *Trap the bastard*. She would have to find a way.

Elizabeth found herself becoming more and more fascinated by the inside operation of the pharmaceutical business.

Bad news was deliberately spread. If there was a report that a patient had died from a competitor's medication, within half an hour a dozen men were placing telephone calls all around the world. 'By the way, did you happen to hear about. . . . ?'

Yet on the surface all the companies appeared to be on the best of terms. The heads of some of the large firms held regular informal get-togethers, and Elizabeth was invited to one. She was the only woman present. They talked about their mutual problems.

The president of one of the large companies, a pompous, middle-aged roué, who had been following Elizabeth around all evening, said, 'Government restrictions get more unreasonable every goddamned day. If some genius invented aspirin tomorrow, the government would never okay it.' He gave Elizabeth a superior smile. 'And do you have any idea, little lady, how long we've had aspirin?'

Little lady replied, 'Since four hundred BC, when Hippocrates discovered salicin in the bark of the willow tree.'

He stared at her a moment, and the smile died. 'Right.' He walked away.

The company heads all agreed that one of their biggest problems was the me-too firms, the copycat houses that stole the formulas of successful products, changed the names and rushed them on to the market. It was costing the reputable drug firms hundreds of millions of dollars a year.

In Italy it was not even necessary to steal.

'Italy is one of the countries that has no patent regulations protecting new drugs,' one of the executives told Elizabeth. 'For a bribe of a few hundred thouand lire, anyone can buy the formulas and pirate them under another name. We spend millions of dollars on research – they walk off with the profits.'

'Is it just Italy?' Elizabeth asked.

'Italy and Spain are the worst. France and West Germany aren't bad. England and the United States are clean.'

Elizabeth looked around at all these indignant, moral men and wondered if any of them was involved in the thefts of the patents of Roffe and Sons.

It seemed to Elizabeth that she spent most of her time in aeroplanes. She kept her passport in the top drawer of her desk. At least once a week there was a frantic call from Cairo or Guatemala or Tokyo, and within a few hours Elizabeth would find herself in a plane with half a dozen members of her staff, to cope with some emergency.

She met factory managers and their families in large cities like Bombay, and at remote outposts like Puerto Vallarta, and gradually Roffe and Sons began to take on a new perspective. It was no longer an impersonal mass of reports and statistics. A report headed 'Guatemala' now meant Emil Nunoz and his fat, happy wife and their twelve children; 'Copenhagen' was Nils Bjorn and the crippled mother with whom he lived; 'Rio de Janeiro' was an evening spent with Alessandro Duval and his exquisite mistress.

Elizabeth kept in regular touch with Emil Joeppli. She always telephoned him on her private line, calling him at his little flat on Aussersihl in the evenings.

She was cautious even over the telephone.

'How are things going?'

'A little slower than I hoped, Miss Roffe.'

'Do you need anything?'

'No. Just time. I ran into a little problem but I think it's solved now.'

'Good. Call me if you need anything – anything at all.'

'I will. Thank you, Miss Roffe.'

Elizabeth hung up. She had an urge to push him, to tell him to hurry, for she knew that her time with the banks was running out. She desperately needed what Emil Joeppli was working on, but pressing him was not the answer, and so she kept her impatience to herself. Elizabeth knew that the experiments could not possibly be completed by the time the bank notes were due. But she had a plan. She intended to let Julius Badrutt into the secret, take him into the laboratory and let him see for himself what was happening. The banks would give them all the time they needed.

Elizabeth found herself working with Rhys Williams more and more closely, sometimes late into the night. They often worked alone, just the two of them, having dinner in her private dining-room at the office, or at the elegant apartment she had taken. It was a modern condominium in Zurichberg, overlooking the Lake of Zurich, and it was large and airy and bright. Elizabeth was more aware than ever of the strong animal magnetism of Rhys, but if he felt an attraction for her, he was careful not to show it. He was always polite and friendly. *Avuncular* was the word that came into Elizabeth's mind, and somehow it had a pejorative sound. She wanted to lean on him, confide in him, and yet she knew she had to be careful. More than once she had found herself on the verge of telling Rhys about the efforts to sabotage the company, but something held her back. She was not ready to discuss it with anyone yet. Not until she knew more.

Elizabeth was gaining more confidence in herself. At a sales meeting they were discussing a new hair conditioner that was selling badly. Elizabeth had tried it, and she knew that it was superior to similar products on the markets.

'We're getting heavy returns from drugstores,' one of the sales executives complained. 'It's just not catching on. We need more advertising.'

'We're already over our advertising budget,' Rhys objected. 'We'll have to find a different approach.'

Elizabeth said, 'Take it out of the drugstores.'

They all looked at her. 'What?'

'It's too available.' She turned to Rhys. 'I think we should continue the advertising campaign, but sell it only at beauty salons. Make it exclusive, hard to get. That's the image it should have.'

Rhys thought for a moment, then nodded and said, 'I like it. Let's try it.'

It became a big seller overnight.

Afterwards Rhys had complimented her. 'You're not just another pretty face,' he had said, grinning.

So he *was* beginning to notice!

TWENTY-SIX

London
Friday, November 2
5 p.m.

Alec Nichols was alone in the club sauna when the door opened and a man walked into the steam-filled room, wearing a towel around his waist. He sat down on the wooden bench, next to Alec. 'Hot as a witch's tit in here, ain't it, Sir Alec?'

Alec turned. It was Jon Swinton. 'How did you get in here?'

Swinton winked. 'I said you were expectin' me.' He looked into Alec's eyes and asked, 'You was expectin' me, wasn't you, Sir Alec?'

'No,' Alec replied. 'I told you I need more time.'

'You also told us your little cousin was going to sell the stock, and you'd give us our money.'

'She – she changed her mind.'

'Ah, then you'd better change it back for her, hadn't you?'

'I'm trying. It's a question of –'

'It's a question of how much more horseshit we're going to take from you.' Jon Swinton was moving closer, forcing Alec to slide along the bench. 'We don't want to get rough with you 'cause it's nice to have a good friend like you in Parliament. You know what I mean? But there's a limit.' He was leaning against Alec now, and Alec slid further away from him. 'We did you a favour. Now it's time to pay us back. You're gonna get hold of a shipment of drugs for us.'

'No! That's impossible,' Alec said. 'I can't. There's no way –'

Alec suddenly found that he had been crowded to the end of the bench, next to the large metal container filled with hot rocks. 'Be careful,' Alec said. 'I –'

Swinton grabbed hold of Alec's arm and twisted it, forcing it towards the bed of rocks. Alec could feel the hair on his arm begin to singe.

'No!'

The next instant his arm was pressed down on to the rocks, and he screamed with pain and fell to the floor in agony. Swinton was standing over him.

'You find a way. We'll be in touch.'

TWENTY-SEVEN

Berlin
Saturday, November 3
6 p.m.

Anna Roffe Gassner did not know how much longer she would be able to stand it.

She had become a prisoner in her own home. Except for the cleaning woman who came in for a few hours once a week, Anna and the children were alone, completely at Walther's mercy. He no longer bothered to conceal his hatred. Anna had been in the children's room as they listened together to one of their favourite records.

'Welch ein Singen, Musizieren,
Pfeifen, Zwitschken, Tiriliern . . .'

Walther had stormed in. 'I'm sick of that!' he had yelled.

And he had smashed the record, while the children cowered in terror.

Anna had tried to placate him. 'I – I'm sorry, Walther. I – I didn't know you were home. Can I do something for you?'

He had walked up to her, his eyes blazing, and he said, 'We're going to get rid of the children, Anna.'

In front of them!

He put his hands on her shoulders. 'What happens in this house must be our secret.' *Our secret. Our secret. Our secret.*

She could feel the words reverberating in her head, and his arms started to crush her until she could not breathe. She fainted.

When Anna woke up, she was lying in her bed. The shades were drawn. She looked at the bedside clock. Six p.m. The house was quiet. Too quiet. Her first thought was of the children, and terror swept through her. She rose from the bed on shaky legs, and stumbled over to the door. It was locked from the outside. She pressed her ear hard against the panel, listening. There should have been the sounds of the children. They should have come up to see her.

If they had been able to. If they were still alive.

Her legs were trembling so hard that she could barely walk to the telephone. She breathed a silent prayer, then picked it up. She heard the familiar dialling tone. She hesitated, dreading the thought of what Walther would do to her if he caught her again.

Without giving herself a chance to think, Anna began to dial 110. Her hands shook so badly that she dialled a wrong number. And another. She began to sob. There was so little time left. Fighting her growing hysteria, she tried again, willing her fingers to move slowly. She heard a ringing, then miraculously a man's voice said, '*Hier ist der Notruf der Polizei.*'

Anna could not find her voice.

'*Hier ist der Notruf der Polizei. Kann ich Ihnen helfen?*'

'*Ja!*' It was a high-pitched sob. '*Ja, bitte! Ich bin in grosser Gefahr. Bitte schicken sie jemanden –*'

Walther loomed in front of her, ripping the telephone out of her hand and hurling her against the bed. He slammed down the receiver, breathing hard, tore the cord out of the wall, and turned to Anna.

'The children,' she whispered. 'What have you done with the children?'

Walther did not answer.

The Central Division of the Berlin Kriminalpolizei was located at 2832 Keithstrasse in a district of ordinary-looking apartment houses and office buildings. The emergency number of the *Deltk ans Mensch* department was equipped with an automatic hold system, so that a caller was unable to disconnect until the line had been electronically released by the switchboard. In this way every number calling in could be traced, no matter how brief the conversation. It was a sophisticated piece of equipment of which the department was proud.

Within five minutes of Anna Gassner's telephone call, Detective Paul Lange walked into the office of his chief, Major Wageman, carrying a cassette player.

'I would like you to listen to this.' Detective Lange pressed a button. A metallic male voice said, '*Heir ist der Notruf der Polizei. Kann ich Ihnen helfen?*'

Then a woman's voice, filled with terror. '*Ja! Ja, bitte! Ich bin in grosser Gefahr. Bitte schicken sie jemanden –*'

There was the sound of a thud, a click, and the line went dead. Major Wageman looked up at Detective Lange. 'You've traced the call?'

'We know whose residence it came from,' Detective Lange replied carefully.

'Then what's the problem?' Major Wageman demanded impatiently. 'Have Central send a car to investigate.'

'I wanted your authority first.' Detective Lange placed a slip of paper on the desk in front of the major.

'*Scheiss!*' Major Wageman stared at him. 'Are you sure?'

'Yes, Major.'

Major Wageman looked down at the slip of paper again. The telephone was listed in the name of Gassner, Walther. Head of the German division of Roffe and Sons, one of the industrial giants of Germany.

There was no need to discuss the implications. Only an idiot could miss them. One wrong move and they would both be walking the streets, looking for a job. Major Wageman thought for a moment and then said, 'All right. Check it out. I want you to go there yourself. And walk on fucking eggs. Do you understand?'

'I understand, Major.'

The Gassner estate was in Wannsee, an exclusive suburb in south-west Berlin. Detective Lange took the longer Hohenzollerndamm instead of the speedier autobahn, because the traffic was lighter. He went through the Clayalle, past the CIA building, hidden behind half a mile of barbed wire fences. He passed the American Army Head-quarters and turned right on what was once known as Road One, the longest road in Germany, run-ning from East Prussia to the Belgian border. On his right was the Brücke der Einheit, the Bridge of Unity, where the spy Abel had been exchanged for the American U-2 pilot Gary Powers. Detective Lange turned the car off the highway into the wooded hills of Wannsee.

The houses were beautiful, impressive. On Sundays, Detective Lange sometimes took his wife out here, just to look at the outsides of the houses and the grounds.

He found the address he was looking for and turned into the long driveway leading to the Gassner estate. The estate represented something more than money: it represented power. The Roffe dynasty was big enough to make governments fall.

Major Wageman had been right: he would be very careful.

Detective Lange drove to the front door of the three-storey stone house, got out of the car, took off his hat and pressed the doorbell. He waited. There was the heavy hanging silence of a house that has been deserted. He knew that was impossible. He rang again. Nothing but that still, oppressive silence. He was debating whether to go round to the back when the door unexpectedly opened. A woman stood in the doorway. She was middle-aged, plain-looking, wearing a wrinkled dressing-gown. Detective Lange took her for the housekeeper. He pulled out his identification. 'I'd like to see Mrs Walther Gassner. Please tell her Detective Lange.'

'I am Mrs Gassner,' the woman said.

Detective Lange tried to conceal his surprise. She was totally unlike his image of the lady of this house.

'I – we received a telephone call at police head-quarters a short time ago,' he began.

She watched him, her face blank, disinterested. Detective Lange felt that he was handling this badly, but he did not know why. He had a feeling that he was missing something important.

'Did you make that call, Mrs Gassner?' he asked.

'Yes,' she answered. 'It was a mistake.'

There was a dead, remote quality to her voice that was disturbing. He remembered the shrill, hysterical voice on the tape recorder half an hour earlier.

'Just for our records, may I ask what kind of mistake?'

Her hesitation was barely perceptible. 'There was – I thought that a piece of my jewellery was missing. I found it.'

The emergency number was for murder, rape, mayhem. *Walk on fucking eggs.*

'I see.' Detective Lange hesitated, wanting to get inside the house, wanting to find out what she was covering up. But there was nothing more he could say or do. 'Thank you, Mrs Gassner. I'm sorry to have troubled you.'

He stood there, frustrated, and watched the door close in his face. He slowly got into his car and drove off.

Behind the door Anna turned.

Walther nodded and said softly, 'You did very well, Anna. Now we're going back upstairs.'

He turned towards the stairway, and Anna pulled out a pair of shears that had been concealed in the folds of her dressing-gown and plunged them into his back.

TWENTY-EIGHT

Rome
Sunday, November 4
Noon

It was a perfect day, Ivo Palazzi thought, for visiting the Villa d'Este with Simonetta and their three beautiful daughters. As Ivo strolled through the fabled Tivoli Gardens arm in arm with his wife, watching the girls race ahead from fountain to splashing fountain, he idly wondered whether Pirro Ligorio, who had built the park for his patrons, the d'Este family, had ever dreamed how much joy he would one day give to millions of sightseers. The Villa d'Este was a short distance north-east of Rome, nestled high in the Sabine Hills. Ivo had been there often, but it always gave him a feeling of special pleasure to stand at the very top level and look down on the dozens of sparkling fountains below, each one cunningly designed, each one different from the others.

In the past Ivo had taken Donatella and his three sons here. How they had adored it! The thought of them made Ivo sad. He had not seen or talked to Donatella since the horrifying afternoon at the apartment. He still remembered vividly the terrible scratches she had inflicted on him. He knew what remorse she must be going through, and how she must be longing for him. Well, it would do her good to suffer for a while, as he had suffered. In his mind he could hear Donatella's voice, and she was saying, 'Come along. This way, boys.'

It was so clear it seemed almost real. He could hear her say, 'Faster, Francesco!' and Ivo turned and Donatella was behind him, with their three boys, moving determinedly towards him and Simonetta and the three girls. Ivo's first thought was that Donatella had happened to be here at the Tivoli Gardens by coincidence, but the instant he saw the expression on her face, he knew better. The *putana* was trying to bring his two families together, trying to destroy him! Ivo rose to the occasion like a madman.

He shouted to Simonetta. 'There's something I must show you. Quickly, everybody.'

And he swept his family down the long, winding stone steps towards a lower level, pushing tourists aside, casting frantic glances over his shoulder. Above, Donatella and the boys were moving towards the steps. Ivo knew that if the boys saw him, everything was lost. All it needed was for one of them to shout 'Papa!' and he might as well drown himself in the fountains. He hurried Simonetta and the girls along, not giving them a chance to pause, not daring to let them stop for an instant.

'Where are we rushing to?' Simonetta gasped. 'What's the hurry?'

'It's a surprise,' Ivo said gaily. 'You'll see.'

He risked another quick glance back. Donatella and the three boys were out of sight for the moment. Ahead was a labyrinth, with one set of stairs leading up and another leading down. Ivo chose the stairs going up.

'Come along,' he called to the girls. 'Whoever gets to the top first gets a prize!'

'Ivo! I'm exhausted!' Simonetta complained. 'Can't we rest a minute?'

He looked at her in shock. '*Rest?* That would spoil the surprise. Hurry!'

He took Simonetta's arm and dragged her up the steep steps, his three daughters racing ahead of them. Ivo found himself gasping for breath. It would serve them all right, he thought bitterly, if I had a heart attack and died right here. Goddamn women! You can't trust any of them. How could she do this to me? She adores me. I'll kill the bitch for this.

He could visualize himself strangling Donatella in her bed. She was wearing nothing but a flimsy negligée. He ripped it off and began to mount her, while she screamed for mercy. Ivo could feel himself getting an erection.

'Can we stop now?' Simonetta begged.

'No! We're almost there!'

They had reached the upper level again. Ivo took a hasty look around. Donatella and the boys were nowhere in sight.

'Where are you taking us?' Simonetta demanded.

'You'll see,' Ivo said hysterically. 'Follow me!' He shoved them towards the exit.

Isabella, the oldest girl, said, 'Are we leaving, Papa? We just got here!'

'We're going to a better place,' Ivo panted. He glanced back. Coming into sight, climbing the stairs, were Donatella and the boys.

'Faster, girls!'

A moment later Ivo and one of his families were outside the gate of the Villa d'Este, racing towards their car on the large square.

'I've never seen you like this,' Simonetta gasped.

'I've never been like this,' Ivo said truthfully. He had the motor going before the car doors were closed, and he raced out of the parking lot as though the devil was pursuing him.

'Ivo!'

He patted Simonetta's hand. 'I want everybody to relax now. As a special treat I'm – I'm taking you to lunch at the Hassler.'

They sat at a picture window overlooking the Spanish Steps, with Saint Peter's looming gloriously in the distance.

Simonetta and the children had a marvellous time. The food was delicious. Ivo could have been eating cardboard. His hands were trembling so badly that he could hardly hold his knife and fork. I can't stand much more of this, he thought. I'm not going to let her ruin my life.

For he had no doubt now that that was exactly what Donatella intended to do. *Il giuoco è stata fatto*. The game was up. Unless he could find a way to give Donatella the money she was demanding.

He had to get it. It did not matter how.

TWENTY-NINE

Paris
Monday, November 5
6 p.m.

The instant Charles Martel arrived home he knew he was in trouble. Hélène was waiting for him, and with her was Pierre Richaud, the jeweller who had made the replicas of her stolen jewellery. Charles stood in the doorway, in a state of shock.

'Come in, Charles,' Hélène said. There was an undercurrent in her voice that terrified him. 'I believe that you and M. Richaud know each other.'

Charles stared, knowing that whatever he said would hang him. The jeweller was studying the floor in embarrassment, obviously ill at ease.

'Sit down, Charles.' It was a command. Charles sat down.

Hélène said, 'What you're facing, *mon cher mari*, is a criminal charge of grand theft. You have been stealing my jewellery and replacing the pieces with clumsy imitation paste, made by M. Richaud.'

To his horror Charles found himself wetting his pants, a thing he had not done since he was a small boy. He blushed. He wished desperately that he could leave the room for a moment to clean himself. No, he wanted to flee and never return.

Hélène knew everything. It did not matter how she had found him out. There would be no escape and no mercy. It was terrifying enough that Hélène had discovered he had been stealing from her. Wait until she learned his motive! Wait until she found out that he had been planning to use the money to run away from her! Hell was going to have a new meaning. No-one knew Hélène as Charles did. She was *une sauvage*, capable of anything. She would destroy him, without a moment's thought, turn him into a *clochard*, one of those sad bums who sleep on the streets of Paris in rags. His life had suddenly turned into an *emmerdement*, a shower of shit.

'Did you really think you could get away with anything so stupid?' Hélène was asking.

Charles remained miserably silent. He could feel his pants getting wetter, but he did not dare look down.

'I have persuaded M. Richaud to give me all the facts.'

Persuaded. Charles dreaded to think how.

'I have photostat copies of the receipts for the money you stole from me. I can put you in prison for the next twenty years.' She paused, and added, 'If I choose to.'

Her words only served to increase Charles's panic. Experience had taught him that a generous Hélène was a dangerous Hélène. Charles was afraid to meet her glance. He wondered what it was she would demand from him. Something monstrous.

Hélène turned to Pierre Richaud. 'You will say nothing of this to anyone until I have made up my mind what I wish to do.'

'Of course, Mme Roffe-Martel, of course, of course.' The man was babbling. He looked hopefully towards the door. 'May I –?'

Hélène nodded, and Pierre Richaud scurried out.

Hélène watched him go, then swung round to study her husband. She could smell his fear. And something else. Urine. She smiled. Charles had pissed himself out of fear. She had taught him well. Hélène was pleased with Charles. It was a very satisfying marriage. She had broken Charles, then made him her creature. The innovations he had brought to Roffe and Sons were brilliant, for they had all come from Hélène. She ruled a small part of Roffe and Sons through her husband, but now it was not enough. She was a Roffe. She was wealthy in her own right; her earlier marriages had made her even wealthier. But it was not money she was interested in. It was the control of the company. She had planned to use her stock to acquire more stock, to buy up the interest of the others. She had already discussed it with them. They were willing to go along with her, to form a minority group. First, Sam had stood in the way of her plan, and now Elizabeth. But Hélène had no intention of allowing Elizabeth or anyone else to keep her from getting what she wanted. Charles was going to get it for her. If anything went wrong, he would be her scapegoat.

Now, of course, he must be punished for his *petite révolte*. She watched his face and said, 'No-one steals from me, Charles. No-one. You're finished. Unless I decide to save you.'

He sat there, silent, wishing her dead, terrified of her. She walked over to where he sat, her thighs brushing against his face.

She said, 'Would you like me to save you, Charles?'

'Yes,' he said hoarsely. She was stepping out of her skirt, her eyes vicious, and he thought, *Oh, my God! Not now!*

'Then listen to me. Roffe and Sons is my company. I want the controlling interest.'

He looked up at her miserably and said, 'You know Elizabeth won't sell.'

Hélène slipped out of her blouse and pants. She stood there, animal naked, her body lean and magnificent, her nipples hard. 'Then you must do something about her. Or spend the next twenty years of your life in prison. Don't worry. I'll tell you what you will do. But first, come here, Charles.'

THIRTY

The following morning, at ten o'clock, Elizabeth's private phone rang. It was Emil Joeppli. She had given him the number so that no one would be aware of their conversations. 'I wonder if I could see you,' he said. He sounded excited.

'I'll be there in fifteen minutes.'

Kate Erling looked up in surprise as Elizabeth came out of her office wearing a coat. 'You have an appointment at –'

'Cancel everything for the next hour,' Elizabeth said, and walked out.

In the Development Building an armed guard examined Elizabeth's pass. 'Last door to the left, Miss Roffe.'

Elizabeth found Joeppli alone in his laboratory. He greeted her with enthusiasm.

'I finished the final tests last night. It works. The enzymes completely inhibit the ageing process. Look.'

He led her to a cage holding four young rabbits,

alert and filled with restless vitality. Next to it was another cage containing four more rabbits, quieter, more mature.

'This is the five hundredth generation to receive the enzyme,' Joeppli said.

Elizabeth stood in front of the cage. 'They look healthy.'

Joeppli smiled. '*That's* part of the control group.' He pointed to the cage on the left. '*Those* are the senior citizens.'

Elizabeth stared at the energetic rabbits, frisking around in the cage like newborn bunnies, and she could not believe it.

'They'll outlive the others by at least three to one,' Joeppli told her.

When you applied that ratio to human beings, the implications were staggering. She could barely contain her excitement.

'When – when will you be ready to start testing it on people?'

'I'm getting my final notes together. After that, another three or four weeks at the most.'

'Emil, don't discuss this with anyone,' Elizabeth warned.

Emil Joeppli nodded. 'I won't, Miss Roffe. I'm working alone. I'm being very careful.'

The entire afternoon had been taken up with a board meeting, and it had gone well. Walther had not appeared. Charles had again brought up the subject of selling the stock, but Elizabeth had firmly vetoed it. After that, Ivo had been his charming self, as had Alec. Charles seemed unusually tense. Elizabeth wished she knew why.

She invited them all to stay in Zurich and have dinner with her. As casually as possible, Elizabeth brought up the problems that had been mentioned in the report, watching for a reaction of some kind, but she could detect no sign of nervousness or guilt. And everyone who could have been involved, except for Walther, was seated at that table.

Rhys had not attended the meeting or the dinner. 'I have some urgent business to take care of,' he had said, and Elizabeth had wondered if it was a girl. Elizabeth was aware that whenever Rhys stayed late at night to work with her, he had had to cancel a date. Once, when he had been unable to reach the girl in time, she had appeared at the office. She was a stunning redhead, with a figure that made Elizabeth feel like a boy. The girl had been furious at being stood up, and she had not bothered to hide her displeasure. Rhys had escorted her to the lift and returned.

'Sorry about that,' he had said.

Elizabeth could not help herself. 'She's charming,' she said sweetly. 'What does she do?'

'She's a brain surgeon,' Rhys had replied earnestly, and Elizabeth had laughed. The following day Elizabeth had learned that the girl *was* a brain surgeon.

There were others, and Elizabeth found herself

resenting all of them. She wished that she understood Rhys better. She knew the gregarious and public Rhys Williams; she wanted to meet the private Rhys Williams, the self he kept hidden. More than once, Elizabeth had thought, Rhys should be running this company instead of taking orders from me. I wonder how he really feels about it?

That evening after dinner, when the members of the board had dispersed to catch trains and planes back to their homes, Rhys walked into Elizabeth's office where she was working with Kate. 'Thought I ought to give you a hand,' Rhys said lightly.

No explanation of where he had been. Why should there be? Elizabeth thought. He doesn't have to account to me.

They all set to work and the time flew. Elizabeth watched Rhys now, bent over some papers, rapidly scanning them, his eyes quick and alert. He had found several flaws in some important contracts that the attorneys had missed. Now Rhys straightened up, stretched and glanced at his watch.

'Oops! It's after midnight. I'm afraid I have an appointment. I'll come in early tomorrow and finish checking these agreements.'

Elizabeth wondered if his appointment was with the brain surgeon or with one of his other – She stopped herself. What Rhys Williams did with his private life was his own business.

'I'm sorry,' Elizabeth said. 'I didn't realize it was

so late. You run along. Kate and I will finish reading these papers.'

Rhys nodded. 'See you in the morning. Good night, Kate.'

'Good night, Mr Williams.'

Elizabeth watched Rhys leave, then forced her mind back to the contracts. But a moment later her thoughts were on Rhys again. She had been eager to tell him about the progress that Emil Joeppli was making on the new drug, to share it with him, yet she had held back. Soon, she told herself.

By one o'clock in the morning, they were finished.

Kate Erling said, 'Will there be anything else, Miss Roffe?'

'No, I think that's all. Thank you, Kate. Come in late tomorrow.'

Elizabeth stood up, and realized how stiff her body felt from sitting so long.

'Thank you. I'll have everything typed for you by tomorrow afternoon.'

'That will be fine.'

Elizabeth got her coat and purse, waited for Kate, and they walked to the door. They went out into the corridor together and headed towards the private express lift that stood there, door open, waiting. The two of them stepped inside the lift. As Elizabeth reached for the lobby button, they heard the sudden ringing of the telephone from the office.

'I'll answer it, Miss Roffe,' Kate Erling said. 'You go on ahead.' She stepped out of the car.

Downstairs the night guard on duty in the lobby looked up at the elevator control board as a red light at the top of the board flashed on and began descending. It was the signal light for the private lift. That meant Miss Roffe was on her way down. Her chauffeur was sitting in a chair in a corner, drowsing over a newspaper.

'The boss is coming,' the guard said.

The chauffeur stretched, and started lazily to his feet.

An alarm bell suddenly shattered the peace of the lobby.

The guard's eyes flashed to the control board. The red light was moving in a quick plunging pattern, gathering speed, marking the descent of the lift.

It was out of control.

'Oh, Jesus!' the guard mumbled.

He hurried to the board, jerked open a panel and pulled the emergency switch to activate the safety brake. The red light continued its downward plunge. The chauffeur had hurried over to the control panel. He saw the look on the guard's face.

'What's going –?'

'Get away!' the guard yelled. 'It's going to crash!'

They ran from the row of lifts towards the farthest wall. The lobby was beginning to vibrate with the speed of the runaway car inside the shaft, and the guard thought, *Don't let her be in it*, and as the plunging lift shot past the lobby, he heard the terrified screams from inside.

An instant later, there was a loud roar, and the building shuddered as though it had been hit by an earthquake.

THIRTY-ONE

Chief Inspector Otto Schmied of the Zurich Kriminalpolizei was seated at his desk, eyes closed, taking deep yoga breaths, trying to calm himself, trying to control the fury that filled him.

In police procedure there were rules that were so basic, so obvious, that no-one had thought it even necessary to put them in the police manual. They were simply taken for granted, like eating, or sleeping, or breathing. For example, when an accident-related fatality occurred, the first thing the investigating detective did – the *very* first thing a detective did, the simple, obvious, you-don't-have-to-draw-it-on-a-fucking-blackboard thing he did – was to visit the scene of the accident. Nothing could be more elementary than that. Yet staring up at Chief Inspector Otto Schmied from his desk was a report from Detective Max Hornung that violated every element of police procedure. I should have expected it, the Inspector told himself bitterly. Why am I even surprised?

Detective Hornung was Inspector Schmied's albatross, his *bête noire*, his – Inspector Schmied was an ardent admirer of Melville – his Moby Dick. The inspector took another deep breath and slowly exhaled. Then, only slightly less agitated, he picked up Detective Hornung's report and read it again from the beginning.

BRANDTOUR OFFIZIER REPORT
Wednesday, November 7

TIME	1.15 AM
SUBJECT	Report from central switch-board of accident at Roffe and Sons administration building at Eichenbahn factory
TYPE OF ACCIDENT	Unknown
CAUSE OF ACCIDENT	Unknown
NUMBER OF INJURED OR DECEASED	Unknown

TIME	1.27 AM
SUBJECT	Second message from central switchboard re accident at Roffe and Sons
TYPE OF ACCIDENT	Lift crash
CAUSE OF ACCIDENT	Unknown
NUMBER OF INJURED OR DECEASED	One female, deceased

I began an immediate investigation. By 1.35 AM I obtained the name of the superintendent of the Roffe and Sons administration building and from him got the name of the chief architect of the building.

2.30 AM I located the chief architect. He was celebrating his birthday at La Puce. He gave me the name of the company that had installed the lifts in the building. Rudolf Schatz, A.G.

At 3.15 AM I telephoned Mr Rudolf Schatz at his home and requested him to immediately locate the plans for the lifts. I also requested the master budget sheets along with preliminary estimates, final estimates and final costs; I also requested a complete inventory of all mechanical and electrical materials used.

At this point Inspector Schmied could feel a familiar twitch starting in his right cheek. He took several deep breaths and read on.

6.15 AM the requested documents were delivered to me at police headquarters by Mr Schatz's wife. After an examination of the preliminary budget and final costs I was satisfied that:
a) no inferior materials were substituted in building the lifts;
b) because of the reputation of the builders, inferior workmanship could be ruled out as a cause of the crash;
c) the safety measures built into the lifts were adequate;

308

d) my conclusion therefore was that the cause of the crash was not an accident.

[Signed] Max Hornung, CID

NB Since my phone calls took place during the course of the night and early morning, it is possible that you may receive one or two complaints from some of the people I might have awakened.

Inspector Schmied savagely slammed the report down on his desk. 'It is possible'! 'Might have awakened'! The chief inspector had been under attack the entire morning by half of the officials of the Swiss government. What did he think he was running – a gestapo? How dare he awaken the president of a respectable building corporation and order him to deliver documents in the middle of the night? How dare he impugn the integrity of a reputable firm like Rudolf Schatz? And on and on and on.

But the thing that was so stunning – that was so incredible – was that Detective Max Hornung had not even *appeared* at the scene of the accident until *fourteen hours* after it was reported! By the time he arrived the victim had been removed, identified and autopsied. Half a dozen other detectives had examined the scene of the accident, had questioned witnesses and had filed their reports.

When Chief Inspector Schmied finished rereading Detective Max Hornung's report, he summoned him to his office.

The very sight of Detective Max Hornung was

anathema to the chief inspector. Max Hornung was a dumpy, wistful-looking man, egg-bald, with a face that had been put together by an absent-minded prankster. His head was too large, his ears were too small, and his mouth was a raisin stuck in the middle of a pudding face. Detective Max Hornung was six inches too short to meet the rigid standards of the Zurich Kriminalpolizei, fifteen pounds too light, and hopelessly nearsighted. To top it all off, he was arrogant. All the men in the force felt unanimously about Detective Hornung: they hated him.

'Why don't you fire him?' the chief inspector's wife had asked, and he had almost struck her.

The reason that Max Hornung was in the Zurich detective force was that he had single-handedly contributed more to the Swiss national income than all the chocolate and watch factories combined. Max Hornung was an accountant, a mathematical genius with an encyclopaedic knowledge of fiscal matters, an instinct for the chicanery of man, and a patience that would have made Job weep with envy. Max had been a clerk in the Betrug Abteilung, the department set up to investigate financial frauds, irregularities in stock sales and banking transactions, and the ebb and flow of currency in and out of Switzerland. It was Max Hornung who had brought the smuggling of illegal money into Switzerland to a standstill, who had ferreted out billions of dollars' worth of ingenious but illicit financial schemes, and who had put half a dozen of the world's respected business leaders in prison. No matter how cunningly assets were concealed, mingled, remingled, sent to the Seychelles to be laundered, transferred and retransferred through a complex series of dummy corporations, in the end Max Hornung would ferret out the truth. In short, he had made himself the terror of the Swiss financial community.

Above all things that they held sacred and dear, the Swiss valued their privacy. With Max Hornung on the loose, there was no privacy.

Max's salary as a financial watchdog was meagre. He had been offered bribes of a million francs in numbered bank accounts, a chalet at Cortina d'Ampezzo, a yacht, and in half a dozen instances beautiful, nubile women. In each case the bribe had been rejected and the authorities promptly notified. Max Hornung cared nothing for money. He could have become a millionaire simply by applying his financial skills to the stock market, but the idea never even occurred to him. Max Hornung was interested in but one thing: catching those who strayed from the path of financial probity. Ah, yes, there was one other wish that consumed Max Hornung, and in the end it proved to be a blessing to the business community. For reasons which no one could fathom, Max Hornung wanted to be a police detective. He envisaged himself as a kind of Sherlock Holmes or Maigret, patiently following a labyrinth of clues, relentlessly stalking the criminal to his lair. When one of Switzerland's leading financiers accidentally learned of Max Hornung's ambitions to be a sleuth, he immediately got together with a few powerful friends and within forty-eight hours Max Hornung was offered a job in the Zurich police force as a detective. Max could not believe his good fortune. He accepted with alacrity, and the entire business community breathed a collective sigh of relief and resumed its arcane activities.

Chief Inspector Schmied had not even been consulted about the matter. He had received a telephone call from the most powerful political leader in Switzerland, had been given his instructions, and there the matter had ended. Or, to be more accurate, there it had begun. For the chief inspector, it was the beginning of a Gethsemane that showed no sign of ending. He had honestly tried to get over his resentment at having a detective – an inexperienced and unqualified one at that – forced upon him. He assumed that there had to be some strong political motivation for such an unheard of move. Very well, he was determined to cooperate, confident that he could handle the situation easily. His confidence was shaken the moment Max Hornung reported to him. The detective's appearance was ridiculous enough. But what stunned Inspector Schmied as he looked at this lump of humanity was the man's attitude of superiority. He exuded an air that said: Max Hornung is here – now you can all relax and stop worrying.

Inspector Schmied's thoughts of any easy cooperation vanished. Instead he devised another approach. He tried to sweep Max Hornung under the rug, as it were, by transferring him from department to department, assigning him unimportant jobs. Max worked in the Kriminal-Tech Abteilung, the fingerprint and identification division, and the Fahndungsabteilung, the division for stolen property and missing persons. But always Max Hornung kept returning, like a bad centime.

There was a rule that every detective had to work as Brandtour Offizier, on the night emergency desk, one week out of every twelve. Without fail, each time Max was on duty, something important would occur, and while Inspector Schmied's other detectives ran around trying to track down clues, Max would solve the case. It was infuriating.

He knew absolutely nothing about police procedure, criminology, forensics, ballistics, or criminal psychology – all the things that the other detectives were experienced in – and yet he kept solving cases that baffled everyone else. Chief Inspector Schmied came to the conclusion that Max Hornung was the luckiest man who ever lived.

In reality, luck had nothing to do with it. Detective Max Hornung solved criminal cases in exactly the same way that accountant Max Hornung had exposed a hundred ingenious schemes to defraud banks and the government. Max Hornung had a single-track mind, and it was a very narrow-gauge track at that. All he needed was one loose thread, one tiny piece that did not fit into the rest of the fabric, and once he had that he would begin to unravel it, until somebody's brilliant, foolproof scheme fell apart at the seams.

The fact that Max had a photographic memory drove his colleagues crazy. Max could instantly recall anything he had ever heard, read or seen.

Another mark against him, if indeed one was needed, was that his expense accounts were an embarrassment to the entire detective squadron. The first time he had turned in an expense sheet, the Oberleutnant had summoned him to his office and said genially, 'You've obviously made a mistake in your figures here, Max.'

The equivalent of informing Capablanca that he had sacrificed his queen through stupidity.

Max blinked. 'A mistake in my figures?'

'Yes. Several, in fact.' The Oberleutnant pointed to the paper in front of him. 'Transportation across town, eighty centimes. Return, eighty centimes.' He looked up and said, 'The minimum taxi fare would be thirty-four francs each way.'

'Yes, sir. That's why I used the bus.'

The Oberleutnant stared at him. 'A *bus*?'

None of the detectives was required to ride buses while on a case. It was unheard of. The only reply he could think of was, 'Well, it's – it's not necessary. I mean – we naturally don't encourage spendthrifts in this department, Hornung, but we do have a decent expense budget. Another thing. You were out in the field on this case for three days. You forgot to include meals.'

'No, Herr Oberleutnant. I only take coffee in the morning and I prepare my own lunches and carry a lunch bag. My dinners are listed there.'

And so they were. Three dinners, total: sixteen francs. He must have eaten at the Salvation Army kitchen.

The Oberleutnant said coldly, 'Detective Hornung, this department existed for a hundred years before you joined it, and it will exist for a hundred years after you leave it. There are certain traditions that we observe here.' He shoved the expense account back to Max. 'You must think about your colleagues, you know. Now take this, revise it, and return it.'

'Yes, Herr Oberleutnant. I – I'm sorry if I did it incorrectly.'

A generous wave of the hand. 'Quite all right. After all, you're new here.'

Thirty minutes later Detective Max Hornung turned in his revised account. He had decreased his expenses by another three per cent.

Now, on this day in November, Chief Inspector Schmied was holding Detective Max Hornung's report in his hand while the author of the report stood before him. Detective Hornung was wearing a bright blue suit, brown shoes and white socks. In spite of his resolves, and the calming yoga breathing exercises, Inspector Schmied found himself yelling. 'You were in charge here when that report came in. It was *your* job to investigate the accident and you arrived on the scene *fourteen hours later*! The whole fucking New Zealand police force could have been flown here and been back home in that time.'

'Oh, no, sir. The flying time from New Zealand to Zurich by jet is –'

315

'Oh, shut up!'

Chief Inspector Schmied ran his hands through his thick, rapidly greying hair, trying to think what to say to this man. You could not insult him, you could not reason with him. He was an idiot, shot with luck.

Chief Inspector Schmied barked, 'I will not tolerate incompetence in my department, Hornung. When the other detectives came on duty and saw the report, they immediately went to the scene to inspect the accident. They called an ambulance, had the body taken to the morgue, identified it –' He knew he was talking too fast again, and he forced himself to calm down. 'In short, Hornung, they did everything a good detective is supposed to do. While you were sitting in your office waking up half of the most important men in Switzerland, in the middle of the night.'

'I thought –'

'Don't! I've been on the phone apologizing the whole damned morning because of you.'

'I had to find out –'

'Oh, get out of here, Hornung!'

'Yes, sir. Is it all right if I attend the funeral? It's this morning.'

'Yes! Go!'

'Thank you, sir. I –'

'Just go!'

It was thirty minutes before Chief Inspector Schmied was breathing normally again.

THIRTY-TWO

The funeral parlour at Sihlfeld was crowded. It was an ornate, old-fashioned building of stone and marble, with preparation rooms and a crematorium. Inside the large chapel two dozen executives and employees of Roffe and Sons occupied the front row of seats. Towards the rear were the friends, the community representatives and the press. Detective Hornung was seated in the last row, thinking that death was illogical. Man reached his prime and then, when he had the most to give, the most to live for, he died. It was inefficient.

The coffin was mahogany and covered with flowers. More waste, Detective Hornung thought. The coffin had been ordered sealed. Max could understand why. The minister was speaking in a doomsday voice, '. . . death in the midst of life, born in sin, ashes to ashes.' Max Hornung paid little attention. He was studying those in the chapel.

'The Lord giveth, and the Lord taketh away,'

and people were beginning to stand and head for the exit. The service was over.

Max stood near the door, and as a man and a woman approached him he stepped in front of the woman and said, 'Miss Elizabeth Roffe? I wonder if I might have a word with you?'

Detective Max Hornung was seated with Elizabeth Roffe and Rhys Williams in a booth at a Konditorei across from the funeral parlour. Through the window they could see the coffin being loaded into a grey hearse. Elizabeth looked away. Her eyes were haunted.

'What's this all about?' Rhys demanded. 'Miss Roffe has already given her statement to the police.'

Detective Max Hornung said, 'Mr Williams, isn't it? There are just a few little details I want to check out.'

'Can't they wait? Miss Roffe has been through a very trying –'

Elizabeth put her hand on Rhys's. 'It's all right. If I can be of any help –' She turned to Max. 'What would you like to know, Detective Hornung?'

Max stared at Elizabeth, and for the first time in his life he was at a loss for words. Women were as foreign to Max as creatures from an alien planet. They were illogical and unpredictable, subject to emotional reactions rather than rational ones. They did not compute. Max had few sexual stirrings, for he was mind-oriented, but he could appreciate the precise logic of sex. It was the mechanical construction of moving parts fitting together into a coordinated, functioning whole that excited him. That, for Max, was the poetry of loving. The sheer dynamics of it. Max felt that the poets had all missed the point. Emotions were imprecise and untidy, a waste of energy that could not move the smallest grain of sand one inch, while logic could move the world. What was puzzling Max now was that he felt comfortable with Elizabeth. It made him uneasy. No woman had ever affected him that way before. She did not seem to think he was an ugly, ridiculous little man, the way other women did. He forced himself to look away from her eyes so that he could concentrate.

'Were you in the habit of working late at night, Miss Roffe?'

'Very often.' Elizabeth said. 'Yes.'

'How late?'

'It varied. Sometimes until ten. Sometimes until midnight, or after.'

'So it was a kind of pattern? That is, people around you would have known about it?'

She was studying him, puzzled. 'I suppose so.'

'On the night the lift crashed, you and Mr Williams and Kate Erling were all working late?'

'Yes.'

'But you didn't leave together?'

Rhys said, 'I left early. I had an engagement.'

Max regarded him a moment, then turned back to Elizabeth. 'How long after Mr Williams left did you leave?'

'I think it was about an hour.'

'Did you and Kate Erling leave together?'

'Yes. We got our coats and went out into the hall.' Elizabeth's voice faltered. 'The – the lift was there, waiting for us.'

The special express lift.

'What happened then?'

'We both got in. The telephone in the office rang. Kate – Miss Erling – said, "I'll answer it," and she started to get out. But I was expecting an overseas call I had placed earlier, so I told her I would answer it.' Elizabeth stopped, her eyes brimming with tears. 'I got out of the lift. She asked if she should wait, and I said, "No, go ahead." She pressed the lobby button. I started back to the office, and as I was opening the door, I heard – I heard the screaming, then –' She was unable to go on.

Rhys turned to Max Hornung, his face clouded with anger. 'That's enough. Will you tell us what this is all about?'

It was about murder, Max thought. Someone had tried to kill Elizabeth Roffe. Max sat there concentrating, recalling everything he had learned in the past forty-eight hours about Roffe and Sons. It was a deeply plagued company, forced to pay astronomical damages in lawsuits, swamped by bad publicity, losing customers, owing enormous sums of money to banks that had grown impatient. A company ripe for a change. Its president, Sam Roffe, who had held the controlling vote, had died. An expert mountain climber who had been killed in a climbing accident. The controlling stock had gone to his daughter, Elizabeth, who had almost died in a jeep accident in Sardinia, and had narrowly missed being killed in a lift that had passed a recent inspection. Someone was playing deadly games.

Detective Max Hornung should have been a happy man. He had found a loose thread. But now he had met Elizabeth Roffe, and she was no longer simply a name, an equation in a mathematical puzzle. There was something very special about her. Max felt an urge to shield her, to protect her.

Rhys said, 'I asked what this –'

Max looked at him and said vaguely, 'Er – police procedure, Mr Williams. Just routine.' He rose. 'Excuse me.'

He had some urgent work to do.

THIRTY-THREE

Chief Inspector Schmied had had a full morning. There had been a political demonstration in front of Iberia Air Lines, three men detained for questioning. A fire of suspicious origin at a paper factory in Brunau. It was being investigated. A girl had been raped in Platzspitz Park. A smash-and-grab job at Guebelin and another at Grima, next to the Baur-au-Lac. And if that weren't enough, Detective Max Hornung was back, filled with some kind of nonsensical theory. Chief Inspector Schmied found himself starting to hyperventilate again.

'The lift cable drum was cracked,' Max was saying. 'When it collapsed, all the safety controls went out. Someone –'

'I saw the reports, Hornung. Normal wear and tear.'

'No, Chief Inspector. I examined the specifications for the cable drum. It should have lasted another five or six years.'

Chief Inspector Schmied felt the tic in his cheek. 'What are you trying to say?'

'Someone tampered with the lift.'

Not, I think someone tampered with the lift, or, In my opinion someone tampered with the lift. Oh, no! Someone tampered with the lift.

'Why would they do that?'

'That's what I would like to find out.'

'You want to go back to Roffe and Sons?'

Detective Max Hornung looked at Inspector Schmied in genuine surprise. 'No, sir. I want to go to Chamonix.'

The town of Chamonix lies forty miles south-east of Geneva, 3400 feet above sea level in the French department of Haute-Savoie, between the Mont Blanc massif and the Aiguille Rouge range, with one of the most breathtaking vistas in the world.

Detective Max Hornung was completely unaware of the scenery as he debouched from the train at the Chamonix station, carrying a battered cardboard suitcase. He waved a taxi away and headed on foot for the local police station, a small building situated on the main square in the centre of town. Max entered, feeling instantly at home, revelling in the warm camaraderie that he shared with the fraternity of policemen all over the world. He was one of *them*.

The French sergeant behind the desk looked up and asked, '*Est-ce qu' on peut vous aider?*'

'*Oui.*' Max beamed. And he started to talk. Max

approached all foreign languages in the same fashion: he slashed his way through the impenetrable thicket of irregular verbs and tenses and participles, using his tongue like a machete. As he spoke, the expression on the desk sergeant's face changed from puzzlement to disbelief. It had taken the French people hundreds of years to develop their tongues and soft palates and larynxes to form the glorious music that was the French language. And now this man standing before him was somehow managing to turn it into a series of horrible incomprehensible noises.

The desk sergeant could bear no more. He interrupted. 'What – what are you trying to *say*?'

Max replied, 'What do you mean? I'm speaking French.'

The desk sergeant leaned forward and asked with unabashed curiosity, 'Are you speaking it *now*?'

The fool doesn't even speak his own language, Max thought. He pulled out his warrant card and handed it to the sergeant. The sergeant read it through twice, looked up to study Max, and then read it again. It was impossible to believe that the man standing before him was a detective.

Reluctantly he handed the identification back to Max. 'What can I do for you?'

'I'm investigating a climbing accident that happened here two months ago. The victim's name was Sam Roffe.'

The sergeant nodded. 'Yes, I remember.'

'I would like to talk to someone who can give me some information about what happened.'

'That would be the mountain-rescue organization. It is called the Société Chamoniarde de Secours en Montagne. You will find it in Placé du Mont Blanc. The telephone number is five-three-one-six-eight-nine. Or they might have some information at the clinic. That's in Rue du Valais. The telephone number there is five-three-zero-one-eight-two. Here. I'll write all this down for you.' He reached for a pen.

'That won't be necessary,' Max said, 'Société Chamoniarde de Secours en Montagne, Place du Mont Blanc, five-three-one-six-eight-nine. Or the clinic in Rue du Valais, five-three-zero-one-eight-two.'

The sergeant was still staring long after Max had disappeared through the door.

The Société Chamoniarde de Secours was in the charge of a dark, athletic-looking young man seated behind a battered pine desk. He looked up as Max walked in, and his instant thought was that he hoped this odd-looking visitor did not plan to climb a mountain.

'Can I help you?'

'Detective Max Hornung.' He showed his warrant card.

'What can I do for you, Detective Hornung?'

'I am investigating the death of a man named Sam Roffe,' Max said.

The man behind the desk sighed. 'Ah, yes. I liked

Mr Roffe very much. It was an unfortunate accident.'

'Did you see it happen?'

A shake of the head. 'No. I took my rescue team up as soon as we received their distress signal, but there was nothing we could do. Mr Roffe's body had fallen into a crevasse. It will never be found.'

'How did it happen?'

'There were four climbers in the party. The guide and Mr Roffe were last. As I understand it, they were traversing an icy moraine. Mr Roffe slipped and fell.'

'Wasn't he wearing a harness?'

'Of course. His rope broke.'

'Does a thing like that happen often?'

'Only once.' He smiled at his little joke, then saw the detective's look and added quickly. 'Experienced climbers always check their equipment thoroughly, but accidents still happen.'

Max stood there a moment, thinking. 'I'd like to speak to the guide.'

'Mr Roffe's regular guide didn't make the climb that day.'

Max blinked, 'Oh? Why not?'

'As I recall, he was ill. Another guide took his place.'

'Do you have his name?'

'If you'll wait a minute, I can look it up for you.'

The man disappeared into an inner office. In a few minutes he returned with a slip of paper in his hand. 'The guide's name was Hans Bergmann.'

'Where can I find him?'

'He's not a local.' He consulted the piece of paper. 'He comes from a village called Lesgets. It's about sixty kilometres from here.'

Before Max left Chamonix, he stopped at the desk of the Kleine Scheidegg hotel and talked to the room clerk. 'Were you on duty when Mr Roffe was staying here?'

'Yes,' the clerk said. 'The accident was a terrible thing, terrible.'

'Mr Roffe was alone here?'

The clerk shook his head. 'No. He had a friend with him.'

Max stared. 'A friend?'

'Yes. Mr Roffe made the reservation for both of them.'

'Could you give me the name of his friend?'

'Certainly,' the clerk said. He pulled out a large ledger from beneath the desk and began to turn back the pages. He stopped, ran his finger down a page and said, 'Ah, here we are . . .'

It took almost three hours for Max to drive to Lesgets in a Volkswagen, the cheapest rental car he could find, and he almost passed through it. It was not even a village. The place consisted of a few shops, a small alpine lodge, and a general store with a single petrol pump in front of it.

Max parked in front of the lodge and walked in. There were half a dozen men seated in front of an open fireplace, talking. The conversation trailed off as Max entered.

'Excuse me,' he said, 'I'm looking for Herr Hans Bergmann.'

'Who?'

'Hans Bergmann. The guide. He comes from this village.'

An elderly man with a face that was a weather map of his years spat into the fireplace and said, 'Somebody's been kidding you, mister. I was born in Lesgets. I never heard of any Hans Bergmann.'

THIRTY-FOUR

It was the first day that Elizabeth had gone to the office since the death of Kate Erling a week earlier. Elizabeth entered the downstairs lobby with trepidation, responding mechanically to the greetings of the doorman and guards. At the far end of the lobby she saw workmen replacing the smashed lift car. She thought about Kate Erling, and Elizabeth could visualize the terror she must have felt as she plunged twelve interminable storeys to her death. She knew that she could never ride in that lift again.

When she walked into her office, her mail had already been opened by Henriette, the second secretary, and neatly placed on her desk. Elizabeth went through it quickly, initialling some memos, writing questions on others, or marking them for various department heads. At the bottom of the pile was a large sealed envelope marked 'Elizabeth Roffe – Personal'. Elizabeth took a letter-opener and slit the envelope across the top. She reached in and took out an 8-by-10 photograph. It was a close-up of a mongoloid child, its bulging eyes staring out of its encephalic head. Attached to the picture was a note printed in crayon: THIS IS MY BEAUTIFUL SON JOHN. YOUR DRUGS DID THIS TO HIM. I AM GOING TO KILL YOU.

Elizabeth dropped the note and the picture, and found that her hands were trembling. Henriette walked in with a handful of papers.

'These are ready to be signed, Miss –' She saw the look on Elizabeth's face. 'Is something wrong?'

Elizabeth said, 'Please – ask Mr Williams to come in here.' Her eyes went back to the picture on her desk.

Roffe and Sons could not be responsible for anything so dreadful.

'It was our fault,' Rhys said. 'A shipment of drugs was mislabelled. We managed to recall most of it, but –' He raised his hands expressively.

'How long ago did this happen?'

'Almost four years ago.'

'How many people were affected?'

'About a hundred.' He saw the expression on her face and added quickly, 'They received compensation. They weren't all like this, Liz. Look, we're damned careful here. We take every safety precaution we can devise, but people are human. Mistakes are sometimes made.'

Elizabeth sat staring at the picture of the child. 'It's horrible.'

'They shouldn't have shown you the letter.' Rhys ran his fingers through his thick black hair and said, 'This is a hell of a time to bring it up, but we have a few other problems more important than this.'

She wondered what could be more important. 'Yes?'

'The FDA just gave a decision against us on our aerosol sprays. There's going to be a complete ban on aerosols within two years.'

'How will that affect us?'

'It's going to hurt us badly. It means we'll have to close down half a dozen factories around the world and lose one of our most profitable divisions.'

Elizabeth thought about Emil Joeppli and the culture he was working on, but she said nothing. 'What else?'

'Have you seen the morning papers?'

'No.'

'A government minister's wife in Belgium, Mme van den Logh, took some Benexan.'

'That's one of our drugs?'

'Yes. It's an antihistamine. It's contra-indicated for anyone with essential hypertension. Our label carries a clear warning. She ignored it.'

Elizabeth felt her body beginning to tense. 'What happened to her?'

Rhys said, 'She's in a coma. She may not live. The newspaper stories mention that it's our product. Cancellations on orders are pouring in from all over the world. The FDA notified us that it's starting an investigation, but that will take at least a year. Until they finish, we can keep selling the drug.'

Elizabeth said, 'I want it taken off the market.'

'There's no reason to do that. It's a damned effective drug for –'

'Have any other people been hurt by it?'

'Hundreds of thousands of people have been helped by it.' Rhys's tone was cool. 'It's one of our most effective –'

'You haven't answered my question.'

'A few isolated cases, I suppose, yes. But –'

'I want it taken off the market. Now.'

He sat there, fighting his anger, then he said, 'Right. Would you like to know what that will cost the company?'

'No,' Elizabeth said.

Rhys nodded. 'So far you've only heard the good news. The bad news is that the bankers want a meeting with you. Now. They're calling in their loans.'

Elizabeth sat in her office alone, thinking about the mongoloid child, and about the woman who lay in a coma because of a drug that Roffe and Sons had sold her. Elizabeth was well aware that these kinds of tragedies involved other pharmaceutical firms as well as Roffe and Sons. There were almost daily stories in the newspapers about similar cases, but they had not touched her as this had. She felt responsible. She was determined to have a talk with the department heads who were in charge of safety measures to see if they could not be improved.

This is my beautiful son John.

Mme van den Logh is in a coma. She may not live.

The bankers want a meeting with you. Now. They've decided to call in their loans.

She felt choked, as though everything was beginning to close in on her at once. For the first time Elizabeth wondered if she was going to be able to cope. The burdens were too heavy, and they were piling up too fast. She swung round in her chair to look up at the portrait of old Samuel hanging on the wall. He looked so competent, so sure. But she knew about his doubts and uncertainties, and his black despairs. Yet he had come through. She would survive somehow, too. She was a Roffe.

She noticed that the portrait was askew. Probably as a result of the lift crash. Elizabeth got up to straighten it. As she tilted the picture, the hook holding it gave way, and the painting crashed to the floor. Elizabeth did not even look at it. She was staring at the place where the painting had hung. Taped to the wall was a tiny microphone.

It was 4 a.m., and Emil Joeppli was working late again. It had become a habit of his recently. Even though Elizabeth Roffe had not given him a specific deadline, Joeppli knew how important this project was to the company and he was pushing to get it finished as quickly as possible. He had heard disturbing rumours about Roffe and Sons lately. He wanted to do everything he could to help the company. It had been good to him. It gave him a handsome salary and complete freedom. He had liked Sam Roffe, and he liked his daughter too. Elizabeth Roffe would never know, but these late hours were Joeppli's gift to her. He was hunched over his small desk, checking out the results of his last experiment. They were even better than he had anticipated. He sat there, deep in concentration, unaware of the foetid smell of the caged animals in the laboratory or the cloying humidity of the room or the lateness of the hour. The door opened, and the guard on the graveyard shift, Sepp Nolan, walked in. Nolan hated this shift. There was something eerie about the deserted experimental laboratories at night. The smell of the caged animals made him ill. Nolan wondered whether all the animals they had killed here had souls and came back to haunt these corridors. I ought to put in for spook pay, he thought. Everyone in the building had long since gone home. Except for this fucking mad scientist with his cages full of rabbits and cats and hamsters.

'How long you gonna be, Doc?' Nolan asked.

Joeppli looked up, aware of Nolan for the first time. 'What?'

'If you're gonna be here awhile, I can bring you back a sandwich or something. I'm gonna run over to the commissary for a quick bite.'

Joeppli said, 'Just coffee, please.' He turned back to his charts.

Nolan said, 'I'll lock the outside door behind me when I leave the building. Be right back.'

Joeppli did not even hear him.

Ten minutes later the door to the laboratory opened, and a voice said, 'You're working late, Emil.'

Joeppli looked up, startled. When he saw who it was, he got to his feet, flustered, and said, 'Yes, sir.' He felt flattered that this man had dropped in to see him.

'The Fountain of Youth project, top secret, eh?'

Emil hesitated. Miss Roffe had said no one was supposed to know about it. But, of course, that did not include his visitor. It was this man who had brought him into the company. So Emil Joeppli smiled and said, 'Yes, sir. Top secret.'

'Good. Let's keep it that way. How is it going?'

'Wonderfully, sir.'

The visitor wandered over to one of the rabbit cages. Emil Joeppli followed him. 'Is there anything I can explain to you?'

The man smiled. 'No, I'm pretty familiar with it, Emil.' As the visitor started to turn away, he brushed against an empty feeding dish on the ledge and it fell to the floor. 'Sorry.'

'Don't worry about it, sir. I'll get it.' Emil Joeppli reached down to pick it up and the back of his head seemed to explode in a shower of red, and the last thing he saw was the floor racing up to meet him.

The insistent ringing of the telephone awakened Elizabeth. She sat up in bed, heavy with sleep, and looked at the digital clock on the little table. Five a.m. She fumbled the telephone off the hook. A frantic voice said, 'Miss Roffe? This is the security guard at the plant. There's been an explosion at one of the laboratories. It was completely destroyed.'

Instantly she was wide awake. 'Was anybody hurt?'

'Yes, ma'am. One of the scientists was burned to death.'

He did not have to tell Elizabeth the name.

THIRTY-FIVE

Detective Max Hornung was thinking. The detective bureau was filled with the noise of typewriters clattering, voices raised in argument, telephones ringing, but Hornung saw and heard nothing of these things. He had the single-minded concentration of a computer. He was thinking about the charter of Roffe and Sons, as old Samuel had set it up, keeping control within the family. Ingenious, Max thought. And dangerous. It reminded him of the tontine, the Italian insurance plan devised by the banker Lorenzo Tonti in 1695. Every member of the tontine put in an equal amount of money, and as each member died, the survivors inherited his share. It provided a powerful motive to eliminate the other members. Like Roffe and Sons. It was too much of a temptation to let people inherit stock worth millions, and then tell them they could not sell it unless everyone agreed.

Max had learned that Sam Roffe had not agreed. He was dead. Elizabeth Roffe had not agreed. She had narrowly escaped death twice. Too many accidents. Detective Max Hornung did not believe in accidents. He went to see Chief Inspector Schmied.

The chief inspector listened to Max Hornung's report on Sam Roffe's climbing accident and growled, 'So there's been a mix-up about the name of a guide. That hardly constitutes a case for murder, Hornung. Not in *my* department, it doesn't.'

The little detective said patiently, 'I think there's more to it. Roffe and Sons is having big internal problems. Perhaps someone thought that getting rid of Sam Roffe would solve them.'

Chief Inspector Schmied sat back and eyed Detective Hornung. He was certain that there was nothing to his theories. But the idea of having Detective Max Hornung out of sight for a while filled Chief Inspector Schmied with a deep pleasure. His absence would be a boost to the morale of the entire department. And there was something else to consider: The people Max Hornung wanted to investigate. No less than the powerful Roffe family. Ordinarily, Schmied would have ordered Max Hornung to keep a million miles away from them. If Detective Hornung irritated them – and how could he not! – they had enough power to have him thrown out of the force. And no one could blame Chief Inspector Schmied. Hadn't the little detective been forced on him? And so he said to Max Hornung, 'The case is yours. Take your time.'

'Thank you,' Max said happily.

* * *

As Max was walking through the corridor towards his office, he ran into the coroner. 'Hornung! Can I borrow your memory for a minute?'

Max blinked. 'I beg your pardon?'

'The river patrol has just fished a girl out of the river. Will you take a look at her?'

Max swallowed and said, 'If you wish.'

This was not a part of the job that Max enjoyed, but he felt that it was his duty.

She lay in the impersonal metal drawer in the chill of the morgue. She had blonde hair and was in her late teens or early twenties. Her body was bloated from the water, and naked, except for a red ribbon knotted around her neck.

'There are signs of sexual intercourse just before death. She was strangled and then dumped into the river,' the coroner said. 'There's no water in her lungs. We can't get any fingerprints on her. Ever seen her before?'

Detective Max Hornung looked down at the girl's face and said, 'No.'

He left to catch his bus to the airport.

THIRTY-SIX

When Detective Max Hornung landed at the Costa Smeralda airport in Sardinia, he rented the cheapest car available, a Fiat 500, and drove into Olbia. Unlike the rest of Sardinia, Olbia was an industrial city, and the outskirts were an ugly sprawl of mills and factories, a city dump and a giant graveyard of once-beautiful automobiles, now useless old hulks, good only for scrap. Every city in the world had its automobile junkyards, Max thought. Monuments to civilization.

Max reached the centre of town and drove up in front of a building with a sign that read: 'QUESTURA DI SASSARI COMMISSARIATO DI POLIZIA OLBIA.' The moment Max entered, he felt that familiar sense of identity, of belonging. He showed his warrant card to the desk sergeant, and a few minutes later he was ushered into the office of the Chief of Police, Luigi Ferraro. Ferraro rose to his feet, a welcoming smile on his face. It died as he saw his visitor. There was something about Max that did not spell 'detective'.

'Could I see your identification?' Chief Ferraro asked politely.

'Certainly,' Max said. He pulled out his warrant card and Chief Ferraro examined both sides of it carefully, then returned it. His immediate conclusion was that Switzerland must be very hard up for detectives. He took a seat behind his desk and said, 'What can I do for you?'

Max started to explain, in fluent Italian. The problem was that it took Chief Ferraro some moments to figure out what language Max was speaking. When he realized what it was supposed to be, he held up a horrified hand and said, '*Basta!* Do you speak English?'

'Of course,' Max replied.

'Then I beg of you! Let us speak in English.'

When Max was through talking, Chief Ferraro said, 'You are mistaken, signor. I can tell you that you are wasting your time. My mechanics have already examined the jeep. Everyone is agreed that it was an accident.'

Max nodded, unperturbed. '*I* haven't looked at it.'

Chief Ferraro said, 'Very well. It is in a public garage now, up for sale. I will have one of my men take you there. Would you like to see the scene of the accident?'

Max blinked and said, 'What for?'

Detective Bruno Campagna was elected as

Max's escort. 'We've already checked it out. It was an accident,' Campagna said.

'No,' Max replied.

The jeep was in a corner of the garage, its front still dented and splashed with dried green sap.

'I haven't had time to work on it yet,' the mechanic explained.

Max walked around the jeep, examining it. 'How were the brakes tampered with?' he asked.

The mechanic said, '*Gesù!* You, too?' A note of irritation crept into his voice. 'I have been a mechanic for twenty-five years, signor. I examined this jeep myself. The last time anyone touched these brakes was when this car left the factory.'

'Someone tampered with them,' Max said.

'How?' The mechanic was spluttering.

'I don't know yet, but I will,' Max assured him confidently. He took a last look at the jeep, then turned and walked out of the garage.

Chief of Police Luigi Ferraro looked at Detective Bruno Campagna and demanded, 'What did you *do* with him?'

'I didn't do anything. I took him to the garage, he made an ass of himself with the mechanic, then he said he wanted to go for a stroll by himself.'

'*Incredibile!*'

Max was standing on the shore, staring out at the emerald Tyrrhenian waters, seeing nothing. He was concentrating, his mind busily putting the pieces together. It was like working on a giant jigsaw puzzle. Everything always went neatly into place when you knew where it fitted. The jeep was a small but important part of the puzzle. Its brakes had been examined by expert mechanics. Max had no reason to doubt either their honesty or competence. He therefore accepted the fact that the brakes of the jeep had not been tampered with. Because Elizabeth had been driving the jeep and someone wanted her dead, he also accepted the fact that they *had* been tampered with. There was no way it could have been done. Yet someone had done it. Max was up against someone clever. It made things more interesting.

Max stepped out on to the sandy beach, sat down on a large rock, closed his eyes and began to concentrate again, focusing on the pieces, shifting, dissecting, rearranging the bits of the puzzle.

Twenty minutes later the last piece clicked into place. Max's eyes flew open and he thought admiringly, Bravo! I must meet the man who thought of this.

After that, Detective Max Hornung had two stops to make, the first just outside Olbia and the second in the mountains. He caught the late afternoon plane back to Zurich.

Economy class.

THIRTY-SEVEN

The head of the security forces of Roffe and Sons said to Elizabeth, 'It all happened too fast, Miss Roffe. There was nothing we could do. By the time the fire-fighting equipment got into action, the whole laboratory was gone.'

They had found the remains of Emil Joeppli's charred body. There was no way of knowing whether his formula had been removed from the laboratory before the explosion.

Elizabeth asked, 'The Development Building was under twenty-four-hour guard, was it not?'

'Yes, ma'am. We –'

'How long have you been in charge of our security department?'

'Five years. I –'

'You're fired.'

He started to say something in protest, then changed his mind. 'Yes, ma'am.'

'How many men are there on your staff?'

'Sixty-five.'

344

Sixty-five! And they could not save Emil Joeppli. 'I'm giving them twenty-four hours' notice,' Elizabeth said. 'I want them all out of here.'

He looked at her a moment. 'Miss Roffe, do you think you're being fair?'

She thought of Emil Joeppli, and the priceless formula that had been stolen, and of the bug that had been planted in her office that she had ground under the heel of her shoe.

'Get out,' Elizabeth said.

She filled every minute that morning, trying to wipe out the vision of the charred body of Emil Joeppli and his laboratory full of burned animals. She tried not to think about what the loss of that formula was going to cost the company. There was a chance a rival company might patent it and there was nothing Elizabeth could do about it. It *was* a jungle. When your competitors thought you were weak, they moved in for the kill. But this wasn't a competitor doing this. This was a friend. A deadly friend.

Elizabeth arranged for a professional security force to take over immediately. She would feel safer with strangers around her.

She phoned the Hôpital Internationale in Brussels to check on the condition of Mme van den Logh, the wife of the Belgian minister. They reported that she was still in a coma. They did not know whether she would live.

Elizabeth was thinking about Emil Joeppli and the mongoloid child and the minister's wife when

Rhys walked in. He looked at her face and said gently, 'As bad as that?'

She nodded, miserably.

Rhys walked over to her and studied her. She looked tired, drained. He wondered how much more she could stand. He took her hands in his and asked gently, 'Is there anything I can do to help?'

Everything, Elizabeth thought. She needed Rhys desperately. She needed his strength and his help and his love. Their eyes met and she was ready to go into his arms, to tell him everything that had happened, that was happening.

Rhys said, 'There's nothing new on Mme van den Logh?'

And the moment had passed.

'No,' Elizabeth said.

He asked, 'Have you had any calls yet on the *Wall Street Journal* story?'

'What story?'

'You haven't seen it?'

'No.'

Rhys sent to his office for a copy. The article enumerated all the recent troubles of Roffe and Sons, but the major theme of the story was that the company needed someone experienced to run it. Elizabeth put the newspaper down. 'How much damage will this do?'

Rhys shrugged. 'The damage has already been done. They're just reporting it. We're beginning to lose a lot of our markets. We –'

The intercom buzzed. Elizabeth pressed the switch. 'Yes?'

'Herr Julius Badrutt is on line two, Miss Roffe. He says it's urgent.'

Elizabeth looked up at Rhys. She had been postponing the meeting with the bankers. 'Put him on.' She picked up the phone. 'Good morning, Herr Badrutt.'

'Good morning.' Over the phone his voice sounded dry and brittle. 'Are you free this afternoon?'

'Well, I'm –'

'Fine. Will four o'clock be satisfactory?'

Elizabeth hesitated. 'Yes. Four o'clock.'

There was a dry, rustling sound over the phone and Elizabeth realized that Herr Badrutt was clearing his throat. 'I was sorry to hear about Mr Joeppli,' he said.

Joeppli's name had not been mentioned in the newspaper accounts of the explosion.

She hung up slowly, and found that Rhys was watching her.

'The sharks smell blood,' Rhys said.

The afternoon was filled with phone calls. Alec telephoned. 'Elizabeth, did you see the story in the newspaper this morning?'

'Yes,' Elizabeth said. '*The Wall Street Journal* was exaggerating.'

There was a pause, and then Alec said, 'I'm not talking about *The Wall Street Journal*. The *Financial*

Times has a headline story on Roffe and Sons. It's not good. My phones haven't stopped ringing. We're getting heavy cancellations. What are we going to do?'

'I'll get back to you, Alec,' Elizabeth promised.

Ivo called. '*Carissima*, I think you'd better prepare yourself for a shock.'

I'm prepared, Elizabeth thought wryly. 'What is it?'

Ivo said, 'An Italian minister was arrested a few hours ago for accepting bribes.'

Elizabeth had a sudden feeling of what was coming. 'Go on.'

There was a note of apology in Ivo's voice. 'It wasn't our fault,' Ivo said. 'He got greedy and he was careless. They caught him at the airport, trying to smuggle money out of Italy. They've traced the money to us.'

Even though Elizabeth was prepared for it, she still felt a shock of disbelief. 'Why were we bribing him?'

Ivo said matter-of-factly, 'So that we could do business in Italy. It's a way of life here. Our crime was not in bribing the minister, *cara* – it was in getting caught.'

She sat back in her chair, her head beginning to pound.

'What happens now?'

'I would suggest that we meet with the company attorney as quickly as possible,' Ivo said. 'Don't worry. Only the poor go to jail in Italy.'

Charles called from Paris, his voice frantic with worry. The French press was full of Roffe and Sons. Charles urged Elizabeth to sell the company while it still had a reputation.

'Our customers are losing faith,' Charles said. 'Without that, there is no company.'

Elizabeth thought about the phone calls, the bankers, her cousins, the press. Too much was happening too quickly. Someone was making it happen. She *had* to find out who.

The name was still in Elizabeth's private telephone book. Maria Martinelli. It brought back long-ago memories of the tall, leggy Italian girl who had been a classmate of Elizabeth's in Switzerland. They had corresponded from time to time. Maria had become a model and she had written to Elizabeth that she was engaged to marry an Italian newspaper publisher in Milan. It took Elizabeth fifteen minutes to reach Maria. When the social amenities had been disposed of, Elizabeth said into the phone, 'Are you still engaged to that newspaper publisher?'

'Of course. The minute Tony gets his divorce, we're going to be married.'

'I want you to do me a favour, Maria.'

'Name it.'

Less than one hour later Maria Martinelli called back. 'I got that information you wanted. The banker who was caught trying to smuggle money out of Italy was set up. Tony says a man tipped off the border police.'

'Was he able to find out the name of the man?'
'Ivo Palazzi.'

Detective Max Hornung had made an interesting discovery. He had learned that not only was the explosion at the Roffe and Sons laboratory arranged deliberately, but that it had been caused by an explosive called Rylar X, made exclusively for the military, and not available to anyone else. What intrigued Max was that Rylar X was manufactured at one of the factories of Roffe and Sons. It took Max only one telephone call to learn which one.

The factory outside Paris.

At exactly 4 p.m. Herr Julius Badrutt lowered his angular figure into a chair and said without preamble, 'As much as we would like to accommodate you, Miss Roffe, I am afraid our responsibility towards our stockholders must take precedence.'

It was the kind of statement, Elizabeth thought, that bankers made to widows and orphans before they foreclosed their mortgages. But this time she was ready for Herr Badrutt.

'. . . My board of directors has therefore instructed me to inform you that our bank is calling in the notes on Roffe and Sons immediately.'

'I was told I had ninety days,' Elizabeth said.

'Unfortunately, we feel that the circumstances have changed for the worse. I should also inform you that the other banks you are dealing with have reached the same decision.'

With the banks refusing to help her, there would be no way to keep the company private.

'I'm sorry to bring you such bad news, Miss Roffe, but I felt that I should tell you personally.'

'You know, of course, that Roffe and Sons is still a very strong and healthy company.'

Herr Julius Badrutt nodded his head, once. 'Of course. It's a great company.'

'Yet you won't give us more time.'

Herr Badrutt looked at her for a moment, then said, 'The bank thinks your problems are manageable, Miss Roffe. But . . .' He hesitated.

'But you don't think there's anyone to manage them?'

'I'm afraid that is correct.' He started to rise.

'What if someone else were president of Roffe and Sons?' Elizabeth asked.

He shook his head. 'We have discussed that possibility. We don't feel that any of the present members of the board have the overall ability to cope with –'

She said, 'I was thinking of Rhys Williams.'

THIRTY-EIGHT

Constable Thomas Hiller of the Thames Marine Police Division was in terrible shape. He was sleepy, hungry, horny and wet; and he could not decide which was the greatest of his miseries.

He was sleepy because his fiancée, Flo, had kept him awake all night, fighting; he was hungry because by the time she was through screaming at him, he was late for duty, and he had had no time to pick up a bite; he was horny because she had refused to let him touch her, and he was wet because the thirty-foot police boat on which he was travelling had been built for service, not comfort, and a rising wind was driving the rain into the small wheelhouse where he stood. On days like this there was bloody little to see and even bloody less to do. The Thames Division covered fifty-four miles of river from Dartford Creek to Staines Bridge, and ordinarily Constable Hiller enjoyed patrol duty. But not when he was in this shape. Damn all women! He thought about Flo in bed, naked as a pouter pigeon, her large tits waving up and down as she yelled at him. He glanced at his watch. Another half-hour and this miserable tour would be finished. The boat had turned and was headed back towards Waterloo Pier. His only problem now was deciding what to do first: sleep, eat, or jump in the kip with Flo. Maybe all three at once, he thought. He rubbed his eyes to force the sleep out of them, and turned to look at the muddy, swollen river pimpled by the rain.

It seemed to loom out of nowhere. It looked like a large white fish floating belly up, and Constable Hiller's first thought was: If we haul it aboard, we're going to stink of it. It was about ten yards to starboard and the boat was moving away from it. If he opened his mouth, the bloody fish was going to delay his getting off duty. They would have to stop and grapple it, and either pull it over the side or tow it in. Whichever they did would delay his getting to Flo. Well, he didn't *have* to report it. What if he had not seen it? What if –? They were moving farther away.

Constable Hiller called out, 'Sergeant, there's a floating fish twenty degrees off starboard. Looks like a big shark.'

The hundred-horsepower diesel engine suddenly changed rhythm, and the boat began to slow. Sergeant Gaskins stepped to one side. 'Where is it?' he asked.

The dim shape was gone now, buried in the rain. 'It was over there.'

Sergeant Gaskins hesitated. He too was anxious to get home. His impulse was to ignore the damned fish.

'Was it big enough to menace navigation?' he asked.

Constable Hiller fought with himself and lost. 'Yes,' he said.

And so the patrol boat turned and slowly headed towards where the object had last been seen. It materialized again unexpectedly, almost under the bow, and they both stood there, staring down at it. It was the body of a young blonde girl.

She was naked, except for a red ribbon tied around her swollen neck.

THIRTY-NINE

At the moment when Constable Hiller and Sergeant Gaskins were fishing the body of the murdered girl out of the Thames, ten miles on the other side of London, Detective Max Hornung was entering a grey and white marble lobby of New Scotland Yard. Just walking through the storied portals gave him a sense of pride. They were all part of the same great fraternity. He enjoyed the fact that the Yard's cable address was HAND-CUFFS. Max was very fond of the English. His only problem concerned their ability to communicate with him. The English spoke their native language so strangely.

The policeman behind the reception desk asked, 'Can I help you, sir?'

Max turned. 'I have an appointment with Inspector Davidson.'

'Name, sir?'

Max said, slowly and distinctly, 'Inspector Davidson.'

The guard looked at him with interest. 'Your name is Inspector Davidson?'

'My name is *not* Inspector Davidson. My name is Max Hornung.'

The policeman behind the desk said apologetically, 'Excuse me, sir, but do you speak any English?'

Five minutes later Max was seated in the office of Inspector Davidson, a large, middle-aged man with a florid face and uneven yellow teeth. Typically British-looking, Max thought happily.

'Over the phone you said you were interested in information on Sir Alec Nichols as a possible suspect in a murder case.'

'He's one of half a dozen.'

Inspector Davidson stared at him. 'His wanted toes are frozen?'

Max sighed. He repeated what he had just said, slowly and carefully.

'Ah.' The inspector thought for a moment. 'Tell you what I'll do. I'll turn you over to C-Four Criminal Records Department. If they have nothing on him, we'll try C-Eleven and C-Thirteen – Criminal Intelligence.'

Sir Alec Nichols' name was not listed in any of the files. But Max Knew where he could get the information he wanted.

Earlier that morning Max had phoned a number of executives who worked in the City, the financial centre of London.

Their reactions were identical. When Max announced his name, they were filled with trepidation, for everyone doing business in the City had *something* to hide, and Max Hornung's reputation as a financial avenging angel was international. The moment that Max informed them that he was seeking information about someone else, they fell over themselves to co-operate with him.

Max spent two days visiting banks and financial companies, credit rating organizations and vital statistics offices. He was not interested in talking to the people at those places: he was interested in talking to their computers.

Max was a genius with computers. He would sit before the console board and play the machines like a virtuoso. It did not matter what language the computer had been taught, for Max spoke all of them. He talked to digital computers and low-level and high-level language computers. He was at ease with FORTRAN and FORTRAN IV, the giant IBM 370s and the PDP 10s and 11s and ALGOL 68.

He was at home with COBOL, programmed for business, and BASIC, used by the police, and the high speed APL, which conversed solely in charts and graphs. Max talked to LISP and APT, and the PL-1. He held conversations in the binary code, and questioned the arithmetic units and the CPV units, and the high-speed printer answered his questions at the rate of eleven hundred lines a minute. The giant computers had spent their lives sucking up information like insatiable pumps, storing it, analysing it, remembering it, and now they were spewing it out in Max's ear, whispering their secrets to him in their secluded air-conditioned crypts.

Nothing was sacred, nothing was safe. Privacy in today's civilization was a delusion, a myth. Every citizen was exposed, his deepest secrets laid bare, waiting to be read. People were on record if they had a social security number, an insurance policy, a driving licence or a bank account. They were listed if they had paid taxes, drawn unemployment benefit or welfare funds. Their names were stored in computers if they were covered by private medical insurance, had made mortgage payments on a house, owned a car or motor bicycle, or had a deposit or current account. The computer knew their names if they had been in hospital, or had done military service; had a gun or a fishing licence; had applied for a passport, a telephone or electricity; or if they had been born, married or divorced.

If one knew where to look, and if one was patient, all the facts were available.

Max Hornung and the computers had a wonderful rapport. They did not laugh at Max's accent, or the way he looked, or dressed. To the computers Max was a giant. They respected his intelligence, admired him, loved him. They happily gave up their secrets to him, sharing their delicious gossip about the fools that mortals made of themselves. It was like old friends chatting.

'Let's talk about Sir Alec Nichols,' Max said.

The computers began. They gave Max a mathematical sketch of Sir Alec, drawn in digits and binary codes and charts. In two hours Max had a composite picture of the man, a financial identi-kit.

Copies of bank receipts and cancelled cheques and bills were all laid before him. The first puzzling item that caught Max's eye was a series of cheques for large amounts, all made out to 'Bearer', cashed by Sir Alec Nichols. Where had the money gone? Max looked to see if it had been reported as a business or personal expense, or as a tax deduction. Negative. He went back over the lists of expenditures again: a cheque to White's club, a meat-market bill, unpaid . . . an evening gown from John Bates . . . the Guinea . . . a dentist's bill, unpaid . . . Annabelle's . . . one challis robe from Saint Laurent in Paris . . . a bill from the White Elephant, unpaid . . . a rates bill . . . John Wyndham, the hairdresser, unpaid . . . four dresses from Yves Saint Laurent, Rive Gauche . . . household salaries . . .

Max asked a question of the computer at the Motor Vehicle Licensing Centre.

Affirmative. *Sir Alec owns a Bentley and a Morris.*

Something was missing. There was no mechanic's bill.

Max had the computers search their memories. In seven years no such bill existed.

Did we forget something? the computers asked.

No, Max replied, *you didn't forget.*

Sir Alec did not use a mechanic. He repaired his own cars. A man with that mechanical ability would have no trouble causing a lift, or a jeep, to crash. Max Hornung pored over the arcane figures that his friends set before him, with the eagerness of an Egyptologist translating a set of newly discovered hieroglyphics. He found further mysteries. Sir Alec was spending a great deal more than his income.

Another loose thread.

Max's friends in the City had connections in many quarters. Within two days Max learned that Sir Alec had been borrowing money from Tod Michaels, the owner of a club in Soho.

Max turned to the police computers and asked questions. They listened, and they replied. *Yes, we have Tod Michaels for you. Has been charged with several crimes, but never convicted. Suspected of being involved in blackmail, dope, prostitution and loan-sharking.*

Max went down to Soho and asked more questions. He found out that Sir Alec Nichols did not gamble. But his wife did.

When Max was finished, there was no doubt in his mind that Sir Alec Nichols was being blackmailed. He had unpaid bills, he needed money fast. He had stock that would be worth millions, if he could sell it. Sam Roffe had stood in his way, and now Elizabeth Roffe.

Sir Alec Nichols had a motive for murder.

* * *

Max checked out Rhys Williams. The machines tried, but the information proved too sketchy.

The computers informed Max that Rhys Williams was male, born in Wales, thirty-four years of age, unmarried. An executive of Roffe and Sons. Salary eighty thousand dollars a year, plus bonuses. A London savings account with a balance of twenty-five thousand pounds, a current account with an average balance of eight hundred pounds. A safe-deposit box in Zurich, contents unknown. All major charge accounts and credit cards. Many of the items purchased with them were for women. Rhys Williams had no criminal record. He had been employed at Roffe and Sons for nine years.

Not enough, Max thought. Not nearly enough. It was as though Rhys Williams was hiding behind the computers. Max remembered how protective the man had been when Max had questioned Elizabeth, after Kate Erling's funeral. Whom had he been protecting? Elizabeth Roffe? Or himself?

At six o'clock that evening Max booked himself on an Alitalia economy flight to Rome.

FORTY

Ivo Palazzi had spent almost ten years carefully and skilfully building an intricate double life that not even his closest associates had penetrated.

It took Max Hornung and his computer friends in Rome less than twenty-four hours. Max held discussions with the computer at the Anagrafe Building, where vital statistics and city-administration data were kept, and he visited the computers at SID, and went to call on the bank computers.

They all welcomed Max.

Tell me about Ivo Palazzi, Max said.

Happily, they replied.

The conversations began.

A grocery bill from Amici . . . a beauty salon bill from Sergio in the Via Condotti . . . one blue suit from Angelo . . . flowers from Carducci . . . two evening dresses from Irene Galitzine . . . shoes from Gucci . . . a Pucci purse . . . utility bills . . .

Max kept reading the print-outs, examining,

analysing, smelling. Something smells wrong. There were tuition fees for six children.

Have you made an error? Max asked.

Sorry. What type of error?

The computers at Anagrafe told me that Ivo Palazzi is registered as the father of three children. Do you verify six tuition fees?

We do.

You show Ivo Palazzi's address as being in Olgiata?

That is correct.

But he is paying for an apartment in Via Montemignaio?

Yes.

Are there two Ivo Palazzis?

No. One man. Two families. Three daughters by his wife. Three sons by Donatella Spolini.

Before Max was through, he knew the tastes of Ivo's mistress, her age, the name of her hairdresser, and the names of Ivo's illegitimate children. He knew that Simonetta was a blonde, and Donatella a brunette. He knew what size dresses and bras and shoes each wore and how much they cost.

Among the expenses several interesting items caught Max's eye. The amounts were small, but they stood out like beacons. There was a receipted cheque for a lathe, a plane and a saw. Ivo Palazzi liked to work with his hands. Max thought about the fact that an architect would probably know something about lifts.

Ivo Palazzi applied for a large bank loan recently, the computers informed Max.

Did he receive it?

No. The bank asked him to have his wife co-sign. He withdrew the request.

Thank you.

Max took a bus to the Polizia Scientifica centre in EUR, where the giant computer was kept in a large round room.

Does Ivo Palazzi have a criminal record? Max asked.

Affirmative. Ivo Palazzi was convicted on an assault and battery charge at age twenty-three. His victim went to hospital. Palazzi went to jail for two months.

Anything else?

Ivo Palazzi keeps a mistress at Via Montemignaio.

Thank you. I know.

There are several police reports of complaints from neighbours.

What sort of complaints?

Disturbing the peace. Fighting, yelling. One night she smashed all the dishes. Is that important?

Very, Max said. *Thank you.*

So Ivo Palazzi had a temper. And Donatella Spolini had a temper. Had something happened between her and Ivo? Was she threatening to expose him? Was that why he had suddenly gone to the bank for a large loan? How far would a man like Ivo Palazzi go to protect his marriage, his family, his way of life?

There was one final item that caught the little detective's attention. A large payment had been made to Ivo Palazzi by the financial section of the Italian security police. It was a reward, a percentage of the money found on the banker whom Ivo had turned in. If Ivo Palazzi was that desperate for money, what else would he do for it?

Max bade farewell to his computers and caught a noon flight to Paris on Air France.

FORTY-ONE

The taxi fare from Charles de Gaulle Airport to the Notre Dame area is seventy francs, not including a tip. The fare by city bus Number 351, to the same area, is seven and a half francs, no tip required. Detective Max Hornung took the bus. He checked into the inexpensive Hôtel Meublé and began making phone calls.

He talked to the people who held in their hands the secrets of the citizens of France. The French were normally more suspicious than even the Swiss, but they were eager to cooperate with Max Hornung. There were two reasons. The first was that Max Hornung was a virtuoso in his field, greatly admired, and it was an honour to co-operate with such a man. The second was that they were terrified of him. There were no secrets from Max. The odd-looking little man with the funny accent stripped everyone naked. 'Certainly,' they told Max. 'You're welcome to use our computers.

Everything to be kept confidential, of course.'

'Of course.'

Max dropped in at the Inspecteurs des Finances, the Crédit Lyonnais, and the Assurance Nationale and chatted with the tax computers. He visited the computers at the *gendarmerie* at Rosny-sous-Bois and the ones at the Prefecture of Police at Île de la Cité.

They started off with the light, easy gossip of old friends. *Who are Charles and Hélène Roffe-Martel?* Max asked.

Charles and Hélène Roffe-Martel, residence Rue François Premier 5, Vésinet, married May 24, 1970, at the Mairie in Neuilly, children none, Hélène three times divorced, maiden name Roffe, bank account at the Crédit Lyonnais in Avenue Montaigne in name of Hélène Roffe-Martel, average balance in excess of twenty thousand francs.

Expenditures?

With pleasure. A bill from Librairie Marceau for books . . . a dental bill for root-canal work for Charles Martel . . . hospital bills for Charles Martel . . . doctor's bill for examination of Charles Martel.

Do you have result of diagnosis?

Can you wait? I will have to speak to another computer.

Yes, please. Max waited.

The machine containing the doctor's report began to speak. *I have the diagnosis.*

Go ahead.

A nervous condition.

Anything else?

Severe bruises and contusions on thighs and buttocks.

Any explanation?

None given.

Go-on, please.

A bill for a pair of men's shoes from Pinet . . . one hat from Rose Valois . . . foie gras from Fauchon . . . Carita beauty salon . . . Maxim's, dinner party for eight . . . flat silver from Christofle . . . a man's robe from Sulka . . . Max stopped the computer. Something was bothering him. Something about the bills. He realized what it was. Every purchase had been signed by Mme Roffe-Martel. The bill for men's clothes, the restaurant bills – all the accounts were in her name. Interesting.

And then the first loose thread.

A company named Belle Paix had purchased a land tax stamp. One of the owners of Belle Paix was named Charles Dessain. Charles Dessain's Social Security number was the same as Charles Martel's. Concealment.

Tell me about Belle Paix, Max said.

Belle Paix is owned by René Duchamps and Charles Dessain, also known as Charles Martel.

What does Belle Paix do?

It owns a vineyard.

How much is the company capitalized at?

Four million francs.

Where did Charles Martel get his share of the money?

From Chez ma tante.

The house of your aunt?

Sorry. A French slang expression. The proper name is Crédit Municipal.

Is the vineyard profitable?

No. It failed.

Max needed more. He kept talking to his friends, probing, cajoling, demanding. It was the insurance computer that confided to Max that there was a warning on file of a possible insurance fraud. Max felt something delicious stir within him.

Tell me about it, he said.

And they talked, like two women gossiping back and forth over the Monday wash.

When Max was through he went to see a jeweller named Pierre Richaud.

In thirty minutes Max knew to a franc how much of Hélène Roffe-Martel's jewellery had been duplicated. It came to just over two million francs, the amount Charles Martel had invested in the vineyard. So Charles Dessain-Martel had been desperate enough to steal his wife's jewellery.

What other acts of desperation had he committed?

There was one other entry that interested Max. It might be of little significance, but Max methodically filed it away in his mind. It was a bill for the purchase of one pair of mountain-climbing boots. It made Max pause, because mountain climbing did not fit in with his image of Charles Martel-Dessain,

369

a man who was so dominated by his wife that he was allowed no charge accounts of his own, had no bank account in his name, and was forced to steal in order to make an investment.

No, Max could not visualize Charles Martel challenging a mountain. Max went back to his computers.

The bill you showed me yesterday from Timwear Sports Shop. I would like to see an itemized statement, please.

Certainly.

It flashed on the screen before him. There was the bill for the boots. Size *36A*. A woman's size. It was Hélène Roffe-Martel who was the mountain climber.

Sam Roffe had been killed on a mountain.

FORTY-TWO

Rue Armengaud was a quiet Paris street lined with
one- and two-storey private residences, each with
its sloping guttered roof. Towering above its neighbours was Number 26, an eight-storey, modern
structure of glass, steel and stone, the headquarters of Interpol, the clearing house for information
on international criminal activities.

Detective Max Hornung was talking to a computer in the huge, air-conditioned basement room
when one of the staff members walked in and said,
'They're running a snuff film upstairs. Want to see
it?'

Max looked up and said, 'I don't know. What
is a snuff film?'

'Come and take a look.'

Two dozen men and women were seated in the
large screening room on the third floor of the
building. There were members of the Interpol staff,
police inspectors from the Sûreté, plainclothes
detectives and a scattering of uniformed policemen.

Standing at the front of the room next to a blank screen, René Almedin, an assistant to the secretary of Interpol, was speaking. Max entered and found a seat in the back row.

René Almedin was saying, '. . . for the last several years we have been hearing increasing rumours of snuff films, pornographic films in which at the end of the sexual act the victim is murdered on camera. There has never been proof that such films actually existed. The reason, of course, is obvious. These films would not have been made for the public. They would have been made to be shown privately to wealthy individuals who got their pleasure in twisted, sadistic ways.' René Almedin carefully removed his glasses. 'As I have said, everything has been rumour and speculation. That has now changed, however. In a moment you are going to see footage from an actual snuff film.' There was an expectant stir from the audience. 'Two days ago, a male pedestrian carrying an attaché case was struck down in a hit-and-run accident in Passy. The man died on the way to the hospital. He is still unidentified. The Sûreté found this reel of film in his attaché case and turned it over to the laboratory, where it was developed.' He gave a signal and the lights began to dim. The film began.

The blonde girl could not have been more than eighteen. There was something unreal about watching that young face and budding woman's body performing fellatio, analingus and a variety of other sexual acts with the large hairless man in bed with her. The camera moved in to a close-up to show his enormous penis driving into her body, then pulled back to show her face. Max Hornung had never seen her face before. But he had seen something else that was familiar. His eyes were fixed on the ribbon that the girl was wearing around her neck. It triggered a memory. A red ribbon. Where? Slowly, the girl on the screen began to build to a peak, and as she started to climax, the man's fingers went around her throat and began to squeeze. The look on the girl's face changed from ecstasy to horror. She fought wildly to escape, but his hands pressed tighter, until at the final moment of orgasm the girl died. The camera moved in for a close-up of her face. The film ended. The lights suddenly came on in the room. Max remembered.

The girl who had been fished out of the river in Zurich.

At Interpol headquarters in Paris, replies from urgent inquiry cables were beginning to arrive from all over Europe. Six similar murders had taken place – in Zurich, London, Rome, Portugal, Hamburg and Paris.

René Almedin said to Max, 'The descriptions match exactly. The victims were all blonde, female, young; they were strangled during sexual intercourse and their bodies were nude except for a red ribbon around their necks. We're dealing with a mass murderer. Someone who has a passport, and is either affluent enough to travel extensively on his own or is on an expense account.'

A man in plain clothes walked into the office and said, 'We ran into some good luck. The raw stock of the film is manufactured by a small outfit in Brussels. This particular batch had a colour-balance problem, which makes it easy for them to identify. We're getting a list of the customers they sold it to.'

Max said, 'I would like to see that list when you have it.'

'Of course,' René Almedin said. He studied the little detective. Max Hornung looked like no detective he had ever seen. And yet it was Max Hornung who had tied the snuff murders together.

'We owe you a debt of gratitude,' Almedin said.

Max Hornung looked at him and blinked. 'What for?' he asked.

FORTY-THREE

Alec Nichols had not wanted to attend the banquet, but he had not wished Elizabeth to go alone. They were both scheduled to speak. The banquet was in Glasgow, a city Alec hated. A car was outside the hotel, waiting to take them to the airport as soon as they could decently make their excuses. He had already given his speech but his mind had been elsewhere. He was tense and nervous, and his stomach was upset. Some fool had had the bad judgement to serve haggis. Alec had barely tasted it. Elizabeth was seated next to him. 'Are you all right, Alec?'

'Fine.' He patted her hand reassuringly.

The speeches were almost finished when a waiter came up to Alec and whispered, 'Excuse me, sir. There's a trunk call for you. You can take it in the office.'

Alec followed the waiter out of the large dining-room into the small office behind the reception desk. He picked up the telephone. 'Hello?'

Swinton's voice said, 'This is your last warning!' The line went dead.

FORTY-FOUR

The last city on Detective Max Hornung's agenda was Berlin.

His friends the computers were waiting for him. Max spoke to the exclusive Nixdorf computer, to which one had access only with a specially punched card. He talked to the great computers at Allianz and Schuffa and to the ones at the Bundeskriminalamt at Wiesbaden, the collection point for all criminal activity in Germany.

What can we do for you? they asked.

Tell me about Walther Gassner.

And they told him. When they were through telling Max Hornung their secrets, Walther Gassner's life was spread out before Max in beautiful mathematical symbols. Max could see the man as clearly as if he were looking at a photograph of him. He knew his taste in clothes, wines, food, hotels. A handsome young ski instructor who had lived off women and had married an heiress much older than himself.

There was one item that Max found curious: a cancelled cheque made out to a Dr Heissen, for two hundred marks. On the cheque was written 'For consultation'. What kind of consultation? The cheque had been cashed at the Dresdener Bank in Düsseldorf. Fifteen minutes later Max was speaking to the branch manager of the bank. Yes, of course the branch manager knew Dr Heissen. He was a valued client of the bank.

What kind of doctor was he?

A psychiatrist.

When Max had hung up, he sat back, his eyes closed, thinking. A loose thread. He picked up the telephone and put through a call to Dr Heissen in Düsseldorf.

An officious receptionist told Max that the doctor could not be disturbed. When Max insisted, Dr Heissen got on the telephone and rudely informed Max that he never revealed any information about his patients, and that he would certainly not dream of discussing such matters over the telephone. He hung up on the detective.

Max went back to the computers. *Tell me about Dr Heissen*, he said.

Three hours later Max was speaking to Dr Heissen on the telephone again.

'I told you before,' the doctor snapped, 'that if you want any information about any of my patients, you will have to come to my office with a court order.'

'It is inconvenient for me to come to Düsseldorf just now,' the detective explained.

'That's your problem. Anything else? I'm a busy man.'

'I know you are. I have in front of me your income tax reports for the past five years.'

'So?'

Max said, 'Doctor, I don't want to make trouble for you. But you are illegally concealing twenty-five per cent of your income. If you prefer, I can just forward your files to the German income tax authorities and tell them where to look. They could start with your safe-deposit box in Munich, or your numbered bank account in Basle.'

There was a long silence, and then the doctor's voice asked, 'Who did you say you were?'

'Detective Max Hornung of the Swiss Kriminalpolizei.'

There was another pause. The doctor said politely, 'And what is it exactly you wish to know?'

Max told him.

Once Dr Heissen began talking, there was no stopping him. Yes, of course he remembered Walther Gassner. The man had barged in without an appointment and had insisted on seeing him. He had refused to give his name. He had used the pretext that he wanted to discuss the problems of a friend.

'Of course, that alerted me instantly,' Dr Heissen confided to Max. 'It is a classic syndrome of people unwilling or afraid to face their problems.'

'What *was* the problem?' Max asked.

'He said his friend was schizophrenic and homicidal, and would probably kill someone unless he could be stopped. He asked if there was some kind of treatment that could help. He said he could not bear to have his friend locked away in an insane asylum.'

'What did you tell him?'

'I told him that first, of course, I would have to examine his friend, that some types of mental illness could be helped with modern drugs and other psychiatric and therapeutic treatments, and that other types were incurable. I also mentioned that in a case such as he described, treatment might be necessary for an extended period of time.'

'What happened then?' Max asked.

'Nothing. That was really all. I never saw the man again. I would like to have helped him. He was very distraught. His coming to me was obviously a cry for help. It is similar to a killer who writes on the wall of his victim's apartment, "Stop me before I kill again!"'

There was one thing still puzzling Max. 'Doctor, you said he wouldn't give you his name, and yet he gave you a cheque and signed it.'

Dr Heissen explained, 'He had forgotten to bring any money with him. He was very upset about that. In the end he had to write a cheque. That's how I happened to learn his name. Is there anything else you need to know, sir?'

'No.'

Something was disturbing Max, a loose thread dangling tantalizingly out of reach. It would come to him – meanwhile, he had finished with the computers. The rest was up to him now.

When Max returned to Zurich the following morning, he found a teletype on his desk from Interpol. It contained a list of customers who had purchased the batch of raw stock used to make the snuff murder film.

There were eight names on the list.

Among them was Roffe and Sons.

Chief Inspector Schmied was listening to Detective Max Hornung make his report. There was no doubt about it. The lucky little detective had stumbled on to another big case.

'It's one of five people,' Max was saying. 'They all have a motive and they had the opportunity. They were all in Zurich for a board meeting the day the lift crashed. Any one of them could have been in Sardinia at the time of the jeep accident.'

Chief Inspector Schmied frowned, 'You said there were five suspects. Aside from Elizabeth Roffe, there are only four members of the board. Who's your other suspect?'

Max blinked and said patiently, 'The man who was in Chamonix with Sam Roffe when he was murdered. Rhys Williams.'

FORTY-FIVE

Mrs Rhys Williams.

Elizabeth could not believe it. The whole thing had
an air of unreality. It was something out of a blissful
girlhood dream. Elizabeth remembered how she had
written in her exercise book, over and over, *Mrs
Rhys Williams, Mrs Rhys Williams*. She glanced
down now at the wedding ring on her finger.

Rhys said, 'What are you grinning about?' He
was seated in an easy chair across from her in the
luxurious Boeing 707-320. They were thirty-five
thousand feet somewhere above the Atlantic ocean,
dining on Iranian caviar and drinking chilled Dom
Perignon, and it was such a cliché of *La Dolce
Vita* that Elizabeth had to laugh aloud.

Rhys smiled. 'Something I said?'

Elizabeth shook her head. She looked at him
and marvelled at how attractive he was. Her husband. 'I'm just happy.'

He would never know how happy. How could

she tell him how much this marriage meant to her? He would not understand, because to Rhys it was not a marriage, it was a business proposition. But she loved Rhys. It seemed to Elizabeth that she had always loved him. She wanted to spend the rest of her life with him, have his children, belong to him, have him belong to her. Elizabeth looked over at Rhys again and thought wryly, But first I have to solve one small problem. I have to find a way to make him fall in love with me.

Elizabeth had proposed to Rhys the day of her meeting with Julius Badrutt. After the banker had left, Elizabeth had carefully brushed her hair, walked into Rhys's office, taken a deep breath and said, 'Rhys – would you marry me?'

She had seen the look of surprise on his face, and before he could speak, she had gone hurriedly on, trying to sound efficient and cool. 'It would be a purely business arrangement. The banks are willing to extend our loans if you take over as president of Roffe and Sons. The only way you can do that' – to Elizabeth's horror her voice had cracked – 'is to marry a member of the family, and I – I seem to be the only one available.'

She felt her face flush. She could not look at him.

'It wouldn't be a real marriage, of course,' Elizabeth had said, 'in the sense that – I mean – you'd be free to – to come and go as you pleased.'

He had watched her, not helping her. Elizabeth wished he would say something. Anything.

'Rhys –'

'Sorry. You took me by surprise.' He had smiled. 'It isn't every day a man gets proposed to by a beautiful girl.'

He was stalling, trying to get out of this without hurting her feelings. *I'm sorry, Elizabeth, but –*

'You have a deal,' Rhys said.

And Elizabeth had suddenly felt as though a heavy burden had been lifted from her. She had not realized until that moment how important this had been. She had bought time now to learn who the enemy was. Together she and Rhys could stop all the terrible things that had been happening. There was one thing she had to make clear to him.

'You will be president of the company,' she had said, 'but the voting control of the stock will remain in my hands.'

Rhys had frowned. 'If I'm running the company –'

'You will be,' Elizabeth had assured him.

'But the controlling stock –'

'Stays in my name. I want to make sure that it can't be sold.'

'I see.'

She could sense his disapproval. She had wanted to tell him that she had reached a decision. She had decided that the company should go public, that the members of the board should be able to sell their shares. With Rhys as president, Elizabeth would no longer have any fears about strangers coming in and taking over. Rhys would be strong enough to handle them. But Elizabeth could not let that happen until she found out who was trying to destroy the company. She had wanted desperately to tell Rhys all these things, but she knew that now was not the time, and so all she said was 'Other than that, you'll have complete control.'

Rhys had stood there, silently studying her for what seemed a long time. When he spoke, he said, 'When would you like to get married?'

'As soon as possible.'

Except for Anna, and Walther, who was at home, ill, they all came to Zurich for the wedding. Alec and Vivian, Hélène and Charles, Simonetta and Ivo. They seemed delighted for Elizabeth, and their pleasure made her feel like a fraud. She had not made a marriage, she had made a business deal.

Alec hugged her and said, 'You know I wish you everything wonderful.'

'I know, Alec. Thank you.'

Ivo waxed ecstatic. '*Carissima, tanti auguri e fig maschi*. "To find riches is a beggar's dream, but to find love is the dream of kings."'

Elizabeth smiled. 'Who said that?'

'I did,' Ivo declared. 'I hope Rhys appreciates what a lucky man he is.'

'I keep telling him,' she said lightly.

Hélène took Elizabeth aside. 'You are full of surprises, *ma chère*. I had no idea that you and Rhys were interested in each other.'

'It happened suddenly.'

Hélène studied her with cool, calculating eyes. 'Yes. I'm sure it did.' And she walked away.

After the ceremony there was a wedding reception at the Baur-au-Lac. On the surface it was gay and festive, but Elizabeth felt the undercurrents. There was something evil in the room, a malediction, but she could not tell from whom it was coming. All she knew was that someone in the room hated her. She could feel it, deep down inside her, yet when she looked around, all she saw were smiles and friendly faces. Charles raising his glass in a toast to her . . . Elizabeth had received a report on the laboratory explosion. *The explosive was manufactured by your factory outside Paris.*

Ivo, a happy grin on his face . . . *The banker who was caught trying to smuggle money out of Italy was set up. A man tipped off the border police. Ivo Palazzi.*

Alec? Walther? Which? Elizabeth wondered.

The following morning a board meeting was held, and Rhys Williams was unanimously elected president and chief operating officer of Roffe and Sons. Charles raised the question that was on everyone's mind. 'Now that you are running the company, are we going to be allowed to sell our stock?'

Elizabeth could feel the sudden tension in the room.

'The controlling stock is still in Elizabeth's hands,' Rhys informed them. 'It's her decision.'

Every head turned towards Elizabeth.

'We're not selling,' she announced.

When Elizabeth and Rhys were alone, he said, 'How would you like to honeymoon in Rio?'

Elizabeth looked at him, and her heart soared. He added matter-of-factly, 'Our manager there is threatening to quit. We cannot afford to lose him. I was planning to fly there tomorrow to straighten things out. It would look a bit strange if I went without my bride.'

Elizabeth nodded and said, 'Yes, of course.' You're a fool, she told herself. This was your idea. It's an arrangement, not a marriage. You have no right to expect anything from Rhys. And still, a small voice, deep inside her, said, Who knows what can happen? . . .

When they got off the plane at the Galeão airport, the air was surprisingly warm, and Elizabeth realized that in Rio it was summer. A Mercedes 600 was waiting for them. The chauffeur was a thin, dark-skinned man in his late twenties. When they got into the car, Rhys asked the driver, 'Where's Luis?'

'Luis is sick, Mr Williams. I'll be driving you and Mrs Williams.'

'Tell Luis I hope he'll be better soon.'

The driver studied them in the rearview mirror and said, 'I will.'

Half an hour later they were driving along the esplanade, over the colourful tiles of the broad avenue along the Copacabana Beach. They pulled up in front of the modern Princessa Sugarloaf Hotel and a moment later, their luggage was being attended to. They were ushered into an enormous suite with four bedrooms, a beautiful living-room, a kitchen, and a huge terrace overlooking the bay. The suite had been stocked with flowers in silver vases, champagne, whisky, and boxes of chocolates. The manager himself had escorted them to their suite.

'If there is anything at all we can do for you – anything – I am personally at your service twenty-four hours a day.' And he bowed himself out.

'They're certainly friendly,' Elizabeth said.

Rhys laughed and replied, 'They should be. You own this hotel.'

Elizabeth felt herself colour. 'Oh. I – I didn't know.'

'Hungry?'

'I – No, thank you,' Elizabeth replied.

'Some wine?'

'Yes, thank you.'

In her own ears her voice sounded stilted and unnatural. She was not certain how she was supposed to behave, or what to expect from Rhys. He had suddenly become a stranger, and she felt terribly conscious of the fact that they were alone in the honeymoon suite of a hotel, that it was getting late, and that it would soon be time for bed.

She watched Rhys as he deftly opened a bottle of champagne. He did everything so smoothly, with the easy assurance of a man who knows exactly what he wants and how to get it. What did he want?

Rhys carried a glass of champagne to Elizabeth and raised his own glass in a toast. 'To beginnings,' he said.

'To beginnings,' Elizabeth echoed. *And happy endings*, she added silently.

They drank.

We should smash our glasses into a fireplace, Elizabeth thought, to celebrate. She gulped down the rest of her champagne.

They were in Rio on their honeymoon, and she wanted Rhys. Not just for now, but forever.

The phone rang. Rhys picked it up and spoke into it briefly. When he finished he hung up and said to Elizabeth, 'It's late. Why don't you get ready for bed?'

It seemed to Elizabeth that the word 'bed' hung heavily in the air.

'Right,' she said weakly. She turned and went into the bedroom where the bellboys had put their luggage. There was a large double bed in the centre of the room. A maid had unpacked their suitcases and prepared the bed. On one side was a sheer silk nightgown of Elizabeth's and on the other side a pair of men's blue pyjamas. She hesitated a moment, then began to undress. When she was naked, she walked into the large mirrored dressing-room and carefully removed her make-up. She wrapped a Turkish towel around her head, went into the bathroom and showered, slowly lathering her body and feeling the warm soapy water running between her breasts and down her belly and thighs, like warm wet fingers.

All the time she was trying not to think about Rhys, and she could think of nothing else. She thought of his arms around her and his body on hers. Had she married Rhys to help save the company, or was she using the company as an excuse because she wanted him? She no longer knew. Her desire had turned into one burning, all-consuming need. It was as though the fifteen-year-old child had been waiting for him all these years without being aware of it, and the need had turned into a hunger. She stepped out of the shower, dried herself with a soft warmed towel, put on the sheer silk nightgown, let her hair fall loose and free and climbed into bed. She lay there waiting, thinking about what was going to happen, wondering what he would be like, and she found that her heart was beginning to pound faster. She heard a sound and looked up. Rhys was standing in the doorway. He was fully dressed.

'I'll be going out now,' he said.

Elizabeth sat up. 'Where – where are you going?'

'It's a business problem I have to take care of.' And he was gone.

Elizabeth lay awake all that night, tossing and turning, filled with conflicting emotions, telling herself how grateful she was that Rhys had kept to their agreement, feeling like a fool for what she had been anticipating, furious with him for rejecting her.

It was dawn when Elizabeth heard Rhys return. His footsteps moved towards the bedroom, and Elizabeth closed her eyes, pretending to be asleep.

She could hear Rhys's breathing as he came over to the bed. He stood there, watching her for a long time. Then he turned and walked into the other room.

A few minutes later Elizabeth was asleep.

In the late morning they had breakfast on the terrace. Rhys was pleasant and chatty, telling her what the city was like at carnival time. But he volunteered no information about where he had spent the night, and Elizabeth did not ask. One waiter took their order for breakfast. Elizabeth noticed that it was a different waiter who served it. She thought no more about it, nor about the maids who were constantly in and out of the suite.

Elizabeth and Rhys were at the Roffe and Sons factory on the outskirts of Rio, seated in the office of the plant manager, Senhor Tumas, a middle-aged, frog-faced man, who perspired copiously.

He was addressing Rhys. 'You must understand how it is. Roffe and Sons is dearer to me than my own life. It is my family. When I leave here, it will be like leaving home. A part of my heart will be torn out. More than anything in the world, I want to stay here.' He stopped to wipe his brow. 'But I have a better offer from another company, and I have my wife and children and mother-in-law to think of. You understand?'

Rhys was leaning back in his chair, his legs casually stretched out before him. 'Of course, Roberto. I know how much this company means to you.

You have spent many years here. Still, a man has to think of his family.'

'Thank you,' Roberto said gratefully. 'I knew I could count on you, Rhys.'

'What about your contract with us?'

Tumas shrugged. 'A piece of paper. We will tear it up, no? What good is a contract if a man is unhappy in his heart?'

Rhys nodded. 'That's why we flew down here, Roberto – to make you happy in your heart.'

Tumas sighed. 'Ah, if only it were not too late. But I have already agreed to go to work for this other company.'

'Do they know you're going to prison?' Rhys asked conversationally.

Tumas gaped at him. 'Prison?'

Rhys said, 'The United States government has ordered every company doing business overseas to turn in a list of all foreign bribes they've paid over the past ten years. Unfortunately, you're heavily involved in that, Roberto. You've broken a few laws here. We had planned to protect you – as a faithful member of the family – but if you're not with us, there's no longer any reason to, is there?'

All the colour had drained from Roberto's face. 'But – but it was for the company that I did it,' he protested. 'I was only following orders.'

Rhys nodded sympathetically. 'Of course. You can explain that to the government at your trial.' He rose to his feet and said to Elizabeth, 'We'd better be starting back.'

'Wait a minute,' Roberto yelled. 'You can't walk out and leave me like this.'

Rhys said, 'I think you're confused. *You're* the one who's leaving.'

Tumas was mopping his brow again, his lips twitching uncontrollably. He walked over to the window and looked out. A heavy silence hung over the room. Finally, without turning, he said, 'If I stay with the company – will I be protected?'

'All the way,' Rhys assured him.

They were in the Mercedes, the thin, dark chauffeur at the wheel, driving back to the city. 'You blackmailed him,' Elizabeth declared.

Rhys nodded. 'We couldn't afford to lose him. He was going over to a competitor. He knows too much about our business. He would have sold us out.'

Elizabeth looked at Rhys and thought, I have so much to learn about him.

That evening they went to Mirander for dinner, and Rhys was charming and amusing and impersonal. Elizabeth felt as though he were hiding behind a façade of words, putting up a verbal smoke-screen to conceal his feelings. When they finished dinner, it was after midnight. Elizabeth wanted to be alone with Rhys. She had hoped they would return to the hotel. Instead he said, 'I'm going to show you some of the night life in Rio.'

They made the rounds of nightclubs, and everyone seemed to know Rhys. Wherever they went, he was the centre of attention, charming everyone. They were invited to join couples at other tables, and groups of people joined them at their table. Elizabeth and Rhys were never alone for a moment. It seemed to Elizabeth that it was intentional, that Rhys was deliberately putting a wall of people between them. They had been friends before, and now they were – what? Elizabeth only knew that there was some unseen barrier between them. What was he afraid of and why?

At the fourth nightclub, where they had joined a table with half a dozen of Rhys's friends, Elizabeth decided she had had enough. She broke into the conversation between Rhys and a lovely-looking Spanish girl. 'I haven't had a chance to dance with my husband. I'm sure you'll excuse us.'

Rhys looked at her in quick surprise, then rose to his feet. 'I'm afraid I've been neglecting my bride,' he said lightly to the others. He took Elizabeth's arm and led her out to the dance floor. She was holding herself stiffly, and he looked at her face and said, 'You're angry.'

He was right, but it was an anger directed at herself. She had made the rules, and was upset now because Rhys would not break them. But it was more than that, of course. It was not knowing how Rhys felt. Was he sticking to their agreement because of a sense of honour, or because he was simply not interested in her? She had to know.

Rhys said, 'Sorry about all these people, Liz, but

they're in the business, and in one way or another they can be helpful to us.'

So he was aware of her feelings. She could feel his arms around her, his body against hers. She thought, It feels right. Everything about Rhys was right for her. They belonged together. She knew it. But did he know how much she wanted him? Elizabeth's pride would not let her tell him. And yet he must feel something. She closed her eyes and pressed closer to him. Time had stopped and there was nothing but the two of them and the soft music and the magic of this moment. She could have gone on dancing forever in Rhys's arms. She relaxed and gave herself up to him completely and she began to feel his male hardness pressing against her thighs. She opened her eyes and looked up at him and there was something in his eyes she had never seen there before, an urgency, a wanting, that was a reflection of her own.

When he spoke, his voice was hoarse. He said, 'Let's go back to the hotel.'

And she could not speak.

When he helped her on with her wrap, his fingers burned her skin. They sat apart in the back of the limousine, afraid to touch. Elizabeth felt as if she were on fire. It seemed to her that it took an eternity for them to reach their suite. She did not think she could wait another moment. As the door closed, they came together in a wonderful wild hunger that swept through both of them. She was in his arms and there was a ferocity in him that she had never known. He picked her up and carried her into the bedroom. They could not get their clothes off quickly enough. We're like eager children, Elizabeth thought, and she wondered why it had taken Rhys all this time. But it did not matter now. Nothing mattered except their nakedness and the wonderful feel of his body against hers. They were in bed, exploring each other, and Elizabeth gently pulled away from his embrace and started kissing him, her tongue moving down his lean, taut body, embracing him with her lips, feeling his velvet hardness inside her mouth. His hands were on her hips, turning her on her side, and his mouth was running down between her thighs, parting them to his tongue and thrusting into the sweetness there, and when neither of them could bear it an instant longer, he moved on top of her and slowly slid inside her, thrusting deep and making gently circling motions and she began to move to his rhythm, their rhythm, the rhythm of the universe, and everything began to move faster and faster, spinning out of control, until there was a vast ecstatic explosion and the earth became still and peaceful again.

They lay there, holding each other close, and Elizabeth thought joyfully, *Mrs Rhys Williams.*

FORTY-SIX

'Excuse me, Mrs Williams,' Henriette's voice said on the intercom, 'there's a Detective Hornung here to see you. He says it's urgent.'

Elizabeth turned to look up at Rhys, puzzled. They had just returned from Rio to Zurich the evening before, and they had only been in the office a few minutes. Rhys shrugged. 'Tell her to send the man in. Let's find out what's so important.'

A few moments later the three of them were seated in Elizabeth's office. 'What did you want to see me about?' Elizabeth asked.

Max Hornung had no small talk. He said, 'Someone is trying to murder you.' As he watched the colour drain from Elizabeth's face, Max was genuinely distressed, wondering if there might have been a more tactful way he could have phrased it.

Rhys Williams said, 'What the hell are you talking about?'

Max continued to address himself to Elizabeth.

'There have already been two attempts on your life. There will probably be more.'

Elizabeth stammered, 'I – you must be mistaken.'

'No, ma'am. That lift crash was meant to kill you.'

She stared at him in silence, her dark eyes filled with bewilderment, and some other emotion buried deeper, that Max could not define. 'So was the jeep.'

Elizabeth found her voice again. 'You're wrong. That was an accident. There was nothing the matter with the jeep. The police in Sardinia examined it.'

'No.'

'I saw them,' Elizabeth insisted.

'No, ma'am. You saw them examine *a* jeep. It wasn't yours.'

They were both staring at him now.

Max went on, 'Your jeep was never in that garage. I found it in an auto junkyard at Olbia. The bolt that sealed the master cylinder had been loosened, and the brake fluid had run out. That's why you had no brakes. The left front fender was still bashed in and there were green markings on it from the sap of the trees you ran into. The lab checked it out. It matches.'

The nightmare was back. Elizabeth felt it sweep through her, as though the floodgates of her hidden fears had suddenly opened, and she was filled again with the terror of that ride down the mountains.

Rhys was saying, 'I don't understand. How could anyone –?'

Max turned to look at Rhys. 'All jeeps look alike. That's what they were counting on. When she crashed instead of going off the mountain, they had to improvise. They couldn't let anyone examine that jeep because it had to look like an accident. They had expected it to be at the bottom of the sea. They probably would have finished her off there, but a maintenance crew came along, found her and took her to the hospital. They got hold of another jeep, smashed it up a little and made the switch before the police came.'

Rhys said, 'You keep saying "they".'

'Whoever was behind it had help.'

'Who – who would want to kill me?' Elizabeth asked.

'The same person who killed your father.'

She had a sudden feeling of unreality, as if none of this was happening. It was all a nightmare that would go away.

'Your father was murdered,' Max went on. 'He was set up with a phony guide who killed him. Your father didn't go to Chamonix alone. There was someone with him.'

When Elizabeth spoke, her voice was a hollow whisper. 'Who?'

Max looked at Rhys and said, 'Your husband.'

The words echoed in her ears. They seemed to come from far away, fading in and out, and she wondered if she was losing her mind.

'Liz,' Rhys said, 'I wasn't there with Sam when he was killed.'

'You were in Chamonix with him, Mr Williams,' Max insisted.

'That's true.' Rhys was talking to Elizabeth now. 'I left before Sam went on his climb.'

She turned to look at him. 'Why didn't you tell me?'

He hesitated a moment, then seemed to make a decision. 'It's something I couldn't discuss with anyone. For the past year someone has been sabotaging Roffe and Sons. It was done very cleverly, so that it seemed to be a series of accidents. But I began to see a pattern. I went to Sam with it, and we decided to hire an outside agency to investigate.'

Elizabeth knew then what was coming, and she was simultaneously filled with a deep sense of relief and a feeling of guilt. Rhys had known about the report all along. She should have trusted him enough to tell him about it, instead of keeping her fears to herself.

Rhys turned to Max Hornung, 'Sam Roffe got a report that confirmed my suspicions. He asked me to go up to Chamonix to discuss it with him. I went. We decided to keep it just between the two of us until we could find out who was responsible for what was happening.' When he continued, there was a note of bitterness in his voice. 'Obviously, it wasn't kept quiet enough. Sam was killed because someone knew we were getting on to him. The report is missing.'

'I had it,' Elizabeth said. Rhys looked at her in surprise. 'It was with Sam's personal effects.' She said to Max, 'The report indicates that it was someone on the board of Roffe and Sons, but they all have stock in the company. Why would they want to destroy it?'

Max explained, 'They're not trying to destroy it, Mrs Williams. They're trying to cause enough trouble to make the banks nervous enough to start calling in their loans. They wanted to force your father to sell the stock and go public. Whoever is behind this hasn't got what he wanted yet. Your life is still in danger.'

'Then you've got to give her police protection,' Rhys demanded.

Max blinked and said tonelessly, 'I wouldn't worry about that, Mr Williams. She hasn't been out of our sight since she married you.'

FORTY-SEVEN

Berlin
Monday, December 1
10 a.m.

The pain was unbearable and he had lived with it
for four weeks.

The doctor had left some pills for him, but
Walther Gassner was afraid to take them. He had
to stay constantly alert to see that Anna did not
try to kill him again, or to escape.

'You should go straight to a hospital,' the doctor
had told him. 'You've lost a good deal of blood –'

'No!' That was the last thing Walther wanted.
Stab wounds were reported to the police. Walther
had sent for the company doctor because he knew
he would not report it. Walther could not afford
to have the police snooping around. Not now.
The doctor had silently stitched up the gaping
wound, his eyes filled with curiosity. When he
had finished, he had asked, 'Would you like me

to send a nurse to the house, Mr Gassner?'

'No. My – my wife will take care of me.'

That had been a month ago. Walther had telephoned his secretary and told her that he had had an accident and would be staying at home.

He thought about that terrible moment when Anna had tried to kill him with the shears. He had turned just in time to catch the blade in his shoulder instead of through the heart. He had almost fainted from the pain and shock, but he had retained consciousness long enough to drag Anna to her bedroom and lock her in. And all the while she was screaming, 'What have you done with the children? What have you done with the children? . . .'

Since then Walther had kept her in the bedroom. He prepared all her meals. He would take a tray up to Anna's room, unlock the door and enter. She would be huddled in a corner, cringing from him, and she would whisper, 'What have you done with the children?'

Sometimes he would open the bedroom door and find her with her ear pressed against the wall, listening for the sounds of their son and daughter. The house was silent now, except for the two of them. Walther knew there was very little time left. His thoughts were interrupted by a faint noise. He listened. And then he heard it again. *Someone was moving around in the hallway upstairs. There was not supposed to be anyone in the house. He had locked all the doors himself.*

* * *

Upstairs, Frau Mendler was dusting. She was a day-worker, and this was only her second time in this house. She did not like it. When she had worked here on Wednesday the week before, Herr Gassner had followed her around as though expecting her to steal something. When she had tried to go upstairs to clean, he had angrily stopped her, given her her wages and sent her away. There was something about his manner that frightened her.

Today he was nowhere in sight, *Gott sei Dank*. Frau Mendler had let herself in with the key she had taken the week before, and she had gone upstairs. The house was unnaturally silent, and she decided that no-one was at home. She had cleaned one bedroom and had found some loose change lying around, and a gold pillbox. She started down the hallway towards the next bedroom and tried to open the door. It was locked. Strange. She wondered if they kept something valuable inside. She turned the handle again, and a woman's voice from behind the door whispered, 'Who is it?'

Frau Mendler jerked her hand away from the knob, startled.

'Who is it? Who's out there?'

'Frau Mendler, the cleaning lady. Do you want me to do your bedroom?'

'You can't. I'm locked in.' The voice was louder now, filled with hysteria. 'Help me! Please! Call the police. Tell them my husband has killed our children. He's going to kill me. Hurry! Get away from here before he –'

A hand spun Frau Mendler around and she found herself staring up into the face of Herr Gassner. He looked as pale as death.

'What are you sneaking around here for?' he demanded. He was holding her arm, hurting it.

'I – I'm not sneaking,' she said. 'Today is my day to clean. The agency –'

'I told the agency I didn't want anyone here. I –' He stopped. Had he telephoned the agency? He had meant to, but he was in such pain that he could no longer remember. Frau Mendler looked into his eyes and she was terrified by what she saw there.

'They never told me,' she said.

He stood still, listening for sounds from behind the locked door. Silence.

He turned to Frau Mendler. 'Get out of here. Don't come back.'

She could not leave the house fast enough. He had not paid her, but she had the gold pillbox and the coins she had found on the dresser. She felt sorry for the poor woman behind the door. She wished she could help her, but she could not afford to get involved. She had a police record.

In Zurich, Detective Max Hornung was reading a teletype from Interpol headquarters in Paris.

INVOICE NUMBER OF SNUFF FILM RAW STOCK USED FOR ROFFE AND SONS GENERAL EXECU-TIVE ACCOUNT. PURCHASING AGENT NO LONGER

WITH COMPANY. TRYING TO TRACE. WILL KEEP
YOU INFORMED. END MESSAGE.

In Paris the police were fishing a nude body out
of the Seine. She was a blonde in her late teens.
She wore a red ribbon around her neck.

In Zurich, Elizabeth Williams had been placed
under twenty-four-hour police protection.

FORTY-EIGHT

The white light flashed, signalling a call on Rhys's private line. Fewer than half a dozen people had the number. He picked up the telephone. 'Hello.'

'Good morning, darling.' There was no mistaking the husky, distinctive voice.

'You shouldn't be calling me.'

She laughed. 'You never used to worry about things like that. Don't tell me that Elizabeth has tamed you already.'

'What do you want?' Rhys asked.

'I want to see you this afternoon.'

'That's impossible.'

'Don't make me cross, Rhys. Shall I come to Zurich or –?'

'No, I can't see you here.' He hesitated. 'I'll come there.'

'That's better. Our usual place, *chéri*.'

And Hélène Roffe-Martel hung up.

Rhys replaced the receiver slowly and sat thinking. As far as he was concerned, he had had a brief physical affair, with an exciting woman, and it had been finished for some time. But Hélène was not a woman who let go easily. She was bored with Charles, and she wanted Rhys. 'You and I would make a perfect team,' she had said, and Hélène Roffe-Martel could be very determined. And very dangerous. Rhys decided the trip to Paris was necessary. He had to make her understand once and for all that there could be nothing further between them.

A few moments later he walked into Elizabeth's office, and her eyes brightened. She put her arms around him and whispered, 'I've been thinking about you. Let's go home and play hooky this afternoon.'

He grinned. 'You're becoming a sex maniac.'

She held him closer. 'I know. Isn't it lovely?'

'I'm afraid I have to fly to Paris this afternoon, Liz.'

She tried to conceal her disappointment. 'Shall I come with you?'

'No point. It's just a minor business problem. I'll be back tonight. We'll have a late supper.'

When Rhys walked into the familiar small hotel on the Left Bank, Hélène was already there, seated in the dining-room, waiting for him. Rhys had never known her to be late. She was organized and efficient, extraordinarily beautiful, intelligent, a wonderful lover; and yet something was missing. Hélène was a woman without compassion. There was a ruthlessness about her, a killer's instinct. Rhys had seen others hurt by it. He had no intention of becoming one of her victims. He sat down at the table.

She said, 'You're looking well, darling. Marriage agrees with you. Is Elizabeth taking good care of you in bed?'

He smiled to take the sting out of his words. 'That's none of your business.'

Hélène leaned forward and took one of his hands, 'Ah, but it is, *chéri*. It is *our* business.'

She began stroking his hand, and he thought of her in bed. A tigress, wild, skilled and insatiable. He withdrew his hand.

Hélène's eyes chilled. She said, 'Tell me, Rhys. How does it feel to be president of Roffe and Sons?'

He had almost forgotten how ambitious she was, how greedy. He remembered the long conversations they had once had. She was obsessed by the idea of taking control of the company. *You and I, Rhys. If Sam were out of the way, we could run it.*

Even in the midst of their lovemaking: *It's my company, darling. Samuel Roffe's blood is in me. It's mine. I want it. Fuck me, Rhys.*

Power was Hélène's aphrodisiac. And danger. 'What did you want to see me about?' Rhys asked.

'I think it's time you and I made some plans.'

'I don't know what you're talking about.'

She said maliciously, 'I know you too well, darling. You're as ambitious as I am. Why did you serve as Sam's shadow all those years when you had dozens of offers to run other companies? Because you knew that one day you would be running Roffe and Sons.'

'I stayed because I liked Sam.'

She grinned. 'Of course, *chéri*. And now you've married his charming little girl.' She took a thin black cigar from her purse and lit it with a platinum lighter. 'Charles tells me that Elizabeth has arranged to keep control of the stock and that she refuses to sell.'

'That's right, Hélène.'

'It's occurred to you, of course, that if she had an accident, you would inherit her estate.'

Rhys stared at her for a long time.

FORTY-NINE

In his home in Olgiata, Ivo Palazzi was casually looking out the window of his living-room when he saw a terrifying sight. Coming up the driveway were Donatella and their three sons. Simonetta was upstairs, taking a nap. Ivo hurried out of the front door and went to meet his second family. He was filled with such rage that he could have killed. He had been so wonderful to this woman, so kind, so loving, and now she was deliberately trying to destroy his career, his marriage, his life. He watched Donatella get out of the Lancia Flavia he had so generously given her. Ivo thought she had never looked more beautiful. The boys climbed out of the car, and were hugging and kissing him. Oh, how Ivo loved them. Oh, how he hoped that Simonetta would not wake up from her nap!

'I came to see your wife,' Donatella said stiffly. She turned to the boys. 'Come on, boys.'

'No!' Ivo commanded.

'How are you going to stop me? If I don't see her today, I'll see her tomorrow.'

Ivo was cornered. There was no way out. Yet he knew that he could not let her or anyone else ruin everything he had worked so hard for. Ivo thought of himself as a decent man, and he hated what he knew he must do. Not just for himself, but for Simonetta and Donatella and all his children.

'You will have your money,' Ivo promised. 'Give me five days.'

Donatella looked into his eyes. 'Five days,' she said.

In London, Sir Alec Nichols was taking part in a serious debate in the House of Commons. He had been chosen to make a major policy speech dealing with the crucial subject of the labour strikes that were crippling the British economy. But it was difficult for him to concentrate. He was thinking about the series of telephone calls he had received over the past few weeks. They had managed to find him wherever he was, at his club, at his barber, restaurants, business meetings. And each time Alec had hung up on them. He knew that what they were asking was only the beginning. Once they controlled him, they would find a way to take over his stock, they would own a piece of a gigantic pharmaceutical company that manufactured drugs of every description. He could not let that happen. They had begun telephoning him four and five times a day until his nerves were stretched to the breaking-point. What worried Alec now was that on this day he had *not* heard from them. He had expected a call at breakfast, and then again when he had lunched at White's. But there were no calls and somehow he could not shake off the feeling that the silence was more ominous than the threats. He tried to push these thoughts away now as he addressed the House.

'No man has been a stauncher friend of labour than I. Our labour force is what makes our country great. Workers feed our mills, turn the wheels in our factories. They are the true élite of this country, the backbone that makes England stand tall and strong among nations.' He paused. 'However, there comes a time in the fortunes of every nation when certain sacrifices must be made . . .'

He spoke by rote. He was wondering whether he had frightened them off by calling their bluff. After all, they were just small-time hoodlums. He was Sir Alec Nichols, MP. What could they do to him? In all probability he would not hear from them again. From now on they would leave him in peace. Sir Alec finished his speech amid vociferous applause from the back benches.

He was on his way out when an attendant came up to him and said, 'I have a message for you, Sir Alec.'

Alec turned. 'Yes?'

'You're to go home as quickly as possible. There has been an accident.'

*   *   *

They were carrying Vivian into the ambulance when Alec arrived at the house. The doctor was at her side. Alec slammed the car against the kerb and was out running before it had stopped. He took one look at Vivian's white, unconscious face and turned to the doctor. 'What happened?'

The doctor said helplessly, 'I don't know, Sir Alec. I received an anonymous call that there had been an accident. When I got here, I found Lady Nichols on the floor of her bedroom. Her – her kneecaps had been hammered to the floor with spikes.'

Alec closed his eyes, fighting off the spasm of nausea that gripped him. He could feel the bile rising in his throat.

'We'll do everything we can, of course, but I think you had better be prepared. It's unlikely that she'll ever walk again.'

Alec felt as though he could not breathe. He started towards the ambulance.

'She's under heavy sedation,' the doctor said. 'I don't think she'll recognize you.'

Alec did not even hear him. He climbed into the ambulance and sat in a jump seat, staring down at his wife, oblivious of the back doors being closed, the sound of the siren, and the ambulance beginning to move. He took Vivian's cold hands in his. Her eyes opened. 'Alec.' Her voice was a slurred whisper.

Alec's eyes filled with tears. 'Oh, my darling, my darling . . .'

'Two men . . . wore masks . . . they held me down

. . . broke my legs . . . I'll never be able to dance again . . . I'm going to be a cripple, Alec . . . Will you still want me?'

He buried his head in her shoulder and wept. They were tears of despair and agony, and yet there was something else, something he hardly dared admit to himself. He felt a sense of relief. If Vivian were crippled, he would be able to take care of her, she could never leave him for anyone else.

But Alec knew that this was not over. They were not finished with him. This was only their warning. The only way he would ever get rid of them was to give them what they wanted.

Quickly.

FIFTY

Zurich
Thursday, December 4

It was exactly noon when the call came through the switchboard at the Kriminalpolizei headquarters in Zurich. It was routed through to Chief Inspector Schmied's office, and when the chief inspector had finished talking he went to find Detective Max Hornung.

'It's all over,' he told Max. 'The Roffe case has been solved. They've found the killer. Get out to the airport. You've just got time to catch your plane.'

Max blinked at him. 'Where am I going?'

'To Berlin.'

Chief Inspector Schmied telephoned Elizabeth Williams. 'I am calling to bring you some good news,' he said. 'You will no longer need a body-guard. The murderer has been caught.'

Elizabeth found herself gripping the telephone.

416

At long last she was going to learn the name of her faceless enemy. 'Who is it?' she asked.

'Walther Gassner.'

They were speeding along the autobahn, heading for Wannsee. Max was in the back seat, next to Major Wageman, and two detectives sat in front. They had met Max at Tempelhof Airport, and Major Wageman had briefed Max on the situation as they drove. 'The house is surrounded, but we have to be careful how we move in. He's holding his wife hostage.'

Max asked, 'How did you get on to Walther Gassner?'

'Through you. That's why I thought you would like to be here.'

Max was puzzled. 'Through me?'

'You told me about the psychiatrist he visited. On a hunch, I sent out Gassner's description to other psychiatrists and found out that he had gone to half a dozen of them, looking for help. Each time he used a different name, then ran away. He knew how ill he was. His wife had phoned us for help a couple of months ago, but when one of our men went out to investigate, she sent him away.'

They were turning off the autobahn now, only a few minutes from the house. 'This morning we received a call from a cleaning woman, a Frau Mendler. She told us she was working at the Gassner house on Monday and that she talked to Mrs Gassner through the locked door of her bedroom.

Mrs Gassner told her that her husband had killed their two children and was going to kill her.'

Max blinked. 'This happened on *Monday*? And the woman didn't call you until this morning?'

'Frau Mendler has a long police record. She was afraid to come to us. Last night she told her boy friend what had happened, and this morning they decided to call us.'

They had reached Wannsee. The car pulled up a block away from the entrance to the Gassner estate, behind an unmarked car. A man got out of the vehicle and hurried towards Major Wageman and Max. 'He's still inside the house, Major. I have men all round the grounds.'

'Do you know if the woman is still alive?'

The man hesitated, 'No, sir. All the blinds are drawn.'

'All right. Let's make it fast and quiet. Get everyone in place. Five minutes.'

The man hurried off. Major Wageman reached into the car and pulled out a small walkie-talkie. He began rapidly to issue orders. Max was not listening. He was thinking of something that Major Wageman had said to him a few minutes ago. Something that made no sense. But there was no time to ask him about it now. Men were starting to move towards the house, using trees and shrubs as cover. Major Wageman turned to Max. 'Coming, Hornung?'

It seemed to Max that there was an army of men infiltrating the garden. Some of them were supplied with telescopic rifles and armoured vests;

others carried snub-nosed tear gas rifles. The operation was carried out with mathematical precision. At a signal from Major Wageman, tear gas grenades were simultaneously hurled through the downstairs and upstairs windows of the house and at the same instant the front and rear doors were smashed in by men wearing gas masks. Behind them came more detectives with drawn guns.

When Max and Major Wageman ran through the open front door, the hallway was filled with acrid smoke, but it was rapidly being dispersed by the open windows and doors. Two detectives were bringing Walther Gassner into the hallway in handcuffs. He was wearing a robe and pyjamas and he was unshaven and his face looked gaunt and his eyes swollen.

Max stared at him, seeing him for the first time in person. Somehow he seemed unreal to Max. It was the *other* Walther Gassner who was real, the man in the computer, whose life had been spelled out in digits. Which was the shadow and which was the substance?

Major Wageman said, 'You're under arrest, Herr Gassner. Where is your wife?'

Walther Gassner said hoarsely, 'She's not here. She's gone! I –'

Upstairs there was the sound of a door being forced open, and a moment later a detective called down, 'I've found her. She was locked in her room.'

The detective appeared on the staircase, supporting a trembling Anna Gassner. Her hair was

419

stringy and her face was streaked and blotchy, and she was sobbing.

'Oh, thank God,' she said. 'Thank God you've come!'

Gently the detective led her downstairs towards the group standing in the enormous reception hall. When Anna Gassner looked up and saw her husband, she began to scream.

'It's all right, Frau Gassner,' Major Wageman said soothingly. 'He can't harm you any more.'

'My children,' she cried. 'He killed my children!'

Max was watching Walther Gassner's face. He was staring at his wife with an expression of utter hopelessness. He looked broken and lifeless.

'Anna,' he whispered. 'Oh, Anna.'

Major Wageman said, 'You have the right to remain silent or to ask for a lawyer. For your own sake I hope you will co-operate with us.'

Walther was not listening. 'Why did you have to call them, Anna?' he pleaded. 'Why? Weren't we happy together?'

'The children are dead,' Anna Gassner shrieked. 'They're dead.'

Major Wageman looked at Walther Gassner and asked, 'Is that true?'

Walther nodded, and his eyes looked old and defeated. 'Yes . . . They're dead.'

'Murderer! Murderer!' his wife was shrieking.

Major Wageman said, 'We would like you to show us the bodies. Will you do that?'

Walther Gassner was crying now, the tears

rolling down his cheeks. He could not speak.

Major Wageman said, 'Where are they?'

It was Max who answered. 'The children are buried in Saint Paul's graveyard.'

Everyone in the room turned to stare at him. 'They died at birth five years ago,' Max explained.

'Murderer!' Anna Gassner screamed at her husband.

And they turned and saw the madness blazing out of her eyes.

FIFTY-ONE

The cold winter night had fallen, snuffing out the brief twilight. It had begun to snow, a soft, wind-blown powder that dusted the city. In the administration building at Roffe and Sons the lights of the deserted offices flowed against the darkness like pale yellow moons.

In her office Elizabeth was alone, working late, waiting for Rhys to return from Geneva, where he had gone for a meeting. She wished that he would hurry. Everyone had long since left the building. Elizabeth felt restless, unable to concentrate. She could not get Walther and Anna out of her mind. She remembered Walther as she had first met him, boyish and handsome and madly in love with Anna. Or pretending to be. It was so hard to believe that Walther was responsible for all those terrible acts. Elizabeth's heart went out to Anna. Elizabeth had tried several times to telephone her, but there had been no answer. She would fly to Berlin, to give her whatever comfort she could. The telephone rang, startling her. She picked it up. It was Alec on the other end of the line, and Elizabeth was pleased to hear his voice.

'You've heard about Walther?' Alec asked.

'Yes. It's horrible. I can't believe it.'

'Don't, Elizabeth.'

She thought she had misunderstood him. 'What?'

'Don't believe it. Walther's not guilty.'

'The police said –'

'They've made a mistake. Walther was the first person Sam and I checked out. We cleared him. He's not the one we are looking for.'

Elizabeth stared at the phone, filled with a sense of confusion. *He's not the one we were looking for.* She said, 'I – I don't understand what you're saying.'

Alec replied hesitantly, 'It's awkward doing this over a telephone, Elizabeth, but I haven't had an opportunity to speak to you alone.'

'Speak to me about what?' Elizabeth asked.

'For the past year,' Alec said, 'someone has been sabotaging the company. There was an explosion in one of our South American factories, patents have been stolen, dangerous drugs have been mislabelled. There isn't time to go into it all now. I went to Sam and suggested that we engage an outside investigating agency to try to find out who

423

was behind it. We agreed not to discuss it with anyone else.'

It was as though the earth had suddenly stopped and time was frozen. A dizzying feeling of *déjà vu* swept through Elizabeth. Alec's words were coming through the telephone, but it was Rhys's voice she was hearing. Rhys saying, *Someone has been sabotaging Roffe and Sons. It was done very cleverly, so that it seemed to be a series of accidents. But I began to see a pattern. I went to Sam with it and we decided to hire an outside agency to investigate.*

Alec's voice was going on. 'They finished their report and Sam took it with him to Chamonix. We discussed it over the telephone.'

Elizabeth could hear Rhys's voice saying, *Sam asked me to come up to Chamonix to discuss it with him . . . We decided to keep it just between the two of us until we could find out who was responsible for what was happening.*

Elizabeth was suddenly finding it hard to breathe. When she spoke, she tried to make her voice sound normal. 'Alec, who – who else knew about the report beside you and Sam?'

'No-one. That was the whole point. According to Sam, the report showed that whoever was guilty had to be someone high up in the company.'

The highest echelon. And Rhys had not mentioned being in Chamonix until the detective had brought it up.

She asked slowly, the words dragged out of her, 'Could Sam have told Rhys about it?'

'No. Why?'

There was only one way Rhys could have known what was in the report. He had stolen it. There was only one reason he could have gone to Chamonix. To kill Sam. Elizabeth did not hear the rest of what Alec was saying. The loud roaring in her ears drowned his words. She dropped the receiver, her head spinning, fighting off the horror that was starting to engulf her. Her mind was a series of chaotic jumbled images. At the time she had had the jeep accident she had left a message for Rhys that she would be in Sardinia. The night of the lift crash, Rhys had not been at the board meeting, but he had appeared later when she and Kate were alone. *Thought I ought to give you a hand.* And soon afterwards he had left the building. *Or had he?* Her body was trembling now. It had to be some terrible mistake. Not Rhys. *No!* It was a scream in her mind.

Elizabeth rose from the desk and on unsteady legs walked through the connecting door to Rhys's office. The room was dark. She turned on the lights and stood looking around uncertainly, not sure what she expected to find. She was not searching for evidence of Rhys's guilt, she was looking for evidence of his innocence. It was unbearable to think that the man she loved, the man who had held her in his arms and made love to her, could be a cold-blooded murderer.

There was an engagement book on Rhys's desk. Elizabeth opened it, turning the pages back to September, to the holiday weekend of the jeep accident. Nairobi was marked on his calendar. She would need to check his passport to see if he had gone there. She started to look through Rhys's desk for the passport, feeling guilty, knowing that somehow there had to be an innocent explanation.

The bottom drawer of Rhys's desk was locked. Elizabeth hesitated. She knew she had no right to break into it. Somehow it was a violation of faith, the crossing of a forbidden boundary, from which there could be no return. Rhys would know that she had done this and she would have to tell him why. And yet Elizabeth had to know. She picked up a letter opener from the desk and broke the lock, splintering the wood.

In the drawer were stacks of notes and memoranda. She lifted them out. There was an envelope addressed to Rhys Williams in a woman's handwriting. It was postmarked a few days earlier, from Paris. Elizabeth hesitated a moment, then opened it. The letter was from Hélène. It began, '*Chéri*, I tried to reach you by phone. It is urgent that we meet again soon to make our plans . . .' Elizabeth did not finish the letter.

She was staring at the stolen report in the drawer.

MR SAM ROFFE
CONFIDENTIAL
NO COPIES

She felt the room begin to spin and she clutched the edge of the desk for support. She stood there for ever, eyes closed, waiting for the dizziness to pass. Her killer had a face now. It was the face of her husband.

The silence was broken by the insistent ringing of a distant telephone. It took Elizabeth a long time to realize where the sound was coming from. Slowly she walked back to her office. She picked up the telephone.

It was the attendant in the lobby, his voice cheerful. 'Just checkin' that you're still there, Mrs Williams. Mr Williams is on his way up to you.'

To stage another accident.

Her life was all that stood between Rhys and the control of Roffe and Sons. She could not face him, could not pretend that nothing was wrong. The moment he saw her, he would know. She had to escape. In a blind panic, Elizabeth grabbed her purse and coat and started out of the office. She stopped. She had forgotten something. Her passport. She had to get far away from Rhys, some place where he could not find her. She hurried back to her desk, found the passport and ran out into the corridor, her heart pounding as though it would burst. The indicator on the private lift was swinging upward.

Eight . . . nine . . . ten . . .

Elizabeth began racing down the stairs, running for her life.

FIFTY-TWO

There was a ferryboat that ran between Civitavecchia and Sardinia, carrying passengers and automobiles. Elizabeth drove aboard in a rental car, lost among a dozen other cars. Airports kept records, but the huge boat was anonymous. Elizabeth was one of a hundred passengers crossing over to the island of Sardinia for a holiday. She was sure she could not have been followed, and yet she was filled with an unreasoning fear. Rhys had gone too far to let anything stop him now. She was the only one who could expose him. He would have to get rid of her.

When Elizabeth had fled from the building, she had had no idea where she was going. She knew only that she must get out of Zurich and hide somewhere, that she would not be safe until Rhys was caught. *Sardinia*. It was the first place she thought of. She had rented a small car and had stopped at a phone booth along the auto route to Italy and had tried to call Alec. He was out. She left a message for him to call her in Sardinia.

Unable to reach Detective Max Hornung, she left the same message for him.

She would be at the villa in Sardinia. But this time she would not be alone. The police would be there to protect her.

When the ferryboat landed in Olbia, Elizabeth found that it would not be necessary to go to the police. They were waiting for her in the person of Bruno Campagna, the detective she had met with Chief of Police Ferraro. It had been Campagna who had taken her to look at the jeep following the accident. The detective hurried over to Elizabeth's car and said, 'We were beginning to get very worried about you, Mrs Williams.'

Elizabeth looked at him, surprised.

'We received a call from the Swiss police,' Campagna explained, 'asking us to keep an eye out for you. We've been covering all the boats and airports.'

Elizabeth was filled with a feeling of gratitude. Max Hornung! He had got her message. Detective Campagna looked at her tired, drawn face. 'Would you like me to drive?'

'Please,' Elizabeth said gratefully.

She slid over to the passenger seat, and the tall detective got behind the wheel. 'Where would you rather wait – the police station or your villa?'

'The villa, if someone could stay with me. I'd – I'd rather not be there alone.'

Campagna nodded reassuringly. 'Don't worry. We have orders to keep you well guarded. I'll stay there with you tonight, and we'll have a radio car stationed at the driveway leading to your place. No-one will be able to get near you.'

His confidence was enough to let Elizabeth relax. Detective Campagna drove swiftly and expertly, winding through the little streets of Olbia, heading up the mountain road that led to the Costa Smeralda. Every place they passed reminded her of Rhys.

Elizabeth asked, 'Has there been any – any news of my husband?'

Detective Campagna gave her a quick, compassionate glance, then turned his eyes back to the road. 'He's on the run, but he won't get far. They expect to have him in custody by morning.'

Elizabeth knew that she should feel a sense of relief, and instead the words brought a terrible, aching pain. It was Rhys they were talking about, Rhys who was being hunted like some animal. He had placed her in this terrible nightmare, and now he was caught up in his own nightmare, fighting for his life, as he had made her fight for hers. And how she had trusted him! How she had believed in his kindness and his gentleness and his love! She shuddered. Detective Campagna asked her, 'Are you cold?'

'No. I'm fine.' She felt feverish. A warm wind seemed to be whistling through the car, setting her nerves on edge. At first she thought it was her imagination until Detective Campagna said, 'I'm afraid we're in for a sirocco. It's going to be a busy night.'

Elizabeth understood what he meant. The sirocco could drive people and animals crazy. The wind blew in from the Sahara, hot and dry and grainy with sand, with a macabre keening sound that had an eerie, unbalancing effect on the nerves. The crime rate always went up during a sirocco, and the judges treated criminals leniently.

An hour later, out of the dark, the villa loomed ahead of them. Detective Campagna turned into the driveway, drove into the empty carport and turned off the engine. He walked round to the side of the car and opened Elizabeth's door. 'I'd like you to stay right behind me, Mrs Williams,' he said. 'Just in case.'

'All right,' Elizabeth replied.

They moved towards the front door of the darkened villa. Detective Campagna said, 'I'm sure he's not here but we won't take any chances. May I have your key?'

Elizabeth handed him the key. He gently edged her to one side of the door, inserted the key and opened the door, his other hand hovering near his gun. He reached inside and flicked on the light switch, and the hallway was suddenly flooded with brilliant light.

'I'd like you to show me the house,' Detective Campagna said. 'Make sure we cover every room. Okay?'

'Yes.'

They started walking through the house, and everywhere they went the huge detective turned the lights on. He looked in all the closets and corners

431

and checked to make sure the windows and doors were locked. There was no-one else in the house. When they returned to the living-room downstairs, Detective Campagna said, 'If you don't mind, I'd like to call headquarters.'

'Of course,' Elizabeth said. She led him into the study.

He picked up the telephone and dialled. A moment later he said, 'Detective Campagna. We're at the villa. I'll camp here for the night. You can send a cruiser up to park at the foot of the driveway.' He listened a moment, then said into the phone, 'She's fine. Just a little tired. I'll check in later.' He replaced the receiver.

Elizabeth sank into a chair. She was feeling tense and nervous, but she knew that it was going to be worse tomorrow. Much worse. She would be safe but Rhys would be either dead or in prison. Somehow, in spite of everything he had done, she could not bear the thought of that.

Detective Campagna was studying her, a look of concern on his face. 'I could use a cup of coffee,' he said. 'How about you?'

She nodded. 'I'll make some.' She started to rise.

'You stay where you are, Mrs Williams. My wife says I make the best coffee in the world.'

Elizabeth managed a smile. 'Thank you.' She sank back gratefully. She had not realized how emotionally drained she felt. For the first time now, Elizabeth admitted to herself that even during the telephone conversation with Alec she had felt that there might be some mistake, some explanation, that Rhys must be innocent. Even while she was fleeing, she had held on to the thought that he could not have done all those terrible things, that he could not have killed her father and then made love to her and tried to kill her. It would take a monster to do those things. And so she had kept that tiny ember of hope flickering in her. It had died when Detective Campagna had said, *He's on the run, but he won't get far. They expect to have him in custody by morning.*

She could not bear to think about it any more, but she could think of nothing else. How long had Rhys been planning to take over the company? Probably from the moment he had met that impressionable fifteen-year-old girl, alone and lonely in a Swiss boarding school. That was when he must have decided how he was going to outwit Sam – through his daughter. How easy it had been for him. The dinner at Maxim's and the long friendly talks during the years, and the charm – oh, the incredible charm! He had been patient. He had waited until she had become a woman, and the greatest irony of all was that Rhys did not even have to woo her. She had wooed *him*. How he must have laughed at her. He and Hélène. Elizabeth wondered whether they were in it together, and she wondered where Rhys was now, and whether the police would kill him when they caught him. She began to weep uncontrollably.

'Mrs Williams . . .' Detective Campagna was standing over her, holding out a cup of coffee.

'Drink this,' he said. 'You'll feel better.'

'I – I'm sorry,' Elizabeth apologized. 'I don't usually carry on this way.'

He said to her gently, 'I think you're doing *molto bene.*'

Elizabeth took a sip of the hot coffee. He had put something in it. She looked up at him, and he grinned. 'I decided a shot of Scotch wouldn't do you any harm.'

He sat down across from her in a companionable silence. She was grateful for his company. She could never have stayed here alone. Not until she knew what had happened to Rhys, not until she knew whether he was dead or alive. She finished her coffee.

Detective Campagna looked at his watch. 'The patrol car should be here any minute. There'll be two men in it on guard duty all night. I'll stay downstairs. I suggest you go up to bed now and try to get some sleep.'

Elizabeth shivered. 'I couldn't sleep.' But even as she said it, her body was filled with an enormous lassitude. The long drive and the tremendous strain she had been under for so long were finally taking their toll.

'Maybe I'll just lie down for a bit,' she said. She found it difficult to get the words out.

Elizabeth lay in her bed, fighting against sleep. Somehow it did not seem fair that she should be asleep while Rhys was being hunted. She visualized

434

him being shot down on some cold, dark street and she shuddered. She tried to keep her eyes open, but they were heavy weights, and the instant they closed she began to feel herself sinking down, down, into a soft cushion of nothingness.

Some time later she was awakened by the screams.

FIFTY-THREE

Elizabeth sat up in bed, her heart beating wildly, not knowing what it was that had awakened her. Then she heard it again. An eerie, high-pitched scream that seemed to come from right outside her window, the sound of someone in the agony of death. Elizabeth arose and stumbled over to the window and looked out into the night. It was a landscape by Daumier, lit by a chill winter moon. The trees were black and stark, their branches whipped by a wild wind. In the distance, far below, the sea was a boiling cauldron.

The scream came again. And again. And Elizabeth realized what it was. The singing rocks. The sirocco had risen in intensity and was blowing through them, making that terrible keening sound, over and over. And it became Rhys's voice she was hearing, crying out for her, begging her to help him. She could not stand it. She covered her ears with her hands, but the sound would not go away.

Elizabeth started towards the bedroom door,

and she was surprised at how weak she was. Her mind was hazy with exhaustion. She walked out into the hallway and started down the stairs. She felt dazed, as though she had been drugged. She tried to call out to Detective Campagna, but her voice was a hoarse croak. She kept descending the long flight of stairs, fighting to keep her balance. She called aloud, 'Detective Campagna.'

There was no answer. Elizabeth stumbled into the living-room. He was not there. She moved from room to room, holding on to furniture to keep from falling down.

Detective Campagna was not in the house.

She was alone.

Elizabeth stood in the hallway, her mind confused, trying to force herself to think. The detective had stepped outside to talk to the policemen in the patrol car. Of course that was it. She walked to the front door and opened it and looked outside.

No-one was there. Only the black night and the screaming wind. With a growing feeling of fear, Elizabeth turned and made her way back to the study. She would call the police station and find out what had happened. She picked up the telephone, and the line was dead.

It was at that instant that all the lights went out.

FIFTY-FOUR

In London, at Westminster Hospital, Vivian Nichols regained consciousness as she was being wheeled out of the operating room, down the long, bleak corridor. The operation had taken eight hours. In spite of everything the skilled surgeons had been able to do, she would never walk again. She woke in agonizing pain, whispering Alec's name over and over. She needed him, she needed to have him at her side, to have him promise that he would still love her.

The hospital staff was unable to locate Alec.

In Zurich, in the communications room of the Kriminalpolizei, an Interpol message was received from Australia. The former film purchasing agent for Roffe and Sons had been located in Sydney. He had died of a heart attack three days earlier. His ashes were being shipped home. Interpol had been unable to obtain any information regarding the purchase of the film. They were awaiting further instructions.

* * *

In Berlin, Walther Gassner was seated in the discreet waiting-room of an exclusive, private sanatorium in a pleasant suburb outside the city. He had been there, motionless, for almost ten hours. From time to time a nurse or an attendant would stop to speak to him and offer him something to eat or drink. Walther paid no attention to them. He was waiting for his Anna.

It would be a long wait.

In Olgiata, Simonetta Palazzi was listening to a woman's voice on the telephone. 'My name is Donatella Spolini,' the voice said. 'We've never met, Mrs Palazzi, but we have a great deal in common. I suggest we meet for luncheon at the Bolognese in the Piazza del Popolo. Shall we say one o'clock tomorrow?'

Simonetta had a conflicting appointment at the beauty parlour the next day, but she adored mysteries. 'I'll be there,' she said. 'How will I know you?'

'I'll have my three sons with me.'

In her villa in Le Vésinet, Hélène Roffe-Martel was reading a note she had found waiting for her on the mantelpiece in the drawing-room. It was from Charles. He had left her, run away. 'You will never see me again,' the note said. 'Don't try to find me.' Hélène tore the note into small pieces. She would see him again. She would find him.

* * *

In Rome, Max Hornung was at Leonardo da Vinci Airport. For the past two hours he had been trying to get a message through to Sardinia, but because of the storm all communications were down. Max went back to the flight operations office to talk to the airport manager again. 'You've *got* to get me on a plane to Sardinia,' Max said. 'Believe me, it's a matter of life and death.'

The airport manager said, 'I believe you, signor, but there is nothing I can do about it. Sardinia is shut up tight. The airports are closed. Even the boats have stopped running. Nothing is going in or out of that island until the sirocco is over.'

'When will that be?' Max asked.

The airport manager turned to study the large weather map on the wall. 'It looks like it's good for at least another twelve hours.'

Elizabeth Williams would not be alive in twelve hours.

FIFTY-FIVE

The dark was hostile, filled with invisible enemies waiting to strike at her. And Elizabeth realized now that she was completely at their mercy. Detective Campagna had brought her here to be murdered. He was Rhys's man. Elizabeth remembered Max Hornung explaining about switching the jeeps. *Whoever did it had help. Someone who knew the island.* How convincing Detective Campagna had been. *We've been covering all the boats and airports.* Because Rhys had known she would come here to hide. *Where would you like to wait – at the police station or your villa?* Detective Campagna had had no intention of letting her go to the police. It had not been headquarters he had phoned. It had been Rhys. *We're at the villa.*

Elizabeth knew she had to flee, but she no longer had the strength. She was fighting to keep her eyes open, and her arms and legs felt heavy. She suddenly realized why. He had drugged her coffee. Elizabeth turned and made her way into the dark kitchen. She opened a cabinet and fumbled around until she found what she wanted. She took down a bottle of vinegar and splashed some into a glass with water and forced herself to drink it. Immediately she began to retch into the sink. In a few minutes she felt a little better, but she was still weak. Her brain refused to function. It was as if all the circuits inside her had already closed down, were preparing for the darkness of death.

'No,' she told herself fiercely. 'You're not going to die like that. You're going to fight. They're going to have to kill you.' She raised her voice and said, 'Rhys, come and kill me,' but her voice was barely a whisper. She turned and headed for the hallway, feeling her way by instinct. She stopped under the portrait of old Samuel, while outside the moaning, alien wind tore against the house, screaming at her, taunting her, warning her. She stood there in the blackness, alone, facing a choice of terrors. She could go outside, into the unknown, and try to escape from Rhys, or she could stay here and try to fight him. But how?

Her mind was trying to tell her something but she was still dazed by the drug. She could not concentrate. Something about an accident.

She remembered then and said aloud, 'He has to make it look like an accident.'

You must stop him, Elizabeth. Had Samuel spoken? Or was it in her mind?

'I can't. It's too late.' Her eyes were closing, and her face was pressed against the coolness of the portrait. It would be so wonderful to go to sleep. But there was something she had to do. She tried to remember what it was, but it kept slipping away.

Don't let it look like an accident. Make it look like murder. Then the company will never belong to him.

Elizabeth knew what she had to do. She walked into the study. She stood there a moment, then reached for a table lamp and hurled it against a mirror. She could hear them both smash. She lifted a small chair and pounded it against the wall until the chair began to splinter. She moved over to the bookcase and began ripping pages out of the books, scattering them around the room. She tore the useless telephone cord out of the wall. Let Rhys explain this to the police, she thought. Do not go gentle into that good night. Well, she would not go gentle. They would have to take her by force.

A sudden gale swept through the room, swirling the papers through the air, then died away. It took Elizabeth a moment to realize what had happened.

She was no longer alone in the house.

At Leonardo da Vinci Airport, near the *merci* area where freight was handled, Detective Max Hornung was watching a helicopter land. By the time the pilot had his door open Max was at his side. 'Can you fly me to Sardinia?' he asked.

The pilot stared at him. 'What's going on? I just flew somebody there. There's a bad storm blowing.'

'Will you take me?'

443

'It'll cost you triple.'

Max did not even hesitate. He climbed into the helicopter. As they took off, Max turned to the pilot and asked, 'Who was the passenger you took to Sardinia?'

'His name was Williams.'

The dark was Elizabeth's ally now, concealing her from her killer. It was too late to get away. She had to try to find a place to hide somewhere in the house. She went upstairs, putting distance between herself and Rhys. At the top of the stairs she hesitated, then turned towards Sam's bedroom. Something leaped at her out of the dark, and she started to scream, but it was only the shadow of a windwhipped tree through the window. Her heart was pounding so hard that she was sure that Rhys would be able to hear it downstairs.

Delay him, her mind said. *But how?* Her head felt heavy. Everything was fuzzy. Think! she told herself. What would old Samuel have done? She walked to the bedroom at the end of the hall, took the key from the inside and locked the door from the outside. Then she locked the other doors and they were the doors of the gates of the ghetto in Krakow, and Elizabeth was not sure why she was doing it, and then she remembered that she had killed Aram and that they must not catch her. She saw the beam of a flashlight below, starting to move up the stairs, and her heart leaped. Rhys was coming for her. Elizabeth began to climb the tower stairs, and halfway up, her knees began to buckle. She slid to the floor and crawled the rest of the way on her hands and knees. She reached the top of the stairs and dragged herself upright. She opened the door to the tower room and went in. *The door*, Samuel said. *Lock the door.*

Elizabeth locked the door, but she knew that that would not keep Rhys out. At least, she thought, he will have to break it down. More violence to explain. Her death was going to look like murder. She pushed furniture against the door, moving slowly, as though the darkness were a heavy sea dragging her down. She pushed a table against the door, then an armchair and another table, working like an automaton, fighting for time, building her pitiable fortress against death. From the floor below she heard a crash and a moment later another and then a third. Rhys was breaking down the bedroom doors, looking for her. Signs of an attack, a trail for the police to follow. She had tricked him, as he had tricked her. Yet something was vaguely bothering her. If Rhys had to make her death look like an accident, why was he breaking down doors? She moved to the French doors and looked outside, listening to the mad wind singing a dirge to her. Beyond the balcony there was a sheer drop to the sea below. There was no escape from this room. This was where Rhys would have to come to get her. Elizabeth felt around for a weapon, but there was nothing that could help her.

She waited in the dark for her killer.

What was Rhys waiting for? Why didn't he break the door down and get it over with? *Break the door down.* Something was wrong. Even if he took her body away from here and disposed of it somewhere else, Rhys would still not be able to explain the violence of the house, the smashed mirror, the broken doors. Elizabeth tried to put herself in Rhys's mind, to figure out what plan he could have that would explain all those things without the police suspecting him of her death. There was only one way.

And even as Elizabeth thought of it, she could smell the smoke.

FIFTY-SIX

From the helicopter Max could see the coast of Sardinia, thickly blanketed by a cloud of swirling red dust. The pilot shouted above the din of the rotor blades, 'It's got worse. I don't know if I can land.'

'You've got to!' Max yelled. 'Head for Porto Cervo.'

The pilot turned to look at Max. 'That's at the top of a fucking mountain.'

'I know,' Max said. 'Can you do it?'

'Our chances are about seventy-thirty.'

'Which way?'

'Against.'

The smoke was seeping in under the door, coming up from below through the floorboards, and a new sound had been added to the shrieking of the wind. The roar of flames. Elizabeth knew now, she had the answer, but it was too late to save her life. She was trapped here. Of course it did not matter whether doors and mirrors and furniture had been smashed, because in a few minutes nothing would be left of this house or of her. Everything would be ruined by the fire, as the laboratory and Emil Joeppli had been destroyed, and Rhys would have an alibi in some other place, so that he could not be blamed. He had beaten her. He had beaten them all.

The smoke was beginning to billow into the room now – yellow, acrid fumes that made Elizabeth choke. She could see the edges of flame start to lick at the cracks of the door, and she began to feel the heat.

It was her anger that gave Elizabeth the strength to move.

Through the blinding haze of smoke she felt her way towards the French doors. She pushed them open and stepped on to the balcony. The instant the doors opened, the flames from the hallway leaped into the room, licking at the walls. Elizabeth stood on the balcony, gratefully gulping in deep breaths of fresh air as the wind tore at her clothes. She looked down. The balcony protruded from the side of the building, a tiny island hanging over an abyss. There was no hope, no escape.

Unless . . . Elizabeth looked up at the sloping slate roof above her head. If there was some way for her to reach the roof and get to the other side of the house that was not burning yet, she might get away. She stretched her arms as high as she could, but the eave of the roof was beyond her reach. The flames were beginning to move closer now, enveloping the room. There was one slender chance. Elizabeth took it. She forced herself to go back into the blazing, smoke-filled room, choking from the acrid fumes. She grabbed the chair behind her father's desk and dragged it on to the balcony. Fighting to keep her balance, she positioned the chair and stood on top of it. Her fingers could reach the roof now, but they could not find a grip. She fumbled blindly, vainly, searching to get a purchase.

Inside, the flames had reached the curtains and were dancing all around the room, attacking the books and the carpet and the furniture, moving towards the balcony. Elizabeth's fingers suddenly found a grip on a protruding slate. Her arms were leaden; she was not sure she could hold on. She started to pull herself up, and the chair began to slip away from her. With her last remaining strength she pulled herself up and held on. She was climbing the walls of the ghetto now, fighting for her life. She kept pulling and straining and suddenly she found herself lying on the sloping roof, gasping for breath. She forced herself to move, inching her way upward, pressing her body hard against the steep pitch of the roof, aware that one slip would hurtle her into the black abyss below. She reached the peak of the roof and paused to catch her breath and take her bearings. The balcony she had just escaped from was blazing. There could be no turning back.

Looking down on the far side of the house, Elizabeth could see the balcony of one of the guest bedrooms. There were no flames there yet. But Elizabeth did not know whether she would be able to reach it. The roof slanted sharply downward, the slates were loose, the wind was pulling madly at her. If she slipped, there would be nothing to stop her fall. She stayed where she was, frozen, afraid to try it. And then, like a sudden miracle, a figure appeared on the guest balcony, and it was Alec, and he was looking up and calling out calmly, 'You can make it, old girl. Nice and easy.'

And Elizabeth's heart soared within her.

'Take it slow,' Alec counselled. 'One step at a time. It's a piece of cake.'

And Elizabeth began to let herself move towards him, carefully, sliding down inch by inch, not letting go of one slate until she had found a firm grip on another. It seemed to take for ever. And all the while she heard Alec's encouraging voice, urging her on. She was almost there now, sliding towards the balcony. A slate loosened, and she started to fall.

'Hold on!' Alec called.

Elizabeth found another hold, grabbing it fiercely. She had reached the edge of the roof now, with nothing below her but endless space. She would have to drop down on to the balcony where Alec stood waiting. If she missed . . .

Alec was looking up at her, his face filled with quiet confidence. 'Don't look down,' he said. 'Close your eyes, and let yourself go. I'll catch you.'

She tried. She took a deep breath, and then another. She knew she had to let go and yet she could not bring herself to do it. Her fingers were frozen to the tiles.

'Now!' Alec called, and Elizabeth let herself drop and she was falling into space, and suddenly she was caught in Alec's arms as he pulled her to safety. She closed her eyes in relief.

'Well done,' Alec said.

And she felt the muzzle of the gun against her head.

FIFTY-SEVEN

The helicopter pilot was flying as low as he dared over the island, skimming the treetops, trying to avoid the punishing winds. Even at that altitude the air was filled with turbulence. In the distance ahead the pilot saw the mountain peak of Porto Cervo. Max saw it at the same moment. 'There it is!' Max shouted. 'I can see the villa.' And then he saw something else that made his heart jump. 'It's on fire!'

On the balcony Elizabeth heard the sound of the approaching helicopter over the wind, and she looked up. Alec paid no attention. He was watching Elizabeth, his eyes filled with pain. 'It was for Vivian. I had to do it for Vivian. You see that, don't you? They have to find you in the fire.'

Elizabeth was not listening. She could only think, *It wasn't Rhys. It wasn't Rhys.* All the time it had been Alec. Alec had killed her father and had tried to kill her. He had stolen the report and then tried to frame Rhys with it. He had terrified her into running away from Rhys because Alec had known that she would come here.

The helicopter had disappeared from sight now, beyond some nearby trees.

Alec said, 'Close your eyes, Elizabeth.'

She said fiercely, 'No!'

And Rhys's voice suddenly called, 'Drop the gun, Alec!'

They both looked down, and on the lawn below, in the light of the flickering flames, they saw Rhys and Chief of Police Luigi Ferraro and half a dozen detectives, armed with rifles.

'It's finished, Alec,' Rhys shouted. 'Let her go.'

One of the detectives with a telescopic rifle said, 'I can't shoot at him unless she moves out of the way.'

Move, Rhys prayed. *Move!*

From behind the trees across the lawn Max Hornung came hurrying up to Rhys. He stopped as he saw the tableau above. Rhys said, 'I got your message. I was too late.'

They were both staring up at the two figures on the balcony, puppets, backlit by the rising flames coming from the far side of the villa. The wind was whipping the house into a gigantic torch, lighting the surrounding mountains, turning the night into an inferno, a blazing Valhalla.

Elizabeth turned and looked into Alec's face, and it was a mask of death, his eyes unseeing. He moved away from her towards the balcony door.

On the ground the detective said, 'I've got him,' and raised his rifle. He fired once. Alec staggered, then disappeared through the door into the house.

One moment there were two figures on the balcony, and then only one.

Elizabeth screamed, 'Rhys!'

But he was already racing towards her.

Everything after that happened in a quick, confused kaleidoscope of motion. Rhys was picking her up and carrying her down to safety, and she clung tightly to him and could not hold him close enough.

She was lying on the grass, with her eyes closed, and Rhys was holding her in his arms, saying, 'I love you, Liz. I love you, my darling.'

She listened to his voice washing over her, caressing her. She could not speak. She looked into his eyes and saw all the love and anguish, and there was so much she wanted to tell him. She was filled with guilt for all of her terrible suspicions. She would spend the rest of her life making it up to him.

She was too weary to think about it now, too weary to think about any of it. It was as though it had all happened to someone else in some other place, at some other time.

The only important thing was that she and Rhys were together. She felt his strong arms holding her close, for ever, and it was enough.

FIFTY-EIGHT

It was like stepping into a blazing corner of hell.
The smoke was getting thicker, filling the room
with dancing chimeras that kept vanishing. The
fire leaped down at Alec, fondling his hair, and the
crackle of the flames became Vivian's voice calling
to him in an irresistible siren song.

In a sudden flare of brightness, he saw her. She
was stretched out on the bed, her beautiful body
naked except for the scarlet ribbon tied around
her neck, the same red ribbon she had worn the
first time he had made love to her. She called his
name again, her voice filled with longing. And this
time she wanted *him*, not the others. He moved
closer, and she whispered, 'You're the only one I
ever loved.'

And Alec believed it. He had had to punish her
because of the things she had done. But he had
been clever – he had made those others pay for her
sins. The terrible things he had done had been for
her. As he moved towards her, Vivian whispered

again, 'You're the only one I ever loved, Alec,' and he knew that it was true.

She was holding out her beckoning arms to him, and he sank down beside her. He embraced her, and they became one. He was inside her, and he *was* her. And this time he was able to satisfy her. And he felt such pleasure that it became an exquisite pain beyond bearing. He could feel the heat from her body consuming him, and even as he watched in wonder, the ribbon around Vivian's neck turned into a vivid tongue of flame caressing him, licking at him. In the next instant, a blazing beam from the ceiling crashed on top of him in a fiery pyre.

Alec died as the others had. In ecstasy.

Nothing Lasts Forever

To Anastasia and Roderick Mann,
with love

The author wishes to express his deep appreciation
to the many doctors, nurses, and medical technicians
who were generous enough
to share their expertise with him.

What cannot be cured with medicaments is cured
by the knife, what the knife cannot cure
is cured with the searing iron, and whatever
this cannot cure must be considered incurable.

HIPPOCRATES, 5th century B.C.

There are three classes of human beings: men,
women, and women physicians.　　SIR WILLIAM OSLER

PROLOGUE

San Francisco
Spring, 1995

District Attorney Carl Andrews was in a fury. 'What the hell is going on here?' he demanded. 'We have three doctors living together and working at the same hospital. One of them almost gets an entire hospital closed down, the second one kills a patient for a million dollars, and the third one is murdered.'

Andrews stopped to take a deep breath. 'And they're all women! Three goddam women doctors! The media is treating them like celebrities. They're all over the tube. *60 Minutes* did a segment on them. Barbara Walters did a special on them. I can't pick up a newspaper or magazine without seeing their pictures, or reading about them. Two to one, Hollywood is going to make a movie about them, and they'll turn the bitches into some kind of heroines! I wouldn't be surprised if the government put their faces on postage stamps, like Presley. Well, by God, I won't have it!' He slammed a fist down against the photograph of a woman on the cover of *Time* magazine. The caption read: *Dr Paige Taylor— Angel of Mercy or the Devil's Disciple?*

1

'Dr Paige Taylor.' The district attorney's voice was filled with disgust. He turned to Gus Venable, his chief prosecuting attorney. 'I'm handing this trial over to you, Gus. I want a conviction. Murder One. The gas chamber.'

'Don't worry,' Gus Venable said quietly. 'I'll see to it.'

Sitting in the courtroom watching Dr Paige Taylor, Gus Venable thought: *She's jury-proof.* Then he smiled to himself. *No one is jury-proof.* She was tall and slender, with eyes that were a startling dark brown in her pale face. A disinterested observer would have dismissed her as an attractive woman. A more observant one would have noticed something else — that all the different phases of her life coexisted in her. There was the happy excitement of the child, superimposed onto the shy uncertainty of the adolescent and the wisdom and pain of the woman. There was a look of innocence about her. *She's the kind of girl*, Gus Venable thought cynically, *a man would be proud to take home to his mother. If his mother had a taste for cold-blooded killers.*

There was an almost eerie sense of remoteness in her eyes, a look that said that Dr Paige Taylor had retreated deep inside herself to a different place, a different time, far from the cold, sterile courtroom where she was trapped.

The trial was taking place in the venerable old San Francisco Hall of Justice on Bryant Street. The building, which housed the Superior Court and County

Jail, was a forbidding-looking edifice, seven stories high, made of square gray stone. Visitors arriving at the courthouse were funneled through electronic security checkpoints. Upstairs, on the third floor, was the Superior Court. In Courtroom 121, where murder trials were held, the judge's bench stood against the rear wall, with an American flag behind it. To the left of the bench was the jury box, and in the center were two tables separated by an aisle, one for the prosecuting attorney, the other for the defense attorney.

The courtroom was packed with reporters and the type of spectators attracted to fatal highway accidents and murder trials. As murder trials went, this one was spectacular. Gus Venable, the prosecuting attorney, was a show in himself. He was a burly man, larger than life, with a mane of gray hair, a goatee, and the courtly manner of a Southern plantation owner. He had never been to the South. He had an air of vague bewilderment and the brain of a computer. His trademark, summer and winter, was a white suit, with an old-fashioned stiff-collar shirt.

Paige Taylor's attorney, Alan Penn, was Venable's opposite, a compact, energetic shark, who had built a reputation for racking up acquittals for his clients.

The two men had faced each other before, and their relationship was one of grudging respect and total mistrust. To Venable's surprise, Alan Penn had come to see him the week before the trial was to begin.

'I came here to do you a favor, Gus.'

Beware of defense attorneys bearing gifts. 'What did you have in mind, Alan?'

3

'Now understand—I haven't discussed this with my client yet, but suppose—just suppose—I could persuade her to plead guilty to a reduced charge and save the State the cost of a trial?'

'Are you asking me to plea-bargain?'

'Yes.'

Gus Venable reached down to his desk, searching for something. 'I can't find my damn calendar. Do you know what the date is?'

'June first. Why?'

'For a minute there, I thought it must be Christmas already, or you wouldn't be asking for a present like that.'

'Gus . . .'

Venable leaned forward in his chair. 'You know, Alan, ordinarily, I'd be inclined to go along with you. Tell you the truth, I'd like to be in Alaska fishing right now. But the answer is no. You're defending a cold-blooded killer who murdered a helpless patient for his money. I'm demanding the death penalty.'

'I think she's innocent, and I—'

Venable gave a short, explosive laugh. 'No, you don't. And neither does anyone else. It's an open-and-shut case. Your client is as guilty as Cain.'

'Not until the jury says so, Gus.'

'They will.' He paused. 'They will.'

After Alan Penn left, Gus Venable sat there thinking about their conversation. Penn's coming to him was a sign of weakness. Penn knew there was no chance he could win the trial. Gus Venable thought about the irrefutable evidence he had, and the witnesses he was going to call, and he was satisfied.

4

There was no question about it. Dr Paige Taylor was going to the gas chamber.

It had not been easy to impanel a jury. The case had occupied the headlines for months. The cold-bloodedness of the murder had created a tidal wave of anger.

The presiding judge was Vanessa Young, a tough, brilliant black jurist rumored to be the next nominee for the United States Supreme Court. She was not known for being patient with lawyers, and she had a quick temper. There was an adage among San Francisco trial lawyers: *If your client is guilty, and you're looking for mercy, stay away from Judge Young's courtroom.*

The day before the start of the trial, Judge Young had summoned the two attorneys to her chambers.

'We're going to set some ground rules, gentlemen. Because of the serious nature of this trial, I'm willing to make certain allowances to make sure that the defendant gets a fair trial. But I'm warning both of you not to try to take advantage of that. Is that clear?'

'Yes, your honor.'

'Yes, your honor.'

Gus Venable was finishing his opening statement. 'And so ladies and gentlemen of the jury, the State will prove—yes, prove beyond a reasonable doubt—that Dr Paige Taylor killed her patient, John Cronin. And not only did she commit murder,

5

she did it for money . . . a lot of money. She killed John Cronin for one million dollars.

'Believe me, after you've heard all the evidence, you will have no trouble in finding Dr Paige Taylor guilty of murder in the first degree. Thank you.'

The jury sat in silence, unmoved but expectant.

Gus Venable turned to the judge. 'If it please your honor I would like to call Gary Williams as the State's first witness.'

When the witness was sworn in, Gus Venable said, 'You're an orderly at Embarcadero County Hospital?'

'Yes, that's right.'

'Were you working in Ward Three when John Cronin was brought in last year?'

'Yes.'

'Can you tell us who the doctor in charge of his case was?'

'Dr Taylor.'

'How would you characterize the relationship between Dr Taylor and John Cronin?'

'Objection!' Alan Penn was on his feet. 'He's calling for a conclusion from the witness.'

'Sustained.'

'Let me phrase it another way. Did you ever hear any conversations between Dr Taylor and John Cronin?'

'Oh, sure. I couldn't help it. I worked that ward all the time.'

'Would you describe those conversations as friendly?'

'No, sir.'

'Really? Why do you say that?'

'Well, I remember the first day Mr Cronin was brought in, and Dr Taylor started to examine him, he said to keep her . . .' He hesitated. 'I don't know if I can repeat his language.'

'Go ahead, Mr Williams. I don't think there are any children in this courtroom.'

'Well, he told her to keep her fucking hands off him.'

'He said *that* to Dr Taylor?'

'Yes, sir.'

'Please tell the court what else you may have seen or heard.'

'Well, he always called her "that bitch." He didn't want her to go near him. Whenever she came into his room, he would say things like "Here comes that bitch again!" and "Tell that bitch to leave me alone" and "Why don't they get me a *real* doctor?"'

Gus Venable paused to look over to where Dr Taylor was seated. The jurors' eyes followed him. Venable shook his head, as though saddened, then turned back to the witness. 'Did Mr Cronin seem to you to be a man who wanted to give a million dollars to Dr Taylor?'

Alan Penn was on his feet again. 'Objection! He's calling for an opinion again.'

Judge Young said, 'Overruled. The witness may answer the question.'

Alan Penn looked at Paige Taylor and sank back in his seat.

'Hell, no. He hated her guts.'

*   *   *

7

Dr Arthur Kane was in the witness box.

Gus Venable said, 'Dr Kane, you were the staff doctor in charge when it was discovered that John Cronin was mur—' He looked at Judge Young. '. . . killed by insulin being introduced into his IV. Is that correct?'

'It is.'

'And you subsequently discovered that Dr Taylor was responsible.'

'That's correct.'

'Dr Kane, I'm going to show you the official hospital death form signed by Dr Taylor.' He picked up a paper and handed it to Kane. 'Would you read it aloud, please?'

Kane began to read. '"John Cronin. Cause of Death: Respiratory arrest occurred as a complication of myocardial infarction occurring as a complication of pulmonary embolus."'

'And in layman's language?'

'The report says that the patient died of a heart attack.'

'And that paper is signed by Dr Taylor?'

'Yes.'

'Dr Kane, was that the true cause of John Cronin's death?'

'No. The insulin injection caused his death.'

'So, Dr Taylor administered a fatal dose of insulin and then falsified the report?'

'Yes.'

'And you reported it to Dr Wallace, the hospital administrator, who then reported it to the authorities.'

'Yes. I felt it was my duty.' His voice rang with righteous indignation. 'I'm a doctor. I don't believe in taking the life of another human being under any circumstances.'

The next witness called was John Cronin's widow. Hazel Cronin was in her late thirties, with flaming red hair, and a voluptuous figure that her plain black dress failed to conceal.

Gus Venable said, 'I know how painful this is for you, Mrs Cronin, but I must ask you to describe to the jury your relationship with your late husband.'

The widow Cronin dabbed at her eyes with a large lace handkerchief. 'John and I had a loving marriage. He was a wonderful man. He often told me I had brought him the only real happiness he had ever known.'

'How long were you married to John Cronin?'

'Two years, but John always said it was like two years in heaven.'

'Mrs Cronin, did your husband ever discuss Dr Taylor with you? Tell you what a great doctor he thought she was? Or how helpful she had been to him? Or how much he liked her?'

'He never mentioned her.'

'Never?'

'Never.'

'Did John ever discuss cutting you and your brothers out of his will?'

'Absolutely not. He was the most generous man in the world. He always told me that there was nothing I couldn't have, and that when he died . . .' her voice broke, '. . . that when he died, I would be a wealthy woman, and . . .' She could not go on.

Judge Young said, 'We'll have a fifteen-minute recess.'

Seated in the back of the courtroom, Jason Curtis was filled with anger. He could not believe what the witnesses were saying about Paige. *This is the woman I love*, he thought. *The woman I'm going to marry*.

Immediately after Paige's arrest, Jason Curtis had gone to visit her in jail.

'We'll fight this,' he assured her. 'I'll get you the best criminal lawyer in the country.' A name immediately sprang to mind. *Alan Penn*. Jason had gone to see him.

'I've been following the case in the papers,' Penn said. 'The press has already tried and convicted her of murdering John Cronin for a bundle. What's more she admits she killed him.'

'I know her,' Jason Curtis told him. 'Believe me, there's no way Paige could have done what she did, for money.'

'Since she admits she killed him,' Penn said, 'what we're dealing with here then is euthanasia. Mercy killings are against the law in California, as in most states, but there are a lot of mixed feelings about them. I can make a pretty good case for Florence Nightingale listening to a Higher Voice and all that shit, but the problem is that your lady love killed a patient who left her a million dollars in his will. Which came first, the chicken or the egg? Did she know about the million before she killed him, or after?'

'Paige didn't know a thing about the money,' Jason said firmly.

10

Penn's tone was noncommittal. 'Right. It was just a happy coincidence. The DA is calling for Murder One, and he wants the death penalty.'

'Will you take the case?'

Penn hesitated. It was obvious that Jason Curtis believed in Dr Taylor. *The way Samson believed in Delilah.* He looked at Jason and thought: *I wonder if the poor son of a bitch had a haircut and doesn't know it.*

Jason was waiting for an answer.

'I'll take the case, as long as you know it's all uphill. It's going to be a tough one to win.'

Alan Penn's statement turned out to be over-optimistic.

When the trial resumed the following morning, Gus Venable called a string of new witnesses.

A nurse was on the stand. 'I heard John Cronin say "I know I'll die on the operating table. You're going to kill me. I hope they get you for murder."'

An attorney, Roderick Pelham, was on the stand. Gus Venable said, 'When you told Dr Taylor about the million dollars from John Cronin's estate, what did she say?'

'She said something like "It seems unethical. He was my patient."'

'She admitted it was unethical?'

'Yes.'

'But she agreed to take the money?'

'Oh yes. Absolutely.'

* * *

11

Alan Penn was cross-examining.

'Mr Pelham, was Dr Taylor expecting your visit?'

'Why, no, I . . .'

'You didn't call her and say, "John Cronin left you one million dollars"?'

'No, I . . .'

'So when you told her, you were actually face to face with her?'

'Yes.'

'In a position to see her reaction to the news.'

'Yes.'

'And when you told her about the money, how did she react?'

'Well—she—she seemed surprised, but . . .'

'Thank you Mr Pelham. That's all.'

The trial was now in its fourth week. The spectators and press had found the prosecuting attorney and defense attorney fascinating to watch. Gus Venable was dressed in white and Alan Penn in black, and the two of them had moved around the courtroom like players in a deadly, choreographed game of chess, with Paige Taylor the sacrificial pawn.

Gus Venable was tying up the loose ends.

'If the court please, I would like to call Alma Rogers to the witness stand.'

When his witness was sworn in, Venable said, 'Mrs Rogers, what is your occupation?'

'It's *Miss* Rogers.'

'I do beg your pardon.'

'I work at the Corniche Travel Agency.'

'Your agency books tours to various countries and

makes hotel reservations and handles other accommodations for your clients?'

'Yes, sir.'

'I want you to take a look at the defendant. Have you ever seen her before?'

'Oh, yes. She came into our travel agency two or three years ago.'

'And what did she want?'

'She said she was interested in a trip to London and Paris, and, I believe, Venice.'

'Did she ask about package tours?'

'Oh, no. She said she wanted everything first-class—plane, hotel. And I believe she was interested in chartering a yacht.'

The courtroom was hushed. Gus Venable walked over to the prosecutor's table and held up some folders. 'The police found these brochures in Dr Taylor's apartment. These are travel itineraries to Paris and London and Venice, brochures for expensive hotels and airlines, and one listing the cost of chartering a private yacht.'

There was a loud murmur from the courtroom.

The prosecutor had opened one of the brochures.

'Here are some of the yachts listed for charter.' He read aloud. 'The *Christina O* . . . twenty-six thousand dollars a week plus ship's expenses . . . the *Resolute Time*, twenty-four thousand five hundred dollars a week . . . the *Lucky Dream*, twenty-seven thousand three hundred dollars a week.' He looked up. 'There's a check mark after the *Lucky Dream*. Paige Taylor had already selected the twenty-seven thousand three hundred a week yacht. She just hadn't selected her victim yet.'

13

'We'd like to have these marked Exhibit A.'
Venable turned to Alan Penn and smiled. Alan
Penn looked at Paige. She was staring down at the
table, her face pale. 'Your witness.'

Penn rose to his feet, stalling, thinking fast.

'How is the travel business these days, Miss
Rogers?'

'I beg your pardon?'

'I asked how business was. Is Corniche a large
travel agency?'

'It's quite large, yes.'

'I imagine a lot of people come in to inquire about
trips.'

'Oh, yes.'

'Would you say five or six people a day?'

'Oh, no!' Her voice was indignant. 'We talk to
as many as fifty people a day about travel
arrangements.'

'Fifty people a day?' He sounded impressed. 'And
the day we're talking about was two or three years
ago. If you multiply fifty by nine hundred days, that's
roughly forty-five thousand people.'

'I suppose so.'

'And yet, out of all those people, you remembered
Dr Taylor. Why is that?'

'Well, she and her two friends were so excited
about taking a trip to Europe. I thought it was lovely.
They were like schoolgirls. Oh, yes. I remember
them very clearly, particularly because they didn't
look like they could afford a yacht.'

'I see. I suppose everyone who comes in and asks
for a brochure goes away on a trip?'

'Well, of course not. But —'

'Dr Taylor didn't actually *book* a trip, did she?'

14

'Well, no. Not with us. She—'

'Nor with anyone else. She merely asked to see some brochures.'

'Yes. She—'

'That's not the same as *going* to Paris or London, is it?'

'Well, no, but—'

'Thank you. You may step down.'

Venable turned to Judge Young. 'I would like to call Dr Benjamin Wallace to the stand . . .'

'Dr Wallace, you're in charge of administration at Embarcadero County Hospital?'

'Yes.'

'So, of course, you're familiar with Dr Taylor and her work?'

'Yes, I am.'

'Were you surprised to learn that Dr Taylor was indicted for murder?'

Penn was on his feet, 'Objection your honor. Dr Wallace's answer would be irrelevant.'

'If I may explain,' interrupted Venable. 'It could be very relevant if you'll just let me . . .'

'Well, let's see what develops,' said Judge Young. 'But no nonsense, Mr Venable.'

'Let me approach the question differently,' continued Venable. 'Dr Wallace, every physician is required to take the Hippocratic oath, is that not so?'

'Yes.'

'And part of that oath is . . . ,' the prosecutor read

from a paper in his hand, ' "That I shall abstain from every act of mischief or corruption"?'

'Yes.'

'Was there anything Dr Taylor did in the past that made you believe she was capable of breaking her Hippocratic oath?'

'Objection.'

'Overruled.'

'Yes, there was.'

'Please explain what it was.'

'We had a patient who Dr Taylor decided needed a blood transfusion. His family refused to grant permission.'

'And what happened?'

'Dr Taylor went ahead and gave the patient the transfusion anyway.'

'Is that legal?'

'Absolutely not. Not without a court order.'

'And then what did Dr Taylor do?'

'She obtained the court order afterward, and changed the date on it.'

'So she performed an illegal act, and falsified the hospital records to cover it up?'

'That is correct.'

Alan Penn glanced over at Paige, furious. *What the hell else has she kept from me?* he wondered.

If the spectators were searching for any tell-tale sign of emotion on Paige Taylor's face, they were disappointed.

Cold as ice, the foreman of the jury was thinking.

Gus Venable turned to the bench. 'Your honor, as you know, one of the witnesses I had hoped to call

16

is a Dr Lawrence Barker. Unfortunately he is still suffering from the effects of a stroke and is unable to be in this courtroom to testify. Instead I will now question some of the hospital staff who have worked with Dr Barker.'

Penn stood up. 'I object. I don't see the relevance. Dr Barker is not here, nor is Dr Barker on trial here. If . . .'

Venable interrupted. 'Your honor, I assure you that my line of questioning is very relevant to the testimony we have just heard. It also has to do with the defendant's competency as a doctor.'

Judge Young said skeptically, 'We'll see. This is a courtroom, not a river. I won't stand for any fishing expeditions. You may call your witnesses.'

'Thank you.'

Gus Venable turned to the bailiff. 'I would like to call Dr Mathew Peterson.'

An elegant-looking man in his sixties approached the witness box. He was sworn in, and when he took his seat, Gus Venable said, 'Dr Peterson, how long have you worked at Embarcadero County Hospital?'

'Eight years.'

'And what is your specialty?'

'I'm a cardiac surgeon.'

'And during the years you've been at Embarcadero County Hospital, did you ever have occasion to work with Dr Lawrence Barker?'

'Oh, yes. Many times.'

'What was your opinion of him?'

'The same as everyone else's. Aside, possibly, from DeBakey and Cooley, Dr Barker is the best heart surgeon in the world.'

'Were you present in the operating room on the

17

morning that Dr Taylor operated on a patient named . . .' he pretended to consult a slip of paper. '. . . Lance Kelly?'

The witness's tone changed. 'Yes, I was there.'

'Would you describe what happened that morning?'

Dr Peterson said reluctantly, 'Well, things started to go wrong. We began losing the patient.'

'When you say, "losing the patient . . ."'

'His heart stopped. We were trying to bring him back, and . . .'

'Had Dr Barker been sent for?'

'Yes.'

'And did he come into the operating room while the operation was going on?'

'Toward the end. Yes. But it was too late to do anything. We were unable to revive the patient.'

'And did Dr Barker say anything to Dr Taylor at that time?'

'Well, we were all pretty upset, and . . .'

'I asked you if Dr Barker said anything to Dr Taylor.'

'Yes.'

'And what did Dr Barker say?'

There was a pause, and in the middle of the pause, there was a crack of thunder outside, like the voice of God. A moment later, the storm broke, nailing raindrops to the roof of the courthouse.

'Dr Barker said, "You killed him."'

The spectators were in an uproar. Judge Young slammed her gavel down. 'That's enough! Do you people live in caves? One more outburst like that and you'll all be standing outside in the rain.'

Gus Venable waited for the noise to die down. In

18

the hushed silence he said, 'Are you sure that's what Dr Barker said to Dr Taylor? "You killed him."'

'Yes.'

'And you have testified that Dr Barker was a man whose medical opinion was valued?'

'Oh, yes.'

'Thank you. That's all, doctor.' He turned to Alan Penn. 'Your witness.'

Penn rose and approached the witness box.

'Dr Peterson, I've never watched an operation, but I imagine there's enormous tension, especially when it's something as serious as a heart operation.'

'There's a great deal of tension.'

'At a time like that, how many people are in the room? Three or four?'

'Oh, no. Always half a dozen or more.'

'Really?'

'Yes. There are usually two surgeons, one assisting, sometimes two anesthesiologists, a scrub nurse, and at least one circulating nurse.'

'I see. Then there must be a lot of noise and excitement going on. People calling out instructions and so on.'

'Yes.'

'And I understand that it's a common practice for music to be playing during an operation.'

'It is.'

'When Dr Barker came in and saw that Lance Kelly was dying, that probably added to the confusion.'

'Well, everybody was pretty busy trying to save the patient.'

'Making a lot of noise?'

'There was plenty of noise, yes.'

'And yet, in all that confusion and noise, and over the music, you could hear Dr Barker say that Dr Taylor had killed the patient. With all that excitement, you could have been wrong, couldn't you?'

'No, sir. I could not be wrong.'

'What makes you so sure?'

Dr Peterson sighed. 'Because I was standing right next to Dr Barker when he said it.'

There was no graceful way out.

'No more questions.'

The case was falling apart, and there was nothing he could do about it. It was about to get worse.

Denise Berry took the witness stand.

'You're a nurse at Embarcadero County Hospital?'

'Yes.'

'How long have you worked there?'

'Five years.'

'During that time, did you ever hear any conversations between Dr Taylor and Dr Barker?'

'Sure. Lots of times.'

'Can you repeat some of them?'

Nurse Berry looked at Dr Taylor and hesitated. 'Well, Dr Barker could be very sharp . . .'

'I didn't ask you that, Nurse Berry. I asked you to tell us some specific things you heard him say to Dr Taylor.'

There was a long pause. 'Well, one time he said she was incompetent, and . . .'

Gus Venable put on a show of surprise. 'You heard Dr Barker say that Dr Taylor was incompetent?'

'Yes, sir. But he was always . . .'

'What other comments did you hear him make about Dr Taylor?'

The witness was reluctant to speak. 'I really can't remember.'

'Miss Berry, you're under oath.'

'Well, once I heard him say . . .' The rest of the sentence was a mumble.

'We can't hear you. Speak up, please. You heard him say what?'

'He said he . . . he wouldn't let Dr Taylor operate on his dog.'

There was a collective gasp from the courtroom.

'But I'm sure he only meant . . .'

'I think we can all assume that Dr Barker meant what he said.'

All eyes were fixed on Paige Taylor.

The prosecutor's case against Paige seemed overwhelming. Yet Alan Penn had the reputation of being a master magician in the courtroom. Now it was his turn to present the defendant's case. Could he pull another rabbit out of his hat?

Paige Taylor was on the witness stand, being questioned by Alan Penn. This was the moment everyone had been waiting for.

'John Cronin was a patient of yours, Dr Taylor?'

'Yes, he was.'

'And what were your feelings toward him?'

'I liked him. He knew how ill he was, but he was

very courageous. He had surgery for a cardiac tumor.'

'You performed the heart surgery?'

'Yes.'

'And what did you find during the operation?'

'When we opened up his chest, we found that he had melanoma that had metastasized.'

'In other words, cancer that had spread throughout his body.'

'Yes. It had metastasized throughout the lymph glands.'

'Meaning that there was no hope for him? No heroic measures that could bring him back to health?'

'None.'

'John Cronin was put on life-support systems?'

'That's correct.'

'Dr Taylor, did you deliberately administer a fatal dose of insulin to end John Cronin's life?'

'I did.'

There was a sudden buzz in the courtroom.

She's really a cool one, Gus Venable thought. *She makes it sound as though she gave him a cup of tea.*

'Would you tell the jury why you ended John Cronin's life?'

'Because he asked me to. He begged me to. He sent for me in the middle of the night, in terrible pain. The medications we were giving him were no longer working.' Her voice was steady. 'He said he didn't want to suffer anymore. His death was only a few days away. He pleaded with me to end it for him. I did.'

'Doctor, did you have any reluctance to let him die? Any feelings of guilt?'

22

Dr Paige Taylor shook her head. 'No. If you could have seen . . . There was simply no point to letting him go on suffering.'

'How did you administer the insulin?'

'I injected it into his IV.'

'And did that cause him any additional pain?'

'No. He simply drifted off to sleep.'

Gus Venable was on his feet. 'Objection! I think the defendant means he drifted off to his death! I —'

Judge Young slammed down her gavel. 'Mr Venable, you're out of order. You'll have your chance to cross-examine the witness. Sit down.'

The prosecutor looked over at the jury, shook his head, and took his seat.

'Dr Taylor, when you administered the insulin to John Cronin, were you aware that he had put you in his will for one million dollars?'

'No. I was stunned when I learned about it.'

Her nose should be growing, Gus Venable thought.

'You never discussed money or gifts at any time, or asked John Cronin for anything?'

A faint flush came to her cheeks. 'Never!'

'But you were on friendly terms with him?'

'Yes. When a patient is that ill, the doctor-patient relationship changes. We discussed his business problems and his family problems.'

'But you had no reason to expect anything from him?'

'No.'

'He left that money to you because he had grown to respect you and trust you. Thank you, Dr Taylor.' Penn turned to Gus Venable. 'Your witness.'

As Penn returned to the defense table, Paige Taylor glanced toward the back of the courtroom. Jason was seated there, trying to look encouraging. Next to him was Honey. A stranger was sitting next to Honey in the seat that Kat should have occupied. *If she were still alive. But Kat was dead*, Paige thought. *I killed her, too.*

Gus Venable rose and slowly shuffled over to the witness box. He glanced at the rows of press. Every seat was filled, and the reporters were all busily scribbling. *I'm going to give you something to write about*, Venable thought.

He stood in front of the defendant for a long moment, studying her. Then he said casually, 'Dr Taylor . . . was John Cronin the first patient you murdered at Embarcadero County Hospital?'

Alan Penn was on his feet, furious. 'Your honor, I—'

Judge Young had already slammed her gavel down. 'Objection sustained!' She turned to the two attorneys. 'There will be a fifteen-minute recess. I want to see counsel in my chambers.'

When the two attorneys were in her chambers, Judge Young turned to Gus Venable. 'You *did* go to law school, didn't you, Gus?'

'I'm sorry, your honor. I—'

'Did you see a tent out there?'

'I beg your pardon?'

Her voice was a whiplash. 'My courtroom is not a circus, and I don't intend to let you turn it into one. How dare you ask an inflammatory question like that!'

24

'I apologize, your honor. I'll rephrase the question and —'

'You'll do more than that!' Judge Young snapped. 'You'll rephrase your attitude. I'm warning you, you pull one more stunt like that and I'll declare a mistrial.'

'Yes, your honor.'

When they returned to the courtroom, Judge Young said to the jury, 'The jury will completely disregard the prosecutor's last question.' She turned to the prosecutor. 'You may go on.'

Gus Venable walked back to the witness box. 'Dr Taylor, you must have been very surprised when you were informed that the man you murdered left you one million dollars.'

Alan Penn was on his feet. 'Objection!'

'Sustained.' Judge Young turned to Venable. 'You're trying my patience.'

'I apologize, your honor.' He turned back to the witness. 'You must have been on *very* friendly terms with your patient. I mean, it isn't every day that an almost complete stranger leaves us a million dollars, is it?'

Paige Taylor flushed slightly. 'Our friendship was in the context of a doctor-patient relationship.'

'Wasn't it a little more than that? A man doesn't cut his beloved wife and family out of his will and leave a million dollars to a stranger without some kind of persuasion. Those talks you claimed to have had with him about his business problems . . .'

Judge Young leaned forward and said warningly, 'Mr Venable . . .' The prosecutor raised his hands in a gesture of surrender. He turned back to the defendant. 'So you and John Cronin had a friendly chat. He told you personal things about himself, and he liked you and respected you. Would you say that's a fair summation, doctor?'

'Yes.'

'And for doing that he gave you a million dollars?'

Paige looked out at the courtroom. She said nothing. She had no answer.

Venable started to walk back toward the prosecutor's table, then suddenly turned to face the defendant again.

'Dr Taylor, you testified earlier that you had no idea that John Cronin was going to leave you any money, or that he was going to cut his family out of his will.'

'That's correct.'

'How much does a resident doctor make at Embarcadero County Hospital?'

Alan Penn was on his feet. 'Objection! I don't see —'

'It's a proper question. The witness may answer.'

'Thirty-eight thousand dollars a year.'

Venable said sympathetically, 'That's not very much these days, is it? And out of that, there are deductions and taxes and living expenses. That wouldn't leave enough to take a luxury vacation trip, say, to London or Paris or Venice, would it?'

'I suppose not.'

'No. So you didn't plan to take a vacation like that, because you knew you couldn't afford it.'

'That's correct.'

Alan Penn was on his feet again. 'Your honor . . .'

Judge Young turned to the prosecutor. 'Where is this leading, Mr Venable?'

'I just want to establish that the defendant could not plan a luxury trip without getting the money from someone.'

'She's already answered the question.'

Alan Penn knew he had to do something. His heart wasn't in it, but he approached the witness box with all the good cheer of a man who had just won the lottery.

'Dr Taylor, do you remember picking up these travel brochures?'

'Yes.'

'Were you planning to go to Europe or to charter a yacht?'

'Of course not. It was all sort of a joke, an impossible dream. My friends and I thought it would lift our spirits. We were very tired, and . . . it seemed like a good idea at the time.' Her voice trailed off.

Alan Penn glanced covertly at the jury. Their faces registered pure disbelief.

Gus Venable was questioning the defendant on re-examination. 'Dr Taylor, are you acquainted with Dr Lawrence Barker?'

She had a sudden memory flash. *I'm going to kill Lawrence Barker. I'll do it slowly. I'll let him suffer first . . . then I'll kill him.* 'Yes. I know Dr Barker.'

'In what connection?'

'Dr Barker and I have often worked together during the past two years.'

27

'Would you say that he's a competent doctor?'

Alan Penn jumped up from his chair. 'I object, your honor. The witness . . .'

But before he could finish or Judge Young could rule, Paige answered, 'He's more than competent. He's brilliant.'

Penn sank back in his chair, too stunned to speak.

'Would you care to elaborate on that?'

'Dr Barker is one of the most renowned cardio-vascular surgeons in the world. He had a large private practice, but he donated three days a week to Embarcadero County Hospital.'

'So you have a high regard for his judgement in medical matters?'

'Yes.'

'And do you feel he would be capable of judging another doctor's competence?'

Penn willed Paige to say, *I don't know*.

She hesitated. 'Yes.'

Gus Venable turned to the jury. 'You've heard the defendant testify that she had a high regard for Dr Barker's medical judgement. I hope she listened carefully to Dr Barker's judgement about her competence . . . Or the lack of it.'

Alan Penn was on his feet, furious. 'Objection!'

'Sustained.'

But it was too late. The damage had been done.

During the next recess, Alan Penn pulled Jason into the men's room.

'What the hell have you gotten me into?' Penn demanded angrily. 'John Cronin hated her, Barker hated her. I insist on my clients telling me the truth,

28

and the whole truth. That's the only way I can help them. Well, I can't help *her*. Your lady friend has given me a snow job so deep I need skis. Every time she opens her mouth she puts a nail in her coffin. The fucking case is in free fall!'

That afternoon, Jason Curtis went to see Paige.

'You have a visitor, Dr Taylor.'

Jason walked into Paige's cell.

'Paige . . .'

She turned to him, and she was fighting back tears. 'It looks pretty bad, doesn't it?'

Jason forced a smile. 'You know what the man said—It's not over till it's over.'

'Jason, you don't believe that I killed John Cronin for his money, do you? What I did, I did only to help him.'

'I believe you,' Jason said quietly. 'I love you.'

He took her into his arms. *I don't want to lose her*, Jason thought. *I can't. She's the best thing in my life.* 'Everything is going to be all right. I promised you we would be together forever.'

Paige held him close and thought, *Nothing lasts forever. Nothing. How could everything have gone so wrong . . . so wrong . . . so wrong . . .*

Book One

Book One

1

San Francisco
July, 1990

'Hunter, Kate.'
  'Here.'
  'Taft, Betty Lou.'
  'I'm here.'
  'Taylor, Paige.'
  'Here.'

They were the only women among the big group of incoming first-year residents gathered in the large, drab auditorium at Embarcadero County Hospital.

Embarcadero County was the oldest hospital in San Francisco, and one of the oldest in the country. During the earthquake of 1989, God had played a joke on the residents of San Francisco and left the hospital standing. It was an ugly complex, occupying more than three square blocks, with buildings of brick and stone, gray with years of accumulated grime.

Inside the front entrance of the main building was a large waiting room, with hard wooden benches for patients and visitors. The walls were flaking from too many decades of coats of paint, and the corridors were worn and uneven from too many thousands of patients in wheelchairs and on crutches and walkers. The entire complex was coated with the stale patina of time.

Embarcadero County Hospital was a city within a city. There were over nine thousand people employed at the hospital, including four hundred staff physicians, one hundred and fifty part-time voluntary physicians, eight hundred residents, and three thousand nurses, plus the technicians, unit aides, and other technical personnel. The upper floors contained a complex of twelve operating rooms, central supply, a bone bank, central scheduling, three emergency wards, an AIDS ward, and over two thousand beds.

Now, on the first day of the arrival of the new residents in July, Dr Benjamin Wallace, the hospital administrator, rose to address them. Wallace was the quintessential politician, a tall, impressive-looking man with small skills and enough charm to have ingratiated his way up to his present position.

'I want to welcome all of you new resident doctors this morning. For the first two years of medical school, you worked with cadavers. In the last two years, you have worked with hospital patients under the supervision of senior doctors. Now, it's *you* who are going to be responsible for your patients. It's an awesome responsibility, and it takes dedication and skill.'

His eyes scanned the auditorium. 'Some of you are planning to go into surgery. Others of you will be going into internal medicine. Each group will be assigned to a senior resident who will explain the daily routine to you. From now on, everything you do could be a matter of life or death.'

They were listening intently, hanging on every word.

'Embarcadero is a county hospital. That means we admit anyone who comes to our door. Most of the patients are indigent. They come here because they can't afford a private hospital. Our emergency rooms are busy twenty-four hours a day. You're going to be overworked and underpaid. In a private hospital, your first year would consist of routine scut work. In the second year, you would be allowed to hand a scalpel to the surgeon, and in your third year, you would be permitted to do some supervised minor surgery. Well, you can forget all that. Our motto here is "Watch one, do one, teach one."

'We're badly understaffed, and the quicker we can get you into the operating rooms, the better. Are there any questions?'

There were a million questions the new residents wanted to ask.

'None? Good. Your first day officially begins tomorrow. You will report to the main reception desk at five-thirty tomorrow morning. Good luck!'

The briefing was over. There was a general exodus toward the doors and the low buzz of excited conversations. The three women found themselves standing together.

'Where are all the other women?'

'I think we're it.'

'It's a lot like medical school, huh? The boys' club. I have a feeling this place belongs to the Dark Ages.'

The person talking was a flawlessly beautiful black woman, nearly six feet tall, large-boned, but

35

intensely graceful. Everything about her, her walk, her carriage, the cool, quizzical look she carried in her eyes, sent out a message of aloofness. 'I'm Kate Hunter. They call me Kat.'

'Paige Taylor.' Young and friendly, intelligent-looking, self-assured.

They turned to the third woman.

'Betty Lou Taft. They call me Honey.' She spoke with a soft Southern accent. She had an open, guile-less face, soft gray eyes, and a warm smile.

'Where are you from?' Kat asked.

'Memphis, Tennessee.'

They looked at Paige. She decided to give them the simple answer. 'Boston.'

'Minneapolis,' Kat said. *That's close enough*, she thought.

Paige said, 'It looks like we're all a long way from home. Where are you staying?'

'I'm at a fleabag hotel,' Kat said. 'I haven't had a chance to look for a place to live.'

Honey said, 'Neither have I.'

Paige brightened. 'I looked at some apartments this morning. One of them was terrific, but I can't afford it. It has three bedrooms . . .'

They stared at one another.

'If the three of us shared . . .' Kat said.

The apartment was in the Marina district, on Filbert Street. It was perfect for them. 3Br/2Ba, nu cpts, lndry, prkg, utils pd. It was furnished in early Sears Roebuck, but it was neat and clean.

When the three women were through inspecting it, Honey said, 'I think it's lovely.'

'So do I!' Kat agreed.

They looked at Paige.

'Let's take it.'

They moved into the apartment that afternoon. The janitor helped them carry their luggage upstairs.

'So you're gonna work at the hospital,' he said. 'Nurses, huh?'

'Doctors,' Kat corrected him.

He looked at her skeptically. 'Doctors? You mean, like *real* doctors?'

'Yes, like real doctors,' Paige told him.

He grunted. 'Tell you the truth, if I needed medical attention, I don't think I'd want a woman examining my body.'

'We'll keep that in mind.'

'Where's the television set?' Kat asked. 'I don't see one.'

'If you want one, you'll have to buy it. Enjoy the apartment, ladies—er, doctors.' He chuckled.

They watched him leave.

Kat said, imitating his voice, 'Nurses, eh?' She snorted. 'Male chauvinist. Well, let's pick out our bedrooms.'

'Any one of them is fine with me,' Honey said softly.

They examined the three bedrooms. The master bedroom was larger than the other two.

Kat said, 'Why don't you take it, Paige? You found this place.'

Paige nodded. 'All right.'

They went to their respective rooms and began to unpack. From her suitcase, Paige carefully removed a framed photograph of a man in his early thirties. He was attractive, wearing black-framed glasses that

37

gave him a scholarly look. Paige put the photograph at her bedside, next to a bundle of letters.

Kat and Honey wandered in. 'How about going out and getting some dinner?'

'I'm ready,' Paige said.

Kat saw the photograph. 'Who's that?'

Paige smiled. 'That's the man I'm going to marry. He's a doctor who works for the World Health Organization. His name is Alfred Turner. He's working in Africa right now, but he's coming to San Francisco so we can be together.'

'Lucky you,' Honey said wistfully. 'He looks nice.'

Paige looked at her. 'Are you involved with anyone?'

'No. I'm afraid I don't have much luck with men.'

Kat said, 'Maybe your luck will change at Embarcadero.'

The three of them had dinner at Tarantino's, not far from their apartment building. During dinner they chatted about their backgrounds and lives, but there was a restraint to their conversation, a holding back. They were three strangers, probing, cautiously getting to know one another.

Honey spoke very little. *There's a shyness about her*, Paige thought. *She's vulnerable. Some man in Memphis probably broke her heart.*

Paige looked at Kat. *Self-confident. Great dignity. I like the way she speaks. You can tell she came from a good family.*

Meanwhile, Kat was studying Paige. *A rich girl who never had to work for anything in her life. She's gotten by on her looks.*

38

Honey was looking at the two of them. *They're so confident, so sure of themselves. They're going to have an easy time of it.*

They were all mistaken.

When they returned to their apartment, Paige was too excited to sleep. She lay in bed, thinking about the future. Outside her window, in the street, there was the sound of a car crash, and then people shouting, and in Paige's mind it dissolved into the memory of African natives yelling and chanting, and guns being fired. She was transported back in time, to the small jungle village in East Africa, caught in the middle of a deadly tribal war.

Paige was terrified. 'They're going to kill us!'

Her father took her in his arms. 'They won't harm us, darling. We're here to help them. They know we're their friends.'

And without warning, the chief of one of the tribes had burst into their hut . . .

Honey lay in bed thinking, *This is sure a long way from Memphis, Tennessee, Betty Lou. I guess I can never go back there. Never again.* She could hear the sheriff's voice saying to her, 'Out of respect for his family, we're going to list the death of the Reverend Douglas Lipton as a "suicide for reasons unknown," but I would suggest that you get the fuck out of this town fast, and stay out . . .'

*   *   *

Kat was staring out the window of her bedroom, listening to the sounds of the city. A voice inside her head whispered, *You made it . . . you made it . . . I showed them all they were wrong. You want to be a doctor? A black woman doctor? And the rejections from medical schools. 'Thank you for sending us your application. Unfortunately our enrollment is complete at this time.'*

'In view of your background, perhaps we might suggest that you would be happier at a smaller university.'

She had top grades, but out of twenty-five schools she had applied to, only one had accepted her. The dean of the school had said, 'In these days, it's nice to see someone who comes from a normal, decent background.'

If he had only known the terrible truth.

2

At five-thirty the following morning, when the new residents checked in, members of the hospital staff were standing by to guide them to their various assignments. Even at that early hour, the bedlam had begun.

The patients had been coming in all night, arriving in ambulances, and police cars, and on foot. The staff called them the 'F and J's'—the flotsam and jetsam that streamed into the emergency rooms, broken and bleeding, victims of shootings and stabbings and automobile accidents, the wounded in flesh and spirit, the homeless and the unwanted, the ebb and flow of humanity that streamed through the dark sewers of every large city.

There was a pervasive feeling of organized chaos, frenetic movements and shrill sounds and dozens of unexpected crises that all had to be attended to at once.

The new residents stood in a protective huddle, getting attuned to their new environment, listening to the arcane sounds around them.

Paige, Kat, and Honey were waiting in the corridor when a senior resident approached them. 'Which one of you is Dr Taft?'

Honey looked up and said, 'I am.'

The resident smiled and held out his hand. 'It's an honor to meet you. I've been asked to look out for you. Our chief of staff says that you have the highest medical school grades this hospital has ever seen. We're delighted to have you here.'

Honey smiled, embarrassed. 'Thank you.'

Kat and Paige looked at Honey in astonishment. *I wouldn't have guessed she was that brilliant*, Paige thought.

'You're planning to go into internal medicine, Dr Taft?'

'Yes.'

The resident turned to Kat. 'Dr Hunter?'

'Yes.'

'You're interested in neurosurgery.'

'I am.'

He consulted a list. 'You'll be assigned to Dr Lewis.'

The resident looked over at Paige. 'Dr Taylor?'

'Yes.'

'You're going into cardiac surgery.'

'That's right.'

'Fine. We'll assign you and Dr Hunter to surgical rounds. You can report to the head nurse's office. Margaret Spencer. Down the hall.'

'Thank you.'

Paige looked at the others and took a deep breath. 'Here I go! I wish us all luck!'

Margaret Spencer was more a battleship than a woman, heavyset and stern-looking, with a brusque manner. She was busy behind the nurses' station when Paige approached.

'Excuse me . . .'

Nurse Spencer looked up. 'Yes?'

'I was told to report here. I'm Dr Taylor.'

Nurse Spencer consulted a sheet. 'Just a moment.' She walked through a door and returned a minute later with some scrubs and a white coat.

'Here you are. The scrubs are to wear in the operating theater, and on rounds. And when you're doing rounds you put a white coat over the scrubs.'

'Thanks.'

'Oh. And here.' She reached down and handed Paige a metal tag that read 'Paige Taylor, M.D.' 'Here's your name tag, doctor.'

Paige held it in her hand and looked at it for a long time. *Paige Taylor, M.D.* She felt as though she had been handed the Medal of Honor. All the long hard years of work and study were summed up in those brief words. *Paige Taylor, M.D.*

Nurse Spencer was watching her. 'Are you all right?'

'I'm fine.' Paige smiled. 'I'm just fine, thank you. Where do I . . . ?'

'Doctors' dressing room is down the corridor to the left. You'll be making rounds, so you'll want to change.'

'Thank you.'

Paige walked down the corridor, amazed at the amount of activity around her. The corridor was crowded with doctors, nurses, technicians, and patients, hurrying to various destinations. The insistent chatter of the public address system added to the din.

'Dr Keenan . . . OR Three . . . Dr Keenan . . . OR Three.'

'Dr Talbot . . . Emergency Room One. Stat . . . Dr Talbot . . . Emergency Room One. Stat.'

'Dr Engel . . . Room 212 . . . Dr Engel . . . Room 212.'

Paige approached a door marked DOCTORS' DRESSING ROOM and opened it. Inside there were a dozen male doctors in various stages of undress. Two of them were totally naked. They turned to stare at Paige as the door opened.

'Oh! I . . . I'm sorry,' Paige mumbled, and quickly closed the door. She stood there, uncertain about what to do. A few feet down the corridor, she saw a door marked NURSES' DRESSING ROOM. Paige walked over to it and opened the door. Inside, several nurses were changing into their uniforms.

One of them looked up. 'Hello. Are you one of the new nurses?'

'No,' Paige said tightly. 'I'm not.' She closed the door and walked back to the doctors' dressing room. She stood there a moment, then took a deep breath and entered. The conversation came to a stop.

One of the men said, 'Sorry, honey. This room is for doctors.'

'I'm a doctor,' Paige said.

They turned to look at one another. 'Oh? Well, er . . . welcome.'

'Thank you.' She hesitated a moment, then walked over to an empty locker. The men watched as she put her hospital clothes into the locker. She looked at the men for a moment, then slowly started to unbutton her blouse.

The doctors stood there, not sure what to do. One of them said, 'Maybe we should—er—give the little lady some privacy, gentlemen.'

The little lady! 'Thank you,' Paige said. She stood there, waiting, as the doctors finished dressing and left the room. *Am I going to have to go through this every day?* she wondered.

In hospital rounds, there is a traditional formation that never varies. The attending physician is always in the lead, followed by the senior resident, then the other residents, and one or two medical students. The attending physician Paige had been assigned to was Dr William Radnor. Paige and five other residents were gathered in the hallway, waiting to meet him.

In the group was a young Chinese doctor. He held out his hand. 'Tom Chang,' he said. 'I hope you're all as nervous as I am.'

Paige liked him immediately.

A man was approaching the group. 'Good morning,' he said. 'I'm Dr Radnor.' He was soft-spoken, with sparkling blue eyes. Each resident introduced himself.

'This is your first day of rounds. I want you to pay close attention to everything you see and hear, but at the same time, it's important to appear relaxed.'

Paige made a mental note. *Pay close attention, but appear to be relaxed.*

'If the patients see that you're tense, *they're* going to be tense, and they'll probably think they're dying of some disease you aren't telling them about.'

Don't make patients tense.

'Remember, from now on, you're going to be responsible for the lives of other human beings.'

45

Now responsible for other lives. Oh, my God!

The longer Dr Radnor talked, the more nervous Paige became, and by the time he was finished, her self-confidence had completely vanished. *I'm not ready for this!* she thought. *I don't know what I'm doing. Who ever said I could be a doctor? What if I kill somebody?*

Dr Radnor was going on, 'I will expect detailed notes on each one of your patients—lab work, blood, electrolytes, everything. Is that clear?'

There were murmurs of 'Yes, doctor.'

'There are always thirty to forty surgical patients here at one time. It's your job to make sure that everything is properly organized for them. We'll start the morning rounds now. In the afternoon, we'll make the same rounds again.'

It had all seemed so easy at medical school. Paige thought about the four years she had spent there. There had been one hundred and fifty students, and only fifteen women. She would never forget the first day of Gross Anatomy class. The students had walked into a large white tiled room with twenty tables lined up in rows, each table covered with a yellow sheet. Five students were assigned to each table.

The professor had said, 'All right, pull back the sheets.' And there, in front of Paige, was her first cadaver. She had been afraid that she would faint or be sick, but she felt strangely calm. The cadaver had been preserved, which somehow removed it one step from humanity.

In the beginning the students had been hushed and

46

respectful in the anatomy laboratory. But, incredibly to Paige, within a week, they were eating sandwiches during the dissections, and making rude jokes. It was a form of self-defense, a denial of their own mortality. They gave the corpses names, and treated them like old friends. Paige tried to force herself to act as casually as the other students, but she found it difficult. She looked at the cadaver she was working on, and thought: *Here was a man with a home and a family. He went to an office every day, and once a year he took a vacation with his wife and children. He probably loved sports and enjoyed movies and plays, and he laughed and cried, and he watched his children grow up and he shared their joys and their sorrows, and he had big, wonderful dreams. I hope they all came true . . .* A bittersweet sadness engulfed her because he was dead and *she* was alive.

In time, even to Paige, the dissections became routine. *Open the chest, examine the ribs, lungs, pericardial sac covering the heart, the veins, arteries, and nerves.*

Much of the first two years of medical school was spent memorizing long lists that the students referred to as the Organ Recital: First the cranial nerves: olfactory, optic, oculomotor, trochlear, trigeminal, abducens, facial, auditory, glossopharyngeal, vagus, spinal, and hypoglossal.

The students used mnemonics to help them remember. The classic one was '*O*n *o*ld *O*lympus's *t*owering *t*ops, *a F*rench *a*nd *G*erman *v*ended *s*ome *h*ops.' The modern male version was '*O*h, *o*h, *o*h, *t*o *t*ouch *a*nd *f*eel *a* girl's *v*agina—*s*uch *h*eaven.'

The last two years of medical school were more

interesting, with courses in internal medicine, surgery, pediatrics, and obstetrics, and they worked at the local hospital. *I remember the time* . . . Paige was thinking.

'Dr Taylor . . .' The senior resident was staring at her.

Paige came to with a start. The others were already halfway down the corridor.

'Coming,' she said hastily.

The first stop was at a large, rectangular ward, with rows of beds on both sides of the room, with a small stand next to each bed. Paige had expected to see curtains separating the beds, but here there was no privacy.

The first patient was an elderly man with a sallow complexion. He was sound asleep, breathing heavily. Dr Radnor walked over to the foot of the bed, studied the chart there, then went to the patient's side and gently touched his shoulder. 'Mr Potter?'

The patient opened his eyes. 'Huh?'

'Good morning. I'm Dr Radnor. I'm just checking to see how you're doing. Did you have a comfortable night?'

'It was okay.'

'Do you have any pain?'

'Yeah. My chest hurts.'

'Let me take a look at it.'

When he finished the examination, he said, 'You're doing fine. I'll have the nurse give you something for the pain.'

'Thanks, doctor.'

'We'll be back to see you this afternoon.'

They moved away from the bed. Dr Radnor turned to the residents. 'Always try to ask questions that have a yes or no answer so the patient doesn't tire himself out. And reassure him about his progress. I want you to study his chart and make notes. We'll come back here this afternoon to see how he's doing. Keep a running record of every patient's chief complaint, present illness, past illnesses, family history, and social history. Does he drink, smoke, etc.? When we make the rounds again, I'll expect a report on the progress of each patient.'

They moved on to the bed of the next patient, a man in his forties.

'Good morning, Mr Rawlings.'

'Good morning, doctor.'

'Are you feeling better this morning?'

'Not so good. I was up a lot last night. My stomach's hurting.'

Dr Radnor turned to the senior resident. 'What did the proctoscopy show?'

'No sign of any problem.'

'Give him a barium enema and an upper GI, stat.'

The senior resident made a note.

The resident standing next to Paige whispered in her ear, 'I guess you know what stat stands for. "Shake that ass, tootsie!"'

Dr Radnor heard. '"Stat" comes from the Latin, *statim*. Immediately.'

In the years ahead, Paige was to hear it often.

The next patient was an elderly woman who had had a by-pass operation.

'Good morning, Mrs Turkel.'

'How long are you going to keep me in here?'

49

'Not very long. The procedure was a success. You'll be going home soon.'

And they moved on to the next patient.

The routine was repeated over and over, and the morning went by swiftly. They saw thirty patients. After each patient, the residents frantically scribbled notes, praying that they would be able to decipher them later.

One patient was a puzzle to Paige. She seemed to be in perfect health.

When they had moved away from her, Paige asked, 'What's her problem, doctor?'

Dr Radnor sighed. 'She has no problem. She's a gomer. And for those of you who forgot what you were taught in medical school, gomer is an acronym for "Get out of my emergency room!" Gomers are people who *enjoy* poor health. That's their hobby. I've admitted her six times in the last year.'

They moved on to the last patient, an old woman on a respirator, who was in a coma.

'She's had a massive heart attack,' Dr Radnor explained to the residents. 'She's been in a coma for six weeks. Her vital signs are failing. There's nothing more we can do for her. We'll pull the plug this afternoon.'

Paige looked at him in shock. 'Pull the plug?'

Dr Radnor said gently, 'The hospital ethics committee made the decision this morning. She's a vegetable. She's eighty-seven years old, and she's brain-dead. It's cruel to keep her alive, and it's breaking her family financially. I'll see you all at rounds this afternoon.'

They watched him walk away. Paige turned to look

at the patient again. She was alive. *In a few hours she will be dead. We'll pull the plug this afternoon.*

That's murder! Paige thought.

3

That afternoon, when the rounds were finished, the new residents gathered in the small upstairs lounge. The room held eight tables, an ancient black-and-white television set, and two vending machines that dispensed stale sandwiches and bitter coffee.

The conversations at each table were almost identical.

One of the residents said, 'Take a look at my throat, will you? Does it look raw to you?'

'I think I have a fever. I feel lousy.'

'My abdomen is swollen and tender. I know I have appendicitis.'

'I've got this crushing pain in my chest. I hope to God I'm not having a heart attack!'

Kat sat down at a table with Paige and Honey. 'How did it go?' she asked.

Honey said, 'I think it went all right.'

They both looked at Paige. 'I was tense, but I was relaxed. I was nervous, but I stayed calm.' She sighed. 'It's been a long day. I'll be glad to get out of here and have some fun tonight.'

'Me, too,' Kat agreed. 'Why don't we have dinner and then go see a movie?'

'Sounds great.'

An orderly approached their table. 'Dr Taylor?'

Paige looked up. 'I'm Dr Taylor.'

'Dr Wallace would like to see you in his office.'

The hospital administrator! *What have I done?* Paige wondered.

The orderly was waiting. 'Dr Taylor . . .'

'I'm coming.' She took a deep breath and got to her feet. 'I'll see you later.'

'This way, doctor.'

Paige followed the orderly into an elevator and rode up to the fifth floor, where Dr Wallace's office was located.

Benjamin Wallace was seated behind his desk. He glanced up as Paige walked in. 'Good afternoon, Dr Taylor.'

'Good afternoon.'

Wallace cleared his throat. 'Well! Your first day and you've already made quite an impression!'

Paige looked at him, puzzled. 'I . . . I don't understand.'

'I hear you had a little problem in the doctors' dressing room this morning.'

'Oh.' *So, that's what this is all about!*

Wallace looked at her and smiled. 'I suppose I'll have to make some arrangements for you and the other girls.'

'We're . . .' *We're not girls*, Paige started to say. 'We would appreciate that.'

'Meanwhile, if you don't want to dress with the nurses . . .'

'I'm not a nurse,' Paige said firmly. 'I'm a doctor.'

'Of course, of course. Well, we'll do something about accommodations for you, doctor.'

'Thank you.'

He handed Paige a sheet of paper. 'Meanwhile, this is your schedule. You'll be on call for the next

53

twenty-four hours, starting at six o'clock.' He looked at his watch. 'That's thirty minutes from now.'

Paige was looking at him in astonishment. Her day had started at five-thirty that morning. *'Twenty-four hours?'*

'Well, thirty-six, actually. Because you'll be starting rounds again in the morning.'

Thirty-six hours! I wonder if I can handle this.

She was soon to find out.

Paige went to look for Kat and Honey.

'I'm going to have to forget about dinner and a movie,' Paige said. 'I'm on a thirty-six-hour call.'

Kat nodded. 'We just got our bad news. I go on it tomorrow, and Honey goes on Wednesday.'

'It won't be so bad,' Paige said cheerfully. 'I understand there's an on-call room to sleep in. I'm going to enjoy this.'

She was wrong.

An orderly was leading Paige down a long corridor.

'Dr Wallace told me that I'll be on call for thirty-six hours,' Paige said. 'Do all the residents work those hours?'

'Only for the first three years,' the orderly assured her.

Great!

'But you'll have plenty of chance to rest, doctor.'

'I will?'

'In here. This is the on-call room.' He opened the door, and Paige stepped inside. The room resembled a monk's cell in some poverty-stricken monastery. It

54

contained nothing but a cot with a lumpy mattress, a cracked washbasin, and a bedside stand with a telephone on it. 'You can sleep here between calls.'

'Thanks.'

The calls began as Paige was in the coffee shop, just starting to have her dinner.

'Dr Taylor . . . ER Three . . . Dr Taylor . . . ER Three.'

And all the time she was pursued by nurses.

'We have a patient with a fractured rib . . .'

'Mr Henegan is complaining of chest pains . . .'

'The patient in Ward Two has a headache. Is it all right to give him an acetaminophen . . . ?'

At midnight, Paige had just managed to fall asleep when she was awakened by the telephone.

'Report to ER One.' It was a knife wound, and by the time Paige had taken care of it, it was one-thirty in the morning. At two-fifteen she was awakened again.

'Dr Taylor . . . Emergency Room Two. Stat.'

Paige said, groggily, 'Right.' *What did he say it meant? Shake that ass, tootsie.* She forced herself up and moved down the corridor to the emergency room. A patient had been brought in with a broken leg. He was screaming with pain.

'Get an X-ray,' Paige ordered. 'And give him Demerol, 50 milligrams.' She put her hand on the patient's arm. 'You're going to be fine. Try to relax.'

Over the PA system, a metallic disembodied voice said, 'Dr Taylor . . . Ward Three. Stat.'

Paige looked at the moaning patient, reluctant to leave him.

The voice came on again, 'Dr Taylor . . . Ward Three. Stat.'

'Coming,' Paige mumbled. She hurried out the door and down the corridor to Ward Three. A patient had vomited, aspirated, and was choking.

'He can't breathe,' the nurse said.

'Suction him,' Paige ordered. As she watched the patient begin to catch his breath, she heard her name again on the PA system. 'Dr Taylor . . . Ward Four. Ward Four.' Paige shook her head and ran down to Ward Four, to a screaming patient with abdominal spasms. Paige gave him a quick examination. 'It could be intestinal dysfunction. Get an ultrasound,' Paige said.

By the time she returned to the patient with the broken leg, the pain reliever had taken effect. She had him moved to the operating room and set the leg. As she was finishing, she heard her name again. 'Dr Taylor, report to Emergency Room Two. Stat.'

'The stomach ulcer in Ward Four is having a pain . . .'

At 3:30 A.M.: 'Dr Taylor, the patient in Room 310 is hemorrhaging . . .'

There was a heart attack in one of the wards, and Paige was nervously listening to the patient's heartbeat when she heard her name called over the PA system: 'Dr Taylor . . . ER Two. Stat . . . Dr Taylor . . . ER Two. Stat.'

I must not panic, Paige thought. *I've got to remain calm and cool.* She panicked. Who was more important, the patient she was examining, or the next patient? 'You stay here,' she said inanely. 'I'll be right back.'

As Paige hurried toward ER Two, she heard her name called again. 'Dr Taylor . . . ER One. Stat . . . Dr Taylor . . . ER One. Stat.'

Oh, my God! Paige thought. She felt as though she were caught up in the middle of some endless terrifying nightmare.

During what was left of the night, Paige was awakened to attend to a case of food poisoning, a broken arm, a hiatal hernia, and a fractured rib. By the time she stumbled back into the on-call room, she was so exhausted that she could hardly move. She crawled onto the little cot and had just started to doze off when the telephone rang.

She reached out for it with her eyes closed. 'H'lo . . .'

'Dr Taylor, we're waiting for you.'

'Wha'?' She lay there, trying to remember where she was.

'Your rounds are starting, doctor.'

'My rounds?' *This is some kind of bad joke*, Paige thought. *It's inhuman. They can't work anyone like this!* But they were waiting for her.

Ten minutes later, Paige was making the rounds again, half asleep. She stumbled against Dr Radnor. 'Excuse me,' she mumbled, 'but I haven't had any sleep . . .'

He patted her on the shoulder sympathetically. 'You'll get used to it.'

When Paige finally got off duty, she slept for fourteen straight hours.

*   *   *

The intense pressure and punishing hours proved to be too much for some of the residents, and they simply disappeared from the hospital. *That's not going to happen to me*, Paige vowed.

The pressure was unrelenting. At the end of one of Paige's shifts, thirty-six grueling hours, she was so exhausted that she had no idea where she was. She stumbled to the elevator and stood there, her mind numb.

Tom Chang came up to her. 'Are you all right?'

'Fine,' Paige mumbled.

He grinned. 'You look like hell.'

'Thanks. Why do they do this to us?' Paige asked.

Chang shrugged. 'The theory is that it keeps us in touch with our patients. If we go home and leave them, we don't know what's happening to them while we're gone.'

Paige nodded. 'That makes sense.' It made no sense at all. 'How can we take care of them if we're asleep on our feet?'

Chang shrugged again. 'I don't make the rules. It's the way all hospitals operate.' He looked at Paige more closely. 'Are you going to be able to make it home?'

Paige looked at him and said haughtily, 'Of course.'

'Take care.' Chang disappeared down the corridor.

Paige waited for the elevator to arrive. When it finally came, she was standing there, sound asleep.

Two days later, Paige was having breakfast with Kat.

'Do you want to hear a terrible confession?' Paige

asked. 'Sometimes when they wake me up at four o'clock in the morning to give somebody an aspirin, and I'm stumbling down the hall, half conscious, and I pass the rooms where all the patients are tucked in and having a good night's sleep, I feel like banging on all the doors and yelling, "Everybody wake up!"'

Kat held out her hand. 'Join the club.'

The patients came in all shapes, sizes, ages, and colors. They were frightened, brave, gentle, arrogant, demanding, considerate. They were human beings in pain.

Most of the doctors were dedicated people. As in any profession, there were good doctors and bad doctors. They were young and old, clumsy and adept, pleasant and nasty. A few of them, at one time or another, made sexual advances to Paige. Some were subtle and some were crude.

'Don't you ever feel lonely at night? I know that I do. I was wondering . . .'

'These hours are murder, aren't they? Do you know what I find gives me energy? Good sex. Why don't we . . . ?'

'My wife is out of town for a few days. I have a cabin near Carmel. This weekend we could . . .'

And the patients.

'So you're my doctor, eh? You know what would cure me . . . ?'

'Come closer to the bed, baby. I want to see if those are real . . .'

Paige gritted her teeth and ignored them all. *When Alfred and I are married, this will stop.* And just the thought of Alfred gave her a glow. He would be returning from Africa soon. *Soon*.

One morning before rounds, Paige and Kat talked about the sexual harassment they were experiencing.

'Most of the doctors behave like perfect gentlemen, but a few of them seem to think we're perks that go with the territory, and that we're there to service them,' Kat said. 'I don't think a week goes by but what one of the doctors hits on me. "Why don't you come over to my place for a drink? I've got some great CDs." Or in the OR, when I'm assisting, the surgeon will brush his arm across my breast. One moron said to me, "You know, whenever I order chicken, I like the dark meat."'

Paige sighed. 'They think they're flattering us by treating us as sex objects. I'd rather they treated us as doctors.'

'A lot of them don't even want us around. They either want to fuck us or they want to fuck us. You know, it's not fair. Women are judged inferior until we prove ourselves, and men are judged superior until they prove what assholes they are.'

'It's the old boys' network,' Paige said. 'If there were more of us, we could start a new girls' network.'

Paige had heard of Arthur Kane. He was the subject of constant gossip around the hospital. His nickname was Dr 007—licensed to kill. His solution to every problem was to operate, and he had a higher rate of operations than any other doctor at the hospital. He also had a higher mortality rate.

He was bald, short, hawk-nosed, with tobacco-stained teeth, and was grossly overweight. Incredibly, he fancied himself a ladies' man. He liked to refer to the new nurses and female residents as 'fresh meat'.

Paige Taylor was fresh meat. He saw her in the upstairs lounge and sat down at her table, uninvited.

'I've been keeping an eye on you.'

Paige looked up, startled. 'I beg your pardon?'

'I'm Dr Kane. My friends call me Arthur.' There was a leer in his voice.

Paige wondered how many friends he had.

'How are you getting along here?'

The question caught Paige off guard. 'I . . . all right, I think.'

He leaned forward. 'This is a big hospital. It's easy to get lost here. Do you know what I mean?'

Paige said warily, 'Not exactly.'

'You're too pretty to be just another face in the crowd. If you want to get somewhere here, you need someone to help you. Someone who knows the ropes.'

The conversation was getting more unpleasant by the minute.

'And you'd like to help me.'

'Right.' He bared his tobacco-stained teeth. 'Why don't we discuss it at dinner?'

'There's nothing to discuss, Dr Kane,' Paige said. 'I'm not interested.'

Arthur Kane watched Paige get up and walk away, and there was a baleful expression on his face.

*   *   *

First-year surgical residents were on a two-month rotation schedule, alternating among obstetrics, orthopedics, urology, and surgery.

Paige learned that it was dangerous to go into a training hospital in the summer for any serious illness, because many of the staff doctors were on vacation and the patients were at the mercy of the inexperienced young residents.

Nearly all surgeons liked to have music in the operating room. One of the doctors was nicknamed Mozart and another Axl Rose because of their tastes in music.

For some reason, operations always seemed to make everyone hungry. They constantly discussed food. A surgeon would be in the middle of removing a gangrenous gallbladder from a patient and say, 'I had a great dinner last night at Bardelli's. Best Italian food in all of San Francisco.'

'Have you eaten the crab cakes at the Cypress Club?'

'If you like good beef, try the House of Prime Rib over on Van Ness.'

And meanwhile, a nurse would be mopping up the patient's blood.

When they weren't talking about food, the doctors talked about baseball or football scores.

'Did you see the 49ers play last Sunday? I bet they miss Joe Montana. He always came through for them in the last two minutes of a game.'

And out would come a ruptured appendix.

Kafka, Paige thought. *Kafka would have loved this.*

*   *   *

At three in the morning when Paige was asleep in the on-call room, she was awakened by the telephone.

A raspy voice said, 'Dr Taylor — Room 419 — a heart attack patient. You'll have to hurry!' The line went dead.

Paige sat on the edge of the bed, fighting sleep, and stumbled to her feet. *You have to hurry!* She went into the corridor, but there was no time to wait for an elevator. She rushed up the stairs and ran down the fourth-floor corridor to Room 419, her heart pounding. She flung open the door and stood there, staring.

Room 419 was a storage room.

Kat Hunter was making her rounds with Dr Richard Hutton. He was in his forties, brusque and fast. He spent no more than two or three minutes with each patient, scanning their charts, then snapping out orders to the surgical residents in a machine-gun, staccato fashion.

'Check her hemoglobin and schedule surgery for tomorrow . . .'

'Keep a close eye on his temperature chart . . .'

'Cross-match four units of blood . . .'

'Remove these stitches . . .'

'Get some chest films . . .'

Kat and the other residents were busily making notes on everything, trying hard to keep up with him.

They approached a patient who had been in the hospital a week and had had a battery of tests for a high fever, with no results.

When they were out in the corridor, Kat asked, 'What's the matter with him?'

'It's a GOK,' a resident said. 'A God only knows. We've done X-rays, CAT scans, MRIs, spinal taps, liver biopsy. Everything. We don't know what's wrong with him.'

They moved into a ward where a young patient, his head bandaged after an operation, was sleeping. As Dr Hutton started to unwrap the head dressing, the patient woke up, startled. 'What . . . what's going on?'

'Sit up,' Dr Hutton said curtly. The young man was trembling.

I'll never treat my patients that way, Kat vowed.

The next patient was a healthy-looking man in his seventies. As soon as Dr Hutton approached the bed, the patient yelled, '*Gonzo!* I'm going to sue you, you dirty son of a bitch.'

'Now, Mr Sparolini . . .'

'Don't Mr Sparolini me! You turned me into a fucking eunuch.'

That's an oxymoron, Kat thought.

'Mr Sparolini, you agreed to have the vasectomy, and—'

'It was my wife's idea. Damn bitch! Just wait till I get home.'

They left him muttering to himself.

'What's his problem?' one of the residents asked.

'His problem is that he's a horny old goat. His young wife has six kids and she doesn't want any more.'

Next was a little girl, ten years old. Dr Hutton looked at her chart. 'We're going to give you a shot to make the bad bugs go away.'

A nurse filled a syringe and moved toward the little girl.

'No!' she screamed. 'You're going to hurt me!'

'This won't hurt, baby,' the nurse assured her.

The words were a dark echo in Kat's mind.

This won't hurt, baby . . . It was the voice of her stepfather whispering to her in the scary dark.

'This will feel good. Spread your legs. Come on, you little bitch!' And he had pushed her legs apart and forced his male hardness into her and put his hand over her mouth to keep her from screaming with the pain. She was thirteen years old. After that, his visits became a terrifying nightly ritual. 'You're lucky you got a man like me to teach you how to fuck,' he would tell her. 'Do you know what a Kat is? A little pussy. And I want some.' And he would fall on top of her and grab her, and no amount of crying or pleading would make him stop.

Kat had never known her father. Her mother was a cleaning woman who worked nights at an office building near their tiny apartment in Gary, Indiana. Kat's stepfather was a huge man who had been injured in an accident at a steel mill, and he stayed home most of the time, drinking. At night, when Kat's mother left for work, he would go into Kat's room. 'You say anything to your mother or brother, and I'll kill him,' he told Kat. *I can't let him hurt Mike*, Kat thought. Her brother was five years younger than she, and Kat adored him. She mothered him and protected him and fought his battles for him. He was the only bright spot in Kat's life.

One morning, terrified as Kat was by her step-father's threats, she decided she had to tell her mother what was happening. Her mother would put a stop to it, would protect her.

'Mama, your husband comes to my bed at night when you're away, and forces himself on me.'

Her mother stared at her a moment, then slapped Kat hard across the face.

'Don't you dare make up lies like that, you little slut!'

Kat never discussed it again. The only reason she stayed at home was Mike. *He'd be lost without me*, Kat thought. But the day she learned she was pregnant, she ran away to live with an aunt in Minneapolis. From then, her life completely changed.

'You don't have to tell me what happened,' her Aunt Sophie had said. 'You know that song they sing on *Sesame Street*? "It's Not Easy Being Green"? Well, honey, it's not easy being black, either. You have two choices. You can keep running and hiding and blaming the world for your problems, or you can stand up for yourself and decide to be somebody important.'

'How do I do that?'

'By *knowing* that you're important. First, you get an image in your mind of who you want to be, child, and what you want to be. And then you go to work, *becoming* that person.'

'I'm not going to have his baby,' Kat decided. 'I want an abortion.'

It was arranged quietly, during a weekend, and it was performed by a midwife who was a friend of Kat's aunt. When it was over, Kat thought fiercely,

I'm never going to let a man touch me again. Never!

Minneapolis was a fairyland for Kat. Within a few blocks of almost every home were lakes and streams and rivers. And there were over eight thousand acres of landscaped parks. She went sailing on the city lakes and took boat rides on the Mississippi.

She visited the Great Zoo with Aunt Sophie and spent Sundays at the Valleyfair Amusement Park. She went on the hay rides at Cedar Creek Farm, and watched knights in armor jousting at the Shakopee Renaissance Festival.

Aunt Sophie watched Kat and thought, *The girl has never had a childhood.*

Kat was learning to enjoy herself, but Aunt Sophie sensed that deep inside her niece was a place that no one could reach, a barrier she had set up to keep her from being hurt again.

She made friends at school. But never with boys. Her girlfriends were all dating, but Kat was a loner, and too proud to tell anyone why. She looked up to her aunt, whom she loved very much.

Kat had taken little interest in school, or in reading books, but Aunt Sophie changed all that. Her home was filled with books, and Sophie's excitement about them was contagious.

'There are wonderful worlds in there,' she told the young girl. 'Read, and you'll learn where you came from and where you're going. I've got a feeling that you're going to be famous one day, baby. But you have to get an education first. This is America. You can become anybody you want to be. You may be black and poor, but so were some of our congresswomen, and movie stars, and scientists, and sports legends. One day we're going to have a black president. You can be anything you want to be. It's up to you.'

It was the beginning.

Kat became the top student in her class. She was an avid reader. In the school library one day, she happened to pick up a copy of Sinclair Lewis's *Arrowsmith*, and she was fascinated by the story of the dedicated young doctor. She read Agnes Cooper's *Promises to Keep*, and *Woman Surgeon* by Dr Else Roe, and it opened up a whole new world for her. She discovered that there were people on this earth who devoted themselves to helping others, to saving lives. When Kat came home from school one day, she said to Aunt Sophie, 'I'm going to be a doctor. A famous one.'

4

On Monday morning, three of Paige's patients' charts were missing, and Paige was blamed.

On Wednesday, Paige was awakened at 4:00 A.M. in the on-call room. Sleepily, she picked up the telephone. 'Dr Taylor.'

Silence.

'Hello . . . hello.'

She could hear breathing at the other end of the line. And then there was a click.

Paige lay awake for the rest of the night.

In the morning, Paige said to Kat, 'I'm either becoming paranoid or someone hates me.' She told Kat what had happened.

'Patients sometimes get grudges against doctors,' Kat said. 'Can you think of anyone who . . . ?'

Paige sighed. 'Dozens.'

'I'm sure there's nothing to worry about.'

Paige wished that she could believe it.

In late summer the magic telegram arrived. It was waiting for Paige when she returned to the apartment late at night. It read: 'Arriving San Francisco noon Sunday. Can't wait to see you. Love, Alfred.'

He was finally on his way back to her! Paige read the telegram again and again, her excitement

growing each time. *Alfred!* His name conjured up
a tumbling kaleidoscope of exciting memories . . .

Paige and Alfred had grown up together. Their
fathers were part of a medical cadre of WHO that
traveled to Third World countries, fighting exotic
and virulent diseases. Paige and her mother accompanied Dr Taylor, who headed the team.

Paige and Alfred had had a fantasy childhood. In
India, Paige learned to speak Hindi. At the age of
two, she knew that the name for the bamboo hut
they lived in was *basha*. Her father was *gorashaib*,
a white man, and she was *nani*, a little sister. They
addressed Paige's father as *abadhan*, the leader, or
baba, father.

When Paige's parents were not around, she drank
bhanga, an intoxicating drink made with hashish
leaves, and ate *chapati* with *ghi*.

And then they were on their way to Africa. Off
to another adventure!

Paige and Alfred became used to swimming and
bathing in rivers that had crocodiles and hippopota-
muses. Their pets were baby zebras and cheetahs
and snakes. They grew up in windowless round
huts made of wattle and daub, with packed dirt
floors and conical thatched roofs. *Someday*, Paige
vowed to herself, *I'm going to live in a real house,
a beautiful cottage with a green lawn and a white
picket fence*.

To the doctors and nurses, it was a difficult, frus-
trating life. But to the two children, it was a constant
adventure, living in the land of lions, giraffes, and
elephants. They went to primitive cinder-block

70

schoolhouses, and when none was available, they had tutors.

Paige was a bright child, and her mind was a sponge, absorbing everything. Alfred adored her.

'I'm going to marry you one day, Paige,' he said when she was twelve, he fourteen.

'I'm going to marry you, too, Alfred.'

They were two serious children, determined to spend the rest of their lives together.

The doctors from WHO were selfless, dedicated men and women who devoted their lives to their work. They often worked under nearly impossible circumstances. In Africa, they had to compete with *wogesha*—the native medical practitioners whose primitive remedies were passed on from father to son, and often had deadly effects. The Masai's traditional remedy for flesh wounds was *olkilorite*, a mixture of cattle blood, raw meat, and essence of a mysterious root.

The Kikuyu remedy for smallpox was to have children drive out the sickness with sticks.

'You must stop that,' Dr Taylor would tell them. 'It doesn't help.'

'Better than having you stick sharp needles in our skin,' they would reply.

The dispensaries were tables lined up under the trees, for surgery. The doctors saw hundreds of patients a day, and there was always a long line, waiting to see them—lepers, natives with tubercular lungs, whooping cough, smallpox, dysentery.

Paige and Alfred were inseparable. As they grew older, they would walk to the market together, to a village miles away. And they would talk about their plans for the future.

71

Medicine was a part of Paige's early life. She learned to care for patients, to give shots and dispense medications, and she anticipated ways to help her father.

Paige loved her father. Curt Taylor was the most caring, selfless man she had ever known. He genuinely liked people, dedicating his life to helping those who needed him, and he instilled that passion in Paige. In spite of the long hours he worked, he managed to find time to spend with his daughter. He made the discomfort of the primitive places they lived in fun.

Paige's relationship with her mother was something else. Her mother was a beauty from a wealthy social background. Her cool aloofness kept Paige at a distance. Marrying a doctor who was going to work in far-off exotic places had seemed romantic to her, but the harsh reality had embittered her. She was not a warm, loving woman, and she seemed to Paige always to be complaining.

'Why did we ever have to come to this godforsaken place, Curt?'

'The people here live like animals. We're going to catch some of their awful diseases.'

'Why can't you practice medicine in the United States and make money like other doctors?'

And on and on it went.

The more her mother criticized him, the more Paige adored her father.

When Paige was fifteen years old, her mother disappeared with the owner of a large cocoa plantation in Brazil.

'She's not coming back, is she?' Paige asked.

'No, darling. I'm sorry.'

'I'm glad!' She had not meant to say that. She was hurt that her mother had cared so little for her and her father that she had abandoned them.

The experience made Paige draw even closer to Alfred Turner. They played games together and went on expeditions together, and shared their dreams.

'I'm going to be a doctor, too, when I grow up,' Alfred confided. 'We'll get married, and we'll work together.'

'And we'll have lots of children!'

'Sure. If you like.'

On the night of Paige's sixteenth birthday, their lifelong emotional intimacy exploded into a new dimension. At a little village in East Africa, the doctors had been called away on an emergency, because of an epidemic, and Paige, Alfred, and a cook were the only ones left in camp.

They had had dinner and gone to bed. But in the middle of the night Paige had been awakened in her tent by the faraway thunder of stampeding animals. She lay there, and as the minutes went by and the sound of the stampede came closer, she began to grow afraid. Her breath quickened. There was no telling when her father and the others would return.

She got up. Alfred's tent was only a few feet away. Terrified, Paige got up, raised the flap of the tent, and ran to Alfred's tent.

He was asleep.

'Alfred!'

He sat up, instantly awake. 'Paige? Is anything wrong?'

'I'm frightened. Could I get into bed with you for a while?'

'Sure.' They lay there, listening to the animals charging through the brush.

In a few minutes, the sounds began to die away.

Alfred became conscious of Paige's warm body lying next to him.

'Paige, I think you'd better go back to your tent.'

Paige could feel his male hardness pressing against her.

All the physical needs that had been building up within them came boiling to the surface.

'Alfred.'

'Yes?' His voice was husky.

'We're getting married, aren't we?'

'Yes.'

'Then it's all right.'

And the sounds of the jungle around them disappeared, and they began to explore and discover a world no one had ever possessed but themselves. They were the first lovers in the world, and they gloried in the wonderful miracle of it.

At dawn, Paige crept back to her tent and she thought, happily, *I'm a woman now*.

From time to time, Curt Taylor suggested to Paige that she return to the United States to live with his brother in his beautiful home in Deerfield, north of Chicago.

'Why?' Paige would ask.

'So that you can grow up to be a proper young lady.'

'I *am* a proper young lady.'

'Proper young ladies don't tease wild monkeys and try to ride baby zebras.'

Her answer was always the same. 'I won't leave you.'

When Paige was seventeen, the WHO team went to a jungle village in South Africa to fight a typhoid epidemic. Making the situation even more perilous was the fact that shortly after the doctors arrived, war broke out between two local tribes. Curt Taylor was warned to leave.

'I can't, for God's sake. I have patients who will die if I desert them.'

Four days later, the village came under attack. Paige and her father huddled in their little hut, listening to the yelling and the sounds of gunfire outside.

Paige was terrified. 'They're going to kill us!'

Her father had taken her in his arms. 'They won't harm us, darling. We're here to help them. They know we're their friends.'

And he had been right.

The chief of one of the tribes had burst into the hut with some of his warriors. 'Do not worry. We guard you.' And they had.

The fighting and shooting finally stopped, but in the morning Curt Taylor made a decision.

He sent a message to his brother. *Sending Paige out on next plane. Will wire details. Please meet her at airport.*

Paige was furious when she heard the news. She was taken, sobbing wildly, to the dusty little airport where a Piper Cub was waiting to fly her to a town where she could catch a plane to Johannesburg.

'You're sending me away because you want to get rid of me!' she cried.

Her father held her close in his arms. 'I love you more than anything in the world, baby. I'll miss you every minute. But I'll be going back to the States soon, and we'll be together again.'

'Promise?'

'Promise.'

Alfred was there to see Paige off.

'Don't worry,' Alfred told Paige. 'I'll come and get you as soon as I can. Will you wait for me?'

It was a pretty silly question, after all those years.

'Of course I will.'

Three days later, when Paige's plane arrived at O'Hare Airport in Chicago, Paige's Uncle Richard was there to greet her. Paige had never met him. All she knew about him was that he was a very wealthy businessman whose wife had died several years earlier. 'He's the successful one in the family,' Paige's father always said.

Paige's uncle's first words stunned her. 'I'm sorry to tell you this, Paige, but I just received word that your father was killed in a native uprising.'

Her whole world had been shattered in an instant. The ache was so strong that she did not think she could bear it. *I won't let my uncle see me cry*, Paige vowed. *I won't. I never should have left. I'm going back there*.

Driving from the airport, Paige stared out the window, looking at the heavy traffic.

'I hate Chicago.'

76

'Why, Paige?'

'It's a jungle.'

Richard would not permit Paige to return to Africa and her father's funeral, and that infuriated her.

He tried to reason with her. 'Paige, they've already buried your father. There's no point in your going back.'

But there was a point: *Alfred was there.*

A few days after Paige arrived, her uncle sat down with her to discuss her future.

'There's nothing to discuss,' Paige informed him. 'I'm going to be a doctor.'

At twenty-one, when Paige finished college, she applied to ten medical schools and was accepted by all of them. She chose a school in Boston.

It took two days to reach Alfred by telephone in Zaire, where he was working part-time with a WHO unit.

When Paige told him the news, he said, 'That's wonderful, darling. I'm nearly finished with my medical courses. I'll stay with WHO for a while, but in a few years we'll be practicing together.'

Together. The magical word.

'Paige, I'm desperate to see you. If I can get out for a few days, could you meet me in Hawaii?'

There wasn't the slightest hesitation. 'Yes.'

And they had both managed it. Later, Paige could only imagine how difficult it must have been for Alfred to make the long journey, but he never mentioned it.

They spent three incredible days at a small hotel in Hawaii, called Sunny Cove, and it was as though they had never been apart. Paige wanted so much to ask Alfred to go back to Boston with her, but she knew how selfish that would have been. The work that he was doing was far more important.

On their last day together, as they were getting dressed, Paige asked, 'Where will they be sending you, Alfred?'

'Gambia, or maybe Bangladesh.'

To save lives, to help those who so desperately need him. She held him tightly and closed her eyes. She never wanted to let him go.

As though reading her thoughts, he said, 'I'll never let you get away.'

Paige started medical school, and she and Alfred corresponded regularly. No matter in what part of the world he was, Alfred managed to telephone Paige on her birthday and at Christmas. Just before New Year's Eve, when Paige was in her second year of school, Alfred telephoned.

'Paige?'

'Darling! Where are you?'

'I'm in Senegal. I figured out it's only eighty-eight hundred miles from the Sunny Cove hotel.'

It took a minute for it to sink in.

'Do you mean . . . ?'

'Can you meet me in Hawaii for New Year's Eve?'

'Oh, yes! Yes!'

Alfred traveled nearly halfway round the world to meet her, and this time the magic was even stronger. Time had stood still for both of them.

'Next year I'll be in charge of my own cadre at WHO,' Alfred said. 'When you finish school, I want us to get married . . .'

They were able to get together once more, and when they weren't able to meet, their letters spanned time and space.

All those years he had worked as a doctor in Third World countries, like his father and Paige's father, doing the wonderful work that they did. And now, at last, he was coming home to her.

As Paige read Alfred's telegram for the fifth time, she thought, *He's coming to San Francisco!*

Kat and Honey were in their bedrooms, asleep. Paige shook them awake. 'Alfred's coming! He's coming! He'll be here Sunday!'

'Wonderful,' Kat mumbled. 'Why don't you wake me up Sunday? I just got to bed.'

Honey was more responsive. She sat up and said, 'That's great! I'm dying to meet him. How long since you've seen him?'

'Two years,' Paige said, 'but we've always stayed in touch.'

'You're a lucky girl,' Kat sighed. 'Well, we're all awake now. I'll put on some coffee.'

The three of them sat around the kitchen table.

'Why don't we give Alfred a party?' Honey suggested. 'Kind of a "Welcome to the Groom" party.'

'That's a good idea,' Kat agreed.

'We'll make it a real celebration—a cake, balloons—the works!'

'We'll cook dinner for him here,' Honey said.

Kat shook her head. 'I've tasted your cooking. Let's send out for food.'

Sunday was four days away, and they spent all their spare time discussing Alfred's arrival. By some miracle, the three of them were off duty on Sunday.

Saturday, Paige managed to get to a beauty salon. She went shopping and splurged on a new dress.

'Do I look all right? Do you think he'll like it?'

'You look sensational!' Honey assured her. 'I hope he deserves you.'

Paige smiled. 'I hope I deserve *him*. You'll love him. He's fantastic!'

On The Sunday, an elaborate lunch they had ordered was laid out on the dining-room table, with a bottle of iced champagne. The women stood around, nervously waiting for Alfred's arrival.

At two o'clock, the doorbell rang, and Paige ran to the door to open it. There was Alfred. A bit tired-looking, a little thinner. But he was her Alfred. Standing next to him was a brunette who appeared to be in her thirties.

'Paige!' Alfred exclaimed.

Paige threw her arms around him. Then she turned to Honey and Kat and said proudly, 'This is Alfred Turner. Alfred, these are my roommates, Honey Taft and Kat Hunter.'

'Pleased to meet you,' Alfred said. He turned to the woman at his side. 'And this is Karen Turner. My wife.'

The three women stood there, frozen.

Paige said slowly, 'Your wife?'

'Yes.' He frowned. 'Didn't . . . didn't you get my letter?'

'Letter?'

'Yes. I sent it several weeks ago.'

'No . . .'

'Oh. I . . . I'm terribly sorry. I explained it all in my . . . but of course, if you didn't get the . . .' His voice trailed off. 'I'm really sorry, Paige. You and I have been apart so long, that I . . . and then I met Karen . . . and you know how it is . . .'

'I know how it is,' Paige said numbly. She turned to Karen and forced a smile. 'I . . . I hope you and Alfred will be very happy.'

'Thank you.'

There was an awkward silence.

Karen said, 'I think we had better go, darling.'

'Yes. I think you had,' Kat said.

Alfred ran his fingers through his hair. 'I'm really sorry, Paige. I . . . well . . . goodbye.'

'Goodbye, Alfred.'

The three women stood there, watching the departing newlyweds.

'That bastard!' Kat said. 'What a lousy thing to do.'

Paige's eyes were brimming with tears. 'I . . . he didn't mean to . . . I mean . . . he must have explained everything in his letter.'

Honey put her arms around Paige. 'There ought to be a law that all men should be castrated.'

'I'll drink to that,' Kat said.

'Excuse me,' Paige said. She hurried to her bedroom and closed the door behind her.

She did not come out for the rest of the day.

5

During the next few months, Paige saw very little of Kat and Honey. They would have a hurried breakfast in the cafeteria and occasionally pass one another in the corridors. They communicated mainly by leaving notes in the apartment.

'Dinner is in the fridge.'

'The microwave is out.'

'Sorry, I didn't have time to clean up.'

'What about the three of us having dinner out Saturday night?'

The impossible hours continued to be a punishment, testing the limits of endurance for all the residents.

Paige welcomed the pressure. It gave her no time to think about Alfred and the wonderful future they had planned together. And yet, she could not get him out of her mind. What he had done filled her with a deep pain that refused to go away. She tortured herself with the futile game of 'what if?'

What if I had stayed with Alfred in Africa?

What if he had come to Chicago with me?

What if he had not met Karen?

What if . . . ?

*   *   *

On a Friday when Paige went into the change room to put on her scrubs, the word 'bitch' had been written on them with a black marker pen.

The following day when Paige went to look for her scut book, it was gone. All her notes had disappeared. *Maybe I misplaced it*, Paige thought.

But she couldn't make herself believe it.

The world outside the hospital ceased to exist. Paige was aware that Iraq was pillaging Kuwait, and that was overshadowed by the needs of a fifteen-year-old patient who was dying of leukemia. The day East and West Germany became united, Paige was busy trying to save the life of a diabetic patient. Margaret Thatcher resigned as prime minister of Great Britain, but more important, the patient in 214 was able to walk again.

What made it bearable were the doctors Paige worked with. With few exceptions, they had dedicated themselves to healing others, relieving pain, and saving lives. Paige watched the miracles they performed every day, and it filled her with a sense of pride.

The greatest stress was working in the ER. The emergency room was constantly overcrowded with people suffering every form of trauma imaginable.

The long hours at the hospital and the pressures placed an enormous strain on the doctors and nurses who worked there. The divorce rate among the doctors was extraordinarily high, and extramarital affairs were common.

Tom Chang was one of those having a problem. He told Paige about it over coffee.

'I can handle the hours,' Chang confided, 'but my wife can't. She complains that she never sees me anymore and that I'm a stranger to our little girl. She's right. I don't know what to do about it.'

'Has your wife visited the hospital?'

'No.'

'Why don't you invite her here for lunch, Tom? Let her see what you're doing here and how important it is.'

Chang brightened. 'That's a good idea. Thanks, Paige. I will. I would like you to meet her. Will you join us for lunch?'

'I'd love to.'

Chang's wife, Sye, turned out to be a lovely young woman with a classic, timeless beauty. Chang showed her around the hospital, and afterward they had lunch in the cafeteria with Paige.

Chang had told Paige that Sye had been born and raised in Hong Kong.

'How do you like San Francisco?' Paige asked.

There was a small silence. 'It's an interesting city,' Sye said politely, 'but I feel as though I am a stranger here. It is too big, too noisy.'

'But I understand Hong Kong is also big and noisy.'

'I come from a small village an hour away from Hong Kong. There, there is no noise and no automobiles, and everyone knows his neighbors.' She looked at her husband. 'Tom and I and our little daughter were very happy there. It is very beautiful on the island of Lamma. It has white beaches and small farms, and nearby is a little fishing village, Sak Kwu Wan. It is so peaceful.'

Her voice was filled with a wistful nostalgia. 'My husband and I were together much of the time, as a family should be. Here, I never see him.'

Paige said, 'Mrs Chang, I know it's difficult for you right now, but in a few years, Tom will be able to set up his own practice, and then his hours will be much easier.'

Tom Chang took his wife's hand. 'You see? Everything will be fine, Sye. You must be patient.'

'I understand,' she said. There was no conviction in her voice.

As they talked, a man walked into the cafeteria, and as he stood at the door, Paige could see only the back of his head. Her heart started to race. He turned around. It was a complete stranger.

Chang was watching Paige. 'Are you all right?'

'Yes,' Paige lied. *I've got to forget him. It's over.* And yet, the memories of all those wonderful years, the fun, the excitement, the love they had for each other . . . *How do I forget all that? I wonder if I could persuade any of the doctors here to do a lobotomy on me.*

Paige ran into Honey in the corridor. Honey was out of breath and looked worried.

'Is everything all right?' Paige asked.

Honey smiled uneasily. 'Yes. Fine.' She hurried on.

Honey had recently been assigned to an attending

physician named Charles Isler, who was known around the hospital as a martinet.

On Honey's first day of rounds, he had said, 'I've been looking forward to working with you, Dr Taft. Dr Wallace has told me about your outstanding record at medical school. I understand you're going to practice internal medicine.'

'Yes.'

'Good. So, we'll have you here for three more years.'

They began their rounds.

The first patient was a young Mexican boy. Dr Isler ignored the other residents and turned to Honey. 'I think you'll find this an interesting case, Dr Taft. The patient has all the classic signs and symptoms: anorexia, weight loss, metallic taste, fatigue, anemia, hyperirritability, and unco-ordination. How would you diagnose it?' He smiled expectantly.

Honey looked at him for a moment. 'Well, it could be several things, couldn't it?'

Dr Isler was watching her, puzzled. 'It's a clear-cut case of—'

One of the other residents broke in, 'Lead poisoning?'

'That's right,' Dr Isler said.

Honey smiled. 'Of course. Lead poisoning.'

Dr Isler turned to Honey again. 'How would you treat it?'

Honey said evasively, 'Well, there are several different methods of treatment, aren't there?'

A second resident spoke up. 'If the patient has had long-term exposure, he should be treated as a potential case of encephalopathy.'

Dr Isler nodded. 'Right. That's what we're doing. We're correcting the dehydration and electrolyte disturbances, and giving him chelation therapy.'

He looked at Honey. She nodded in agreement.

The next patient was a man in his eighties. His eyes were red and his eyelids were nearly stuck together.

'We'll have your eyes taken care of in a moment,' Dr Isler assured him. 'How are you feeling?'

'Oh, not too bad for an old man.'

Dr Isler pulled aside the blanket to reveal the patient's swollen knee and ankle. There were lesions on the soles of his feet.

Dr Isler turned to the residents. 'The swelling is caused by arthritis.' He looked at Honey. 'Combined with the lesions and the conjunctivitis, I'm sure you know what the diagnosis is.'

Honey said slowly, 'Well, it could be . . . you know . . .'

'It's Reiter's syndrome,' one of the residents spoke up. 'The cause is unknown. It's usually accompanied by low-grade fever.'

Dr Isler nodded. 'That's right.' He looked at Honey. 'What is the prognosis?'

'The prognosis?'

The resident replied. 'The prognosis is unclear. It can be treated with anti-inflammation drugs.'

'Very good,' Dr Isler said.

They made the rounds of a dozen more patients, and when they were finished, Honey said to Dr Isler, 'Could I see you for a moment alone, Dr Isler?'

'Yes. Come into my office.'

When they were seated in his office, Honey said, 'I know you're disappointed in me.'

'I must admit that I was a little surprised that you —'

Honey interrupted. 'I know, Dr Isler. I didn't close my eyes last night. To tell you the truth, I was so excited about working with you that I . . . I just couldn't sleep.'

He looked at her in surprise. 'Oh. I see. I knew there had to be a reason for . . . I mean, your medical school record was so fantastic. What made you decide to become a doctor?'

Honey looked down for a moment, then said softly, 'I had a younger brother who was injured in an accident. The doctors did everything they could to try to save him . . . but I watched him die. It took a long time, and I felt so helpless. I decided then that I was going to spend my life helping other people get well.' Her eyes welled up with tears.

She's so vulnerable, Isler thought. 'I'm glad we had this little talk.'

Honey looked at him and thought, *He believed me*.

88

6

Across town, in another part of the city, reporters and TV crews were waiting in the street for Lou Dinetto as he left the courtroom, smiling and waving, the greeting of royalty to the peasants. There were two bodyguards at his side, a tall, thin man known as the Shadow, and a heavyset man called Rhino. Lou Dinetto was, as always, dressed elegantly and expensively, in a gray silk suit with a white shirt, blue tie, and alligator shoes. His clothes had to be carefully tailored to make him look trim, because he was short and stout, with bandy legs. He always had a smile and a ready quip for the press, and they enjoyed quoting him. Dinetto had been indicted and tried three times on charges ranging from arson to racketeering to murder, and each time he had gone free.

Now as he left the courtroom, one of the reporters yelled out, 'Did you know you were going to be acquitted, Mr Dinetto?'

Dinetto laughed. 'Of course I did. I'm an innocent businessman. The government has got nothing better to do than to persecute me. That's one of the reasons our taxes are so high.'

A TV camera was aimed at him. Lou Dinetto stopped to smile into it.

'Mr Dinetto, can you explain why two witnesses

who were scheduled to testify against you in your murder trial failed to appear?'

'Certainly I can explain it,' Dinetto said. 'They were honest citizens who decided not to perjure themselves.'

'The government claims that you're the head of the West Coast mob, and that it was you who arranged for—'

'The only thing I arrange for is where people sit at my restaurant. I want everybody to be comfortable.' He grinned at the milling crowd of reporters. 'By the way, you're all invited to the restaurant tonight for a free dinner and drinks.'

He was moving toward the curb, where a black stretch limousine was waiting for him.

'Mr Dinetto . . .'

'Mr Dinetto . . .'

'Mr Dinetto . . .'

'I'll see you at my restaurant tonight, boys and girls. You all know where it is.'

And Lou Dinetto was in the car, waving and smiling. Rhino closed the door of the limousine and got into the front seat. The Shadow slipped behind the wheel.

'That was great, boss!' Rhino said. 'You sure know how to handle them bums.'

'Where to?' the Shadow asked.

'Home. I can use a hot bath and a good steak.'

The car started off.

'I don't like that question about the witnesses,' Dinetto said. 'You sure they'll never . . . ?'

'Not unless they can talk underwater, boss.'

Dinetto nodded. 'Good.'

The car was speeding along Fillmore Street.

Dinetto said, 'Did you see the look on the DA's face when the judge dismissed . . . ?'

A small dog appeared out of nowhere, directly in front of the limousine. The Shadow swung the wheel hard to avoid hitting it and jammed on the brakes. The car jumped the curb and crashed into a lamp-post. Rhino's head flew forward into the windshield.

'What the *fuck* are you doing?' Dinetto screamed. 'You trying to kill me?'

The Shadow was trembling. 'Sorry, boss. A dog ran in front of the car . . .'

'And you decided his life was more important than mine? You stupid asshole!'

Rhino was moaning. He turned around, and Dinetto saw blood pouring from a large cut in his forehead.

'For Christ's sake!' Dinetto screamed. 'Look what you've done!'

'I'm all right,' Rhino mumbled.

'The hell you are!' Dinetto turned to the Shadow. 'Get him to a hospital.'

The Shadow backed the limousine off the curb.

'The Embarcadero is only a couple of blocks down. We'll take him to the emergency ward there.'

'Right, boss.'

Dinetto sank back in his seat. 'A dog,' he said disgustedly. 'Jesus!'

Kat was in the emergency ward when Dinetto, the Shadow, and Rhino walked in. Rhino was bleeding heavily.

Dinetto called out to Kat, 'Hey, you!'

Kat looked up. 'Are you talking to me?'

91

'Who the hell do you think I'm talking to? This man is bleeding. Get him fixed up right away.'

'There are half a dozen others ahead of him,' Kat said quietly. 'He'll have to wait his turn.'

'He's not waiting for anything,' Dinetto told her. 'You'll take care of him now.'

Kat stepped over to Rhino and examined him. She took a piece of cotton and pressed it against the cut. 'Hold it there. I'll be back.'

'I said to take care of him *now*,' Dinetto snapped.

Kat turned to Dinetto. 'This is an emergency hospital ward. I'm the doctor in charge. So either keep quiet or get out.'

The Shadow said, 'Lady, you don't know who you're talking to. You better do what the man says. This is Mr Lou Dinetto.'

'Now that the introductions are over,' Dinetto said impatiently, 'take care of my man.'

'You have a hearing problem,' Kat said. 'I'll tell you once more. Keep quiet or get out of here. I have work to do.'

Rhino said, 'You can't talk to—'

Dinetto turned to him. 'Shut up!' He looked at Kat again, and his tone changed. 'I would appreciate it if you could get to him as soon as possible.'

'I'll do my best.' Kat sat Rhino down on a cot. 'Lie down. I'll be back in a few minutes.' She looked at Dinetto. 'There are some chairs over there in the corner.'

Dinetto and the Shadow watched her walk to the other end of the ward to take care of the waiting patients.

'Jesus,' the Shadow said. 'She has no idea who you are.'

'I don't think it would make any difference. She's got balls.'

Fifteen minutes later, Kat returned to Rhino and examined him. 'No concussion,' she announced. 'You're lucky. That's a nasty cut.'

Dinetto stood watching as Kat skillfully put stitches in Rhino's forehead.

When Kat was finished, she said, 'That should heal nicely. Come back in five days, and I'll take out the stitches.'

Dinetto walked over and examined Rhino's forehead. 'That's a damn good job.'

'Thanks,' Kat said. 'Now, if you'll excuse me . . .'

'Wait a minute,' Dinetto called. He turned to the Shadow. 'Give her a C-note.'

The Shadow took a hundred-dollar bill out of his pocket. 'Here.'

'The cashier's office is outside.'

'This isn't for the hospital. It's for you.'

'No, thanks.'

Dinetto stared as Kat walked away and began working on another patient.

The Shadow said, 'Maybe it wasn't enough, boss.'

Dinetto shook his head. 'She's an independent broad. I like that.' He was silent for a moment. 'Doc Evans is retiring, right?'

'Yeah.'

'Okay. I want you to find out everything you can about this doctor.'

'What for?'

'Leverage. I think she might come in very handy.'

7

Hospitals are run by nurses. Margaret Spencer, the chief nurse, had worked at Embarcadero County Hospital for twenty years and knew where all the bodies—literally and figuratively—were buried. Nurse Spencer was in charge of the hospital, and doctors who did not recognize it were in trouble. She knew which doctors were on drugs or addicted to alcohol, which doctors were incompetent, and which doctors deserved her support. In her charge were all the student nurses, registered nurses, and operating room nurses. It was Margaret Spencer who decided which of them would be assigned to the various surgeries, and since the nurses ranged from indispensable to incompetent, it paid the doctors to get along with her. She had the power to assign an inept scrub nurse to assist on a complicated kidney removal, or, if she liked the doctor, to send her most competent nurse to help him with a simple tonsillectomy. Among Margaret Spencer's many prejudices was an antipathy to woman doctors and to blacks.

Kat Hunter was a black woman doctor.

Kat was having a hard time. Nothing was overtly said or done, and yet prejudice was at work in ways too subtle to pin down. The nurses she asked for were unavailable, those assigned to her were close to incompetent. Kat found herself frequently being sent to examine male clinic patients with venereal diseases. She accepted the first few cases as routine, but when she was given half a dozen to examine in one day, she became suspicious.

At a lunch break she said to Paige, 'Have you examined many men with venereal disease?'

Paige thought for a moment. 'One last week. An orderly.'

I'm going to have to do something about this, Kat thought.

Nurse Spencer had planned to get rid of Dr Hunter by making her life so miserable that she would be forced to quit, but she had not counted on Kat's dedication or her ability. Little by little, Kat was winning over the people she worked with. She had a natural skill that impressed her fellow workers as well as her patients. But the real breakthrough happened because of what came to be known around the hospital as the famous pig blood caper.

On morning rounds one day, Kat was working with a senior resident named Dundas. They were at the bedside of a patient who was unconscious.

'Mr Levy was in an automobile accident,' Dundas informed the younger residents. 'He's lost a great deal of blood, and he needs an immediate transfusion. The hospital is short of blood right now. This man has a family, and they refuse to donate any blood to him. It's infuriating.'

Kat asked, 'Where is his family?'

'In the visitors' waiting room,' Dr Dundas said.

'Do you mind if I talk to them?' Kat asked.

'It won't do any good. I've already spoken to them. They've made up their minds.'

When the rounds were over, Kat went into the visitors' waiting room. The man's wife and grown son and daughter were there. The son wore a yarmulke and ritual tallis.

'Mrs Levy?' Kat asked the woman.

She stood up. 'How is my husband? Is the doctor going to operate?'

'Yes,' Kat said.

'Well, don't ask us to give any of our blood. It's much too dangerous these days, with AIDS and all.'

'Mrs Levy,' Kat said, 'you can't get AIDS by donating blood. It's not poss—'

'Don't tell me! I read the papers. I know what's what.'

Kat studied her a moment. 'I can see that. Well, it's all right, Mrs Levy. The hospital is short of blood right now, but we've solved the problem.'

'Good.'

'We're going to give your husband pig's blood.'

The mother and son were staring at Kat, shocked. *'What?'*

'Pig's blood,' Kat said cheerfully. 'It probably won't do him any harm.' She turned to leave.

'Wait a minute!' Mrs Levy cried.

Kat stopped. 'Yes?'

'I, uh . . . just give us a minute, will you?'

'Certainly.'

Fifteen minutes later, Kat went up to Dr Dundas. 'You don't have to worry about Mr Levy's family anymore. They're all happy to make a blood donation.'

The story became an instant legend around the hospital. Doctors and nurses who had ignored Kat before made a point of speaking to her.

A few days later, Kat went into the private room of Tom Leonard, an ulcer patient. He was eating an enormous lunch that he had had brought in from a nearby delicatessen.

Kat walked up to his bed. 'What are you doing?'

He looked up and smiled. 'Having a decent lunch for a change. Want to join me? There's plenty here.'

Kat rang for a nurse.

'Yes, doctor?'

'Get this food out of here. Mr Leonard is on a strict hospital diet. Didn't you read his chart?'

'Yes, but he insisted on—'

'Remove it, please.'

'Hey! Wait a minute!' Leonard protested. 'I can't eat the pap this hospital is giving me!'

'You'll eat it if you want to get rid of your ulcer.' Kat looked at the nurse. 'Take it out.'

Thirty minutes later, Kat was summoned to the office of the administrator.

'You wanted to see me, Dr Wallace?'

'Yes. Sit down. Tom Leonard is one of your patients, isn't he?'

'That's right. I found him eating a hot pastrami sandwich with pickles and potato salad for lunch today, full of spices and—'

'And you took it away from him.'

'Of course.'

Wallace leaned forward in his chair. 'Doctor, you probably were not aware that Tom Leonard is on the hospital's supervisory board. We want to keep him happy. Do you get my meaning?'

Kat looked at him and said stubbornly, 'No, sir.'

He blinked. 'What?'

'It seems to me that the way to keep Tom Leonard happy is to get him healthy. He's not going to be cured if he tears his stomach apart.'

Benjamin Wallace forced a smile. 'Why don't we let him make that decision?'

Kat stood up. 'Because *I'm* his doctor. Is there anything else?'

'I . . . er . . . no. That's all.'

Kat walked out of the office.

Benjamin Wallace sat there stunned. *Woman doctors!*

Kat was on night duty when she received a call. 'Dr Hunter, I think you had better come up to 320.'

'Right away.'

The patient in Room 320 was Mrs Molloy, a cancer patient in her eighties, with a poor prognosis. As Kat neared the door she heard voices inside, raised in argument. Kat stepped inside the room.

Mrs Molloy was in bed, heavily sedated, but conscious. Her son and two daughters were in the room.

The son was saying, 'I say we split the estate up three ways.'

'No!' one of the daughters said. 'Laurie and I are the ones who have been taking care of Mama. Who's been doing the cooking and cleaning for her? We have! Well, we're entitled to her money and—'

'I'm as much her flesh and blood as you are!' the man yelled.

Mrs Molloy lay in bed, helpless, listening.

Kat was furious. 'Excuse me,' she said.

One of the women glanced at her. 'Come back later, nurse. We're busy.'

Kat said angrily, 'This is my patient. I'm giving you all ten seconds to get out of this room. You can wait in the visitors' waiting room. Now get out before I call security and have you thrown out.'

The man started to say something, but the look in Kat's eyes stopped him. He turned to his sisters and shrugged. 'We can talk outside.'

Kat watched the three of them leave the room. She turned to Mrs Molloy in bed and stroked her head. 'They didn't mean anything by it,' Kat said softly. She sat at the bedside, holding the old woman's hand, and watched her drop off to sleep.

We're all dying, Kat thought. *Forget what Dylan Thomas said. The real trick is to go gentle into that good night.*

Kat was in the middle of treating a patient when an orderly came into the ward. 'There's an urgent call for you at the desk, doctor.'

Kat frowned. 'Thank you.' She turned to the patient, who was in a full body cast, with his legs suspended on a pulley. 'I'll be right back.'

In the corridor, at the nurses' station, Kat picked up the desk telephone. 'Hello?'

'Hi, sis.'

'Mike!' She was excited to hear from him, but her excitement immediately turned to concern. 'Mike, I told you never to call me here. You have the number at the apartment if—'

'Hey, I'm sorry. This couldn't wait. I have a little problem.'

Kat knew what was coming.

'I borrowed some money from a fellow to invest in a business . . .'

Kat didn't bother asking what kind of business. 'And it failed.'

'Yeah. And now he wants his money.'

'How much, Mike?'

'Well, if you could send five thousand . . .'

'What?'

The desk nurse was looking at Kat curiously.

Five thousand dollars. Kat lowered her voice. 'I don't have that much. I . . . I can send you half now and the rest in a few weeks. Will that be all right?'

'I guess so. I hate to bother you, sis, but you know how it is.'

Kat knew exactly how it was. Her brother was twenty-two years old and was always involved in mysterious deals. He ran with gangs, and God only knew what they were up to, but Kat felt a deep responsibility toward him. *It's all my fault*, Kat thought. *If I hadn't run away from home and deserted him . . .* 'Stay out of trouble, Mike. I love you.'

'I love you, too, Kat.'

I'll have to get that money, somehow, Kat thought. *Mike's all I have in the world.*

Dr Isler had been looking forward to working with Honey Taft again. He had forgiven her inept performance and, in fact, was flattered that she was in such awe of him. But now, on rounds with her once

100

more, Honey stayed behind the other residents and never volunteered an answer to his questions.

Thirty minutes after rounds, Dr Isler was seated in Benjamin Wallace's office.

'What's the problem?' Wallace asked.

'It's Dr Taft.'

Wallace looked at him in genuine surprise. 'Dr Taft? She has the best recommendations I've ever seen.'

'That's what puzzles me,' Dr Isler said. 'I've been getting reports from some of the other residents. She's misdiagnosing cases and making serious mistakes. I'd like to know what the hell is going on.'

'I don't understand. She went to a fine medical school.'

'Maybe you should give the dean of the school a call,' Dr Isler suggested.

'That's Jim Pearson. He's a good man. I'll call him.'

A few minutes later, Wallace had Jim Pearson on the telephone. They exchanged pleasantries, and then Wallace said, 'I'm calling about Betty Lou Taft.'

There was a brief silence. 'Yes?'

'We seem to be having a few problems with her, Jim. She was admitted here with your wonderful recommendation.'

'Right.'

'In fact, I have your report in front of me. It says she was one of the brightest students you ever had.'

'That's right.'

'And that she was going to be a credit to the medical profession.'

'Yes.'

101

'Was there any doubt about . . . ?'

'None,' Dr Pearson said firmly. 'None at all. She's probably a little nervous. She's high-strung, but if you just give her a chance, I'm sure she'll be fine.'

'Well, I appreciate your telling me. We'll certainly give her every chance. Thank you.'

'Not at all.' The line went dead.

Jim Pearson sat there, hating himself for what he had done.

But my wife and children come first.

8

Honey Taft had the bad fortune to have been born into a family of overachievers. Her handsome father was the founder and president of a large computer company in Memphis, Tennessee, her lovely mother was a genetic scientist, and Honey's older twin sisters were as attractive, as brainy, and as ambitious as their parents. The Tafts were among the most prominent families in Memphis.

Honey had inconveniently come along when her sisters were six years old.

'Honey was our little accident,' her mother would tell their friends. 'I wanted to have an abortion, but Fred was against it. Now he's sorry.'

Where Honey's sisters were stunning, Honey was plain. Where they were brilliant, Honey was average. Her sisters had started talking at nine months. Honey had not uttered a word until she was almost two.

'We call her "the dummy",' her father would laugh. 'Honey is the ugly duckling of the Taft family. Only I don't think she's going to turn into a swan.'

It was not that Honey was ugly, but neither was she pretty. She was ordinary-looking, with a thin, pinched face, mousy blond hair, and an unenviable figure. What Honey *did* have was an extraordinarily sweet, sunny disposition, a quality not particularly prized in a family of competitive overachievers.

From the earliest time Honey could remember, her greatest desire was to please her parents and sisters and make them love her. It was a futile effort. Her parents were busy with their careers, and her sisters were busy winning beauty contests and scholarships. To add to Honey's misery, she was inordinately shy. Consciously or unconsciously, her family had implanted in her a feeling of deep inferiority.

In high school, Honey was known as the Wallflower. She attended school dances and parties by herself, and smiled and tried not to show how miserable she was, because she did not want to spoil anyone's fun. She would watch her sisters picked up at the house by the most popular boys at school, and then she would go up to her lonely room to struggle with her homework.

And try not to cry.

On weekends and during the summer holidays, Honey made pocket money by baby-sitting. She loved taking care of children, and the children adored her.

When Honey was not working, she would go off and explore Memphis by herself. She visited Graceland, where Elvis Presley had lived, and walked down Beale Street, where the blues started. She wandered through the Pink Palace Museum, and the Planetarium, with its roaring, stomping dinosaur. She went to the aquarium.

And Honey was always alone.

She was unaware that her life was about to change drastically.

* * *

Honey knew that many of her classmates were having love affairs. They discussed it constantly at school.

'Have you gone to bed with Ricky yet? He's the best . . . !'

'Joe is really into orgasms . . .'

'I was out with Tony last night. I'm exhausted. What an animal! I'm seeing him again tonight . . .'

Honey stood there listening to their conversations and she was filled with a bittersweet envy, and a feeling that she would never know what sex was like. *Who would want me?* Honey wondered.

One Friday night, there was a school prom. Honey had no intention of going, but her father said, 'You know, I'm concerned. Your sisters tell me that you're a wallflower, and that you're not going to the prom because you can't get a date.'

Honey blushed. 'That's not true,' she said. 'I do have a date, and I *am* going.' *Don't let him ask who my date is*, Honey prayed.

He didn't.

Now Honey found herself at the prom, seated in her usual corner, watching the others dancing and having a wonderful time.

And that was when the miracle occurred.

Roger Merton, the captain of the football team and the most popular boy at school, was on the dance floor, having a fight with his girlfriend. He had been drinking.

'You're a no-good, selfish bastard!' she said.

'And you're a dumb bitch!'

'You can go screw yourself.'

'I don't have to screw myself, Sally. I can screw somebody else. Anyone I want to.'

'Go ahead!' She stormed off the dance floor.

Honey could not help but overhear.

Merton saw her looking at him. 'What the hell are you staring at?' He was slurring his words.

'Nothing,' Honey said.

'I'll show the bitch! You think I won't show her?'

'I . . . yes.'

'Damn right. Let's have a li'l drink.'

Honey hesitated. Merton was obviously drunk. 'Well, I don't . . .'

'Great. I have a bottle in the car.'

'I really don't think I . . .'

And he had Honey's arm and was steering her out of the room. She went along because she did not want to make a scene and embarrass him.

Outside, Honey tried to pull away. 'Roger, I don't think this is a good idea. I . . .'

'What the hell are you—chicken?'

'No, I . . .'

'Okay, then. Come on.'

He led her to his car and opened the door. Honey stood there a moment.

'Get in.'

'I can only stay a moment,' Honey said.

She got in the car because she did not want to upset Roger. He climbed in beside her.

'We're going to show that dumb broad, aren't we?' He held out a bottle of bourbon. 'Here.'

Honey had had only one drink of alcohol before

and she had hated it. But she did not want to hurt Roger's feelings. She looked at him and reluctantly took a small sip.

'You're okay,' he said. 'You're new at school, huh?'

Honey was in three of his classes. 'No,' Honey said. 'I . . .'

He leaned over and began to play with her breasts.

Startled, Honey pulled away.

'Hey! Come on. Don't you want to please me?' he said.

And that was the magic phrase. Honey wanted to please everybody, and if this was the way to do it . . .

In the uncomfortable backseat of Merton's car, Honey had sex for the first time, and it opened an incredible new world to her. She did not particularly enjoy the sex, but that was not important. The important thing was that Merton enjoyed it. In fact, Honey was amazed by how *much* he enjoyed it. It seemed to make him ecstatic. She had never seen anyone enjoy anything so much. *So this is how to please a man*, Honey thought.

It was an epiphany.

Honey was unable to get the miracle of what had occurred out of her mind. She lay in bed, remembering Merton's hard maleness inside her, thrusting faster and faster, and then his moans, 'Oh, yes, yes . . . Jesus, you're fantastic, Sally . . .'

And Honey had not even minded that. She had pleased the captain of the football team! The most popular boy in school! *And I really didn't even know*

107

what I was doing, Honey thought. *If I truly learned how to please a man . . .*

And that was when Honey had her second epiphany.

The following morning, Honey went to the Pleasure Chest, a porno bookstore on Poplar Street, and bought half a dozen books on eroticism. She smuggled them home and read them in the privacy of her room. She was astounded by what she was reading.

She raced through the pages of *The Perfumed Garden* and the *Kama Sutra*, the *Tibetan Arts of Love*, the *Alchemy of Ecstasy*, and then went back for more. She read the words of Gedun Chopel and the arcane accounts by Kanchinatha.

She studied the exciting photographs of the thirty-seven positions of lovemaking, and she learned the meaning of the Half Moon and the Circle, the Lotus Petal, and the Pieces of Cloud, and the way of churning.

Honey became an expert on the eight types of oral sex, and the paths of the sixteen pleasures, and the ecstasy of the string of marbles. She knew how to teach a man to perform *karuna*, to intensify his pleasure. In theory, at least.

Honey felt she was now ready to put her knowledge into practice.

The *Kama Sutra* had several chapters on aphrodisiacs to arouse a man, but since Honey had no idea where she could obtain *Hedysarum gangeticum*, the *kshirika* plant, or the *Xanthochymus pictorius*, she figured out her own substitutes.

108

When Honey saw Roger Merton in class the following week, she walked up to him and said, 'I really enjoyed the other night. Can we do it again?'

It took him a moment to remember who Honey was. 'Oh. Sure. Why not? My folks are out tonight. Why don't you come by about eight o'clock?'

When Honey arrived at Merton's house that night, she had a small jar of maple syrup with her.

'What's that for?' Merton said.

'I'm going to show you,' Honey said.

She showed him.

The next day, Merton was telling his buddies at school about Honey.

'She's incredible,' he said. 'You wouldn't believe what she can do with a little warm syrup!'

That afternoon, half a dozen boys were asking Honey for dates. From that time on, she started going out every night. The boys were very happy, and that made Honey very happy.

Honey's parents were delighted by their daughter's sudden popularity.

'It took our girl a little while to bloom,' her father said proudly, 'but now she's turned into a real Taft!'

Honey had always had poor grades in mathematics, and she knew she had failed badly on her final test. Her mathematics teacher, Mr Janson, was a bachelor and lived near the school. Honey paid him a visit one evening. He opened the door and looked at her in surprise.

'Honey! What are you doing here?'

'I need your help,' Honey said. 'My father will kill me if I fail your course. I brought some math problems, and I wonder if you would mind going over them with me.'

He hesitated a moment. 'This is unusual, but . . . very well.'

Mr Janson liked Honey. She was not like the other girls in his class. They were raucous and indifferent, while Honey was sensitive and caring, always eager to please. He wished that she had more of an aptitude for mathematics.

Mr Janson sat next to Honey on the couch and began to explain the arcane intricacies of logarithms.

Honey was not interested in logarithms. As Mr Janson talked, Honey moved closer and closer to him. She started breathing on his neck and into his ear, and before he knew what was happening, Mr Janson found that his pants were unzipped.

He was looking at Honey in astonishment. 'What are you doing?'

'I've wanted you since the first time I saw you,' Honey said. She opened her purse and took out a small can of whipped cream.

'What's that?'

'Let me show you . . .'

Honey received an A in math.

It was not only the accessories Honey used that made her so popular. It was the knowledge she had gleaned from all the ancient books on erotica she had read. She delighted her partners with techniques they had never dreamed of, that were thousands of years old, and long forgotten. She brought a new meaning to the word 'ecstasy'.

Honey's grades improved dramatically, and she

was suddenly even more popular than her sisters had been in their high school days. Honey was dined at the Private Eye and the Bombay Bicycle Club, and taken to the Ice Capades at the Memphis Mall. The boys took her skiing at Cedar Cliff and sky diving at Landis Airport.

Honey's years at college were just as successful socially. At dinner one evening, her father said, 'You'll be graduating soon. It's time to think about your future. Do you know what you want to do with your life?'

She answered immediately. 'I want to be a nurse.'

Her father's face reddened. 'You mean a doctor.'

'No, Father. I —'

'You're a Taft. If you want to go into medicine, you'll be a doctor. Is that understood?'

'Yes, Father.'

Honey had meant it when she told her father she wanted to be a nurse. She loved taking care of people, helping them and nurturing them. She was terrified by the idea of becoming a doctor, and being responsible for people's lives, but she knew that she must not disappoint her father. *You're a Taft.*

Honey's college grades were not good enough to get her into medical school, but her father's influence was. He was a heavy contributor to a medical school in Knoxville, Tennessee. He met with Dr Jim Pearson, the dean.

'You're asking for a big favor,' Pearson said, 'but I'll tell you what I'll do. I'll admit Honey on a probationary basis. If at the end of six months we feel she's not qualified to continue, we'll have to let her go.'

'Fair enough. She's going to surprise you.'

He was right.

Honey's father had made arrangements for her to stay in Knoxville with a cousin of his, the Reverend Douglas Lipton.

Douglas Lipton was the minister of the Baptist Church. He was in his sixties, married to a woman ten years older.

The minister was delighted to have Honey in the house.

'She's like a breath of fresh air,' he told his wife.

He had never seen anyone so eager to please.

Honey did fairly well in medical school, but she lacked dedication. She was there only to please her father.

Honey's teachers liked her. There was a genuine niceness about her that made her professors want her to succeed.

Ironically, she was particularly weak in anatomy. During the eighth week, her anatomy teacher sent for her. 'I'm afraid I'm going to have to fail you,' he said unhappily.

I can't fail, Honey thought. *I can't let my father down. What would Boccaccio have advised?*

Honey moved closer to the professor. 'I came to this school because of you. I have heard so much about you.' She moved closer to him. 'I want to be like you.' And closer. 'Being a doctor means everything to me.' And closer. 'Please help me . . .'

One hour later, when Honey left his office, she had the answers to the next examination.

Before Honey was finished with medical school, she had seduced several of her professors. There was a helplessness about her that they were unable to resist. They were all under the impression that it was *they* who were seducing *her*, and they felt guilty about taking advantage of her innocence.

Dr Jim Pearson was the last to succumb to Honey. He was intrigued by all the reports he had heard about her. There were rumors of her extraordinary sexual skills. He sent for Honey one day to discuss her grades. She brought a small box of powdered sugar with her, and before the afternoon was over, Dr Pearson was as hooked as all the others. Honey made him feel young and insatiable. She made him feel that he was a king who had subjugated her and made her his slave.

He tried not to think of his wife and children.

Honey was genuinely fond of the Reverend Douglas Lipton, and it upset her that his wife was a cold, frigid woman who was always criticizing him. Honey felt sorry for the minister. *He doesn't deserve that*, Honey thought. *He needs comforting*.

In the middle of the night, when Mrs Lipton was out of town visiting a sister, Honey walked into the minister's bedroom. She was naked. 'Douglas . . .'

His eyes flew open. 'Honey? Are you all right?'

'No,' she said. 'Can I talk to you?'

113

'Of course.' He reached for the lamp.

'Don't turn on the light.' She crept into bed beside him.

'What's the matter? Aren't you feeling well?'

'I'm worried.'

'About what?'

'You. You deserve to be loved. I want to make love to you.'

He was wide awake. 'My God!' he said. 'You're just a child. You can't be serious.'

'I am. Your wife's not giving you any love . . .'

'Honey, this is impossible! You'd better get back to your room now, and . . .'

He could feel her naked body pressing against his. 'Honey, we can't do this. I'm . . .'

Her lips were on his, and her body was on top of him, and he was completely swept away. She spent the night in his bed.

At six o'clock in the morning, the door to the bedroom opened and Mrs Lipton walked in. She stood there, staring at the two of them, then walked out without a word.

Two hours later, the Reverend Douglas Lipton committed suicide in his garage.

When Honey heard the news, she was devastated, unable to believe what had happened.

The sheriff arrived at the house and had a talk with Mrs Lipton.

When he was through, he went to find Honey. 'Out of respect for his family, we're going to list the death of the Reverend Douglas Lipton as a "suicide for reasons unknown," but I would suggest that you get the fuck out of this town fast, and stay out.'

Honey had gone to Embarcadero County Hospital in San Francisco.

With a glowing recommendation from Dr Jim Pearson.

9

Time had lost all meaning for Paige. There was no beginning and no end, and the days and nights flowed into one another in a seamless rhythm. The hospital had become her whole life. The outside world was a foreign, faraway planet.

Christmas came and went, and a new year began. In the world outside, US troops liberated Kuwait from Iraq.

There was no word from Alfred. *He'll find out he made a mistake*, Paige thought. *He'll come back to me.*

The early morning crank telephone calls had stopped as suddenly as they had started. Paige was relieved that no new mysterious or threatening incidents had befallen her. It was almost as if they had all been a bad dream . . . except, of course, they hadn't been.

The routine continued to be frantic. There was no time to know patients. They were simply gallbladders and ruptured livers, fractured femurs and broken backs.

The hospital was a jungle filled with mechanical demons — respirators, heart rate monitors, CAT scan equipment, X-ray machines. And each had its own peculiar sound. There were whistles, and buzzers, and the constant chatter on the PA

116

system, and they all blended into a loud, insane cacophony.

The second year of residency was a rite of passage. The residents moved up to more demanding duties and watched the new group come in, feeling a mixture of scorn and arrogance toward them.

'Those poor devils,' Kat said to Paige. 'They have no idea what they're in for.'

'They'll find out soon enough.'

Paige and Honey were becoming worried about Kat. She was losing weight, and seemed depressed. In the middle of conversations, they would find Kat looking off into space, her mind preoccupied. From time to time, she would receive a mysterious phone call, and after each one her depression seemed to worsen.

Paige and Honey sat down to have a talk with her.

'Is everything all right?' Paige asked. 'You know we love you, and if there's a problem, we'd like to help.'

'Thanks. I appreciate it, but there's nothing you can do. It's a money problem.'

Honey looked at her in surprise. 'What do you need money for? We never go anyplace. We haven't any time to buy anything. We—'

'It's not for me. It's for my brother.' Kat had not mentioned her brother before.

'I didn't know you had a brother,' Paige said.

'Does he live in San Francisco?' Honey asked.

Kat was hesitant. 'No. He lives back East. In Detroit. You'll have to meet him one day.'

'We'd like to. What does he do?'

'He's kind of an entrepreneur,' Kat said vaguely. 'He's a little down on his luck right now, but Mike will bounce back. He always does.' *I hope to God I'm right*, Kat thought.

Harry Bowman had transferred from a residency program in Iowa. He was a good-humored, happy-go-lucky fellow who went out of his way to be pleasant to everyone.

One day, he said to Paige, 'I'm giving a little party tomorrow night. If you and Dr Hunter and Dr Taft are free, why don't you come? I think you'll have a good time.'

'Fine,' Paige said. 'What shall we bring?'

Bowman laughed. 'Don't bring anything.'

'Are you sure?' Paige asked. 'A bottle of wine, or . . .'

'Forget it! It's going to be at my little apartment.'

Bowman's little apartment turned out to be a ten-room penthouse, filled with antique furniture.

The three women walked in and stared in amazement.

'My God!' Kat said. 'Where did all this come from?'

'I was smart enough to have a clever father,' Bowman said. 'He left all his money to me.'

'And you're working?' Kat marveled.

Bowman smiled. 'I like being a doctor.'

The buffet consisted of Beluga Malossol caviar, *pâté de campagne*, smoked Scottish salmon, oysters on the half shell, backfin lump crabmeat, *crudités* with a shallot vinaigrette dressing, and Cristal champagne.

Bowman had been right. The three of them did have a wonderful time.

'I can't thank you enough,' Paige told Bowman at the end of the evening when they were leaving.

'Are you free Saturday?' he asked.

'Yes.'

'I have a little motorboat. I'll take you out for a spin.'

'Sounds great.'

At four o'clock in the morning, Kat was awakened out of a deep sleep in the on-call room. 'Dr Hunter, Emergency Room Three . . . Dr Hunter, Emergency Three.'

Kat got out of bed, fighting exhaustion. Rubbing sleep from her eyes, she took the elevator down to the ER.

An orderly greeted her at the door. 'He's over on the gurney in the corner. He's in a lot of pain.'

Kat walked over to him. 'I'm Dr Hunter,' she said sleepily.

He groaned. 'Jesus, doc. You've got to do somethin'. My back is killin' me.'

Kat stifled a yawn. 'How long have you been in pain?'

'About two weeks.'

Kat was looking at him, puzzled. 'Two weeks? Why didn't you come in sooner?'

He tried to move, and winced. 'To tell you the truth, I hate hospitals.'

'Then why are you coming in now?'

He brightened. 'There's a big golf tournament coming up, and if you don't fix my back, I won't be able to enjoy it.'

Kat took a deep breath. 'A golf tournament.'

'Yeah.'

She was fighting to control herself. 'I'll tell you what. Go home. Take two aspirins, and if you aren't feeling better in the morning, give me a call.' She turned and stormed out of the room, leaving him gaping after her.

Harry Bowman's little motorboat was a sleek fifty-foot motor cruiser.

'Welcome aboard!' he said as he greeted Paige, Kat, and Honey at the dock.

The women looked at the boat admiringly.

'It's beautiful,' Paige said.

They cruised around the bay for three hours, enjoying the warm, sunny day. It was the first time any of them had relaxed in weeks.

While they were anchored off Angel Island, eating a delicious lunch, Kat said, 'This is the life. Let's not go back to shore.'

'Good thinking,' Honey said.

All in all, it was a heavenly day.

When they returned to the dock, Paige said, 'I can't tell you how much I've enjoyed this.'

'It's been my pleasure.' Bowman patted her arm. 'We'll do it again. Anytime. You three are always welcome.'

What a lovely man, Paige thought.

Honey liked working in obstetrics. It was a ward filled with new life and new hope, in a timeless, joyful ritual.

The first-time mothers were eager and apprehensive. The veterans could not wait to get it over with.

One of the women who was about to deliver said to Honey, 'Thank God! I'll be able to see my toes again.'

If Paige had kept a diary, she would have marked the fifteenth of August as a red-letter day. That was the day Jimmy Ford came into her life.

Jimmy was a hospital orderly, with the brightest smile and the sunniest disposition Paige had ever seen. He was small and thin, and looked seventeen. He was twenty-five, and moved around the hospital corridors like a cheerful tornado. Nothing was too much trouble for him.

He was constantly running errands for everyone. He had absolutely no sense of status and treated doctors, nurses, and janitors alike.

Jimmy Ford loved to tell jokes.

'Did you hear about the patient in a body cast? The fellow in the bed next to him asked him what he did for a living.

'He said, "I was a window washer at the Empire State Building."

'The other fellow said, "When did you quit?"

'"Halfway down."'

And Jimmy would grin and hurry off to help somebody.

He adored Paige. 'I'm going to be a doctor one day. I want to be like you.'

He would bring her little presents—candy bars, and stuffed toys. A joke went with each gift.

'In Houston, a man stopped a pedestrian and asked, "What's the quickest way to the hospital?"

121

The other man said, "Say something bad about Texas."'

The jokes were terrible, but Jimmy made them sound funny.

He would arrive at the hospital the same time as Paige, and he would race up to her on his motorcycle.

'The patient asked, "Will my operation be dangerous?" And the surgeon said, "No. You can't get a dangerous operation for two hundred dollars."'

And he would be gone.

Whenever Paige, Kat, and Honey were free on the same day, they went out exploring San Francisco. They visited the Dutch Mill and the Japanese Tea Garden. They went to Fisherman's Wharf and rode the cable car. They went to see plays at the Curran Theater, and had dinner at the Maharani on Post Street. All the waiters were Indian, and to the astonishment of Kat and Honey, Paige addressed them in Hindi.

'*Hum Hindustani baht bahut ocho bolta hi.*' And from that moment, the restaurant was theirs.

'Where in the world did you learn to talk Indian?' Honey asked.

'Hindi,' Paige said. She hesitated. 'We . . . I lived in India for a while.' It was still so vivid. She and Alfred were at Agra, staring at the Taj Mahal. *Shah Jahan built that in memory of his wife. It took twenty years, Alfred.*

I'm going to build you a Taj Mahal. I don't care how long it takes!

This is Karen Turner. My wife.

She heard her name called, and turned.

122

'Paige . . .' There was a look of concern on Kat's face. 'Are you all right?'

'Fine. I'm fine.'

The impossible hours continued. Another New Year's Eve came and went, and the second year slid into the third, and nothing had changed. The hospital was untouched by the outside world. The wars and famines and disasters of far-off countries paled by comparison with the life-and-death crises they coped with twenty-four hours a day.

Whenever Kat and Paige met in the hospital corridors, Kat would grin and say, 'Having a good time?'

'When did you sleep last?' Paige asked.

Kat sighed. 'Who can remember?'

They stumbled through the long days and nights, trying to keep up with the incessant, demanding pressure, grabbing sandwiches when they had time, and drinking cold coffee out of paper cups.

The sexual harassment seemed to have become a part of Kat's life. There were the constant innuendos not only from the doctors, but also from patients who tried to get her into bed. They got the same response as the doctors. *There's not a man in the world I'll let touch me.*

And she really believed it.

In the middle of a busy morning, there was another telephone call from Mike.

'Hi, sis.'

And Kat knew what was coming. She had sent him all the money she could spare, but deep down inside, she knew that whatever she sent would never be enough.

'I hate like hell to bother you, Kat. I really do. But I got into a small jam.' His voice sounded strained.

'Mike . . . are you all right?'

'Oh, yeah. It's nothing serious. It's just that I owe somebody who needs his money back right away, and I was wondering . . .'

'I'll see what I can do,' Kat said wearily.

'Thanks. I can always count on you, can't I, sis? I love you.'

'I love you, too, Mike.'

One day, Kat said to Paige and Honey, 'Do you know what we all need?'

'A month's sleep?'

'A vacation. That's where we should be, strolling down the Champs-Elysées, looking in all those expensive shop windows.'

'Right. First-class all the way!' Paige giggled. 'We'll sleep all day and play all night.'

Honey laughed. 'Sounds good.'

'We have some vacation time coming up in a few months,' Paige observed. 'Why don't we make some plans for the three of us to go away somewhere?'

'That's a great idea,' Kat said enthusiastically. 'Saturday, let's stop in at a travel agency.'

They spent the next three days excitedly making plans.

'I'm dying to see London. Maybe we'll run into the queen.'

'Paris is where I want to go. It's supposed to be the most romantic city in the world.'

'I want to ride a gondola in the moonlight in Venice.'

Maybe we'll go to Venice on our honeymoon, Paige, Alfred had said. *Would you like that?*

Oh, yes!

She wondered if Alfred had taken Karen to Venice on their honeymoon.

Saturday morning the three of them stopped in at the Corniche Travel Agency on Powell Street.

The woman behind the counter was polite. 'What kind of trip are you interested in?'

'We'd like to go to Europe—London, Paris, Venice . . .'

'Lovely. We have some economical package tours that—'

'No, no, no.' Paige looked at Honey and grinned. 'First-class.'

'Right. First-class air travel,' Kat chimed in.

'First-class hotels,' Honey added.

'Well, I can recommend the Ritz in London, the Crillon in Paris, the Cipriani in Venice, and—'

Paige said, 'Why don't we just take some brochures with us? We can study them and make up our minds.'

'That will be fine,' the travel agent said.

Paige was looking at a brochure. 'You arrange yacht charters, too?'

'Yes.'

'Good. We may be chartering one.'

'Excellent.' The travel agent collected a handful of brochures and handed them to Paige. 'Whenever you're ready, just let me know and I'll be happy to make your reservations.'

'You'll hear from us,' Honey promised.

When they got outside, Kat laughed and said, 'Nothing like dreaming big, is there?'

'Don't worry,' Paige assured her. 'One day we'll be able to go to all those places.'

10

Seymour Wilson, the chief of medicine at Embarcadero County Hospital, was a frustrated man with an impossible job. There were too many patients, too few doctors and nurses, and too few hours in a day. He felt like the captain of a sinking ship, running around vainly trying to plug up the holes.

At the moment, Dr Wilson's immediate concern was Honey Taft. While some doctors seemed to like her a great deal, reliable residents and nurses kept reporting that Dr Taft was incapable of doing her job.

Wilson finally went to see Ben Wallace. 'I want to get rid of one of our doctors,' he said. 'The residents she makes rounds with tell me she's incompetent.'

Wallace remembered Honey. She was the one who had the extraordinarily high grades and glowing recommendation. 'I don't understand it,' he said. 'There must be some mistake.' He was thoughtful for a moment. 'I'll tell you what we'll do, Seymour. Who's the meanest son of a bitch on your staff?'

'Ted Allison.'

'All right. Tomorrow morning, send Honey Taft out on rounds with Dr Allison. Have him give you a report on her. If he says she's incompetent, I'll get rid of her.'

'Fair enough,' Dr Wilson said. 'Thanks, Ben.'

* * *

At lunch, Honey told Paige that she had been assigned to make the rounds with Dr Allison the following morning.

'I know him,' Paige said. 'He has a miserable reputation.'

'That's what I hear,' Honey said thoughtfully.

At that moment, in another part of the hospital, Seymour Wilson was talking to Ted Allison. Allison was a hard-bitten veteran of twenty-five years. He had served as a medical officer in the navy, and he still took pride in 'kicking ass'.

Seymour Wilson was saying, 'I want you to keep a close eye on Dr Taft. If she can't cut it, she's out. Understood?'

'Understood.'

He was looking forward to this. Like Seymour Wilson, Ted Allison despised incompetent doctors. In addition, he had a strong conviction that if women wanted to be in the medical profession, they should be nurses. If it was good enough for Florence Nightingale, it was good enough for the rest of them.

At six o'clock the following morning, the residents gathered in the corridor to begin their rounds. The group consisted of Dr Allison, Tom Benson, who was his chief assistant, and five residents, including Honey Taft.

Now, as Allison looked at Honey, he thought, *Okay, sister, let's see what you've got*. He turned to the group. 'Let's go.'

The first patient in Ward One was a teenage girl lying in bed, covered with heavy blankets. She was asleep when the group approached her.

'All right,' Dr Allison said. 'I want you all to take a look at her chart.'

The residents began to study the patient's chart. Dr Allison turned to Honey. 'This patient has fever, chills, general malaise, and anorexia. She has a temperature, a cough, and pneumonia. What's your diagnosis, Dr Taft?'

Honey stood there, frowning, silent.

'*Well?*'

'Well,' Honey said thoughtfully, 'I would say she probably has psittacosis—parrot fever.'

Dr Allison was looking at her in surprise. 'What . . . what makes you say that?'

'Her symptoms are typical of psittacosis, and I noticed that she works part-time as a clerk in a pet shop. Psittacosis is transmitted by infected parrots.'

Allison nodded slowly. 'That's . . . that's very good. Do you know what the treatment is?'

'Yes. Tetracycline for ten days, strict bed rest, and plenty of fluids.'

Dr Allison turned to the group, 'Did you all hear that? Dr Taft is absolutely right.'

They moved on to the next patient.

Dr Allison said, 'If you'll examine his chart, you'll find that he has mesothelial tumors, bloody effusion, and fatigue. What's the diagnosis?'

One of the residents said, hopefully, 'It sounds like some form of pneumonia.'

A second resident spoke up, 'It could be cancer.'

Dr Allison turned to Honey. 'What is your diagnosis, doctor?'

Honey looked thoughtful. 'Offhand, I'd say it was fibrous pneumoconiosis, a form of asbestos poisoning. His chart shows that he works in a carpet mill.'

Ted Allison could not conceal his admiration. 'Excellent! Excellent! Do you happen to know what the therapy is?'

'Unfortunately, no specific therapy is available yet.'

It became even more impressive. In the next two hours, Honey diagnosed a rare case of Reiter's syndrome, osteitis deformans polycythemia, and malaria.

When the rounds were over, Dr Allison shook Honey's hand. 'I'm not easily impressed, doctor, but I want to tell you that you have a tremendous future!'

Honey blushed. 'Thank you, Dr Allison.'

'And I intend to tell Ben Wallace so,' he said as he walked away.

Tom Benson, Allison's senior assistant, looked at Honey and smiled. 'I'll meet you in half an hour, baby.'

Paige tried to stay out of the way of Dr Arthur Kane—007. But at every opportunity, Kane asked for Paige to assist him with operations. And each time, he would become more offensive.

'What do you mean, you won't go out with me? You must be getting it from someone else.'

And, 'I may be short, honey, but not everywhere. You know what I mean?'

She came to dread the occasions she had to work with him. Time after time, Paige watched Kane perform unnecessary surgery and take out organs that were healthy.

One day, as Paige and Kane were walking toward

the operating room, Paige asked, 'What are we going to operate on, doctor?'

'His wallet!' He saw the look on Paige's face. 'Just kidding, honey.'

'He should be working in a butcher shop,' Paige later said angrily to Kat. 'He has no right to be operating on people.'

After a particularly inept liver operation, Dr Kane turned to Paige and shook his head. 'Too bad. I don't know if he's going to make it.'

It was all Paige could do to contain her anger. She decided to have a talk with Tom Chang.

'Someone should report Dr Kane,' Paige said. 'He's murdering his patients!'

'Take it easy.'

'I can't! It's not right that they let a man like that operate. It's criminal. He should be brought up before the credentials committee.'

'What good would it do? You'd have to get other doctors to testify against him, and no one would be willing to do that. This is a close community, and we all have to live in it, Paige. It's almost impossible to get one doctor to testify against another. We're all vulnerable and we need each other too much. Calm down. I'll take you out and buy you lunch.'

Paige sighed. 'All right, but it's a lousy system.'

At lunch, Paige asked, 'How are you and Sye doing?'

He took a moment to answer. 'I . . . we're having problems. My work is destroying our marriage. I don't know what to do.'

'I'm sure it will work out,' Paige said.

Chang said fiercely, 'It had better.'

131

Paige looked up at him.

'I would kill myself if she left me.'

The following morning, Arthur Kane was scheduled
to perform a kidney operation. The chief of surgery
said to Paige, 'Dr Kane asked for you to assist him
in OR Four.'

Paige's mouth was suddenly dry. She hated the
thought of being near him.

Paige said, 'Couldn't you get someone else
to . . . ?'

'He's waiting for you, doctor.'

Paige sighed. 'Right.'

By the time Paige had scrubbed up, the operation
was already in progress.

'Give me a hand here, darling,' Kane said to Paige.

The patient's abdomen had been painted with an
iodine solution and an incision had been made in the
right upper quadrant of the abdomen, just below the
rib cage. *So far, so good*, Paige thought.

'Scalpel!'

The scrub nurse handed Dr Kane a scalpel.

He looked up. 'Put some music on.'

A moment later a CD began to play.

Dr Kane kept cutting. 'Let's have something a
little peppier.' He looked over at Paige. 'Start the
bovie, sweetheart.'

Sweetheart. Paige gritted her teeth and picked up
a bovie — an electric cautery tool. She began to cauterize the arteries to reduce the amount of blood in
the abdomen. The operation was going well.

Thank God, Paige thought.

'Sponge.'

The scrub nurse handed Kane a sponge.

'Good. Let's have some suction.' He cut around the kidney until it was exposed. 'There's the little devil,' Dr Kane said. 'More suction.' He lifted up the kidney with forceps. 'Right. Let's sew him back up.'

For once, everything had gone well, yet something was bothering Paige. She took a closer look at the kidney. It looked healthy. She frowned, wondering if . . .

As Dr Kane began sewing up the patient, Paige hurried over to the X-ray in the lighted wall frame. She studied it for a moment and said softly, 'Oh, my God!'

The X-ray had been put up backward. Dr Kane had removed the wrong kidney.

Thirty minutes later, Paige was in Ben Wallace's office.

'He took out a healthy kidney and left in a diseased one!' Paige's voice was trembling. 'The man should be put in jail!'

Benjamin Wallace said soothingly, 'Paige, I agree with you that it's regrettable. But it certainly wasn't intentional. It was a mistake, and —'

'A *mistake*? That patient is going to have to live on dialysis for the rest of his life. Someone should pay for that!'

'Believe me, we're going to have a peer review evaluation.'

Paige knew what that meant: a group of physicians would review what had happened, but it would be done in confidence. The information would be withheld from the public and the patient.

'Dr Wallace . . .'

'You're part of our team, Paige. You've got to be a team player.'

'He has no business working in this hospital. Or any other hospital.'

'You've got to look at the whole picture. If he were removed, there would be bad publicity and the reputation of the hospital would be hurt. We'd probably face a lot of malpractice suits.'

'What about the patients?'

'We'll keep a closer eye on Dr Kane.' He leaned forward in his chair. 'I'm going to give you some advice. When you get into private practice, you're going to need the goodwill of other doctors for referrals. Without that, you'll go nowhere, and if you get the reputation of being a maverick and blowing the whistle on your fellow doctors, you won't get any referrals. I can promise you that.'

Paige rose. 'So you aren't going to do anything?'

'I told you, we're going to do a peer review evaluation.'

'And that's it?'

'That's it.'

'It's not fair,' Paige said. She was in the cafeteria having lunch with Kat and Honey.

Kat shook her head. 'Nobody said life has to be fair.'

Paige looked around the antiseptic white-tiled room. 'This whole place depresses me. Everybody is sick.'

'Or they wouldn't be here,' Kat pointed out.

'Why don't we give a party?' Honey suggested.

'A party? What are you talking about?'

Honey's voice was suddenly filled with enthusiasm. 'We could order up some decent food and liquor, and have a celebration! I think we could all use a little cheering up.'

Paige thought for a second. 'You know,' she said, 'that's not a bad idea. Let's do it!'

'It's a deal. I'll organize things,' Honey told them. 'We'll do it tomorrow after rounds.'

Arthur Kane approached Paige in the corridor. There was ice in his voice. 'You've been a naughty girl. Someone should teach you to keep your mouth shut!' And he walked away.

Paige looked after him in disbelief. *Wallace told him what I said. He shouldn't have done that. 'If you get the reputation of being a maverick and blowing the whistle on your fellow doctors . . .' Would I do it again?* Paige pondered. *Darned right I would!*

News of the forthcoming party spread rapidly. All the residents chipped in. A lavish menu was ordered from Ernie's restaurant, and liquor was delivered from a nearby store. The party was set for five o'clock in the doctors' lounge. The food and drinks arrived at four-thirty. There was a feast: seafood platters with lobster and shrimp, a variety of pâtés, Swedish meatballs, hot pasta, fruit, and desserts. When Paige, Kat, and Honey walked into the lounge at five-fifteen, it was already crowded with eager residents, interns, and nurses, eating and having a wonderful time.

Paige turned to Honey. 'This was a great idea!'

Honey smiled. 'Thank you.'

An announcement came over the loudspeaker. 'Dr Finley and Dr Ketler to the ER. Stat.' And the two doctors, in the middle of downing shrimp, looked at each other, sighed, and hurriedly left the room.

Tom Chang came up to Paige. 'We ought to do this every week,' he said.

'Right. It's—'

The loudspeaker came on again. 'Dr Chang . . . Room 317 . . . Dr Chang . . . Room 317.'

And a minute later, 'Dr Smythe . . . ER Two . . . Dr Smythe to ER Two.'

The loudspeaker never stopped. Within thirty minutes, almost every doctor and nurse had been called away on some emergency. Honey heard her name called, and then Paige's, and Kat's.

'I can't believe what's happening,' Kat said. 'You know how people talk about having a guardian angel? Well, I think the three of us are under the spell of a guardian devil.'

Her words proved to be prophetic.

The next Monday morning, when Paige got off duty and went to get into her car, two of the tires had been slashed. She stared at them in disbelief. *Someone should teach you to keep your mouth shut!*

When she got back to the apartment she said to Kat and Honey, 'Watch out for Arthur Kane. He's crazy.'

11

Kat was awakened by the ring of the telephone. Without opening her eyes, she reached out for it and put the receiver to her ear.

'H'lo?'

'Kat? It's Mike.'

She sat up, her heart suddenly pounding. 'Mike, are you all right?' She heard him laugh.

'Never better, sis. Thanks to you and your friend.'

'My friend?'

'Mr Dinetto.'

'Who?' Kat tried to concentrate, groggy with sleep.

'Mr Dinetto. He really saved my life.'

Kat had no idea what he was talking about. 'Mike . . .'

'You know the fellows I owed money to? Mr Dinetto got them off my back. He's a real gentleman. And he thinks the world of you, Kat.'

Kat had forgotten the incident with Dinetto, but now it suddenly flashed into her mind: *Lady, you don't know who you're talking to. You better do what the man says. This is Mr Lou Dinetto.*

Mike was going on. 'I'm sending you some cash, Kat. Your friend arranged for me to get a job. It pays real good money.'

Your friend. Kat was nervous. 'Mike, listen to me. I want you to be careful.'

She heard him laugh again.

'Don't worry about me. Didn't I tell you everything would be coming up roses? Well, I was right.'

'Take care of yourself, Mike. Don't —'

The connection was broken.

Kat was unable to go back to sleep. *Dinetto! How did he find out about Mike, and why is he helping him?*

The following night, when Kat left the hospital, a black limousine was waiting for her at the curb. The Shadow and Rhino were standing beside it.

As Kat started to pass, Rhino said, 'Get in, doctor. Mr Dinetto wants to see you.'

She studied the man for a moment. Rhino was ominous-looking, but it was the Shadow who frightened Kat. There was something deadly about his stillness. Under other circumstances, Kat would never have gotten into the car, but Mike's telephone call had puzzled her. And worried her.

She was driven to a small apartment on the outskirts of the city, and when she arrived, Dinetto was waiting for her.

'Thanks for coming, Dr Hunter,' he said. 'I appreciate it. A friend of mine had a little accident. I want you to take a look at him.'

'What are you doing with Mike?' Kat demanded.

'Nothing,' he said innocently. 'I heard he was in a little trouble, and I got it taken care of.'

'How did . . . how did you find out about him? I mean, that he was my brother and . . .'

Dinetto smiled. 'In my business, we're all friends. We help each other. Mike got mixed up with some bad boys, so I helped him out. You should be grateful.'

'I am,' Kat said. 'I really am.'

'Good! You know the saying "One hand washes the other"?'

Kat shook her head. 'I won't do anything illegal.'

'Illegal?' Dinetto said. He seemed hurt. 'I wouldn't ask you to do anything like that. This friend of mine was in a little accident and he hates hospitals. Would you take a look at him?'

What am I letting myself in for? Kat wondered. 'Very well.'

'He's in the bedroom.'

Dinetto's friend had been badly beaten up. He was lying in bed, unconscious.

'What happened to him?' Kat asked.

Dinetto looked at her and said, 'He fell down a flight of stairs.'

'He should be in a hospital.'

'I told you, he doesn't like hospitals. I can get whatever hospital equipment you need. I had another doctor who took care of my friends, but he had an accident.'

The words sent a chill through Kat. She wanted nothing more than to run out of the place and go home, and never hear Dinetto's name again, but nothing in life was free. *Quid pro quo*. Kat took off her coat and went to work.

12

By the beginning of her fourth year of residency, Paige had assisted in hundreds of operations. They had become second nature to her. She knew the surgery procedures for the gallbladder, spleen, liver, appendix, and, most exciting, the heart. But Paige was frustrated because she was not doing the operations herself. *Whatever happened to 'Watch one, do one, teach one'?* she wondered.

The answer came when George Englund, chief of surgery, sent for her.

'Paige, there's a hernia operation scheduled for tomorrow in OR Three, seven-thirty A.M.'

She made a note. 'Right. Who's doing the operation?'

'You are.'

'Right. I . . .' The words suddenly sank in. '*I* am?'

'Yes. Any problem with that?'

Paige's grin lit up the room. 'No, sir! I . . . thanks!'

'You're ready for it. I think the patient's lucky to have you. His name is Walter Herzog. He's in 314.'

'Herzog. Room 314. Right.'

And Paige was out the door.

Paige had never been so excited. *I'm going to do my first operation! I'm going to hold a human being's life in my hands. What if I'm not ready? What if I make a mistake? Things can go wrong. It's Murphy's Law.* By the time Paige was through arguing with herself, she was in a state of panic.

She went into the cafeteria and sat down to have a cup of black coffee. *It's going to be all right*, she told herself. *I've assisted in dozens of hernia operations. There's nothing to it. He's lucky to have me.* By the time she finished her coffee, she was calm enough to face her first patient.

Walter Herzog was in his sixties, thin, bald, and very nervous. He was in bed, clutching his groin, when Paige walked in, carrying a bouquet of flowers. Herzog looked up.

'Nurse . . . I want to see a doctor.'

Paige walked over to the bed and handed him the flowers. 'I'm the doctor. I'm going to operate on you.'

He looked at the flowers, and looked at her. 'You're *what*?'

'Don't worry,' Paige said reassuringly. 'You're in good hands.' She picked up his chart at the foot of the bed and studied it.

'What does it say?' the man asked anxiously. *Why did she bring me flowers?*

'It says you're going to be just fine.'

He swallowed. 'Are you really going to do the operation?'

'Yes.'

'You seem awfully . . . awfully young.'

Paige patted his arm. 'I haven't lost a patient yet.' She looked around the room. 'Are you comfortable?

Can I get you anything to read? A book or magazine?'

He was listening, nervously. 'No, I'm okay.' *Why was she being so nice to him? Was there something she wasn't telling him?*

'Well, then, I'll see you in the morning,' Paige said cheerfully. She wrote something on a piece of paper and handed it to him. 'Here's my home number. You call me if you need me tonight. I'll stay right by the phone.'

By the time Paige left, Walter Herzog was a nervous wreck.

A few minutes later, Jimmy found Paige in the lounge. He walked up to her with his wide grin. 'Congratulations! I hear you're going to do a procedure.'

Word gets around fast, Paige thought. 'Yes.'

'Whoever he is, he's lucky,' Jimmy said. 'If anything ever happened to me, you're the only one I'd let operate on me.'

'Thanks, Jimmy.'

And, of course, with Jimmy, there was always a joke.

'Did you hear the one about the man who had a strange pain in his ankles? He was too cheap to go to a doctor, so when his friend told him he had exactly the same pain, he said, "You'd better get to a doctor right away. And tell me exactly what he says."

'The next day, he learns his friend is dead. He rushes to a hospital and has five thousand dollars' worth of tests. They can't find anything wrong. He

142

calls his friend's widow, and says, "Was Chester in a lot of pain before he died?"

'"No," she says. "He didn't even see the truck that hit him!"'

And Jimmy was gone.

Paige was too excited to eat dinner. She spent the evening practicing tying surgical knots on table legs and lamps. *I'm going to get a good night's sleep*, Paige decided, *so I'll be nice and fresh in the morning*.

She was awake all night, going over the operation again and again in her mind.

There are three types of hernias: reducible hernia, where it's possible to push the intestines back into the abdomen; irreducible hernia, where adhesions prevent returning the contents to the abdomen; and the most dangerous, strangulated hernia, where the blood flow through the hernia is shut off, damaging the intestines. Walter Herzog's was a reducible hernia.

At six o'clock in the morning, Paige drove to the hospital parking lot. A new red Ferrari was next to her parking space. Idly, Paige wondered who owned it. Whoever it was had to be rich.

At seven o'clock, Paige was helping Walter Herzog change from pajamas to a blue hospital gown. The nurse had already given him a sedative to relax him while they waited for the gurney that would take him to the operating room.

'This is my first operation,' Walter Herzog said.

Mine, too, Paige thought.

The gurney arrived and Walter Herzog was on his way to OR Three. Paige walked down the corridor beside him, and her heart was pounding so loudly that she was afraid he could hear it.

OR Three was one of the larger operating rooms, able to accommodate a heart monitor, a heart-lung machine, and an array of other technical paraphernalia. When Paige walked into the room, the staff were already there, preparing the equipment. There was an attending physician, the anesthesiologist, two residents, a scrub nurse, and two circulating nurses.

The staff were watching her expectantly, eager to see how she would handle her first operation.

Paige walked up to the operating table. Walter Herzog had had his groin shaved and scrubbed with an antiseptic solution. Sterile drapes had been placed around the operating area.

Herzog looked up at Paige and said drowsily, 'You're not going to let me die, are you?'

Paige smiled. 'What? And spoil my perfect record?'

She looked over at the anesthesiologist, who would give the patient an epidural anesthesia, a saddle block. Paige took a deep breath and nodded.

The operation began.

'Scalpel.'

As Paige was about to make the first cut through the skin, the circulating nurse said something.

'What?'

'Would you like some music, doctor?'

144

It was the first time she had been asked that question. Paige smiled. 'Right. Let's have some Jimmy Buffett.'

The moment Paige made the first incision, her nervousness vanished. It was as though she had done this all her life. Skillfully, she cut through the first layers of fat and muscle, to the site of the hernia. All the while, she was aware of the familiar litany that was echoing through the room.

'Sponge . . .'

'Give me a bovie . . .'

'There it is . . .'

'Looks like we got there just in time . . .'

'Clamp . . .'

'Suction, please . . .'

Paige's mind was totally focused on what she was doing. Locate the hernial sac . . . free it . . . place the contents back into the abdominal cavity . . . tie off the base of the sac . . . cut off the remainder . . . inguinal ring . . . suture it . . .

One hour and twenty minutes after the first incision, the operation was finished.

Paige should have felt drained, but instead she felt wildly exhilarated.

When Walter Herzog had been sewn up, the scrub nurse turned to Paige. 'Dr Taylor . . .'

Paige looked up. 'Yes?'

The nurse grinned. 'That was beautiful, doctor.'

It was Sunday and the three women had the day off.

'What should we do today?' Kat asked.

Paige had an idea. 'It's such a lovely day, why

145

don't we drive out to Tree Park? We can pack a picnic lunch and eat outdoors.'

'That sounds lovely,' Honey said.

'Let's do it!' Kat agreed.

The telephone rang. The three of them stared at it.

'Jesus!' Kat said. 'I thought Lincoln freed us. Don't answer it. It's our day off.'

'We *have* no days off,' Paige reminded her.

Kat walked over to the telephone and picked it up. 'Dr Hunter.' She listened for a moment and handed the telephone to Paige. 'It's for you, Dr Taylor.'

Paige said resignedly, 'Right.' She picked up the receiver. 'Dr Taylor . . . Hello, Tom . . . What? . . . No, I was just going out . . . I see . . . All right. I'll be there in fifteen minutes.' She replaced the receiver. *So much for the picnic*, she thought.

'Is it bad?' Honey asked.

'Yes, we're about to lose a patient. I'll try to be back for dinner tonight.'

When Paige arrived at the hospital, she drove into the doctors' parking lot and parked next to the new bright red Ferrari. *I wonder how many operations it took to pay for that?*

Twenty minutes later, Paige was walking into the visitors' waiting room. A man in a dark suit was seated in a chair, staring out the window.

'Mr Newton?'

He rose to his feet. 'Yes.'

'I'm Dr Taylor. I was just in to see your little

146

boy. He was brought in suffering abdominal pains.'

'Yes. I'm going to take him home.'

'I'm afraid not. Peter has a ruptured spleen. He needs an immediate transfusion and an operation, or he'll die.'

Mr Newton shook his head. 'We are Jehovah's Witnesses. The Lord will not let him die, and I will not let him be tainted with someone else's blood. It was my wife who brought him here. She will be punished for that.'

'Mr Newton, I don't think you understand how serious the situation is. If we don't operate right away, your son is going to die.'

The man looked at her and smiled. 'You don't know God's ways, do you?'

Paige was angry. 'I may not know a lot about God's ways, but I do know a lot about a ruptured spleen.' She took out a piece of paper. 'He's a minor, so you'll have to sign this consent form for him.' She held it out.

'And if I don't sign it?'

'Why . . . then we can't operate.'

He nodded. 'Do you think your powers are stronger than the Lord's?'

Paige was staring at him. 'You're not going to sign, are you?'

'No. A higher power than yours will help my son. You will see.'

When Paige returned to the ward, six-year-old Peter Newton had lapsed into unconsciousness.

'He's not going to make it,' Chang said. 'He's lost too much blood. What do you want to do?'

Paige made her decision. 'Get him into OR One. Stat.'

Chang looked at her in surprise. 'His father changed his mind?'

Paige nodded. 'Yes. He changed his mind. Let's move it.'

'Good for you! I talked to him for an hour and I couldn't budge him. He said God would take care of it.'

'God is taking care of it,' Paige assured him.

Two hours and four pints of blood later, the operation was successfully completed. All the boy's vital signs were strong.

Paige gently stroked his forehead. 'He's going to be fine.'

An orderly hurried into the operating room. 'Dr Taylor? Dr Wallace wants to see you right away.'

Benjamin Wallace was so angry his voice was cracking. 'How could you do such an outrageous thing? You gave him a blood transfusion and operated without permission? You broke the law!'

'I saved the boy's life!'

Wallace took a deep breath. 'You should have gotten a court order.'

'There was no time,' Paige said. 'Ten minutes more and he would have been dead. God was busy elsewhere.'

Wallace was pacing back and forth. 'What are we going to do now?'

'Get a court order.'

'What for? You've already *done* the operation.'

148

'I'll backdate the court order one day. No one will ever know the difference.'

Wallace looked at her and began to hyperventilate. 'Jesus!' He mopped his brow. 'This could cost me my job.'

Paige looked at him for a long moment. Then she turned and started toward the door.

'Paige . . . ?'

She stopped. 'Yes?'

'You'll never do anything like this again, will you?'

'Only if I have to,' Paige assured him.

13

All hospitals have problems with drug theft. By law, each narcotic that is taken from the dispensary must be signed for, but no matter how controlled the security is, drug addicts almost invariably find a way to circumvent it.

Embarcadero County Hospital was having a major problem. Margaret Spencer went to see Ben Wallace.

'I don't know what to do, doctor. Our fentanyl keeps disappearing.'

Fentanyl is a highly addictive narcotic and anesthetic drug.

'How much is missing?'

'A great deal. If it were just a few bottles, there could be an innocent explanation for it, but it's happening now on a regular basis. More than a dozen bottles a week are disappearing.'

'Do you have any idea who might be taking it?'

'No, sir. I've talked to security. They're at a loss.'

'Who has access to the dispensary?'

'That's the problem. Most of the anesthetists have pretty free access to it, and most of the nurses and surgeons.'

Wallace was thoughtful. 'Thank you for coming to me. I'll take care of it.'

'Thank you, doctor.' Nurse Spencer left.

I don't need this right now, Wallace thought

150

angrily. A hospital board meeting was coming up, and there were already enough problems to be dealt with. Ben Wallace was well aware of the statistics. More than 10 percent of the doctors in the United States became addicted, at one time or another, to either drugs or alcohol. The easy accessibility of the drugs made them a temptation. It was simple for a doctor to open a cabinet, take out the drug he wanted, and use a tourniquet and syringe to inject it. An addict could need a fix as often as every two hours.

Now it was happening at his hospital. Something had to be done about it before the board meeting. *It would look bad on my record.*

Ben Wallace was not sure whom he could trust to help him find the culprit. He had to be careful. He was certain that neither Dr Taylor nor Dr Hunter was involved, and after a great deal of thought, he decided to use them.

He sent for the two of them. 'I have a favor to ask of you,' he told them. He explained about the missing fentanyl. 'I want you to keep your eyes open. If any of the doctors you work with has to step out of the OR for a moment, in the middle of an operation, or shows any other signs of addiction, I want you to let me know. Look for any changes in personality — depression or mood swings — or tardiness, or missed appointments. I would appreciate it if you would keep this strictly confidential.'

When they left the office, Kat said, 'This is a big hospital. We're going to need Sherlock Holmes.'

'No, we won't,' Paige said unhappily. 'I know who it is.'

*   *   *

151

Mitch Campbell was one of Paige's favorite doctors. Dr Campbell was a likable gray-haired man in his fifties, always good-humored, and one of the hospital's best surgeons. Paige had noticed lately that he was always a few minutes late for an operation, and that he had developed a noticeable tremor. He used Paige to assist him as often as possible, and he usually let her do a major part of the surgery. In the middle of an operation, his hands would begin to shake and he would hand the scalpel to Paige.

'I'm not feeling well,' he would mumble. 'Would you take over?'

And he would leave the operating room.

Paige had been concerned about what could be wrong with him. Now she knew. She debated what to do. She was aware that if she brought her information to Wallace, Dr Campbell would be fired, or worse, his career would be destroyed. On the other hand, if she did nothing, she would be putting patients' lives in danger. *Perhaps I could talk to him*, Paige thought. *Tell him what I know, and insist that he get treatment.* She discussed it with Kat.

'It's a problem,' Kat agreed. 'He's a nice guy, and a good doctor. If you blow the whistle, he's finished, but if you don't, you have to think about the harm he might do. What do you think will happen if you confront him?'

'He'll probably deny it, Kat. That's the usual pattern.'

'Yeah. It's a tough call.'

*   *   *

The following day, Paige had an operation scheduled with Dr Campbell. *I hope I'm wrong*, Paige prayed. *Don't let him be late, and don't let him leave during the operation.*

Campbell was fifteen minutes late, and in the middle of the operation, he said, 'Take over, will you, Paige? I'll be right back.'

I must talk to him, Paige decided. *I can't destroy his career.*

The following morning, as Paige and Honey drove into the doctors' parking lot, Harry Bowman pulled up next to them in the red Ferrari.

'That's a beautiful car,' Honey said. 'How much does one of those cost?'

Bowman laughed. 'If you have to ask, you can't afford it.'

But Paige wasn't listening. She was staring at the car, and thinking about the penthouse, the lavish parties, and the boat. *I was smart enough to have a clever father. He left all his money to me.* And yet Bowman worked at a county hospital. Why?

Ten minutes later, Paige was in the personnel office, talking to Karen, the secretary in charge of records.

'Do me a favor, will you, Karen? Just between us, Harry Bowman has asked me to go out with him and I have a feeling he's married. Would you let me have a peek at his personnel file?'

'Sure. Those horny bastards. They never get enough, do they? You're darn right I'll let you look at his file.' She went over to a cabinet and found what she was looking for. She brought some papers back to Paige.

Paige glanced through them quickly. Dr Harry Bowman's application showed that he had come from a small university in the Midwest and, according to the records, had worked his way through medical school. He was an anesthesiologist.

His father was a barber.

Honey Taft was an enigma to most of the doctors at Embarcadero County Hospital. During the morning rounds, she appeared to be unsure of herself. But on the afternoon rounds, she seemed like a different person. She was surprisingly knowledgeable about each patient, and crisp and efficient in her diagnoses.

One of the senior residents was discussing her with a colleague.

'I'll be damned if I understand it,' he said. 'In the morning, the complaints about Dr Taft keep piling up. She keeps making mistakes. You know the joke about the nurse who gets everything wrong? A doctor is complaining that he told her to give the patient in Room 4 three pills, and she gave the patient in Room 3 four pills, and just as he's talking about her, he sees her chasing a naked patient down the hall, holding a pan of boiling water. The doctor says, "Look at that! I told her to prick his boil!"'

His colleague laughed.

'Well, that's Dr Taft. But in the afternoon she's absolutely brilliant. Her diagnoses are correct, her notes are wonderful, and she's as sharp as hell. She must be taking some kind of miracle pill that only works afternoons.' He scratched his head. 'It beats the hell out of me.'

Dr Nathan Ritter was a pedant, a man who lived and worked by the book. While he lacked the spark of brilliance, he was capable and dedicated, and he expected the same qualities from those who worked with him.

Honey had the misfortune to be assigned to his team.

Their first stop was a ward containing a dozen patients. One of them was just finishing breakfast. Ritter looked at the chart at the foot of the bed. 'Dr Taft, the chart says this is your patient.'

Honey nodded. 'Yes.'

'He's having a bronchoscopy this morning.'

Honey nodded. 'That's right.'

'And you're allowing him to *eat*?' Dr Ritter snapped. '*Before* a bronchoscopy?'

Honey said, 'The poor man hasn't had anything to eat since —'

Nathan Ritter turned to his assistant. 'Postpone the procedure.' He started to say something to Honey, then controlled himself. 'Let's move on.'

The next patient was a Puerto Rican who was coughing badly. Dr Ritter examined him. 'Whose patient is this?'

'Mine,' Honey said.

He frowned. 'His infection should have cleared up before now.' He took a look at the chart. 'You're giving him fifty milligrams of ampicillin four times a day?'

'That's right.'

'That's *not* right. It's *wrong*! That's supposed to be *five hundred* milligrams four times a day. You left off a zero.'

'I'm sorry, I . . .'

'No wonder the patient's not getting any better! I want it changed immediately.'

'Yes, doctor.'

When they came to another patient of Honey's, Dr Ritter said impatiently, 'He's scheduled for a colonoscopy. Where is the radiology report?'

'The radiology report? Oh. I'm afraid I forgot to order one.'

Ritter gave Honey a long speculative look.

The morning went downhill from there.

The next patient they saw was moaning tearfully. 'I'm in such pain. What's wrong with me?'

'We don't know,' Honey said.

Dr Ritter glared at her. 'Dr Taft, may I see you outside for a moment?'

In the corridor, he said, 'Never, *never* tell a patient that you don't know. You're the one they're looking to for help! And if you don't know the answer, make one up. Do you understand?'

'It doesn't seem right to . . .'

'I didn't ask you whether it seemed right. Just do as you're told.'

They examined a hiatal hernia, a hepatitis patient, a patient with Alzheimer's disease, and two dozen others. The minute the rounds were over, Dr Ritter went to Benjamin Wallace's office.

'We have a problem,' Ritter said.

'What is it, Nathan?'

'It's one of the residents here. Honey Taft.'

Again! 'What about her?'

'She's a disaster.'

'But she had such a wonderful recommendation.'

'Ben, you'd better get rid of her before the hospital gets in real trouble, before she kills a patient or two.'

Wallace thought about it for a moment, then made his decision. 'Right. She'll be out of here.'

Paige was busy in surgery most of the morning. As soon as she was free, she went to see Dr Wallace, to tell him of her suspicions about Harry Bowman.

'Bowman? Are you sure? I mean . . . I've seen no signs of any addiction.'

'He doesn't use it,' Paige explained. 'He sells it. He's living like a millionaire on a resident's salary.'

Ben Wallace nodded. 'Very well. I'll check it out. Thank you, Paige.'

Wallace sent for Bruce Anderson, head of security. 'We may have identified the drug thief,' Wallace told him. 'I want you to keep a close watch on Dr Harry Bowman.'

'Bowman?' Anderson tried to conceal his surprise. Dr Bowman was constantly giving the guards Cuban cigars and other little gifts. They all loved him.

'If he goes into the dispensary, search him when he comes out.'

'Yes, sir.'

Harry Bowman was headed for the dispensary. He had orders to fill. A *lot* of orders. It had started as a lucky accident. He had been working in a small hospital in Ames, Iowa, struggling to get by on a resident's salary. He had champagne taste and a beer pocketbook, and then Fate had smiled on him.

One of his patients who had been discharged from the hospital telephoned him one morning.

'Doctor, I'm in terrible pain. You have to give me something for it.'

'Do you want to check back in?'

'I don't want to leave the house. Couldn't you bring something here for me?'

Bowman thought about it. 'All right. I'll drop by on my way home.'

When he visited the patient, he brought with him a bottle of fentanyl.

The patient grabbed it. 'That's wonderful!' he said. He pulled out a handful of bills. 'Here.'

Bowman looked at him, surprised. 'You don't have to pay me for that.'

'Are you kidding? This stuff is like gold. I have a lot of friends who will pay you a fortune if you bring them this stuff.'

That was how it had begun. Within two months, Harry Bowman was making more money than he had ever dreamed possible. Unfortunately, the head of the hospital got wind of what was going on. Fearing a public scandal, he told Bowman that if he left quietly, nothing would appear on his record.

I'm glad I left, Bowman thought. *San Francisco has a much bigger market.*

He reached the dispensary. Bruce Anderson was standing outside. Bowman nodded to him. 'Hi, Bruce.'

'Good afternoon, Dr Bowman.'

Five minutes later when Bowman came out of the dispensary, Anderson said, 'Excuse me. I'm going to have to search you.'

158

Harry Bowman stared at him. 'Search me? What are you talking about, Bruce?'

'I'm sorry, doctor. We have orders to search everyone who uses the dispensary,' Anderson lied.

Bowman was indignant. 'I've never heard of such a thing. I absolutely refuse!'

'Then I'll have to ask you to come along with me to Dr Wallace's office.'

'Fine! He's going to be furious when he hears about this.'

Bowman stormed into Wallace's office. 'What's going on, Ben? This man wanted to search me, for God's sake!'

'And did you refuse to be searched?'

'Absolutely.'

'All right.' Wallace reached for the telephone. 'I'll let the San Francisco police do it, if you prefer.' He began to dial.

Bowman panicked. 'Wait a minute! That's not necessary.' His face suddenly cleared. 'Oh! I know what this is all about!' He reached in his pocket and took out a bottle of fentanyl. 'I was taking these to use for an operation, and . . .'

Wallace said quietly, 'Empty your pockets.'

A look of desperation came over Bowman's face. 'There's no reason to . . .'

'Empty your pockets.'

Two hours later, the San Francisco office of the Drug Enforcement Agency had a signed confession and the names of the people to whom Bowman had been selling drugs.

*   *   *

When Paige heard the news, she went to see Mitch Campbell. He was sitting in an office, resting. His hands were on the desk when Paige walked in, and she could see the tremor in them.

Campbell quickly moved his hands to his lap. 'Hello, Paige. How're you doing?'

'Fine, Mitch. I wanted to talk to you.'

'Sit down.'

She took a seat opposite him. 'How long have you had Parkinson's?'

He turned a shade whiter. 'What?'

'That's it, isn't it? You've been trying to cover it up.'

There was a heavy silence. 'I . . . I . . . yes. But I . . . I can't give up being a doctor. I . . . I just can't give it up. It's my whole life.'

Paige leaned forward and said earnestly, 'You don't have to give up being a doctor, but you shouldn't be operating.'

He looked suddenly old. 'I know. I was going to quit last year.' He smiled wanly. 'I guess I'll have to quit now, won't I? You're going to tell Dr Wallace.'

'No,' Paige said gently. '*You're* going to tell Dr Wallace.'

Paige was having lunch in the cafeteria when Tom Chang joined her.

'I heard what happened,' he said. 'Bowman! Unbelievable. Nice work.'

She shook her head. 'I almost had the wrong man.'

Chang sat there, silent.

'Are you all right, Tom?'

'Do you want the "I'm fine", or do you want the truth?'

'We're friends. I want the truth.'

'My marriage has gone to hell.' His eyes suddenly filled with tears. 'Sye has left. She's gone back home.'

'I'm so sorry.'

'It's not her fault. We didn't have a marriage anymore. She said I'm married to the hospital, and she's right. I'm spending my whole life here, taking care of strangers, instead of being with the people I love.'

'She'll come back. It will work out,' Paige said soothingly.

'No. Not this time.'

'Have you thought about counseling, or . . . ?'

'She refuses.'

'I'm sorry, Tom. If there's anything I . . .' She heard her name on the loudspeaker.

'Dr Taylor, Room 410 . . .'

Paige felt a sudden pang of alarm. 'I have to go,' she said. Room 410. That was Sam Bernstein's room. He was one of her favorite patients, a gentle man in his seventies who had been brought in with inoperable stomach cancer. Many of the patients at the hospital were constantly complaining, but Sam Bernstein was an exception. Paige admired his courage and his dignity. He had a wife and two grown sons who visited him regularly, and Paige had grown fond of them, too.

He had been put on life-support systems with a note, DNR — Do Not Resuscitate — if his heart stopped.

When Paige walked into his room, a nurse was at the bedside. She looked up as Paige entered. 'He's

161

gone, doctor. I didn't start emergency procedures, because . . .' Her voice trailed off.

'You were right not to,' Paige said slowly. 'Thank you.'

'Is there anything I . . . ?'

'No. I'll make the arrangements.' Paige stood by the bedside and looked down at the body of what had been a living, laughing human being, a man who had a family and friends, someone who had spent his life working hard, taking care of the ones he loved. And now . . .

She walked over to the drawer where he kept his possessions. There was an inexpensive watch, a set of keys, fifteen dollars in cash, dentures, and a letter to his wife. All that remained of a man's life.

Paige was unable to shake the feeling of depression that hung over her. 'He was such a dear man. Why . . . ?'

Kat said, 'Paige, you can't let yourself get emotionally involved with your patients. It will tear you apart.'

'I know. You're right, Kat. It's just that . . . it's over so quickly, isn't it? This morning he and I were talking. Tomorrow is his funeral.'

'You're not thinking of going to it?'

'No.'

The funeral took place at the Hills of Eternity Cemetery.

In the Jewish religion, burial must take place as soon as possible following the death, and the service usually takes place the next day.

The body of Sam Bernstein was dressed in a *takhri-*

162

khim, a white robe, and wrapped in a *talit*. The family was gathered around the graveside. The rabbi was intoning, '*Hamakom y'nathaim etkhem b'tokh sh'ar availai tziyon veeyerushalayim*.'

A man standing next to Paige saw the puzzled expression on her face, and he translated for her. '"May the Lord comfort you with all the mourners of Zion and Jerusalem."'

To Paige's astonishment, the members of the family began tearing at the clothes they were wearing as they chanted, '*Baruch ata adonai elohainu melech haolam dayan ha-emet*.'

'What . . . ?'

'That's to show respect,' the man whispered. '"From dust you are and to dust you have returned, but the spirit returns to God who gave it."'

The ceremony was over.

The following morning, Kat ran into Honey in the corridor. Honey looked nervous.

'Anything wrong?' Kat asked.

'Dr Wallace sent for me. He asked me to be in his office at two o'clock.'

'Do you know why?'

'I think I messed up at rounds the other day. Dr Ritter is a monster.'

'He can be,' Kat said. 'But I'm sure everything will be all right.'

'I hope so. I just have a bad feeling.'

Promptly at two o'clock, she arrived at Benjamin Wallace's office, carrying a small jar of honey in her

163

purse. The receptionist was at lunch. Dr Wallace's door was open. 'Come in, Dr Taft,' he called.

Honey walked into his office.

'Close the door behind you, please.'

Honey closed the door.

'Take a seat.'

Honey sat down across from him. She was almost trembling.

Benjamin Wallace had been putting this off as long as he could. He looked across at her and thought, *It's like kicking a puppy. But what has to be done has to be done.* 'I'm afraid I have some unfortunate news for you,' he said.

One hour later, Honey met Kat in the solarium. Honey sank into a chair next to her, smiling.

'Did you see Dr Wallace?' Kat asked.

'Oh, yes. We had a long talk. Did you know that his wife left him last September? They were married for fifteen years. He has two grown children from an earlier marriage, but he hardly ever sees them. The poor darling is so lonely.'

Book Two

14

It was New Year's Eve again, and Paige, Kat and Honey ushered in 1994 at Embarcadero County Hospital. It seemed to them that nothing in their lives had changed except the names of their patients.

As Paige walked through the parking lot, she was reminded of Harry Bowman and his red Ferrari. *How many lives were destroyed by the poison Harry Bowman was selling?* she wondered. Drugs were so seductive. And, in the end, so deadly.

Jimmy Ford showed up with a small bouquet of flowers for Paige.

'What's this for, Jimmy?'

He blushed. 'I just wanted you to have it. Did you know I'm getting married?'

'No! That's wonderful. Who's the lucky girl?'

'Her name is Betsy. She works at a dress shop. We're going to have half a dozen kids. The first girl is going to be named Paige. I hope you don't mind.'

'Mind? I'm flattered.'

He was embarrassed. 'Did you hear the one about the doctor who gave a patient two weeks to live? "I can't pay you right now," the man said. "All right, I'll give you another two weeks."'

And Jimmy was gone.

Paige was worried about Tom Chang. He was having violent mood swings from euphoria to deep depression.

One morning during a talk with Paige, he said, 'Do you realize that most of the people in here would die without us? We have the power to heal their bodies and make them whole again.'

And the next morning: 'We're all kidding ourselves, Paige. Our patients would get better faster without us. We're hypocrites, pretending that we have all the answers. Well, we don't.'

Paige studied him a moment. 'What do you hear from Sye?'

'I talked to her yesterday. She won't come back here. She's going ahead with the divorce.'

Paige put her hand on his arm. 'I'm so sorry, Tom.'

He shrugged. 'Why? It doesn't bother me. Not anymore. I'll find another woman.' He grinned. 'And have another child. You'll see.'

There was something unreal about the conversation.

That night Paige said to Kat, 'I'm worried about Tom Chang. Have you talked to him lately?'

'Yes.'

'Did he seem normal to you?'

'No man seems normal to me,' Kat said.

Paige was still concerned. 'Let's invite him out for dinner tomorrow night.'

'All right.'

168

The next morning when Paige reported to the hospital, she was greeted with the news that a janitor had found Tom Chang's body in a basement equipment room. He had died of an overdose of sleeping pills.

Paige was near hysteria. 'I could have saved him,' she cried. 'All this time he was calling out for help, and I didn't hear him.'

Kat said firmly, 'There's no way you could have helped him, Paige. You were not the problem, and you were not the solution. He didn't want to live without his wife and child. It's as simple as that.'

Paige wiped the tears from her eyes. 'Damn this place!' she said. 'If it weren't for the pressure and the hours, his wife never would have left him.'

'But she did,' Kat said gently. 'It's over.'

Paige had never been to a Chinese funeral before. It was an incredible spectacle. It began at the Green Street Mortuary in Chinatown early in the morning, where a crowd started gathering outside. A parade was assembled, with a large brass marching band, and at the head of the parade, mourners carried a huge blowup of a photograph of Tom Chang.

The march began with the band loudly playing, winding through the streets of San Francisco, with a hearse at the end of the procession. Most of the mourners were on foot, but the more elderly rode in cars.

To Paige, the parade seemed to be moving around the city at random. She was puzzled. 'Where are they going?' she asked one of the mourners.

He bowed slightly and said, 'It is our custom to

take the departed past some of the places that have meaning in his life—restaurants where he ate, shops that he used, places he visited . . .'

'I see.'

The parade ended in front of Embarcadero County Hospital.

The mourner turned to Paige and said, 'This is where Tom Chang worked. This is where he found his happiness.'

Wrong, Paige thought. *This is where he lost his happiness.*

Walking down Market Street one morning, Paige saw Alfred Turner. Her heart started pounding. She had not been able to get him out of her mind. He was starting to cross the street as the light was changing. When Paige got to the corner, the light had turned to red. She ignored it and ran out into the street, oblivious to the honking horns and the outraged cries of motorists.

Paige reached the other side and hurried to catch up with him. She grabbed his sleeve. 'Alfred . . .'

The man turned. 'I beg your pardon?'

It was a total stranger.

Now that Paige and Kat were fourth-year residents, they were performing operations on a regular basis.

Kat was working with doctors in neurosurgery, and she never ceased to be amazed at the miracle of the hundred billion complex digital computers called neurons that lived in the skull. The work was exciting.

Kat had enormous respect for most of the doctors she worked with. They were brilliant, skilled surgeons. There were a few doctors who gave her a hard time. They tried to date her, and the more Kat refused to go out with them, the more of a challenge she became.

She heard one doctor mutter, 'Here comes old ironpants.'

She was assisting Dr Kibler at a brain operation. A tiny incision was made in the cortex, and Dr Kibler pushed the rubber cannula into the left lateral ventricle, the cavity in the center of the left half of the brain, while Kat held the incision open with a small retractor. Her entire concentration was focused on what was happening in front of her.

Dr Kibler glanced at her and, as he worked, said, 'Did you hear about the wino who staggered into a bar and said, "Give me a drink, quick!" "I can't do that," the bartender said. "You're already drunk."'

The burr was cutting in deeper.

'"If you don't give me a drink, I'll kill myself."'

Cerebral spinal fluid flowed out of the cannula from the ventricle.

'"I'll tell you what I'll do," the bartender said. "There are three things I want. You do them for me, and I'll give you a bottle."'

As he went on talking, fifteen milliliters of air were injected into the ventricle, and X-rays were taken of the anterior-posterior view and the lateral view.

'"See that football player sitting in the corner? I can't get him out of here. I want you to throw him out. Next, I have a pet crocodile in my office with a bad tooth. He's so mean I can't get a vet to go near

171

him. Lastly, there's a lady doctor from the Department of Health who's trying to close up this place. You fuck her, and you get the bottle."'

A scrub nurse was using suction to reduce the amount of blood in the field.

'The wino throws out the football player, and goes into the office where the crocodile is. He comes out fifteen minutes later, all bloody, and his clothes torn, and he says, "Where's the lady doctor with the bad tooth?"'

Dr Kibler roared with laughter. 'Do you get it? He fucked the crocodile instead of the doctor. It was probably a better experience!'

Kat stood there, furious, wanting to slap him.

When the operation was over, Kat went to the on-call room to try to get over her anger. *I'm not going to let the bastards beat me down. I'm not.*

From time to time, Paige went out with doctors from the hospital, but she refused to get romantically involved with any of them. Alfred Turner had hurt her too deeply, and she was determined never to go through that again.

Most of her days and nights were spent at the hospital. The schedule was grueling, but Paige was doing general surgery and she enjoyed it.

One morning, George Englund, the chief of surgery, sent for her.

'You're starting your specialty this year. Cardiovascular surgery.'

She nodded. 'That's right.'

'Well, I have a treat for you. Have you heard of Dr Barker?'

172

Paige looked at him in surprise. 'Dr *Lawrence* Barker?'

'Yes.'

'Of course.'

Everyone had heard of Lawrence Barker. He was one of the most famous cardiovascular surgeons in the world.

'Well, he returned last week from Saudi Arabia, where he operated on the king. Dr Barker's an old friend of mine, and he's agreed to give us three days a week here. *Pro bono*.'

'That's fantastic!' Paige exclaimed.

'I'm putting you on his team.'

For a moment, Paige was speechless. 'I . . . I don't know what to say. I'm very grateful.'

'It's a wonderful opportunity for you. You can learn a lot from him.'

'I'm sure I can. Thank you, George. I really appreciate this.'

'You'll start your rounds with him tomorrow morning at six o'clock.'

'I'm looking forward to it.'

'Looking forward to it' was an understatement. It had been Paige's dream to work with someone like Dr Lawrence Barker. *What do I mean, 'someone like Dr Lawrence Barker'? There's only one Dr Lawrence Barker.*

She had never seen a photograph of him, but she could visualize what he looked like. He would be tall and handsome, with silver-gray hair, and slender, sensitive hands. A warm and gentle man. *We'll be working closely together*, Paige thought, *and I'm*

173

going to make myself absolutely indispensable. I wonder if he's married?

That night, Paige had an erotic dream about Dr Barker. They were performing an operation in the nude. In the middle of it, Dr Barker said, 'I want you.' A nurse moved the patient off the operating table and Dr Barker picked Paige up and put her on the table, and made love to her.

When Paige woke up, she was falling off the bed.

At six o'clock the following morning, Paige was nervously waiting in the second-floor corridor with Joel Philips, the senior resident, and five other residents, when a short, sour-faced man stormed toward them. He leaned forward as he walked, as though battling a stiff wind.

He approached the group. 'What the hell are you all standing around for? Let's go!'

It took Paige a moment to regain her composure. She hurried along to catch up with the rest of the group. As they moved along the corridor, Dr Barker snapped, 'You'll have between thirty and thirty-five patients to care for every day. I'll expect you to make detailed notes on each one of them. Clear?'

There were murmurs of 'Yes, sir.'

They had reached the first ward. Dr Barker walked over to the bed of a patient, a man in his forties. Barker's gruff and forbidding manner went through an instant change. He touched the patient gently on the shoulder and smiled. 'Good morning. I'm Dr Barker.'

'Good morning, doctor.'

'How are you feeling this morning?'

'My chest hurts.'

Dr Barker studied the chart at the foot of the bed, then turned to Dr Philips. 'What do his X-rays show?'

'No change. He's healing nicely.'

'Let's do another CBC.'

Dr Philips made a note.

Dr Barker patted the man on the arm and smiled. 'It's looking good. We'll have you out of here in a week.' He turned to the residents and snapped, 'Move it! We have a lot of patients to see.'

My God! Paige thought. *Talk about Dr Jekyll and Mr Hyde!*

The next patient was an obese woman who had had a pacemaker put in. Dr Barker studied her chart. 'Good morning, Mrs Shelby.' His voice was soothing. 'I'm Dr Barker.'

'How long are you going to keep me in this place?'

'Well, you're so charming, I'd like to keep you here forever, but I have a wife.'

Mrs Shelby giggled. 'She's a lucky woman.'

Barker was examining her chart again. 'I'd say you're just about ready to go home.'

'Wonderful.'

'I'll stop by to see you this afternoon.'

Lawrence Barker turned to the residents. 'Move on.'

They obediently trailed behind the doctor to a semiprivate room where a young Guatemalan boy lay in bed, surrounded by his anxious family.

'Good morning,' Dr Barker said warmly. He scanned the patient's chart. 'How are you feeling this morning?'

'I am feeling good, doctor.'

Dr Barker turned to Philips. 'Any change in the electrolytes?'

'No, doctor.'

'That's good news.' He patted the boy's arm. 'You hang in there, Juan.'

The mother asked anxiously, 'Is my son going to be all right?'

Dr Barker smiled. 'We're going to do everything we can for him.'

'Thank you, doctor.'

Dr Barker stepped out into the corridor, the others trailing behind him. He stopped. 'The patient has myocardiopathy, irregular fever tremors, headaches, and localized edema. Can any of you geniuses tell me what the most common cause of it is?'

There was a silence. Paige said hesitantly, 'I believe it's congenital . . . hereditary.'

Dr Barker looked at her and nodded encouragingly.

Pleased, Paige went on. 'It skips . . . wait . . .' She was struggling to remember. 'It skips a generation and is passed along by the genes of the mother.' She stopped, flushed, proud of herself.

Dr Barker stared at her a moment. 'Horseshit! It's Chagas' disease. It affects people from Latin American countries.' He looked at Paige with disgust. 'Jesus! Who told you you were a doctor?'

Paige's face was flaming red.

The rest of the rounds was a blur to her. They saw twenty-four patients and it seemed to Paige that Dr Barker spent the morning trying to humiliate her. She was always the one Barker addressed his questions to, testing, probing. When she was right, he never complimented her. When she was wrong, he

176

yelled at her. At one point, when Paige made a mistake, Barker roared, 'I wouldn't let you operate on my dog!'

When the rounds were finally over, Dr Philips, the senior resident, said, 'We'll start rounds again at two o'clock. Get your scut books, make notes on each patient, and don't leave anything out.'

He looked at Paige pityingly, started to say something, then turned away to join Dr Barker.

Paige thought, *I never want to see that bastard again.*

The following night, Paige was on call. She ran from one crisis to the next, frantically trying to stem the tide of disasters that flooded the emergency rooms.

At 1:00 A.M., she finally fell asleep. She did not hear the sound of a siren screaming out its warning as an ambulance roared to a stop in front of the emergency entrance of the hospital. Two paramedics swung open the ambulance door, transferred the unconscious patient from his stretcher to a gurney, and ran it through the entrance doors of ER One.

The staff had been alerted by radiophone. A nurse ran alongside the patient, while a second nurse waited at the top of the ramp. Sixty seconds later, the patient was transferred from the gurney to the examination table.

He was a young man, and he was covered with so much blood that it was difficult to tell what he looked like.

A nurse went to work, cutting his torn clothes off with large shears.

'It looks like everything's broken.'

'He's bleeding like a stuck pig.'

'I'm not getting a pulse.'

'Who's on call?'

'Dr Taylor.'

'Get her. If she hurries, he may still be alive.'

Paige was awakened by the ringing of the telephone.

'H'lo . . .'

'We have an emergency in ER One, doctor. I don't think he's going to make it.'

Paige sat up on the cot. 'Right. I'm coming.'

She looked at her wristwatch. 1:30 A.M. She stumbled out of bed and made her way to the elevator.

A minute later, she was walking into ER One. In the middle of the room, on the examining table, was the blood-covered patient.

'What do we have here?' Paige asked.

'Motorcycle accident. He was hit by a bus. He wasn't wearing a helmet.'

Paige moved toward the unconscious figure, and even before she saw his face, she somehow knew.

She was suddenly wide awake. 'Get three IV lines in him!' Paige ordered. 'Get him on oxygen. I want some blood sent down, stat. Call Records to get his blood type.'

The nurse looked at her in surprise. 'You know him?'

'Yes.' She had to force herself to say the words. 'His name is Jimmy Ford.'

Paige ran her fingers over his scalp. 'There's heavy edema. I want a head scan and X-rays. We're going to push the envelope on this one. I want him alive!'

'Yes, doctor.'

Paige spent the next two hours making sure that everything possible was being done for Jimmy Ford. The X-rays showed a fractured skull, a brain contusion, a broken humerus, and multiple lacerations. But everything would have to wait until he was stabilized.

At 3:30 A.M., Paige decided there was nothing more she could do for the present. He was breathing better, and his pulse was stronger. She looked down at the unconscious figure. *We're going to have half a dozen kids. The first girl is going to be named Paige. I hope you don't mind.*

'Call me if there's any change at all,' Paige said.

'Don't worry, doctor,' one of the nurses said. 'We'll take good care of him.'

Paige made her way back to the on-call room. She was exhausted, but she was too concerned about Jimmy to go back to sleep.

The telephone rang again. She barely had the energy to pick it up. 'H'lo.'

'Doctor, you'd better come up to the third floor. Stat. I think one of Dr Barker's patients is having a heart attack.'

'Coming,' Paige said. *One of Dr Barker's patients.* Paige took a deep breath, staggered out of bed, threw cold water on her face, and hurried to the third floor.

A nurse was waiting outside a private room. 'It's Mrs Hearns. It looks like she's having another heart seizure.'

Paige went into the room.

Mrs Hearns was a woman in her fifties. Her face

179

still held the remnants of a onetime beauty, but her body was fat and bloated. She was holding her chest and moaning. 'I'm dying,' she said. 'I'm dying. I can't breathe.'

'You're going to be all right,' Paige said reassuringly. She turned to the nurse. 'Did you do an EKG?'

'She won't let me touch her. She said she's too nervous.'

'We must do an EKG,' Paige told the patient.

'No! I don't want to die. Please don't let me die . . .'

Paige said to the nurse, 'Call Dr Barker. Ask him to get down here right away.'

The nurse hurried off.

Paige put a stethoscope to Mrs Hearns's chest. She listened. The heartbeat seemed normal, but Paige could not afford to take any chances.

'Dr Barker will be here in a few minutes,' she told Mrs Hearns. 'Try to relax.'

'I've never felt this bad. My chest feels so heavy. Please don't leave me.'

'I'm not going to leave you,' Paige promised her.

While she was waiting for Dr Barker to arrive, Paige telephoned the intensive care unit. There was no change in Jimmy Ford's condition. He was still in a coma.

Thirty minutes later, Dr Barker appeared. He had obviously dressed in haste. 'What's going on?' he demanded.

Paige said, 'I think Mrs Hearns is having another heart attack.'

Dr Barker moved over to the bedside. 'Did you do an EKG?'

'She wouldn't let us.'

'Pulse?'

'Normal. No fever.'

Dr Barker put a stethoscope against Mrs Hearns's back. 'Take a deep breath.'

She obliged.

'Again.'

Mrs Hearns let out a loud belch. 'Excuse me.' She smiled. 'Oh. That's better.'

He studied her a moment. 'What did you have for dinner, Mrs Hearns?'

'I had a hamburger.'

'Just a hamburger? That's all? One?'

'Two.'

'Anything else?'

'Well, you know . . . onions and french fries.'

'And to drink?'

'A chocolate milk shake.'

Dr Barker looked down at the patient. 'Your heart is fine. It's your appetite we have to worry about.' He turned to Paige. 'What you're seeing here is a case of heartburn. I'd like to see you outside, doctor.'

When they were in the corridor, he roared, 'What the hell did they teach you in medical school? Don't you even know the difference between heartburn and a heart attack?'

'I thought . . .'

'The problem is, you *didn't*! If you ever wake me up again in the middle of the night for a heartburn case, I'll have your ass. You understand that?'

Paige stood there stiffly, her face grim.

'Give her some antacid, *doctor*,' Lawrence Barker said sarcastically, 'and you'll find that she's cured. I'll see you at six o'clock for rounds.'

181

Paige watched him storm out.

When Paige stumbled back to her cot in the on-call room, she thought, *I'm going to kill Lawrence Barker. I'll do it slowly. He'll be very ill. He'll have a dozen tubes in his body. He'll beg me to put him out of his misery, but I won't. I'll let him suffer, and then when he feels better . . . that's when I'll kill him!*

15

Paige was on morning rounds with the Beast, as she secretly referred to Dr Barker. She had assisted him in three cardiothoracic surgeries, and in spite of her bitter feelings toward him, she could not help but admire his incredible skill. She watched in awe as he opened up a patient, deftly replaced the old heart with a donor heart, and sewed him up. The operation took less than five hours.

Within a few weeks, Paige thought, *that patient will be able to return to a normal life. No wonder surgeons think they're gods. They bring the dead back to life.*

Time after time, Paige watched a heart stop and turn to an inert piece of flesh. And then the miracle would occur, and a lifeless organ would begin to pulsate again and send blood through a body that had been dying.

One morning, a patient was scheduled for a procedure to insert an intra-aortic balloon. Paige was in the operating room assisting Dr Barker. As they were about to begin, Dr Barker snapped, 'Do it!'

Paige looked at him. 'I beg your pardon?'

'It's a simple procedure. Do you think you can handle it?' There was contempt in his voice.

'Yes,' Paige said tightly.

'Well, then, get on with it!'

He was infuriating.

Barker watched as Paige expertly inserted a hollow tube into the patient's artery and threaded it up into the heart. It was done flawlessly. Barker stood there, without saying a word.

To hell with him, Paige thought. *Nothing I could ever do would please him.*

Paige injected a radiopaque dye through the tube. They watched the monitor as the dye flowed into the coronary arteries. Images appeared on a fluoroscopy screen and showed the degree of blockage and its location in the artery, while an automatic motion-picture camera recorded the X-rays for a permanent record.

The senior resident looked at Paige and smiled. 'Nice job.'

'Thank you.' Paige turned to Dr Barker.

'Too damned slow,' he growled.

And he walked out.

Paige was grateful for the days that Dr Barker was away from the hospital, working at his private practice. She said to Kat, 'Being away from him for a day is like a week in the country.'

'You really hate him, don't you?'

'He's a brilliant doctor, but he's a miserable human being. Have you ever noticed how some people fit their names? If Dr Barker doesn't stop barking at people, he's going to have a stroke.'

'You should see some of the beauties I have to put up with.' Kat laughed. 'They all think they're

God's gift to pussies. Wouldn't it be great if there were no men in the world!'

Paige looked at her, but said nothing.

Paige and Kat went to check on Jimmy Ford. He was still in a coma. There was nothing they could do.

Kat sighed. 'Dammit. Why does it happen to the good guys?'

'I wish I knew.'

'Do you think he'll make it?'

Paige hesitated. 'We've done everything we can. Now it's up to God.'

'Funny. I thought *we* were God.'

The following day when Paige was in charge of afternoon rounds, Kaplan, a senior resident, stopped her in the corridor. 'This is your lucky day.' He grinned. 'You're getting a new medical school student to take around.'

'Really?'

'Yeah, the IN.'

'IN?'

'Idiot nephew. Dr Wallace's wife has a nephew who wants to be a doctor. They threw him out of his last two schools. We've all had to put up with him. Today it's your turn.'

Paige groaned. 'I don't have time for this. I'm up to my . . .'

'It's not an option. Be a good girl and Dr Wallace will give you brownie points.' Kaplan moved off.

Paige sighed and walked over to where the new residents were waiting to start the rounds. *Where's the IN?* She looked at her watch. He was already three minutes late. *I'll give him one more minute*, Paige decided, *and then to hell with him*. She saw him then, a tall, lean-looking man, hurrying toward her, down the hall.

He walked up to Paige, out of breath, and said, 'Excuse me. Dr Wallace asked me to—'

'You're late,' Paige said curtly.

'I know. I'm sorry. I was held up at—'

'Never mind. What's your name?'

'Jason. Jason Curtis.' He was wearing a sport jacket.

'Where's your white coat?'

'My white coat?'

'Didn't anyone tell you to wear a white coat on rounds?'

He looked flustered. 'No. I'm afraid I . . .'

Paige said irritably, 'Go back to the head nurse's office and tell her to give you a white coat. And you don't have a scut book.'

'No.'

'Idiot nephew' doesn't begin to describe him. 'Meet us in Ward One.'

'Are you sure? I . . .'

'Just do it!' Paige and the others started off, leaving Jason Curtis staring after them.

They were examining their third patient when Jason Curtis came hurrying up. He was wearing a white coat. Paige was saying, '. . . tumors of the heart can be primary, which is rare, or secondary, which is much more common.'

She turned to Curtis. 'Can you name the three types of tumors?'

He stared at her. 'I'm afraid I . . . I can't.'

Of course not. 'Epicardial. Myocardial. Endo-cardial.'

He looked at Paige and smiled. 'That's really interesting.'

My God! Paige thought. *Dr Wallace or no Dr Wallace, I'm going to get rid of him fast.*

They moved on to the next patient, and when Paige was through examining him, she took the group into the corridor, out of earshot. 'We're dealing here with a thyroid storm, with fever and extreme tachycardia. It came on after surgery.' She turned to Jason Curtis. 'How would you treat him for that?'

He stood there, thoughtful for a moment. Then he said, 'Gently?'

Paige fought for self-control. 'You're not his mother, you're his doctor! He needs continuous IV fluids to combat dehydration, along with IV iodine and antithyroid drugs and sedatives for convulsions.'

Jason nodded. 'That sounds about right.'

The rounds got no better. When they were over, Paige called Jason Curtis aside. 'Do you mind my being frank with you?'

'No. Not at all,' he said agreeably. 'I'd appreciate it.'

'Look for another profession.'

He stood there, frowning. 'You don't think I'm cut out for this?'

'Quite honestly, no. You don't enjoy this, do you?'

'Not really.'

'Then why did you choose to go into this?'

'To tell you the truth, I was pushed into it.'

'Well, you tell Dr Wallace that he's making a mistake. I think you should find something else to do with your life.'

'I really appreciate your telling me this,' Jason

187

Curtis said earnestly. 'I wonder if we could discuss this further. If you aren't doing anything for dinner tonight . . . ?'

'We have nothing further to discuss,' Paige said curtly. 'You can tell your uncle . . .'

At that moment Dr Wallace came into view. 'Jason!' he called. 'I've been looking all over for you.' He turned to Paige. 'I see you two have met.'

'Yes, we've met,' Paige said grimly.

'Good. Jason is the architect in charge of designing the new wing we're building.'

Paige stood there, motionless. 'He's . . . *what*?'

'Yes. Didn't he tell you?'

She felt her face getting red. *Didn't anyone tell you to wear a white coat on rounds? Why did you go into this? To tell you the truth, I was pushed into it. By me!*

Paige wanted to crawl into a hole. He had made a complete fool of her. She turned to Jason. 'Why didn't you tell me who you were?'

He was watching her, amused. 'Well, you really didn't give me a chance.'

'She didn't give you a chance to what?' Dr Wallace asked.

'If you'll excuse me . . .' Paige said tightly.

'What about dinner tonight?'

'I don't eat. And I'm busy.' And Paige was gone.

Jason looked after her, admiringly. 'That's quite a woman.'

'She is, isn't she? Shall we go to my office and talk about the new designs?'

'Fine.' But his thoughts were on Paige.

* * *

It was July, time for the ritual that took place every twelve months at hospitals all over the United States, as new residents came in to begin their journey toward becoming real doctors.

The nurses had been looking forward to the new crop of residents, staking out claims on the ones they thought would make good lovers or husbands. On this particular day, as the new residents appeared, nearly every female eye was fixed on Dr Ken Mallory.

No one knew why Ken Mallory had transferred from an exclusive private hospital in Washington, DC, to Embarcadero County Hospital in San Francisco. He was a fifth-year resident, and a general surgeon. There were rumors that he had had to leave Washington in a hurry because of an affair with a congressman's wife. There was another rumor that a nurse had committed suicide because of him and he had been asked to leave. The only thing the nurses were sure of was that Ken Mallory was, without doubt, the best-looking man they had ever seen. He had a tall, athletic body, wavy blond hair, and a face that would have looked great on a movie screen.

Mallory blended into the hospital routine as though he had been there forever. He was a charmer, and almost from the beginning, the nurses were fighting for his attention. Night after night, the other doctors would watch Mallory disappear into an empty on-call room with a different nurse. His reputation as a stud was becoming legendary around the hospital.

Paige, Kat, and Honey were discussing him.

'Can you believe all those nurses throwing

themselves at him?' Kat laughed. 'They're actually fighting to be the flavor of the week!'

'You have to admit, he *is* attractive,' Honey pointed out.

Kat shook her head. 'No. I don't.'

One morning, half a dozen residents were in the doctors' dressing room when Mallory walked in.

'We were just talking about you,' one of them said. 'You must be exhausted.'

Mallory grinned. 'It was not a bad night.' He had spent the night with two nurses.

Grundy, one of the residents, said, 'You're making the rest of us look like eunuchs, Ken. Isn't there anyone in this hospital you can't lay?'

Mallory laughed. 'I doubt it.'

Grundy was thoughtful for a moment. 'I'll bet I can name someone.'

'Really? Who's that?'

'One of the senior residents here. Her name is Kat Hunter.'

Mallory nodded. 'The black doll. I've seen her. She's very attractive. What makes you think I can't take her to bed?'

'Because we've all struck out. I don't think she likes men.'

'Or maybe she just hasn't met the right one,' Mallory suggested.

Grundy shook his head. 'No. You wouldn't have a chance.'

It was a challenge. 'I'll bet you're wrong.'

One of the other residents spoke up. 'You mean you're willing to bet on it?'

Mallory smiled. 'Sure. Why not?'

'All right.' The group began to crowd around Mallory. 'I'll bet you five hundred dollars you can't lay her.'

'You're on.'

'I'll bet you three hundred.'

Another one spoke up. 'Let me in on it. I'll bet you six hundred.'

In the end, five thousand dollars was bet.

'What's the time limit?' Mallory asked.

Grundy thought for a moment. 'Let's say thirty days. Is that fair?'

'More than fair. I won't need that much time.'

Grundy said, 'But you have to prove it. She has to admit that she went to bed with you.'

'No problem.' Mallory looked around the group and grinned. 'Suckers!'

Fifteen minutes later, Grundy was in the cafeteria where Kat, Paige, and Honey were having breakfast. He walked over to their table. 'Can I join you ladies—you doctors—for a moment?'

Paige looked up. 'Sure.'

Grundy sat down. He looked at Kat and said apologetically, 'I hate to tell you this, but I'm really mad, and I think it's only fair that you should know . . .'

Kat was looking at him, puzzled. 'Know what?'

Grundy sighed. 'That new senior resident who came in—Ken Mallory?'

'Yes. What about him?'

Grundy said, 'Well, I . . . God, this is embarrassing. He bet some of the doctors five thousand dollars

191

that he could get you into bed in the next thirty days.'

Kat's face was grim. 'He did, did he?'

Grundy said piously, 'I don't blame you for being angry. It made me sick when I heard about it. Well, I just wanted to warn you. He'll be asking you out, and I thought it was only right that you should know why he was doing it.'

'Thanks,' Kat said. 'I appreciate your telling me.'

'It was the least I could do.'

They watched Grundy leave.

In the corridor outside the cafeteria, the other residents were waiting for him.

'How did it go?' they asked.

Grundy laughed. 'Perfect. She's as mad as hell. The son of a bitch is dead meat!'

At the table, Honey was saying, 'I think that's just terrible.'

Kat nodded. 'Someone should give him a dickotomy. They'll be ice skating in hell before I go out with that bastard.'

Paige sat there thinking. After a moment, she said, 'You know something, Kat? It might be interesting if you *did* go out with him.'

Kat looked at her in surprise. *'What?'*

There was a glint in Paige's eye. 'Why not? If he wants to play games, let's help him — only he'll play *our* game.'

Kat leaned forward. 'Go on.'

'He has thirty days, right? When he asks you out, you'll be warm and loving and affectionate. I mean, you'll be absolutely *crazy* about the man. You'll drive him out of his mind. The only thing you *won't*

192

do, bless your heart, is to go to bed with him. We'll teach him a five-thousand-dollar lesson.'

Kat thought of her stepfather. It was a way of getting revenge. 'I like it,' she said.

'You mean you're going to do it?' Honey said.

'I am.'

And Kat had no idea that with those words, she had signed her death warrant.

16

Jason Curtis had been unable to get Paige Taylor out of his mind. He telephoned Ben Wallace's secretary. 'Hi. This is Jason Curtis. I need a home telephone number for Dr Paige Taylor.'

'Certainly, Mr Curtis. Just a moment.' She gave him the number.

Honey answered the telephone. 'Dr Taft.'

'This is Jason Curtis. Is Dr Taylor there?'

'No, she's not. She's on call at the hospital.'

'Oh. That's too bad.'

Honey could hear the disappointment in his voice. 'If it's some kind of emergency, I can . . .'

'No, no.'

'I could take a message for her and have her call you.'

'That will be fine.' Jason gave her his telephone number.

'I'll give her the message.'

'Thank you.'

'Jason Curtis called,' Honey said when Paige returned to the apartment. 'He sounded cute. Here's his number.'

'Burn it.'

'Aren't you going to call him back?'

194

'No. Never.'

'You're still hung up on Alfred, aren't you?'

'Of course not.'

And that was all Honey could get out of her.

Jason waited two days before he called again.

This time Paige answered the telephone. 'Dr Taylor.'

'Hello there!' Jason said. 'This is Dr Curtis.'

'Doctor . . . ?'

'You may not remember me,' Jason said lightly. 'I was on rounds with you the other day, and I asked you to have dinner with me. You said—'

'I said I was busy. I still am. Goodbye, Mr Curtis.' She slammed the receiver down.

'What was that all about?' Honey asked.

'About nothing.'

At six o'clock the following morning, when the residents gathered with Paige for morning rounds, Jason Curtis appeared. He was wearing a white coat.

'I hope I'm not late,' he said cheerfully. 'I had to get a white coat. I know how upset you get when I don't wear one.'

Paige took a deep, angry breath. 'Come in here,' she said. She led Jason into the deserted doctors' dressing room. 'What are you doing here?'

'To tell you the truth, I've been worried about some of the patients we saw the other day,' he said earnestly. 'I came to see if everyone is all right.'

The man was infuriating. 'Why aren't you out building something?'

Jason looked at her and said, quietly, 'I'm trying to.' He pulled out a handful of tickets. 'Look, I don't know what your tastes are, so I got tickets for tonight's Giants game, the theater, the opera, and a concert. Take your choice.'

The man was exasperating. 'Do you always throw your money away like this?'

'Only when I'm in love,' Jason said.

'Wait a min—'

He held the tickets out to her. 'Take your choice.'

Paige reached out and took them all. 'Thank you,' she said sweetly. 'I'll give them to my outpatients. Most of them don't have a chance to go to the theater or opera.'

He smiled. 'Great! I hope they enjoy it. Will you have dinner with me?'

'No.'

'You have to eat, anyway. Won't you change your mind?'

Paige felt a small frisson of guilt about the tickets. 'I'm afraid I wouldn't be very good company. I was on call last night, and . . .'

'We'll make it an early evening. Scout's honor.'

She sighed. 'All right, but . . .'

'Wonderful! Where shall I pick you up?'

'I'll be through here at seven.'

'I'll pick you up here then.' He yawned. 'Now I'm going home and going back to bed. What an ungodly hour to be up! What makes you do it?'

Paige watched him walk away, and she could not help smiling.

*   *   *

At seven o'clock that evening when Jason arrived at the hospital to pick up Paige, the supervising nurse said, 'I think you'll find Dr Taylor in the on-call room.'

'Thanks.' Jason walked down the corridor to the on-call room. The door was closed. He knocked. There was no answer. He knocked again, then opened the door and looked inside. Paige was on the cot, in a deep sleep. Jason walked over to where she lay and stood there for a long time, looking down at her. *I'm going to marry you, lady*, he thought. He tiptoed out of the room and quietly closed the door behind him.

The following morning, Jason was in a meeting when his secretary came in with a small bouquet of flowers. The card read: *I'm sorry. RIP.* Jason laughed. He telephoned Paige at the hospital. 'This is your date calling.'

'I really am sorry about last night,' Paige said. 'I'm embarrassed.'

'Don't be. But I have a question.'

'Yes?'

'Does RIP stand for Rest in Peace or Rip Van Winkle?'

Paige laughed. 'Take your choice.'

'My choice is dinner tonight. Can we try again?'

She hesitated. *I don't want to become involved. You're not still hung up on Alfred, are you?*

'Hello. Are you there?'

'Yes.' *One evening won't do any harm*, Paige decided. 'Yes. We can have dinner.'

'Wonderful.'

*   *   *

As Paige was getting dressed that evening, Kat said, 'It looks like you have a heavy date. Who is it?'

'He's a doctor-architect,' Paige said.

'A *what*?'

Paige told her the story.

'He sounds like fun. Are you interested in him?'

'Not really.'

The evening went by pleasantly. Paige found Jason easy to be with. They talked about everything and nothing, and the time seemed to fly.

'Tell me about you,' Jason said. 'Where did you grow up?'

'You won't believe me.'

'I promise I will.'

'All right. The Congo, India, Burma, Nigeria, Kenya . . .'

'I don't believe you.'

'It's true. My father worked for WHO.'

'Who? I give up. Is this going to be an Abbott and Costello rerun?'

'The World Health Organization. He was a doctor. I spent my childhood traveling to most of the Third World countries with him.'

'That must have been difficult for you.'

'It was exciting. The hardest part was that I was never able to stay long enough to make friends.' *We don't need anyone else, Paige. We'll always have each other . . . This is my wife, Karen.* She shook off the memory. 'I learned a lot of strange languages, and exotic customs.'

'For instance?'

'Well, for instance, I . . .' She thought for a

moment. 'In India they believe in life after death, and that the next life depends on how you behaved in this one. If you were bad, you would come back as an animal. I remember that in one village, we had a dog, and I used to wonder who he used to be and what he did that was bad.'

Jason said, 'He probably barked up the wrong tree.'

Paige smiled. 'And then there was the *gherao*.'

'The *gherao*?'

'It's a very powerful form of punishment. A crowd surrounds a man.' She stopped.

'And?'

'That's it.'

'That's it?'

'They don't say anything or do anything. But he can't move, and he can't get away. He's trapped until he gives in to what they want. It can last for many, many hours. He stays inside the circle, but the crowd keeps changing shifts. I saw a man try to escape the *gherao* once. They beat him to death.'

The memory of it made Paige shudder. The normally friendly people had turned into a screaming frenzied mob. 'Let's get away from here,' Alfred had yelled. He had taken her arm and led her to a quiet side street.

'That's terrible,' Jason said.

'My father moved us away the next day.'

'I wish I could have known your father.'

'He was a wonderful doctor. He would have been a big success on Park Avenue, but he wasn't interested in money. His only interest was in helping people.' *Like Alfred*, she thought.

'What happened to him?'

'He was killed in a tribal war.'

'I'm sorry.'

'He loved doing what he did. In the beginning, the natives fought him. They were very superstitious. In the remote Indian villages, everyone has a *jatak*, a horoscope done by the village astrologer, and they live by it.' She smiled. 'I loved having mine done.'

'And did they tell you that you were going to marry a handsome young architect?'

Paige looked at him and said firmly, 'No.' The conversation was getting too personal. 'You're an architect, so you'll appreciate this. I grew up in huts made of wattle, with earthen floors and thatched roofs which mice and bats liked to inhabit. I lived in *tukuls* with grass roofs and no windows. My dream was to live one day in a comfortable two-story house with a veranda and a green lawn and a white picket fence, and . . .' Paige stopped. 'Sorry. I didn't mean to go on like this, but you *did* ask.'

'I'm glad I asked,' Jason said.

Paige looked at her watch. 'I had no idea it was so late.'

'Can we do this again?'

I don't want to lead him on, Paige thought. *Nothing is going to come of this*. She thought of something Kat had said to her. *You're clinging to a ghost. Let go*. She looked at Jason and said, 'Yes.'

Early the following morning, a messenger arrived with a package. Paige opened the door for him.

'I have something for Dr Taylor.'

'I'm Dr Taylor.'

The messenger looked at her in surprise. 'You're a doctor?'

'Yes,' Paige said patiently. 'I'm a doctor. Do you mind?'

He shrugged. 'No, lady. Not at all. Would you sign here, please?'

The package was surprisingly heavy. Curious, Paige carried it to the living-room table and unwrapped it. It was a miniature model of a beautiful white two-story house with a veranda. In front of the house was a little lawn and garden, surrounded by a white picket fence. *He must have stayed up all night, making it*. There was a card that read:

> *Mine*   [ ]
> *Ours*   [ ]
> *Please check one*.

She sat there looking at it for a long time. It was the right house, but it was the wrong man.

What's the matter with me? Paige asked herself. *He's bright and attractive and charming*. But she knew what the matter was. He was not Alfred.

The telephone rang. It was Jason. 'Did you get your house?' he asked.

'It's beautiful!' Paige said. 'Thank you so much.'

'I'd like to build you the real thing. Did you fill in the box?'

'No.'

'I'm a patient man. Are you free for dinner tonight?'

'Yes, but I have to warn you, I'm going to be operating all day, and by this evening I'll be exhausted.'

'We'll make it an early evening. By the way, it's going to be at my parents' home.'

Paige hesitated a moment. 'Oh?'

'I've told them all about you.'

'That's fine,' Paige said. Things were moving too quickly. It made her nervous.

When Paige hung up, she thought: *I really shouldn't be doing this. By tonight I'm going to be too tired to do anything but go to sleep.* She was tempted to telephone Jason back and cancel their date. *It's too late to do that now. We'll make it an early evening.*

As Paige was getting dressed that night, Kat said, 'You look exhausted.'

'I am.'

'Why are you going out? You should be going to bed. Or is that redundant?'

'No. Not tonight.'

'Jason again?'

'Yes. I'm going to meet his parents.'

'Ah.' Kat shook her head.

'It's not like that at all,' Paige said. *It's really not.*

Jason's mother and father lived in a charming old house in the Pacific Heights district. Jason's father was an aristocratic-looking man in his seventies. Jason's mother was a warm, down-to-earth woman. They made Paige feel instantly at home.

'Jason has told us so much about you,' Mrs Curtis said. 'He didn't tell us how beautiful you are.'

'Thank you.'

They went into the library, filled with miniature models of buildings that Jason and his father had designed.

'I guess that between us, Jason, his great-grandfather, and I have done a lot of the landscape of San Francisco,' Jason's father said. 'My son is a genius.'

'That's what I keep telling Paige,' Jason said.

Paige laughed. 'I believe it.' Her eyes were getting heavy and she was fighting to stay awake.

Jason was watching her, concerned. 'Let's go in to dinner,' he suggested.

They went into the large dining room. It was oak-paneled, furnished with attractive antiques and portraits on the wall. A maid began serving.

Jason's father said, 'That painting over there is Jason's great-grandfather. All the buildings he designed were destroyed in the earthquake of 1906. It's too bad. They were priceless. I'll show you some photographs of them after dinner if you . . .'

Paige's head had dropped to the table. She was sound asleep.

'I'm glad I didn't serve soup,' Jason's mother said.

Ken Mallory had a problem. As word of the wager about Kat had spread around the hospital, the bets had quickly increased to ten thousand dollars. Mallory had been so confident of his success that he had bet much more than he could afford to pay off.

If I fail, I'm in a hell of a lot of trouble. But I'm not going to fail. Time for the master to go to work.

Kat was having lunch in the cafeteria with Paige and Honey when Mallory approached the table.

'Mind if I join you doctors?'

Not ladies, not girls. Doctors. The sensitive type, Kat thought cynically. 'Not at all. Sit down,' she said.

Paige and Honey exchanged a look.

'Well, I have to get going,' Paige said.

'Me, too. See you later.'

Mallory watched Paige and Honey leave.

'Busy morning?' Mallory asked. He made it sound as though he really cared.

'Aren't they all?' Kat gave him a warm, promising smile.

Mallory had planned his strategy carefully. *I'm going to let her know I'm interested in her as a person, not just as a woman. They hate the sex-object thing. Discuss medicine with her. I'll take it slow and easy. I have a whole month to get her in the sack.*

'Did you hear about the postmortem on Mrs Turnball?' Mallory began. 'The woman had a Coca-Cola bottle in her stomach! Can you imagine how . . . ?'

Kat leaned forward. 'Are you doing anything Saturday night, Ken?'

Mallory was caught completely off guard. 'What?'

'I thought you might like to take me out to dinner.'

He found himself almost blushing. *My God!* he thought. *Talk about shooting fish in a barrel! This is no lesbian. The guys said that because they couldn't get into her pants. Well, I'm going to. She's actually asking for it!* He tried to remember with whom he had a date on Saturday. *Sally, the little nurse in OR. She can wait.*

'Nothing important,' Mallory said. 'I'd love to take you to dinner.'

Kat put her hand over his. 'Wonderful,' she said softly. 'I'll really be looking forward to it.'

He grinned. 'So will I.' *You have no idea how much, baby. Ten thousand dollars' worth!*

That afternoon, Kat reported back to Paige and Honey.

'His mouth dropped open!' Kat laughed. 'You should have seen the look on his face! He looked like the cat that swallowed the canary.'

Paige said, 'Remember, you're the Kat. He's the canary.'

'What are you going to do Saturday night?' Honey asked.

'Any suggestions?'

'I have,' Paige answered. 'Here's the plan . . .'

Saturday evening, Kat and Ken Mallory had dinner at Emilio's, a restaurant on the bay. She had dressed carefully for him, in a white cotton dress, off the shoulder.

'You look sensational,' Mallory said. He was careful to strike just the right note. *Appreciative, but not pressing. Admiring, but not suggestive.* Mallory had determined to be at his most charming, but it was not necessary. It quickly became obvious to him that Kat was intent on charming *him*.

Over a drink, she said, 'Everyone talks about what a wonderful doctor you are, Ken.'

'Well,' Mallory said modestly, 'I've had fine training, and I care a lot about my patients. They're very important to me.' His voice was filled with sincerity.

Kat put her hand over his. 'I'm sure they are.

Where are you from? I want to know all about you. The *real* you.'

Jesus! Mallory thought. *That's the line I use.* He could not get over how easy this was going to be. He was an expert on the subject of women. His radar knew all the signals they put out. They could say yes with a look, a smile, a tone of voice. Kat's signals were jamming his radar.

She was leaning close to him, and her voice was husky. 'I want to know everything.'

He talked about himself during dinner, and every time he tried to change the subject and bring it around to Kat, she said, 'No, no. I want to hear more. You've had such a fascinating life!'

She's crazy about me, Mallory decided. He wished now that he had taken more bets. *I might even win tonight*, he thought. And he was sure of it when Kat said, as they were having coffee, 'Would you like to come up to my apartment for a nightcap?'

Bingo! Mallory stroked her arm and said softly, 'I'd love to.' *The guys were all crazy*, Mallory decided. *She's the horniest broad I've ever met.* He had a feeling that he was about to be raped.

Thirty minutes later, they were walking into Kat's apartment.

'Nice,' Mallory said, looking around. 'Very nice. Do you live here alone?'

'No. Dr Taylor and Dr Taft live with me.'

'Oh.' She could hear the note of regret in his voice.

Kat gave him a beguiling smile. 'But they won't be home until much later.'

Mallory grinned. 'Good.'

'Would you like a drink?'

'Love one. Scotch and soda, please.' He watched as Kat walked over to the little bar and mixed two drinks. *She's got great buns*, Mallory thought. *And she's damned good-looking, and I'm getting ten thousand dollars to lay her*. He laughed aloud.

Kat turned. 'What's so funny?'

'Nothing. I was just thinking how lucky I am to be here alone with you.'

'I'm the lucky one,' Kat said warmly. She handed him his drink.

Mallory raised his glass and started to say, 'Here's to . . .'

Kat beat him to it. 'Here's to us!' she said.

He nodded. 'I'll drink to that.'

He started to say, 'How about a little music?' and as he opened his mouth, Kat said, 'Would you like some music?'

'You're a mind reader.'

Kat put on an old Cole Porter standard. She surreptitiously glanced at her watch, then turned to Mallory. 'Do you like to dance?'

Mallory moved closer to her. 'It depends on whom I'm dancing with. I'd love to dance with you.'

Kat moved into his arms, and they began to dance to the slow and dreamy music. He felt Kat's body pressing hard against his, and he could feel himself getting aroused. He held her tighter, and Kat smiled up at him.

Now is the time to go in for the kill, he thought.

'You're lovely, you know,' Mallory said huskily. 'I've wanted you since the first moment I saw you.'

Kat looked into his eyes. 'I've felt the same way

about you, Ken.' His lips moved toward hers, and he gave her a warm, passionate kiss.

'Let's go into the bedroom,' Mallory said. There was a sudden urgency in him.

'Oh, yes!'

He took her by the arm and she started leading him toward her bedroom. And at that moment, the front door opened and Paige and Honey walked in.

'Hi, there!' Paige called. She looked at Ken Mallory in surprise. 'Oh, Dr Mallory! I didn't expect to see you here.'

'Well, I . . . I . . .'

'We went out to dinner,' Kat said.

Mallory was filled with a dark rage. He fought to control it. He turned to Kat. 'I should go. It's late and I have a big day tomorrow.'

'Oh. I'm sorry you're leaving,' Kat said. There was a world of promise in her eyes.

Mallory said, 'What about tomorrow night?'

'I'd love to . . .'

'Great!'

'. . . but I can't.'

'Oh. Well, what about Friday?'

Kat frowned. 'Oh, dear. I'm afraid Friday isn't good, either.'

Mallory was getting desperate. 'Saturday?'

Kat smiled. 'Saturday would be lovely.'

He nodded, relieved. 'Good. Saturday it is, then.'

He turned to Paige and Honey. 'Good night.'

'Good night.'

Kat walked Mallory to the door. 'Sweet dreams,' she said softly. 'I'm going to dream about you.'

Mallory squeezed her hand. 'I believe in making dreams come true. We'll make up for this Saturday night.'

'I can't wait.'

That night, Kat lay in her bed thinking about Mallory. She hated him. But to her surprise, she had enjoyed the evening. She was sure that Mallory had enjoyed it too, in spite of the fact that he was playing a game. *If only this were real*, Kat thought, *and not a game*. She had no idea how dangerous a game it was.

Maybe it's the weather, Paige thought wearily. It was cold and dreary outside, with a heavy fog that depressed the spirits. Her day had begun at six o'clock in the morning, and it was filled with constant problems. The hospital seemed to be full of gomers, all complaining at once. The nurses were surly and careless. They drew blood from the wrong patients, lost X-rays that were urgently needed, and snapped at the patients. In addition, there was a staff shortage because of a flu epidemic. It was that kind of day.

The only bright spot was the telephone call from Jason Curtis.

'Hello,' he said cheerily. 'Just thought I'd check in and see how all our patients are doing.'

'They're surviving.'

'Any chance of our having lunch?'

Paige laughed. 'What's lunch? If I'm lucky, I'll be able to grab a stale sandwich about four o'clock this afternoon. It's pretty hectic around here.'

'All right. I won't keep you. May I call you again?'

'All right.' *No harm in that*.

'Bye.'

Paige worked until midnight without a moment to rest, and when she was finally relieved, she was almost too tired to move. She briefly debated staying at the hospital and sleeping on the cot in the on-call room, but the thought of her warm, cozy bed at home was too tempting. She changed clothes and lurched her way to the elevator.

Dr Peterson came up to her. 'My God!' he said. 'Where's the cat that dragged you in?'

Paige smiled wearily. 'Do I look that bad?'

'Worse.' Peterson grinned. 'You're going home now?'

Paige nodded.

'You're lucky. I'm just starting.'

The elevator arrived. Paige stood there half asleep.

Peterson said gently, 'Paige?'

She shook herself awake. 'Yes?'

'Are you going to be able to drive home?'

'Sure,' Paige mumbled. 'And when I get there, I'm going to sleep for twenty-four hours straight.'

She walked to the parking lot and got into her car. She sat there drained, too tired to turn on the ignition. *I mustn't go to sleep here. I'll sleep at home.*

Paige drove out of the parking lot and headed toward the apartment. She was unaware of how erratically she was driving until a driver yelled at her, 'Hey, get off the road, you drunken broad!'

She forced herself to concentrate. *I must not fall asleep . . . I must not fall asleep.* She snapped the radio on and turned the volume up loudly. When she reached her apartment building, she sat in the car for a long time before she was able to summon enough strength to go upstairs.

Kat and Honey were in their beds, asleep. Paige looked at the clock at her bedside. *One o'clock.* She

211

stumbled into her bedroom and started to get undressed, but the effort was too much for her. She fell into bed with her clothes on, and in an instant was sound asleep.

She was awakened by the shrill ringing of a telephone that seemed to be coming from some far-off planet. Paige fought to stay asleep, but the ringing was like needles penetrating her brain. She sat up groggily and reached for the phone. 'H'lo?'

'Dr Taylor?'

'Yes.' Her voice was a hoarse mumble.

'Dr Barker wants you in OR Four to assist him, stat.'

Paige cleared her throat. 'There must be some mistake,' she mumbled. 'I just got off duty.'

'OR Four. He's waiting.' The line went dead.

Paige sat on the edge of the bed, numb, her mind clouded by sleep. She looked at the clock on the bedside table. Four-fifteen. Why was Dr Barker asking for her in the middle of the night? There was only one answer. Something had happened to one of her patients.

Paige staggered into the bathroom and threw cold water on her face. She looked in the mirror and thought, *My God! I look about eighty.*

Ten minutes later, Paige was making her way back to the hospital. She was still half asleep when she took the elevator to the fourth floor to OR Four. She went into the dressing room and changed, then scrubbed up and stepped into the operating room.

There were three nurses and a resident assisting Dr Barker.

He looked up as Paige entered and yelled, 'For Christ's sake, you're wearing a hospital gown! Didn't anyone ever inform you that you're supposed to wear *scrubs* in an operating room?'

Paige stood there, stunned, jolted wide awake, her eyes blazing. 'You listen to me,' she said, furiously. 'I'm supposed to be off duty. I came in as a favor to you. I don't—'

'Don't argue with me,' Dr Barker said curtly. 'Get over here and hold this retractor.'

Paige walked over to the operating table and looked down. It was not her patient on the table. It was a stranger. *Barker had no reason to call me. He's trying to force me to quit the hospital. Well, I'll be damned if I will!* She gave him a baleful look, picked up the retractor, and went to work.

The operation was an emergency coronary artery bypass graft. The skin incision had already been made down the center of the chest to the breastbone, which had been split with an electric saw. The heart and major blood vessels were exposed.

Paige inserted the metal retractor between the cut sides of the breastbone, forcing the edges apart. She watched as Dr Barker skillfully opened the pericardial sac, exposing the heart.

He indicated the coronary arteries. 'Here's the problem,' Barker said. 'We're going to do some grafting.'

He had already removed a long strip of vein from one leg. He sewed a piece of it into the main artery coming out of the heart. The other end he attached to one of the coronary arteries, beyond the obstructed area, sending the blood through the vein graft, bypassing the obstruction.

Paige was watching a master at work. *If only he weren't such a bastard!*

The operation took three hours. By the time it was over, Paige was only half conscious. When the incision had been closed, Dr Barker turned to the staff and said, 'I want to thank all of you.' He was not looking at Paige.

Paige stumbled out of the room without a word and went upstairs to the office of Dr Benjamin Wallace.

Wallace was just arriving. 'You look exhausted,' he said. 'You should get some rest.'

Paige took a deep breath to control her anger. 'I want to be transferred to another surgical team.'

Wallace studied her a moment. 'You're assigned to Dr Barker, right?'

'Right.'

'What's the problem?'

'Ask *him*. He hates me. He'll be glad to get rid of me. I'll go with anyone else. Anyone.'

'I'll talk to him,' Wallace said.

'Thank you.'

Paige turned and walked out of the office. *They'd better take me away from him. If I see him again, I'll kill him.*

Paige went home and slept for twelve hours. She woke up with a feeling that something wonderful had happened, and then she remembered. *I don't have to see the Beast anymore!* She drove to the hospital, whistling.

As Paige was walking down the corridor, an orderly came up to her. 'Dr Taylor . . .'

'Yes?'

'Dr Wallace would like to see you in his office.'

214

'Thank you,' Paige said. She wondered who the new senior surgeon would be. *Anybody will be an improvement*, Paige thought. She walked into Benjamin Wallace's office.

'Well, you look much better now, Paige.'

'Thanks. I feel much better.' And she did. She felt great, filled with an enormous sense of relief.

'I talked to Dr Barker.'

Paige smiled. 'Thank you. I really appreciate it.'

'He won't let you go.'

Paige's smile faded. *What?*

'He said you're assigned to his team and you'll stay there.'

She could not believe what she was hearing. 'But *why*?' She knew why. The sadistic bastard needed a whipping girl, someone to humiliate. 'I'm not going to stand for it.'

Dr Wallace said ruefully, 'I'm afraid you have no choice. Unless you want to leave the hospital. Would you like to think about it?'

Paige did not have to think about it. 'No.' She was not going to let Barker force her to quit. That was his plan. 'No,' she repeated slowly. 'I'll stay.'

'Good. Then that's settled.'

Not by a long shot, Paige thought. *I'm going to find some way to pay him back*.

In the doctors' dressing room, Ken Mallory was getting ready to make his rounds. Dr Grundy and three other doctors walked in.

'There's our man!' Grundy said. 'How are you doing, Ken?'

'Fine,' Mallory said.

215

Grundy turned to the others. 'He doesn't look like he just got laid, does he?' He turned back to Mallory. 'I hope you have our money ready. I plan to make a down payment on a little car.'

Another doctor joined in. 'I'm buying a whole new wardrobe.'

Mallory shook his head pityingly. 'I wouldn't count on it, suckers. Get ready to pay me off!'

Grundy was studying him. 'What do you mean?'

'If she's a lesbian, I'm a eunuch. She's the horniest broad I ever met. I practically had to hold her off the other night!'

The men were looking at one another, worried.

'But you didn't get her into the sack?'

'The only reason I didn't, my friends, is because we were interrupted on the way to the bedroom. I have a date with her Saturday night, and it's already over but the shouting.' Mallory finished dressing. 'Now, if you gentlemen will excuse me . . .'

An hour later, Grundy stopped Kat in the corridor.

'I've been looking for you,' he said. He looked angry.

'Is something wrong?'

'It's that bastard Mallory. He's so sure of himself that he's telling everyone that he's going to get you into bed by Saturday night.'

'Don't worry,' Kat said grimly. 'He's going to lose.'

When Ken Mallory picked Kat up Saturday night, she had on a low-cut dress that accentuated her voluptuous figure.

'You look gorgeous,' he said admiringly.

She put her arms around him. 'I want to look good for you.' She was clinging to him.

God, she really wants it! When Mallory spoke, his voice was husky. 'Look, I have an idea, Kat. Before we go out to dinner, why don't we slip into the bedroom and . . .'

She was stroking his face. 'Oh, darling, I wish we could. Paige is home.' Paige was actually at the hospital, working.

'Oh.'

'But after dinner . . .' She let the suggestion hang in the air.

'Yes?'

'We could go to your place.'

Mallory put his arms around her and kissed her. 'That's a wonderful idea!'

He took her to the Iron Horse, and they had a delicious dinner. In spite of herself, Kat was having a wonderful time. He was charming and amusing, and incredibly attractive. He seemed genuinely interested in knowing everything about her. She knew he was flattering her, but the look in his eye made the compliments seem real.

If I didn't know better . . .

Mallory had hardly tasted his food. All he could think was, *In two hours I will be making ten thousand dollars . . . In one hour, I will be making ten thousand dollars . . . In thirty minutes . . .*

They finished their coffee.

'Are you ready?' Mallory asked.

Kat put her hand over his. 'You have no idea how ready, darling. Let's go.'

They took a taxi to Mallory's apartment. 'I'm

217

absolutely crazy about you,' Mallory murmured. 'I've never known anyone like you.'

And she could hear Grundy's voice: *He's so sure of himself that he says he's going to get you into bed by Saturday night.*

When they arrived at the apartment, Mallory paid the taxi driver and led Kat into the elevator. It seemed to Mallory to take forever to get up to his apartment. He opened the door and said eagerly, 'Here it is.'

Kat stepped inside.

It was an ordinary little bachelor's apartment that desperately needed a woman's touch.

'Oh, it's lovely,' Kat breathed. She turned to Mallory. 'It's *you*.'

He grinned. 'Let me show you *our* room. I'll put some music on.'

As he went over to the tape deck, Kat glanced at her watch. The voice of Barbra Streisand filled the room.

Mallory took her hand. 'Let's go, honey.'

'Wait a minute,' Kat said softly.

He was looking at her, puzzled. 'What for?'

'I just want to enjoy this moment with you. You know, before we . . .'

'Why don't we enjoy it in the bedroom?'

'I'd love a drink.'

'A drink?' He tried to hide his impatience. 'Fine. What would you like?'

'A vodka and tonic, please.'

He smiled. 'I think we can handle that.' He went over to the little bar and hurriedly mixed two drinks.

Kat looked at her watch again.

Mallory returned with the drinks and handed one to Kat. 'Here you are, baby.' He raised his glass. 'To togetherness.'

'To togetherness,' Kat said. She took a sip of the drink. 'Oh, my God!'

He looked at her, startled. 'What's the matter?'

'This is vodka!'

'That's what you asked for.'

'Did I? I'm sorry. I hate vodka!' She stroked his face. 'May I have a scotch and soda?'

'Sure.' He swallowed his impatience and went back to the bar to mix another drink.

Kat glanced at her watch again.

Ken Mallory returned. 'Here you are.'

'Thank you, darling.'

She took two sips of her drink. Mallory took the glass from her and set it on a table. He put his arms around Kat and held her close, and she could feel that he was aroused.

'Now,' Ken said softly, 'let's make history.'

'Oh, yes!' Kat said. 'Yes!'

She let him lead her into the bedroom.

I've done it! Mallory exulted. *I've done it! Here go the walls of Jericho!* He turned to Kat. 'Get undressed, baby.'

'You first, darling. I want to watch you get undressed. It excites me.'

'Oh? Well, sure.'

As Kat stood there watching, Mallory slowly took his clothes off. First his jacket, then his shirt and tie, then his shoes and stockings, and then his trousers. He had the firm figure of an athlete.

'Does this excite you, baby?'

'Oh, yes. Now take off your shorts.'

Slowly Mallory let his shorts fall to the floor. He had a turgid erection.

'That's beautiful,' Kat said.

'Now it's your turn.'

'Right.'

And at that moment, Kat's beeper went off.

Mallory was startled. 'What the hell . . . ?'

'They're calling me,' Kat said. 'May I use your telephone?'

'*Now?*'

'Yes. It must be an emergency.'

'*Now?* Can't it wait?'

'Darling, you know the rules.'

'But . . .'

As Mallory watched, Kat walked over to the telephone and dialed a number. 'Dr Hunter.' She listened. 'Really? Of course. I'll be right there.'

Mallory was staring at her, stupefied. 'What's going on?'

'I have to get back to the hospital, angel.'

'*Now?*'

'Yes. One of my patients is dying.'

'Can't he wait until . . . ?'

'I'm sorry. We'll do this another night.'

Ken Mallory stood there, buck naked, watching Kat walk out of his apartment, and as the door closed behind her, he picked up her drink and slammed it into the wall. *Bitch . . bitch . . . bitch . . .*

When Kat got back to the apartment, Paige and Honey were eagerly waiting for her.

'How did it go?' Paige asked. 'Was I on time?'

Kat laughed. 'Your timing was perfect.'

220

She began to describe the evening. When she came to the part about Mallory standing in the bedroom naked, with an erection, they laughed until tears came to their eyes.

Kat was tempted to tell them how enjoyable she really found Ken Mallory, but she felt foolish. After all, he was seeing her only so he could win a bet.

Somehow, Paige seemed to sense how Kat felt. 'Be careful of him, Kat.'

Kat smiled. 'Don't worry. But I will admit that if I didn't know about that bet . . . He's a snake, but he gives good snake oil.'

'When are you going to see him again?' Honey asked.

'I'm going to give him a week to cool off.'

Paige was studying her. 'Him or you?'

Dinetto's black limousine was waiting for Kat outside the hospital. This time, the Shadow was alone. Kat wished that Rhino were there. There was something about the Shadow that petrified her. He never smiled and seldom spoke, but he exuded menace.

'Get in,' he said as Kat approached the car.

'Look,' Kat said indignantly, 'you tell Mr Dinetto that he can't order me around. I don't work for him. Just because I did him a favor once . . .'

'Get in. You can tell him yourself.'

Kat hesitated. It would be easy to walk away and not get involved any further, but how would it affect Mike? Kat got into the car.

*   *   *

The victim this time had been badly beaten, whipped with a chain. Lou Dinetto was there with him.

Kat took one look at the patient and said, 'You've got to get him to a hospital right away.'

'Kat,' Dinetto said, 'you have to treat him here.'

'Why?' Kat demanded. But she knew the answer, and it terrified her.

18

It was one of those clear days in San Francisco when there was a magic in the air. The night wind had swept away the rainclouds, producing a crisp, sunny Sunday morning.

Jason had arranged to pick up Paige at the apartment. When he arrived, she was surprised at how pleased she was to see him.

'Good morning,' Jason said. 'You look beautiful.'

'Thank you.'

'What would you like to do today?'

Paige said, 'It's your town. You lead, I'll follow.'

'Fair enough.'

'If you don't mind,' Paige said, 'I'd like to make a quick stop at the hospital.'

'I thought this was your day off.'

'It is, but there's a patient I'm concerned about.'

'No problem.' Jason drove her to the hospital.

'I won't be long,' Paige promised as she got out of the car.

'I'll wait for you here.'

Paige went up to the third floor and into Jimmy Ford's room. He was still in a coma, attached to an array of tubes feeding him intravenously.

A nurse was in the room. She looked up as Paige entered. 'Good morning, Dr Taylor.'

'Good morning.' Paige walked over to the boy's bedside. 'Has there been any change?'

'I'm afraid not.'

Paige felt Jimmy's pulse and listened to his heartbeat.

'It's been several weeks now,' the nurse said. 'It doesn't look good, does it?'

'He's going to come out of it,' Paige said firmly. She turned to the unconscious figure on the bed and raised her voice. 'Do you hear me? You're going to get well!' There was no reaction. She closed her eyes a moment and said a silent prayer. 'Have them beep me at once if there's any change.'

'Yes, doctor.'

He's not going to die, Paige thought. *I'm not going to let him die . . .*

Jason got out of the car as Paige approached. 'Is everything all right?'

There was no point in burdening him with her problems. 'Everything's fine,' Paige said.

'Let's play real tourists today,' Jason said. 'There's a state law that all tours have to start at Fisherman's Wharf.'

Paige smiled. 'We mustn't break the law.'

Fisherman's Wharf was like an outdoor carnival. The street entertainers were out in full force. There were mimes, clowns, dancers and musicians. Vendors were selling steaming caldrons of Dungeness crabs and clam chowder with fresh sourdough bread.

'There's no place like this in the world,' Jason said warmly.

Paige was touched by his enthusiasm. She had seen Fisherman's Wharf before and most of the other tourist sites of San Francisco, but she did not want to spoil his fun.

'Have you ridden a cable car yet?' Jason asked.

'No.' *Not since last week.*

'You haven't lived! Come along.'

They walked to Powell Street and boarded a cable car. As they started up the steep grade, Jason said, 'This was known as Hallidie's Folly. He built it in 1873.'

'And I'll bet they said it wouldn't last!'

Jason laughed. 'That's right. When I was going to high school, I used to work weekends as a tour guide.'

'I'm sure you were good.'

'The best. Would you like to hear some of my spiel?'

'I'd love to.'

Jason adopted the nasal tone of a tour guide. 'Ladies and gentlemen, for your information, the oldest street in San Francisco is Grant Avenue, the longest is Mission Street—seven and a half miles long—the widest is Van Ness Avenue at one hundred twenty-five feet, and you'll be surprised to know that the narrowest, DeForest Street, is only four and a half feet. That's right, ladies and gentlemen, four and a half feet. The steepest street we can offer you is Filbert Street, with a thirty-one and a half percent grade.' He looked at Paige and grinned. 'I'm surprised that I still remember all that.'

When they alit from the cable car, Paige looked up at Jason and smiled. 'What's next?'

'We're going to take a carriage ride.'

Ten minutes later, they were seated in a horse-drawn carriage that took them from Fisherman's Wharf to Ghirardelli Square to North Beach. Jason pointed out the places of interest along the way, and Paige was surprised at how much she was enjoying herself. *Don't let yourself get carried away.*

They went up to Coit Tower for a view of the city. As they ascended, Jason asked, 'Are you hungry?'

The fresh air had made Paige very hungry. 'Yes.'

'Good. I'm going to take you to one of the best Chinese restaurants in the world—Tommy Toy's.'

Paige had heard the hospital staff speak of it.

The meal turned out to be a banquet. They started with lobster pot stickers with chili sauce, and hot and sour soup with seafood. That was followed by filet of chicken with snow peas and pecans, veal filet with Szechuan sauce, and four-flavored fried rice. For dessert, they had a peach mousse. The food was wonderful.

'Do you come here often?' Paige asked.

'As often as I can.'

There was a boyish quality about Jason that Paige found very attractive.

'Tell me,' Paige said, 'did you always want to be an architect?'

'I had no choice.' Jason grinned. 'My first toys were Erector sets. It's exciting to dream about something and then watch that dream become concrete and bricks and stone, and soar up into the sky and become a part of the city you live in.'

I'm going to build you a Taj Mahal. I don't care how long it takes!

'I'm one of the lucky ones, Paige, spending my life doing what I love to do. Who was it who said, "Most people live lives of quiet desperation"?'

Sounds like a lot of my patients, Paige thought.

'There's nothing else I would want to do, or any other place I would want to live. This is a fabulous city.' His voice was filled with excitement. 'It has everything anyone could want. I never get tired of it.'

Paige studied him for a moment, enjoying his enthusiasm. 'You've never been married?'

Jason shrugged. 'Once. We were both too young. It didn't work out.'

'I'm sorry.'

'No need to be. She's married to a very wealthy meat packer. Have you been married?'

I'm going to be a doctor, too, when I grow up. We'll get married, and we'll work together.

'No.'

They took a bay cruise under the Golden Gate and Bay Bridge. Jason assumed his tour guide's voice again. 'And there, ladies and gentlemen, is the storied Alcatraz, former home of some of the world's most infamous criminals—Machine Gun Kelly, Al Capone, and Robert Stroud, known as the Birdman! "Alcatraz" means pelican in Spanish. It was originally called Isla de los Alcatraces, after the birds that were its only inhabitants. Do you know why they had hot showers every day for the prisoners here?'

227

'No.'

'So that they wouldn't get used to the cold bay water when they were trying to escape.'

'Is that true?' Paige asked.

'Have I ever lied to you?'

It was late afternoon when Jason said, 'Have you ever been to Noe Valley?'

Paige shook her head. 'No.'

'I'd like to show it to you. It used to be farms and streams. Now it's filled with brightly colored Victorian homes and gardens. The houses are very old, because it was about the only area spared in the 1906 earthquake.'

'It sounds lovely.'

Jason hesitated. 'My home is there. Would you like to see it?' He saw Paige's reaction. 'Paige, I'm in love with you.'

'We hardly know each other. How could you . . . ?'

'I knew it from the moment you said, "Don't you know you're supposed to wear a white coat on rounds?" That's when I fell in love with you.'

'Jason . . .'

'I'm a firm believer in love at first sight. My grandfather saw my grandmother riding a bicycle in the park and he followed her, and they got married three months later. They were together for fifty years, until he died. My father saw my mother crossing a street, and he knew she was going to be his wife. They've been married for forty-five years. You see, it runs in the family. I want to marry you.'

It was the moment of truth.

Paige looked at Jason and thought, *He's the first man I've been attracted to since Alfred. He's adorable and bright and genuine. He's everything a woman could want in a man. What's the matter with me? I'm holding on to a ghost.* Yet deep inside her, she still had the overpowering feeling that one day Alfred was going to come back to her.

She looked at Jason and made her decision. 'Jason . . .'

And at that moment, Paige's beeper went off.

'Paige . . .'

'I have to get to a telephone.' Two minutes later, she was talking to the hospital.

Jason watched Paige's face turn pale.

She was shouting into the telephone, 'No! Absolutely not! Tell them I'll be right there.' She slammed the phone down.

'What is it?' Jason asked.

She turned to him, and her eyes were filled with tears. 'It's Jimmy Ford, my patient. They're going to take him off the respirator. They're going to let him die.'

When Paige reached Jimmy Ford's room, there were three people there beside the comatose figure in bed: George Englund, Benjamin Wallace, and a lawyer, Silvester Damone.

'What's going on here?' Paige demanded.

Benjamin Wallace said, 'At the hospital ethics committee meeting this morning, it was decided that Jimmy Ford's condition is hopeless. We've decided to remove —'

'No!' Paige said. 'You can't! I'm his doctor. I say

229

he has a chance to come out of it! We're *not* going to let him die.'

Silvester Damone spoke up. 'It's not your decision to make, doctor.'

Paige looked at him defiantly. 'Who are you?'

'I'm the family's attorney.' He pulled out a document and handed it to Paige. 'This is Jimmy Ford's living will. It specifically states that if he has a life-threatening trauma, he's not to be kept alive by mechanical means.'

'But I've been monitoring his condition,' Paige pleaded. 'He's been stabilized for weeks. He could come out of the coma any moment.'

'Can you guarantee that?' Damone asked.

'No, but . . .'

'Then you'll have to do as you're ordered, doctor.'

Paige looked down at the figure of Jimmy. 'No! You have to wait a little longer.'

The lawyer said smoothly, 'Doctor, I'm sure it benefits the hospital to keep patients here as long as possible, but the family cannot afford the medical expenses any longer. I'm ordering you now to take him off the respirator.'

'Just another day or two,' Paige said desperately, 'and I'm sure . . .'

'No,' Damone said firmly. 'Today.'

George Englund turned to Paige. 'I'm sorry, but I'm afraid we have no choice.'

'Thank you, doctor,' the lawyer said. 'I'll leave it to you to handle it. I'll notify the family that it will be taken care of immediately, so they can begin to make the funeral arrangements.' He turned to Benjamin Wallace. 'Thank you for your cooperation. Good day.'

They watched him walk out of the room.

'We can't do this to Jimmy!' Paige said.

Dr Wallace cleared his throat. 'Paige . . .'

'What if we got him out of here and hid him in another room? There must be something we haven't thought of. Something . . .'

Benjamin Wallace said, 'This isn't a request. It's an order.' He turned to George Englund. 'Do you want to . . . ?'

'No!' Paige said. 'I'll . . . I'll do it.'

'Very well.'

'If you don't mind, I'd like to be alone with him.'

George Englund squeezed her arm. 'I'm sorry, Paige.'

'I know.'

Paige watched the two men leave the room.

She was alone with the unconscious boy. She looked at the respirator that was keeping him alive and the IVs that were feeding his body. It would be so simple to turn the respirator off, to snuff out a life. But he had had so many wonderful dreams, such high hopes.

I'm going to be a doctor one day. I want to be like you.

Did you know I'm getting married? . . . Her name is Betsy . . . We're going to have half a dozen kids. The first girl is going to be named Paige.

He had so very much to live for.

Paige stood there looking down at him, tears blurring the room. 'Damn you!' she said. 'You're a quitter!' She was sobbing now. 'What happened to those dreams of yours? I thought you wanted to become a doctor! Answer me! Do you hear me? Open your eyes!' She looked down at the pale figure.

There was no reaction. 'I'm sorry,' Paige said. 'I'm so sorry.' She leaned down to kiss him on the cheek, and as she slowly straightened up, she was looking into his open eyes.

'Jimmy! *Jimmy!*'

He blinked and closed his eyes again. Paige squeezed his hand. She leaned forward and said through her sobs, 'Jimmy, did you hear the one about the patient who was being fed intravenously? He asked the doctor for an extra bottle. He was having a guest for lunch.'

19

Honey was happier than she had ever been in her life. She had a warm relationship with patients that few of the other doctors had. She genuinely cared about them. She worked in geriatrics, in pediatrics, and in various other wards, and Dr Wallace saw to it that she was given assignments that kept her out of harm's way. He wanted to make sure that she stayed at the hospital and was available to him.

Honey envied the nurses. They were able to nurture their patients without worrying about major medical decisions. *I never wanted to be a doctor*, Honey thought. *I always wanted to be a nurse.*

There are no nurses in the Taft family.

In the afternoon when Honey left the hospital, she would go shopping at the Bay Company, and Streetlight Records, and buy gifts for the children in pediatric care.

'I love children,' she told Kat.

'Are you planning to have a large family?'

'Someday,' Honey said wistfully. 'I have to find their father first.'

One of Honey's favorite patients in the geriatric ward was Daniel McGuire, a cheerful man in his nineties who was suffering from a diseased liver condition. He had been a gambler in his youth, and he liked to make bets with Honey.

'I'll bet you fifty cents the orderly is late with my breakfast.'

'I'll bet you a dollar it's going to rain this afternoon.'

'I'll bet you the Giants win.'

Honey always took his bets.

'I'll bet you ten to one I beat this thing,' he said.

'This time I'm not going to bet you,' Honey told him. 'I'm on your side.'

He took her hand. 'I know you are.' He grinned. 'If I were a few months younger . . .'

Honey laughed. 'Never mind. I like older men.'

One morning a letter came for him at the hospital. Honey took it to him in his room.

'Read it to me, would you?' His eyesight had faded.

'Of course,' Honey said. She opened the envelope, looked at it a moment, and let out a cry. 'You've won the lottery! Fifty thousand dollars! Congratulations!'

'How about that?' He yelled. 'I always knew I'd win the lottery one day! Give me a hug.'

Honey leaned down and hugged him.

'You know something, Honey? I'm the luckiest man in the world.'

When Honey came back to visit him that afternoon, he had passed away. He had lost the most important bet of all.

Honey was in the doctors' lounge when Dr Stevens walked in. 'Is there a Virgo here?'

One of the doctors laughed. 'If you mean a virgin, I doubt it.'

'A *Virgo*,' Stevens repeated. 'I need a Virgo.'

'I'm a Virgo,' Honey said. 'What's the problem?'

He walked up to her. 'The problem is that I have a goddam maniac on my hands. She won't let anyone near her but a Virgo.'

Honey got up. 'I'll go see her.'

'Thanks. Her name is Frances Gordon.'

Frances Gordon had just had a hip replacement. The moment Honey walked into the room, the woman looked up and said, 'You're a Virgo. Born on the cusp, right?'

Honey smiled. 'That's right.'

'Those Aquarians and Leos don't know what the hell they're doin'. They treat patients like they're meat.'

'The doctors here are very good,' Honey protested. 'They —'

'Ha! Most of them are in it for the money.' She looked at Honey more closely. 'You're different.'

Honey scanned the chart at the foot of the bed, a surprised look on her face.

'What's the matter? What are you lookin' at?'

Honey blinked. 'It says here that your occupation is a . . . a psychic.'

Frances Gordon nodded. 'That's right. Don't you believe in psychics?'

Honey shook her head. 'I'm afraid not.'

'That's too bad. Sit down a minute.'

Honey took a chair.

'Let me hold your hand.'

Honey shook her head. 'I really don't . . .'

'C'mon, give me your hand.'

Reluctantly, Honey let her take her hand.

Frances Gordon held it for a moment, and closed her eyes. When she opened them, she said, 'You've had a difficult life, haven't you?'

Everyone has had a difficult life, Honey thought. *Next she'll be telling me that I'll be taking a trip across the water.*

'You've used a lot of men, haven't you?'

Honey felt herself stiffen.

'There's been some kind of change in you—just recently—hasn't there?'

Honey could not wait to get out of the room. The woman was making her nervous. She started to pull away.

'You're going to fall in love.'

Honey said, 'I'm afraid I really have to . . .'

'He's an artist.'

'I don't know any artists.'

'You will.' Frances Gordon let go of her hand. 'Come back and see me,' she commanded.

'Sure.'

Honey fled.

Honey stopped in to visit Mrs Owens, a new patient, a thin woman who appeared to be in her late forties. Her chart noted that she was twenty-eight. She had a broken nose and two black eyes, and her face was puffy and bruised.

Honey walked up to the bed. 'I'm Dr Taft.'

The woman looked at her with dull, expressionless eyes. She remained silent.

'What happened to you?'

'I fell down some stairs.' When she opened her mouth, she revealed a gap where two front teeth were missing.

Honey glanced at the chart. 'It says here that you have two broken ribs and a fractured pelvis.'

'Yeah. It was a bad fall.'

'How did you get the black eyes?'

'When I fell.'

'Are you married?'

'Yeah.'

'Any children?'

'Two.'

'What does your husband do?'

'Let's leave my husband out of this, okay?'

'I'm afraid it's not okay,' Honey said. 'Is he the one who beat you up?'

'No one beat me up.'

'I'm going to have to file a police report.'

Mrs Owens was suddenly panicky. 'No! Please don't!'

'Why not?'

'He'll kill me! You don't know him!'

'Has he beaten you up before?'

'Yes, but he . . . he doesn't mean anything by it. He gets drunk and loses his temper.'

'Why haven't you left him?'

Mrs Owens shrugged, and the movement caused her pain. 'The kids and I have nowhere to go.'

Honey was listening, furious. 'You don't have to take this, you know. There are shelters and agencies that will take care of you and protect you and the children.'

The woman shook her head in despair. 'I have no

money. I lost my job as a secretary when he started . . .' She could not go on.

Honey squeezed her hand. 'You're going to be fine. I'll see that you're taken care of.'

Five minutes later Honey marched into Dr Wallace's office. He was delighted to see her. He wondered what she had brought with her this time. At various times, she had used warm honey, hot water, melted chocolate, and — his favorite — maple syrup. Her ingenuity was boundless.

'Lock the door, baby.'

'I can't stay, Ben. I have to get back.'

She told him about her patient.

'You'll have to file a police report,' Wallace said. 'It's the law.'

'The law hasn't protected her before. Look, all she wants to do is get away from her husband. She worked as a secretary. Didn't you say you needed a new file clerk?'

'Well, yes, but . . . wait a minute!'

'Thanks,' Honey said. 'We'll get her on her feet, and find her a place to live, and she'll have a new job!'

Wallace sighed. 'I'll see what I can do.'

'I knew you would,' Honey said.

The next morning, Honey went back to see Mrs Owens.

'How are you feeling today?' Honey asked.

'Better, thanks. When can I go home? My husband doesn't like it when —'

'Your husband is not going to bother you anymore,' Honey said firmly. 'You'll stay here until we find a place for you and the children to live, and when you're well enough, you're going to have a job here at the hospital.'

Mrs Owens stared at her unbelievingly. 'Do . . . do you mean that?'

'Absolutely. You'll have your own apartment with your children. You won't have to put up with the kind of horror you've been living through, and you'll have a decent, respectable job.'

Mrs Owens clutched Honey's hand. 'I don't know how to thank you,' she sobbed. 'You don't know what it has been like.'

'I can imagine,' Honey said. 'You're going to be fine.'

The woman nodded, too choked up to speak.

The following day when Honey returned to see Mrs Owens, the room was empty.

'Where is she?' Honey asked.

'Oh,' the nurse said, 'she left this morning with her husband.'

Her name was on the PA system again. 'Dr Taft . . . Room 215 . . . Dr Taft . . . Room 215.'

In the corridor Honey ran into Kat. 'How's your day going?' Kat asked.

'You wouldn't believe it!' Honey told her.

Dr Ritter was waiting for her in Room 215. In bed was an Indian man in his late twenties.

Dr Ritter said, 'This is your patient?'

'Yes.'

'It says here that he speaks no English. Right?'

'Yes.'

He showed her the chart. 'And this is your writing? Vomiting, cramps, thirst, dehydration . . .'

'That's right,' Honey said.

'. . . absence of peripheral pulse . . .'

'Yes.'

'And what was your diagnosis?'

'Stomach flu.'

'Did you take a stool sample?'

'No. What for?'

'Because your patient has cholera, that's what for!' He was screaming. 'We're going to have to close down the fucking hospital!'

20

'*Cholera?* Are you telling me this hospital has a patient with *cholera?*' Benjamin Wallace yelled.

'I'm afraid so.'

'Are you absolutely *sure?*'

'No question,' Dr Ritter said. 'His stool is swarming with vibrios. He has low arterial pH, with hypotension, tachycardia, and cyanosis.'

By law, all cases of cholera and other infectious diseases must immediately be reported to the state health board and to the Center for Disease Control in Atlanta.

'We're going to have to report it, Ben.'

'They'll close us down!' Wallace stood up and began to pace. 'We can't afford that. I'll be goddamned if I'm going to put every patient in this hospital under quarantine.' He stopped pacing for a moment. 'Does the patient know what he has?'

'No. He doesn't speak English. He's from India.'

'Who has had contact with him?'

'Two nurses and Dr Taft.'

'And Dr Taft diagnosed it as stomach flu?'

'Right. I suppose you're going to dismiss her.'

'Well, no,' Wallace said. 'Anyone can make a mistake. Let's not be hasty. Does the patient's chart read stomach flu?'

'Yes.'

Wallace made his decision. 'Let's leave it that way.

241

Here's what I want you to do. Start intravenous rehydration—use lactated Ringer's solution. Also give him tetracycline. If we can restore his blood volume and fluid immediately, he could be close to normal in a few hours.'

'We aren't going to report this?' Dr Ritter asked.

Wallace looked him in the eye. 'Report a case of stomach flu?'

'What about the nurses and Dr Taft?'

'Give them tetracycline, too. What's the patient's name?'

'Hari Singh.'

'Put him in quarantine for forty-eight hours. He'll either be cured by then or dead.'

Honey was in a panic. She went to find Paige.

'I need your help.'

'What's the problem?'

Honey told her. 'I wish you would talk to him. He doesn't speak English, and you speak Indian.'

'Hindi.'

'Whatever. Will you talk to him?'

'Of course.'

Ten minutes later, Paige was talking to Hari Singh.

'*Aap ki tabyat kaisi hai?*'

'*Karab hai.*'

'*Aap jald acha ko hum kardenge.*'

'*Bhagwan aap ki soney ga.*'

'*Aap ka ilaj hum jalb shuroo kardenge.*'

'*Shukria.*'

'*Dost kiss liay hain?*'

*   *   *

242

Paige took Honey outside in the corridor.

'What did he say?'

'He said he feels terrible. I told him he's going to get well. He said to tell it to God. I told him we're going to start treatment immediately. He said he's grateful.'

'So am I.'

'What are friends for?'

Cholera is a disease that can cause death within twenty-four hours from dehydration, or that can be cured within a few hours.

Five hours after his treatment began, Hari Singh was nearly back to normal.

Paige stopped in to see Jimmy Ford.

His face lit up when he saw her. 'Hi.' His voice was weak, but he had improved miraculously.

'How are you feeling?' Paige asked.

'Great. Did you hear about the doctor who said to his patient, "The best thing you can do is give up smoking, stop drinking, and cut down on your sex life"? The patient said, "I don't deserve the best. What's the second best?"'

And Paige knew Jimmy Ford was going to get well.

Ken Mallory was getting off duty and was on his way to meet Kat when he heard his name being paged. He hesitated, debating whether or not simply to slip out. His name was paged once more. Reluctantly, he picked up a telephone. 'Dr Mallory.'

'Doctor, could you come to ER Two, please? We have a patient here who—'

'Sorry,' Mallory said, 'I just checked out. Find someone else.'

'There's no one else available who can handle this. It's a bleeding ulcer, and the patient's condition is critical. I'm afraid we're going to lose him if . . .'

Damn! 'All right. I'll be right there.' *I'll have to call Kat and tell her I'll be late.*

The patient in the emergency room was a man in his sixties. He was semiconscious, ghost-pale, perspiring, and breathing hard, obviously in enormous pain. Mallory took one look at him and said, 'Get him into an OR, stat!'

Fifteen minutes later, Mallory had the patient on an operating table. The anesthesiologist was monitoring his blood pressure. 'It's dropping fast.'

'Pump some more blood into him.'

Ken Mallory began the operation, working against time. It took only a moment to cut through the skin, and after that, the layer of fat, the fascia, the muscle, and finally the smooth, translucent peritoneum, the lining of the abdomen. Blood was pouring into the stomach.

'Bovie!' Mallory said. 'Get me four units of blood from the blood bank.' He began to cauterize the bleeding vessels.

The operation took four hours, and when it was over, Mallory was exhausted. He looked down at the patient and said, 'He's going to live.'

One of the nurses gave Mallory a warm smile. 'It's a good thing you were here, Dr Mallory.'

He looked over at her. She was young and pretty and obviously open to an invitation. *I'll get to you later, baby*, Mallory thought. He turned to a junior resident. 'Close him up and get him into the recovery room. I'll check on him in the morning.'

Mallory debated whether to telephone Kat, but it was midnight. He sent her two dozen roses.

When Mallory checked in at 6:00 A.M., he stopped by the recovery room to see his new patient.

'He's awake,' the nurse said.

Mallory walked over to the bed. 'I'm Dr Mallory. How do you feel?'

'When I think of the alternative, I feel fine,' the patient said weakly. 'They tell me you saved my life. This was the damnedest thing. I was in the car on my way to a dinner party, and I got this sudden pain and I guess I blacked out. Fortunately, we were only a block away from the hospital, and they brought me to the emergency room here.'

'You were lucky. You lost a lot of blood.'

'They told me that in another ten minutes, I would have been gone. I want to thank you, doctor.'

Mallory shrugged. 'I was just doing my job.'

The patient was studying him carefully. 'I'm Alex Harrison.'

The name meant nothing to Mallory. 'Glad to know you, Mr Harrison.' He was checking Harrison's pulse. 'Are you in any pain now?'

'A bit, but I guess they have me pretty well doped up.'

'The anesthetic will wear off,' Mallory assured him. 'So will the pain. You're going to be fine.'

'How long will I have to be in the hospital?'

'We should have you out of here in a few days.'

245

A clerk from the business office came in, carrying some hospital forms. 'Mr Harrison, for our records, the hospital needs to know whether you have medical coverage.'

'You mean you want to know if I can pay my bill.'

'Well, I wouldn't put it like that, sir.'

'You might check with the San Francisco Fidelity Bank,' he said dryly. 'I own it.'

In the afternoon, when Mallory stopped by to see Alex Harrison, there was an attractive woman with him. She was in her early thirties, blond and trim, and elegant-looking. She was wearing an Adolfo dress that Mallory figured must have cost more than his monthly salary.

'Ah! Here's our hero,' Alex Harrison said. 'It's Dr Mallory, isn't it?'

'Yes. Ken Mallory.'

'Dr Mallory, this is my daughter, Lauren.'

She held out a slim, manicured hand. 'Father tells me you saved his life.'

He smiled. 'That's what doctors are for.'

Lauren was looking over him approvingly. 'Not all doctors.'

It was obvious to Mallory that these two did not belong in a county hospital. He said to Alex Harrison, 'You're coming along fine, but perhaps you'd feel more comfortable if you called your own doctor.'

Alex Harrison shook his head. 'That won't be necessary. He didn't save my life. You did. Do you like it here?'

It was a strange question. 'It's interesting, yes. Why?'

Harrison sat up in bed. 'Well, I was just thinking. A good-looking fellow as capable as you are could have a damned bright future. I don't think you have much of a future in a place like this.'

'Well, I . . .'

'Maybe it was fate that brought me here.'

Lauren spoke up. 'I think what my father is trying to say is that he would like to show you his appreciation.'

'Lauren is right. You and I should have a serious talk when I get out of here. I'd like you to come up to the house for dinner.'

Mallory looked at Lauren and said slowly, 'I'd like that.'

And it changed his life.

Ken Mallory was having a surprisingly difficult time getting together with Kat.

'How's Monday night, Kat?'

'Wonderful.'

'Good. I'll pick you up at—'

'Wait! I just remembered. A cousin from New York is coming to town for the night.'

'Well, Tuesday?'

'I'm on call Tuesday.'

'What about Wednesday?'

'I promised Paige and Honey that we'd do something together Wednesday.'

Mallory was getting desperate. His time was running out too fast.

'Thursday?'

'Thursday is fine.'

'Great. Shall I pick you up?'

'No. Why don't we meet at Chez Panisse?'

'Very well. Eight o'clock?'

'Perfect.'

Mallory waited at the restaurant until nine o'clock and then telephoned Kat. There was no answer. He waited another half hour. *Maybe she misunderstood*, he thought. *She wouldn't deliberately break a date with me.*

The following morning, he saw Kat at the hospital. She ran up to him.

'Oh, Ken, I'm so sorry! It was the silliest thing. I decided to take a little nap before our date. I fell asleep and when I woke up it was the middle of the night. Poor darling. Did you wait for me long?'

'No, no. It's all right.' *The stupid woman!* He moved closer to her. 'I want to finish what we started, baby. I go crazy when I think about you.'

'Me, too,' Kat said. 'I can't wait.'

'Maybe next weekend we can . . .'

'Oh, dear. I'm busy over the weekend.'

And so it went.

The clock was running.

Kat was reporting events to Paige when her beeper went off.

'Excuse me.' Kat picked up a telephone. 'Dr Hunter.' She listened a moment. 'Thanks. I'll be right there.' She replaced the receiver. 'I have to go. Emergency.'

Paige sighed. 'What else is new?'

Kat strode down the corridor and took an elevator

248

down to the emergency room. Inside were two dozen cots, all of them occupied. Kat thought of it as the suffering room, filled day and night with victims of automobile accidents, gunshots or knife wounds, and twisted limbs. A kaleidoscope of broken lives. To Kat it was a small corner of hell.

An orderly hurried up to her. 'Dr Hunter . . .'

'What have we got?' Kat asked. They were moving toward a cot at the far end of the room.

'He's unconscious. It looks as though someone beat him up. His face and head are battered, he has a broken nose, a dislocated shoulder blade, at least two different fractures to his right arm, and . . .'

'Why did you call me?'

'The paramedics think there's a head injury. There could be brain damage.'

They had reached the cot where the victim lay. His face was caked with blood, swollen and bruised. He was wearing alligator shoes and . . . Kat's heart skipped a beat. She leaned forward and took a closer look. It was Lou Dinetto.

Kat ran skillful fingers over his scalp and examined his eyes. There was a definite concussion.

She hurried over to a telephone and dialed. 'This is Dr Hunter. I want a head CAT scan done. The patient's name is Dinetto. Lou Dinetto. Send down a gurney, stat.'

Kat replaced the receiver and turned her attention back to Dinetto. She said to the orderly, 'Stay with him. When the gurney arrives, take him to the third floor. I'll be waiting.'

Thirty minutes later on the third floor, Kat was studying the CAT scan she had ordered. 'He has some brain hemorrhaging, he has a high fever, and he's in shock. I want him stabilized for twenty-four hours. I'll decide then when we'll operate.'

Kat wondered whether what had happened to Dinetto might affect Mike.

And how.

Paige stopped by to see Jimmy. He was feeling much better.

'Did you hear about the flasher in the garment district? He walked up to a little old lady and opened up his raincoat. She studied him a moment and said, "You call *that* a lining?"'

Kat was having dinner with Mallory at an intimate little restaurant near the bay. Seated across from Mallory, studying him, Kat felt guilty. *I should never have started this*, she thought. *I know what he is, and yet I'm having a wonderful time. Damn the man! But I can't stop our plan now.*

They had finished their coffee.

Kat leaned forward. 'Can we go to your place, Ken?'

'You bet!' *Finally*, Mallory thought.

Kat shifted in her chair uncomfortably and frowned. 'Uh, oh!'

'Are you all right?' Mallory asked.

'I don't know. Would you excuse me for a moment?'

'Certainly.' He watched her get up and head for the ladies' room.

When she returned, she said, 'It's bad timing, darling. I'm so sorry. You'd better get me home.'

He stared at her, trying to conceal his frustration. The damned fates were conspiring against him.

'Right,' Mallory said curtly. He was ready to explode.

He was going to lose a precious five days.

Five minutes after Kat returned to the apartment, the front doorbell rang. Kat smiled to herself. Mallory had found an excuse to come back, and she hated herself for being so pleased. She walked over to the door and opened it.

'Ken . . .'

Rhino and the Shadow were standing there. Kat felt a sudden sense of fear. The two men pushed past her into the apartment.

Rhino spoke. 'You doin' the operation on Mr Dinetto?'

Kat's throat was dry. 'Yes.'

'We don't want anything to happen to him.'

'Neither do I,' Kat said. 'Now, if you'll excuse me. I'm tired and—'

'Is there a chance he'll die?' the Shadow asked.

Kat hesitated. 'In brain surgery there's always a risk of—'

'You better not let it happen.'

'Believe me, I—'

'Don't let it happen.' He looked at Rhino. 'Let's go.'

Kat watched them start to leave.

At the door, the Shadow turned and said, 'Say hello to Mike for us.'

Kat was suddenly very still. 'Is . . . is this some kind of threat?'

'We don't threaten people, doc. We're telling you. If Mr Dinetto dies, you and your fucking family are gonna be wiped out.'

21

In the doctors' dressing room, half a dozen doctors were waiting for Ken Mallory to appear.

When he walked in, Grundy said, 'Hail the conquering hero! We want to hear all the lurid details.' He grinned. 'But the catch is, buddy, we want to hear them from *her*.'

'I ran into a little bad luck.' Mallory smiled. '*But you can all start getting your money ready.*'

Kat and Paige were getting into scrubs.

'Have you ever done a procedure on a doctor?' Kat asked.

'No.'

'You're lucky. They're the worst patients in the world. They know too much.'

'Who are you operating on?'

'Dr Mervyn "Don't Hurt Me" Franklin.'

'Good luck.'

'I'll need it.'

Dr Mervyn Franklin was a man in his sixties, thin, bald, and irascible.

When Kat walked into his room, he snapped, 'It's about time you got here. Did the damned electrolyte reports come back?'

'Yes,' Kat said. 'They're normal.'

'Who says so? I don't trust the damn lab. Half the time they don't know what they're doing. And make sure there's no mix-up on the blood transfusion.'

'I'll make sure,' Kat said patiently.

'Who's doing the operation?'

'Dr Jurgenson and I. Dr Franklin, I promise you, there's nothing for you to worry about.'

'Whose brain are they operating on, yours or mine? All operations are risky. You know why? Because half of the damned surgeons are in the wrong profession. They should have been butchers.'

'Dr Jurgenson is very capable.'

'I know he is, or I wouldn't let him touch me. Who's the anesthesiologist?'

'I believe it's Dr Miller.'

'That quack? I don't want him. Get me someone else.'

'Dr Franklin . . .'

'Get me someone else. See if Haliburton is available.'

'All right.'

'And get me the names of the nurses in the OR. I want to check them out.'

Kat looked him in the eye. 'Would you prefer to do the operation yourself?'

'What?' He stared at her a moment, then smiled sheepishly. 'I guess not.'

Kat said gently, 'Then why don't you let us handle it?'

'Okay. You know something? I like you.'

'I like you, too. Did the nurse give you a sedative?'

'Yes.'

'All right. We'll be ready in a few minutes. Is there anything I can do for you?'

'Yeah. Teach my stupid nurse where my veins are located.'

In OR Four, the brain surgery on Dr Mervyn Franklin was going perfectly. He had complained every step of the way from his room to the operating theater.

'Now mind you,' he said, 'minimal anesthetic. The brain has no feeling, so once you get in there, you won't need much.'

'I'm aware of that,' Kat said patiently.

'And see that the temperature is kept down to forty degrees. That's maximum.'

'Right.'

'Let's have some fast music on during the operation. Keep you all on your toes.'

'Right.'

'And make sure you have a top scrub nurse in there.'

'Right.'

And on and on it went.

When the opening in Dr Franklin's skull was drilled, Kat said, 'I see the clot. It doesn't look too bad.' She went to work.

Three hours later as they were beginning to close the incision, George Englund, the chief of surgery, came into the operating room and went up to Kat.

'Kat, are you almost through here?'

'We're just wrapping it up.'

'Let Dr Jurgenson take over. We need you fast. There's an emergency.'

Kat nodded. 'Coming.' She turned to Jurgenson. 'Will you finish up here?'

'No problem.'

Kat walked out with George Englund. 'What's happening?'

'You were scheduled to do an operation later, but your patient has started to hemorrhage. They're taking him to OR Three now. It doesn't look as though he's going to make it. You'll have to operate right away.'

'Who — ?'

'A Mr Dinetto.'

Kat looked at him aghast. '*Dinetto?*' *If Mr Dinetto dies, you and your fucking family are gonna be wiped out.*

Kat hurried down the corridor that led to OR Three. Approaching her were Rhino and the Shadow.

'What's going on?' Rhino demanded.

Kat's mouth was so dry that it was difficult to speak. 'Mr Dinetto started hemorrhaging. We must operate right away.'

The Shadow grabbed her arm. 'Then do it! But remember what we told you. Keep him alive.'

Kat pulled away and hurried into the operating room.

Dr Vance was doing the operation with Kat. He was a good surgeon. Kat began the ritual scrub: a half minute on each arm first, then a half minute on each hand. She repeated it and then scrubbed her nails.

Dr Vance stepped in beside her and started his scrub. 'How are you feeling?'

'Fine,' Kat lied.

Lou Dinetto was wheeled semiconscious into the operating room on a gurney, and carefully transferred to the operating table. His shaven head was scrubbed and painted with Merthiolate solution that gleamed a bright orange under the operating lights. He was as pale as death.

The team was in place: Dr Vance, another resident, an anesthesiologist, two scrub nurses, and a circulating nurse. Kat checked to make sure that everything they might require was there. She glanced at the wall monitors—oxygen saturation, carbon dioxide, temperature, muscle stimulators, precordial stethoscope, EKG, automatic blood pressure, and disconnect alarms. Everything was in order.

The anesthesiologist strapped a blood pressure cuff on Dinetto's right arm, then placed a rubber mask over the patient's face. 'All right, now. Breathe deeply. Take three big breaths.'

Dinetto was asleep before the third breath.

The procedure began.

Kat was reporting aloud. 'There's an area of damage in the middle of the brain, caused by a clot that's broken off the aorta valve. It's blocking a small blood vessel on the right side of the brain and extending slightly into the left half.' She probed deeper. 'It's at the lower edge of the aqueduct of Sylvius. Scalpel.'

A tiny burr hole about the size of a dime was made

257

by an electric drill to expose the dura mater. Next, Kat cut open the dura to expose a segment of the cerebral cortex that lay underneath. 'Forceps!'

The scrub nurse handed her the electric forceps.

The incision was held open by a small retractor which maintained itself in place.

'There's a hell of a lot of bleeding,' Vance said.

Kat picked up the bovie and started to cauterize the bleeders. 'We're going to control it.'

Dr Vance started suction on soft cotton patties that were placed on the dura. The oozing veins on the surface of the dura were identified and coagulated.

'It looks good,' Vance said. 'He's going to make it.'

Kat breathed a sigh of relief.

And at that instant, Lou Dinetto stiffened and his body went into spasm. The anesthesiologist called out, 'Blood pressure's dropping!'

Kat said, 'Get some more blood into him!'

They were all looking at the monitor. The curve was rapidly flattening out. There were two quick heartbeats followed by ventricular fibrillation.

'Shock him!' Kat snapped. She quickly attached the electric pads to his body and turned on the machine.

Dinetto's chest heaved up once and then fell.

'Inject him with epinephrine! Quick!'

'No heartbeat!' the anesthesiologist called out a moment later.

Kat tried again, raising the dial.

Once again, there was a quick convulsive movement.

'No heartbeat!' the anesthesiologist cried. 'Asystole. No rhythm at all.'

Desperately, Kat tried one last time. The body rose higher this time, then fell again. Nothing.

'He's dead,' Dr Vance said.

Code Red is an alert that immediately brings all-out medical assistance to try to save the life of a patient. When Lou Dinetto's heart stopped in the middle of his operation, the operating room Code Red team rushed to give aid.

Over the public address system Kat could hear, 'Code Red, OR Three . . . Code Red . . .' *Red rhymes with dead.*

Kat was in a panic. She applied the electroshock again. It was not only his life she was trying to save — it was Mike's and her own. Dinetto's body leaped into the air, then fell back, inert.

'Try once more!' Dr Vance urged.

We don't threaten people, doc. We're telling you. If Mr Dinetto dies, you and your fucking family are gonna be wiped out.

Kat turned on the switch and applied the machine to Dinetto's chest again. Once more his body rose a few inches into the air and then fell back.

'Again!'

It's not going to happen, Kat thought despairingly. *I'm going to die with him.*

The operating room was suddenly filled with doctors and nurses.

'What are you waiting for?' someone asked.

Kat took a deep breath and pressed down once

again. For an instant, nothing happened. Then a faint blip appeared on the monitor. It faltered a moment, then appeared again and faltered, and then began to grow stronger and stronger, until it became a steady, stabilized rhythm.

Kat stared at it unbelievingly.

There was a cheer from the crowded room. 'He's going to make it!' someone yelled.

'Jesus, that was close!'

They have no idea how close, Kat thought.

Two hours later, Lou Dinetto was off the table and on a gurney, on his way back to intensive care. Kat was at his side. Rhino and the Shadow were waiting in the corridor.

'The operation was successful,' Kat said. 'He's going to be fine.'

Ken Mallory was in deep trouble. It was the last day to make good on his bet. The problem had been growing so gradually that he had hardly been aware of it. From almost the first night, he had been positive that he would have no trouble getting Kat into bed. *Trouble? She's eager for it!* Now his time was up, and he was facing disaster.

Mallory thought about all the things that had gone wrong — Kat's roommates coming in just as she was about to go to bed with him, the difficulty of getting together for a date, Kat's being called away by her beeper and leaving him standing naked, her cousin coming to town, her oversleeping, her period. He stopped suddenly and thought, *Wait a minute! They couldn't have all been coincidences!* Kat was doing this to him deliberately! She had somehow gotten wind of the bet, and had decided to make a fool of him, to play a joke on him, a joke that was going to cost him ten thousand dollars that he didn't have. *The bitch!* He was no closer to winning than he had been at the beginning. She had deliberately led him on. *How the hell did I let myself get into this?* He knew there was no way he could come up with the money.

When Mallory walked into the doctors' dressing room, they were waiting for him.

'Payoff day!' Grundy sang out.

Mallory forced a smile. 'I have until midnight, right? Believe me, she's ready, fellows.'

There was a snicker. 'Sure. We'll believe you when we hear it from the lady herself. Just have the cash ready in the morning.'

Mallory laughed. 'You'd better have *yours* ready!'

He *had* to find a way. And suddenly he had the answer.

Ken Mallory found Kat in the lounge. He sat down opposite her. 'I hear you saved a patient's life.'

'And my own.'

'What?'

'Nothing.'

'How would you like to save my life?'

Kat looked at him quizzically.

'Have dinner with me tonight.'

'I'm too tired, Ken.' She was weary of the game she was playing with him. *I've had enough*, Kat thought. *It's time to stop. It's over. I've fallen into my own trap*. She wished he were a different kind of man. If only he had been honest with her. *I really could have cared for him*, Kat thought.

There was no way Mallory was going to let Kat get away. 'We'll make it an early night,' he coaxed. 'You have to have dinner somewhere.'

Reluctantly, Kat nodded. She knew it was going to be the last time. She was going to tell him she knew about the bet. She was going to end the game. 'All right.'

Honey finished her shift at 4:00 P.M. She looked at her watch and decided that she had just enough time to do some quick shopping. She went to the Candelier to buy some candles for the apartment, then to the San Francisco Tea and Coffee Company so there would be some drinkable coffee for breakfast, and on to Chris Kelly for linens.

Loaded down with packages, Honey headed for the apartment. *I'll fix myself some dinner at home*, Honey decided. She knew that Kat had a date with Mallory, and that Paige was on call.

Fumbling with her packages, Honey entered the apartment and closed the door behind her. She switched on the light. A huge black man was coming out of the bathroom, dripping blood on the white carpet. He was pointing a gun at her.

'Make one sound, and I'll blow your fucking head off!'

Honey screamed.

23

Mallory was seated across from Kat at Schroeder's restaurant on Front Street.

What was going to happen when he couldn't pay the ten thousand dollars? Word would spread quickly around the hospital, and he would become known as a welcher, a sick joke.

Kat was chatting about one of her patients, and Mallory was looking into her eyes, not hearing a word she said. He had more important things on his mind.

Dinner was almost over, and the waiter was serving coffee. Kat looked at her watch. 'I have an early call, Ken. I think we'd better go.'

He sat there, staring down at the table. 'Kat . . .' He looked up. 'There's something I have to tell you.'

'Yes?'

'I have a confession to make.' He took a deep breath. 'This isn't easy for me.'

She watched him, puzzled. 'What is it?'

'I'm embarrassed to tell you.' He was fumbling for words. 'I . . . I made a stupid bet with some of the doctors that . . . that I could take you to bed.'

Kat was staring at him. 'You . . .'

'Please don't say anything yet. I'm so ashamed of what I did. It started out as a kind of joke, but the joke is on me. Something happened that I didn't count on. I fell in love with you.'

'Ken . . .'

'I've never been in love before, Kat. I've known a lot of women, but never felt anything like this. I haven't been able to stop thinking about you.' He took a shaky breath. 'I want to marry you.'

Kat's mind was spinning. Everything was being turned topsy-turvy. 'I . . . I don't know what to . . .'

'You're the only woman I've ever proposed to. Please say yes. Will you marry me, Kat?'

So he had really meant all the lovely things he had said to her! Her heart was pounding. It was like a wonderful dream suddenly come true. All she had wanted from him was honesty. And now he was being honest with her. All this time he had been feeling guilty about what he had done. He was not like other men. He was genuine, and sensitive.

When Kat looked at him, her eyes were glowing. 'Yes, Ken. Oh, yes!'

His grin lit up the room. 'Kat . . .' He leaned over and kissed her. 'I'm so sorry about that stupid bet.' He shook his head in self-derision. 'Ten thousand dollars. We could have used that money for our honeymoon. But it's worth losing it to have you.'

Kat was thinking, *Ten thousand dollars*.

'I was such a fool.'

'When is your deadline up?'

'At midnight tonight, but that's not important anymore. The important thing is us. That we're going to be married. We —'

'Ken?'

'Yes, darling?'

'Let's go to your place.' There was a mischievous

265

glint in Kat's eyes. 'You still have time to win your bet.'

Kat was a tigress in bed.

My God! This was worth waiting for, Mallory thought. All the feelings that Kat had kept bottled up over the years suddenly exploded. She was the most passionate woman Ken Mallory had ever known. At the end of two hours, he was exhausted. He held Kat in his arms. 'You're incredible,' he said.

She lifted herself up on her elbows and looked down at him. 'So are you, darling. I'm so happy.'

Mallory grinned. 'So am I.' *Ten thousand dollars' worth!* he thought. *And great sex.*

'Promise me it will always be like this, Ken.'

'I promise,' Mallory said in his sincerest voice.

Kat looked at her watch. 'I'd better get dressed.'

'Can't you spend the night here?'

'No, I'm riding to the hospital with Paige in the morning.' She gave him a warm kiss. 'Don't worry. We'll have all our iives to spend together.'

He watched her get dressed.

'I can't wait to collect on that bet. It will buy us a great honeymoon.' He frowned. 'But what if the boys don't believe me? They aren't going to take my word for it.'

Kat was thoughtful for a moment. Finally, she said, 'Don't worry. I'll let them know.'

Mallory grinned. 'Come on back to bed.'

24

The black man with the gun pointed at Honey screamed, 'I told you to shut up!'

'I . . . I'm sorry,' Honey said. She was trembling. 'Wh . . . what do you want?'

He was pressing his hand against his side, trying to stop the flow of blood. 'I want my sister.'

Honey looked at him, puzzled. He was obviously insane. 'Your sister?'

'Kat.' His voice was becoming faint.

'Oh, my God! You're Mike!'

'Yeah.'

The gun dropped, and he slipped to the floor. Honey rushed to him. Blood was pouring out from what looked like a gunshot wound.

'Lie still,' Honey said. She hurried into the bathroom and gathered up some peroxide and a large bath towel. She returned to Mike. 'This is going to hurt,' she warned.

He lay there, too weak to move.

She poured peroxide into the wound and pressed the towel against his side. He bit down on his hand to keep from screaming.

'I'm going to call an ambulance and get you to the hospital,' Honey said.

He grabbed her arm. 'No! No hospitals. No police.' His voice was getting weaker. 'Where's Kat?'

'I don't know,' Honey said helplessly. She knew Kat was out somewhere with Mallory, but she had no idea where. 'Let me call a friend of mine.'

'Paige?' he asked.

Honey nodded. 'Yes.' *So Kat told him about the two of us.*

It took the hospital ten minutes to reach Paige.

'You'd better come home,' Honey said.

'I'm on call, Honey. I'm in the middle of —'

'Kat's brother is here.'

'Oh, well, tell him —'

'He's been shot.'

'He *what*?'

'He's been shot!'

'I'll send the paramedics over and —'

'He says no hospitals and no police. I don't know what to do.'

'How bad is it?'

'Pretty bad.'

There was a pause. 'I'll find someone to cover for me. I'll be there in half an hour.'

Honey replaced the receiver and turned to Mike. 'Paige is coming.'

Two hours later, on her way back to the apartment, Kat was filled with a glorious sense of well-being. She had been nervous about making love, afraid that she would hate it after the terrible experience she had had, but instead, Ken Mallory had turned it into something wonderful. He had unlocked emotions in her that she had never known existed.

Smiling to herself at the thought of how they had outwitted the doctors at the last moment and won the bet, Kat opened the door to the apartment and stood there in shock. Paige and Honey were kneeling beside Mike. He was lying on the floor, a pillow under his head, a towel pressed against his side, his clothes soaked with blood.

Paige and Honey looked up as Kat entered.

'Mike! My God!' She rushed over to Mike and knelt beside him. 'What happened?'

'Hi, sis.' His voice was barely a whisper.

'He's been shot,' Paige said. 'He's hemorrhaging.'

'Let's get him to the hospital,' Kat said.

Mike shook his head. 'No,' he whispered. 'You're a doctor. Fix me up.'

Kat looked over at Paige.

'I've stopped as much of the bleeding as I can, but the bullet is still inside him. We don't have the instruments here to—'

'He's still losing blood,' Kat said. She cradled Mike's head in her arms. 'Listen to me, Mike. If you don't get help, you're going to die.'

'You . . . can't . . . report . . . this . . . I don't want any police.'

Kat asked quietly, 'What are you involved in, Mike?'

'Nothing. I was in a . . . a business deal . . . and it went sour . . . and this guy got mad and shot me.'

It was the kind of story Kat had been listening to for years. Lies. All lies. She had known that then, and she knew it now, but she had tried to keep the truth from herself.

Mike held on to her arm. 'Will you help me, sis?'

'Yes. I'm going to help you, Mike.' Kat leaned down and kissed him on the cheek. Then she rose and went to the telephone. She picked up the receiver and dialed the emergency room at the hospital. 'This is Dr Hunter,' she said in an unsteady voice. 'I need an ambulance right away . . .'

At the hospital, Kat asked Paige to perform the operation to remove the bullet.

'He's lost a lot of blood,' Paige said. She turned to the assisting surgeon. 'Give him another unit.'

It was dawn when the operation was finished. The surgery was successful.

When it was over, Paige called Kat aside. 'How do you want me to report this?' she asked. 'I could list it as an accident, or . . .'

'No,' Kat said. Her voice was filled with pain. 'I should have done this a long time ago. I want you to report it as a gunshot wound.'

Mallory was waiting for Kat outside the operating theater.

'Kat! I heard about your brother and . . .'

Kat nodded wearily.

'I'm so sorry. Is he going to be all right?'

Kat looked at Mallory and said, 'Yes. For the first time in his life, Mike is going to be all right.'

Mallory squeezed Kat's hand. 'I just want you to know how wonderful last night was. You were a miracle. Oh. That reminds me. The doctors I bet with are in the lounge waiting, but I suppose with all that has happened, you wouldn't want to go in and . . .'

'Why not?'

She took his arm and the two of them walked

into the lounge. The doctors watched them as they approached.

Grundy said, 'Hi, Kat. We need to have your word on something. Dr Mallory claims that you and he spent the night together, and it was great.'

'It was better than great,' Kat said. 'It was *fantastic*!' She kissed Mallory on the cheek. 'I'll see you later, lover.'

The men sat there, gaping, as Kat walked away.

In their dressing room, Kat said to Paige and Honey, 'In all the excitement, I haven't had a chance to tell you the news.'

'What news?' Paige asked.

'Ken asked me to marry him.'

There were looks of disbelief on their faces.

'You're joking!' Paige said.

'No. He proposed to me last night. I accepted.'

'But you can't marry him!' Honey exclaimed. 'You know what he's like. I mean, he tried to get you to go to bed on a bet!'

'He succeeded.' Kat grinned.

Paige looked at her. 'I'm confused.'

Kat said, 'We were wrong about him. Completely wrong. Ken told me about that bet himself. All this time, it's been bothering his conscience. Don't you see what happened? I went out with him to punish him, and he went out with me to win some money, and we ended up falling in love with each other. Oh, I can't tell you how happy I am!'

Honey and Paige looked at each other. 'When are you getting married?' Honey asked.

'We haven't discussed it yet, but I'm sure it will

271

be soon. I want you two to be my bridesmaids.'

'You can count on it,' Paige said. 'We'll be there.'
But there was a nagging doubt in the back of her
mind. She yawned. 'It's been a long night. I'm going
home and get some sleep.'

'I'll stay here with Mike,' Kat said. 'When he
wakes up, the police want to talk to him.' She took
their hands in hers. 'Thank you for being such good
friends.'

On the way home, Paige thought about what had
happened that night. She knew how much Kat loved
her brother. It had taken a lot of courage to turn
him over to the police. *I should have done this a long
time ago.*

The telephone was ringing as Paige walked into
the apartment. She hurried to pick it up.

It was Jason. 'Hi! I just called to tell you how
much I miss you. What's going on in your life?'

Paige was tempted to tell him, to share it with
somebody, but it was too personal. It belonged to
Kat.

'Nothing,' Paige said. 'Everything is fine.'

'Good. Are you free for dinner tonight?'

Paige was aware that it was more than an invitation
to dinner. *If I see him any more, I'm going to get
involved*, she thought. She knew that it was one of
the most important decisions of her life.

She took a deep breath. 'Jason . . .' The doorbell
rang. 'Hold it a minute, will you, Jason?'

Paige put the telephone down and went to the
door and opened it.

Alfred Turner was standing there.

25

Paige stood there, frozen.

Alfred smiled. 'May I come in?'

She was flustered. 'Of . . . of course. I'm s . . . sorry.' She watched Alfred walk into the living room, and she was filled with conflicting emotions. She was happy and excited and angry at the same time. *Why am I going on like this?* Paige thought. *He probably dropped by to say hello.*

Alfred turned to her. 'I've left Karen.'

The words were a shock.

Alfred moved closer to her. 'I made a big mistake, Paige. I never should have let you go. Never.'

'Alfred . . .' Paige suddenly remembered. 'Excuse me.'

She hurried to the telephone and picked it up. 'Jason?'

'Yes, Paige. About tonight, we could—'

'I . . . I can't see you.'

'Oh. If tonight is bad, what about tomorrow night?'

'I . . . I'm not sure.'

He sensed the tension in her voice. 'Is anything wrong?'

'No. Everything is fine. I'll call you tomorrow and explain.'

'All right.' He sounded puzzled.

Paige replaced the receiver.

'I've missed you, Paige,' Alfred said. 'Have you missed me?'

No. I just follow strangers on the street and call them Alfred. 'Yes,' Paige admitted.

'Good. We belong together, you know. We always have.'

Have we? Is that why you married Karen? Do you think you can walk in and out of my life anytime you please?

Alfred was standing close to her. 'Haven't we?'

Paige looked at him and said, 'I don't know.' It was all too sudden.

Alfred took her hand in his. 'Of course you do.'

'What happened with Karen?'

Alfred shrugged. 'Karen was a mistake. I kept thinking about you and all the great times we had. We were always good for each other.'

She was watching him, wary, guarded. 'Alfred . . .'

'I'm here to stay, Paige. When I say "here", I don't exactly mean that. We're going to New York.'

'New York?'

'Yes. I'll tell you all about it. I could use a cup of coffee.'

'Of course. I'll make a fresh pot. It will just take a few minutes.'

Alfred followed her into the kitchen, where Paige began to prepare the coffee. She was trying to get her thoughts in order. She had wanted Alfred back so desperately, and now that he was here . . .

Alfred was saying, 'I've learned a lot in the last few years, Paige. I've grown up.'

'Oh?'

'Yes. You know I've been working with WHO all these years.'

'I know.'

'Those countries haven't changed any since we were kids. In fact, some of them are worse. There's more disease down there, more poverty . . .'

'But you were there, helping,' Paige said.

'Yes, and I suddenly woke up.'

'Woke up?'

'I realized I was throwing my life away. I was down there, living in misery, working twenty-four hours a day, helping those ignorant savages, when I could have been making a bundle of money over here.'

Paige was listening in disbelief.

'I met a doctor who has a practice on Park Avenue in New York. Do you know how much he makes a year? Over five hundred thousand dollars! Did you hear me? Five hundred thousand a year!'

Paige was staring at him.

'I said to myself, "Where has that kind of money been all of my life?" He offered me a position as an associate,' Alfred said proudly, 'and I'm going in with him. That's why you and I are going to New York.'

Paige stood there, numbed by what she was hearing.

'I'll be able to afford a penthouse apartment for us, and to get you pretty dresses, and all the things I've always promised you.' He was grinning. 'Well, are you surprised?'

Paige's mouth was dry. 'I . . . I don't know what to say, Alfred.'

He laughed. 'Of course you don't. Five hundred

thousand dollars a year is enough to make anyone speechless.'

'I wasn't thinking of the money,' Paige said slowly.

'No?'

She was studying him, as though seeing him for the first time. 'Alfred, when you were working for WHO, didn't you feel you were helping people?'

He shrugged. 'Nothing can help those people. And who the hell really cares? Would you believe that Karen wanted me to stay down there in Bangladesh? I told her no way, so she went back.' He took Paige's hand. 'So here I am . . . You're a little quiet. I guess you're overwhelmed by all this, huh?'

Paige thought of her father. *He would have been a big success on Park Avenue, but he wasn't interested in money. His only interest was in helping people.*

'I've already divorced Karen, so we can get married right away.' He patted her hand. 'What do you think of the idea of living in New York?'

Paige took a deep breath. 'Alfred . . .'

There was an expectant smile on his face. 'Yes?'

'Get out.'

The smile slowly faded. 'What?'

Paige rose. 'I want you to get out of here.'

He was confused. 'Where do you want me to go?'

'I won't tell you,' Paige said. 'It would hurt your feelings.'

After Alfred had gone, Paige sat lost in thought. Kat had been right. She had been clinging to a ghost. *Helping those ignorant savages, when I could have*

*been making a bundle over here . . . Five hundred
thousand a year!*

And that's what I've been hanging on to, Paige
thought wonderingly. She should have felt depressed, but instead she was filled with a feeling of
elation. She suddenly felt free. She knew now what
she wanted.

She walked over to the telephone and dialed
Jason's number.

'Hello.'

'Jason, it's Paige. Remember telling me about
your house in Noe Valley?'

'Yes . . .'

'I'd love to see it. Are you free tonight?'

Jason said quietly, 'Do you want to tell me what's
going on, Paige? I'm very confused.'

'*I'm* the one who's confused. I thought I was in
love with a man I knew a long time ago, but he's not
the same man. I know what I want now.'

'Yes?'

'I want to see your house.'

Noe Valley belonged to another century. It was a
colorful oasis in the heart of one of the most cosmo-
politan cities in the world.

Jason's house was a reflection of him—comfortable, neat, and charming. He escorted Paige through
the house. 'This is the living room, the kitchen, the
guest bathroom, the study . . .' He looked at her and
said, 'The bedroom is upstairs. Would you like to
see it?'

Paige said quietly, 'Very much.'

They went up the stairs into the bedroom. Paige's

heart was pounding wildly. But what was happening seemed inevitable. *I should have known from the beginning*, she thought.

Paige never knew who made the first move, but somehow they were in each other's arms and Jason's lips were on hers, and it seemed the most natural thing in the world. They started to undress each other, and there was a fierce urgency in both of them. And then they were in bed, and he was making love to her.

'God,' he whispered. 'I love you.'

'I know,' Paige teased. 'Ever since I told you to put on the white coat.'

After they made love, Paige said, 'I'd like to spend the night here.'

Jason smiled. 'You won't hate me in the morning?'

'I promise.'

Paige spent the night with Jason, talking . . . making love . . . talking. In the morning, she cooked breakfast for him.

Jason watched her, and said, 'I don't know how I got so lucky, but thank you.'

'I'm the lucky one,' Paige told him.

'You know something? I never got an answer to my proposal.'

'You'll have an answer this afternoon.'

That afternoon, a messenger arrived at Jason's office, with an envelope. Inside was the card that Jason had sent with the model house.

Mine   [ ]
Ours   [x]
Please check one.

26

Lou Dinetto was ready to check out of the hospital. Kat went to his room to say goodbye. Rhino and the Shadow were there.

As Kat walked in, Dinetto turned to them and said, 'Get lost.'

Kat watched them leave the room.

Dinetto looked at Kat and said, 'I owe you one.'

'You don't owe me anything.'

'Is that what you think my life is worth? I hear you're getting married.'

'That's right.'

'To a doctor.'

'Yes.'

'Well, tell him to take good care of you, or he'll have to answer to me.'

'I'll tell him.'

There was a small pause. 'I'm sorry about Mike.'

'He'll be all right,' Kat said. 'I had a long talk with him. He'll be fine.'

'Good.' Dinetto held out a bulky manila envelope. 'A little wedding present for you.'

Kat shook her head. 'No. Thank you.'

'But . . .'

'Take care of yourself.'

'You, too. You know something? You're a real stand-up broad. I'm going to tell you something I

want you to remember. If you ever need a favor—
anything—you come to me. You hear me?'

'I hear you.'

She knew that he meant it. And she knew that she
would never go to him.

During the weeks that followed, Paige and Jason
spoke on the phone three and four times a day, and
were together every time Paige was not on night call.

The hospital was busier than ever. Paige had been
on a thirty-six-hour shift that had been filled with
emergencies. She had just gone to sleep in the on-call
room when she was awakened by the urgent shrill
of the telephone.

She fumbled the phone to her ear. 'H'lo?'

'Dr Taylor, will you come to Room 422, stat?'

Paige tried to clear her mind. *Room 422. One of
Dr Barker's patients. Lance Kelly.* He had just had
a mitral valve replaced. *Something must have gone
wrong.* Paige stumbled off the cot and walked out
into the deserted corridor. She decided not to wait
for the elevator. She ran up the stairs. *Maybe it's
just a nervous nurse. If it's serious, I'll call Dr Barker,*
she thought.

She walked into Room 422 and stood in the doorway, staring. The patient was fighting for breath and
moaning. The nurse turned to Paige in obvious relief.
'I didn't know what to do, doctor. I . . .'

Paige hurried to the bedside. 'You're going to
be fine,' she said reassuringly. She took his wrist
between two fingers. His pulse was jumping wildly.
The mitral valve was malfunctioning.

'Let's sedate him,' Paige ordered.

The nurse handed Paige a syringe, and Paige injected it into a vein. Paige turned to the nurse. 'Tell the head nurse to get an operating team together, stat. And send for Dr Barker!'

Fifteen minutes later, Kelly was on the operating table. The team consisted of two scrub nurses, a circulating nurse, and two residents. A television monitor was perched high in a corner of the room to display the heart rate, EKG, and blood pressure.

The anesthesiologist walked in, and Paige felt like cursing. Most of the anesthesiologists at the hospital were skilled doctors, but Herman Koch was an exception. Paige had worked with him before and tried to avoid him as much as possible. She did not trust him. Now she had no choice.

Paige watched him secure a tube to the patient's throat, while she unfolded a paper drape with a clear window and placed it over the patient's chest.

'Put a line into the jugular vein,' Paige said.

Koch nodded. 'Right.'

One of the residents asked, 'What's the problem here?'

'Dr Barker replaced the mitral valve yesterday. I think it's ruptured.' Paige looked over at Dr Koch. 'Is he out?'

Koch nodded. 'Sleeping like he's in bed at home.'

I wish you were, Paige thought. 'What are you using?'

'Propofol.'

She nodded. 'All right.'

She watched Kelly being connected to the heart-lung machine so she could perform a cardio-pulmonary bypass. Paige studied the monitors on the wall. Pulse 140 . . . blood oxygen saturation 92 percent . . . blood pressure 80 over 60. 'Let's go,' she said.

One of the residents put on music.

Paige stepped up to the operating table under eleven hundred watts of hot white light and turned to the scrub nurse. 'Scalpel, please . . .'

The operation began.

Paige removed all the sternal wires from the operation the day before. She then cut from the base of the neck to the lower end of the sternum, while one of the residents blotted away the blood with gauze pads.

She carefully went through the layers of fat and muscle, and in front of her was the erratically beating heart. 'There's the problem,' Paige said. 'The atrium is perforated. Blood is collecting around the heart and compressing it.' Paige was looking at the monitor on the wall. The pump pressure had dropped dangerously.

'Increase the flow,' Paige ordered.

The door to the operating room opened and Lawrence Barker stepped in. He stood to one side, watching what was happening.

Paige said, 'Dr Barker. Do you want to . . . ?'

'It's your operation.'

Paige took a quick look at what Koch was doing. 'Be careful. You'll overanesthetize him, dammit! Slow it down!'

'But I . . .'

'He's in V-tach! His pressure is dropping!'

'What do you want me to do?' Koch asked helplessly.

He should know, Paige thought angrily. 'Give him lidocaine and epinephrine! *Now!*' She was yelling.

'Right.'

Paige watched as Koch picked up a syringe and injected it into the patient's IV.

A resident looked at the monitor and called out, 'Blood pressure is falling.'

Paige was working frantically to stop the flow of blood. She looked up at Koch. 'Too much flow! I told you to . . .'

The noise of the heartbeat on the monitor suddenly became chaotic.

'My God! Something's gone wrong!'

'Give me the defibrillator!' Paige yelled.

The circulating nurse reached for the defibrillator on the crash cart, opened two sterile paddles, and plugged them in. She turned the buttons up to charge them and ten seconds later handed them to Paige.

She took the paddles and positioned them directly over Kelly's heart. Kelly's body jumped, then fell back.

Paige tried again, *willing* him to come back to life, willing him to breathe again. Nothing. The heart lay still, a dead, useless organ.

Paige was in a fury. Her part of the operation had been successful. Koch had overanesthetized the patient.

As Paige was applying the defibrillator to Lance Kelly's body for the third futile time, Dr Barker stepped up to the operating table and turned to Paige.

'You killed him.'

27

Jason was in the middle of a design meeting when his secretary said, 'Dr Taylor is on the phone for you. Shall I tell her you'll call back?'

'No. I'll take it.' Jason picked up the phone. 'Paige?'

'Jason . . . I need you!' She was sobbing.

'What happened?'

'Can you come to the apartment?'

'Of course. I'll be right there.' He stood up. 'The meeting is over. We'll pick it up in the morning.'

Half an hour later, Jason was at the apartment. Paige opened the door and threw her arms around him. Her eyes were red from crying.

'What happened?' Jason asked.

'It's awful! Dr Barker told me I . . . I killed a patient, and honestly, it . . . it wasn't my fault!' Her voice broke. 'I can't take any more of his . . .'

'Paige,' Jason said gently, 'you've told me how mean he always is. That's the man's character.'

Paige shook her head. 'It's more than that. He's been trying to force me out since the day I started working with him. Jason, if he were a bad doctor and didn't think I was any good, I wouldn't mind so much, but the man is brilliant. I have to respect his opinion. I just don't think I'm good enough.'

'Nonsense,' Jason said angrily. 'Of course you are. Everyone I talk to says you're a wonderful doctor.'

'Not Lawrence Barker.'

'Forget Barker.'

'I'm going to,' Paige said. 'I'm quitting the hospital.'

Jason took her in his arms. 'Paige, I know you love the profession too much to give it up.'

'I won't give it up. I just never want to see that hospital again.'

Jason took out a handkerchief and dried Paige's tears.

'I'm sorry to bother you with all of this,' Paige said.

'That's what husbands-to-be are for, isn't it?'

She managed a smile. 'I like the sound of that. All right.' Paige took a deep breath. 'I feel better now. Thanks for talking to me. I telephoned Dr Wallace and told him I was quitting. I'm going over to the hospital to see him now.'

'I'll see you at dinner tonight.'

Paige walked through the corridors of the hospital, knowing that she was seeing them for the last time. There were the familiar noises and the people hurrying up and down the corridors. It had become more of a home to her than she'd realized. She thought of Jimmy and Chang, and all the wonderful doctors she had worked with. Darling Jason going on rounds with her in his white coat. She passed the cafeteria where she and Honey and Kat had had a hundred breakfasts, and the lounge, where they had tried to have a party. The corridors and rooms were full of so many memories. *I'm going to miss it*, Paige thought, *but I refuse to work under the same roof as that monster*.

She went up to Dr Wallace's office. He was waiting for her.

'Well, I must say, your telephone call surprised me, Paige! Have you definitely made up your mind?'

'Yes.'

Benjamin Wallace sighed. 'Very well. Before you go, Dr Barker would like to see you.'

'I want to see him.' All of Paige's pent-up anger boiled to the surface.

'He's in the lab. Well . . . good luck.'

'Thanks.' Paige headed for the lab.

Dr Barker was examining some slides under a microscope when Paige entered. He looked up. 'I'm told you've decided to quit the hospital.'

'That's right. You finally got your wish.'

'And what was that?' Barker asked.

'You've wanted me out of here from the first moment you saw me. Well, you've won. I can't fight you anymore. When you told me I killed your patient, I . . .' Paige's voice broke. 'I . . . I think you're a sadistic, cold-hearted son of a bitch, and I hate you.'

'Sit down,' Dr Barker said.

'No. I have nothing more to say.'

'Well, I have. Who the hell do you think you . . . ?'

He suddenly stopped and began to gasp.

As Paige watched in horror, he clutched his chest and toppled over in his chair, his face twisted to one side in a horrible rictus.

Paige was at his side instantly. 'Dr Barker!' She

286

grabbed the telephone and shouted into it, 'Code Red! Code Red!'

Dr Peterson said, 'He's suffered a massive stroke. It's too early to tell whether he's going to come out of it.'

It's my fault, Paige thought. *I wanted him dead.* She felt miserable.

She went back to see Ben Wallace. 'I'm sorry about what happened,' Paige said. 'He was a good doctor.'

'Yes. It's regrettable. Very . . .' Wallace studied her a moment. 'Paige, if Dr Barker can't practice here anymore, would you consider staying on?'

Paige hesitated. 'Yes. Of course.'

28

His chart read, 'John Cronin, white male, age 70. Diagnosis: Cardiac tumor.'

Paige had not yet met John Cronin. He was scheduled to have heart surgery. She walked into his room, a nurse and staff doctor at her side. She smiled warmly and said, 'Good morning, Mr Cronin.'

They had just extubated him, and there were the marks of adhesive tape around his mouth. IV bottles hung overhead, and the tubing had been inserted in his left arm.

Cronin looked over at Paige. 'Who the hell are you?'

'I'm Dr Taylor. I'm going to examine you and—'

'Like hell you are! Keep your fucking hands off me. Why didn't they send in a *real* doctor?'

Paige's smile died. 'I'm a cardiovascular surgeon. I'm going to do everything I can to get you well again.'

'*You're* going to operate on my heart?'

'That's right. I . . .'

John Cronin looked at the staff doctor and said, 'For Christ's sakes, is this the best this hospital can do?'

'I assure you, Dr Taylor is thoroughly qualified,' the staff doctor said.

'So is my ass.'

Paige said stiffly, 'Would you rather bring in your own surgeon?'

'I don't have one. I can't afford those high-priced quacks. You doctors are all alike. All you're interested in is money. You don't give a damn about people. We're just pieces of meat to you, aren't we?'

Paige was fighting to control her temper. 'I know you're upset right now, but—'

'Upset? Just because you're going to cut my heart out?' He was screaming. 'I know I'll die on the operating table. You're going to kill me, and I hope they get you for murder!'

'That's enough!' Paige said.

He was grinning at her maliciously. 'It wouldn't look good on your record if I died, would it, doctor? Maybe I *will* let you operate on me.'

Paige found that she was hyperventilating. She turned to the nurse. 'I want an EKG and a chemistry panel.' She took one last look at John Cronin, then turned and left the room.

When Paige returned an hour later with the reports on the tests, John Cronin looked up. 'Oh, the bitch is back.'

Paige operated on John Cronin at six o'clock the following morning.

The moment she opened him up, she knew that there was no hope. The major problem was not the heart. Cronin's organs showed signs of melanoma.

A resident said, 'Oh, my God! What are we going to do?'

'We're going to pray that he doesn't have to live with this too long.'

When Paige stepped out of the operating room into the corridor, she found a woman and two men waiting for her. The woman was in her late thirties. She had bright red hair and too much makeup, and she wore a heavy, cheap perfume. She had on a tight dress that accentuated a voluptuous figure. The men were in their forties, and both had red hair. To Paige, they looked like a circus troupe.

The woman said to Paige, 'You Dr Taylor?'

'Yes.'

'I'm Mrs Cronin. These are my brothers. How's my husband?'

Paige hesitated. She said carefully, 'The operation went as well as could be expected.'

'Oh, thank God!' Mrs Cronin said melodramatically, dabbing at her eyes with a lace handkerchief. 'I'd die if anything happened to John!'

Paige felt as if she were watching an actress in a bad play.

'Can I see my darling now?'

'Not yet, Mrs Cronin. He's in the recovery room. I suggest that you come back tomorrow.'

'We'll be back.' She turned to the men. 'Come along, fellas.'

Paige watched as they walked away. *Poor John Cronin*, she thought.

Paige was given the report the next morning. The cancer had metastasized throughout Cronin's body. It was too late for radiation treatment.

The oncologist said to Paige, 'There's nothing to do but try to keep him comfortable. He's going to be in a hell of a lot of pain.'

'How much time does he have?'

'A week or two at the most.'

Paige went to visit John Cronin in intensive care. He was asleep. He was no longer a bitter, vitriolic man, but a human being, fighting desperately for his life. He was on a respirator, and being fed intravenously. Paige sat down at his bedside, watching him. He looked tired and defeated. *He's one of the unlucky ones*, Paige thought. *Even with all the modern medical miracles, there's nothing we can do to save him.* Paige touched his arm gently. After a while, she left.

Later that afternoon, Paige stopped by to see John Cronin again. He was off the respirator now. When he opened his eyes and saw Paige, he said drowsily, 'The operation's over, huh?'

Paige smiled reassuringly. 'Yes. I just came by to make sure that you're comfortable.'

'Comfortable?' he snorted. 'What the hell do you care?'

Paige said, 'Please. Let's not fight.'

Cronin lay there, silently studying her. 'The other doctor told me you did a good job.'

Paige said nothing.

'I have cancer, don't I?'

'Yes.'

'How bad is it?'

The question posed a dilemma that all surgeons

were faced with sooner or later. Paige said, 'It's pretty bad.'

There was a long silence. 'What about radiation or chemotherapy?'

'I'm sorry. It would make you feel worse, and it wouldn't help.'

'I see. Well . . . I've had a good life.'

'I'm sure you have.'

'You may not think so, looking at me now, but I've had a lot of women.'

'I believe it.'

'Yeah. Women . . . thick steaks . . . good cigars . . . You married?'

'No.'

'You ought to be. Everyone should be married. I've been married. Twice. First, for thirty-five years. She was a wonderful lady. She died of a heart attack.'

'I'm sorry.'

'It's okay.' He sighed. 'Then I got sucked into marrying a bimbo. Her and her two hungry brothers. It's my fault for being so horny, I guess. Her red hair turned me on. She's some piece of work.'

'I'm sure she . . .'

'No offense, but do you know why I'm in this cockamamie hospital? My wife put me here. She didn't want to waste money on me for a private hospital. This way there'll be more to leave to her and her brothers.' He looked up at Paige. 'How much time *do* I have left?'

'Do you want it straight?'

'No . . . yes.'

'A week or two.'

'Jesus! The pain is going to get worse, isn't it?'

'I'll try to keep you as comfortable as possible, Mr Cronin.'

'Call me John.'

'John.'

'Life is a bitch, isn't it?'

'You said you've had a good life.'

'I did. It's kinda funny, knowing it's about over. Where do you think we go?'

'I don't know.'

He forced a smile. 'I'll let you know when I get there.'

'Some medication is on the way. Can I do anything to make you more comfortable?'

'Yeah. Come back and talk to me tonight.'

It was Paige's night off, and she was exhausted. 'I'll come back.'

That night when Paige went back to see John Cronin, he was awake.

'How are you feeling?'

He winced. 'Terrible. I was never very good about pain. I guess I've got a low threshold.'

'I understand.'

'You met Hazel, huh?'

'Hazel?'

'My wife. The bimbo. She and her brothers were here to see me. They said they talked to you.'

'Yes.'

'She's something, ain't she? I sure got myself into a bundle of trouble there. They can't wait for me to kick the bucket.'

'Don't say that.'

'It's true. The only reason Hazel married me was

for my money. To tell you the truth, I didn't mind that so much. I really had a good time with her in bed, but then she and her brothers started to get greedy. They always wanted more.'

The two of them sat there in a comfortable silence.

'Did I tell you I used to travel a lot?'

'No.'

'Yeah. I've been to Sweden . . . Denmark . . . Germany. Have you been to Europe?'

She thought about the day at the travel agency. *I'm dying to see London. Paris is where I want to go. I want to ride a gondola in the moonlight in Venice.*

'No. I haven't.'

'You ought to go.'

'Maybe one day I will.'

'I guess you don't make much money working at a hospital like this, huh?'

'I make enough.'

He nodded to himself. 'Yeah. You have to go to Europe. Do me a favor. Go to Paris . . . stay at the Crillon, have dinner at Maxim's, order a big, thick steak and a bottle of champagne, and when you eat that steak and drink that champagne, I want you to think of me. Will you do that?'

Paige said slowly, 'I'll do that one day.'

John Cronin was studying her. 'Good. I'm tired now. Will you come back tomorrow and talk to me again?'

'I'll come back,' Paige said.

John Cronin slept.

Ken Mallory was a great believer in Lady Luck, and after meeting the Harrisons, he believed even more firmly that she was on his side. The odds against a man as wealthy as Alex Harrison being brought to Embarcadero County Hospital were enormous. *And I'm the one who saved his life, and he wants to show his gratitude*, Mallory thought gleefully.

He had asked a friend of his about the Harrisons.

'Rich doesn't even begin to cover it,' his friend had said. 'He's a millionaire a dozen times over. And he has a great-looking daughter. She's been married three or four times. The last time to a count.'

'Have you ever met the Harrisons?'

'No. They don't mingle with the *hoi polloi*.'

On a Saturday morning, Alex Harrison telephoned Ken Mallory. 'Ken, do you think I'll be in shape to give a dinner party a week from now?'

'If you don't overdo it, I don't see why not,' Mallory said.

Alex Harrison smiled. 'Fine. You're the guest of honor.'

Mallory felt a sudden thrill. *The old man really meant what he said*. 'Well . . . thank you.'

'Lauren and I will expect you at seven-thirty next Saturday night.' He gave Mallory an address on Nob Hill.

'I'll be there,' Mallory said. *Will I ever!*

Mallory had promised to take Kat to the theater that evening, but it would be easy to cancel. He had collected his winnings, and he enjoyed having sex with her. Several times a week they had managed to get together in one of the empty on-call rooms, or a deserted hospital room, or at her apartment or his. *Her fires were banked a long time*, Mallory thought happily, *but when the explosion came — wow! Well, one of these days, it will be time to say arrivederci.*

On the day he was to have dinner with the Harrisons, Mallory telephoned Kat. 'Bad news, baby.'

'What's the matter, darling?'

'One of the doctors is sick and they've asked me to cover for him. I'm afraid I'm going to have to break our date.'

She did not want to let him know how disappointed she was, how much she needed to be with him. Kat said lightly, 'Oh well, that's the doctor business, isn't it?'

'Yeah. I'll make it up to you.'

'You don't have to make anything up to me,' she said warmly. 'I love you.'

'I love you, too.'

'Ken, when are we going to talk about us?'

'What do you mean?' He knew exactly what she meant. A commitment. They were all alike. *They use their pussies for bait, hoping to hook a sucker into spending his life with them.* Well, he was too smart for that. When the time came, he would regretfully bow out, as he had done a dozen times before.

Kat was saying, 'Don't you think we should set a date, Ken? I have a lot of plans to make.'

'Oh, sure. We'll do that.'

296

'I thought maybe June. What do you think?'

You don't want to know what I think. If I play my cards right, there's going to be a wedding, but it won't be with you. 'We'll talk about it, baby. I really have to go now.'

The Harrisons' home was a mansion out of a motion picture, situated on acres of manicured grounds. The house itself seemed to go on forever. There were two dozen guests, and in the huge drawing room a small orchestra was playing. When Mallory walked in, Lauren hurried over to greet him. She was wearing a silky clinging gown. She squeezed Mallory's hand. 'Welcome, guest of honor. I'm so glad you're here.'

'So am I. How is your father?'

'Very much alive, thanks to you. You're quite a hero in this house.'

Mallory smiled modestly. 'I only did my job.'

'I suppose that's what God says every day.' She took his hand and began introducing him to the other guests.

The guest list was blue-ribbon. The governor of California was there, the French ambassador, a justice of the Supreme Court, and a dozen assorted politicians, artists, and business tycoons. Mallory could feel the power in the room, and it thrilled him. *This is where I belong*, he thought. *Right here, with these people*.

The dinner was delicious and elegantly served. At the end of the evening, when the guests started to leave, Harrison said to Mallory, 'Don't rush off, Ken. I'd like to talk to you.'

'I'd be delighted.'

Harrison, Lauren, and Mallory sat in the library. Harrison was seated in a chair next to his daughter.

'When I told you at the hospital that I thought you had a great future before you, I meant it.'

'I really appreciate your confidence, sir.'

'You should be in private practice.'

Mallory laughed self-deprecatingly. 'I'm afraid it's not that easy, Mr Harrison. It takes a long time to build up a practice, and I'm . . .'

'Ordinarily, yes. But you're not an ordinary man.'

'I don't understand.'

'After you finish your residency, Father wants to set you up in your own practice,' Lauren said.

For a moment, Mallory was speechless. It was too easy. He felt as though he were living in some kind of wonderful dream. 'I . . . I don't know what to say.'

'I have a lot of very wealthy friends. I've already spoken to some of them about you. I can promise you that you'll be swamped the minute you put up your shingle.'

'Father, lawyers put up shingles,' Lauren said.

'Whatever. In any case, I'd like to finance you. Are you interested?'

Mallory was finding it difficult to breathe. 'Very much so. But I . . . I don't know when I would be able to repay you.'

'You don't understand. I'm repaying *you*. You won't owe me anything.'

Lauren was looking at Mallory, her eyes warm. 'Please say yes.'

'I'd be stupid to say no, wouldn't I?'

'That's right,' Lauren said softly. 'And I'm sure you're not stupid.'

On his way home, Ken Mallory was in a state of euphoria. *This is as good as it gets*, he thought. But he was wrong. It got better.

Lauren telephoned him. 'I hope you don't mind mixing business with pleasure.'

He smiled to himself. 'Not at all. What did you have in mind?'

'There's a charity ball next Saturday night. Would you like to take me?'

Oh, baby, I'm going to take you all right. 'I'd love to.' He was on duty Saturday night, but he would call in sick and they would have to find someone to take his place.

Mallory was a man who believed in planning ahead, and what was happening to him now went beyond his wildest dreams.

Within a few days he was swept up in Lauren's social circle, and life took on a dizzying pace. He would be out with Lauren dancing half the night, and stumble through his days at the hospital. There were mounting complaints about his work, but he didn't care. *I'll be out of here soon*, he told himself.

The thought of getting away from the dreary county hospital and having his own practice was exciting enough, but Lauren was the bonus that Lady Luck had given him.

Kat was becoming a nuisance. Mallory had to keep finding pretexts to avoid seeing her. When she would press him, he would say, 'Darling, I'm crazy about you . . . of course I want to marry you, but right now, I . . .' and he would go into a litany of excuses.

It was Lauren who suggested that the two of them spend the weekend at the family lodge at Big Sur. Mallory was elated. *Everything is coming up roses,* he thought. *I'm going to own the whole damned world!*

The lodge was spread across pine-covered hills, an enormous structure built of wood and tile and stone, overlooking the Pacific Ocean. It had a master bedroom, eight guest bedrooms, a spacious living room with a stone fireplace, an indoor swimming pool, and a large hot tub. Everything smelled of old money.

When they walked in, Lauren turned to Mallory and said, 'I let the servants go for the weekend.'

Mallory grinned. 'Good thinking.' He put his arms around Lauren and said softly, 'I'm wild about you.'

'Show me,' Lauren said.

They spent the day in bed, and Lauren was almost as insatiable as Kat.

'You're wearing me out!' Mallory laughed.

'Good. I don't want you to be able to make love to anyone else.' She sat up in bed. 'There *is* no one else, is there, Ken?'

'Absolutely not,' Mallory said sincerely. 'There's no one in the world for me but you. I'm in love with you, Lauren.' Now was the time to take the plunge, to wrap his whole future up in one neat package. It would be one thing to be a successful doctor in private practice. It would be something else to be Alex Harrison's son-in-law. 'I want to marry you.'

He held his breath, waiting for her answer.

'Oh, yes, darling,' Lauren said. 'Yes.'

At the apartment, Kat was frantically trying to reach Mallory. She telephoned the hospital.

'I'm sorry, Dr Hunter, Dr Mallory is not on call, and doesn't answer his page.'

'Didn't he leave word where he could be reached?'

'We have no record of it.'

Kat replaced the receiver and turned to Paige. 'Something's happened to him, I know it. He would have called me by now.'

'Kat, there could be a hundred reasons why you haven't heard from him. Perhaps he had to go out of town suddenly, or . . .'

'You're right. I'm sure there's some good excuse.' Kat looked at the phone and *willed* it to ring.

When Mallory returned to San Francisco, he telephoned Kat at the hospital.

'Dr Hunter is off duty,' the receptionist told him.

'Thank you.' Mallory called the apartment. Kat was there.

'Hi, baby!'

'Ken! Where have you been? I've been worried about you. I tried everywhere to reach—'

'I had a family emergency,' he said smoothly. 'I'm sorry. I didn't have a chance to call you. I had to go out of town. May I come over?'

'You know you may. I'm so glad you're all right. I—'

'Half an hour.' He replaced the receiver and

thought happily, *'The time has come,' the Walrus said, 'To talk of many things.' Kat, baby, it was great fun, but it was just one of those things.*

When Mallory arrived at the apartment, Kat threw her arms around him. 'I've missed you!' She could not tell him how desperately worried she had been. Men hated that kind of thing. She stood back. 'Darling, you look absolutely exhausted.'

Mallory sighed. 'I've been up for the last twenty-four hours.' *That part is true*, he thought.

Kat hugged him. 'Poor baby. Can I fix something for you?'

'No, I'm fine. All I really need is a good night's sleep. Let's sit down, Kat. We have to have a talk.' He sat on the couch next to her.

'Is anything wrong?' Kat asked.

Mallory took a deep breath. 'Kat, I've been thinking a lot about us lately.'

She smiled. 'So have I. I have news for you —'

'No, wait. Let me finish. Kat, I think we're rushing into things too fast. I . . . I think I proposed too hastily.'

She paled. 'What . . . what are you saying?'

'I'm saying that I think we should postpone everything.'

She felt as though the room were closing in on her. She was finding it difficult to breathe. 'Ken, we can't postpone anything. I'm having your baby.'

30

Paige got home at midnight, drained. It had been an exhausting day. There had been no time for lunch, and dinner had consisted of a sandwich between operations. She fell into her bed and was asleep instantly. She was awakened by the ringing of the telephone. Groggily, she reached for the instrument and automatically glanced at the bedside clock. It was three in the morning. 'H'lo?'

'Dr Taylor? I'm sorry to disturb you, but one of your patients is insisting on seeing you right away.'

Paige's throat was so dry she could hardly talk. 'I'm off duty,' she mumbled. 'Can't you get someone . . . ?'

'He won't talk to anyone else. He says he needs *you*.'

'Who is it?'

'John Cronin.'

She sat up straighter. 'What's happened?'

'I don't know. He refuses to speak with anyone but you.'

'All right,' she said wearily. 'I'm on my way.'

Thirty minutes later, Paige arrived at the hospital. She went directly to John Cronin's room. He was lying in bed, awake. Tubes were protruding from his nostrils and his arms.

303

'Thanks for coming.' His voice was weak and hoarse.

Paige sat down in a chair next to the bed. She smiled. 'That's all right, John. I had nothing to do, anyway, but sleep. What can I do for you that no one else here at this great big hospital couldn't have done?'

'I want you to talk to me.'

Paige groaned. 'At this hour? I thought it was some kind of emergency.'

'It is. I want to leave.'

She shook her head. 'That's impossible. You can't go home now. You couldn't get the kind of treatment —'

He interrupted her. 'I don't want to go home. I want to leave.'

She looked at him and said slowly, 'What are you saying?'

'You know what I'm saying. The medication isn't working anymore. I can't stand this pain. I want out.'

Paige leaned over and took his hand. 'John, I can't do that. Let me give you some —'

'No. I'm tired, Paige. I want to go wherever it is I'm going, but I don't want to hang around here like this. Not anymore.'

'John . . .'

'How much time do I have left? A few more days? I told you, I'm not good about pain. I'm lying here like a trapped animal, filled with all these goddam tubes. My body is being eaten away inside. This isn't living — it's dying. For God's sake, help me!'

He was racked by a sudden spasm of pain. When he spoke again, his voice was even weaker. 'Help me . . . please . . .'

Paige knew what she had to do. She had to report John Cronin's request to Dr Benjamin Wallace. He would pass it on to the administration committee. They would assemble a panel of doctors to assess Cronin's condition, and then make a decision. After that, it would have to be approved by . . .

'Paige . . . it's *my* life. Let me do with it as I like.'

She looked over at the helpless figure locked in his pain.

'I'm begging you . . .'

She took his hand and held it for a long time. When she spoke, she said, 'All right, John. I'll do it.'

He managed a trace of a smile. 'I knew I could count on you.'

Paige leaned over and kissed him on the forehead. 'Close your eyes and go to sleep.'

'Good night, Paige.'

'Good night, John.'

John Cronin sighed and closed his eyes, a beatific smile on his face.

Paige sat there watching him, thinking about what she was about to do. She remembered how horrified she had been on her first day of rounds with Dr Radnor. *She's been in a coma for six weeks. Her vital signs are failing. There's nothing more we can do for her. We'll pull the plug this afternoon.* Was it wrong to release a fellow human being from his misery?

Slowly, as though she were moving under water, Paige rose and walked to a cabinet in the corner, where a bottle of insulin was kept for emergency use. She removed the bottle and stood there, staring at it. Then she uncapped the bottle. She filled a syringe with the insulin and walked back to John Cronin's bedside. There was still time to go back. *I'm lying here like a trapped animal . . . This isn't living—it's dying. For God's sake, help me!*

Paige leaned forward and slowly injected the insulin into the IV attached to Cronin's arm.

'Sleep well,' Paige whispered. She was unaware that she was sobbing.

Paige drove home and stayed awake the rest of the night, thinking about what she had done.

At six o'clock in the morning, she received a telephone call from one of the residents at the hospital.

'I'm sorry to give you bad news, Dr Taylor. Your patient John Cronin died of cardiac arrest early this morning.'

The staff doctor in charge that morning was Dr Arthur Kane.

31

The one other time Ken Mallory had gone to an opera, he had fallen asleep. On this night he was watching *Rigoletto* at the San Francisco Opera House and enjoying every minute of it. He was seated in a box with Lauren Harrison and her father. In the lobby of the opera house during intermission, Alex Harrison had introduced him to a large number of friends.

'This is my future son-in-law and a brilliant doctor, Ken Mallory.'

Being Alex Harrison's son-in-law was enough to *make* him a brilliant doctor.

After the performance, the Harrisons and Mallory went to the Fairmont Hotel for supper in the elegant main dining room. Mallory enjoyed the deferential greeting that the maître d' gave to Alex Harrison as he led them to their booth. *From now on, I'll be able to afford places like this*, Mallory thought, *and everyone is going to know who I am*.

After they had ordered, Lauren said, 'Darling, I think we should have a party to announce our engagement.'

'That's a good idea!' her father said. 'We'll make it a big one. What do you say, Ken?'

A warning bell sounded in Mallory's mind. An

engagement party would mean publicity. *I'll have to set Kat straight first. A little money should take care of that.* Mallory cursed the stupid bet he had made. For a mere ten thousand dollars, his whole shining future might now be in jeopardy. He could just imagine what would happen if he tried to explain Kat to the Harrisons.

By the way, I forgot to mention that I'm already engaged to a doctor at the hospital. She's black . . .

Or: *Do you want to hear something funny? I bet the boys at the hospital ten thousand dollars I could fuck this black doctor . . .*

Or: *I already have one wedding planned . . .*

No, he thought, *I'll have to find a way to buy Kat off.*

They were looking at Mallory expectantly.

Mallory smiled. 'A party sounds like a wonderful idea.'

Lauren said enthusiastically, 'Good. I'll get things started. You men have no idea what it takes to give a party.'

Alex Harrison turned to Mallory. 'I've already started the ball rolling for you, Ken.'

'Sir?'

'Gary Gitlin, the head of North Shore Hospital, is an old golf buddy of mine. I talked to him about you, and he doesn't think there will be any problem about having you affiliated with his hospital. That's quite prestigious, you know. And at the same time, I'll get you set up in your own practice.'

Mallory listened, filled with a sense of euphoria. 'That's wonderful.'

'Of course it will take a few years to build up a really lucrative practice, but I think you should be

308

able to make two or three hundred thousand dollars the first year or two.'

Two or three hundred thousand! My God! Mallory thought. *He makes it sound like peanuts.* 'That . . . that would be very nice, sir.'

Alex Harrison smiled. 'Ken, since I'm going to be your father-in-law, let's get off this "sir" business. Call me Alex.'

'Right, Alex.'

'You know, I've never been a June bride,' Lauren said. 'Is June all right with you, darling?'

He could hear Kat's voice saying: *Don't you think we should set a date? I thought maybe June.*

Mallory took Lauren's hand in his. 'That sounds great.' *That will give me plenty of time to handle Kat*, Mallory decided. He smiled to himself. *I'll offer her some of the money I won getting her into bed.*

'We have a yacht in the south of France,' Alex Harrison was saying. 'Would you two like to honeymoon on the French Riviera? You can fly over in our Gulfstream.'

A yacht. The French Riviera. It was like a fantasy come true. Mallory looked at Lauren. 'I'd honeymoon anywhere with Lauren.'

Alex Harrison nodded. 'Well, it looks like everything is settled.' He smiled at his daughter. 'I'm going to miss you, baby.'

'You're not losing me, Father. You're gaining a doctor!'

Alex Harrison nodded. 'And a damn good one. I can never thank you enough for saving my life, Ken.'

Lauren stroked Mallory's hand. 'I'll thank him for you.'

'Ken, why don't we have lunch next week?' Alex

Harrison said. 'We'll pick out some decent office space for you, maybe in the Post Building, and I'll make a date for you to see Gary Gitlin. A lot of my friends are dying to meet you.'

'I think you might rephrase that, Father,' Lauren suggested. She turned to Ken. 'I've been talking to *my* friends about you and they're eager to meet you, too, only I'm not going to let them.'

'I'm not interested in anyone but you,' Mallory said warmly.

When they got into their chauffeur-driven Rolls-Royce, Lauren asked, 'Where can we drop you, darling?'

'The hospital. I've got to check on a few patients.' He had no intention of seeing any patients. Kat was on duty at the hospital.

Lauren stroked his cheek. 'My poor baby. You work much too hard.'

Mallory sighed. 'It doesn't matter. As long as I'm helping people.'

Mallory went quickly to the doctors' dressing room and changed out of his dinner jacket.

He found Kat in the geriatric ward.

'Hi, Kat.'

She was in an angry mood. 'We had a date last night, Ken.'

'I know. I'm sorry. I wasn't able to make it, and—'

'That's the third time in the last week. What's going on?'

She was becoming a boring nag. 'Kat, I have to talk to you. Is there an empty room around here?'

She thought for a moment. 'A patient checked out of 315. Let's go in there.'

They started down the corridor. A nurse walked up to them. 'Oh, Dr Mallory! Dr Peterson has been looking for you. He —'

'Tell him I'm busy.' He took Kat by the arm and led her to the elevator.

When they arrived at the third floor, they walked silently down the corridor and went into Room 315. Mallory closed the door behind them. He was hyperventilating. His whole golden future depended on the next few minutes.

He took Kat's hand in his. It was time to be sincere. 'Kat, you know I'm crazy about you. I've never felt about anyone the way I feel about you. But, honey, the idea of having a baby right now . . . well . . . can't you see how wrong it would be? I mean . . . we're both working day and night, we aren't making enough money to . . .'

'But we can manage,' Kat said. 'I love you, Ken, and I —'

'Wait. All I'm asking is that we put everything off for a little while. Let me finish my term at the hospital and get started in private practice somewhere. Maybe we'll go back East. In a few years we'll be able to afford to get married and have a baby.'

'*In a few years?* But I told you, I'm pregnant.'

'I know, darling, but it's been what, now . . . two months? There's still plenty of time to abort it.'

Kat looked at him, shocked. 'No! I won't abort it. I want us to get married right away. Now.'

We have a yacht in the south of France. Would you

311

two like to honeymoon on the French Riviera? You can fly over in our Gulfstream.

'I've already told Paige and Honey that we're getting married. They're going to be my bridesmaids. And I told them about the baby.'

Mallory felt a cold chill go through him. Things were getting out of hand. If the Harrisons got wind of this, he would be finished. 'You shouldn't have done that.'

'Why not?'

Mallory forced a smile. 'I want to keep our private lives private.' *I'll get you set up in your own practice . . . You should be able to make two or three hundred thousand dollars the first year or two.* 'Kat, I'm going to ask you this for the last time. Will you have an abortion?' He was *willing* her to say yes, trying to keep the desperation out of his voice.

'No.'

'Kat . . .'

'I can't, Ken. I told you how I felt about the abortion I had as a girl. I swore I could never live through such a thing again. Don't ask me again.'

And it was at that moment that Ken Mallory realized he could not take a chance. He had no choice. He was going to have to kill her.

32

Honey looked forward every day to seeing the patient in Room 306. His name was Sean Reilly, and he was a good-looking Irishman, with black hair and black sparkling eyes. Honey guessed that he was in his early forties.

When Honey first met him on her rounds, she had looked at his chart and said, 'I see you're here for a cholecystectomy.'

'I thought they were going to remove my gall-bladder.'

Honey smiled. 'Same thing.'

Sean fixed his black eyes on her. 'They can cut out anything they want except my heart. That belongs to you.'

Honey laughed. 'Flattery will get you everywhere.'

'I hope so, darlin'.'

When Honey had a few minutes to spare, she would drop by and chat with Sean. He was charming and amusing.

'It's worth bein' operated on just to have you around, little darlin'.'

'You aren't nervous about the operation, are you?' she asked.

'Not if you're going to operate, love.'

'I'm not a surgeon. I'm an internist.'

'Are internists allowed to have dinner with their patients?'

'No. There's a rule against it.'

'Do internists ever break rules?'

'Never.' Honey was smiling.

'I think you're beautiful,' Sean said.

No one had ever told Honey that before. She found herself blushing. 'Thank you.'

'You're like the fresh mornin' dew in the fields of Killarney.'

'Have you ever been to Ireland?' Honey asked.

He laughed. 'No, but I promise you we'll go there together one day. You'll see.'

It was ridiculous Irish blarney, and yet . . .

That afternoon when Honey went in to see Sean, she said, 'How are you feeling?'

'The better for seeing you. Have you thought about our dinner date?'

'No,' Honey said. She was lying.

'I was hoping after my operation, I could take you out. You're not engaged, or married, or anything silly like that, are you?'

Honey smiled. 'Nothing silly like that.'

'Good! Neither am I. Who would have me?'

A lot of women, Honey thought.

'If you like home cooking, I happen to be a great cook.'

'We'll see.'

When Honey went to Sean's room the following morning, he said, 'I have a little present for you.' He handed her a sheet of drawing paper. On it was a softened, idealized sketch of Honey.

'I love it!' Honey said. 'You're a wonderful artist!' And she suddenly remembered the psychic's words:

314

You're going to fall in love. He's an artist. She was looking at Sean strangely.

'Is anything wrong?'

'No,' Honey said slowly. 'No.'

Five minutes later, Honey walked into Frances Gordon's room. The psychic was constantly being readmitted for a series of tests.

'Here comes the Virgo!'

Honey said, 'Do you remember telling me that I was going to fall in love with someone—an artist?'

'Yes.'

'Well, I . . . I think I've met him.'

Frances Gordon smiled. 'See? The stars never lie.'

'Could . . . could you tell me a little about him? About us?'

'There are some tarot cards in that drawer over there. Could you give them to me, please?'

As Honey handed her the cards, she thought, *This is ridiculous! I don't believe in this!*

Frances Gordon was laying out the cards. She kept nodding to herself, and nodding and smiling, and suddenly she stopped. Her face went pale. 'Oh, my God!' She looked up at Honey.

'What . . . what's the matter?' Honey asked.

'This artist. You say you've already met him?'

'I think so. Yes.'

Frances Gordon's voice was filled with sadness. 'The poor man.' She looked up at Honey. 'I'm sorry . . . I'm so sorry.'

* * *

Sean Reilly was scheduled to have his operation the following morning.

8:15 A.M. Dr William Radnor was in OR Two, preparing for the operation.

8:25 A.M. A truck containing a week's supply of bags of blood pulled up at the emergency entrance to Embarcadero County Hospital. The driver carried the bags to the blood bank in the basement. Eric Foster, the resident doctor on duty, was sharing coffee and a danish with a pretty young nurse, Andrea.

'Where do you want these?' the driver asked.

'Just set them down there.' Foster pointed to a corner.

'Right.' The driver put the bags down and pulled out a form. 'I need your John Hancock.'

'Okay.' Foster signed the form. 'Thanks.'

'No sweat.' The driver left.

Foster turned to Andrea. 'Where were we?'

'You were telling me how adorable I am.'

'Right. If you weren't married, I'd really go after you,' the resident said. 'Do you ever fool around?'

'No. My husband is a boxer.'

'Oh. Do you have a sister?'

'As a matter of fact, I do.'

'Is she as pretty as you are?'

'Prettier.'

'What's her name?'

'Marilyn.'

'Why don't we double-date one night?'

As they chatted, the fax machine began to click. Foster ignored it.

8:45 A.M. Dr Radnor began the operation on Sean Reilly. The beginning went smoothly. The operating room functioned like a well-oiled machine, run by capable people doing their jobs.

9:05 A.M. Dr Radnor reached the cystic duct. A textbook operation up until then. As he started to excise the gallbladder, his hand slipped and the scalpel nicked an artery. Blood began to pour out.

'Jesus!' He tried to stop the flow.

The anesthesiologist called out, 'His blood pressure just dropped to 95. He's going into shock!'

Radnor turned to the circulating nurse. 'Get some more blood up here, stat!'

'Right away, doctor.'

9:06 A.M. The telephone rang in the blood bank.

'Don't go away,' Foster told Andrea. He walked past the fax machine, which had stopped clicking, and picked up the telephone. 'Blood supply.'

'We need four units of Type O in OR Two, stat.'

'Right.' Foster replaced the receiver and went to the corner where the new blood had been deposited. He pulled out four bags and placed them on the top shelf of the metal cart used for such emergencies. He double-checked the bags. 'Type O,' he said aloud. He rang for an orderly.

'What's going on?' Andrea asked.

317

Foster looked at the schedule in front of him. 'It looks like one of the patients is giving Dr Radnor a bad time.'

9:10 A.M. The orderly came into the blood bank. 'What have we got?'

'Take this to OR Two. They're waiting for it.'

He watched the orderly wheel out the cart, then turned to Andrea. 'Tell me about your sister.'

'She's married, too.'

'Aw . . .'

Andrea smiled. 'But she fools around.'

'Does she really?'

'I'm only kidding. I have to go back to work, Eric. Thanks for the coffee and danish.'

'Anytime.' He watched her leave and thought, *What a great ass!*

9.12 A.M. The orderly was waiting for an elevator to take him to the second floor.

9.13 A.M. Dr Radnor was doing his best to minimize the catastrophe. 'Where's the damned blood?'

9:15 A.M. The orderly pushed at the door to OR Two and the circulating nurse opened it.

'Thanks,' she said. She carried the bags into the room. 'It's here, doctor.'

'Start pumping it into him. Fast!'

* * *

318

In the blood bank, Eric Foster finished his coffee, thinking about Andrea. *All the good-looking ones are married.*

As he started toward his desk, he passed the fax machine. He pulled out the fax. It read:

Recall Warning Alert #687, June 25: Red Blood Cells, Fresh Frozen Plasma. Units CB83711, CB800007. Community Blood Bank of California, Arizona, Washington, Oregon. Blood products testing repeatedly reactive for Antibody HIV Type 1 were distributed.

He stared at it a moment, then walked over to his desk and picked up the invoice he had signed for the bags of blood that had just been delivered. He looked at the number on the invoice. The number on the warning was identical.

'Oh, my God!' he said. He grabbed the telephone. 'Get me OR Two, fast!'

A nurse answered.

'This is the blood bank. I just sent up four units of Type O. Don't use it! I'm sending up some fresh blood immediately.'

The nurse said, 'Sorry, it's too late.'

Dr Radnor broke the news to Sean Reilly.

'It was a mistake,' Radnor said. 'A terrible mistake. I would give anything if it had not happened.'

Sean was staring at him, in shock. 'My God! I'm going to die.'

'We won't know whether you're HIV-positive for six or eight weeks. And even if you are, that does not necessarily mean you will get AIDS. We're going to do everything we can for you.'

'What the hell can you do for me that you haven't already done?' Sean said bitterly. 'I'm a dead man.'

When Honey heard the news, she was devastated. She remembered Frances Gordon's words. *The poor man.*

Sean Reilly was asleep when Honey walked into his room. She sat at his bedside for a long time, watching him.

He opened his eyes and saw Honey. 'I dreamed that I was dreaming, and that I wasn't going to die.'

'Sean . . .'

'Did you come to visit the corpse?'

'Please don't talk that way.'

'How could this happen?' he cried.

'Someone made a mistake, Sean.'

'God, I don't want to die of AIDS!'

'Some people who get HIV may never get AIDS. The Irish are lucky.'

'I wish I could believe you.'

She took his hand in hers. 'You've got to.'

'I'm not a praying man,' Sean said, 'but I sure as hell am going to start now.'

'I'll pray with you,' Honey said.

He smiled wryly. 'I guess we can forget about that dinner, huh?'

'Oh, no. You don't get out of it that easily. I'm looking forward to it.'

He studied her a moment. 'You really mean that, don't you?'

'You bet I do! No matter what happens. Remember, you promised to take me to Ireland.'

33

'Are you all right, Ken?' Lauren asked. 'You seem tense, darling.'

They were alone in the huge Harrison library. A maid and a butler had served a six-course dinner, and during dinner he and Alex Harrison — *Call me Alex* — had chatted about Mallory's brilliant future.

'Why are you tense?'

Because this pregnant black bitch expects me to marry her. Because any minute word is going to leak out about our engagement and she'll hear about it and blow the whistle. Because my whole future could be destroyed.

He took Lauren's hand in his. 'I guess I'm working too hard. My patients aren't just patients to me, Lauren. They're people in trouble, and I can't help worrying about them.'

She stroked his face. 'That's one of the things I love about you, Ken. You're so caring.'

'I guess I was brought up that way.'

'Oh, I forgot to tell you. The society editor of the *Chronicle* and a photographer are coming here Monday to do an interview.'

It was like a blow to the pit of his stomach.

'Is there any chance you could be here with me, darling? They want a picture of you.'

'I . . . I wish I could, but I have a busy day scheduled at the hospital.' His mind was racing. 'Lauren, do you think it's a good idea to do an interview now? I mean, shouldn't we wait until . . . ?'

Lauren laughed. 'You don't know the press, darling. They're like bloodhounds. No, it's much better to get it over with now.'

Monday!

The following morning, Mallory tracked down Kat in a utility room. She looked tired and haggard. She had no makeup on and her hair was uncurled. *Lauren would never let herself go like that*, Mallory thought.

'Hi, honey!'

Kat did not answer.

Mallory took her in his arms. 'I've been thinking a lot about us, Kat. I didn't sleep at all last night. There's no one else for me. You were right, and I was wrong. I guess the news came as kind of a shock to me. I want you to have our baby.' He watched the sudden glow on Kat's face.

'Do you really mean that, Ken?'

'You bet I do.'

She put her arms around him. 'Thank God! Oh, darling. I was so worried. I don't know what I would do without you.'

'You don't have to worry about that. From now on, everything is going to be wonderful.' *You'll never know how wonderful*. 'Look, I have Sunday night off. Are you free?'

She grasped his hand. 'I'll make myself free.'

'Great! We'll have a nice quiet dinner and then

323

we'll go back to your place for a nightcap. Do you think you can get rid of Paige and Honey? I want us to be alone.'

Kat smiled. 'No problem. You don't know how happy you've made me. Did I ever tell you how much I love you?'

'I love you, too. I'll show you how much Sunday night.'

Thinking it over, Mallory decided it was a foolproof plan. He had worked it out to the smallest detail. There was no way Kat's death could ever be blamed on him.

It was too risky to get what he needed from the hospital pharmacy because security had been tightened after the Bowman affair. Instead, early Sunday morning, Mallory went looking for a pharmacy far away from the neighborhood where he lived. Most of them were closed on Sunday, and he went to half a dozen before he found one that was open.

The pharmacist behind the counter said, 'Morning. Can I help you?'

'Yes. I'm going to see a patient in this area, and I want to take a prescription to him.' He pulled out his prescription pad and wrote on it.

The pharmacist smiled. 'Not many doctors make house calls these days.'

'I know. It's a pity, isn't it? People just don't care anymore.' He handed the slip of paper to the pharmacist.

The pharmacist looked at it and nodded. 'This will only take a few minutes.'

'Thank you.'
Step one.

That afternoon, Mallory made a stop at the hospital. He was there no more than ten minutes, and when he left, he was carrying a small package.

Step two.

Mallory had arranged to meet Kat at Trader Vic's for dinner, and he was waiting for her when she arrived. He watched her walking toward the table and thought, *It's the Last Supper, bitch*.

He rose and gave her a warm smile. 'Hello, doll. You look beautiful.' And he had to admit that she did. She looked sensational. *She could have been a model. And she's great in bed. All she lacks*, Ken thought, *is about twenty million dollars, give or take a few million*.

Kat was aware again of how the other women in the restaurant were eyeing Ken, envying her. But he only had eyes for her. He was the old Ken, warm and attentive.

'How was your day?' he asked.

She sighed. 'Busy. Three operations in the morning and two this afternoon.' She leaned forward. 'I know it's too early, but I swear I could feel the baby kicking when I was getting dressed.'

Mallory smiled. 'Maybe it wants to get out.'

'We should do an ultrasound test and find out if it's a boy or a girl. Then I can start buying clothes for it.'

'Great idea.'

'Ken, can we set a wedding date? I'd like to have our wedding as soon as possible.'

'No problem,' Mallory said easily. 'We can apply for a license next week.'

'That's wonderful!' She had a sudden thought. 'Maybe we could get a few days off and go somewhere on our honeymoon. Somewhere not too far away—up to Oregon or Washington.'

Wrong, baby. I'll be honeymooning in June, on my yacht on the French Riviera.

'That sounds great. I'll talk to Wallace.'

Kat squeezed his hand. 'Thank you,' she said huskily. 'I'm going to make you the best wife in the whole world.'

'I'm sure of it.' Mallory smiled. 'Now eat your vegetables. We want the baby to be healthy, don't we?'

They left the restaurant at 9:00 P.M. As they approached Kat's apartment building, Mallory said, 'Are you sure Paige and Honey won't be home?'

'I made sure,' Kat said. 'Paige is at the hospital, on call, and I told Honey you and I wanted to be alone here.'

Shit!

She saw the expression on his face. 'Is anything wrong?'

'No, baby. I told you, I just like our private times to be private.' *I'll have to be careful*, he thought. *Very careful*. 'Let's hurry.'

His impatience warmed Kat.

* * *

Inside the apartment, Mallory said, 'Let's go into the bedroom.'

Kat grinned. 'That sounds like a great idea.'

Mallory watched Kat undress, and he thought, *She still has a great figure. A baby would ruin it.*

'Aren't you going to get undressed, Ken?'

'Of course.' He remembered the time she had gotten him to undress and then walked out on him. Well, now she was going to pay for that.

He took his clothes off slowly. *Can I perform?* he wondered. He was almost trembling with nervousness. *What I'm going to do is her fault. Not mine. I gave her a chance to back out and she was too stupid to take it.*

He slipped into bed beside her and felt her warm body against his. They began to stroke each other, and he felt himself getting aroused. He entered her and she began to moan.

'Oh, darling . . . it feels so wonderful . . .' She began to move faster and faster. 'Yes . . . yes . . . oh, my God! . . . Don't stop . . .' And her body began to jerk spasmodically, and she shuddered and then lay still in his arms.

She turned to him anxiously. 'Did you . . . ?'

'Of course,' Mallory lied. He was much too tense. 'How about a drink?'

'No. I shouldn't. The baby . . .'

'But this is a celebration, honey. One little drink isn't going to hurt.'

Kat hesitated. 'All right. A small one.' Kat started to get up.

Mallory stopped her. 'No, no. You stay in bed, Mama. You have to get used to being pampered.'

Kat watched Mallory as he walked into the living

327

room and she thought, *I'm the luckiest woman in the world!*

Mallory walked over to the little bar and poured scotch into two glasses. He glanced toward the bedroom to make sure he could not be seen, then went over to the couch, where he had placed his jacket. He took a small bottle from his pocket and poured the contents into Kat's drink. He returned to the bar and stirred Kat's drink and smelled it. There was no odor. He took the two glasses back to the bedroom, and handed Kat her drink.

'Let's drink a toast to our baby,' Kat said.

'Right. To our baby.'

Ken watched as Kat took a swallow of her drink.

'We'll find a nice apartment somewhere,' Kat said dreamily. 'I'll fix up a nursery. We're going to spoil our child rotten, aren't we?' She took another sip.

Mallory nodded. 'Absolutely.' He was watching her closely. 'How do you feel?'

'Wonderful. I've been so worried about us, darling, but I'm not, not anymore.'

'That's good,' Mallory said. 'You have nothing to worry about.'

Kat's eyes were getting heavy. 'No,' she said. 'There's nothing to worry about.' Her words were beginning to slur. 'Ken, I feel funny.' She was beginning to sway.

'You should never have gotten pregnant.'

She was staring up at him stupidly. 'What?'

'You spoiled everything, Kat.'

'Spoiled . . . ?' She was having trouble concentrating.

'You got in my way.'

'Wha'?'

'No one gets in my way.'

'Ken, I feel dizzy.'

He stood there, watching her.

'Ken . . . help me, Ken . . .' Her head fell back onto the pillow.

Mallory looked at his watch again. There was plenty of time.

34

It was Honey who arrived at the apartment first and stumbled across Kat's mutilated body, lying in a pool of blood on the floor of the bathroom, obscenely sprawled against the cold white tiles. A bloodstained curette lay beside her. She had hemorrhaged from her womb.

Honey stood there in shock. 'Oh, my God!' Her voice was a strangled whisper. She knelt beside the body and placed a trembling finger against the carotid artery. There was no pulse. Honey hurried back into the living room, picked up the telephone and dialed 911.

A male voice said, 'Nine-one-one Emergency.'

Honey stood there paralyzed, unable to speak.

'Nine-one-one Emergency . . . Hello . . . ?'

'H . . . help! I . . . there's . . .' She was choking over her words. 'Sh . . . she's dead.'

'Who is dead, miss?'

'Kat.'

'Your cat is dead?'

'*No!*' Honey screamed. '*Kat's* dead. Get someone over here right away.'

'Lady . . .'

Honey slammed down the receiver. With shaking fingers, she dialed the hospital. 'Dr T . . . Taylor.' Her voice was an agonized whisper.

'One moment, please.'

Honey gripped the telephone and waited two minutes before she heard Paige's voice. 'Dr Taylor.'

'Paige! You . . . you've got to come home right away!'

'Honey? What's happened?'

'Kat's . . . dead.'

'*What?*' Paige's voice was filled with disbelief. 'How?'

'It . . . it looks like she tried to abort herself.'

'Oh, my God! All right. I'll be there as soon as I can.'

By the time Paige arrived at the apartment, there were two policemen, a detective, and a medical examiner there. Honey was in her bedroom, heavily sedated. The medical examiner was leaning over Kat's naked body. The detective looked up as Paige entered the bloody bathroom.

'Who are you?'

Paige was staring at the lifeless body. Her face was pale. 'I'm Dr Taylor. I live here.'

'Maybe *you* can help me. I'm Inspector Burns. I was trying to talk to the other lady who lives here. She's hysterical. The doctor gave her a sedative.'

Paige looked away from the awful sight on the floor. 'What . . . what do you want to know?'

'She lived here?'

'Yes.'

I'm going to have Ken's baby. How good can it get?

'It looks like she tried to get rid of the kid, and messed it up,' the detective said.

Paige stood there, her mind spinning. When she spoke, she said, 'I don't believe it.'

Inspector Burns studied her a moment. 'Why don't you believe it, doctor?'

'She wanted that baby.' She was beginning to think clearly again. 'The father didn't want it.'

'The father?'

'Dr Ken Mallory. He works at Embarcadero County Hospital. He didn't want to marry her. Look, Kat is—*was*—' it was so painful to say *was*—'a doctor. If she had wanted to have an abortion, there's no way she would try to do it herself in a bathroom.' Paige shook her head. 'There's something wrong.'

The medical examiner rose from beside the body. 'Maybe she tried it herself because she didn't want anyone else to know about the baby.'

'That's not true. She told us about it.'

Inspector Burns was watching Paige. 'Was she alone here this evening?'

'No. She had a date with Dr Mallory.'

Ken Mallory was in bed, carefully going over the events of the evening. He replayed every step of the way, making sure there were no loose ends. *Perfect*, he decided. He lay in bed, wondering why it was taking the police so long, and even as he was thinking it, the doorbell rang. Mallory let it ring three times, then got up, put on a robe over his pajamas, and went into the living room.

He stood in front of the door. 'Who's there?' He sounded sleepy.

A voice said, 'Dr Mallory?'

'Yes.'

'Inspector Burns. San Francisco Police Department.'

'Police Department?' There was just the right note of surprise in his voice. Mallory opened the door.

The man standing in the hall showed his badge. 'May I come in?'

'Yes. What's this all about?'

'Do you know a Dr Hunter?'

'Of course I do.' A look of alarm crossed his face. 'Has something happened to Kat?'

'Were you with her earlier this evening?'

'Yes. My God! Tell me what's happened! Is she all right?'

'I'm afraid I have some bad news. Dr Hunter is dead.'

'*Dead*? I can't believe it. *How?*'

'Apparently she tried to perform an abortion on herself and it went wrong.'

'Oh, my God!' Mallory said. He sank into a chair. 'It's my fault.'

The inspector was watching him closely. 'Your fault?'

'Yes. I . . . Dr Hunter and I were going to be married. I told her I didn't think it was a good idea for her to have a baby now. I wanted to wait, and she agreed. I suggested she go to the hospital and have them take care of it, but she must have decided to . . . I . . . I can't believe it.'

'What time did you leave, Dr Hunter?'

'It must have been about ten o'clock. I dropped her off at her apartment and left.'

'You didn't go into the apartment?'

'No.'

'Did Dr Hunter talk about what she planned to do?'

'You mean about the . . . ? No. Not a word.'

Inspector Burns pulled out a card. 'If you think of anything else that might be helpful, doctor, I'd appreciate it if you gave me a call.'

'Certainly. I . . . you have no idea what a shock this is.'

Paige and Honey stayed up all night, talking about what had happened to Kat, going over it and over it, in shocked disbelief.

At nine o'clock, Inspector Burns came by.

'Good morning. I wanted to tell you that I spoke to Dr Mallory last night.'

'And?'

'He said they went out to dinner, and then he dropped her off and went home.'

'He's lying,' Paige said. She was thinking. 'Wait! Did they find any traces of semen in Kat's body?'

'Yes, as a matter of fact.'

'Well, then,' Paige said excitedly, 'that *proves* he's lying. He did take her to bed and—'

'I went to talk to him about that this morning. He says they had sex *before* they went out to dinner.'

'Oh.' She would not give up. 'His fingerprints will be on the curette he used to kill her.' Her voice was eager. 'Did you find fingerprints?'

'Yes, doctor,' he said patiently. 'They were hers.'

'That's imp—Wait! Then he wore gloves, and when he was finished, he put her prints on the curette. How does that sound?'

'Like someone's been watching too many *Murder, She Wrote* television programs.'

'You don't believe Kat was murdered, do you?'

'I'm afraid I don't.'

'Have they done an autopsy?'

'Yes.'

'And?'

'The medical examiner is listing it as an accidental death. Dr Mallory told me she decided not to have the baby, so apparently she —'

'Went into the bathroom and butchered herself?' Paige interrupted. 'For God's sakes, inspector! She was a doctor, a surgeon! There's no way in the world she would have done that to herself.'

Inspector Burns said thoughtfully, 'You think Mallory persuaded her to have an abortion, and tried to help her, and then left when it went wrong?'

Paige shook her head. 'No. It couldn't have happened that way. Kat would never have agreed. He deliberately murdered her.' She was thinking out loud. 'Kat was strong. She would have had to be unconscious for him to . . . to do what he did.'

'The autopsy showed no signs of any blows or anything that would have caused her to become unconscious. No bruises on her throat . . .'

'Were there any traces of sleeping pills or . . . ?'

'Nothing.' He saw the expression on Paige's face. 'This doesn't look to me like a murder. I think Dr Hunter made an error in judgement, and . . . I'm sorry.'

She watched him start toward the door. 'Wait!' Paige said, 'You have a motive.'

He turned. 'Not really. Mallory says she agreed to have the abortion. That doesn't leave us much, does it?'

'It leaves you with a murder,' Paige said stubbornly.

'Doctor, what we *don't* have is any evidence. It's his word against the victim's and she's dead. I'm really sorry.'

Paige watched him leave.

I'm not going to let Ken Mallory get away with it, she thought despairingly.

Jason came by to see Paige. 'I heard what happened,' he said. 'I can't believe it! How could she have done that to herself?'

'She didn't,' Paige said. 'She was murdered.' She told Jason about her conversation with Inspector Burns. 'The police aren't going to do anything about it. They think it was an accident. Jason, it's my fault that Kat is dead.'

'Your fault?'

'I'm the one who persuaded her to go out with Mallory in the first place. She didn't want to. It started out as a silly joke, and then she . . . she fell in love with him. Oh, Jason!'

'You can't blame yourself for that,' he said firmly.

Paige looked around in despair. 'I can't live in this apartment anymore. I have to get out of here.'

Jason took her in his arms. 'Let's get married right away.'

'It's too soon. I mean, Kat isn't even . . .'

'I know. We'll wait a week or two.'

'All right.'

'I love you, Paige.'

'I love you, too, darling. Isn't it stupid! I feel guilty because Kat and I both fell in love, and she's dead and I'm alive.'

The photograph appeared on the front page of the *San Francisco Chronicle* on Tuesday. It showed a smiling Ken Mallory with his arm around Lauren Harrison. The caption read: 'Heiress to Wed Doctor.'

Paige stared at it in disbelief. Kat had been dead for only two days, and Ken Mallory was announcing his engagement to another woman! All the time he had been promising to marry Kat, he had been planning to marry someone else. *That's why he killed Kat. To get her out of the way!*

Paige picked up the telephone and dialed police headquarters.

'Inspector Burns, please.'

A moment later, she was talking to the inspector.

'This is Dr Taylor.'

'Yes, doctor.'

'Have you seen the photograph in this morning's *Chronicle*?'

'Yes.'

'Well, there's your motive!' Paige exclaimed. 'Ken Mallory had to shut Kat up before Lauren Harrison found out about her. You've got to arrest Mallory.' She was almost yelling into the telephone.

'Wait a minute. Calm down, doctor. We may have a motive, but I told you, we don't have a shred of evidence. You said yourself that Dr Hunter would have had to be unconscious before Mallory could perform an abortion on her. After I spoke to you, I talked to our forensic pathologist again. There was no sign of any kind of blow that could have caused unconsciousness.'

'Then he must have given her a sedative,' Paige said stubbornly. 'Probably chloral hydrate. It's fast-acting and—'

Inspector Burns said patiently, 'Doctor, there was no trace of chloral hydrate in her body. I'm sorry— I really am—but we can't arrest a man because he's going to get married. Was there anything else?'

Everything else. 'No,' Paige said. She slammed down the receiver and sat there thinking. *Mallory has to have given Kat some kind of drug. The easiest place for him to have gotten it would be the hospital pharmacy.*

Fifteen minutes later, Paige was on her way to Embarcadero County Hospital.

Pete Samuels, the chief pharmacist, was behind the counter. 'Good morning, Dr Taylor. How can I help you?'

'I believe Dr Mallory came by a few days ago and picked up some medication. He told me the name of it, but I can't remember what it was.'

Samuels frowned. 'I don't remember Dr Mallory coming by here for at least a month.'

'Are you sure?'

Samuels nodded. 'Positive. I would have remembered. We always talk football.'

Paige's heart sank. 'Thank you.'

He must have written a prescription at some other

338

pharmacy. Paige knew that the law required that all prescriptions for narcotics be made out in triplicate—one copy for the patient, one to be sent to the Bureau of Controlled Substances, and the third for the pharmacy's files.

Somewhere, Paige thought, *Ken Mallory had a prescription filled. There are probably two or three hundred pharmacies in San Francisco*. There was no way she could track down the prescription. It was likely that Mallory had gotten it just before he murdered Kat. That would have been on Saturday or Sunday. *If it was Sunday, I might have a chance*, Paige thought. *Very few pharmacies are open on Sunday. That narrows it down*.

She went upstairs to the office where the assignment sheets were kept and looked up the roster for Saturday. Dr Ken Mallory had been on call all day, so the chances were that he had had the presciption filled on Sunday. How many pharmacies were open on Sunday in San Francisco?

Paige picked up the telephone and called the state pharmaceutical board.

'This is Dr Taylor,' Paige said. 'Last Sunday, a friend of mine left a prescription at a pharmacy. She asked me to pick it up for her, but I can't remember the name of the pharmacy. I wonder if you could help me.'

'Well, I don't see how, doctor. If you don't know . . .'

'Most drugstores are closed on Sunday, aren't they?'

'Yes, but . . .'

'I'd appreciate it if you could give me a list of those that were open.'

339

There was a pause. 'Well, if it's important . . .'
'It's very important,' Paige assured her.
'Hold on, please.'

There were thirty-six stores on the list, spread all over the city. It would have been simple if she could have gone to the police for help, but Inspector Burns did not believe her. *Honey and I are going to have to do this ourselves*, Paige thought. She explained to Honey what she had in mind.

'It's a real long shot, isn't it?' Honey said. 'You don't even know if he filled the prescription on Sunday.'

'It's the only shot we have.' *That Kat has.* 'I'll check out the ones in Richmond, the Marina, North Beach, Upper Market, Mission, and Potrero, and you check out the Excelsior, Ingleside, Lake Merced, Western Addition, and Sunset areas.'

'All right.'

At the first pharmacy Paige went into, she showed her identification and said, 'A colleague of mine, Dr Ken Mallory, was in here Sunday for a prescription. He's out of town, and he asked me to get a refill, but I can't remember the name of it. Would you mind looking it up, please?'

'Dr Ken Mallory? Just a moment.' He came back a few minutes later. 'Sorry, we didn't fill any prescriptions Sunday for a Dr Mallory.'

'Thank you.'

Paige got the same response at the next four pharmacies.

340

Honey was having no better luck.

'We have thousands of prescriptions here, you know.'

'I know, but this was last Sunday.'

'Well, we have no prescriptions here from a Dr Mallory. Sorry.'

The two of them spent the day going from pharmacy to pharmacy. They were both getting discouraged. It was not until late afternoon, just before closing time, that Paige found what she was looking for in a small pharmacy in the Potrero district.

The pharmacist said, 'Oh, yes, here we are. Dr Ken Mallory. I remember him. He was on his way to make a house call on a patient. I was impressed, because not many doctors do that these days.'

No resident ever makes house calls. 'What's the prescription for?'

Paige found she was holding her breath.

'Chloral hydrate.'

Paige was almost trembling with excitement. 'You're sure?'

'It says so right here.'

'What was the patient's name?'

He looked at the copy of the prescription. 'Spyros Levathes.'

'Would you mind giving me a copy of that prescription?' Paige asked.

'Not at all, doctor.'

One hour later, Paige was in Inspector Burns's office. She laid the prescription on his desk.

'Here's your proof,' Paige said. 'On Sunday, Dr Mallory went to a pharmacy miles away from where

341

he lives, and had this prescription for chloral hydrate filled. He put the chloral hydrate in Kat's drink, and when she was unconscious, he butchered her to make it look like an accident.'

'There's only one problem with that, Dr Taylor. There *was* no chloral hydrate in her body.'

'There has to be. Your pathologist made a mistake. Ask him to check again.'

He was losing his patience. 'Doctor . . .'

'Please! I know I'm right.'

'You're wasting everybody's time.'

Paige sat across from him, her eyes fixed on his face.

He sighed. 'All right. I'll call him again. Maybe he *did* make a mistake.'

Jason picked Paige up for dinner. 'We're having dinner at my house,' he said. 'There's something I want you to see.'

During the drive there, Paige brought Jason up to date on what was happening.

'They'll find the chloral hydrate in her body,' Paige said. 'And Ken Mallory will get what's coming to him.'

'I'm so sorry about all this, Paige.'

'I know.' She pressed his hand against her cheek. 'Thank God for you.'

The car pulled up in front of Jason's home.

Paige looked out of the window and she gasped. Around the green lawn in front of the house was a new white picket fence.

*   *   *

She was alone in the dark apartment. Ken Mallory used the key that Kat had given him and moved quietly toward the bedroom. Paige heard his footsteps coming toward her, but before she could move, he had leaped at her, his hands tight around her throat.

'You bitch! You're trying to destroy me. Well, you aren't going to snoop around anymore.' He began squeezing harder. 'I outsmarted all of you, didn't I?' His fingers squeezed tighter. 'No one can ever prove I killed Kat.'

She tried to scream, but it was impossible to breathe. She struggled free, and was suddenly awake. She was alone in her room. Paige sat up in bed trembling.

She stayed awake the rest of the night, waiting for Inspector Burns's phone call. It came at 10:00 A.M.

'Dr Taylor?'

'Yes.' She was holding her breath.

'I just got the *third* report from the forensic pathologist.'

'And?' Her heart was pounding.

'There was no trace of chloral hydrate or any other sedative in Dr Hunter's body. None.'

That was impossible! There had to be. There was no sign of any blow or anything that would have caused her to become unconscious. No bruises on her throat. It didn't make sense. Kat had to have been unconscious when Mallory killed her. The forensic pathologist was wrong.

Paige decided to go talk to him herself.

*   *   *

Dr Dolan was in an irritable mood. 'I don't like to be questioned like this,' he said. 'I've checked it three times. I told Inspector Burns that there was no trace of chloral hydrate in any of her organs, and there wasn't.'

'But . . .'

'Is there anything else, doctor?'

Paige looked at him helplessly. Her last hope was gone. Ken Mallory was going to get away with murder. 'I . . . I guess not. If you didn't find any chemicals in her body, then I don't . . .'

'I didn't say I didn't find *any* chemicals.'

She looked at him a moment. 'You found something?'

'Just a trace of trichloroethylene.'

She frowned. 'What would that do?'

He shrugged. 'Nothing. It's an analgesic drug. It wouldn't put anyone to sleep.'

'I see.'

'Sorry I can't help you.'

Paige nodded. 'Thank you.'

She walked down the long, antiseptic corridor of the morgue, depressed, feeling that she was missing something. She had been so sure Kat had been put to sleep with chloral hydrate.

All he found was a trace of trichloroethylene. It wouldn't put anyone to sleep. But why would trichloroethylene be in Kat's body? Kat had not been taking any medications. Paige stopped in the middle of the corridor, her mind working furiously.

When Paige arrived at the hospital, she went directly to the medical library on the fifth floor. It took her less than a minute to find trichloroethylene. The description read: *A colorless, clear, volatile liquid with a specific gravity of 1.47 at 59 degrees F. It is a halogenated hydrocarbon, having the chemical formula CCl₂, CHCl.*

And there, on the last line, she found what she was looking for. *When chloral hydrate is metabolized, it produces trichloroethylene as a by-product.*

'Inspector, Dr Taylor is here to see you.'

'Again?' He was tempted to turn her away. She was obsessed with the half-baked theory she had. He was going to have to put a stop to it. 'Send her in.'

When Paige walked into his office, Inspector Burns said, 'Look, doctor, I think this has gone far enough. Dr Dolan called to complain about—'

'I know how Ken Mallory did it!' Her voice was charged with excitement. 'There was trichloroethylene in Kat's body.'

He nodded. 'Dr Dolan told me that. But he said it couldn't have made her unconscious. He—'

'Chloral hydrate turns into trichloroethylene!' Paige said triumphantly. 'Mallory lied when he said he didn't go back into the apartment with Kat. He put chloral hydrate in her drink. It has no taste when you mix it with alcohol, and it only takes a few minutes for it to work. Then when she was unconscious, he killed her and made it look like a bungled abortion.'

'Doctor, if you'll forgive my saying so, that's a hell of a lot of speculation.'

'No, it isn't. He wrote the prescription for a patient named Spyros Levathes, but he never gave it to him.'

'How do you know that?'

'Because he *couldn't* have. I checked on Spyros Levathes. He has erythropoietic porphyria.'

'What's that?'

'It's a genetic metabolic disorder. It causes photosensitivity and lesions, hypertension, tachycardia, and a few other unpleasant symptoms. It's the result of a defective gene.'

'I still don't understand.'

'Dr Mallory didn't give his patient chloral hydrate because it would have killed him! Chloral hydrate is contra-indicated for porphyria. It would have caused immediate convulsive seizures.'

For the first time, Inspector Burns was impressed. 'You've really done your homework, haven't you?'

Paige pressed on. 'Why would Ken Mallory go to a remote pharmacy and fill a prescription for a patient he knew he couldn't *give* it to? You've *got* to arrest him.'

His fingers were drumming on his desk. 'It's not that simple.'

'You've got to . . .'

Inspector Burns raised a hand. 'All right. I'll tell you what I'll do. I'll talk to the district attorney's office and see whether they think we have a case.'

Paige knew she had gone as far as she could. 'Thank you, inspector.'

'I'll get back to you.'

After Paige Taylor left, Inspector Burns sat there thinking about their conversation. There was no hard evidence against Dr Mallory, only the suspicions of a persistent woman. He reviewed the few facts that he had. Dr Mallory had been engaged to Kat Hunter. Two days after she died, he was engaged to Alex

Harrison's daughter. Interesting, but not against the law.

Mallory had said that he dropped Dr Hunter off at her front door and did not go into the apartment. Semen was found in her body, but he had a plausible explanation for that.

Then there was the matter of the chloral hydrate. Mallory had written a prescription for a drug that could have killed his patient. Was he guilty of murder? Not guilty?

Burns buzzed his secretary on the intercom. 'Barbara, get me an appointment with the district attorney this afternoon.'

There were four men in the office when Paige walked in: the district attorney, his assistant, a man named Warren, and Inspector Burns.

'Thank you for stopping by, Dr Taylor,' the district attorney said. 'Inspector Burns has been telling me of your interest in the death of Dr Hunter. I can appreciate that. Dr Hunter was your roommate, and you want to see justice done.'

So they're going to arrest Ken Mallory after all!

'Yes,' Paige said. 'There's no doubt about it. Dr Mallory killed her. When you arrest him, he—'

'I'm afraid we can't do that.'

Paige looked at him blankly. 'What?'

'We can't arrest Dr Mallory.'

'But why?'

'We have no case.'

'Of course you have!' Paige exclaimed. 'The trichloroethylene proves that—'

348

'Doctor, in a court of justice, ignorance of the law is no excuse. But ignorance in medicine *is*.'

'I don't understand.'

'It's simple. It means that Dr Mallory could claim he made a mistake, that he didn't know what effect chloral hydrate would have on a patient with porphyria. No one could prove he was lying. It might prove that he's a lousy doctor, but it wouldn't prove that he's guilty of murder.'

Paige looked at him in frustration. 'You're going to let him get away with this?'

He studied her a moment. 'I'll tell you what I'm prepared to do. I've discussed this with Inspector Burns. With your permission, we're going to send someone to your apartment to pick up the glasses in the bar. If we find any traces of chloral hydrate, we'll take the next step.'

'What if he rinsed them out?'

Inspector Burns said dryly, 'I don't imagine he took the time to use a detergent. If he just rinsed out the glasses, we'll find what we're looking for.'

Two hours later, Inspector Burns was on the phone with Paige.

'We did a chemical analysis of all the glasses in the bar, doctor,' Burns said.

Paige steeled herself for disappointment.

'We found one with traces of chloral hydrate.'

Paige closed her eyes in a silent prayer of thanks.

'And there were fingerprints on that glass. We're going to check them against Dr Mallory's prints.'

Paige felt a surge of excitement.

The inspector went on, 'When he killed her—

if he did kill her—he was wearing gloves, so his fingerprints wouldn't be on the curette. But he couldn't very well have served her a drink while he wore gloves, and he might not have worn them when he put the glass back on the shelf after rinsing it out.'

'No,' Paige said. 'He couldn't, could he?'

'I have to admit that in the beginning, I didn't believe your theory was going anywhere. I think now maybe Dr Mallory could be our man. But proving it is going to be another matter.' He continued, 'The district attorney is right. It would be a tricky business to bring Mallory to trial. He can still say that the prescription was for his patient. There's no law against making a medical mistake. I don't see how we—'

'Wait a minute!' Paige said excitedly. 'I think I know how!'

Ken Mallory was listening to Lauren on the telephone. 'Father and I found some office space that you're going to adore, darling! It's a beautiful suite in the 490 Post Building. I'm going to hire a receptionist for you, someone not too pretty.'

Mallory laughed. 'You don't have to worry about that, baby. There isn't anyone in the world for me but you.'

'I'm dying for you to come see it. Can you get away now?'

'I'm off in a couple of hours.'

'Wonderful! Why don't you pick me up at the house?'

'All right. I'll be there.' Mallory replaced the telephone. *It doesn't get any better than this*, he thought. *There is a God, and She loves me.*

He heard his name called over the PA system, 'Dr Mallory . . . Room 430 . . . Dr Mallory . . . Room 430.' He sat there daydreaming, thinking about the golden future that lay ahead of him. *A beautiful suite in the 490 Post Building, filled with rich old ladies, eager to throw their money at him.* He heard his name called again. 'Dr Mallory . . . Room 430.' He sighed and got to his feet. *I'll be out of this goddam madhouse soon*, he thought. He headed toward Room 430.

A resident was waiting for him in the corridor, outside the room. 'I'm afraid we have a problem here,' he said. 'This is one of Dr Peterson's patients, but Dr Peterson isn't here. I'm having an argument with one of the other doctors.'

They stepped inside. There were three people in the room—a man in bed, a male nurse, and a doctor Mallory had not met before.

The resident said, 'This is Dr Edwards. We need your advice, Dr Mallory.'

'What's the problem?'

The resident explained. 'This patient is suffering from erythropoietic porphyria, and Dr Edwards insists on giving him a sedative.'

'I don't see any problem with that.'

'Thank you,' Dr Edwards said. 'The man hasn't slept in forty-eight hours. I've prescribed chloral hydrate for him so he can get some rest and . . .'

Mallory was looking at him in astonishment. 'Are you out of your mind? That could kill him! He'd have a convulsive seizure, tachycardia, and he'd probably die. Where in hell did you study medicine?'

351

The man looked at Mallory and said quietly, 'I didn't.' He flashed a badge. 'I'm with the San Francisco Police Department, Homicide.' He turned to the man in bed. 'Did you get that?'

The man pulled out a tape recorder from under the pillow. 'I got it.'

Mallory was looking from one to the other, frowning. 'I don't understand. What is this? What's going on?'

The inspector turned to Mallory. 'Dr Mallory, you're under arrest for the murder of Dr Kate Hunter.'

36

The headline in the *San Francisco Chronicle* read, DOCTOR ARRESTED IN LOVE TRIANGLE. The story beneath it went on at length to detail the lurid facts of the case.

Mallory read the newspaper in his cell. He slammed it down.

His cellmate said, 'Looks like they got you cold, pal.'

'Don't you believe it,' Mallory said confidently. 'I've got connections, and they're going to get me the best goddam lawyer in the world. I'll be out of here in twenty-four hours. All I have to do is make one phone call.'

The Harrisons were reading the newspaper at breakfast.

'My God!' Lauren said. 'Ken! I can't believe it!'

A butler approached the breakfast table. 'Excuse me, Miss Harrison. Dr Mallory is on the telephone for you. I believe he's calling from jail.'

'I'll take it.' Lauren started to get up from the table.

'You'll stay here and finish your breakfast,' Alex

Harrison said firmly. He turned to the butler. 'We don't know any Dr Mallory.'

Paige read the newspaper as she was getting dressed. Mallory was going to be punished for the terrible thing he had done, but it gave Paige no satisfaction. Nothing they did to him could ever bring Kat back.

The doorbell rang, and Paige went to answer it. A stranger stood there. He was wearing a dark suit and carried a briefcase.

'Dr Taylor?'

'Yes . . .'

'My name is Roderick Pelham. I'm an attorney with Rothman and Rothman. May I come in?'

Paige studied him, puzzled. 'Yes.'

He entered the apartment.

'What did you want to see me about?'

She watched him open the briefcase and take out some papers.

'You are aware, of course, that you are the principal beneficiary of John Cronin's will?'

Paige looked at him blankly. 'What are you talking about? There must be some mistake.'

'Oh, there's no mistake. Mr Cronin has left you the sum of one million dollars.'

Paige sank into a chair, overwhelmed, remembering.

You have to go to Europe. Do me a favor. Go to Paris . . . stay at the Crillon, have dinner at Maxim's, order a big, thick steak and a bottle of champagne, and when you eat that steak and drink that champagne, I want you to think of me.

'If you'll just sign here, we'll take care of all the necessary paperwork.'

Paige looked up. 'I . . . I don't know what to say. I . . . he had a family.'

'According to the terms of his will, they get only the remainder of his estate, not a large amount.'

'I can't accept this,' Paige told him.

Pelham looked at her in surprise. 'Why not?'

She had no answer. John Cronin had wanted her to have this money. 'I don't know. It . . . it seems unethical, somehow. He was my patient.'

'Well, I'll leave the check here with you. You can decide what you want to do with it. Just sign here.'

Paige signed the paper in a daze.

'Goodbye, doctor.'

She watched him leave and sat there thinking of John Cronin.

The news of Paige's inheritance was the talk of the hospital. Somehow, Paige had hoped it could be kept quiet. She still had not made up her mind about what to do with the money. *It doesn't belong to me*, she thought. *He had a family.*

Paige was not emotionally ready to go back to work, but her patients had to be taken care of. An operation was scheduled for that morning. Arthur Kane was waiting for Paige in the corridor. They had not spoken to each other since the incident of the reversed X-rays. Although Paige had no proof it was Kane, the tire-slashing episode had scared her.

'Hello, Paige. Let's let bygones be bygones. What do you say?'

Paige shrugged. 'Fine.'

'Wasn't that a terrible thing about Ken Mallory?' he asked.

'Yes,' Paige said.

Kane was looking at her slyly. 'Can you imagine a doctor deliberately killing a human being? It's horrible, isn't it?'

'Yes.'

'By the way,' he said, 'congratulations. I hear that you're a millionairess.'

'I can't see . . .'

'I have tickets for the theater tonight, Paige. I thought that the two of us could go.'

'Thanks,' Paige said. 'I'm engaged to someone.'

'Then I suggest you get unengaged.'

She looked at him, surprised. 'I beg your pardon?'

Kane moved closer to her. 'I ordered an autopsy on John Cronin.'

Paige found her heart beginning to beat faster. 'Yes?'

'He didn't die of heart failure. Someone gave him an overdose of insulin. I guess that particular someone never figured on an autopsy.'

Paige's mouth was suddenly dry.

'You were with him when he died, weren't you?'

She hesitated. 'Yes.'

'I'm the only one who knows that, and I'm the only one who has the report.' He patted her arm. 'And my lips are sealed. Now, about those tickets tonight . . .'

Paige pulled away from him. 'No!'

'Are you sure you know what you're doing?'

She took a deep breath. 'Yes. Now, if you'll excuse me . . .' And she walked away. Kane looked after her, and his face hardened. He turned and headed toward Dr Benjamin Wallace's office.

The telephone awakened her at 1:00 A.M. at her apartment.

'You have been a naughty girl again.'

It was the same raspy voice disguised in a breathy whisper, but this time Paige recognized it. *My God*, she thought, *I was right to be scared*.

The following morning, when Paige arrived at the hospital, two men were waiting for her.

'Dr Paige Taylor?'

'Yes.'

'You'll have to come with us. You're under arrest for the murder of John Cronin.'

It was the final day of Paige's trial. Alan Penn, the defense attorney, was making his summation to the jury.

'Ladies and gentlemen, you have heard a lot of testimony about Dr Taylor's competence or incompetence. Well, Judge Young will instruct you that's not what this trial is about. I'm sure that for every doctor who did not approve of her work, we could produce a dozen doctors who did. But that is not the issue.

'Paige Taylor is on trial for the death of John Cronin. She has admitted helping him die. She did so because he was in great pain, and he asked her to do so. That is euthanasia, and it's being accepted more and more throughout the world. In the past year, the California Supreme Court has upheld the right of a mentally competent adult to refuse or demand the withdrawal of medical treatment of any form. It is the individual who must live or die with the course of treatment chosen or rejected.'

He looked into the faces of the jurors. 'Euthanasia is a crime of compassion, of mercy, and I daresay it takes place in some form or another in hospitals all over the world. The prosecuting attorney is asking for a death sentence. Don't let him confuse the issue. There has never been a death sentence for euthanasia. Sixty-three percent of Americans believe euthanasia should be legal, and in eighteen states in this country, it *is* legal. The question is, do we have the right to compel helpless patients to live in pain, to force them to stay alive and suffer? The question has become complicated because of the great strides we've made in medical technology. We've turned the care of patients over to machines. Machines have no mercy. If a horse breaks a leg, we put it out of its misery by shooting it. With a human being, we condemn him or her to a half life that is hell.

'Dr Taylor didn't decide when John Cronin would die. John Cronin decided. Make no mistake about it, what Dr Taylor did was an act of mercy. She has taken full responsibility for that. But you can rest assured that she knew nothing about the money that was left to her. What she did, she did in a spirit of compassion. John Cronin was a man with a failing heart and an untreatable, fatal cancer that had spread through his body, causing him agony. Just ask yourself one question. Under those circumstances, would you like to go on living? Thank you.' He turned, walked back to the table, and sat next to Paige.

Gus Venable rose and stood before the jury. '*Compassion? Mercy?*' He looked over at Paige, shook his head, then turned back to the jury. 'Ladies and gentlemen, I have been practicing law in courtrooms for more than twenty years, and I must tell you that in all those years, I have never—never—seen a more clear-cut case of cold-blooded, deliberate murder for profit.'

Paige was hanging on every word, tense and pale.

'The defense talked about euthanasia. Did Dr Taylor do what she did out of a feeling of compassion? I don't think so. Dr Taylor and others have testified that Mr Cronin had only a few more days to live. Why didn't she let him live those few days? Perhaps it was because Dr Taylor was afraid Mrs Cronin might learn about her husband changing his will, and put a stop to it.

'It's a most remarkable coincidence that immediately after Mr Cronin changed his will and left Dr Taylor the sum of one million dollars, she gave him an overdose of insulin and murdered him.

'Again and again, the defendant has convicted herself with her own words. She said that she was on friendly terms with John Cronin, that he liked and respected her. But you have heard witnesses testify that he hated Dr Paige, that he called her "that bitch" and told her "to keep her fucking hands off him".'

Gus Venable glanced at the defendant again. There was a look of despair on Paige's face. He turned back to the jury. 'An attorney has testified that Dr Taylor said, about the million dollars that was left to her, "It's unethical. He was my patient." But she grabbed the money. She needed it. She had a drawerful of travel brochures at home—Paris, London, the Riviera. And bear in mind that she didn't go to the travel agency *after* she got the money. Oh, no. She planned those trips earlier. All she needed was the money and the opportunity, and John Cronin supplied both. A helpless, dying man she could control. She had at her mercy a man who she admitted was in enormous pain—agony, in fact, according to her own admission. When you're in that kind of pain, you can imagine how difficult it must be to think clearly. We don't know *how* Dr Taylor persuaded John Cronin to change his will, to cut out the family he loved and to make her his main beneficiary. What we *do* know is that he summoned her to his bedside on that fatal night. What did they talk about? Could he have offered her a million dollars to put him out of his misery? It's a possibility we must face. In either case, it was cold-blooded murder.

'Ladies and gentlemen, during this trial, do you know who was the most damaging witness of all?' He pointed a dramatic finger at Paige. 'The defendant herself! You've heard her testify that she never violated the sacred Hippocratic oath that she took, but she lied. We've heard testimony that she gave an illegal blood transfusion and then falsified the record. She said that she never killed a patient except John Cronin, but we've heard testimony that Dr Barker, a physician respected by everybody, accused her of killing his patient.

'Unfortunately, ladies and gentlemen, Lawrence Barker suffered a stroke and can't be here with us today to testify against the defendant. But let me remind you of Dr Barker's opinion of the defendant. This is Dr Peterson, testifying about a patient Dr Taylor was operating on.'

He read from the transcript.

'"Dr Barker came into the operating room during the operation?"

'"Yes." And did Dr Barker say anything?'

'Answer: "He turned to Dr Taylor and said, 'You killed him.'"'

'This is from Nurse Berry. "Tell me some specific

things you heard Dr Barker say to Dr Taylor."

'Answer: "He said she was incompetent . . . Another time he said he wouldn't let her operate on his dog."'

Gus Venable looked up. 'Either there is some kind of conspiracy going on, where all these reputable doctors and nurses are lying about the defendant, or Dr Taylor is a liar. Not *just* a liar, but a pathological . . .'

The rear door of the courtroom had opened and an aide hurried in. He paused in the doorway a moment, trying to make a decision. Then he moved down the aisle toward Gus Venable.

'Sir . . .'

Gus Venable turned, furious. 'Can't you see I'm . . . ?'

The aide whispered in his ear.

Gus Venable looked at him, stunned. '*What? That's* wonderful!'

Judge Young leaned forward, her voice ominously quiet. 'Forgive me for interrupting you two, but what exactly do you think you're doing?'

Gus Venable turned to the judge excitedly. 'Your honor, I've just been informed that Dr Lawrence Barker is outside this courtroom. He's in a wheelchair, but he's able to testify. I'd like to call him to the stand.'

There was a loud buzz in the courtroom.

Alan Penn was on his feet. 'Objection!' he yelled. 'The prosecuting attorney is in the middle of his summation. There's no precedent for calling a new witness at this late hour. I —'

Judge Young slammed her gavel down. 'Would counsel please approach the bench.'

362

Penn and Venable moved up to the bench.

'This is highly irregular, your honor. I object . . .'

Judge Young said, 'You're right about its being irregular, Mr Penn, but you're wrong about its being without precedent. I can cite a dozen cases around the country where material witnesses were allowed to testify under special circumstances. In fact, if you're so interested in precedent, you might look up a case that took place in this courtroom five years ago. I happened to be the judge.'

Alan Penn swallowed. 'Does this mean you're going to allow him to testify?'

Judge Young was thoughtful. 'Since Dr Barker is a material witness to this case, and was physically unable to testify earlier, in the interest of justice, I'm going to rule that he be allowed to take the stand.'

'Exception! There is no proof that the witness is competent to testify. I demand a battery of psy-chiatrists —'

'Mr Penn, in this courtroom, we don't demand. We request.' She turned to Gus Venable. 'You may bring in your witness.'

Alan Penn stood there, deflated. *It's all over*, he thought. *Our case is down the drain*.

Gus Venable turned to his aide. 'Bring Dr Barker in.'

The door opened slowly, and Dr Lawrence Barker entered the courtroom. He was in a wheelchair. His head was tilted, and one side of his face was drawn up in a slight rictus.

Everyone watched the pale and fragile figure being wheeled to the front of the courtroom. As he moved past Paige, he looked over at her.

There was no friendliness in his eyes, and Paige remembered his last words: *Who the hell do you think you . . . ?*

When Lawrence Barker was in front of the bench, Judge Young leaned forward and said gently, 'Dr Barker, are you able to testify here today?'

When Barker spoke, his words were slurred. 'I am, your honor.'

'Are you fully aware of what is going on in this courtroom?'

'Yes, your honor.' He looked over to where Paige was seated. 'That woman is being tried for the murder of a patient.'

Paige winced. *That woman!*

Judge Young made her decision. She turned to the bailiff. 'Would you swear the witness in, please?'

When Dr Barker had been sworn in, Judge Young said, 'You may stay in the chair, Dr Barker. The prosecutor will proceed, and I will allow the defense to cross-examine.'

Gus Venable smiled. 'Thank you, your honor.' He strolled over to the wheelchair. 'We won't keep you very long, doctor, and the court deeply appreciates your coming in to testify under these trying circumstances. Are you familiar with any of the testimony that has been given here over the past month?'

Dr Barker nodded. 'I've been following it on television and in the newspapers, and it made me sick to my stomach.'

Paige buried her head in her hands.

It was all Gus Venable could do to hide his feeling of triumph. 'I'm sure a lot of us feel the same way, doctor,' the prosecutor said piously.

'I came here because I want to see justice done.'

Venable smiled. 'Exactly. So do we.'

Lawrence Barker took a deep breath, and when he spoke, his voice was filled with outrage. 'Then how the hell could you bring Dr Taylor to trial?'

Venable thought he had misunderstood him. 'I beg your pardon?'

'This trial is a farce!'

Paige and Alan Penn exchanged a stunned look.

Gus Venable turned pale. 'Dr Barker . . .'

'Don't interrupt me,' Barker snapped. 'You've used the testimony of a lot of biased, jealous people to attack a brilliant surgeon. She —'

'Just a minute!' Venable was beginning to panic. 'Isn't it true that you criticized Dr Taylor's ability so severely that she was finally ready to quit Embarcadero Hospital?'

'Yes.'

Gus Venable was starting to feel better. 'Well, then,' he said patronizingly, 'how can you say that Paige Taylor is a brilliant doctor?'

'Because it happens to be the truth.' Barker turned to look at Paige, and when he spoke again, he was talking to her as though they were the only two people in the courtroom: 'Some people are born to be doctors. You were one of those rare ones. I knew from the beginning how capable you were. I was hard on you — maybe too hard — because you were good. I was tough on you because I wanted you to be tougher on yourself. I wanted you to be perfect, because in our profession, there's no room for error. None.'

Paige was staring at him, mesmerized, her mind spinning. It was all happening too fast.

The courtroom was hushed.

'I wasn't about to let you quit.'

Gus Venable could feel his victory slipping away. His prize witness had become his worst nightmare. 'Dr Barker—it has been testified that you accused Dr Taylor of killing your patient Lance Kelly. How . . . ?'

'I told her that because she was the surgeon in charge. It was her ultimate responsibility. In fact, the anesthetist caused Mr Kelly's death.'

By now the court was in an uproar.

Paige sat there stunned.

Dr Barker went on speaking slowly, with an effort. 'And as for John Cronin leaving her that money, Dr Taylor knew nothing about it. I talked to Mr Cronin myself. He told me that he was going to leave Dr Taylor that money because he hated his family, and he said he was going to ask Dr Taylor to release him from his misery. I agreed.'

There was an uproar from the spectators. Gus Venable was standing there, a look of total bewilderment on his face.

Alan Penn leaped to his feet. 'Your honor, I move for a dismissal!'

Judge Young was slamming her gavel down. 'Quiet!' she yelled. She looked at the two attorneys. 'Into my chambers.'

Judge Young, Alan Penn, and Gus Venable were seated in Judge Young's chambers.

Gus Venable was in a state of shock. 'I . . . I don't know what to say. He's obviously a sick man, your honor. He's confused. I want a battery of psychiatrists to examine him and—'

'You can't have it both ways, Gus. It looks like your case just went up in smoke. Let's save you any further embarrassment, shall we? I'm going to grant a dismissal on the murder charge. Any objection?'

There was a long silence. Finally, Venable nodded. 'I guess not.'

Judge Young said, 'Good decision. I'm going to give you some advice. Never, *never* call a witness unless you know what he's going to say.'

The court was in session again. Judge Young said, 'Ladies and gentlemen of the jury, thank you for your time and your patience. The court is going to grant a dismissal on all charges. The defendant is free.'

Paige turned to blow Jason a kiss, then hurried over to where Dr Barker was seated. She slid down to her knees and hugged him.

'I don't know how to thank you,' she whispered.

'You never should have gotten into this mess in the first place,' he growled. 'Damned fool thing to do. Let's get out of here and go somewhere where we can talk.'

Judge Young heard. She stood up and said, 'You may use my chambers if you like. That's the least we can do for you.'

Paige, Jason, and Dr Barker were in the judge's chambers, alone.

Dr Barker said, 'Sorry they wouldn't let me come here to help you sooner. You know what goddam doctors are like.'

Paige was near tears. 'I can't tell you how much I . . .'

'Then don't!' he said gruffly.

Paige was studying him, suddenly remembering something. 'When did you speak to John Cronin?'

'*What?*'

'You heard me. When did you speak to John Cronin?'

'*When?*'

She said slowly, 'You never even *met* John Cronin. You didn't know him.'

There was the trace of a smile on Barker's lips. 'No. But I know you.'

Paige leaned over and threw her arms around him.

'Don't get sloppy,' he growled. He looked over at Jason. 'She gets sloppy sometimes. You'd better take good care of her, or you'll have to answer to me.'

Jason said, 'Don't worry, sir. I will.'

Paige and Jason were married the following day. Dr Barker was their best man.

EPILOGUE

Paige Curtis went into private practice and is affiliated with the prestigious North Shore Hospital. Paige used the million dollars John Cronin left her to set up a medical foundation in her father's name in Africa.

Lawrence Barker shares an office with Paige, as a surgical consultant.

Arthur Kane had his license revoked by the Medical Board of California.

Jimmy Ford fully recovered and married Betsy. They named their first daughter Paige.

Honey Taft moved to Ireland with Sean Reilly, and works as a nurse in Dublin.

Sean Reilly is a successful artist, and shows no symptoms of AIDS, as yet.

Mike Hunter was sentenced to state prison for armed robbery and is still serving time.

Alfred Turner joined a practice on Park Avenue and is enormously successful.

Benjamin Wallace was fired as administrator of Embarcadero County Hospital.

Lauren Harrison married her tennis pro.

Lou Dinetto was sentenced to fifteen years in the penitentiary for tax evasion.

Ken Mallory was sentenced to life imprisonment.

One week after Dinetto arrived at the penitentiary, Mallory was found stabbed to death in his cell.

The Embarcadero Hospital is still there, awaiting the next earthquake.

Are You Afraid of the Dark?

Sidney Sheldon

In New York, Denver, Paris and Berlin, four people have died in what appear to be random accidents.

When two women – widows of the dead – find themselves under merciless attack, their fear and confusion help them to form an unlikely alliance. But why are they being targeted? Is there a connection to their husbands' mysterious deaths?

Meanwhile, the Chief Executive of an international Think Tank is on the cusp of a discovery which could change the world – and deliver unbelievable power into the company's hands. Could the mysterious deaths be connected to this volatile secret?

Taut with suspense and vivid characterization, and with an unnervingly realistic premise, *Are You Afraid of the Dark?* is a *tour de force* from a master storyteller.

ISBN 0 00 716516 1

Rage of Angels

Sidney Sheldon

At the heart of the story stands the woman who is Sheldon's most unforgettable creation . . .

Jennifer Parker is brilliant, beautiful and indomitable – the most glamorous lawyer in America and one of the most successful.

Her life is shadowed by two men. Both of them powerful and both drawn irresistibly to her.

One is the politician, destined for greatness who fathers her son. The other is the Mafia boss, her only ally when crisis strikes and the man who brings her world crashing down . . .

'The fast moving plot . . . with new surprises on every page . . . will keep his fans enthralled.'   *Publishers Weekly*

0 00 617873 1

The Stars Shine Down
Sidney Sheldon

A magnificent story of passion, intrigue, ambition and revenge – Sidney Sheldon at his compelling, provocative best.

Lara Cameron seems to possess everything that life has to offer. Young, beautiful, a self-made tycoon, she has outshone her competitors to reach the pinnacle of international fortune and renown. But the real Lara is a lonely figure, driven by a childhood obsession, trying, at all costs to bury the ghosts of her terrible past . . .

With her glittering marriage to a world-famous concert pianist, Lara is sure she has fulfilled her destiny. But what she cannot foresee is that terrifying, uncontrollable forces from her secret past are bent on destroying everything she has created, everything she values in life . . .

'Sheldon shines again . . . a compelling read' *Today*

ISBN 0 00 617871 5

Bloodline
Sidney Sheldon

A daughter of privilege: Elizabeth Roffe possessed beauty, intelligence, youth, the adored daughter of a rich and powerful father.

At his death she had to obey his behest and take command of his mighty global empire. It made Elizabeth the richest girl in the world. But someone, somewhere, was determined that she must die . . .

In this story that spans three continents, Sidney Sheldon spins a hypnotic, exotic web – of love and ambition, of danger and death.

'Sheldon is a writer working at the height of his power . . . powerful enough to drag us along with him. I hung on till the very end.'   *New York Times*

ISBN 0 00 617501 5

The Doomsday Conspiracy
Sidney Sheldon

A devastatingly topical novel from
the world's master storyteller

Robert Bellamy of US naval intelligence, a disillusioned man
recovering from a broken marriage, is despatched on a top
secret mission. A weather balloon, he is told, carrying
sensitive military information, has crashed in Switzerland
and Bellamy must locate the ten witnesses to the incident.
But when he arrives in Switzerland he discovers that it wasn't
a weather balloon that crashed after all, but a UFO with two
dead aliens aboard, whose remains have since vanished . . .
As the story unfolds, Bellamy gradually discovers the full,
terrible nature of Operation Doomsday, a conspiracy of such
magnitude as to threaten the destruction of the earth's
environment. He also rebuilds his own shattered life, finding
true love and hope for the future again.

ISBN 0 00 647208 7

Morning, Noon and Night

Sidney Sheldon

The Stanford family is one of the most respected in America - but behind the facade of fame and glamour lies a hidden web of blackmail, drugs and murder . . .

When Harry Stanford, one of the wealthiest men in the world, mysteriously drowns while cruising on his yacht, it sets off a chain of events that reverberates around the globe . . . At the family gathering following the funeral in Boston, a strikingly beautiful young woman appears. She claims to be Stanford's daughter and entitled to a share of the tycoon's estate. Is she genuine or is she an imposter?

Sweeping from the splendours of the Italian Riviera, to the fashion salons of Paris and New York, and the élite opulence of Boston and Florida, *Morning, Noon and Night* twists and turns its way through intrigue, smoke and mirrors to a surprise ending you'll never forget . . .

'Sheldon is a writer working at the height of his power . . . I hung on till the very end'   *New York Times*

ISBN 0 00 649806 X